ACHILLA THE STRONG

G. MILLER

Illustrated by
RYAN WITH BEST CHOICES

Genesis 6:4

"The Nephilim were on the earth in those days, and also afterward, when the sons of God came in to the daughters of man and they bore children to them. These were the mighty men who were of old, the men of renown." –Genesis 6:4

Provers 22:6

"Train a child in the way he should go, and when he is old he will not turn from it." –Proverbs 22:6

Prologue

HARLEM OF THE WEST. That was what they called the Five Points neighborhood of Denver, but as far as Achilla Johnson could tell, they should think of a new name. A few weeks out there, and Achilla Johnson saw enough white women jogging with baby strollers to think she was in Castle Rock nearly an hour south. But that was America, wasn't it? People were always migrating and setting up shop.

Achilla knew all about that. Denver was her fourth city this year. She got a great deal in an apartment in Montbello where her entire floor had black residents. Achilla expected to see more of the same in the Five Points, but a few weeks of scoping it out showed her how gentrification really changes a city. Looking at it now, who would've thought it was one of Miles Davis' stomping grounds? She did find at least some of what she wanted though. Achilla sat on a stoop in a red dress and matching heels as she stared out at the Victorian-style homes lining East 23rd Street. They were mere shadows where the streetlights couldn't reach, but they were big enough to obstruct her view of the mountains.

Achilla loved those mountains. In her hometown, there was no comparison, and she couldn't get enough of them. That view whenever she drove on the highway or looked out the window of a LoDo apartment compelled her to stay, but she couldn't. Sitting still was not an option. That rolling stone life was the best thing for her right now, and Achilla had to move on to her fifth city soon.

But first, she had to go back inside and say goodbye to Mr. Sidney Christie, one of the few black men who transplanted into the Five Points. They met at La Rumba, a salse club Downtown, and he was quite the dancer. Sidney had a strong lead and a gentle caress, the kind of hands that tempt a woman to see what else he could do with them. And here she was sitting outside on his steps in her red dress. Achilla sighed and stood up. Time to get this over with.

She opened the front door and stepped inside, grabbing a black bag to her right and strolling down the hall to his bathroom. In there, she changed out of her dress into a pair of blue jeans and a black t-shirt. Achilla looked at herself in the mirror and gave the brown-eyed, dark-skinned woman looking back at her a flirty smile. Then she blew a kiss before pulling out a hair tie and smoothing her hair into a ponytail. Once her hair was completely pulled back, she pulled out her contacts, revealing a pair of green eyes so intense they looked like they might crack the glass. Achilla hated her eyes. They reminded her of a past she couldn't escape. So she glared at them until she forced herself to look away.

After shoving her bag into her car outside, Achilla strolled back in and down to the basement where Sidney was waiting. He sat naked in a chair in the middle of a concrete floor with his hands tied behind his back and his feet tied to the chair legs. His dark, bald head dripped with sweat at the sight of her, but he didn't scream because about half an hour ago Achilla stuffed his mouth with the black panties he pulled off of her. The poor idiot thought he was getting some. Achilla shook her head as she walked up to him and kneeled by his face.

"You can tell who I am now, right?" Achilla asked as she pointed at her eyes. "By now it's obvious?"

Sidney nodded his head.

"Good," Achilla said as she pulled her panties out of his mouth

2

and shook the saliva off of them. "Then you know what happens next."

"You don't have to do this," Sidney said. "You can just go home and live a normal life, just like me."

Achilla's left eye twitched as she stared at him. Go home? Yeah, that sounded nice, but it wasn't possible. Not anymore. Achilla couldn't face her family anymore after all she had done, and this man was a big part of that. No, he deprived her of that, and now he was going to pay for it.

"Actually, Sidney, I do have to do this," Achilla sighed as she reached behind her back and pulled a knife from her belt loop, tapping the blade on his nose. "And we both know why."

"I thought you hated her," Sidney said with a breaking voice. "But you're just like her. You're no different than--"

"Do not mention her name in front of me," Achilla snapped. "She does this kind of thing because she enjoys it. I'm doing it because I'm pissed."

Achilla stood up and paced the basement. Now that she had her man, what was she going to do with him? What did he deserve? How could Achilla send the right message to those who would see this? But what if the wrong people saw it? Her family, friends, everyone she loved, what if they knew what she was doing out here? Achilla had no doubt in her mind that they would be crushed, and that thought jerked tears from her eyes. How did things get this far? Why did they have to be this way? Achilla didn't know if she was right or wrong anymore. All she knew was that this was the best solution she could come up with, and it would have to do until the job was finished. Achilla examined the sharpness of her blade before looking at Sidney's tear-drenched, sweaty face.

She didn't have time for guilt. Not anymore.

Chapter One

ACHILLA JOHNSON:20

Despite what she told her family, Achilla was not a Marine. She was not traveling to Iraq. She hadn't even left her home state of Connecticut. The pictures she sent, the letters she wrote, and the phone calls she made were all a ruse doctored by the United States government to keep her family safe and ignorant. She hated lying to them, but it was necessary.

Achilla was a CIA Agent. At least that was what she told herself for the past four years. It was better than listening to her inner impatient twenty-year-old who constantly nagged at her that all she got was grunt work and training exercises. She ignored that nagging voice as she stared out of the window of a studio apartment in Downtown Hartford watching a drug transaction across the street. Any other person would need binoculars, but she watched with her naked eyes as a heavyset black male with back-length dreadlocks walked into a one bedroom apartment. He wore a black t-shirt with a skull and crossbones on the front. Achilla still couldn't believe those shirts, pirate shirts as she called them, were in style. There were few things she found less sexy in a man than a reminder that he might have scurvy and frequently spent his weekends at Davy

Jones' Locker. She shook her head as she watched him shove his hands into the pockets of his baggy black jeans.

The man Achilla identified as the owner of the home, a tall, thin, bald Hispanic wearing a pink button-down shirt and dark blue jeans, walked into the main area from the kitchen to the right and extended his hand. Though she hated pink on men, at least this guy avoided the pirate shirt. He wasn't overwhelmingly sexy but doable if she hadn't had any in a while. Achilla's thoughts snapped back to the task at hand when the black male pulled out a gallon-sized ziplock bag full of white powder from under his t-shirt and handed it to the owner. Achilla smirked as she rose to her feet. They made the drop. Now all she had to do was trail the black male's car, interrogate him, and find the source. Achilla had reason to believe his supplier was connected to a Chinese diplomat. That kind of intel could give the U.S. a lot of leverage in future negotiations. The first step of her mission was a success. Now all she had to do was get downstairs in time to--

Achilla's ears twitched when she heard three men of average height and weight approaching her location. She leaped across the apartment and leaned against the wall next to the door. The entire studio had bare white walls with black furniture, and Achilla wore a white t-shirt with black sweatpants and black sneakers. There was no way she could hide from her intruders. She had to fight them. That was what she told herself as she grinned from ear-to-ear at the thought of trying out some new combinations.

As expected, they busted the door wide open. The second Achilla saw a gun protruding past the door, she grabbed the shooter's wrist, pulled him toward her and struck his elbow with the heel of her hand, snapping his arm with a pop. As he screamed, she shoved him into his partner and lunged for the third guy behind them, diving low and upper-cutting his groin before rising up and punching his face. He flew across the hall and landed on the floor with a slump as Achilla turned and kicked one of the original two in the temple. She grabbed the first shooter's head by his blond hair and was about to knee his face when she heard the click of a gun behind her. Achilla sighed and raised her hands.

"You got me," Achilla said. "But you never said you'd be involved."

"Expect the unexpected," the man behind her said. "Want to explain how you heard them coming but not me?"

"I was too focused on the fight," Achilla said as she rolled her eyes. "And not focused enough on the escape."

"Too focused is right," the guy from across the hall grunted. "Jesus, Achilla, you crushed my balls, and I'm wearing a cup."

"Sorry, I tried to go easy," Achilla said with a shrug and a weak smile. "I guess I got caught up in the moment."

"You tried to kill me!"

"No, I didn't," Achilla sighed. "If I wanted to kill you I would've hit your groin a lot harder than that, or I would've reached into your chest and pulled out your heart, or finger-jabbed your jugular vein, or elbowed your solar plexus--"

"We specifically said no contact," the first shooter said as he rose to his feet and pointed at his arm. "That means you don't break my arm. I'm not doing any more of these training exercises with you if you expect me to be your punching bag. That's not what I signed up for."

"You pointed a gun at me," Achilla shot back. "What did you expect? And by the way, we did not discuss firearms before we started this, so I guess we're even, buddy."

"It's not even loaded!" the first shooter growled as he pointed at the pistol on the floor.

"How the hell should I know that?" Achilla replied.

"You tell me," the first shooter said. "You're the freak!"

Achilla swallowed and blinked back tears at those words before glaring at him.

"Call me that again," Achilla snarled, "and I will break your other arm, I swear to God!"

"Both of you shut up," said the man standing behind Achilla as he grabbed her shoulder. "Achilla, you should know by now that nobody here plans on shooting you, but that's beside the point. The fact of the matter is you should be long gone by now, and you're still here. You made a mistake. Own up to it."

Achilla closed her eyes and hung her head.

"Yeah that's true," Achilla groaned. "I messed up. Mr. Jones, can I put my hands down now?"

"It's Agent Jones, for the umpteenth time," Agent Jones snapped. "And yes."

Achilla dropped her hands to her sides and leaned over to help up the man she kicked in the head just a few moments ago. She studied his motionless body and checked his pulse. He was alive, but he wasn't going anywhere for a while. Achilla leaned him against the wall in the apartment until the first shooter came to his side and gave her a curt wave with his hand; the kind you give a child you know is about to break something if you don't step in and stop her. Achilla pouted before she stepped back into the hallway and faced a black male with cul-de-sac hair wearing a black t-shirt, jeans, and black boots. Achilla shook her head at herself as she stared at his clunky, black, steel-toed boots. She knew she should have heard him coming. Achilla pinched herself in the thigh. She had to get better at this. Her supervisor, Agent Freeman Jones, was a strict teacher, and Achilla hated to lose.

"Your destructive force is obvious," Agent Jones said with his arms crossed. "But your assignment was to get in and out unnoticed by the general public even if your enemy finds you. How can you do that if you throw a man across the hall?"

"She punched me across the hall," the man said from the hallway floor. "I wish she threw me. God, I think she cracked my cheekbone too."

"You waste a lot of time, Johnson," Agent Jones continued over his groaning. "Someone with your strength and speed should be able to escape something like this in seconds. I, the fourth and unexpected person, wouldn't have been able to arrive in time. We don't need you to be an exhibitionist. We need you to be efficient. This isn't a kung fu movie."

"Understood," Achilla said as she forced herself to look Agent Jones in the eye.

"All right," Agent Jones replied before he turned his back and walked down the hall. "I need to show you something. Let's go."

"What about them?" Achilla asked as she pointed at her victims. "It's my fault they're injured."

"They knew what they were getting into when they volunteered," Agent Jones said. "That's why they got paid overtime, and that's why there's a medical station on standby outside."

Achilla walked out with Agent Jones as the medical staff walked in. She also watched as the black male with dreads and the Hispanic male in the pink t-shirt stood across the street and placed their fingers on their earpieces. When they both saw Achilla walking out, they walked past her into the building. The black male with dreads gave Achilla a knowing look as he walked by. Like most agents in her division, he most likely heard about her. Like most of the black agents, he always nodded at her like they were part of a secret club within the CIA. Achilla knew that head nod well. It was the good-to-see-another-one-of-us look, and it made Achilla smile.

As she stepped into Agent Jones' tan sedan that he used to blend in with urban areas like Hartford, Achilla smirked at the carpeted seating. Though he could probably afford something fancier, it would only stick out in neighborhoods where people worked three jobs and still struggled to make the rent. Hartford was indicative of most of Connecticut's major cities with a gap between rich and poor that was hard to fathom unless you saw it for yourself. Looking like you belong on the rich side of town could draw unnecessary attention. That was what Agent Jones reminded Achilla over and over before she went on one of her training exercises. No matter where you are, learn the culture and find a way to go unnoticed. If only he knew how difficult that was for someone like her, with or without a beat-up car.

While they drove past a few high rises and brick buildings, Achilla leaned her head on her hand and stared out the window. Up until now, the CIA had only given her measly assignments; most of which helped them watch her. While she attended boarding school, they made her bug her teachers' classrooms and the principal's office and taught her how to hack into the school's network. They also made her date a student they believed could blow her cover. Now that she graduated with high honors, they were putting her through all sorts of simulations to test her abilities. Sometimes Achilla felt like they were just keeping her occupied until Ailina Harris reappeared.

And just where was Ailina? Achilla hadn't seen her biological mother in years; not that she missed her. Achilla regularly asked Agent Jones if he had heard of any changes in Ailina's behavior or if she had come near her family. The answer was always the same. If she did, somebody would notify him, and then he would notify her. As cool as her job was, Achilla really hated the secrecy of it; especially when she wanted more information.

Agent Jones pulled into a parking garage and parked on the first floor. He then stepped out of the car and walked away without waiting. Achilla speed walked to keep up as he used his key to open an elevator door. The elevator descended to a basement level with a door that opened from behind. Achilla shook her head. She was a CIA agent for four years now, and she still couldn't believe how they hid in plain sight. Achilla followed Agent Jones down a hallway with white walls and steel doors with eye-level windows.

"Is this a nuthouse or something?" Achilla asked. "Or is it a jail for rogue agents?"

"Neither," Agent Jones said as he turned to the last room on the left and opened the door. "This is a research center."

"Yet I didn't have to show ID or get scanned with some weird gadget?" Achilla asked.

"Like most people, you watch too many movies," Agent Jones replied as they walked into a dark room with a dim light over a table and two chairs. Agent Jones beckoned for Achilla to sit down and she followed suit. He then sat across from her with his hands folded. Achilla leaned back and crossed her arms.

"I'm too old for kid lectures," Achilla said.

"Good because I'm not giving one," Agent Jones replied. "It's time I shared some information about you. As you know, you're not like the rest of us. Your body is a remarkable specimen."

"Now I feel like you're hitting on me," Achilla replied with a grin. "Keep it coming."

"Your juvenile humor aside," Agent Jones sighed. "Your mind

and body are advanced on levels that we cannot quantify. Your mother tested your I.Q. at 200. I estimate that it's much higher. So far I've seen you push or pull objects that Olympic weightlifters couldn't budge. Add your advanced martial arts training, and you're quite dangerous. I won't lie to you, the CIA recruited you to make sure you're on the side of the United States."

"I gathered that much," Achilla said with a nod of her head. "But why all the busy work? What are you hiding?"

Agent Jones frowned.

"Don't look at me like that," Achilla said with a smirk. "Come on, I know busy work when I see it. Someone else with my qualifications would be in Afghanistan by now, but you're holding me here in Connecticut. Like anything substantial actually happens here that concerns national security."

"Ailina concerns national security," Agent Jones replied. "And she's a much greater potential threat than Bin Laden."

"Then send me looking for her," Achilla demanded. "Come on, what are we waiting for?"

"I get your assignments from higher up," Agent Jones said with a shrug. "That's all. To be honest, I wish I knew more. I would've sent you out a long time ago."

"Dodging my question and flattering me," Achilla said. "Not bad."

"Anyway, I was assigned to you because I've been monitoring Ailina for the past twenty years," Agent Jones said. "From a distance of course. A few agents who got too close ended up dead."

"That tends to happen," Achilla replied with a shrug. "You should send female agents. She doesn't try to kill women unless they're raising me to be a decent person. Oh wait, I'm a female agent! You could send me. What a coincidence."

"Yes, Ailina's ruthless," Agent Jones said. "But believe it or not, brute strength is not her calling card. Her strengths are investigation and manipulation, and we can't engage her without a foolproof plan and a little patience on your part. I have reason to suspect that her intelligence is even greater than yours, but at your peak, you will be twice as strong. You're one of the brutes of your kind."

Achilla flexed her bicep and tightened her abs at that thought. Achilla knew her strength was abnormal. However, she wouldn't have guessed that she was predestined to be stronger than Ailina. Just a few more years in the CIA and Achilla may be able to protect her family on her own. She kissed her bicep and smiled as Agent Jones stared at her as if she were wasting his time.

"I don't like the word brute," Achilla said with a grin. "How about a warrior?"

"You're physically advancing at a faster rate than she did," Agent Jones continued as if she never spoke. "I would estimate that even right now, you two are equal in raw power."

"You haven't told me anything new," Achilla said. "Can I go home now?"

"You've never been given a name for your subspecies," Agent Jones replied as he stood up and walked away from the table. "We've given you the acronym N.E.P.H.; newly evolved posthumanoids. We prefer to call you Nephilim. It's more poetic."

"Even the CIA reads the Bible," Achilla chuckled. "Good thing I can't tell Mom or she'll make me go to church again."

"I've studied both you and Ailina and found lots of similarities," Agent Jones said with a deep breath as if to power through Achilla's side comments. "You have heightened senses and physical capabilities. You're also aggressive breeders."

"Whoa, stop," Achilla said with her hand raised. "Please don't talk about me like I'm some endangered species of frog. I like guys just like anyone else. It really isn't any more complicated than that."

"The correct animalistic sexual innuendo would be a rabbit--"

"Whatever, just don't talk to me like I'm anything less than a human being," Achilla snapped. "And besides, you haven't shown me anything outside of what I've already learned; except that you see me as Thumper apparently."

"How about this?" Agent Jones asked as he walked across the room and flipped a switch. The lights in the room illuminated the white walls and a large interrogation window. On the other side of the window was an even larger room with a twenty-foot-tall tank full of blue liquid on the other side. Inside that liquid floated a large white male with black, shaggy hair.

Achilla placed him at 6-foot-5 and 230 pounds of muscle.

"Who's he?" Achilla asked with a frown.

"Your grandfather," Agent Jones said. "Meet Ares Harris; our first known, present-day Nephilim."

Achilla gazed at this man with the same nose and facial structure as her, but with much lighter, Mediterranean skin. His neck muscles looked like shoulder pads and his biceps were as large as Achilla's head. Even his abs looked like ropes wrapped around his midsection. Achilla frowned at Agent Jones when she noticed two small scars on his forehead.

"What happened to his head?" Achilla asked. "I'd like to meet whoever managed to land a hit on someone like him."

"You already have," Agent Jones replied. "That's a gunshot wound from Gregory Price."

Gregory Price was the chief of police in her hometown. He was also her half-brother's grandfather, and an overall asshole, but he did take his job seriously. Perhaps a little too seriously considering how little he saw his own family. Despite being so closed off, he shared this story with Achilla as a pitch to get her to join the CIA.

"That's right, he did mention that," Achilla said with a nod of her head. "Price shot the guy before he got a car thrown at him. I'm impressed."

"It was a domestic violence call," Agent Jones said. "Rosa, your grandmother, called the police on Ares. Of course, it was too late by the time Greg got there. He literally tore her in half right in front of Ailina."

Achilla crossed her arms to keep her composure. In a rare moment of empathy, Achilla actually felt sorry for Ailina. It didn't last long. Achilla dug her nails into her biceps at the thought of seeing Ailina again. She always did.

"It's not the kind of scene any officer wants to walk into," Agent Jones continued. "Once Price got there, he tried to piece together the crime while keeping the little girl away from the bloody mess that used to be her mother. Ailina was only eleven at the time."

"That's...horrible," Achilla said with a shudder. "Where was Ares during all of this?"

"Waiting across the street," Agent Jones said. "When Price was just about to leave the scene, he appeared carrying Rosa's upper body in his arms. He then killed nine officers with his bare hands before picking up Price's squad car to crush him with it. Price shot him in the head, and the car landed on Price's legs. It took him years of physical and psychological therapy to recover. In return for his silence, we paid for everything. We also pulled strings to make sure he moved up in the ranks."

"Bridgeport's youngest police chief," Achilla said. "Now it makes sense. He thinks he owes you something, and in return, you use him to monitor Ailina and me."

"That's a very cynical way of looking at it."

"Yeah, you haven't denied it though," Achilla quipped. "What happened to Ailina?"

"She moved into a foster home in Boston not far from where she lived as a small child," Agent Jones replied. "Price took extra care to visit her and make sure she was turning out OK. She had a destructive temper, but she functioned well until she returned to Bridgeport and joined the police academy. After that, she met your father."

"Where?" Achilla asked. "My father never told me where they met."

"Mr. P's in Stratford," Agent Jones sighed. "It's a bar--"

"I know what it is," Achilla snapped. "I lived in Stratford remember?"

Agent Jones took another deep breath. Achilla could tell that she was testing his patience, and it made her laugh inside; served him right for calling her a rabbit.

"Your father was always a good man," Agent Jones said with a hard stare. "But like any pure-minded defense attorney in the making, he saw the good in people even when it wasn't there. As you know, Ailina's a textbook a sociopath. She pegged Brendan for a provider the second she laid eyes on him, but there was no love there. Like all of the other men in her life, he was a possession, nothing more. To this day, I don't understand why she kept him alive."

"What do you mean?" Achilla asked. "My father didn't do anything wrong."

"But she could've killed him, and she never hesitates," Agent Jones replied. "She never does anything by accident. She didn't keep him alive for an emotional reason. It's impossible."

"Maybe she wanted me to experience what she did," Achilla said. "With the story you just told me, it makes sense."

"But again, why didn't she go through with it?" Agent Jones asked. "I'm not advocating your parents' deaths, but she had to have a reason."

"My brother," Achilla said. "She said that he was so bold that it would take the fun out of killing him. She said she wanted to be his friend. Creepy considering he was like fourteen."

"I see," Agent Jones said as he crossed his arms and paced the room. "Ailina never keeps a man in good health unless she plans on using him. Your brother may be a new target. I'll pass the word along--"

"Price said the same thing," Achilla said. "Target for what?"

"Breeding," Agent Jones said. "There's a reason you like guys so much. It advances your next generation at a rapid rate, and you're living proof that mixing a Nephilim with a human being bears positive results. Ailina's too smart to miss that."

"No," Achilla snarled. "She can't have Samuel."

"Like I said, I'll talk to the proper people," Agent Jones replied. "Your brother's life isn't in danger yet, but if he resists her--"

"I'll kill her myself!" Achilla barked. "My brother isn't her toy."

"We don't want you near her yet," Agent Jones said. "Not without a plan."

"We agreed that you would protect my family," Achilla said with a sideways glance. "If I find out she comes anywhere near him, the plan's over. Just keep that in mind."

Agent Jones stared at Achilla and she glared right back. Agent Jones took a deep breath and looked at Ares.

"Ares only had one child as far as we know," Agent Jones said.

continued. "A danger that only I can handle, right? So how do I kill him?"

"Like you said, Nephilim are still human," Agent Jones replied. "Your bodies have the same weak spots as anyone else's. You just have to have the strength and speed to strike them. Aside from that, another gunshot to the head should do it."

"Sounds right," Achilla said as she walked toward the door. "Unless you have anything else to tell me, I'm grabbing dinner. You're welcome to join me."

"I keep business and pleasure separate, Achilla," Agent Jones replied.

"Wasn't exactly looking for pleasure," Achilla chuckled as she opened the door. "But if you're not coming, more steak for me. Later."

Achilla found her way to Trumbull Kitchen, a restaurant on Trumbull Street in Hartford that served a mean grilled filet mignon. Achilla always ordered one on the government's dime. After that, she took the bus to her apartment building. As she looked out the window, she watched the dark gray clouds roll in and sighed. Another storm was rolling through.

July in Connecticut was always tumultuous, but it followed a pattern. There was a heatwave for about a week, and then a storm would hit with thunder that set off the car alarms on Achilla's block; a noise made doubly annoying to someone with her advanced hearing. Judging from the black clouds with a faint purple lining, this one might have thunder of that caliber. When the bus dropped her off in front of her gray apartment building, Achilla yawned and stretched her arms. Of course, that was her way of pretending to be distracted as she listened for any trails. So far, nobody followed her; or at least they kept their distance. Achilla shrugged her shoulders and walked inside.

When she entered her one bedroom apartment on the twentieth floor with black and cream decor, Achilla checked for any listening devices. The more she worked with the CIA, the less she trusted their respect for her privacy. She was their secret weapon, and they couldn't afford to lose sight of her. Still, Achilla needed her space, and her apartment was her sanctuary. The CIA would just have to wait until she checked into work the next morning like they would for any other agent. After searching every crevice of her apartment and finding nothing, Achilla kicked off her sneakers and strolled to the bathroom for a shower. Despite the old wives tale that showering during a storm was dangerous, Achilla was in no mood to wait. She needed to let off some steam, and going out was the perfect way to do it. If she got struck by lightning before that, well then it was just her time.

After her shower, Achilla threw on a red dress that she bought a few months ago for an undercover training exercise. She hooked up with her partner that night, and ever since then this dress was her secret weapon in the Hartford night scene. No man could resist it. Achilla threw on a pair of black, red bottom heels and walked out of her building to the sounds of people laughing as they strolled down the sidewalk. The pavement carried the scent of fresh rain as she strolled to the bar down the street knowing that CIA agents were most likely watching her. They knew her range of hearing and would stay out of it; spying her with binoculars and radar sensors if need be. When she found a fun guy, Achilla would give them something to report.

She gave the bouncer her fake ID, and walked inside as the big screen televisions that lined the wall behind the polished wood bar showed a baseball game. Achilla scanned the room for prospects until she found wide-backed, brown-skinned male in a teal button-down shirt drinking a beer as he leaned against the bar and watched the game. Achilla sauntered across the room, ignoring the stares from the other men. She stood next to her new beau and poked his shoulder with her index finger; taking extra care to be soft about it. The last time she poked too hard, the guy thought she was another man picking a fight and took a swing. The next morning, she had to explain to Agent Jones why she still belonged in the CIA after breaking a civilian's jaw.

When her new beau turned and faced her without any animosity, Achilla breathed a sigh of relief and smiled.

"Hey," Achilla said as she stood with her hands on her hips.

"Hello," the man said as he looked Achilla up and down before beckoning for the bartender.

"No," Achilla chuckled as she stepped closer, grabbed his wrist, and set his hand on the bar. "I don't want a drink. I want you to stay focused on me. What's your name?"

"Dhiraj," the man replied as he stood up and leaned on the counter with his elbow. "Yours?"

"You can call me Sikta," Achilla said as she caressed Dhiraj's hand with her thumb.

"So if you don't want a drink, I guess you want to talk a little?" Dhiraj asked.

"Not really," Achilla replied as she intertwined their fingers and squeezed her palm against his with one hand and pointed at the dance floor with another. "We're going to have a date. Right now."

"Wait a minute--"

"Hear me out," Achilla interrupted Dhiraj with a finger on his lips. "And if you have any questions beyond what I'm going to say, ask me after I'm done."

Dhiraj nodded his head.

"Good," Achilla said as a grin grew on her lips and she pointed with her free hand at the dance floor. "You're going to dance with me. If and after I've had a sufficiently good time, I'll take you back to my place."

Dhiraj nodded his head again.

"Now," Achilla said as she removed her finger. "Any questions?"

"Not anymore."

"Good," Achilla replied with a head nod as she led him toward the dance floor. "Oh, I love this song. Date starts now!"

When they reached the dance floor, Ray Jay's "Sexy Can I" blasted throughout the bar and Achilla smirked and pulled Dhiraj close by his belt. Dhiraj held her arms and she grabbed his face, leaning in close for a kiss before turning away at the last minute and backing into him; grinding between his legs. Achilla then craned her neck and kissed him on the lips. She spent the next three songs dancing with Dhiraj until their evening actually felt like a date; the kind of date Dahntay would've taken her on. She wondered how

Dahntay was doing for a split second before the third song ended. She hadn't seen him in four years, but she still thought about his smile. Achilla shook him out of her head, grabbed Dhiraj's hand, and led him out the door. It was time for some aggressive breeding.

The next morning, Achilla yawned and stretched under her black bed sheets before looking over at Dhiraj. She could tell by the dark window behind his head that it was exactly four in the morning. Like most of the men she slept with, Achilla was up long before him. She pouted before sliding her legs out of bed, leaving Dhiraj asleep on the other side.

If Achilla's father knew she was having one-night stands, he would blow his lid, and Achilla knew it wouldn't be because his daughter was sleeping around. It would be the way she picked up men, screwed them, and cast them aside just like Ailina. The thought of resembling a Harris in any way made Achilla scowl at herself as she stepped into a handstand. She then lifted one arm and split her legs before lifting them straight up and performing a set of one-handed handstand pushups. After hitting two hundred, she switched arms. When she finished her upper body morning workout, she hopped into the shower and threw on a pair of gray basketball shorts and a white t-shirt. She then tied her hair into a ponytail as she grabbed a bottle of water out of her refrigerator and stood in her living room watching her view of the city.

Hartford was a city divided. Even from her apartment window, Achilla could determine the wealthy areas from the poor. She could see robberies in progress and rival gangs fighting in the street. Other times, she watched socialites drive their fancy cars to high-class restaurants. Sometimes Achilla just wanted to change things. She wanted to give the homeless man the fancy car and throw the socialite on a street corner just to see how they would handle it. That thought left her head when she heard Dhiraj shift in bed in her room. He would probably wake up in another ten minutes or so. Achilla strolled into the kitchen and grabbed a carton of eggs from her fridge. The only positive to waking up earlier than her partners was watching the looks on their faces when they ate her special scrambled eggs with a side of turkey bacon.

Achilla ignored the steps she heard in the hallway. By now the serious clubbers were coming home so they could sleep all day, but she frowned when the steps arrived at her door and knocked. The only people who knew her address were CIA agents, and they usually didn't make house calls. Achilla opened a drawer next to her black oven, lifted the tray, and pulled out a hunting knife before tip-toeing to the door. When she looked in the peephole, Agent Jones stood in the hallway wearing a button down and jeans with a black blazer. His head was completely bald and shined under the hallway lights. Achilla giggled and opened the door wide, setting her knife on the kitchen counter.

"Aren't we fresh today," Achilla said with her eyebrows raised. "Did you have a breakfast date, or are you taking me on one?"

"No date,"Agent Jones replied. "But you'll like the gift I've brought you. I have a new assignment. A real one."

"Yes!" Achilla hissed as she pumped her first. "Now we're talk-ing. Let me get rid of my guest, and we can get started."

"I can come back at a better time," Agent Jones replied.

"Nope," Achilla said with a wave of her hand as she turned and walked in. "I've been waiting for this."

"Don't you think it'll be awkward?" Agent Jones asked.

"No, this'll be easy," Achilla said. "But I need you to step into the hall."

Agent Jones stepped away from the doorway. Achilla smiled and nodded her head before speed-walking into the bedroom. She pulled her hair out of the ponytail and mussed it around her shoul-ders. She then found Dhiraj's clothes and kicked them into a pile in front of the bed. When Achilla was ready, she stood in front of the man in her bed and cleared her throat before she began.

"Hey, get up," Achilla said in a hurried voice as she shook him awake. "My boyfriend's coming up the stairs! Get up! Oh my God! Oh my God!"

"Boy…friend?" Dhiraj asked as he opened his eyes. "You never mentioned--"

"I didn't think he'd be home so early!" Achilla replied as she paced the room. "He didn't tell me he got out today!"

"Got out?"

"Prison!" Achilla snapped. "Look, I'm wrong, but there's no reason for you to get hurt because of me! You need to go!"

"But wait--"

"Now!" Achilla said as she pulled him out of bed, shoved his clothes in his chest, and pushed him out of the room. He struggled to put his shirt on as she pushed him toward the door. By the time he reached the hallway, he ran on his own in his boxers. Achilla looked both ways and noticed Agent Jones was gone. She frowned at first and lowered her head when she heard movement in her living room.

"You shouldn't do that," Achilla said before closing her door and turning around. "What if he saw you?"

"After that line?" Agent Jones chuckled as he strolled into the kitchen behind her. "Not a chance. If you told me that, all I would see was the door. I wonder if Mrs. Johnson would've approved of that little story."

"I do a lot of things she wouldn't approve of," Achilla sighed as she opened her refrigerator. "For example, lying to my family about joining the Marines."

"Fair enough," Agent Jones replied with a raised hand. "I'll back off."

"What's the assignment?" Achilla asked as she sat at the table with a bottle of water. "Where am I going?"

"It's in-state--"

"Seriously?"

"Hold on," Agent Jones said. "We'll be sending you to New Haven. We need information from a man named Roberto Gabrielli. His friends call him Blue Eyes."

"Criminal defense attorney?" Achilla asked before taking a swig of water.

"You know who he is?"

"Yeah," Achilla said. "He was a classmate of my dad's. They never speak, and anything my dad had to say about him was negative: immoral, money hungry, doesn't care about his clients, stuff like that."

"Well Brendan's right," Agent Jones said. "But he missed an important detail. We have reason to believe that Blue Eyes is involved in an international sex-trafficking ring shipping girls from all over the U.S. to Brazil. He's a United States contact, and if you look at his file, you'll notice that the majority of his clients as of late have been charged with sex trafficking under-aged girls. We think his clients are also his coworkers."

Achilla's free hand clenched into a fist but kept her eyes trained on Agent Jones as she fought the urge to ask for Blue Eyes' address so she could find him and give him a much deserved corporal punishment.

"There's no telling how lucrative this business is," Agent Jones said. "There's also no telling how far they'll go to keep it a secret. You could be killed. My higher-ups aren't happy about this assignment, but I pushed for it."

"Why would you do that?" Achilla asked.

"We brought you in to stop Ailina," Agent Jones said. "This guy might be just as dangerous to your father as she is. How could you handle her if you can't handle him?"

"That's fair," Achilla said with a shrug.

"You're going to be a real estate agent from Los Angeles looking to get her feet wet with a sale," Agent Jones said. "Specifically the home of one of Blue Eyes' clients, Mayor Berger. From there, you'll have to find a way to get close to him. How good is your L.A. accent?"

"Hella proficient," Achilla replied with a grin.

"Achilla, I grew up in L.A.," Agent Jones replied. "Please don't use the words 'hella' and 'proficient' in the same sentence."

"Got it," Achilla said. "Anything else I should know?"

"If you can, sneak in and out with no casualties," Agent Jones said. "If you can't, we doubt anybody will actually miss Blue Eyes all that much. He's the descendant of New Haven mobsters and apparently wants to keep up the tradition. After years of working the kind of criminal defense that police officers hate, no one's going to lead a serious manhunt for him if they suspect he's dead."

"You're telling me to kill him if need be?" Achilla asked.

"Only if need be," Agent Jones replied. "I'm also telling you to make it quick and clean."

"I don't think the higher-ups would approve of that," Achilla said with a frown.

"Then they won't know," said Agent Jones. "Anything goes bad, I'm your superior anyway. I'll take the fall."

"Understood," Achilla said. "When do we start?"

"You start in three days," Agent Jones said as he rose from the table. "Good luck."

"Wait," Achilla blurted as he made his way toward the door.

Agent Jones looked at Achilla and raised his eyebrows.

"Well, um, do you want some scrambled eggs and turkey bacon for the road?" Achilla asked with a smile as she pointed at the carton of eggs next to the stove. "It's my specialty, and I was going to make it anyway."

"For your guest, correct?" Agent Jones replied. "The guy you just kicked out?"

"Well, yeah," Achilla replied. "But he's gone now. No reason why you can't have some, right?"

"No thanks, Achilla," Agent Jones said before reaching for the doorknob. "Contact me when you've gathered enough intel to meet Blue Eyes. I know you'll do well."

Achilla swallowed hard as Agent Jones left her apartment. Why couldn't that man relax and have some food for once? Why did he always have to be so professional all the time? Whatever. Achilla would just have to eat his share too. If he changed his mind, he was just too damn late. After wolfing down ten eggs and twelve slices of turkey bacon, Achilla tried to wash her plate but snapped it in half by accident. She sighed and shook her head as she threw it out and ambled around her kitchen.

This was it. Achilla had her first serious assignment. She took a deep breath and leaned against her kitchen counter as she recounted her own qualifications: trained in nine martial arts, surgical with handguns and sniper rifles, fluent in five languages and conversant in six. Achilla was more ready for espionage and combat than anyone ten years her senior. But as her heart beat out of her chest, Achilla didn't feel ready. She had never killed a man before despite coming close as a teenager. She had no doubt in her mind that she would be able to take a life, but would she be able to stop? Or will she get one step closer to becoming as sick as Ailina? Achilla walked into her bedroom and opened her nightstand drawer. Inside was her .22 caliber Glock pistol equipped with a silencer and six cartridges. She took another deep breath as she loaded her gun.

Preparation begins now.

Chapter Two

ACHILLA JOHNSON: 10

Trigonometry, Spanish, Portuguese, Physiology, those were the subjects Achilla studied on a daily basis for eight hours a day. She read the vocabulary, listened to the tapes, watched the videos, practiced in the mirror, and learned them all. When she wasn't studying, she was training: pushups, body squats, handstand pushups, chin ups, pullups, calf raises. If it made her strong, Achilla had to learn it and do it. But of all the subjects she had to learn, fighting was the easiest. Sure, she could watch more videos and practice her punches and kicks, but sparring was when she really absorbed the information.

Nothing teaches you better than pain. That's what Achilla learned most of all since she was five years old. When mistakes hurt, you don't make them too often. When hesitation hurts, you strike fast. No video, no book, no pamphlet, and no tape could compete with pain. So as Achilla stood in her basement wearing gray sweatpants and a green sweatshirt, she prepared herself. She took deep breaths and wiggled her toes on the cold concrete as she waited. Pain was coming. It always did.

Achilla heard footsteps dashing toward her and ducked without opening her eyes. She slipped to the right and the left as she felt the air shift around her head. She listened for the signs that her opponent was on the attack: keys jingling, clothes shifting, feet sliding. Achilla ducked and sidestepped with each sound until a lightning bolt struck her right side. Achilla gasped and opened her eyes before cringing and falling to the floor as her body curled into the fetal position.

An olive-skinned woman with green eyes wearing a white blouse with suspenders and gray pants stood over Achilla and curled her lip before kicking her in the gut, making Achilla grit her teeth. This was the pain Achilla learned from every day, and Ailina Harris was the source.

She was also her mother.

"Who told you to open your eyes?" Ailina asked. "Close them and find your way up."

Achilla forced her eyes shut right before another blow hit her chest and rocked her whole body. She sobbed and coughed until she felt Ailina yanking her hair. She screamed and a blow struck her mouth.

"No crying," Ailina snarled. "No weakness! You will not cry in front of me!"

Achilla pushed Ailina's hand away and blocked a punch aimed at her gut before rolling away and hopping to her feet with her hands raised and her eyes closed. She huffed and licked sweat from her lips, but she fought the tears as her hands trembled.

"Good," Ailina said. "Open your eyes."

Achilla opened them but kept her hands raised as she eyed Ailina standing across the room. When Ailina stalked forward, Achilla stepped back, but when she blinked, Ailina darted in front of her and kneed her gut; lifting Achilla's feet off the ground. Achilla grunted, but she forced herself to not cry. Instead, she pushed Ailina's knee away and sidestepped before throwing a kick. Ailina blocked, grabbed her leg and threw her across the basement, slamming her against a wall.

"I have company tonight," Ailina said as she walked up to

Achilla. "We're done for now, but you've improved your reaction timing. That's good."

Ailina kicked Achilla's gut again, and Achilla cried out and coughed.

"Your pain tolerance is another story," Ailina said. "I'm going upstairs to change. Clean yourself up. Your dinner will be on the table by the time you're out of the shower. You will have exactly fifteen minutes to eat. Understood?"

"Yes, ma'am," Achilla replied as Ailina walked upstairs. She leaned against the wall and pushed herself to her feet before taking a break, wincing from the throbbing throughout her midsection. Achilla didn't let her get her face this time. Next time she had to protect her body more.

Pain taught her that lesson.

Achilla made her way up the steps and ambled down the hall to her room with white walls, a twin-sized bed with red bedsheets, a wooden dresser, and an attached bathroom. Achilla's room was her quiet place. Ailina never knocked and never walked in, and Achilla had her bed and shower all to herself as long as she was up by five in the morning every day to start cleaning and cooking. No cleaning and cooking meant more pain.

But in her room, she was safe. Achilla smiled as she closed her door behind her and dragged her feet past her dresser to the bathroom. After her five-minute shower, Achilla wiped fog away from her mirror as she stared at her green eyes. They looked so much like Ailina's, but something was different about them. They didn't make her look at the floor and tremble. Achilla sighed and walked out of the bathroom to change into a pair of long, red basketball shorts and an oversized black t-shirt Ailina gave her a couple weeks back. She walked down the hall to the yellow linoleum-floored kitchen with white countertops where Ailina was waiting in a black, strapless dress. Ailina applied lip gloss and checked a pocket mirror as Achilla sat down in front of a t-bone steak and a steaming pile of vegetables. The glass next to it was a protein shake and next to that a bottle of water.

"You know the drill," Ailina said without looking up from her mirror. "I need you to eat before my company arrives so chop chop."

Achilla grabbed her fork and knife and cut the steak into small pieces before tossing the bone into the trash. She then wolfed down the vegetables and meat, taking the precious few seconds she had to enjoy the seasoning.

"I gave you fifteen minutes, Achilla," Ailina sighed. "Not thirty seconds. Protein can't fuel your body if you don't digest it properly. Chew it."

Achilla slowed down.

"Good," Ailina said. "Now that you've hit puberty, I'm going to intensify your regimen and increase your food intake. Your body will take care of the rest, but we need to work on your mental and emotional strength. Too much crying."

Achilla nodded her head as she chewed.

"I suppose it's good you entered puberty so early," Ailina sighed as she examined herself in the pocket mirror and flipped her hair. "The faster your body develops, the faster you'll get strong. I just worry you might get distracted by boys, but I can take care of that. By the way, no males in this house unless they're guests of mine. Are we clear?"

"Yes, ma'am," Achilla said before eating her last morsel of food and swigging down her protein shake. The chocolate flavor was the only one that tasted decent. Achilla then opened her bottle of water and chugged as she watched Ailina play with her hair and kiss at herself in the pocket mirror.

"What are you staring at?" Ailina asked.

"Sorry," Achilla said.

"I didn't ask for an apology," Ailina barked as she snapped her mirror shut. "I asked what you were staring at."

"It's just that…"

"Fucking spit it out," Ailina said with a hard stare that made Achilla look at her plate.

"You look pretty," Achilla muttered before glancing at Ailina. "Your hair's really nice too."

Ailing shrugged and reopened her mirror.

"Thanks," Ailina said. "When you get older, I'll teach you how to do this. Just the basics. After that, you're on your own."

Achilla suppressed her smile as she studied Ailina's rouged cheeks and pink lips. Maybe if she learned how to use makeup as well as her she could hide the bruises. But why did Ailina wear so much? She didn't have any cuts or bumps on her face.

"Can I ask a question?" Achilla muttered again.

"You already have," Ailina said. "Might as well ask two."

"Why do you wear makeup?" Achilla asked.

Ailing frowned before setting the pocket mirror in her purse on the floor. She leaned back and crossed her legs, flipping her hair before looking Achilla in the eye. Achilla breathed a sigh of relief. On some days, Ailina answered the wrong question with a punch in the eye.

"It helps me meet your next father," Ailina said. "I usually don't need it, but this next guy has a lot of potential. Hopefully, he can replace your real father."

Ailina stared off across the room as she scowled.

"That asshole," Ailina said. "Leaves me with a kid and doesn't even send a damn birthday card. Have you seen a birthday card?"

"No, ma'am," Achilla replied.

"Not a penny of child support," Ailina said. "Your father doesn't give a shit about you, Achilla. Remember that. He's rich lawyer, but he's still a fucking deadbeat bastard. Maybe this guy will be better. Fingers crossed."

Ailina raised her fingers and crossed them with a grin. Achilla raised hers and crossed them as well. Both of their faces changed when Achilla heard a car pull into their driveway.

"That's him," Ailina said as she stood up and marched across the kitchen in her heels, exposing defined calves under her dress. "Room. Now."

Achilla hopped out of her chair and jogged down the hall to her room. She crawled onto her bed as she heard Ailina open the front door. She always did that when company arrived. Achilla wondered why she never let them ring the doorbell. When she heard a deep voice walk into the house, Achilla pulled her knees to her chest and closed her eyes. Then the usual happened. They laughed, joked, ate, and then walked to Ailina's bedroom. Achilla scratched her head when she heard Ailina's bed knocking and the moans and grunts echoing through the house. She did this with every man she brought over, and every night it ended the same. Achilla waited and counted down the seconds.

She sighed when a crash rang out from the hallway. This was the part when they argued, Ailina beat him down and physically threw him out of the house, and then Ailina grabbed a glass of wine and complained about Achilla's father again. Achilla waited, but she didn't throw him out. Maybe this guy was different.

"Achilla, come out here," Ailina called. "Now."

Achilla frowned and hopped off the bed before opening her door. She walked down the hall and past the kitchen to their living room where Ailina stood in a black, short, see-through chemise that barely made it to her thighs. Achilla wasn't used to seeing Ailina dressed like that. She flinched when Ailina kicked a black male with a short haircut in the ribs. She then stomped on his head, holding him still as he winced. Achilla examined his muscular body, turning her head away when she realized he was naked.

"Look at him," Ailina snapped. "You'll see it eventually. Might as well look now."

Achilla forced herself to look at the man.

"Good," Ailina said. "Achilla, this asshole was supposed to be your next father, but apparently, he's decided to renege on our agreement."

"I never said that," the man said. "Man, I said I wanted to meet your kid. I didn't say nothing about taking care of her."

"Well, this is fucking news to me," Ailina growled as she yanked his ear. "And it's news to my daughter. Achilla, come here."

Achilla stepped forward.

"Kick him," Ailina said as she pointed at the man under her foot. "He's just like your asshole of a father."

Achilla frowned until Ailina backhanded her face so hard Achilla's cheek burned.

"Do as I say!" Ailina roared. "Kick him!"

Achilla swung her hips into a kick to the man's gut, making him grunt and cough.

"Again," Ailina said as she flipped him onto his back. "Go for the liver."

Achilla kicked his right side, and the man cried out and curled into a ball. Ailina forced him to lie straight and straddled his chest.

"You don't get to do what you want in here," Ailina said. "And you don't get to go back on your word. You will give me what I want, and what I want is what we agreed."

"Look, I can't be a father," the man cried out. "I'm sorry, Ailina. What do you want me to say?"

Ailina glared at the man before glancing at Achilla.

"Achilla, go back to your room," Ailina said as she stood up. "It's time he and I went for a ride."

Achilla waited in her room for an hour before walking back out to get a glass of water. She saw Ailina wearing a dark blue t-shirt and jeans while sitting at the kitchen table again with a bottle of wine and noticed her fingertips were red. When Ailina poured white wine into her glass, Achilla frowned. Ailina gulped down her wine before glaring at Achilla.

"What?" Ailina asked. "You think you can judge me? He deserved it."

"No," Achilla replied with her hands raised. "I don't--"

"You know you're just like me, right?" Ailina asked. "He was inferior to us and forgot his place. I need you to learn that you're above men like him and your father. They must learn the order of things or suffer the consequences. Do you understand?"

"Yes, ma'am," Achilla said.

"Go to bed," Ailina said. "You have an early morning tomorrow."

Achilla ambled back to her room and closed the door behind her. She sighed and threw herself onto her bed. Ailina wouldn't bother her in here. Nobody spoke to her in here. Achilla's room was her quiet place. No pain allowed until tomorrow.

Chapter Three

ACHILLA JOHNSON:20

Achilla researched Roberto "Blue Eyes" Gabrielli and found that he was a direct descendant of the late William "Billy" Grasso; a New Haven mobster who was notorious for his cruelty in the seventies and eighties. Unlike Grasso, Blue Eyes had no criminal record; not officially. Achilla found a couple assault and battery charges as a minor. At sixteen, he was arrested for sexual assault, but he was never charged despite the mountain of evidence against him. His record was expunged when he turned eighteen and remained spotless ever since.

Despite his felonious streak in high school, Blue Eyes was brilliant. He maintained a 4.0 GPA at Hopkins School; a prestigious private school in New Haven. He then earned a full ride to Albertus Magnus where he posted straight A's for two semesters before transferring to Connecticut College. There his GPA dropped to 3.9. Still, a perfect LSAT earned him a scholarship to Yale Law School.

Though it had nothing to do with her assignment, Achilla looked into when he met her father. They were assigned to the same section and held the top two GPAs of their class. Achilla smiled with giddy pride when she saw that Brendan was first, and maintained that ranking for the rest of law school. No matter how smart Blue Eyes may have thought he was, he couldn't compare to Achilla's dad. Her instincts told her that he probably knew that, and that was the real reason they didn't get along.

He couldn't compare to Achilla's father, but Blue Eyes still maintained stellar grades and landed some juicy internships for his resumé; the Federal Defender Program, The Public Defender, and a few big-time law firms, including his father's, Gabrielli & Baldino. Gabrielli & Baldino was an international law firm in New Haven that specialized in business law, civil litigation, and criminal defense; white collar or not. All through law school, and as an associate for Gabrielli & Baldino, Blue Eyes stayed above the law and most of his competition until he made partner. Blue Eyes' record in court was stellar, but of course, he didn't win nearly as many not-guilties as Brendan. Achilla had no doubt that he noticed that as well. She wondered if her father ever realized how much Blue Eyes most likely envied him; perhaps even hated him. Achilla concluded that he must have.

After Blue Eyes made partner, a few blips of fraud and malpractice popped up, but nothing substantial. Blue Eyes was too well connected to ever get punished for anything. Achilla looked up the crowds he associated with. They were mobsters, politicians, judges, and big-time lawyers from across the country; New York, Boston, Philadelphia, Kansas City, Chicago, Seattle, and Salt Lake City to name a few. Achilla remembered spying on a party held by one of the rich kids from boarding school who had ties to a similar crowd. He rented a hotel room and then filled it with beer, wine, shots of tequila, and a slalom of cocaine. Throw in the ecstasy pills that he handed out to the girls, and there was enough evidence there to send him to prison for life. Instead, Achilla reported what she saw to her superiors and they used it to turn him into an informant. If that kid had access to all that, Achilla could only imagine what Blue Eyes, an attorney who was required to keep his business confidential, could get with a simple phone call. He most likely had enough secrets in his head to shut down most of New Haven's criminal and political element.

Normally, Blues Eyes was the FBI's problem. The Feds knew he was involved in illegal activity, and they always sent undercover agents to investigate every corner of his life, but geniuses of his kind are always too paranoid to fall for that. Blue Eyes paid so much attention to detail that every file was in perfect order, and he made it a point to cooperate with the Feds when they openly questioned him. Even when they arrested him and charged him, he always escaped indictment. Blue Eyes had yet to set foot in a courtroom as a defendant in a real trial. Achilla frowned at that. Beating that many cases on the federal level was unheard of.

Of course, it was Achilla's job to change that situation. The CIA had just tied him to a terrorist in Brazil known only as Xerxes. Nobody knew his true identity, or why he was called Xerxes, but that name constantly came up in connection with international crimes such as murder, weapons dealing, and sex trafficking. In the United States, the defendants to these allegations were often Blue Eyes' clients. The CIA noticed that they were Blue Eyes' clients a little too often. There might have been a connection, and that connection could lead to a physical identification of Xerxes who somehow managed to stay hidden. Blue Eyes was the missing link that the CIA needed to take Xerxes down.

Infiltrating Blue Eyes' law firm was Achilla's first task. If she could get a hold of some confidential records exposing his clients as his coworkers in Xerxes' operation, she could figure out their next move, intercept it, stop it, and find Xerxes. That meant getting close to Blue Eyes. In order to do that, she had to learn his every move. She could not afford to make any mistakes about his routine. One mistimed step and the mission was over, and countless innocent children would go unsaved from a life of involuntary prostitution and slave labor.

No pressure.

Achilla wasted no time with her surveillance. She followed Blue Eyes from his firm Downtown to his blue and white, three-story colonial home in Woodbridge; a wealthy suburb west of New Haven. Achilla made sure to use a different car every day when she followed him to work. Sometimes she didn't use a car at all. Being a Nephilim with stronger senses than any police dog opened up options that no paranoid criminal would expect. She watched from the tops of trees three blocks away. She listened as she lay down in the woods down the street. As a result, she learned that he had a wife and three daughters that he never mentioned in the papers and who he never brought to court to watch his trials or even to company parties. Like a smart lawyer/thug, he kept his family away from his business, but he couldn't keep them away from Achilla's eavesdropping.

According to Achilla's research, Blue Eyes' wife, Daniela Gabrielli, was a former waitress at Pepe's on New Haven's Wooster Street. She also modeled to pay for school until she got her bachelor's in nursing at Southern Connecticut State University. Now she was a stay-at-home mom with blonde hair, blue eyes, and perfect measurements. She was as Stepford as a wife could get but not nearly as faithful. Achilla watched the house a few times when Blue Eyes was at work and the kids were away. Juan, her private personal trainer, was giving her one hell of a work out five times a week, and it involved a lot more than stretching and plyometrics. Achilla couldn't help but snicker every time Juan visited on Blue Eyes' dime.

The girls were more innocent. They all attended Hopkins' School; the youngest in seventh grade and the oldest in ninth. Lorien was the oldest; a tall, rail-thin blonde who sang in the choir at mass every Sunday and routinely joined talent shows and singing competitions and won most of them. Jenna was the youngest; every bit as blonde but nowhere near as vocally inclined. She played soccer for Hopkins but needed lots of individual coaching from what Achilla observed at one of her summer league games. There were moments when Achilla literally wanted to march on the field, grab her by the arm, and force her into the right position. She settled for muttering "God, you suck" under her breath.

The middle child, Esther, was Achilla's favorite. She was a natural blonde who dyed her hair jet black and only wore jeans and sneakers. Achilla heard countless arguments between her and Daniela over how she dressed like one of those "ghetto black girls". Esther would then leave her mother fuming in the kitchen as she hitched a ride for AAU basketball practice. Achilla doubted that Roberto and Daniela were aware that Esther had a rather dark-skinned Puerto Rican boyfriend from the Tre neighborhood who waited for her after practice and watched her games; during which she averaged around thirty points a contest.

Achilla did some surveillance in the Tre whenever Esther visited her boyfriend. Though there was a heavy presence of Tre Bloods, nobody bothered her as long as her boyfriend was around and they held hands as they sat on his porch or played basketball in his drive-way. Esther always let him win. Judging from his lack of talent, allowing him to score was probably a greater challenge than beating him.

Achilla wondered if Esther would ever come clean about her relationship. Sure, her boyfriend was nice enough and showed no evidence of gang affiliation, but even Achilla's parents would be alarmed if their children were hanging out in a gang territory. Still, Esther smiled and played in the Tre so much you would never guess the Feds were investigating her boyfriend's neighbors. Achilla stopped wondering when one of Daniela's and Esther's arguments was more passionate than usual.

"Esther, if your father found out, he would strangle you!" Daniela shouted. "I won't tell him if you stop now. Just stop."

"No!"

"Esther, your father--!"

"I don't care!" Esther shrieked. "Why is it such a big deal?"

"These ghetto people are below you!" Daniela snapped. "Why would you ever--"

"You don't even know him!" Esther shot back. "He's nice to me, and he cares about me, and you don't see that because he's Puerto Rican!"

"It's not his race," Daniela said. "That boy is not safe to be around."

"Oh, bullshit, Ma!" Esther screamed. "He runs track and plays on his school's chess team for Christ sake! Besides, Dad's family isn't exactly the boy scouts of fucking America, so don't tell me about picking the right crowd!"

"Watch your language in this house!"

"Why? You and Dad swear at us all the time!"

"This is my house," Daniela yelled. "I can speak any way I want."

"Your house?" Esther shot back. "Yeah, like you pay any of the bills!"

"Esther, you will listen to your mother!"

That argument lasted an hour before Esther stormed off to her room. Later that night, Blue Eyes came home and Daniela told him the news. He marched to Esther's room and screamed a lot louder than Daniela with a voice nearly as strong as Brendan's, but with no love in it. When Brendan yelled at Achilla during her childhood, there was authority and direction; sometimes mixed with concern. Achilla noticed that Blue Eyes' screams were about control and nothing more, the way Ailina's sounded when Achilla was a little girl. That lack of love was probably the reason Esther yelled back until the rest of the family rushed toward their location.

Achilla listened from her sedan down the street and jolted when she heard a smack ring out of the house. She then heard Esther scream just before another slap popped through Achilla's ears. She heard Daniela and her other two daughters sobbing while the slapping continued. Blue Eyes cursed and Esther wailed with each blow. After hearing a lamp crash on the floor, Achilla jumped out of her car and marched toward the house as she pulled out her cell phone.

"Yeah?" Agent Jones answered.

"I need the green light," Achilla said as she held the phone with a trembling hand.

"For what?"

"To engage Blue Eyes," Achilla growled. "He is beating that little girl--"

"Easy, Achilla--"

"She can't defend herself--"

"Stay. On. Task."

"He's nothing but a fucking punk," Achilla snapped with blood-shot eyes. "He's only doing it because she can't make him stop! I'll make him stop if nobody else will! I'll fuck his ass up!"

"NO!" Agent Jones commanded. "No green light! Right now, your role is surveillance. You will stay put and monitor him. That's all."

Achilla stopped in the middle of the street and held her free fist at her side. Her body shook as she listened to the beating that echoed from the Gabrielli household. She knew that only she could hear it. Those walls were too thick for normal human hearing, but every slap and punch tugged at her ears as if Blue Eyes knew she was listening. Each smack and thud was a clear invitation, begging Achilla to snap his neck. Achilla clenched her eyes shut as Esther's cries and pleas filled her head.

"Calm down, Achilla," Agent Jones said. "I know it's tough for you."

"She's defenseless," Achilla replied as her eyes watered. "Someone has to help her."

"You can't help her right now."

"Then someone has to make him pay!" Achilla snarled.

"When the time is right, and we have him, you can hit him where it hurts by destroying everything he has," Agent Jones said with a low voice. "Don't get derailed from your assignment. Keep your emotions in check. Come on, you're stronger than this."

"So we just sit back and do nothing?" Achilla demanded. "I thought we were on the side of the children; of innocent girls like her."

"Achilla, that's enough," Agent Jones stated with a fatherly edge to his voice. "You're making this about yourself."

"How the hell am I--?"

"She isn't you, Achilla," Agent Jones said. "And Blue Eyes isn't Ailina. Strike now, and other little girls will get hurt way worse than her. Do you want your past to ruin someone else's life? Use your head."

Achilla clenched her eyes shut when Blue Eyes smacked his daughter again. Her body tensed at the thought of grabbing him by his tie and clocking him one good time. It wouldn't take much. Achilla was strong enough to knock him unconscious with a simple tap to the temple. Still, she knew that if Blue Eyes saw her face now, the mission was over. Achilla relaxed her body and took deep breaths; breaths that still skipped whenever she heard Blue Eyes strike again.

"Fine, but I want him all to myself when this is over," Achilla replied as she snapped her phone shut, took a deep breath and walked back to the car. She sat in the driver's seat as she listened to Blue Eyes hitting his daughter until she heard Daniela finally speak up.

"Stop!" Daniela sobbed. "Don't hit my baby anymore! She's sorry! She's sorry, Roberto!"

Achilla crossed her arms and tapped her foot as the urge to strangle Daniela surged through her veins. It didn't make sense to beg someone to stop abusing your family; not to Achilla. She wouldn't have begged. No, she would've made him stop and then made him apologize. After that, she would've made him beg for mercy. Achilla crossed her arms and bit her thumb at the thought of Agent Jones leaving her alone with Blue Eyes for just a few minutes. He would never touch Esther again.

The hitting stopped and Achilla breathed a sigh of relief.

"You should thank your mother," Blue Eyes huffed. "Go on."

"Thank you," Esther muttered.

"And you tell that boy it's over," Blue Eyes said. "No daughter of mine..."

"Yes, sir," Esther replied through her sniffling as Achilla heard Blue Eyes' leather shoes march into their kitchen. Achilla halfway hoped that he was getting her a bag of ice. He didn't. Instead, he asked Daniela what was for dinner, and the family ate in silence, except for Esther. From what Achilla could hear, she never moved from where Blue Eyes left her until the rest of the family went to bed. She then shuffled to her feet and ambled into the kitchen where she fixed her own plate. After that, she crept up the stairs and closed her bedroom door. Achilla wiped her tears away before walking back to her car.

For the next few days, no more Puerto Rican boyfriend and no more visits to the Tre. Esther sulked to practice and sulked back home with only a bruise on her face and a scratch under her eye to keep her company; both of which Blue Eyes explained away when a school administrator called. He told them that she fell in the driveway playing basketball and that these darn kids always get hurt. Achilla scoffed at how they just accepted his answer and hung up the phone. She knew those phone calls were just a formality. Blue Eyes was so connected that they would listen to anything he told them or suffer the consequences in the form of lawsuits, terminations, blackballing, and lost pensions.

The following week, Esther's hair was blonde and her striking resemblance to her sisters became more apparent; as was the difference in her demeanor. Her sisters always smiled and kissed their father on the cheek when he came home and asked him how his day went. Esther just stayed in her room and only came out for dinner. When Achilla watched Blue Eyes try to kiss her goodbye before she left for her next game, Esther pecked him on the cheek and darted off to Daniela's car. Achilla could tell from the cold glare in her eyes that they were filled with the unreleased anger and bitterness of someone who had her individuality beaten out of her. Achilla knew that look well. It was the look Achilla held as a child when she stared in her bathroom mirror in Ailina's house before she licked her wounds every night. The sight of it in a girl so young and innocent made her heart drop to her sneakers, and the very thought of Blue Eyes' grin made Achilla clench her fist so tight that her fingernails dug into her palms.

Achilla wanted to hit Blue Eyes so bad it kept her up at night. She had dreams about cornering him in an alley and grabbing his throat or breaking into his bedroom, dragging him out of bed, and stomping his spine in half in front of his wife. One night, she tossed and turned until she rolled out of bed and held her chest as her heart pounded and sweat broke on her forehead. This urge to maim and humiliate the man she watched abuse and disrespect his family over and over made her tremble as she paced her apartment.

She needed an outlet, so Achilla wandered to the roof of her building where she normally worked out. On top of running throughout the city at night, Achilla created her own mini-gym on the rooftop with a heavy bag, weights, and a pull-up bar. Tonight, she shadowboxed around the roof, side-stepping the weight machines as if they were the trees, trash cans, buildings, and other obstacles she would encounter in a real fight. She then approached her heavy bag and she exhaled with each punch and kick, maintaining perfect balance and form. She grunted as she pictured Blue Eyes' face squishing from the impact of each blow as the bag swung and rattled. The urge to hurt Blue Eyes wouldn't subside, so she punched and kicked until daylight crept out onto the horizon. Achilla stared at her hands, clenching and releasing them and seeing no signs of exhaustion after punching for six straight hours. She then watched the sunrise over the city before she wiped her forehead and went back inside. She had learned something new about her body and her mind. Achilla wasn't quite sure if she liked her discovery.

Daniela and the girls left to visit her mother in Syracuse for a couple weeks before they started school. Work prevented Blue Eyes from leaving, and Achilla watched him wave goodbye as the four blonde ladies of his house piled into their black sedan and drove off. For the next three weeks, Achilla watched him bring home nine different women from bars Downtown; all of them as stunning as his wife. They were also all black women with skin tones ranging from sandy brown to midnight. The hypocrisy of the moans echoing from his upstairs bedroom made Achilla want to kick down his door, but she forced herself to stay put. He and Daniela, they were like male and female versions of each other; hating people of color unless they had the opportunity to use them for their own pleasures. The urge to strangle them both pushed beads of sweat out of Achilla's pores as she listened to Blue Eyes adulteries. Fortunately, Blue Eyes' flings never lasted long. When the women left Blue

Eyes' home, Achilla snapped pictures from the top of an oak tree down the street.

Achilla frowned when she noticed something else about Blue Eyes' women. Yes, they were all women of color. They were also tall and kept themselves in good shape, evidenced by their toned legs and flat stomachs. No wonder the CIA agreed to select Achilla for this mission. Every genius was paranoid, but no one was without a vice, and Achilla had the perfect complexion and body to get close to Blue Eyes in a way that he would never make public. Achilla sucked her teeth and shook her head. It would've been nice if she was informed of this part of the plan before she started.

When Achilla was ready to move forward to the next stage, she contacted Agent Jones to meet on her rooftop and emailed him the photos. The next day as she finished her six hundredth one-handed pull-ups, she heard the roof door slam behind her. Achilla grunted into a triple somersault over the bar, landed on her feet, and stretched her arms as she paced the roof wearing a two hundred pound weighted vest over her sleeveless shirt. She saw Agent Jones shake his head and chuckle at her, and she cracked a smile.

"I don't think I'll ever get used to seeing that," Agent Jones said. "I don't think I'd believe it if someone described it to me."

Achilla struggled to contain her laughter. Compliments from Agent Jones were about as rare as his apologies, and they always made her shuffle her feet as a grin grew on her lips.

"Thanks," Achilla said as she wiped a strand of hair from her face. "I have to find a secret place to work out or fans like you might take pictures."

"The CIA has facilities, Achilla," Agent Jones replied. "Facilities with top-secret clearance."

"I prefer my freedom," Achilla said. "Besides, do you know how many heavy bags I used to destroy a week? If I didn't keep this special one from home, I'd buy a new one every day; which means the CIA would have to buy me a new one every day."

"Point taken," Agent Jones sighed. "I hope Blue Eyes is alive enough for us to learn something about him."

"Of course," Achilla replied with a nod of her head. "I stayed on task."

"And what have you found?"

"I know Blue Eyes like the back of my hand," Achilla said with a shrug. "But I need to know him better. Nothing I've found ties him to Xerxes yet. I'll have to meet him and turn him into an informant."

"That's not easy for a first-timer," Agent Jones replied as he adjusted his navy blue tie. "Lawyers have a sharp eye for manipulation; especially defense attorneys."

"Maybe," Achilla replied. "But I get the feeling I have an unfair advantage. Did you know Blue Eyes had a thing for black girls?"

"I suspected," Agent Jones said as he looked down and flicked dust from his gray t-shirt. "Most bigots do when no one's looking."

"Nice to know I'm being objectified," Achilla said while raising her nose.

"Achilla, it's the name of the game," Agent Jones replied. "I've been assigned missions where I had to use my race to get close to a target too. It's called using what you have. Come on, if you had to play a potential victim to stop a sex trafficker, wouldn't you do it?"

"I suppose," Achilla said with her hands on her hips. "I'm not expected to sleep with him, am I?"

"I've slept with targets," Agent Jones replied.

"That was not my question," Achilla barked as she pointed at the floor. "And you know it."

"Do whatever you have to," Agent Jones said. "Sometimes what you do on a regular basis can help shape the effectiveness of--"

"That's got to be the most subtle way of calling me a slut that I've ever heard," Achilla snapped. "You guys really do watch my every move! Look, what I do in my personal time is none of your damn business. If you want me to fight Ailina for you, you will respect that."

"It's not that simple--"

"And for your information, I won't be sleeping with anyone unless I want to," Achilla continued as she turned her back on Agent Jones. "And the only way I'm touching that man's crotch is if

I'm punching it! There are other ways to get information, and I'm not the CIA's hooker. Let's get that straight."

"I don't care how you get the information we need," Agent Jones said. "Just get it. That's all."

Achilla glared at Agent Jones before she paced the rooftop. There he went worrying about the mission and nothing else. No consideration for how she might've felt about getting set up as a sexual object. Nope, she just had to grin and bear it because it was the name of the game. Achilla looked out at her view of the city and let out an exaggerated sigh.

"What's wrong?" Agent Jones asked. "Look, I didn't say you were required to screw the guy, but if your physical appearance gets you close--"

"Something about Blue Eyes bugs me," Achilla cut him off before he said something else that would tempt her to punch a hole in his face. "He reminds me of Ailina. He thinks he's so…superior. People like him have no problem doing some pretty terrible things. I almost attacked him before we got any intel. I don't know how much longer I'll last before I hurt him, or worse."

"Taking a life isn't easy to deal with the first time around," Agent Jones said. "Especially for someone with no law enforcement experience. It should only be a last resort."

"I understand that," Achilla replied before turning and facing Agent Jones with her head low. "It's just that he has three daughters; one of them…she's a good kid. She just doesn't really fit in, but if I kill her father and take away her resources, I'm afraid it'll mess her up."

"I understand that you don't want to ruin the lives of the inno-cent people connected to him," Agent Jones replied. "But that was a choice that he made. Try this perspective. Despite having three little girls, he still chooses to take other people's daughters and sell them as sex slaves. He's an attorney who makes more money than ninety percent of the men his age in New Haven. He had other options, but he chose to victimize innocent children. You're right to associate him with Ailina. If he dies and leaves his family to struggle, it's his fault, not yours."

"You may think I'm soft for saying this," Achilla said as she looked Agent Jones in the eye. "But I want his girls taken care of if Blue Eyes dies. Look my biological mother was horrible to me when I was a kid, but I had someone to take me in. They should at least have that; especially Esther. I'd ask my mom to do it, but I know it isn't safe. Let's just make sure they have a good home after this."

"I don't think that's soft at all," Agent Jones replied. "I think it's humane. What about his wife?"

"Jury's out on her," Achilla replied with a shrug. "Children don't see a whole lot. Adults see what they want to. For all I know, she might not care what he does as long as the check arrives. The fact that she's having an affair tells me all I need to know about her real feelings for him anyway. He's a bank account and nothing more."

"Love isn't that simple," Agent Jones said. "I don't expect someone so young to know that."

"Love is real simple," Achilla retorted. "And I don't expect a jaded spy to see that. Blue Eyes needs Daniela to be his trophy and fulfill whatever fantasies he has for himself. Daniela needs Blue Eyes for financial security and a reason to brag to her girlfriends about what her husband buys her. Neither of those reasons has anything to do with love. They have a marriage of means and social status. That's all."

"You know that for sure?" Agent Jones chuckled. "You haven't said anything that any other cynical young person couldn't think of."

"It's not cynicism" Achilla snapped. "It's accurate intel. When Blue Eyes is at work, they never call or text each other. Never. Blue Eyes just focuses on his work. Daniela works out, screws her trainer, and watches T.V. until she picks the girls up from school or practice. Blue Eyes calls his girlfriends, meets them after work, and then comes home late. Daniela never questions him. She doesn't even ask how his day went. They literally spend over twelve hours a day not talking and then they act like roommates. They don't even have sex. Their marriage is like a business. They only talk about the bills and their next vacation. Do you know who does talk to Blue Eyes?"

"Who?" Agent Jones sighed.

"His little girls," Achilla said. "They ask him how work went. They ask him about his next trial. Well, they all used to. Esther doesn't anymore, but I can understand why."

"The girl he beat up," Agent Jones added. "Got it."

"Yes," Achilla hissed. "The only love in that house is coming from the children, and if Blue Eyes keeps abusing them, even that will fade too. God, it's like he's grooming them to be like his selfish, status-grabbing, money-grubbing, piss-poor excuse for a wife. I want those kids out of there when this is over. I don't care what happens to Blue Eyes or Daniela. Satisfied?"

Agent Jones crossed his arms and paced the roof. He looked up at Achilla momentarily before lowering his head and furrowing his brow. Achilla wiped a strand of hair from her face as she watched him. The last time he paced like this, it was after her bar fight fiasco. Did she mess up again?

"You sound emotionally invested," Agent Jones said with his hands on his hips as he stared out at the city.

"Is that a bad thing?" Achilla replied. "I mean you asked me a question."

"Not when it's based on that much knowledge," Agent Jones said as he turned to walk inside. "You're more ready for this assignment than I anticipated. You'll be staying in New Haven for the duration. Your hotel reservation, driver's license, and passport are all in your mailbox downstairs. Your name will be Terri Blake. Understood?"

"Got it," said Achilla as she walked toward her pull-up bar.

"Oh, and Achilla."

"Yeah," Achilla replied just as she jumped up and grabbed the bar to finish her next set of six hundred on her right arm.

"You may want to call your father."

"What happened?" Achilla asked as she dropped to the ground and whirled around to face Agent Jones' back.

"Nothing," Agent Jones replied as he opened the door. "You just haven't called him in over a month. Once you start this assignment, you won't be able to contact your family for an extended period of time. Just a little advice. Considering what you've just told me, it might be nice to hear from a more positive family environment."

"Thanks?" Achilla said with a frown. "If I didn't know any better, I'd suspect that you were a family man; or at least used to be."

"Used to be," Agent Jones replied. "Long story."

"You don't say much about yourself," Achilla muttered. "But you know everything about me, even more than I know."

"I've researched you," Agent Jones replied.

"And I've done my own research on you," Achilla said she stepped toward him. "You're authoritative with a hard exterior, but I'm not fooled."

"What does that mean?" Agent Jones asked with a frown.

"It means you and my little brother have a lot in common," Achilla replied as she set a hand on Agent Jones' shoulder. "I'm not a teenage girl anymore. I can handle adult things, and you don't have to shield them from me. If you need someone to talk to, I've got you."

"I've got it covered, Achilla," Agent Jones said as he removed Achilla's hand. He then turned his back and walked toward the door.

"The lone soldier," Achilla sighed. "You don't need my help. Or maybe that's because you already have some? What's her name?"

Agent Jones looked back at Achilla before walking through the door and slamming it shut. She forgot to add that he was evasive. Achilla shrugged and strolled across the roof to her phone sitting on top of her gym bag. She sat cross-legged on the ground as she called her father's cell phone number. It only rang once before he picked up.

"Well, it's about time," Brendan said. "I was starting to wonder if you lost your phone or broke your fingers."

"Hey, Dad," Achilla replied. "I know it's been a while. How are you?"

"Good and busy," Brendan said with a tired expression. "But you know how that is. Clients need representation."

"And you're the man for the job," Achilla said as she smiled at the fact that he didn't mention money despite the fact that he was without question making plenty of it.

"You know I am," Brendan chuckled. "How're the Marines?"

"Oh," Achilla sighed as she crossed her arms. "It's good."

"That didn't sound good."

"Yeah, well, it's a little boring," Achilla replied with a cringe at the thought of maintaining her cover. "The only good thing about it is the hot men."

"Oh, is there a boyfriend in the picture?" Brendan asked.

"No," Achilla said. "You know I don't do boyfriends anymore."

"Oh boy, you're at that phase," Brendan said with a chuckle.

"It's not a phase, Dad," Achilla replied. "It's a conscious decision. My work doesn't give me much time for a relationship. It's just not a priority right now."

"Achilla, that's a phase if I've ever heard one," Brendan replied. "Hell, even I used that line before I met your mother."

Achilla paused and frowned.

"I meant Sam," Brendan said with a deadpan tone as if he could see her face. "Look, if there's anything I know it's that there's always time for someone. It's hard doing this thing on your own. You've got to have somebody in your corner."

"Well, I doubt I'll find someone like that anytime soon," Achilla muttered.

"Sure you will," Brendan replied. "I don't know when, but you will. We all do. The key is not to pass that person up when you meet him. That's where a lot of us screw up. I didn't pass Sam up, and look at our lives now."

Dahntay's smile filled Achilla's brain until she shook it out.

"I...I just need to focus on work right now," Achilla stammered.

"Achilla, when are you going to learn to live for yourself?" Brendan asked. "You're always checking on us or teaching your brother something. What about you? I just want you to be happy, and it's sounding like you're not. All I'm saying is, you know, start doing what makes you feel good."

"It's not that simple," Achilla said as she looked at the ground and rubbed her thigh with her free hand.

"Yes it is--"

"So how's Mom doing?" Achilla asked.

"You always change the subject when something makes you uncomfortable," Brendan said with a slight snarl. "Why can't you see that I'm just trying to help you?"

"And you always let things drag on when they don't have to," Achilla snapped. "I won't be bringing home any boyfriends anytime soon. I won't be getting married. I won't be having your grandkids. I'm just not one of those people who gets to do that. Sorry to burst your bubble, but don't get any ideas. Now can we drop the subject or do you plan on preaching some more?"

There was silence on the other end of the phone. Achilla sighed and stared at the sky. For as long as she had known him, she had never spoken to Brendan that way. Perhaps Agent Jones was right about her emotional investment.

"Sorry," Achilla said. "That was a poor choice of words."

"Your mother's doing fine," Brendan replied. "She just got an award for best teacher, and she's getting her principal's license."

"Sounds like she's busy too," Achilla said with a lump in her throat. "She's doing well for herself."

"She is," Brendan said. "And I couldn't be any prouder of her. You know your brother's going to Duke."

"That's good," Achilla said with a smile.

"Yeah, we hoped he would stay closer to home," Brendan sighed. "But it's up to him."

"Got to leave the nest sometime," Achilla replied. "I'll try to catch his games."

"Good," Brendan said. "Look, I have to go. It was nice hearing from you."

"You too," Achilla moused as she stared at the floor. "Again, I'm sorry. It's been a while since we spoke and I just let you have it. My emotions got the best of me. "

"It's all right," Brendan chuckled. "Stress'll do that to you. You should hear how I talk to my interns before a trial. I wonder if I'll have to pay for their therapy one day. Hey, I love you."

"I love you too, Dad."

"Before I go," Brendan said. "I want you to know something."

"Yeah?"

"No matter what you do," Brendan said. "You're more than your job, Achilla. Don't forget who you are. That's all I want for you."

"Thanks, Dad," Achilla said with a smile. "I'll keep that in mind."

"That's my girl," Brendan replied. "I'm so proud of you it's crazy. Hey, don't forget to call your mom she should be getting out of school."

"I will," Achilla said before they hung up. She then dialed her mom's phone. She took a little longer to pick up than Brendan.

"Achilla, hey!" Sam said. "Girl, how've you been?"

"Good," Achilla laughed. "You sound so happy!"

"Girl, I am on cloud nine," Sam replied. "I just came out of a meeting with the superintendent. We're going to add a brand-new curriculum across all Bridgeport Public Schools, and I'm so excited! That's enough about me. How're the Marines?"

"It's...fine."

"Well, it doesn't sound like you enjoy it, honey," Sam said. "Do you pray on it?"

Achilla rolled her eyes. She should've known Sam would say that. Prayer was her answer to everything that she couldn't figure out. Meanwhile, Achilla hadn't attended a church service in over four years. Outside of her knowledge of religions for the purposes of her work, spirituality was foreign to her, and the idea of praying to someone for answers that she believed she could figure out on her own sounded so weak that it sent a chill up her spine.

"I'll take that silence as a no," Sam said. "And that's just fine. Just take five minutes out of your day. God has everything else. He doesn't need much from you."

"I can give it a shot," Achilla replied.

"We need one of you to start praying," Sam said. "I think Samuel's a little lost. He's going all the way to Duke."

"Why is that a problem?" Achilla asked. "Duke's one of the best schools and basketball programs in the country. It practically has a pipeline to the NBA."

"We want him close to home," Sam said. "College isn't easy without your family supporting you. Trust me."

"Yeah, but he can call you just like I'm doing right now," Achilla replied with her arms crossed.

"But we know you can take care of yourself," Sam said in a hushed tone. "We want him close. You know, in case she shows up."

"I see," Achilla sighed as she scrambled to think of a way to reassure her without exposing her deal with the CIA. "You know, Ailina can't dictate your life. If she wants to hurt you, she'll hurt you regardless of what you do. So you might as well live your lives as if she doesn't exist. You can't let her bully you into hovering over your son."

"Hm, maybe you're right," Sam said.

"Besides, Dad tells me you're doing big things," Achilla said. "Why not let your son do big things too? Not everyone gets to play for Coach K, and as a 6-foot-2 combo guard, his system fits Samuel perfectly. I know. I trained him."

"I believe it," Sam sighed. "I can't wait until you finish your term. We'll have so much to talk about. Is there an address where I can send you some food?"

"No address yet, Mom," Achilla said. "When we stay at a base for a little longer, they'll tell us where you can mail the stuff."

"Sounds good," Sam replied. "Well, I have to run to another meeting. You have a good one and stay safe."

"You too, Mom."

"Love you."

"Love you too."

Achilla hung up the phone and stared out at the Hartford skyline as she rose to her feet. Agent Jones was right. Hearing from her family cleared her mind a little bit. She watched the horizon turn pinkish-orange and felt a cool breeze massage her hair. The high rises Downtown weren't much taller than her apartment building, but they blocked out the setting sun just the same. Still, the sunset was always astonishing to watch from up here. While the sky turned deep red, Achilla crossed her arms as she walked the rooftop and contemplated her next move.

How could she get close to a man who lived the American dream? Blue Eyes was a senior partner who had the perfect wife and three perfect kids who lived in the proverbial white house with a picket fence. He had constructed an image of himself that even the FBI couldn't dismantle with the right family, the right home, the right cars, and he lived in the right neighborhood. He was every-thing that American culture loved and accepted. Destroying that façade would take years; maybe a lifetime.

To the outside world, Blue Eyes looked as good as Brendan Johnson, but he wasn't. Achilla knew from the moment she saw her first photo of him that he was bad news, and her observations confirmed her belief. No matter how much he smiled, no matter how much he kissed his children, his eyes gave him away. He didn't have warm eyes like Brendan and Sam. He didn't have cheerful, naïve, bright eyes like Samuel, whose pupils shined like brown light bulbs whenever he smiled. No, Blue Eyes had the same frigid orbs in his head as Ailina; eyes that Achilla grew up fearing as a child. Those eyes committed malpractice and escaped punishment. Those eyes helped criminals and corporations steal money from people who could barely make ends meet. Those eyes cheated on his family with reckless abandon. Those eyes beat the hell out of his own daughter. Achilla had a feeling that those eyes also helped traffickers kidnap innocent children and send them into slavery, and she wanted nothing more than to gouge them out. As she walked toward the door, she stopped and stared at the setting sun for a moment. It glared back at her like a parent expecting a trained response. Achilla sighed.

"Fine, look, I don't know what good this would do," Achilla said. "But I pray tomorrow will be productive."

The sun continued to stare at her. Achilla crossed her arms and looked away before walking toward her heavy bag.

"And I also pray that my family will be safe," Achilla said. "Though I'm pretty sure I can take care of that myself, you never know what can happen. Make sure my family's safe. I don't care about much else. As for Blue Eyes..."

Achilla exhaled hard as she threw her weight into a sidekick. Her leg popped off the bag with perfect form and snap, and it burst open like it had been stabbed with a sword; releasing steel ball bearings that littered the rooftop floor. As the chain that held the bag crumbled and fell, Achilla flexed her leg before strolling toward the door. Tomorrow she would meet Blue Eyes, and just like that bag, he wouldn't know what hit him until it was too late. He was finished.

"Amen," Achilla snarled before walking inside and slamming the door shut.

Chapter Four

ACHILLA JOHNSON: 11

Ailina didn't find Achilla a new father. Based on her dating streak over the past year, she wasn't even trying anymore. Take the man home, sleep with him, kick him out, that was her thing now, and Achilla stopped crossing her fingers. Achilla didn't know much about marriage outside of the legal definition and how often it leads to divorce, but she knew Ailina wasn't getting married. If only her real father had just stuck around...

Who and where was he anyway? Ailina had no photos in the house outside of her police academy graduation and a family portrait with her as a little girl, a tiny tan-skinned woman and a massive, barrel-chested white male with olive skin like Ailina's. Achilla waited until she was away at work to check the house. There was no sign that Achilla's father even existed outside of her own reflection, but Achilla gathered some clues.

Achilla's father was definitely dark. She had brown skin, a flatter nose, and coarser hair than Ailina, just like the men Ailina always brought over for her one-night affairs. That meant Ailina was attracted to black men, so why wouldn't she get pregnant by one? Achilla knew if she saw her father, he would have dark skin, but since they lived in Bridgeport, that didn't narrow down her search very much. For all Achilla knew, her father could be the postman or her next door neighbor. Maybe the next door neighbor. The postman actually stopped by.

Achilla's father made a lot of money. All of the men Ailina brought over the house showed signs of wealth: fancy watches, clean wing-tipped shoes, big rings, expensive sneakers, savory colognes. Achilla heard a few of them mention their jobs. They worked in insurance, education, even Wall Street. So it stood to reason that Ailina liked dark men with money.

Achilla's father must have been tall and muscular. No man Ailina brought home stood under six feet, and they all looked like they trained as hard as Achilla. Yet whenever Ailina asked Achilla to hit one of them, they were so *weak*. One hit and they fell to their knees. What made them so fragile even with all those big muscles? Was Achilla's father this weak too? She hoped not.

At around midnight, Achilla walked out of her room in gray pajama pants and a white t-shirt making sure to walk with soft steps so as not to wake up Ailina. She frowned when she saw a man standing in their living room in front of the door wearing a black tank top and dark blue jeans. When he turned and saw her, he jumped before holding his hand on his chest.

"Shit," he whispered. "You walk as quiet as your mother."

"Why are you still here?" Achilla whispered. "Didn't she kick you out?"

"Nah," the man replied. "Look, we didn't want to do it like this, but I've been seeing your mother for a while now, and we love each other. She says your father isn't around, but I can be here for you."

Achilla frowned as the man smiled and kneeled in front of her. He looked and smelled like he just got his waved hair shaped up, and his goatee was perfect. He wasn't her real father, but maybe he would do for now. The man nodded his head at Achilla before standing up and walking past her into the kitchen. Achilla heard rustling, and he returned with a white plastic bag.

"Look, between you and me," he whispered while maintaining

his smile. "I know who your father is. I played against him in college, and you look just like him."

Achilla covered her mouth as tears welled up in her eyes.

"What's his name?" Achilla asked.

"Now I have to respect Ailina's wishes," the man continued as he reached into the bag. "But she didn't say anything about giving clues."

Achilla grabbed the man and pinned him against the door. Tears streamed down her face as he cringed, and she yanked him closer.

"No clues," Achilla growled. "His *name!*"

"Hey!"

Achilla looked over her shoulder and saw Ailina standing behind them with her arms crossed over her green t-shirt. She scratched herself inside her gray thigh-high shorts before rubbing her eyes and walking toward them.

"I'm sorry," Achilla said. "I--"

"Want something, and he's playing games," Ailina snapped. "Don't give me an apology. Make him talk."

"What?" the man blurted.

"Answer her question, or she'll beat you," Ailina said before nodding at Achilla. "He has ten seconds to learn his place."

"Ailina, I thought we were cool," the man said. "I thought--"

Achilla cupped his throat, making him gag. He coughed until he nodded his head.

"Brendan," he said with a breaking voice as tears streamed down his face. "Damn, man…"

"Get out," Ailina snapped as she pushed Achilla aside and grabbed the man. She opened the door and dragged him by his shirt onto the porch. When she stepped in and closed the door behind her, she picked up the white bag and pulled out a video cassette case with basketball players on it. When she opened it, forms fell out. Achilla picked them up and saw that they were registration forms for a basketball league in two months. At the top, the forms read: "Johnson Law Group Presents: Ball for Bridgeport's Kids."

"Fucking asshole can afford to organize this, but he can't send a check?" Ailina growled.

Achilla kept a straight face as she handed Ailina the forms. So his last name was Johnson?

Brendan. Johnson.

Achilla raised her hand to speak.

"What is it, Achilla?" Ailina snapped as she read the forms.

"I like basketball," Achilla said.

"Thanks for sharing," Ailina replied with rolling eyes.

"Can I play in the league?" Achilla asked.

Ailina cocked her eyebrow at Achilla before punching her gut. Achilla grunted and fell to the floor. Then she gritted her teeth and forced herself to stand. No tears this time. She just raised her chin and looked Ailina in the eye.

"Seems you've developed the mental toughness I'm looking for," Ailina said. "And sports will only help your competitive spirit. Sure, kid. You can play on one condition."

"Yes, ma'am."

"You are not to go near your father," Ailina said. "I will speak to him first. He's done nothing for you. He doesn't deserve you. Understand?"

"Yes, ma'am," Achilla muttered.

"Go to bed," Ailina said. "You have an early morning."

Achilla turned on her heels and strolled to her room, making sure not to show her smile until she closed her door. The next morning, she cleaned the house with a spring in her step and finished her chores early. Then she popped in the video and watched the basketball clips in the living room. After watching it three times, Achilla mimicked Michael Jordan's shooting form, then his footwork, then his defensive stance. Then she frowned as she stood in her living room with her hands on her hips.

She needed a ball.

Achilla jogged down the hall to the basement door and bounded down the steps in two leaps before searching every box and plastic container. When she found an orange men's basketball, Achilla raised it over her head and laughed until she squeezed it flat.

Air.

The ball needed air.

Achilla dug through more boxes, throwing them across the room. She found a red hand pump and squealed before poking it into the basketball and pushing the handle. She pumped and pumped and pumped until the ball was full. Achilla laughed and bounced the ball on the floor, but it rocketed into the ceiling. She caught it and bounced softer. Then she switched hands.

An hour later, Achilla practiced all the moves she learned from Michael Jordan. They were a lot harder with an actual ball in her hands, but they weren't impossible. Next, Achilla needed a hoop. She sulked when she realized there was no hoop in their basement. Achilla knew there was a hoop somewhere outside, but she wasn't allowed to leave the house without Ailina. So Achilla hung her head and cleaned up the basement before carrying the ball and pump up the steps. She looked at the kitchen clock and noticed Ailina wouldn't be home from work for approximately four hours.

It shouldn't take that long to look for a hoop.

Achilla grinned and jogged to the front door, but she hesitated and shuddered at the thought of what Ailina might do if she caught her outside. But Achilla wanted to play basketball, and she wanted her father to see her shoot like Michael Jordan. Achilla took a deep breath and opened the door, stepping onto the porch. She looked to her right and left as cars passed by and kids walked down the sidewalk past her house. Achilla walked off the porch and looked up her driveway.

There stood a basketball hoop with a glass backboard.

Achilla bounced the ball twice and held it like Michael Jordan: feet shoulder width, shooting hand under, guide hand on the side. Then she pushed the ball with her right hand and flicked her wrist. It sailed through the air and into the hoop. Achilla jumped and pumped her fist before running to pick up the rolling ball. She grabbed her ball and whirled around when she heard footsteps in the driveway. A dark brown-skinned boy with cornrows wearing a sleeveless black shirt, black shorts, and black sneakers approached. He smiled, exposing braces. Achilla didn't smile back.

"Yo, you made that?" the boy asked. "That was like NBA range."

Achilla frowned and shook her head. What was so special about that?

"Shoot it again," the boy said. "I bet you can't do it again."

Achilla scowled before shaking her head and carrying her ball to the other end of the driveway. She shot the ball again, and it was nothing but net.

"Oh, shit!" the boy said with a laugh. "What school do you play for?"

"I don't play for a school," Achilla said.

"You should," the boy replied. "What school do you go to?"

"I'm homeschooled," Achilla said before pointing at her hoop. "I play here."

"I'll put money on it if our girls coach sees you, she'll pick you up," the boy said. "What's your name?"

"Achilla."

"Tyron," the boy said. "Harding High School."

"I might be a little young for your school," Achilla said. "I'm only eleven."

"What?" Tyron replied as he stepped back. "You look mad old for your age. I would've thought you were like fifteen or something. Look, man...let's do this. One-on-one."

"I'm sorry?" Achilla asked with a frown as Tyron marched around her and stood in a defensive position between her and the hoop.

"First one to eleven," Tyron said.

"Oh," Achilla replied with a shrug. "Sure."

Achilla shot the ball again and it sailed through the hoop. Tyron jogged back and grabbed the ball. He passed it to her, and she turned to shoot.

"Wait!" Tyron yelled before laughing. "Nah, you have to pass it back. That's checking the ball."

Achilla passed it back and Tyron swung the ball around before dribbling right. Achilla followed him until she looked up, and he was gone. When she looked behind her, he was already shooting the ball.

It bounced off the rim into Achilla's hands and she shot it off the backboard into the hoop.

"Your defense needs work," Tyron said. "You can't guard a crossover. You can shoot though."

"I can too guard a crossover!" Achilla snapped as she adopted a defensive position. Tyron dribbled and faked left, but Achilla didn't budge. He faked right, and she held her ground. So Tyron dribbled past her and whipped the ball back, but Achilla stayed in front of him, holding her forearm against his side like Michael Jordan did in those videos. When Tyron grunted from the contact, she reached for the ball and took it.

"How the hell are you that strong, man?" Tyron asked. "Ah, that shit hurt."

"Maybe you're just weak," Achilla said. "Inferior."

"I can bench my body weight," Tyron replied as he looked her in the eye. "Nothing's weak about me."

"Can you do this?" Achilla asked as she flipped into a handstand and busted out three handstand clap pushups. "How many?"

Tyron stared at her and shook his head. Achilla grinned and flipped to her feet, kneeling as she watched him dribble.

"You're pretty good at that,"Achilla said as she pointed at the ball. "Better than me right now, but that's because I just started. Give me a month, and I'll show you. I can do this better than you."

"You real cocky," Tyron replied with a chuckle.

"She's superior," Ailina said from behind, making Achilla gasp as she turned around and saw her standing in a black business suit and white blouse. "Afternoon, kids. Achilla, who's our guest?"

"Um…"

"Tyron, Miss," Tyron said as he approached and extended his hand. "Tyron Higgins."

"Would you happen to be Jared Higgins' son?" Ailina replied as she shook his hand.

"Yeah," Tryon said with a frown. "You know my dad?"

"Yes, I do," Ailina said. "I'm the reason he's in prison."

Tyron flinched before his lower lip quivered and tears streamed down his face. He stepped back as he wiped his face, but he stopped and dropped the ball as he sobbed. Achilla frowned and look at Ailina. If she broke down and cried like that, she would get a beating for it. Why was he doing it? Why show so much weakness?

"That was you?" Tyron asked before he glared at Ailina. "My father can't walk anymore! He didn't even do anything! Why'd you do that to him?"

"Tell your father I said hello next time you visit," Ailina said with a smile as she waved her fingers. "But Achilla isn't allowed to have guests without my permission, so I need you to leave for now."

Tyron looked at Achilla and shook his head before jogging away. Achilla watched him run until Ailina blocked her view of him and picked up the ball.

"Found it, huh?" Ailina sighed as she bounced the ball and shot it.

Nothing but net.

"I...I'm sorry," Achilla said. "I know you said--"

"Inside," Ailina said. "Now."

Achilla's hands trembled as she walked with her head lowered past Ailina onto the porch. She looked behind her and noticed Ailina didn't follow, but she heard her bouncing the ball and shooting it again. Achilla stepped inside and sat on the couch. What was Tyron talking about? Did Ailina paralyze his father, and why? Achilla knew Ailina was a detective, but she didn't know much else about her work. Achilla shook her head. She was curious, but she didn't want to ask and incur her wrath.

When Achilla stood up to walk to her room, she heard the front door open and saw Ailina stepping inside. She threw the ball at Achilla's head, and she ducked. Ailina then darted forward and uppercut her face, sending Achilla flying onto her back. Achilla tried to stand, but Ailina stomped her gut, pinning her to the floor.

"I told you no boys without my approval," Ailina growled. "Did you really think I was going to let you slide?"

Achilla grunted and coughed as Ailina straddled her and punched her in the head. When Achilla covered her face with her forearms, Ailina ripped them down and pounded on her cheekbones. Achilla whimpered at first, and she wondered what she did to deserve this. It was just a boy. They weren't even doing anything, not like Ailina and her boyfriends. Couldn't she stop hitting her long enough to understand that?

Then she wondered where her father was.

Could he stop her?

No, he couldn't. He was too *weak*.

Achilla had to do it. She had to save herself. She growled and grabbed Ailina's arm. Ailina frowned and shook her arm, but Achilla gritted her teeth as she squeezed. It wasn't much, but it stopped the hitting. Ailina grinned, lifted her off the floor, and slammed her down, knocking the wind out of her. Achilla coughed and rolled on her stomach, and Ailina stomped her back.

"You've improved," Ailina said as she stepped over Achilla and walked down the hall to her room. "Good. I was worried that boy rubbed off on you. Clean yourself up. I have company in a couple hours."

Achilla glared at Ailina's door just as she closed it. She then forced herself to her feet. After catching her breath, she lifted her shirt and checked her midsection. She had fewer bruises than usual. She was also able to walk better than before. Achilla tapped her cheekbone and winced from the sharp sting. Nothing a shower and some alcohol couldn't fix. She could do this. She could survive this. She didn't need her father. He wasn't going to save her anyway.

Chapter Five

ACHILLA JOHNSON:20

Saturday morning cartoons. For the next two weeks, Achilla lived as Terri Blake, the real estate agent from Los Angeles who earned her Juris Doctor from Stanford University and just got her Connecticut real estate license. As Terri Blake, Achilla walked around New Haven asking questions about the market; what was hot, what was not. Like a method actor, Achilla thought like Terri Blake, walked like Terri Blake, spoke like Terri Blake, and even ate like Terri Blake(vegetarian). The only part of her life that she held onto to maintain her true self in the privacy of her hotel room was Saturday morning cartoons. They were actually old DVDs that Agent Jones sent her before she got started, but they still served their purpose. Achilla's favorite was the entire DVD collection of Dragonball Z; though she couldn't understand why the characters took so long to fight. She loved Android 18; a female fighter capable of dismantling one of the strongest characters in the series.

Every morning after watching an hour of cartoons, Achilla worked out in her hotel room before reviewing the data on her black laptop. So far, she learned that Gabrielli & Baldino went to trial an average of 4 times a year and seldom lost. Their clients included drug dealers, high-ranking gang leaders, union officials, CEOs, and politicians. Even now they were involved in litigation that made the Hartford Courant. New Haven's Mayor, Jon Berger, was arrested and charged with possessing and distributing child pornography. Berger resigned from his seat and hired Blue Eyes to personally oversee his defense. Rumors that Berger planned on leaving New Haven prompted Achilla to visit him. Perhaps Terri Blake could help him sell his new home.

Achilla hopped into her rented black sedan and drove out to Berger's four-floor brick home in New Haven's Westville Village; a well-to-do section of New Haven that neighbored Woodbridge. Berger's street in Westville was especially wealthy with plush green lawns, three-floor(minimum) homes, and driveways occupied by cars that cost no less than a college education. It was just as rich as Blue Eyes' neighborhood but without the woodsy suburban feel. Surveillance there was a little more difficult to pull off.

Luckily, she didn't have to wait long before Berger's red Lamborghini pulled into his brick driveway. Achilla sighed, checked her makeup in the mirror and adjusted her black skirt suit and white blouse. She then frowned as she twisted her feet into her black heels. She seldom saw the need to wear a dress and heels unless she was going out to pick up a guy, and even that wasn't always required. Still, she understood that this blouse and skirt served a purpose just the same. Achilla fought the urge to bust out a pair of sneakers as she stepped out of the car, closed the door, and strolled across the street. As a white male with grayish brown, but perfectly styled, hair wearing a black suit and gold tie stepped out, Achilla waved her hand.

"Mayor Berger!" Achilla called out as she trotted across the street. "Mayor Berger, can I speak to you for a minute?"

"No comment," Berger replied with a wave of his hand as Achilla stood in front of him.

"I'm not a reporter," Achilla said as she smiled and extended her card. "I'm a real estate agent. Terri Blake."

"How can I help you, Ms. Blake?" Berger asked with a smile and eye contact that reeked of forced sincerity.

"I hear you're moving," Achilla said. "I'd like to help you expedite that process."

"How did you hear that?"

"Everybody knows about it," Achilla said with a shrug. "I'm sorry about your situation, Mayor--"

"Mr.," Berger replied. "I've resigned. No need to flatter me."

"Mr. Berger," Achilla continued. "I'm here to help."

"This card says that you're from L.A.," Berger said with a cocked eyebrow. "What brings you to New Haven?"

"Business," Achilla said with a smile. "I believe New Haven has a bright future, and I want to be a part of helping it grow."

"You talk a good game," Berger said with a nod. "You should run for mayor in my stead. Come inside. I'd rather we talk where reporters can't see and take pictures. God only knows what they'll say when they see me in the company of a pretty woman in her twenties such as yourself."

"Considering the circumstances, my presence might help you," Achilla replied, and she clamped her hand over her mouth as Berger stared at her. "Sorry. Bad joke."

"I like you already," Berger said with a chuckle. "Come on in."

The image of Blue Eyes bringing home so many stray women flashed in Achilla's mind as she followed Berger into his house. No doubt someone as wealthy as Berger also had his fair share of female visitors, and they likely did not want to leave once they entered. The foyer, the staircase, the kitchen, everything was deep mahogany. His refrigerator was the silver titanium exception. Achilla sat at the kitchen table as Mr. Berger grabbed a bottle of red wine from a cabinet just left of the fridge. He poured himself a glass and offered her one.

"No thank you," Achilla said with a raised hand. "One year sober."

"I commend you," Berger replied as he sat at the table with a glass of wine. "Perhaps you shouldn't run for mayor. It'll send you right back to the bottle."

"I've never been the political sort anyway," Achilla said. "Selling houses is just as hard but lacks the public scrutiny. I applaud you for sticking it out so long."

"Again the flattery is unnecessary," Berger replied. "The truth is I should've quit a long time ago."

"I'm sorry to hear that you feel that way," Achilla said with a slight pout. "Well, on the bright side, I can help you get rid of this house and move on with your life."

"That I can agree with," Berger said before taking a sip. "So how much do you think my house is worth? Based on first impressions of course."

"Right to the nitty gritty," Achilla said with a slight laugh. "I haven't seen the entire home, but considering the property value alone in this neighborhood, you're raking in a cool three million. Of course with bottles of wine that expensive lying around, you probably have a lot of accessories that raise the value of your home. Make that three and a half."

"I bought this home for one million," Berger said. "And you're telling me that it tripled in value in this market?"

"Yes," Achilla said. "Political affiliation tends to raise the value of a home; especially when you're surrounded by other public officials, and Yale professors here and the next town over."

"Political scandal tends to lower it," Berger replied. "Especially when everyone knows you want to skip town. If a newcomer from California found that out so quickly, then I don't have much leverage in negotiations. Since you're the only real estate agent to bother speaking to me about it, I'll hire you, but I determine the price. We'll go two million to start with the expectation that we'll have to go way down."

"Mr. Berger, with all due respect--"

"Look, you're new," Berger said as he pointed down at the table. "I know this city. I know its political machine and its real estate market. I can help you get your feet wet, but it'll have to be on my terms. Two million."

"You really want to leave," Achilla said with a frown.

"You think Los Angeles is rough?" Berger asked with a strained stare at his glass of wine. "Try Connecticut politics. It'll make you do things that'll keep you up at night; make you ignore things you shouldn't. All of it, for what? To be the mayor of a city of people who already expect you to fail them."

"So you're telling me that you're done with politics for good?" Achilla asked.

"I'm telling you that politics out here will make you hate the human race more than you ever thought possible," Berger said as his eyes turned red. "You won't believe the things these people will do; the things they'll make you do for the sake of a political agenda. If you don't follow the program, you're run out of town. Or worse."

"Understood," Achilla replied with her hands up in submission. "You know this place better than I. Two million it is. I'll set up a sign and--"

"No sign," Berger said with curt tone. "We'll keep this under wraps as much as possible for both our sakes."

Achilla suppressed her grin. She had a feeling he would want everything kept secret. If she pushed him, he might tell her to consult his attorney. That would give her the ticket inside that she was looking for. Achilla leaned forward on the table and intertwined her fingers.

"Mr. Berger, how can I help you sell your house?" Achilla asked. "People have to know it's for sale before they buy it."

"Speak to my attorney," Berger said. "His name is Roberto Gabrielli at Gabrielli & Baldino Downtown. Senior Partner. Send him the price, and he'll instruct you from there."

"Isn't he the criminal defense attorney working on your trial?" Achilla asked.

"Yes," Berger replied with a frown. "You really are quite informed."

"What does he know about real estate, Mr. Berger?"

"I trust him to keep this confidential," Berger said with a wink as he took another sip of wine.

"Again, Mr. Berger, with all due respect," Achilla said. "I don't think that confidentiality is the issue. It's unethical for an attorney to advise you on an area of the law in which he has no expertise. As a real estate attorney myself I--"

"Like I told you," Berger said with a slight raise of his hand. "I know how the political machine works in New Haven. I know how to get things done around here. You don't. Not yet. But you will. Please, for now, just send him the price at two million."

"Sure," Achilla said as she stood up and extended her hand. "I'll see what I can do, Mr. Berger."

"Thank you, Ms. Blake," Berger replied as he shook her hand. "I think you have a bright future in New Haven."

"I certainly hope so," Achilla said with a smile before walking out the door. As she walked to her car, Achilla sighed and stared at the house. It didn't take a genius to figure out what just happened. He low balled the price and had her send it to his attorney. He was trading real estate for Blue Eyes' services; most likely because he was running out of money. Still, there was something odd about his insistence on her going, even if it worked in favor of her mission. Achilla stepped into her car and checked her face in the mirror again. Her cell phone vibrated. It was Agent Jones.

"What?" Achilla asked as she picked up.

"How's the market?"

"Not bad," Achilla said. "I have a potential buyer; a big lawyer at this firm Downtown. I'm running over right now."

"Good."

Achilla hung up her phone and drove to Gabrielli & Baldino. It was located in a gray building with glass windows on the corner of Church Street and Elm Street; right across from the green. Typical of New Haven, it took Achilla about twenty minutes of driving around one-way streets until she found a parking space two blocks away. She walked inside the building, and the receptionist sent her to the twelfth floor. When she stepped out of the elevator, Achilla stepped into an office with all glass doors and windows. Everything was so transparent that she could see the receptionist, the conference room behind her, and the view of New Haven Green from the conference room window. She took a deep breath as she stepped forward and opened the first door. The red-haired receptionist wearing a red, sleeveless dress gave Achilla the evil eye before forcing a smile.

"How may I help you?" she asked with forced friendliness.

"Good morning," Achilla replied in kind. "I'm looking for Mr. Gabrielli. His client, Mr. Berger, sent me to speak with him."

"Regarding what may I ask?" the receptionist asked with a smile and slight squint. "Mr. Gabrielli's a very busy man and may not have time."

"Regarding Mr. Berger," Achilla said. "Please, it's urgent."

Achilla struggled not to smirk as the receptionist picked up the phone. She always noticed a lot of the things her parents taught her about race, and one of them was the apparent refusal to provide a black person decent service. Sam would demand help until she got it. Brendan was always calm but immovable just the same. Achilla decided to take his approach for now. She stood with her hands on her hips and a smile on her face as the receptionist waited with the receiver on her ear.

"He's not available," the receptionist said as she hung up the phone. "I can give you his card--"

"Maybe you'll get him if you dial his extension," Achilla said with a soft voice. "Or if your phone's not working, I'd be happy to walk back there and find him and inform him that an associate of his most important client needs his undivided attention."

The receptionist cut her eyes at Achilla before picking up the phone and dialing some numbers.

"Mr. Gabrielli, there's someone here to see you on behalf of Mr. Berger," the receptionist groaned before looking down at her desk. "He said to come on back. Room 1206."

"He must be expecting me," Achilla replied as she walked past the reception desk to another clear door. "Thank you for your help."

Achilla looked both ways before reading a sign that led her toward 1206. She passed by numerous offices with light wood doors; some smaller than others. One office had the door cracked and Achilla could hear and smell the labored breathing and typing of an attorney who had very little sleep and lots of coffee. He must be a first-year associate. Another door held a female voice arguing with a client about their payment schedule. Achilla wouldn't be surprised if that dispute turned into another fraud claim. As Achilla strolled down the hall to a corner office with a clear door, she saw a tan-skinned man with gelled slicked back hair wearing a white shirt with thin blue lines forming squares across it. His tie matched the blue lines and the navy blue jacket hanging on a coat rack behind him. Achilla knocked on the glass door, and he looked up at her with those piercing blue eyes. Achilla fought the urge to wring his neck as he stood up and opened the door.

"Please, come in," Blue Eyes said with a crooked smile. "Mr. Berger told me you were coming. My name is Roberto Gabrielli."

"Terri Blake," Achilla said as she shook his hand. "Nice to meet you, Mr. Gabrielli."

"Roberto, please," Blue Eyes replied as he walked to a desk piled with papers and beckoned for her to sit in the wooden, blue cushioned chair across from him. "Excuse the mess. I'm busy working on a whale, as I'm sure you know. What can I do for you?"

"Mr. Berger asked me to inform you that the price of his home is set at two million dollars," Achilla said as she sat down. "He then said that you would instruct me further."

"Very well," Blue Eyes said as he leaned back in his leather seat. "Tell him that I'll be taking the house."

"Great," Achilla replied with a clap of her hands. "I'll get you the paperwork and--"

"Oh, no," Blue Eyes said with a chuckle and a wave of his hand. "I only wanted to know what the house was worth. I won't be paying for it. I'm taking the house. We'll consider it compensation for all of my hard work on this trial."

This was the part when Achilla gave him what he wanted so she could get closer. She knew that. She knew it was what Agent Jones would want. But as she glared at Blue Eyes' grin, she just couldn't help herself.

"I don't think attorneys should take houses in return for legal services," Achilla said with a frown. "That's not exactly a reasonable fee. Now that I know what's going on, I would rather my name not be involved in this."

"All right," Blue Eyes said with a nod of his head. "I suppose you want me to take care of you then. No reason for your silence to go uncompensated. How much would you like?"

"Hush money?" Achilla asked with a snort. "And I thought L.A. was bad. How about I walk out of here and you talk to Mr. Berger yourself?"

Blue Eyes stared at her with an intensity that made the whole room disappear. Achilla stared back. She was used to eyes like his; eyes that paralyze the weak and make them submit. She refused to back down. Blue Eyes maintained his stare as he stood up from his desk. He then walked past her and closed the blinds to the glass window to his office. The hairs on the back of Achilla's neck stood on end as she heard him walking behind her, and she ran her hand over her thigh until she felt the pistol hidden under her skirt.

Achilla thought she might have to kill him sooner than expected, but this was not the place for it. They were on the far end of a hallway full of witnesses, and Achilla would have to evade twelve floors of security. To escape without getting caught, she would have to wipe out the entire office before they called the cops. Not only was the likelihood of success for such an act without exposing herself as a Nephilim very low, but it was also the last thing that she wanted to do to innocent people. Achilla heard Blue Eyes' breathing as he stood behind her and she stiffened as he spoke.

"You know, Berger said you were new in town," Blue Eyes said. "Looking to get your feet wet. Well around here, this is how we do things. If you want any business in this city, you have to be a team player."

"I don't believe we're on the same team," Achilla replied. "I work for Mr. Berger, not you, and you're not going to pressure me into doing anything unethical. I didn't leave L.A. to deal with more of this."

"Oh, you're on my team all right," Blue Eyes said.

Achilla gasped when she felt his crotch against the back of her head. She bit her lip as her face burned and tears filled her eyes. She had to maintain her cover. She couldn't punch him in the neck, or grab his throat, or snap his arm, or crack his sternum, or break his legs, or any of the multitude of things she could do to him right now without batting an eye. She had to be a frightened, green, real estate agent for the sake of gathering intel. She had to maintain--

"You know the real reason he sent you over here?" Blue Eyes continued. "He could've called me himself. You're part of the deal too."

"What do you mean?" Achilla asked knowing full well what the answer was.

"It means I could have my way with you right now," Blue Eyes said. "And there's nothing you can do about it; not if you want to make it big."

Blue Eyes pushed his crotch harder into the back of Achilla's head before he stroked her hair. Achilla pinched her thigh and clenched her eyes shut. He had the nerve to sexually harass her and pet her like a dog at the same time? Achilla clenched her fists as she fought the urge to crotch-punch him hard enough to slam his underwhelming manhood into his rib cage. She had to maintain her cover. How would Terri Blake react? She would react the same way any honest, hardworking, professional woman would. Achilla rose from her seat and stepped back.

"I am a professional, Mr. Gabrielli," Achilla hissed as she wiped her eyes. "I want to get ahead with my work only!"

"Look, baby, if you want to cross the bridge," Blue Eyes said as he stepped closer, "you'll have to pay the toll. I know every millionaire in New Haven. I can bring you business, but you've got to be willing to give me something too. You scratch my back, I scratch yours."

"No thanks," Achilla snapped as she walked past him toward the door. She had to find another way to get close to him because there was no way she was having sex with this pig. As soon as she left the building, she was going to call Agent Jones and think of a new strategy. Perhaps there was a way to sneak into the building and steal the records. Maybe she could get the keys from the cleaning crew. Something, anything, was better than even the notion of sleeping with Blue Eyes. Just before Achilla reached the door, Blue Eyes grabbed her arm. His grip was tight; too tight for any man to grab a woman.

It was also too tight for Achilla to hold off her temper any longer.

She whirled around and pounded his temple with a left hook before grabbing his shirt, kneeing his groin, and slamming him to the floor; making sure to go just easy enough to keep him conscious. She then pulled him up by his shirt and pinned him to his desk with a crash that sent all of his paperwork flying. Blue Eyes raised his hands in submission as Achilla glared at him.

"I could have my way with you right now," Achilla snarled. "And there's nothing you can do about it; not if you want to live. So I will."

"What?"

"Keep your hands where I can see them the entire time I talk," Achilla said. "I don't want you pressing any silent alarms in here like a dumb-ass, and judging by your grades at Connecticut College and Yale, you're not a dumb-ass, right, Roberto; or should I say Blue Eyes?"

"How the hell do you know that name?" asked Blue Eyes as he kept his hands up.

"Never mind that," Achilla said as she grabbed his neck with one hand and pulled the computer monitor forward with the other. "You will give me the names of all of your clients over the past twelve years."

"It's all on a flash drive at Patricia's desk," gurgled Blue Eyes.

"Patricia?" Achilla asked with a frown. "Who's that?"

"The receptionist up front," Blue Eyes said. "She's my niece."

"That explains why she has no class," Achilla replied. "Clearly it runs in the family. Maybe I should go out there and deal with her too."

"No, relax," Blue Eyes said. "That's my wife's family, all right, and I can get divorced on my own without your help. Look, you got me, now what do you want?"

"After listening to you beat Esther," Achilla growled. "What I really want is to shove my foot very far up your ass!"

"I would consider it a great favor if you didn't," Blue Eyes stammered. "Come on, look, I can give you my contacts. How can I get them to you?"

"Call Patricia and tell her to leave the flash drive on her desk so that you can pick it up," Achilla said. "Then tell her to go to lunch. If you don't…"

Achilla pulled her Glock .22 out from her under her skirt and pushed it against his Adam's apple.

"Do it," Achilla said as she let go of his neck and let Blue Eyes pick up the phone. "Make it quick."

"Trish," Blue Eyes said. "Yeah, could you leave my flash drive on your desk? And go pick me up some pizzas, would you? I've got some clients coming in. Thanks."

"Good," Achilla said as he hung up the phone. "And for the record, if I find anything missing on that flash drive, I'm coming back."

"You're no real estate agent," Blue Eyes replied with wide eyes. "You're a Fed. You just violated the fourth amendment with an unconstitutional search and seizure."

"I tell you what," Achilla said as she grabbed Blue Eyes' throat again and waved her pistol in front of his eyes like a loaded metronome. "How about you keep quiet about this, and I'll keep quiet about those girls you have over whenever your wife's away."

"She already knows," Blue Eyes replied.

"How about your daughters?" Achilla asked. "Maybe they'd like to know that someone else's been calling you Daddy."

"You…wouldn't," Blue Eyes grunted as sweat glistened on his forehead before a grin crept onto his lips. "You wouldn't tell…three little girls that. Would you? No, you don't have it in you. No, you're too straight-laced for that, I can tell. If you were that cold, you'd've taken the money. "

"Maybe I won't tell all three," Achilla said with a sneer. "Maybe I'll just tell Esther how dark your girlfriends are. Oh, she'll just love that. She might even run back to her ex-boyfriend in the Tre to celebrate."

"No!" Blue Eyes growled as his face swelled and reddened.

"Just keep quiet, and we won't have to worry about it," Achilla replied. "I'm going to leave now. If you follow me or have me followed, I will notice. I will kill whoever's trailing me, and then, I will come back for you."

Achilla lifted Blue Eyes off of the desk and carried him overhead before choke-slamming him into the pile of papers on the floor. She then shoved her gun back under her skirt before turning toward the door. When she heard him rise to his feet, she looked over her shoulder. Blue Eyes stared at her with cold intensity as his face maintained its brick red complexion. Achilla smirked and shrugged her shoulders as she heard the sound of high-heeled shoes approaching the office. This time, she would listen to Agent Jones' advice and focus on the escape.

Achilla mussed up her hair and loosened her blouse.

"Clean yourself up," Achilla hissed at Blue Eyes before she opened the door. Patricia stood in the doorway with a pen and pad and walked past her.

"Uncle Rob, you didn't say what kind of pizza--"

Patricia looked at Blue Eyes, then back at Achilla. Achilla smirked as she readjusted her skirt and fanned her neck. She then patted her hair down until it was somewhat presentable and buttoned her blouse. Patricia lowered her head and gripped the notepad in her hand. When Blue Eyes stood up and walked toward her, she turned her back on him.

"Your uncle's quite the negotiator," Achilla said with a grin as she fanned her neck before waving at Blue Eyes with her fingertips. "Bye, Roberto."

Patricia stared at Achilla with her mouth open as her cheeks and eyes turned crimson, and Achilla smirked at her before she sauntered down the hallway to the reception desk. A black flash drive sat on top of the desk, and she snatched it up before walking out the front door. Once Achilla gave those files to Agent Jones, they could learn how many clients were involved in the sex trafficking ring. From there, they could decide who to hit next. Achilla sighed as she walked out the front door and pressed the button for the elevator.

"God, that felt amazing," Achilla said to herself as the elevator doors opened to the first floor. She walked back out to New Haven

Green and into a store across the street where she bought a pair of jeans, a black t-shirt that said "CT: We go Hard" over a map of the state, and a pair of black and purple sneakers. Finally, she could wear the clothes she actually enjoyed on a Monday afternoon. She changed in the back of the store and grabbed a blackout fitted cap to cover her face. She then crossed the street and lowered the brim of her cap over her eyes as she leaned against a tree at the edge of the green to watch the festivities. An Earth, Wind & Fire Concert rang throughout the park, and she nodded her head to the band.

Achilla sent a text to Agent Jones' phone that read "Closed Escrow" and lowered her head when she heard police cars drive by toward the law firm. If anyone asked, she was no longer Terri Blake from Los Angeles. She was Kerry Daniels from New Haven. Achilla grinned and shook with laughter when she saw Blue Eyes marching down the street with three New Haven police officers. When Blue Eyes passed by without even noticing her, she giggled to herself and watched the festival. She would renege on her promise to kill him. At this point, it served no purpose. However, there was one visit Achilla needed to make. She closed her eyes, focused her hearing and smelled the air for the scent of Blue Eyes' cologne mixed with perspiration. No dice. By now he must have been far enough away for her to move without him finding her. She strolled out of the park and found her black sedan before driving back to Westville.

Achilla stopped at the corner of Berger's street when she saw the scene. Five police cars surrounded his home, and there was yellow tape everywhere. She had intended on paying Berger a visit as a hysterical Terri Blake declaring her resignation as his real estate agent, but as she focused her ears on the conversation between two New Haven police detectives wearing white shirts black ties in front of her, she decided to keep her distance.

"Clear suicide," the bald, tan-skinned detective wearing a black tie said. "Bastard slit his own wrists. I guess all the press got to him."

"Press?" the heavyset blonde detective wearing a blue tie snorted. "Did you see his house? He had kiddy porn all over the place. This guy had a guilty conscience. Look, he even left a note."

"What's it say?"

"Eh," the heavyset blonde muttered before he read. "'Tell Ms. Blake I'm sorry. There's a special place in hell for me.' Who the hell's Ms. Blake?"

"That's what we'll find out next," the tan detective said. "Though, I agree with the special place in hell line. Man, I hate child abusers."

"Well, we won't have to worry about that anymore," the blond detective quipped. "If you ask me, he just made my job easy. I wish all these sick bastards would do this."

"Oh, Jesus, Riley! Keep saying that and internal affairs'll be breathing down your neck!"

"Yeah, you're probably right."

Achilla turned the car around and drove the opposite way. Now she understood what Mayor Berger meant about hating the human race. He included himself. Her anger at him died down to a wave of pity that she forced out of her head. No. She had no pity for a man who set her up, no matter what kinds of letters he wrote for her. She forced out any empathy for Berger as she watched the roads for state police and drove the speed limit so as not to draw attention to herself. When she arrived in Hartford, she abandoned her car, leaving it to for another agent to return. She then strolled down the street to the parking garage where she knew Agent Jones was waiting and tossed the flash drive between her hands as she whistled the sweet tunes of "September" and grinned at the afternoon sky.

Mission accomplished.

Chapter Six

ACHILLA JOHNSON:11

Brendan Johnson:37

Brendan Johnson sat in the bleachers inside the Central High School gym in Bridgeport. He tied the laces on his black and white sneakers that matched his black and white windbreakers and a black t-shirt as "California Love" blasted through the speakers. Brendan closed his eyes and nodded to the music as more people filed in carrying the smell of fried chicken and McDonald's fries and the wails of crying babies with them. Today was a rare day off, and he wanted to enjoy it in his hometown. As the best criminal defense attorney in Fairfield County, he worked seven days a week for his startup firm, Johnson Law Group, and he often worked twelve hour days. Serving the Bridgeport was his dream, and he pursued it like a man possessed, but not today. Right now, he was enjoying some good basketball.

Bridgeport was not an easy city to grow up in. As a product of Father Panik Village, Brendan watched his friends grow from innocent school kids into drug dealers and stick-up kids; some even resorted to murder. However, it wasn't just his friends doing wrong. Brendan never forgot how many times he was stopped in the street by police officers looking to get their kicks from picking on him despite the fact that he had a clean record and was just walking home from school. He never forgot the day an officer pinned him down on the sidewalk and maced the back of his head because he "fit the description". Watching relatives get arrested for seemingly no reason and sent to prison for things Brendan knew they would never do drove him to tears. By the time he graduated from high school, four of his friends died from violent crime, and ten were serving a prison sentence; only half of whom actually committed the crime.

Still, Brendan considered himself lucky. He was lucky because his mother and father refused to let him run the streets. They ran their household with the sort of relentless, sickening, authoritarian control necessary when your child's environment could kill him the second he walks out the door; whether the perpetrators were criminals or cops. That controlling nature rubbed off on Brendan and enabled him to graduate at the top of his class at Fairfield University, earn a scholarship to Yale Law School, and graduate at the top of his class there too. Despite the job offers he got from the top law firms in Connecticut, Brendan chose to start his own business in his community and fight for the wrongfully accused. His passion made him an amazing litigator; the kind who won motions nobody else would win, who challenged judges nobody else wanted to challenge and cared more about holding his city accountable than playing the political games. Such dedication to his dreams and morals kept Brendan busy. Luckily, he still found time to pursue his hobbies and keep giving back.

Basketball was one of those hobbies. Brendan was a star shooting guard for Central High School and came off the bench for Fairfield University. During his summers as a Yale law student, he coached and refereed boys and girls. Now all he could do was sponsor a team and watch, but that came with the criminal defense profession; all work and very little play. This year, he started a twelve-and-under summer league and sponsored a girls and a boys team. It took a bit of planning and convincing, but he got enough people on board to raise the money. After all the ticket sales were collected, Brendan was donating it to the local YMCA.

Today, Brendan's undefeated girls team played opposite his former classmate Roberto Gabrielli; another defense attorney who wanted to work with Brendan when he started his own firm. Brendan refused his partnership. Johnson and Gabrielli didn't sound very good, but he couldn't put his finger on why. After hearing Roberto speak about his clients with condescension and disdain, Brendan figured it out. Gabrielli had no interest in justice. All he cared about was money, and he would always work for the highest bidder. Brendan couldn't partner with a man like that, not if he intended to maintain his integrity.

Brendan spotted Gabrielli approaching with his dark brown hair slicked back and wearing blue jeans and a green polo shirt. He held a crooked grin under his pointy nose as Brendan rose to shake his hand. When Gabrielli tried to turn his wrist, he resisted and kept his hand upright. He had a habit of trying to dominate everyone around him, and Brendan refused to allow it for a second.

"Ready for the game?" Gabrielli asked with his typical crooked smile and cold blue eyes that made Brendan want to look away. "I hope you're ready to lose."

"They're twelve," Brendan replied with a chuckle. "Let's be competitive about the things that matter. Like our clients for example. Did I really hear that you let your last guy plead not guilty when you had a deal?"

"Yeah, he had no case," Gabrielli said with a shrug. "But he wanted to go to trial. Far be it from me to stop him."

"You let him get twenty years when he could have gotten five," Brendan said. "I could've gotten the sentence down to five."

"And that's why we should work together," Gabrielli said with his arms wide. "You're a visionary."

"Flattery gets you nowhere with me," Brendan replied. "Especially when you don't fight for your clients. You let him go to trial so you could bill him for more hours before he went to prison."

"When will you understand that this thing is a business?" Gabrielli hissed as he stood closer to Brendan. "I know people.

Look, you're a Bridgeport guy. My family's been in New Haven for generations. We could combine our connections. I could bring you business--"

"I get plenty of business on my own--"

"Punks out of P.T. Barnum who can't pay you what you're worth?" Gabrielli said with a snort. "Is that what you want to do; work with lower people?"

Brendan chuckled a little before wiping his hand on his pants.

"I work with clients who need representation," Brendan snapped as he stared Gabrielli down. "And time and again, you have proven incapable of providing it. Now I am done talking to you about this. Get out of my face with that "lower people" bullshit. You don't want me to say that again."

"Yeah, or what?" Gabrielli snapped back.

"Like you just said," Brendan replied as he stepped forward. "I'm from Bridgeport. You want to find out what that means?"

Gabrielli stared at Brendan for a moment before turning to walk away. Brendan shook his head as his heart beat out of his chest. Something about Gabrielli always made Brendan's skin crawl. His heart leaped out of his chest again when he passed by his wife and son on his way out the door. Gabrielli was the last person he wanted around his family.

Brendan's wife, Samantha "Sam" Johnson, approached wearing blue jeans and a red t-shirt. Their son Samuel held her hand as he trailed behind her wearing a matching outfit and red sneakers. Sam kissed Brendan on the cheek as she sat next to him.

"I saw Gabrielli on the way out," Sam said. "He's not sitting with us, is he? I don't want him around Samuel."

"Me neither," Brendan said. "Don't worry."

"Good," Sam sighed. "Well, it was good of you to sponsor these girls."

"Thanks," Brendan said. "And thank you for bringing Samuel. I want him to learn the importance of giving back early on."

"Of course," Sam replied with a smile as the teams ran out onto the court for their layup lines. "Days like today remind me that I married good."

"You always had a way with words," Brendan said. "Maybe you should be the lawyer."

"Oh no, teaching's much better," Sam said as she nudged him with her elbow. "But if I do it well enough, you won't have too many clients."

"Which is why we should go into business together."

"Nope," Sam quipped with a grin. "I'll just be the breadwinner, that's all."

Brendan and Sam laughed as Samuel walked across them and sat next to Brendan. Samuel's birth was the happiest day of Brendan's life, and his career achievements paled in comparison to watching him grow. He had light brown skin, big ears, and a wide smile like his mother, but Brendan saw himself in everything Samuel did. Much like Brendan at his age, he was very sensitive and impressionable. Growing up in Bridgeport knocked the vulnerability out of Brendan, but now that they lived in Stratford, a neighboring suburb with much less crime and heartache. Samuel didn't have to be so hard so early, and Brendan would teach him how to be tough when he was ready for it. He smiled and patted his son's head before he turned and looked at him with curiosity oozing from his eyes.

"Dad, why are we watching girls play basketball?" Samuel asked as he crossed his arms.

"Son, girls play ball just as well as anybody else," Brendan replied. "Sometimes better in my opinion. Besides, I sponsored this team because I believe in giving back to people who need it."

"How are you giving back if they didn't give you anything?" Samuel replied.

"Samuel, that's not what your father means," Sam said. "He's doing something nice for someone who can't pay for a team themselves."

"Like when you give money to bums on the street?" Samuel asked.

"They're not bums, Samuel," Sam said. "They're homeless people. Don't call them bums anymore."

"Your mother's right," Brendan added. "Don't let me hear you say that again."

"Yes, sir," Samuel groaned.

"I don't know where he learned that from," Sam said to Brendan. "It certainly wasn't us."

Brendan's team was up, and they wore red and white t-shirts with black shorts as they walked on the court. Most of the girls shook hands and introduced themselves. One brown-skinned girl with long black hair stood by herself until one of her opponents wearing a blue t-shirt approached her. When she tapped her shoulder, the girl on Brendan's team just stared at her.

Brendan frowned. Who raised her to be so damn rude?

"Brendan," Sam said as she tapped his shoulder, making him snap back to their conversation. "Do you have any idea where Sam learned to talk like that?"

"He probably overheard your father on the phone with one of his cop buddies," Brendan said as he watched the opening tip. "Among other things. I told you it was a bad idea to let Samuel ride with him--"

"Please, Brendan, not in front of Samuel--"

"That hasn't stopped him," Brendan growled before his eyes settled on the loner on his team. She wasn't any taller than the other girls, but something about the way she carried herself seemed older. Brendan frowned when he watched her catch the ball, dribble twice, and shoot a three-pointer. The ball sailed through the red rim and snapped the net. She then jogged down the court and adjusted her t-shirt as she stood in a defensive stance. After deflecting a pass that the other girls bobbled around, she picked up the loose ball and sprinted down the court faster than all of the other girls, stopped and shot another three-pointer. That shot also dropped through the net without touching the rim.

"We said we wouldn't talk about that in front of Samuel," Sam muttered. "We agreed--"

"Fine, you're right, and I'm done," Brendan said with a wave of his hand before pointing at the girl. "Do you notice anything different about that girl?"

"Aside from a future in the WNBA, no," Sam replied with a shrug. "She sure can shoot."

"No," Brendan said as he watched the girl's every move. "I mean, yes, she has a good jumper, but that's not it. Something about her seems familiar."

"She looks like you, Dad," Samuel said as he pointed at the court. "That girl kind of looks like you. Is she my sister?"

"No, Samuel," Sam giggled.

"No, she's not, son," Brendan said, but as he watched the girl some more, he could see the resemblance. Her face looked nothing like his, but her demeanor was a spitting image. The way she stared at her opponents, the way she exhaled and took long strides as she sprinted down court, the way she tied her shoes without bending her knees. Brendan felt like he was watching his miniature, female self on the court. When she looked up at the stands for a moment, Brendan nearly rose to his feet.

Her eyes were as green as a pair of jade earrings.

Brendan had not seen eyes like those in over eleven years.

"I think I know why she looks familiar," Brendan said as he leaned close to Sam. "Look at those eyes."

"She's got green eyes," Sam said. "So what?"

"Look again."

"No," Sam replied as she rolled her eyes at Brendan. "What are the odds, Brendan? Do you really think she's Ailina's kid?"

"I think it's very possible," Brendan said.

What he didn't tell her was that he was doing the math in his head. Ailina Harris was a tall, brunette woman from Bridgeport's North End who Brendan dated during his senior year of college. When they first met, her green eyes held a hypnotizing gaze that Brendan couldn't stay away from. Brendan was a bit of a player in college, but Ailina had a way of making him focus on her alone; especially when they became physically intimate. Having sex with Ailina was like losing his virginity over and over, and it consumed his mind every day until the next time he saw her.

They broke up when Brendan graduated from Fairfield, but they remained sexually involved during law school; mostly because Ailina would not let Brendan go and because Brendan couldn't resist her advances. The closer he came to graduation, the more she called, and the more jealous she became around other women. Despite her striking beauty and sexual prowess, Brendan started to feel uneasy around her; the same way he often felt around Gabrielli. The more Brendan backed away, the more controlling and manipulative her tactics. After she pretended to have a mental breakdown and called him over to her apartment "just to see if he would come" as she put it, Brendan decided to cut her off cold turkey. He told her wanted no more sex and no more games. They were done, and it was best they both moved on.

Ailina disagreed.

Physically.

Trying to restrain Ailina was like holding off a grizzly bear. Every smack and punch sent shockwaves through his body until all he could do was cover his head and hope that she would stop. She grabbed his arm when he tried to run away and yanked so hard that she broke it at the forearm just as he reached the door. As Brendan crawled out of the apartment, he watched her run to the bathroom. Thinking she was grabbing something to throw at him, Brendan rushed to his feet. He was expecting a pot, pan, maybe a shoe. Brendan's jaw dropped when Ailina pulled her sink out of the bathroom wall and carried it over her head as she stalked toward him.

He would never forget the look in her eyes as she carried that sink through the house; so cold and intense that they seemed to change into a different shade of green as tears streamed down her face. She screamed as she cocked the sink back, but he didn't wait for her to throw it. Brendan never ran so fast from anyone in his entire life. He made it to his beat up, brown Celica out front and gunned the engine to his parents' house on the East End. From there, they called an ambulance to the emergency room. Brendan had nightmares for weeks, and they all involved the shine in Ailina's eyes when she carried that sink.

For the first time, Brendan questioned if she was human. He lived in the weight room in college. He met and hooked up with plenty of athletic women. None of them could beat him up so bad, and they certainly didn't use bathroom sinks as weapons of opportunity. But also, none of them had eyes that glowed like Ailina's.

Those eyes kept him awake at night, and he vowed that if he ever saw her again, he would cross the street and hide unless he had a gun on his person; in which case, he would shoot her between those eyes to make sure they didn't glow anymore.

That was eleven years ago. After recovering in the hospital and graduating from law school, Brendan moved to Stratford where he reconnected with Sam at an old butcher on the South Side of town. Though she was still a tomboy, she was no longer the girl Brendan played tag with as kids in the Father Panik Village. She was a brown-skinned woman with braids and a white smile from ear-to-ear who haggled the butcher down to a lower price for a pound of beef. She also had soft, brown eyes that made Brendan smile back. They were married two years later.

It was possible that this girl, who looked like Ailina and acted like Brendan, was around eleven years old. Brendan held his face in his hands and prayed that he was just being paranoid. Surely, there was no way that he had a child with Ailina. He used protection every time, but condoms were not infallible. Knowing Ailina, she could have found a way to conceive a child without Brendan's knowledge if she wanted one. The question was would she, and why?

"Honey, what's wrong?" Sam asked as she rubbed Brendan's back.

"I'm fine."

"You say that every time something's wrong," Sam replied. "Like during your last trial. Why don't we talk about it later? "

"Yeah," Brendan sighed. "Yeah, maybe later."

Brendan watched the girl's movements the entire game. She carried herself just like a Johnson. She also didn't miss. Brendan estimated that she shot a good sixty percent from the field; a rare percentage for anyone, let alone a girl so young. Samuel played basketball too. He was good for his age and had a future in the sport, but judging from what Brendan was watching right now, this girl had more athletic potential than him.

Come to think of it, she was more athletic than Tyron Higgins, the son of his client who just got convicted of armed robbery. That whole trial made no sense. No video footage. No witnesses. Just money gone missing, a signed written confession, and a defendant in a wheelchair swearing he didn't do it. Right before they wheeled him off to prison, he told Brendan his son would go to college. Brendan watched Tyron play in this tournament with the older kids. He was Division I material.

Unless Brendan's eyes were playing tricks on him, this girl was even faster than Tyron.

"I think we should have a talk about this girl to the coach," Sam said with a frown. "She doesn't look like a twelve-year-old."

"Yes she does," Brendan said. "And she's probably eleven."

"No, she looks eleven in the face maybe," Sam said as she pointed a finger at the game. "But she doesn't play like it. I mean look at her. She would dominate high schoolers. I don't like when people scout older kids to win. It ruins it for the other kids. Somebody did that in Samuel's league, and it cost them the game. It just broke his little heart."

"I honestly don't think she's old, babe," Brendan said as he watched the girl jog down the court. He frowned when another girl tried to push her and bounced off. The green-eyed girl didn't seem to notice. When another player on the opposing team pulled her hair, she stumbled backward. As the referee blew his whistle and ran toward them, the crowd stood up. Brendan stood to see over the crowd and watched the green-eyed girl on his team stomp her opponents foot, back her into a wall, elbow her gut twice, and then turn to punch her in the nose. She then grabbed her head and kneed her face, sending her to the floor in a heap. When the referee grabbed her arm, the girl kicked his groin and tripped him to the floor before punching his throat and face.

Brendan frowned as Al, the coach for his team, ran onto the floor and stepped between the green-eyed girl and the referee. Al was a short, stocky man with curly, black hair wearing khakis and a black polo who must have weighed around two hundred pounds. When Al tried to push her away, she pushed him back and sent him sliding on the floor. How could an eleven-year-old girl knock him down with a simple push? Al got back up for another try. This time, the girl grabbed his shirt and hip tossed him to the floor. He rolled away and rose to his feet as she glared at him.

"What's going on?" Sam asked as she tugged at Brendan's shirt. "Is there a fight?"

"Don't let Samuel see," Brendan said as he watched the girl shove her coach aside like a rag doll.

"See what?"

"That girl's definitely Ailina's kid," Brendan said. "I've never seen a little girl fight like that. God, she hits like a train--"

"Fight like what, Brendan?" Sam demanded with a stomp of her foot. "Can I get some details please?"

"She just beat down a girl on the opposite team and the ref," Brendan said. "And she almost threw the coach across the court."

"Oh, please don't exaggerate," Sam replied with a cocked eyebrow.

"I wish I was," Brendan said as he watched parents rush the floor to grab their daughters. "This game's over. Could you take Samuel to the car?"

"Sure," Sam said as she grabbed Samuel's hand. "What about you?"

"I'll be there in a minute," Brendan said while stepping down the bleachers. He didn't wait for a response from his wife as he moved toward this dangerous girl. She stood at half court and wiped sweat from her face with her shirt. The coach stood next to her but not too close. Brendan tapped his shoulder.

"I've got it from here, Al," Brendan said.

"This girl's crazy," Al replied in his thick Greek accent. "I sign her up because her mother is a nice Greek woman, but this I did not sign up for."

Ailina was Greek and Portuguese and fluent in both languages. Brendan remembered her trying to teach him a few phrases when they were young. This was definitely Ailina's child.

"I've got it," Brendan told Al. "I deal with crazy every day."

Al nodded his head and walked away. Brendan stood with his hands on his hips in front of the girl. She stared at him with green eyes that shot lasers through his head, the same way Ailina's did whenever she was angry, but she was different. Her eyes were intense, but they lacked the coldness that sent shivers up Brendan's spine. He stared her in the eye right back without hesitation.

"Looks like Ailina's taught you some things," Brendan said.

"How do you know my mom?" the girl asked with the voice of a teenager. "Who are you?"

"My name's Brendan," Brendan said. "And Ailina and I used to be friends."

The girl frowned and stepped closer.

"Friends?" the girl asked. "Is that what you're calling it?"

"What would you prefer?" Brendan replied.

"The truth" the girl demanded Brendan flinch. "She doesn't have friends. The last guy was gone in a week. He tried to tell me they were friends too."

"Maybe they were just friends."

"No, friends don't have sex," the girl said. "And they had sex a lot. You had sex with her too."

"I don't think you're old enough to talk about that--"

"Yeah?" the girl replied. "Then how come I just said it?"

"If you lived in my house you wouldn't be," Brendan replied. "I don't...do that in front of my kid."

"Why not?" the girl asked with a shrug. "It's only natural. It's what adults are supposed to do."

"Is that what your mom tells you?" Brendan asked before point his thumb over his shoulder at the girl from the blue team who still hadn't gotten up. "Did she also tell you how to do that?"

"You ask a lot of questions," the girl said. "You're good at pretending to care."

"And I answered yours," Brendan said through gritted teeth. "Now I need you to answer mine."

THE GIRL SQUINTED her eyes at Brendan as if she were searching for something on his face.

"I guess that's fair," the girl said she walked to the scorer's table.

"Yes, she told me that. She taught me how to fight too. Oh wow, I had forty points all by myself! Yes!"

"You're quite the ballplayer," Brendan chuckled. "I was impressed."

"Thanks," the girl replied with a smile. "Not bad for a first time, right?"

"What?"

"Yeah, she never lets me play," the girl said with a slight pout. "But she knows I like basketball and said it helped with competitive nature, and some other stuff I can't really say, but she let me play basketball!"

"How did you know to do all that?" Brendan asked. "Most kids your age don't have a jump shot that good."

"Basketball games are all the television I'm allowed to watch," the girl replied. "I watch Michael Jordan. He's my favorite."

"That explains why you don't pass very often," Brendan said. "Tell you what, I played basketball in high school and college, and I think you have a ton of potential. Why don't you let me coach you?"

"No way," the girl replied as she shook her head. "I'm not allowed."

"Obviously playing basketball isn't a problem if she let--"

"No, I'm not allowed to talk to you," the girl said. "I'm pretty sure you're my dad."

Brendan's heart jumped.

"How would you know that?"

"Well, Mom says my father's a big fancy lawyer who can afford a fancy car, a new house, and a family, but won't send me anything on my birthday," the girl said. "Does that sound like you?"

Brendan's jaw dropped and he stepped back. When did Ailina get pregnant? Ailina became a Bridgeport cop after Brendan graduated from college. She had to have taken time off for maternity leave. Sam's father was the police chief. Why didn't he tell him? Brendan struggled to stay on his feet as he stared at his daughter with tears welling up in his eyes. How could his flesh and blood walk around for eleven years without anyone telling him?

"What's wrong with you?" the girl asked. "You look like you're going to cry. You're not going to cry, are you? Because that would be really weak."

"I'm fine," Brendan said as he wiped his eyes. "What's your name?"

"Achilla."

"Achilla?" Brendan asked knowing that only Ailina would think of such a harsh name for a girl. "How old are you, Achilla?"

"Eleven and a half."

"Does Ailina take good care of you?" Brendan asked as he stepped closer. "What school do you go to? Do you have any friends--?"

"Achilla, what did I tell you?"

Brendan turned and saw a tall brunette with lightning green eyes wearing a tight, green t-shirt that hugged her breasts and jeans step past him and stand behind Achilla. Ailina's appearance hadn't changed much. She still had olive skin, her hair still flowed past her shoulders, and she wore very little make-up. Her eyes set on Brendan and she grinned before patting Achilla's shoulder. She then stepped around Achilla and stood between them. Flashbacks of that day ran through Brendan's mind, and his throat dried up, but Brendan clenched his fists to stop their trembling. If this little girl was their child, Brendan couldn't imagine what kind of abuse she was suffering while living with Ailina. No matter the risk, Brendan had to confront her. He thanked God that Sam and Samuel were outside as he forced himself to look Ailina in the eye.

"Ailina," Brendan said. "Don't play with me. Is she...ours?"

"No, she's mine," Ailina replied. "She'll always be mine, Brendan."

"*Am I the father*, Ailina?" Brendan asked. "She just told me that her dad was a big fancy lawyer."

"You're not the only lawyer in town," Ailina laughed as she wiped a strand of her hair away from her forehead. "I know lots of lawyers; mainly prosecutors. They tend to be more of a challenge. They don't run away and hide like defense attorneys."

"Don't dodge my question--"

"How do you plan on getting me to answer, Brendan?" Ailina

asked with a slight tilt of her head. "You know, I forgot how cute you could be when you think you're in control."

"I'll find a way," Brendan said as he watched Achilla peek around Ailina's waist. "After what I just saw and heard, you are not a fit parent."

"Oh, come on," Ailina replied with a snort. "The girl defended herself--"

"She incapacitated a sixth grader and a grown man," Brendan snapped. "She shouldn't even know how to do that or be able to. You're raising her to be as violent as you."

"Kids and their cartoons," Ailina said with a shrug. "I don't know where she gets it from--"

"You said I couldn't watch cartoons," Achilla said with a frown.

"Not now, Achilla," Ailina said with a sharp stare. "I'm having an adult conversation. Be. Quiet."

Ailina glared at Achilla until she lowered her head. The intensity of her stare showed Brendan everything he needed to see. After working years in criminal defense, Brendan knew the abusers when he saw them. Brendan would bet money that if a doctor examined Achilla right now, she would find all kinds of bruises on her body. It was settled.

He had to get this girl away from Ailina and soon.

"I'm not falling for your games, Ailina," Brendan replied. "If she's my daughter, I'm taking her from you. God knows what kind of damage you've done already. I won't let you do any more to her!"

"I told you," Ailina said as her eyes zeroed in on Brendan with such intensity that his view of the entire court faded away. "She will always be mine."

"Not anymore," Brendan said before he pointed his finger. "I'll see you in court, Ailina; in my domain! And I guarantee you I won't run or *lose* there!"

Brendan stormed off the court, glancing behind him to see Achilla staring at him with wide eyes and an open mouth. He walked out of the gym and saw Sam parking his black sedan just beyond the sidewalk. As soon as she parked the car, Sam walked out and approached Brendan with her arms crossed. Her brown eyes were a refreshing sight. Brendan sighed and embraced her before kissing her forehead.

"What's wrong?" Sam asked. "Is everything all right?"

"I don't know how else to say this," Brendan said. "But that girl's name is Achilla."

"Who names their daughter Achilla?" Sam asked with a scowl. "That sounds so mean."

"Ailina did," Brendan sighed. "She's her mother."

"Oh, so I guess you were right--"

"And I'm pretty sure I'm the father."

Sam jolted and stepped away from Brendan. Her eyes teared up as she held her hand on her chest. As she turned to walk away, Brendan bounded to cut off her path. In his rush to break the news, he forgot to explain the details. He scrambled for a way to get it out before she served him with divorce papers.

"She would've been born before we got together," Brendan said with his hands raised. "I had no clue. I promise I've never cheated on you. I wouldn't do that, Sam. I love you. I would never hurt you like that. You have to believe me."

"Right," Sam said after taking a deep breath. "I trust you. Knowing that we're dealing with Ailina, I can believe that you didn't know about your own child for...at least ten years. I can...I can work with that."

"I know this is sudden," Brendan said, "And it's not your responsibility, but--"

"I agree that she needs to live with us," Sam said. "No way can that woman raise a child; especially your child. Whatever you need, I support you one hundred percent."

"Thanks," Brendan said as they walked to the car. "You're an amazing wife, Sam."

"I know," Sam said. "Just let me know what I can do to help."

"Absolutely."

"Just one question."

"Sure," Brendan said as he stepped into the driver's seat and checked on Samuel behind them. He was fast asleep and spread across the back seat. Normally, he would tell Samuel to get his sneakers off of the leather but now wasn't the right time. Right then a fleeting thought passed through Brendan's head. How did Samuel know Achilla was his daughter? Brendan shook that thought out of his mind as Sam stepped into the car.

"Did my father mention anything to you about this?" Sam asked in a low voice. "She had to take maternity leave at some point, right? So he would know something, but he never told me. He never told me that my husband might have another kid walking around Bridgeport. Did he at least tell you?"

"I'm sorry, Sam," Brendan replied as he pulled off the curb. "He didn't. Maybe he wasn't sure."

"Yeah, but he could connect the dots, right?" Sam said. "He could've at least told one of us to check."

"I don't know what to say, Sam," Brendan said. "But you know your father hasn't spoken much to either of us since we got married. As harsh as this may sound, I'm not surprised that he didn't say anything."

Brendan watched Sam look out the window. She reached into the glove compartment and grabbed a handful of tissues. She ripped a tissue loose and wiped her eyes with it as she sniffed. She continued to look out the window as he reached over and massaged her shoulder. Sam let out a short whimper as she wiped her eyes.

"Sam, I'm sorry--"

"If you ever want Samuel to visit him, I understand," Sam said with a catch in her voice. "Samuel needs to see his grandfather, but I won't be going. No real father keeps that from his daughter."

"I'll talk to him," Brendan said with a set jaw. "I've had a few words for him anyway."

"No, please don't," Sam replied. "Let's take care of this first. You deserve to see your daughter. It can wait."

"Thank you, Sam," Brendan said as he stopped at a red light that shined into the windshield and illuminated the dashboard like a red sun. Brendan gritted his teeth at the thought of his daughter living with Ailina; the same woman who tried to kill him. He would do whatever was necessary to keep all of his children under his roof and away from her. He wasn't running away this time. He had to do something.

Brendan's first step was proving that Ailina was an unfit mother. If he could get DCFS to take Achilla way, he could then prove his paternity. He paid Perry, one the firm's investigators, overtime to stake out Ailina's house in Bridgeport's North End. He warned him that Ailina was a detective who could spot subpar surveillance a mile away. He also told him about Ailina's freakish strength. In response, Perry charged him double time before going out. It took the investigator three weeks to call. They met at Brendan's house in the South End of Stratford. Brendan and Sam sat at the kitchen table as Perry handed him an envelope with photos inside.

"I'm going to need that check a.s.a.p.," Perry said as he ran his hand through his ruffled brown hair and stuff his hands in his khakis. "I don't like getting too close to that woman's house. Something about her just isn't right."

"We appreciate it, Perry," Brendan said as he studied the photos. "Sam, hand him the check please."

As Sam pulled out a check from her purse, Brendan noticed that there wasn't a single photo of Achilla by the house. They were all photos of Ailina pulling in the driveway, leaving for work, bringing home groceries, and even mowing the lawn. Not a single photo of Achilla could be found. Brendan frowned and raised his hand. Sam pulled the check back just before Perry could reach it. Brendan slammed the photos down on the table.

"Where's the girl, Perry?" Brendan asked. "You can't even prove Ailina's a mother in these photos, let alone an unfit one."

"Oh, there's proof," Perry replied. "See this is the difference between a lawyer and a private eye. Look at the driveway. What do you see?"

"Look, honey," Sam said. "There's a basketball hoop with a ball under it."

"That proves nothing," Brendan barked. "Ailina could just say that she plays basketball in her spare time."

"Yeah, what about the pictures with her trunk open?" Perry asked. "See those gloves and pads. I practiced and taught martial arts for thirty years, and the way you described this girl, she's already proficient in krav maga, Muay Thai, and western boxing. Those gloves and pads are training tools. And as you can see in the next picture, she carries them into the house."

"Is she an instructor too?" Sam asked.

"No," Perry replied. "This chick's work is her life. Aside from grocery shopping and bar hopping, she lives at the Police Department. She's training someone and whoever it is; she's got really small hands to fit those gloves. Those are the gloves I used for kids."

"I believe you now, Perry," Brendan said. "But it doesn't necessarily prove that she's unfit."

"Did you forget your own words, Brendan?" Perry chuckled. "How come the kid's never outside? Where are her friends? Look, she's not even in the windows. This kid is inside all day, and I bet she only comes out when she's sure her mother won't be home for a while. I'll bet money she's locked up in a basement."

"The girl had to learn how to shoot somehow," Brendan said. "She had to come outside before that tournament."

"Well, you did tell Ailina you'd take her away," Perry replied. "Maybe she's hyper-vigilant. Maybe she's keeping her inside because she knows you've got investigators."

"Wait, there's more than one car in these pictures," Sam said. "Who else is over there?"

"There's something else," Perry said. "She's got at least four different fellas coming over."

"What kind of guys are they?" Brendan asked. "Those are some expensive cars."

"Good question," Sam said. "I wouldn't have just any man around my child. Brendan's the lawyer, but I bet you can find her unfit if her men are dangerous."

"You'd win the bet," Brendan said before kissing his wife on the cheek. "Sam's right. We need to know what kind of people she's bringing around. We also need to know if any neighbors have seen the girl, and if they have, how often? What have they seen, heard, even smelled coming out of that house?"

"Look, you told me to get as close as I could without getting noticed," Perry said with his hands raised. "No cop with half a brain isn't going notice that someone's snooping around their friends and neighbors. I like you guys, but I'm not trying to get a kitchen sink thrown at me or worse."

"It was a bathroom sink," Brendan said. "And I'll pay whatever it takes."

"You can't afford what I would ask for," Perry replied. "Not with a wife and kid. I'm selfish, but I'm not an asshole. I won't do that to you."

"Will this help?" Sam asked as she ripped off her champagne strapped, white-faced watch. "It's got to be worth at least a thousand dollars."

"Sam, your father bought you that watch," Brendan muttered. "I can't ask you to do that. Achilla's--"

"Not my responsibility?" Sam asked with a cocked eyebrow. "Let me tell you something. I'm not sitting back while a child lives with her. Besides, you have your own firm now. You can afford to buy me a new one."

"I don't think the monetary value of the watch is the issue," Brendan replied.

"Oh, to hell with what my father thinks," Sam snapped. "If he finds out, he'll just have to tell us the truth, won't he? I told you I was going to help you save your daughter. That's what I'm doing."

Brendan sighed. That was Sam. She was always pushing.

"Perry?" Brendan asked with his arms crossed. "Will you take the watch?"

"You've got a good woman, Brendan," Perry said as he took the watch from Sam's extended hand. "My ex-wife takes money from me every month and makes it hard to see my kids even if I pay on time. Yours gives stuff away at a moment's notice to save another woman's kid. I envy you."

"Well, she is amazing," Brendan said with a smile and a wink at Sam. "How soon can we hear back?"

"You'll hear back from me in a week," Perry replied. "If I snoop around any longer than that I'm probably in deep shit."

A week went by and Brendan and Sam waited at home for

Perry's arrival. They even sat in the same seats at the kitchen table as if their last meeting never ended. Samuel, wearing a navy blue Stratford Academy t-shirt, brought them glasses of water and sat at the table with them. Sam smiled and kissed him on the forehead before she guzzled her drink with a trembling hand and spilled some water on her yellow dress. Brendan sighed and rose from his seat. He toyed with his red tie as he paced the kitchen.

"Something's wrong," Brendan said. "I can feel it."

"Samuel, go upstairs, honey," Sam whispered to Samuel. "We have to talk about something."

Samuel nodded his head and walked out of the kitchen. Brendan paced in front of the refrigerator with his hands on his hips. He noticed Sam studying him, but he paced anyway. When he turned his back, he felt her hug him from behind and kiss his neck. Brendan kissed her back as she rubbed his chest. The sweet smell of her perfume gave him a slight relief.

"Relax, baby," Sam said. "It'll work out."

"Perry's never late," Brendan said. "What if Ailina found him?"

"Then he's in God's hands," Sam replied as she patted Brendan's chest. "Just like Achilla and everything else."

"Yeah," Brendan sighed. "It's just that you didn't see what I saw that day. I'm lucky to be alive."

"Lord God," Sam prayed as she gripped Brendan's waist and rested her head against his back. "We thank you that Brendan is alive and well, and we thank you for Achilla. We ask for your favor tonight as--"

They jumped when the doorbell rang.

Brendan looked at Sam and she nodded her head at him. He took a deep breath and turned the corner. As he walked toward the door, Brendan continued his wife's prayer under his breath. He opened the door and saw a tall, brown-skinned man with salt-and-pepper hair wearing a navy blue and yellow uniform. It was Chief Gregory Price; Sam's father and the chief of the Bridgeport Police Department. Brendan crossed his arms at the sight of him.

"Can I help you, Chief?" Brendan asked.

"May I come in?"

"My boy's upstairs, so I guess it's fine," Brendan said as he turned and walked into the kitchen.

"Is that a shot?" Chief Price asked as he stepped inside.

"Yeah, but we can talk about it later," Brendan replied as he strolled into the kitchen. "What brings you here?"

"I'd like to know that too," Sam said as she leaned against the kitchen counter.

"Samantha," Chief Price said with the slightest of nods before facing Brendan. "I understand that you've been conducting an investigation in my city."

"You mean the one you should've conducted?" Sam snarled before sipping her water and slamming the glass down.

"I don't know what you're trying to say," Chief Price replied.

"You should've told us," Sam said with a catch in her voice. "You should've told me. How could you hide something like that from your own daughter?"

"I get that we're on opposite sides of the system," Brendan said. "But my daughter, Chief? I don't have to tell you how bad this looks."

"It wasn't up to me," Chief Price said. "Your blame is misplaced."

"Oh, that's debatable," Sam said with a snort. "This isn't the first time you've put your job over your family. God, you were always so selfish--"

"I paid for your school, Samantha," Chief Price barked. "Even if you wasted it to become a schoolteacher--"

"Wasted?" Brendan asked with a scowl as he walked toward Chief Price. "She didn't *waste* anything! Look, I don't care if you're the police chief. You can't talk to my wife like that in my house, and you can't yell at her either--"

"Oh, is that right?" Chief Price replied as he looked Brendan in the eye.

"Yeah, it is!" Brendan snapped. "Test me if you want to find out!"

"Who do you think you're talking to?" Chief Price barked.

"You!" Brendan roared back as the two men converged on another until Sam darted across the room.

"Babe, no," Sam sighed as she stood between them and held her hands against Brendan's chest. "No, it's fine."

"No, it's not," Brendan said before staring at Chief Price. "Get out."

"Fine, I'll leave," Chief Price said. "But before I go, you may want to hear about Perry."

Brendan and Sam looked at each other before they faced him. Chief Price cleared his throat as he pulled out the watch that Sam gave Perry a week ago. He walked past them and set it on the kitchen table. He then pulled out a roll of hundreds wrapped in a rubber band and set it next to the watch. Sam snatched up the money and the watch and extended it back.

"Sam read my mind," Brendan said. "We don't need you reimbursing us."

"I'm not," Chief Price said. "Perry's in the hospital. He got in a car accident and broke both of his legs in the course of his investigation. Still, he felt so strongly about this case that he decided to do it pro bono."

"I work in criminal defense, Chief," Brendan said. "People lie to me every day. You can't bullshit me. Ailina got to him and broke his legs, didn't she?"

Chief Price stared at Brendan before turning to Sam. That confirmed everything. Perry got close. Perry got caught. Perry got hurt or worse. Brendan held his hands on his hips. One day, he would pay him back for his dedication.

"He wanted you to have the money and the watch back," Chief Price said to Sam before looking back at Brendan. "You can ask him yourself. He also took the liberty of reporting Ailina to DCFS a few days ago. Apparently, he felt like what he had learned warranted immediate action. However, Perry plans to retire after he recovers. He's been dying to take a trip to Puerto Rico."

"What did he tell you, Chief?" Brendan asked. "You wouldn't be over here if it didn't make you concerned, and I doubt it had anything to do with retirement."

"You want the girl, right?" Chief Price replied with a wave of his hand. "Consider it done. I've made arrangements to have her escorted to your home by tomorrow morning."

"This is way too easy," Brendan said.

"Yeah," Sam said. "If someone came to take Samuel, they couldn't have him without a fight. Lord knows what she would do."

"Sam, by now you should know that every mother isn't as caring as you are," Chief Price replied. "Ailina will not be a problem. In return, no DCFS, and no lawsuit."

"You're protecting her," Brendan said as Chief Price walked toward the door. "Why? What are you hiding, Chief?"

Chief Price stopped just short of the door and took a deep breath. When he looked at Brendan, his eyes were moist. Brendan also noticed his hand was shaking the doorknob. There was a lot that Brendan didn't know, but he knew this. Chief Price grew up in the same Bridgeport streets as Brendan. He then spent his life fighting crime in them. It took a lot to frighten him, and Brendan highly doubted that he or Sam was the reason he was trembling so much.

He was afraid of Ailina.

"You may not believe this," Chief Price said as he opened the door. "But I'm protecting all of you."

"I've heard that before," Sam said. "You always say it's for my own good."

"I'm afraid that it is," Chief Price replied. "Maybe one day I'll be able to tell you why. Achilla will be here in the morning. I suggest that you prepare for her. You'll find her to be very different from your son."

Chief Price walked out and Brendan frowned as he stared at the door. If Ailina was abusing Achilla and injured Perry in an effort to cover it up, this whole arrangement protected her from any civil or criminal liability. But had Chief Price just fired Ailina, her legal issues would no longer be his problem. Why did he keep protecting her no matter how much she blatantly violated the law? And why would Perry suddenly retire and leave the state? The sole reason he worked for Brendan was that he could hardly afford his alimony and child support payments. Chief Price had to have paid him off, but why go through so much effort to protect a cop who could tarnish the reputation of the entire department? Why would a man with so much power fear Ailina? Before Brendan had time to ponder further, Sam rubbed his shoulder and kissed his cheek.

"Well, I guess we'll get ready," Brendan said. "Something doesn't feel right, Sam. I don't like how this was done."

"Me neither," Sam replied before smiling. "But we got your daughter. Sometimes God makes a way that we don't understand."

"I get the feeling that God had nothing to do with this," Brendan said as he walked to the window next to the front door and watched with his hands on his hips as Chief Price's Range Rover drove down the street. "That's the part that bothers me."

"I believe that God always has a plan," Sam replied with her hands on her hips.

"Me too," Brendan said before turning around and passing by Sam into the kitchen. "I just doubt that this is a part of it."

Chapter Seven

ACHILLA JOHNSON:20

"You can't return to New Haven," Agent Jones said as he sat across from Achilla in a green cardigan sweater. He sighed as he ran his hands over his face and Achilla crossed her arms over the same "CT We Go Hard" t-shirt she wore at the New Haven Green as she leaned back into her chair. She adjusted the brim to her blackout fitted cap and looked to her left at the room where Ares was floating in his liquid tank. Though he was unconscious, Achilla couldn't help but wonder if he was listening to their conversation.

"What have I told you about getting in and getting out?" Agent Jones growled. "How could you be so careless?"

"The opportunity presented itself," Achilla said with a shrug. "So I took it. I really don't see how that was careless, I mean, I got the job done."

"You blew your cover, Achilla."

"And created a new one," Achilla replied. "He thinks I'm a Fed."

"And then he'll sue the FBI," Agent Jones snapped. "And you know that's a farce for the papers. Now that he's seen your face, he has goons all over the state looking to do you in. On top of that, the

Feds are looking for someone impersonating an agent, and New Haven Police are searching for a Ms. Blake for questioning. You have both sides of the law on your ass, Achilla!"

"Then I guess my next assignment's out of the state?" Achilla said with a smile. "I'm willing to try Miami, Florida, or maybe Brazil--"

"No," Agent Jones replied. "Every checkpoint and airport will be looking for you. You can't leave the state just yet. You can't show your face in public either."

"Am I fired or something?" Achilla asked.

"No," Agent Jones sighed. "My superiors have actually handed out a new assignment for you. They wanted me to tell you as soon as possible."

"Well that was quick," Achilla said as she rose from the table and walked toward the window. She just couldn't keep her eyes off of Ares. Something about his presence in this building upset her stomach. Why didn't they just kill him off? Why didn't they just kill Ailina as well? Why did they need Achilla for that? The more Achilla thought about it, the less her presence in the CIA made sense; especially after earlier today. One minute, they recruited her to fight Ailina. The next, she's strong-arming intel from Blue Eyes.

What was really going on?

"On the bright side, you brought us some good intel," Agent Jones said. "Most of Blue Eyes' clients who were accused of sex trafficking have ties to Xerxes in Brazil."

"See?" Achilla asked with a wink. "Progress."

"Of course there is something troubling on that flash drive," Agent Jones replied.

"What?"

"He has the contact info of a former agent," Agent Jones said. "One we sent to Brazil years ago to investigate Xerxes. Her name is Nina Dos Santos. Codenamed Gumby. The phone number and email lead nowhere. Your assignment is to question her as soon as we nail down her location. We have reason to believe that she is in the states. "

"How can I question someone without showing my face in

public?" Achilla asked with a cocked eyebrow.

"In secret," Agent Jones said. "And by force if necessary. Move at night, find her, get her to talk."

"You want me to torture a former CIA agent?" Achilla replied as she glared at Agent Jones' reflection on the glass. "This doesn't sound like a job for a rookie. Are you guys setting me up to fail?"

"Achilla--"

"No, that's what they do at other jobs," Achilla said. "You're setting me up to get killed. You're hoping that I'll get sloppy and get shot."

"I wouldn't agree to that," Agent Jones sighed. "Achilla, you have to trust me."

"I don't have to do anything," Achilla snapped and turned around. "Last I checked, you need *me* to fight Ailina! Or so you said."

"*So I said?*" Agent Jones demanded. "What are you implying, Achilla? That I've lied to you?"

"Why not just shoot her and make it look like she died in action?" Achilla asked as she leaned forward and glared at Agent Jones' reflection under her cap. "Why did you let her get this far? Why do you require that I fight her? That call to duty worked when I was sixteen and worried about my family, but you can't fool me anymore. What's the real reason I'm here?"

"I've already told you that--"

"Sticking to your guns?" Achilla asked as she walked toward the door. "Fine. I need a job and I can't be seen in public anyway. Just keep in mind that you can't keep the veil over my eyes forever. Just know that if you slip up, I'm gone no matter the risk, and you'll never be able to stop me."

"Agent Johnson," Agent Jones replied while he followed her. "Do you accept your assignment or not?"

"Yes!" Achilla screamed and whirled to face him. "Yes, I accept *my assignment*! What the fuck else am I going to do?"

"Take the week off," Agent Jones said with a wave of his hand. "You're in no condition to start yet. You're young, and this is your first time working at this level of stress. It's understandable."

"Don't patronize me," Achilla growled before catching her breath and turning toward the door. "You know what, just call me when you need me to start. I'm going home."

"You'll be staying here," Agent Jones replied. "It's not safe for you to return to your apartment."

"You took away my apartment?" Achilla asked through gritted teeth as she faced him again.

"Yes," Agent Jones said. "It's for your safety. Your belongings have already been moved to your room. It's just down the hall--"

"What?" Achilla bellowed as she lunged at Agent Jones and pinned him against the glass window by his shirt. Agent Jones struggled, but Achilla forearm pinned him by his collarbone and raised her fist.

How dare they touch her belongings! They were all she had left now; the remainders of the freedom and personal space that she sacrificed to keep her family alive. One good punch ought to teach him not to touch her things. Achilla glared at Agent Jones with her trembling fist aimed at his face until she took a deep breath, lowered her hand and released him. She raised her hands and backed away as Agent Jones stared at her with wide eyes.

"Sorry," Achilla said. "I lost my cool. Just don't touch my stuff anymore. It's all I have."

"Your testosterone levels have skyrocketed," Agent Jones huffed as he adjusted his shirt. "For a while, you'll be more aggressive than usual. Ailina showed the same symptoms when she was your age."

"So now I have roid rage?" Achilla asked with her hands on her hips. "Wow, that's even worse than blaming my period. You can't be serious."

"I wasn't kidding about taking a week off," Agent Jones said. "In your current state, you'll clobber the next person who bumps into you."

"No," Achilla snapped with a raised hand. "You violated my privacy. I'm pissed. That's it. I'll take the few days off, and you'd better have a punching bag in here."

"We brought several for you."

"Good," Achilla said as she walked past Agent Jones and opened the door. "I'm going to need them after talking to you."

"Go for it."

"And there'd better be a television," Achilla continued as she walked down the hallway. "If any of your buddies took my cartoon collection, I will hunt them down and kick them all in the throats one-by-one, and that is a *promise*."

Achilla didn't wait for Agent Jones' response. She searched the hallway until she found a room behind a white door with a window at eye-level. Achilla felt like she was committed to a funny farm as she turned the doorknob and walked in. Her new room was about the same size as a studio apartment with a white floor and a queen sized mattress with white sheets. Her DVD collection was stacked under a sixty-inch platinum television that sat on the white wall across from her bed. Achilla stared at the screen with her hands on her hips. At least her television was an upgrade. She watched the next episode of Dragonball Z on her couch before leaving her room and wandering the halls until she found the fitness center. Inside the one-hundred yard room, the floor was marked like a football field. To Achilla's left were pull-up bars, tires, and weight sets. To her right was a line of punching bags.

She approached one bag and tapped it with her knuckle. She frowned at how much it felt like an actual person. She tested the bag with a light side-kick and watched the bag shake and swing. She then grunted as she swung a left hook with all of her might. Her fist ripped through the bag and water splashed all over her clothes and on the floor. Achilla growled and side-kicked the next bag behind it, causing another water explosion. By the time she ran through all of the bags, Achilla stood in a puddle of water with her clothes so wet that her t-shirt clung to her shoulders. She stared at her hands, soaked with stale water, and felt her blood pulsing through each finger, demanding freedom.

Who were they to tell her where to live? Who were they to tell her who to fight and defend? They were lying to her and keeping her held up in this basement like some weird science experiment. They were treating her no different than Ares. Achilla clenched her fist as she looked down the hall. Tonight, she would sneak out and protect her family on her own.

No more Agent Jones. No more CIA. No more *deal*.

Achilla changed into a plain gray t-shirt and jeans in her room and grabbed her pistol. She tucked her gun into the back of her belt as she walked into the hallway. It was dark except for a light coming from the interrogation room. Achilla tip-toed down the hall without a sound until she was about fifty feet away. She recognized Agent Jones' voice, but the female voice was new. Her voice was soft but stern and short. If it were not for her slight Japanese accent, Achilla would have thought she was Sam.

"What do you mean?" the female voice asked.

"She doesn't trust us," Agent Jones said. "And I don't blame her. What's going on, Kate? Why is she here?"

Achilla frowned. He wasn't in the loop? This Kate was his boss, and she was withholding information from him. Why would she assign him to watch Achilla without giving him all of the facts? Achilla remembered how she assaulted him just a few hours ago and stared at her feet. If she were to look at herself objectively, she was a danger to everyone around her. How could someone be assigned to work with her without knowing everything he needed to know?

Achilla shook her head and kept listening.

"I told you that we need her," Kate replied. "Ailina's a security risk that we can't neutralize without Achilla's help."

"I've always had a hard time buying that," Agent Jones said. "And now Achilla doesn't buy it either. She's too smart to deceive, Kate. You can't expect me to train her properly without all of the information, and if she learns something I don't, she'll assume I was keeping it from her, and I'll have no way of refuting that. She'll be out the door, and we'll have no way of stopping her without killing her."

"We need her alive."

"And I want her alive," Agent Jones stated. "She's a good kid. I just need more."

"You have all of the information you need," Kate snapped. "And as for Achilla, get her to buy into the program."

"We've worked together for a long time, Kate," Agent Jones said. "I deserve better than this."

"Freeman, you know how serious this is," Kate replied with a deadpan tone. "You know what could happen if you fail. Don't fail."

Achilla pressed herself against the wall as she heard high-heels walking toward the hallway. She saw a short, thin woman with shoulder-length, straight black hair wearing a gray dress turn and march down the hall in the opposite direction. Achilla waited for her to disappear before strolling down the hall to the interrogation room. She found Agent Jones sitting at the table with his hands over his face with the hood of his black sweatshirt over his head. Achilla bit her lip and leaned against the doorway as she watched him lean back in his chair without removing his hands. Agent Jones looked up and nearly jumped out of his seat.

"Jesus, Achilla!" Agent Jones gasped before regaining his composure. "What are you doing awake?"

"Nephilim only need three hours of sleep a night," Achilla said as she picked lint from her jeans. "Or at least I do. I won't be tired for about an hour or so."

"How much did you hear?"

"Enough that I can trust you now," Achilla said with a grin as she walked into the room. "It sounds like you're going through a lot. You're stressed. Talk to me."

"It's nothing."

"Nephilim can also tell when you're lying," Achilla said as she stood behind Agent Jones and caressed his shoulders. "Or at least I can. You're stressed. Your body screams it. Talk to me. It's all right."

"I guess so," Agent Jones replied as Achilla massaged his back. "You'll move up in this field, Achilla. You have more than enough potential, but don't let it destroy you. Never forget yourself."

"You sound like my Dad," Achilla said as she moved back to his shoulders. "You remind me of him, actually."

"Is that so?" Agent Jones asked with a frown.

"Yeah," Achilla said as she wrapped her arms around him and leaned forward, turning his head by his chin. "You're real stern and strong. Honest too. It's kind of sexy."

Achilla tried to kiss Agent Jones, but he turned his head away. He then stood up and reached behind her back. When he snatched Achilla's gun and aimed it at her, she raised her hands. Agent Jones' eyes set on her as he pointed the gun at her face. Achilla grinned as she stared down the barrel.

"Why are you strapped?" Agent Jones asked.

"It's not what you think, *Freeman*," Achilla replied. "I was going to sneak out of here until I heard your conversation with Kate. After that, I decided to stay."

"And kill me?" Agent Jones snapped.

"Or maybe have a little fun," Achilla said with a shrug. "Looks like we could both blow off some steam."

"You seduce then you kill," Agent Jones said. "That's Ailina's calling card, and you got it from her."

"You're only half right" Achilla sighed. "I have no interest in killing you. Look, you have no reason to fear me. Just put the gun down."

"No," Agent Jones barked. "Stay right there and keep your hands where I can see them."

Achilla hung her head. She then dashed forward and snatched the gun out of Agent Jones' hand before he could pull the trigger, tripped his feet, lifted him by his shirt, and pinned him down on the table with one arm. As she gripped his shirt with her left hand, she pressed down on his chest and straddled him. Achilla could feel Agent Jones' heartbeat against her palm as she leaned forward and set her face a few inches from his.

"If I wanted to kill you, you'd be dead," Achilla whispered. "Got it? Now, I haven't been with a man in weeks. You're a man. You need to do what you're supposed to do."

"No," Agent Jones replied. "I told you--"

"Right, business and pleasure," Achilla said as she rubbed the crotch of her jeans against his. "Though right about now, it feels like you want this as much as I do."

"That aside, I refuse," Agent Jones said as he looked away. "It's not a good idea."

"It's a perfect idea," Achilla breathed as she gripped his shirt.

"We have been through so much together for four years now. All the training and studying, you're practically my new boyfriend, and boyfriends screw."

"I'm not your boyfriend," Agent Jones muttered. "I'm your mentor."

"I'm willing to mix the two," Achilla replied. "Now I am tired of you ducking me every time I get close to you. No more. Let me give myself to you, Freeman. Don't you want me?"

"No, Achilla," Agent Jones said. "I don't."

Achilla's lower lip quivered before she glared at him.

"What am I not good enough?" Achilla snarled. "Am I just some *freak* to you, or am I too much of an *aggressive breeder*? I don't forget when you say shit like that--"

"You're not my woman," Agent Jones shot back. "You're my responsibility, and nothing more. Our work is too important to lose focus on what matters, and I don't want to jeopardize our progress on this mission."

"Well, I do," Achilla said as she looked Agent Jones up and down as she continued to rock back and forth against him. Just a little more coaxing, and he would be hers for the night. Sure, he resisted now, but that wouldn't last long. No man could refuse her. Achilla stroked her free hand against his stomach before moving down to his belt.

"Stop it, Achilla," Agent Jones said as he grabbed her wrist and sat up. "This isn't the time or the place."

"No," Achilla breathed as she pinned him to the table. "Now is the time. Now is the place. I need you now!"

"Control yourself, dammit!" Agent Jones yelled.

"I'm in complete control," Achilla replied as she leaned in for a kiss. "And you will give me what I want."

She stopped when she saw the look on Agent Jones' face. He didn't hold the relaxed, euphoric face of a man in the throes of ecstasy. Nor could he even look at her like most of the men who were blown away by Achilla's body at first sight. Instead, he looked away as beads of sweat rolled down his face and tears welled up in his eyes. Was he afraid? No, he was more than that.

He was helpless. Agent Jones looked no different than any frightened, vulnerable, victim. He was completely at Achilla's mercy, and if she wanted, she could have her way with him. Achilla frowned at that thought. The idea of taking what she wanted from a man, without him wanting her in return, made her heart sink. What was the difference between her and Ailina? No. Achilla was different. She was nothing like her. She had to believe that. Her family believed it. So did Dahntay. Achilla started wondering how he was doing again. Was he in college? Did he have a girlfriend? She shook those thoughts out of her head.

Achilla lifted her hand, sat up, and stopped rocking against Agent Jones' body.

"You're right," Achilla said. "This is *not* a good idea. What am I doing?"

"You won't want to hear this, but it's your testosterone levels," Agent Jones replied. "It doesn't just make you violently aggressive. You're sexually aggressive as well. There's a reason Ailina had so many men over when you were a child. Some of them were more prisoners than willing partners. I've heard this scenario played over and over. Shit gave me nightmares."

Achilla set both of her hands on either side of Agent Jones' head. She then lifted herself into a handstand and flipped off the table onto the floor. She frowned at herself and what she just did. Testosterone or not, she could never do that again.

"Sorry about that," Achilla said as she looked over her shoulder. "I promise that'll never happen again. No one deserves what I almost did."

"You have morals," said Agent Jones as he hopped off the table and stood with his hands on his hips. "No doubt Brendan's upbringing influenced you, but you seem to have the natural empathy of any other human being."

"You sound surprised," Achilla muttered.

"I am," Agent Jones chuckled. "It's a trait you don't share with Ailina or Ares. Aside from rushing to defend the weak like Blue Eyes' daughter--"

"Esther," corrected Achilla.

"Esther," Agent Jones audibled with a raised hand. "I've never seen you make a purely moral decision. The fact that it involved resisting an impulse is even more impressive."

"I've never received such a condescending and degrading assessment of my character in my entire life," Achilla grumbled. "But at this point, I'm too much in the wrong to be offended. Can we just forget that this happened?"

"In terms of repercussions, yes," Agent Jones sighed. "But we can't ignore it altogether. We have to work together, Achilla. Anything sexual will only compromise our performance."

"Well, if you won't get me off, somebody has to," Achilla said. "Get a man in here; a willing one."

"I'm afraid that's impossible," Agent Jones said. "Only CIA agents can come down here, and even then they need permission."

"Then get an agent," Achilla replied as she strolled out of the room. "If you're going to hold me in here, I'll need everything I had access to on the outside. Otherwise, I'll go get it myself. Good luck stopping me."

"You drive a hard bargain," Agent Jones said. "I'll see what I can do."

"Oh, and I'll do the mission," Achilla replied. "As long as you ask for it. I'd rather not speak to Kate. We wouldn't get along very well."

"I agree, but at some point, you'll have to speak to her," Agent Jones said. "She hands me your assignments."

"Fine, I'll get it over with," Achilla asked. "Where can I find her?"

"Fiftieth floor of this building," Agent Jones replied. "I'm sure you can figure out how to get there."

"Thanks," Achilla said before walking down the hallway. She went to bed an hour later and woke up at seven a.m. She then threw on a black hoody and sweatpants before jogging down the hall to the elevator. When she arrived on the fiftieth floor, Achilla pressed the closed door button and the back of the elevator opened up to an all-glass office space; similar in design to Blue Eyes' firm. Achilla ignored the receptionist and walked straight to the back past the hustle and bustle of men and women wearing business attire. She strolled past a fancy office with a group of men staring at a computer screen with one of the men scanning it with a laser pointer. When Achilla found an office that said Katherine Hanzo on the door, she entered without knocking. Inside a tan woman with straight black hair wearing a black sleeveless dress with black and blue heels stood by a window with a full view of the city.

"I figured you would come up here eventually," Kate said without turning to face her. "I told everyone to let you through on sight. I wouldn't want them getting hurt."

"That's sweet of you," Achilla replied. "But I wasn't going to hurt anyone."

"Your people are an aggressive breed," Kate said as she faced Achilla with thin brown eyes that bore into Achilla's face. "I have to take precautions; especially at your current age. I'm sure Agent Jones made that clear; especially after your little encounter downstairs."

He already told her. Great, now that Achilla's highest superior knows that she sexually accosted her boss, she wondered how quickly she could pack her bags. It looked like she might be leaving anyway. No reason to bite her tongue.

"Why am I here?" Achilla asked.

"Didn't Agent Jones tell you?" Kate replied with a frown. "He informed me that you had difficulty accepting your purpose here, but I expect that he made things clear."

"He told me what you told him," Achilla said.

"Then that's all you need."

"Don't decide what I need *for me*," Achilla replied. "I'm not a child, and you're not my mother."

"No, your mother is back home in Stratford worried sick about you," Kate sighed as she looked at her nails. "It would be a shame if something were to happen to her--"

Achilla leaped across the room and pinned Kate against the wall of her office before slamming her to the floor, but she flinched at Kate's lack of resistance. Kate didn't draw a gun, a knife, not even a taser. She just stared back at Achilla as she held her to the floor by her dress. If she knew Achilla was coming and worried about her coworkers' safety, shouldn't she be armed? Achilla heard seven agents rush into the room with their guns loaded. Kate raised her hands at them.

"Stand down," Kate commanded. "If she wanted to kill me, she would've done it by now. She knows she needs me alive. Stand down. That's an order!"

"You think you can threaten my family?" Achilla snarled as the agents lowered their guns.

"It's no threat," Kate replied. "The truth is without our help, Ailina kills them all, and our help is contingent on your cooperation."

"You planned on hooking me all along," Achilla said. "Ever since that day..."

"Achilla, I've been planning this since you were born," Kate replied. "You are just as much a security risk as Ailina, and the only reason we've kept you alive is--"

"To fight Ailina--"

"Your conscience," Kate spoke over Achilla. "You're not a sociopath like the rest of your kind. You're different. You're one of the good guys, I can tell. That's why we need you."

"For what?" Achilla asked. "And I need the truth."

"Ares had the ability to create a following," Kate replied. "On top of his unreal strength and speed, he was a master manipulator. Someone with his abilities was a tremendous threat to national security. I believe Ailina was indoctrinated by him at a young age. As long as you're alive, she will continue to try to recruit you to her side so you can follow in Ares' footsteps."

"Agent Jones never mentioned that," Achilla said.

"He doesn't know everything," Kate replied. "It's not required for his role in your development."

"My...development?" Achilla asked.

"Yes," Kate said. "Someone with your capabilities would be the perfect foil to Ailina's plan to overthrow the government just like her father wanted. We need you to be effective at gathering intel and eliminating a target if need be. That's why we used Blue Eyes as a test-run for you. Even if you were like a bull in a china shop, you got the job done as expected. We know your next assignment will go even better. Your kind seldom repeats mistakes. We've learned that the hard way with Ailina."

"Why not just kill her yourself?" Achilla asked. "You could've done it a long time ago."

"That was my fault," Kate replied as she looked away. "I underestimated Ares' brainwashing and hoped that we could reform her. We couldn't. Ares created her worldview and she never wavered, even when she pretended to change."

"How do you know you can reform me?" Achilla snarled as she pulled Kate close by the collar of her dress. "What makes you think I'm any easier to control?"

"We don't have to control you," Kate said. "The Johnsons were an unexpected variable in our favor."

"Don't talk about them like some *experiment*--"

"Fine, I'm not a very emotional person," Kate snapped. "But I know good parents when I see them, and Brendan and Samantha were damn good ones. They taught you love and morals and social responsibility and displayed a shining example with few contradictions. As a result, you have no concept of ruling the world as a superior class of human. If you did, you would've killed me and every agent in this room right now."

"What are you--"

"Don't. Play. Dumb," Kate continued. "I've seen Ares in action first hand. Ailina has eliminated over twenty agents who got too close. Nobody is stupid enough to come near her without a weapon, but they still died unless she chose to keep them alive. Your kind is *lethal*, and you are no exception. You could snap my neck and unarm every man in this room if you wanted."

"Yeah," Achilla said with a head nod. "The thought crossed my mind."

"But you didn't because you have a conscience," Kate said with a softer voice. "You value human life. You may be a Nephilim, but you have the heart of every homo-sapien in this room. In my opinion, that makes you more like us than Ailina. That makes you our ally."

"So all this time, even when I was a kid, you saw me as a potential ally?" Achilla asked. "You expect me to believe that?"

"I have no control over what you believe," Kate replied. "I can't control you at all, but I'm confident that you'll do the right thing."

With all of the knowledge that she had on Nephilim, Achilla half-expected Kate to call her the devil. Instead, she spoke to her with the same confidence and high regard as her parents. There was a very high possibility that Kate was gaming her to save her own life, but with seven agents in the room pointing guns at her, Achilla doubted that was necessary. Besides, Achilla saw no signs of dishonesty in Kate's demeanor. Unless she was better than the average CIA agent at lying, she was telling the truth.

Achilla let go of Kate and rose to her feet. As she readjusted her hoody, she looked around the room at all of the agents staring at her with faces that ranged from amazement to contempt. They still looked at her like some freak show. She sighed and walked toward the door. At least she got her conversation with Kate over with.

One of the agents reached for Achilla's arm, and she grabbed his wrist and pulled him into a punch to the chest; sending him flying through the glass and into the wall across the hall. The six other agents drew their weapons, but Achilla bent over and donkey kicked the agent behind her across the office, slamming him against the wall. She then turned and used her arms to cuff two agents behind the knees and force them to fall back on the floor. Achilla dipped behind the remaining two agents, stepped between them, and elbowed them both in the midsection before snatching their guns and pistol-whipping them at the base of their heads.

By the time the last agent aimed his gun, Achilla had already aimed two pistols his face. He held his firearm steady, but she noticed his trembling hands and knees, and her eyes zeroed in on him. He was a harmless non-threat who most likely held his gun to save his own life and nothing more. Her conscience told her to disarm him but keep him alive, but her growling instinct demanded to shoot him before he gained any courage. That instinct rumbled throughout her body as she focused more on him, staring into his eyes until he looked away for a split second.

That was it. That was all she needed to see. He belonged to her now. She could do whatever she pleased. Achilla grimaced as her fingers hovered over the triggers. Just one short pull and it was over.

"Stop!" Kate screamed as she stepped between them. "God, what part about stand down didn't you idiots understand? She let me go."

Achilla snapped back to normal and watched the agent lower his gun as Kate let out a loud sigh before facing her. She looked around at the six trained CIA agents writhing on the floor. Her first opponent wasn't moving. Achilla looked down at the guns in her hands, and the others she stuffed in her hoody pocket and piled them on Kate's desk. At this point, Achilla was so adept at disarming her opponent that she did it without thinking, but that didn't bother her. The fact that she had to fight the urge to kill someone, and almost lost control, made her heart pound in her chest. Was she really going to shoot another agent? Achilla shook her head before facing Kate.

"Still think I'm human?" Achilla asked as she handed her the guns.

"Yes," Kate said as she took the guns and set them in her desk drawer. "I'm still standing here, aren't I?"

"What about him?" Achilla asked with a pointed thumb at the man across the hall.

"*He* knew better," Kate said with a raised chin. "As far as I'm concerned, he's buying me a new wall."

"Not very empathetic," Achilla quipped with her hands on her hips.

"I don't suffer the company of fools," Kate said as she walked around her desk. "Especially the overzealous kind who pick fights with opponents ten times their strength. I believe I gave you an assignment?"

"Nina Dos Santos," Achilla said. "Force information out of her."

"You got it," Kate replied. "Go get ready."

"On it," Achilla said as she turned to leave.

"Oh, and Achilla."

"Yeah?"

"Leave Agent Jones alone," Kate said with a stern look. "I'll make arrangements for your unique needs."

"Unique?" Achilla chuckled. "What's so unique about wanting sex?"

"If you're anything like Ailina, you're unique," Kate replied. "And I get the impression that you are in that regard."

"I don't like that comparison," stated Achilla with a hard stare.

"That's too bad," replied Kate. "Because that conscience we just talked about is the only thing that separates you from her."

"So what *arrangements* are you making?" Achilla asked.

"Top secret arrangements," Kate answered. "We have plenty of male agents around your age who would jump at this sort of assignment I'm sure, but Agent Jones is off-limits. Understood?"

"You guys are more than co-workers, aren't you?" Achilla pressed. "I'm sensing some female territorialism here. Maybe you should piss on his leg so everyone knows how serious you guys are."

"Like I said," Kate said with a hand raised. "I will make arrangements for you. Is that clear?"

"Yeah, sure,"Achilla said with a slight chuckle as she turned to leave the office. She smirked as she watched a crowd gather around the unconscious man in the hallway. He lay in a pile of shattered glass as a female agent with dirty blonde hair checked his pulse. Achilla didn't bother checking his vitals as she strolled past them. She knew her punch was more push than power. He would survive even if it hurt to breathe for a while.

Kate had a point. Achilla didn't kill if it wasn't necessary, no matter how tempting. When the time came, she knew she would have to kill Ailina. Her face popped into Achilla's head, and she smacked her fist into the palm of her hand, clapping so loud that the agents around her jumped. When that time came, Achilla would be more than ready. But first, Nina Dos Santos was her next target. Achilla boarded the elevator to her new home to prepare for her assignment.

Chapter Eight

ACHILLA JOHNSON:11

Ailina wasn't kidding about intensifying Achilla's training, but after that basketball game, the beatings came even harder and more often than usual. Achilla stood in the middle of the concrete floor basement wearing black basketball shorts and a black t-shirt. She huffed and heaved as sweat drenched her entire body. In front of her stood Ailina wearing gray sweatpants and a white t-shirt. She glared at Achilla with green eyes that locked onto her like a heat-seeking missile. As Ailina stalked toward her, Achilla held a fighting stance with her left hand in front and her right hand by her cheek. She took a deep breath as she tried to calm her trembling fists.

"I haven't gotten over my anger with you," Ailina said. "It's been three weeks, and I still can't forgive you. You really pissed me off."

Achilla forced herself to not cry out with another excuse. She forced herself not to ask why she couldn't talk to people and why she couldn't defend herself when attacked. What was the big deal? Why was she so angry? Why did Achilla have to fight all the time, and when would it stop? When would she be good enough for her mother to stop hitting her? Achilla shook those thoughts out of her head. She had to focus on the task at hand.

Just as Achilla calmed her body, Ailina lunged forward with a knee that she blocked with both forearms. Stars burst out of Achilla's eyes when Ailina struck the back of her head. Achilla hit the floor face first with her forearms out and rolled out of the way just in time to avoid her mother's foot. By the time she made it to her feet, Achilla blocked a kick that sent her bouncing against the concrete wall and falling to her knees. She gritted her teeth and rose to her feet as Ailina stood with her hands on her hips.

"You reacted faster against that inferior girl," Ailina said with a slight snarl. "You were so quick! Do you think you can half-ass with me? Do you?!"

Before Achilla could respond, Ailina rushed her with a punch to the gut that knocked the air out of her body. Achilla gasped and held her midsection as she fell to her knees again. Ailina then lifted her up by her shirt and pinned her against the wall; staring into Achilla's eyes with a gaze that made her look away. Achilla's feet dangled in mid-air as Ailina held her fast. Her heart beat out of her shirt and her face flushed as she held her Ailina's forearm.

"It's going to take a lot of beating for me to feel better," Ailina said with a hard stare. "I'm still angry."

Achilla decided that if she was going to get her ass kicked, she could at least fight back. She gritted her teeth and kicked Ailina's midsection, but it caused no effect. Achilla kicked again with the same result, and Ailina punched her in the head before throwing her to the floor. Achilla hopped up and threw a punch that missed wide-left before receiving a knee to the gut and a kick to the face. Achilla held her nose as she stumbled forward, but she shook off the pain as she whirled to face her mother. She then uttered a growl and sprinted toward her opponent.

Achilla threw a flurry of punches and kicks. They all missed their mark. Every last one. It was like Ailina was made of a special gas that only solidified itself when it punched Achilla in the face. Tears streamed down her cheeks as she bared her teeth and swung. Why did Ailina always have to make her suffer? What was so great about being superior? Those questions replayed in Achilla's mind as she threw a left hook, a right straight, a left side kick, a right front kick. Her attack was relentless but ineffective.

After another missed punch, Ailina grabbed her wrist and pulled Achilla behind her; sending her toward a wall face first. Instead of letting her nose crash into the concrete, Achilla lifted her foot and stopped herself before propelling her body at Ailina. She shoulder rammed Ailina's left side and threw a looping punch at her head. It connected to Ailina's chin, and Achilla dropped to the floor as her opponent stumbled back.

It was a small victory, but Achilla was now on all fours with sweat dripping down her face while her mother remained standing.

"Not bad," Ailina said she rubbed her chin. "That was better reaction time. Now I can proudly say you're a superior being like me and actually mean it. I think you're ready."

Achilla raised her hand, and her arm trembled as she held it over her head, waiting for Ailina to grant her the right to speak. If she didn't wait, the sparring would continue, and her trembling limbs could no longer last another five minutes after four hours of fighting.

"Speak," Ailina said with her chin raised. "But only if you have a question."

"Ready for what?" Achilla asked as she dropped her arm.

"You'll be living with your father," Ailina said. "Apparently your little skirmish caught his attention and he pulled some strings. I have to give you up."

"When?" Achilla huffed and swallowed before finishing her statement. "When were you going to tell me?"

"Raise your hand!" Ailina roared as she charged across the basement and punted Achilla's ribcage. Achilla cried out and rolled on the floor. Her mouth gaped and tears rolled down her cheeks, and she struggled to catch her breath as she held her throbbing left side. She tried to stop crying. She knew it was wrong to cry in a fight, but she couldn't help it as her sides stabbed at her. Ailina rolled her over with her foot. She then kneeled over her as she sobbed.

"Achilla, you know crying makes you look weak," Ailina said. "I only broke three ribs, but at least I feel better now. You leave in the morning. Clean yourself up and pack your things."

Achilla lay on her side as she watched her mother turn her back and walk to the stairs across the basement. She then marched up the stairs without a sound except her feet pounding against the wooden steps. After an hour of writhing on the floor and inhaling the dust they kicked up during their sparring session, Achilla rose to her feet. The pain in her ribs still stabbed at her, but she was able to walk. Like every night in this house, Achilla would stumble to the bathroom, disinfect any cuts, shower, then ice any bruises or lumps, and then go to sleep. As much as Ailina said that this training would help her realize that she was a superior being, the pain in Achilla's ribs told her a different story. Achilla didn't know how to identify how she felt right now, but superior didn't quite cut it.

Achilla winced as she walked toward the basement steps. When she made it upstairs into their kitchen she leaned against the wall to keep her balance as her legs trembled under her weight. Her head was a little hazy from all of those punches, but Achilla knew she would be fine. She always managed to wake up the next morning. As she made her way down the blue carpeted hallway, she passed by Ailina's dark, mahogany door and stopped for a break.

Behind the door, Achilla could hear the creaking and knocking of a queen-sized bed taking serious punishment. Ailina apparently called one of her boyfriends over, but she didn't bother telling Achilla she would have company. Achilla shook her head and walked past the doorway until she heard the bed stop. Achilla frowned. They usually didn't quit that quickly. Achilla flinched when she saw the door burst open and a naked, black male with dreadlocked hair flew across the hallway, banged against the wall, and fell on the floor in a heap. Ailina stepped out wearing nothing but her glistening skin and mussed up hair as she stood over him.

"What the hell do you mean you have to go?" Ailina snarled as she stepped on the man's neck. "You don't leave without giving me what I want!"

"Babe, I got a flight in the morn--"

"Reschedule your flight!" Ailina snapped as she kicked the man in the face with a flick of her ankle. "I am your priority, and don't you forget it."

"OK!" the man said with his hands raised. "OK, fine!"

"I'm getting some water," Ailina said before pointing at the bedroom. "When I get back, you'd better be in there, and you'd better be ready to do what I called you here to do. Got it?"

"Yes, of course," the man said as he scrambled to his feet and stumbled back into the bedroom. Achilla wanted to walk away, but her feet refused to move. She always froze when she watched how Ailina kept her men in line. It was almost comforting to know that someone else suffered as much as she did. When Ailina looked at her, Achilla turned her back to walk away. She stopped when she felt a hand grab her shoulder and looked behind her at her mother.

"It's all he's good for, and he needs to know that," Ailina said. "It's all they're all good for. One day, you'll see I'm right."

"Yes, ma'am," Achilla replied

"You have to remind him who's in charge," Ailina said as she squeezed Achilla's shoulder. "It's good for him. I haven't let you have a boyfriend yet, but I want you to remember that."

"Yes, ma'am," Achilla said.

"Now go pack up your things and go to bed," Ailina said as she turned her back and strolled to the kitchen. "Your ride should be here early."

"You're not driving me?" Achilla asked before clamping her hand over her mouth. Ailina stopped in her tracks. Achilla wanted to sprint to her room and lock the door, but all her legs managed was a small step back. She clenched her eyes shut in preparation for another hit, but it didn't come. Achilla opened her eyes and saw Ailina looking over her bare shoulder. Her eyes glowed in the dark hallway as she stared at her.

"No," Ailina said with a slight grin before stretching her arms and scratching her side. "I have work in the morning. Besides, I think it's about time you stretched your legs a little. The more independent you are the better."

Ailina walked into the kitchen, and Achilla caught her breath. She then turned and ambled down the hallway to her room. She looked out into the hallway and saw Ailina returning to her bedroom with an orange bowl. A few minutes later, the bed creaking began again. Achilla sighed and ambled to the bathroom. The sooner she got started, the sooner she could get some sleep. The next day, she would leave this house. That thought made a smile creep onto Achilla's lips as she opened her bathroom door and stepped inside.

Two Bridgeport police officers picked up Achilla at around eight the next morning, and she stepped out of her house wearing a green, oversized t-shirt and black basketball shorts. As expected, Ailina wasn't home when they came. Ailina never acted like those touchy-feely mothers Achilla watched hug their children from her bedroom window. As Achilla handed a tall, blonde police officer her gym bag full of clothes, a lump grew in her throat as she looked back at her house and realized she would never have her room again. She fought back the tears in her eyes and hung her head as she followed the police to their navy blue cruiser and stepped in the backseat.

As she watched the smokestacks and high rises of Bridgeport pass by, Achilla thought about Brendan again. She noticed that he was different from all of the other men Ailina brought home. He had a voice that boomed like a trumpet, and he spoke with a clarity that made Achilla want to listen to him. What stuck out to Achilla the most about him was his rippled hair that held a peculiar scent that Achilla had never smelled before; it reminded her of an unlit scented candle. That smell and his voice lingered in Achilla's mind as she watched the street signs change from blue to green. Within a few minutes, the police stopped their car.

When Achilla stepped out, the blonde police officer took her bag out of the trunk and dropped it on the ground. Achilla never forgot how he just dropped her stuff like it didn't belong to another person. It made Achilla wonder if other police officers actually liked her or her mother. She frowned as she picked up the bag and carried it up the driveway while the officers drove off without another word. If she never saw them again it would be too soon.

Upon arrival, the first thing Achilla noticed about Brendan's house was how normal it was. It was a two-story colonial home with green siding and black shutters; not the big fancy mansion that Ailina always claimed it was. There was a fancy black sedan in the driveway, but it looked at least five years old. Achilla also noticed that the car was spotless, the grass was well-mowed all around with an adult oak tree in the middle of the backyard, and the garden on the side of the house grew without a single weed. Brendan may not have been any richer than Ailina at first glance, but he certainly kept up his house better. At Ailina's house, Achilla did all of the cleaning.

Achilla rang the doorbell outside of a dark green painted door. It had hardly finished its tune when the door swung open and a brown-skinned woman with ear-length hair wearing a blue t-shirt with a denim jacket and jeans stepped outside. Achilla dropped her bag and stepped back as the woman stared at her with brown eyes and a smile on her face. Something about the way she smiled made Achilla avert her gaze at first, but she forced herself to stare back. The woman held her hands on her hips and shook her head.

"Brendan was right," the woman said. "You do look just like Ailina, but that face you just made at me, that's a Johnson face. You've got Brendan written all over you, girl."

"Who are you?" Achilla asked.

"I'm Samantha," the woman replied with a soft voice. "But please call me Sam. Let me take your bag--"

Achilla snatched her bag away when Sam stepped forward. Sam recoiled but her movements were slow. If she were as fast as Ailina, she would have taken the bag already. Achilla took note of that as she clutched her bag and stared at her. Sam held her hands on her hips again and sighed before rubbing the palm of her hand on her forehead. She then turned and opened the door.

"You poor thing," Sam sighed. "You must have been through so much. Well, if it makes you more comfortable, you can carry your own bag."

"Where's Brendan?" Achilla asked without moving an inch. "The cops said this was Brendan's house. Do you know Brendan?"

"Yeah, I think I know Brendan pretty well," Sam replied. "I'm his wife."

"Where is he?" Achilla asked with a stronger tone than she intended as she looked past Sam's shoulder into the house.

"You don't trust me," Sam replied.

"I don't know you," Achilla said.

"Right," Sam replied with a nod of her head. "I should've known this would be difficult. Your father had no clue when exactly you would be here. He walked to the corner store to grab some ice cream."

"For what?"

"For you," Sam said. "Most girls your age like ice cream, and he wanted to make you feel at home; kind of like I'm trying to do right now--"

"I don't eat ice cream," Achilla replied. "Too much sugar."

"Wow," Sam said with wide eyes. "I'm impressed. Then what kind of food do you like? Do you have a favorite?"

"Steak," Achilla said. "T-bone. With steamed vegetables."

"Luckily, we have some steaks in the fridge," Sam smiled and pointed into the house with her thumb. "I'll leave it up to you. If you need to see Brendan before you do anything else, you can wait out here for him to come back; or you can come inside and get settled first. Your call."

Her call? It was her decision? Whoever this woman was, she was nothing like Ailina. Achilla looked at her feet for a split second before extended the bag toward Sam. When she felt Sam take the bag out of her hand, she followed her into the house. Achilla's eyes adjusted to the change of light as she watched Sam's back and trailed her into a kitchen with an off-white tiled floor and white countertops. Achilla's head snapped to her right when she noticed someone sitting at a table on the other end of the kitchen. It was a boy with a strong resemblance to Sam, but with waved hair like Brendan. Achilla picked up the same scent of unscented candles from his hair and noticed he had the same waves flowing around his head.

"Samuel, this is your sister," Sam said as she stood next to Achilla. "Though she hasn't given us her name yet."

Achilla raised her hand, and the boy snorted.

"Don't laugh, Samuel," Sam said with a stern tone before smiling at Achilla. "You don't have to raise your hand to speak in here. What's your question?"

"If you knew I was coming, don't you already know my name?" Achilla asked.

"Yes, but it's rude to walk into someone's house and not introduce yourself," Sam replied with a smile and gritted teeth.

"Oh," Achilla said. "Sorry, I'm Achilla."

"Cool, I'm Samuel," Samuel replied as he hopped out of his chair and extended his hand.

"You're also supposed to shake his hand," Sam chuckled. "Did Ailina teach you any manners?"

"I can do a handshake," Achilla said with a shrug as she gripped Samuel's hand. Samuel cringed and dropped to one knee as Achilla shook his hand. She let go when she saw a tear leak out of his left eye. Samuel stayed on the ground and held his hand as Sam rushed to his side. Achilla frowned and stared at her own hand before looking back at him.

"Are you injured?" Achilla asked. "Why are you crying?"

"He'll be fine," Sam said. "He's just a sensitive boy, that's all--"

"Mom, my hand hurts!" Samuel whined. "I think she broke my hand."

"No, I didn't break anything," Achilla said to Sam. "I would know if I did."

"Your hand isn't broken, honey," Sam said to her son with a soft voice as she rubbed his hand. "Look, I'll shake her hand and show you."

Sam extended her hand to Achilla, and she gripped Sam's hand just the same. She didn't fall to her knees, but Sam yanked her hand away. She then massaged her hand as she stared at Achilla. Achilla looked back with a blank face.

What was the big deal?

"Achilla, honey, you may want to loosen your grip," Sam said with a frown. "If I didn't know any better, I'd think you could beat your father in an arm wrestling match."

"I'll do better next time," Achilla replied with a shrug before she turned and walked toward the black refrigerator to her left. "When do you want me to cook those steaks?"

"I don't," Sam replied. "I'll cook. What made you think I would ask you to do something like that?"

"I always cooked at home unless she was preparing for company," Achilla said.

"Well, this is your new home," Sam said. "It's going to be a lot different around here."

"So, what do you need me to do?" Achilla asked. "Maybe I can clean these countertops?"

"I already cleaned them."

"You did?" Achilla asked as she ran her finger across the counter next to the refrigerator and flicked a speck of dust.

"Is my cleaning not up to your standards?" Sam asked as she stood up with her hands on her hips.

"I don't know," Achilla said with a shrug. "But last time I left a counter looking like this, I got a broken nose."

"Well there won't be any broken noses around here," Sam replied with a soft voice. "And I'm sorry Ailina did that to you."

"I'm used to it," Achilla sighed as she heard the front door open. She followed Sam's gaze as she smiled and stood in the kitchen doorway. Achilla heard the sound of sneakers stepping on the hardwood floor as Sam wiped a strand of her hair and stepped back. Brendan walked into the kitchen wearing a white t-shirt and navy blue basketball shorts over his navy-blue Air Jordan sneakers. The look on Sam's face made Achilla frown. She stared at Brendan with a wide smile and bright eyes; a look Ailina never held when a man came to visit her. Sam kissed Brendan's cheek and leaned against his shoulder as she pointed at Achilla.

"You got her, baby," Sam said. "She's here."

"Is she staying, Dad?" Samuel asked with a smile that Achilla did not expect considering the pain she inflicted on his hand.

"Yeah," Brendan replied before kissing his wife and stepping forward. "Achilla, we would like you to stay here. We'll be taking care of you from now on. You won't be going back to Ailina's house anymore."

"OK," Achilla said with a smile she couldn't suppress.

"I'm sure Sam has already tried her best to help you feel at home," Brendan said as he pulled out a grocery bag from behind his back. "I figured I'd surprise you with this, but obviously I wasn't home in time. For that, I do apologize. You'll find that I'm not late very often."

"She doesn't eat ice cream, honey," Sam whispered.

"I figured," Brendan replied as he pulled out a box of strawberries and a handful of bananas. "Which is why I'll be making everyone fruit smoothies for dessert. How does that sound, Achilla?"

"I've never had one, but I can try it," Achilla said with a shrug. "What's dessert?"

"It's what you eat after dinner," Samuel snickered. "Where've you been?"

"Samuel, stop it," Sam snapped.

"Samuel," Brendan replied with a slight growl. "We discussed this."

"Sorry," Samuel said with his head low.

"Well dinner isn't for another ten hours or so," Brendan said with a shrug that Achilla noticed looked just like her own. "Why don't we take the day to set some grounds rules and give you a tour of the neighborhood?"

"I counted eight houses and around four children on my way here," Achilla said. "But there could be more because of the six basketball hoops and five bikes; two with training wheels."

"You don't know what dessert is?" Sam asked. "But you noticed all of that?"

"We discussed this too, Sam," Brendan whispered.

"Right," Sam replied as she grabbed Achilla's bag. "Come on, Achilla. I'll show you your room."

After getting acclimated to her surroundings, Achilla realized that Sam was right. The Johnson house certainly was different from anything she was used to. In fact, the more time that Achilla spent with the Johnsons, the more she realized that her life with Ailina wasn't normal. The Johnsons gave Achilla a set of chores to do every week and expected them to be done by a certain time. Ailina just expected Achilla to clean everything without having to be told. The Johnsons gave Achilla an allowance every week. Ailina would have thought that giving her money was preposterous. Since she was a high school English teacher for Central High School and off for the summer, Sam made breakfast, lunch, and dinner almost every day, and Brendan cooked whenever he was home early enough. Ailina usually left food in the fridge and told Achilla to figure it out. Whenever Achilla's new brother, Samuel, talked back, he got grounded. Achilla received bare-knuckle punches, elbows, and kicks from Ailina when she didn't follow instructions. She still had bruises and scars on her back for every time she did not do something exactly the way Ailina liked it. The concept of grounding a child, without physically shoving his face into the ground, confused Achilla.

Still, there was one glaring difference above all. Ailina made Achilla train every day until she could barely walk. She taught Achilla how to hit, when to hit, and where to hit someone for almost any situation, and forced her to spar with her until she got it right. She told Achilla every day that she was a superior being above everyone else and that she should use her hands to keep the lower people in their place. She was destined to rule everyone around her.

Achilla learned more by watching how Ailina treated her men. She had a steady rotation of at least three men a month, but if one of them didn't follow instructions, he received a terrible beating. Achilla once watched her choke slam a man to the kitchen floor when she suspected him of sleeping with another woman. Another man tried to rob her of sixty dollars and suffered a jaw fracture so extreme that he couldn't close his mouth without using his hands. Ailina never bothered to hide her partners, nor her victims, from Achilla, and in turn, Achilla learned how to deal with an enemy. That girl during the charity basketball game didn't know what hit her. Literally. Achilla overheard her new parents talking about it. The girl suffered a concussion and couldn't remember what happened.

Achilla's new parents did not expect her to train. Achilla once waited in the basement all night only to find that they had gone to sleep. They didn't call her a superior being. Instead, they expected her to behave, never talk back to adults, and play with the neighborhood kids. Achilla did as she was told and introduced herself to her neighbors. They let her play basketball with them and invited her to play every day after they saw how well she could shoot. Ailina's superiority never left Achilla's mind, but Brendan's lack of it made her smile a lot more.

Though they were not all that close yet, Achilla had an intense desire to protect Samuel from all harm. He was so sensitive that he would cry from the slightest bump, and all Achilla could think about were ways to stop him from crying. Achilla once stood over him in their driveway when he started crying again during a game of one-on-one. He tried to steal the ball from her, and she turned her body to protect the ball. She ended up ramming her shoulder into his chest and knocking him to the ground. Achilla sighed as Samuel sat in the driveway, wailing as he held his head.

"Why are you crying?" Achilla groaned.

"I hit my head!" Samuel cried.

"I saw that," Achilla said. "So what?"

"So it hurts!"

"Just because something hurts doesn't mean you have to cry," Achilla said as she walked up to their basketball hoop. "Watch this."

Achilla cocked her head back and slammed her forehead against the pole so hard that she shook the rim. A sharp pain rang throughout her head, but it was mild compared to an elbow to the temple from Ailina. She turned and smiled at Samuel as blood seeped down her forehead from the lump she knew she would have to ice later. She held her smile as Samuel stared at her through his tears.

"See?" Achilla said as she forced herself to not wince from the throbbing sensation in her forehead. "I'm not crying, and that really hurt. Trust me."

Samuel stopped crying. He then pointed and laughed. Achilla smiled at the sound of his laughter; so gentle and playful. When Samuel laughed so hard that he held his side and rolled on the ground, Achilla held her mouth and giggled under her breath. Within a few seconds, they laughed together.

One day Samuel went off to play with the neighborhood kids. Achilla didn't feel like it and stayed at home. She sat on the porch in her jean shorts and gray t-shirt and basked in the quietness of her new neighborhood. It wasn't much different from her old neighborhood with colonial homes lining the street, dogs napping on their porches, blue jays screeching from the rooftops, and the smells of lunch and dinner wafting through the air. Still, something about it was more peaceful. There was no fear of Ailina coming home early and catching her outside playing basketball. There were no miles to run on the treadmill or number of punches to throw before her next sparring session. Instead, the scent of barbecue chicken filled Achilla's nose as she stared at the cumulus clouds sitting in the blue sky and smiled.

She could get used to this.

Achilla stood up when she saw Samuel ambling up the sidewalk. When he looked up at her, she saw that his left eye was blackish-purple. Achilla jumped off the porch and rushed toward him. She held his shoulders as he started crying. This time, she felt no need to make him stop.

"Samuel, what happened to your eye?" Achilla asked.

"He took my basketball," Samuel sniffed as he rubbed his black eye until Achilla pulled his arm away from it.

"Who did?" Achilla demanded.

"Marty O'Brien," Samuel said. "Some big kid down the street."

"You just let him take it?" Achilla asked with a stern tone.

"No, I punched him in the face!" Samuel said with a slight snarl as more tears fell down his cheeks. "But he's bigger than me."

"Good," Achilla replied as she patted Samuel's shoulder. "You did well, Samuel."

When Samuel sobbed into Achilla's shoulder, she felt a lump in her throat. Tears welled up in her eyes as her face burned, and her hands balled into fists. Achilla had never met Marty, but she heard about him from the other kids. Marty was the oldest boy on their block, and from what the other boys said, he was at least twice

Samuel's size. The thought of him picking on Samuel made Achilla grind her teeth.

"Samuel," Achilla said as she held him by his shoulders and looked him in the eyes. "I want you to show me where he lives. We're getting your ball back."

Samuel led the way as they marched to Marty's house; a plain yellow home with black shutters and a driveway with lots of dips and cracks. The lawn had brown grass and a water hose strewed across it like a snake that succumbed to the summer heat. Achilla noticed a group of boys wearing matching red "Ralphola-Taylor Center" t-shirts playing with Samuel's basketball in front of a hoop attached to their garage. Two of them were tall and skinny with blacktop dark skin and identical short haircuts with diagonal dashes etched in the sides. One of them was shorter but pudgy with pale skin and oily, dark brown hair that fell over his forehead. He also had a small scratch under his eye.

"Which one's Marty?" Achilla said to Samuel as she stepped forward.

Samuel pointed at the pale kid just as one of his friends pointed at Achilla and Samuel. Achilla clenched her fist as she walked up the driveway. Marty held the basketball on his hip as Achilla stood under his nose. Based on Ailina's training, Achilla assessed her opponent. He had four inches of height on her and at least fifty pounds. However, his midsection looked soft and doughy, and as he stood with the ball in his hand, he didn't bother to protect himself. This would be an easy fight.

"That's Samuel's ball," Achilla said. "Give it back. Now."

"Your brother's beat for his ball," Marty replied as his blue eyes stared down at Achilla. "Just because your brother's a punk doesn't mean you can come over here asking for shit."

"I didn't *ask* for anything," Achilla snarled as her eyes turned bloodshot. "I *told* you to give my brother his ball back, and I'm not going to tell you again!"

Marty chuckled as he threw the ball back to one of his friends who caught it. The other one stepped forward with a frown on his face. As his twin shot another jump shot, the look on his face puzzled Achilla. He just looked back and forth at Achilla and then behind her, probably at Samuel. He hesitated and then placed his hand on Marty's shoulder.

"Hey, man, just give them the ball," he said.

"Nah, punks get no respect," Marty snapped. "I thought you were my boy. Why can't you back me up?"

"They're little kids, man," the twin said.

"So what?"

"Fuck this, I can't hang with you no more, man, this is crazy," the twin replied before turning to the other. "Yo, we out, man!"

"But--"

"I said, we out!" the twin snapped. "Put the ball down! You know that ain't right!"

The other twin sucked his teeth and dropped the ball before they both walked past Achilla's shoulder. Achilla kept her eyes trained on Marty as his friends left the driveway. She continued to stare at him as she stepped toward the ball. Marty blocked her path. When Achilla stepped forward again, he blocked her path again.

"That's my ball now," Marty said. "Go buy a new one."

Achilla faced him with a hard stare, and Marty chuckled and pushed her shoulder. Achilla grabbed his arm and pulled him forward as she poked his right eye with a finger jab. Marty cried out as she held him in place, and she kicked his groin twice before shoving him against the house. He bounced against the yellow siding and slumped to the ground while holding his hands between his legs. His face turned red and tears rolled down his cheeks as Achilla stalked toward him. When Marty tried to get up, Achilla kicked him in his gut, causing him to grunt and fall back to the ground. She then gritted her teeth and stomped his ribcage. She continued to stomp him as she thought about Samuel getting beat up for his basketball. She stomped him as she remembered Samuel's black eye and the tears leaking from his eyes. Samuel was a good kid. He didn't deserve that. Marty wasn't a good kid. He deserved this beating. So Achilla was going to stomp him until--

"Stop!" Samuel screamed as he grabbed her shoulder. "Look at him!"

Achilla looked down at the red-faced, pudgy boy who held his hands over his head. When Marty looked up at her with one eye shut, and the other blue eye squinted, she raised her chin and stared back. Achilla then shoved Samuel aside and lifted Marty upright by his shirt. She held his shirt with one hand and punched his nose with the other, bouncing his head against the house. Marty groaned and held his face as he rolled on the ground.

"Achilla!" Samuel yelled. "Stop it!"

"That was for my brother," Achilla snarled as she kicked sand into Marty's face. "You stay away from him from now on, or I'll come back."

Achilla walked up the driveway and picked up the basketball. She bounced it a couple times before making a lay-up on Marty's hoop. She then picked up the ball and carried it against her hip as she approached Samuel. She handed him the ball and he took it. Achilla then wrapped her arm around his shoulder and led him toward Marty.

"Next time he bothers you," Achilla told Samuel as she pointed at the writhing, moaning, chubby boy on the ground. "Hit him in his eyes and groin, just like I did. After that, he's yours to do whatever you want. If that doesn't work, come get me. I'll take care of him again until he learns to keep his hands to himself."

Samuel nodded his head and bounced the basketball between his legs. After they walked home, Samuel ran straight to his room without as much as a thank you. Achilla frowned and watched him run up the stairs before lowering her head and walking outside. She didn't leave the porch until Sam called them in for lunch and then grilled Samuel on why he had a black eye before Achilla explained that she handled it. After that, she went back out until her father came home. Something about the way Samuel avoided her made her want to sit outside for the rest of the day.

The neighborhood kids stopped playing with Achilla after her incident with Marty. Marty's parents threatened to call the police until Sam gave them the whole story and reminded them that this wasn't the first time Marty had picked on Samuel or the other neighborhood kids. After that, nothing came of their complaint, but

Achilla noticed that the O'Briens crossed the street whenever they saw her. After a few weeks, the Johnsons were the only people who would give Achilla the time of day. On the bright side, all of the kids were extra nice to Samuel from that point on, or so Achilla heard.

Sam was especially different from Ailina. She was warm and gentle to the point that it made Achilla wary of her intentions. Unlike Ailina, Sam always smiled when she saw Brendan come home unless she was angry at him; even then they argued behind closed doors. She also always asked Achilla how her day went and if she had made any new friends. When Achilla told her that nobody spoke to her after she beat up Marty, she laughed. Even her laughter was softer than Ailina's cackle in a way that always felt like she was mocking your very existence. After yet another day of playing basketball by herself, Achilla came inside wearing her white t-shirt and black basketball shorts and joined Sam for lunch. Sam rubbed her hands on her jeans before she patted Achilla's shoulder and walked away from the kitchen table to the cabinets above the refrigerator.

"Everyone acts all up in arms after you beat up a boy," Sam said as Achilla read the Price family reunion list of names on the back of her purple t-shirt. "After I beat up a boy in seventh grade people thought I was from outer space."

"You can fight?" Achilla asked.

"Always could," Sam replied as she pulled out a pair of mugs. "I had a mean temper growing up. It's not a good thing though, especially as a black woman. You'll learn that sooner or later."

"What do you mean?"

"Oh, you're so young," Sam sighed. "I'm actually glad that I have to explain this, and I hope you never have to deal with it. As a black woman, the world doesn't like it when you get angry, even if you're right. You know, they'll say you have an attitude and all that. It's not fair, and if I could change it on my own, I would, but that's our situation--"

"Wait, you're calling me black?" Achilla asked; a question that made Sam jolt and almost drop a plate.

"Girl, have you looked in the mirror lately?" Sam asked as she faced Achilla with her hands on her hips. "Honey, you are darker than Samuel. That's that Johnson blood in you. Brendan's dark as midnight just like his father, and you take after him. I don't know what Ailina's been telling you, but when you walk out the door, you're black. "

Achilla looked at her hands. Her skin was now chestnut brown and only a few shades lighter than Brendan's. She normally spent so much time inside while living with Ailina that she never noticed how dark she could get. Ailina never called her black. She just called her superior. At that very moment, Achilla realized that there were a lot of things Ailina never bothered to teach her about herself. From that day forward, she pressed Sam with questions until her twelfth birthday when Sam walked into Achilla's room with a box full of books. Achilla ruffled through them and noticed that they were all biographies, starting with Martin Luther King Jr.

"That's every Black History book I could find in a week," Sam huffed as she wiped her hands on her jeans and rubbed her sweaty forehead. "Did Ailina at least teach you how to read? Lord knows she didn't bother to tell you much else."

Achilla was starting to notice that whenever Sam made comments like that, they were not intended to insult her. They were demonstrations of her frustration with Ailina's lack of parenting. Achilla shared in that frustration as she stared at all the books that she could have read by now. Achilla snatched up the biography of Malcolm X and tossed it between her hands. She smiled as she ran her fingers through the pages.

"Yeah, she taught me how to read," Achilla said. "I read better than most kids my age. At least that's what my last test said."

"You were homeschooled?" Sam asked. "At least she did that right."

"It was really hard," Achilla said with a frown. "We left off on trigonometry, Portuguese, Russian, and Greek."

"You know trigonometry?" Sam asked with her hands on her hips. "And three foreign languages?"

"My Russian sucks--"

"Achilla, in this house--"

"My Russian needs work," Achilla corrected herself with a snap of her fingers. "But I'm conversant in Portuguese and Greek because Ailina spoke both languages around the house. After Russian, we were going to move on to Farsi."

"You're still moving on to Farsi," Sam replied with a nod of her head. "I'm starting to think that public school may not be much of a challenge for you. If you were in my classroom, I would move you up a couple grades. Let me talk to your father. Maybe we can hire a tutor for you."

"Thanks," Achilla said. "I was actually excited for Farsi."

"Did Ailina ever tell you why she wanted you to learn so many languages?" Sam asked as she leaned against the doorway. "Or why she insisted that you learn how to fight so...well? Did she explain any of her reasoning for teaching you anything?"

"No," Achilla replied as she ruffled through her new book. "She just said I was superior."

"Hm," Sam hummed as she crossed her arms. "She used that word a lot, didn't she?"

Sam walked out without waiting for an answer. Achilla shrugged and turned to the first page of Malcolm X's biography. She ran through all of her books before the first day of middle school and read even more in her free time. As promised, her parents hired language tutors for her, and Sam drove Achilla to their homes three times a week after school. America's treatment of black people didn't sound much different than Ailina's behavior toward her boyfriends; the expectation of obedience, the inferior services and treatment, the assumption that one set of people was superior to another. Achilla saw her mother in these books and wondered if she was just like the Ku Klux Klan and the lynch mobs. She found herself wandering in her school library looking for more books so often that the librarians had books waiting for her as she walked through the doors.

One day, Achilla was going to play basketball outside after school when Sam made her stay in and take a test. After she was done, Sam took it to her bedroom and told Achilla to go play. Achilla shot jump shots and performed handstand pushups by herself for hours until Samuel came home. Then she played him in one-on-one again. Achilla loved the feeling of playing outside in October; a time of year when Ailina usually clamped down on their training. The air was just cool enough to give her goosebumps but warm enough for her hands to feel the ball as she dribbled around Samuel. One play, Samuel reached for the ball and Achilla turned her shoulder and bumped him again. This time he didn't cry when he fell. Instead, he rose to his feet and kept playing. Even though she beat him every time, watching Samuel play so much stronger made Achilla smile. She was still smiling when she came in the house and saw Sam and Brendan looking at her test at the kitchen table. Sam had changed out of her blue dress and wore a white t-shirt and sweatpants as she tugged Brendan's white button-down shirt. She smiled at the test and kissed him on the cheek before looking up at Achilla.

"Achilla, baby," Sam said. "Why don't you take a shower and come downstairs? We need to speak with you."

Achilla showered and changed into a pair of black sweatpants and a baggy, blue "Bridgeport Bluefish" t-shirt before scampering back downstairs in her bare feet. She sat at the kitchen table in front of her father, who still wore his white shirt and sky blue tie. Brendan frowned as he read the test, and Sam patted his shoulder as if he missed his queue to start speaking. Brendan cleared his throat.

"Achilla, I know I haven't been home much," Brendan said. "Your father works very hard."

"It's fine," Achilla said. "You're actually home during the day more than my mom ever was."

"Oh God, I was afraid of that," Sam said as she rolled her eyes.

"Yeah," Brendan replied as he nodded his head at Sam. "So Sam gave you an IQ test. Your IQ is…over 200."

"Is that high?" Achilla asked.

"It's the highest I've ever seen," Sam said with a giddy smile. "You're extremely gifted."

"What's Samuel's IQ?" Achilla asked. "Is he gifted?"

"Samuel's gifted too," Sam replied with a nod before her smile faded. "He's actually scheduled to start advanced classes for his grade next year, but he hasn't had the…training that you've had. We're concerned that you never had much of a childhood."

"What do you mean?" Achilla asked.

"From this point forward we're going to put you through some training of our own," Brendan said. "You'll still learn foreign languages and martial arts if you wish, but we'll also find a few other things for you to do that involve making friends."

"I've never taken martial arts," Achilla said. "My mom just taught me how to fight."

"Oh, boy," Sam sighed as she shook her head. "She treated her like a little slave and didn't tell her anything."

"Huh?" Achilla uttered with a frown as she remembered the devastating conditions of the Trans-Atlantic Slave Trade. Surely, Ailina's parenting didn't compare to that. Did it? Achilla shook her head before looking up at her parents. Brendan gave Sam a side-eye before taking a deep breath.

"Ailina never explained this to you," Brendan said with a raised hand. "But do you remember that basketball game where we first met?"

"Yes."

"Well on that day, along with your incident with Marty," Brendan continued, "you demonstrated advanced knowledge of at least three forms of fighting. I didn't want to tell you this yet, but I think Sam has a point. You're intelligent enough to understand."

"Understand what?"

"We don't know why," Brendan said. "But Ailina seems to have trained you the same way you would train someone for combat or espionage. I still can't believe I'm saying this--"

"Think about it, honey," Sam chimed in as she leaned forward. "You know how to speak foreign languages, and you know how to hurt people, but you've had a hard time making friends, and up until now you knew next to nothing about your culture or even yourself. I'm glad your father acted when he did."

"Oh," Achilla said as she looked at the table. "So what do I do?"

"Developmentally, it'll be difficult to change what she's done,"

Sam sighed. "But it's not impossible. We'll guide you every step of the way. I do have one thing to ask of you."

"Yes?" Achilla replied.

"Whenever you get angry," Sam said as she looked Achilla in the eye without blinking. "Whenever you think you're about to get angry, call one of us, OK? Talk to us."

"I'm giving you a cell phone," Brendan said. "Call either of us when that time comes. I'm sure there are things you would rather talk to Sam about, but I'm your father. I'll love you no matter what you tell me."

"Why are you talking like this?" Achilla asked. "You act like I'm going to kill someone."

Brendan and Sam passed a glance at each other that Achilla would never forget for the rest of her life. Achilla frowned as they stared at her. Sam's eyes moistened a little. Brendan looked down at the table. Then they both smiled at her. Sam stood up and walked toward the kitchen doorway.

"Sorry," Sam said with a slight crack in her voice as she walked out of the kitchen to the front door. "I just…have to step outside for something."

Achilla frowned as Sam stepped outside and closed the door behind her. What was she going outside for? It was almost dark and both Samuel and Achilla were home. Why did they look at her like that? What did Achilla say? Achilla swallowed hard as she scrambled to think of what she did wrong.

"Sam's had a long day," Brendan said as he watched the door. "But she cares a lot about you, and she knows a lot about child psychology. Whatever she tells you to do, do it. Understood?"

"Yes, sir," Achilla muttered.

"All right," Brendan said as he rose from the table. "I think I'm cooking tonight. Want some steak and fries?"

"Yes!" Achilla said as she pumped her fist. "I love your steak and fries!"

"Steak and fries it is," Brendan said as he leaned over and kissed Achilla on the forehead. "You'll be all right, baby girl. I promise."

Achilla flinched as he walked toward the refrigerator. She stared at her hands. They still had scars from her days of living in Ailina's house. By now her hands were so hard that she could hit any part of the human body without the slightest pain, but the look that past between Brendan and Sam stung her. It was the same look Samuel held when he stepped in to stop her from beating on Marty. It was the same look Marty's parents held when they saw her and crossed the street. It was the look of fear, and Achilla was becoming all too familiar with it.

Chapter Nine

ACHILLA JOHNSON:20

It took two months for the CIA to narrow down Nina Dos Santos' location. Her last assignment was in São Paulo under the codename "Gumby." After being blacklisted for acting as a double-agent with the Brazilian government, Gumby disappeared. She was last seen in Mexico City, but she disappeared again for a couple years. However, when someone bought a house under the name Aline Gilberto in the Bunker Hill section of Waterbury, Connecticut, the CIA grew suspicious. Aline Barros was a famous gospel singer from Rio de Janeiro. Bebel Gilberto was bossa nova singer from Rio de Janeiro. The average American real estate agent wouldn't even blink twice, but a CIA agent, or anyone with any familiarity with Brazilian culture, would not have fallen for such a poorly crafted false identity. It almost seemed like she wanted the CIA to find her.

Agent Jones agreed to deliver the intel as soon as he got it. So Achilla knew it was him when she heard two knocks on her door on a Saturday morning. Before she got up, a file slid under the door. Achilla hopped out of bed, leaving a black male agent sleeping under her white bed sheets.

Kate made good on her promise.

"Hey," Achilla said as she shook his shoulder. "I need to be alone for this."

"Yeah sure," he yawned as he rolled out of bed and grabbed his pants. "When do you need me back?"

"Tonight," Achilla replied as she picked up a black t-shirt and handed it to him. "Then not for a while. I have to stay focused."

"Cool," he said as he threw on his shirt. Kelly Bryant was his name, and he was a rookie agent just like Achilla. Kate told her that he had a bright future in the CIA; especially if he kept Achilla satisfied. Achilla went along for a while to satiate her own desires, but those words made her shudder. What if someone told her that she would go far if she slept with Blue Eyes?

Wait, someone did.

Blue Eyes.

Achilla shook her head at the hypocrisy in her relationship with Bryant. Even if the advancement aspect wasn't her idea, she was responsible for her knowledge of it. What would her father say? She already knew he would flip at her one-night stands, but allowing someone to sleep with her as a job requirement? Achilla patted Bryant's arm when he turned to the door.

"You know," Achilla sighed. "You don't have to do this. You don't have to come back if you don't want to."

"First time I've heard a woman say that."

"You don't have to posture," Achilla replied. "And I'm not rejecting you. I normally *wouldn't* reject you, but you're being used. Are you really good with this?"

"Am I good with having sex with a beautiful woman as often as I can handle it?" Agent Bryant asked with a cocked eyebrow. "And doing it on the government's dime? Is that your question?"

"More succinctly my question is if a man of your education level is comfortable working as a prostitute," Achilla replied. "It's not that I haven't hooked up with an agent before, but this is different. It's literally your job. Again, are you good with that?"

"Am I really getting used when I get all the sex that I want without any strings?" Agent Bryant replied.

"When you word it that way, I see you have no problem with the arrangement," Achilla said. "But I do. Enough is enough. This is our last time, all right? I don't want you coming back."

"I didn't picture you as the sentimental type," said Agent Bryant as he shrugged his shoulders. "But if you're done, you're done, and my assignment's over. I'll report to Kate."

"Good," Achilla replied with a smile. "I'm sure you'll find everything you want somewhere else. In my opinion, you're more than qualified to make a woman happy."

"You know," Agent Bryant said with a frown. "That's a hell of a compliment."

"I don't hold back when it's true," Achilla said as she led Bryant to the door and opened it. "Go out there, date, and do it for free."

"Date she says,"Agent Bryant chuckled and shook his head. "That part's only free for the woman."

Achilla giggled a little. Had she known he had such a sense of humor, she might have considered dating him, but now it was too late. Their interaction was not only physical but arranged in such a way that Achilla couldn't live with. She found herself wishing they had met under better circumstances. Still, it was fun while it lasted. Before he walked out, Achilla pulled him back by his belt and gave him a kiss goodbye before playfully shoving him into the hallway and shutting her door. She then made some breakfast in her tiny kitchen and ate in silence alone.

Again.

When Achilla read Gumby's file, she found out that she was born in Waterbury and raised on its East End by her Brazilian immigrant parents. Waterbury's crime rate rivaled that of Bridgeport, New Haven, and Hartford. It was not an easy place for a child. Despite all of that, Gumby had a completely clean record in her early years; much unlike Blue Eyes who grew up wealthy and still managed to get in trouble. Judging from her grades in elementary and middle school, Gumby was a good kid who studied hard and seldom gave her parents any reason to discipline her. Achilla furrowed her brow as she chomped a piece of toast. How does a kid like that end up becoming a double agent suspected of treason?

Also unlike Blue Eyes, Gumby switched high schools. A lot. She started as a freshman at Crosby High School; a basketball power-house in Waterbury's East End. Gumby transferred as a sophomore to Wilby High School and then attended Naugatuck High School by the end of the year. Since by law she could not attend school in the suburb of Naugatuck while living in Waterbury, her stint there was short. Still, Gumby never returned to Waterbury public schools. For her junior year, she transferred to Sacred Heart Academy, a private school in Waterbury's Downtown.

Achilla noticed a photo of Gumby attending a funeral and a newspaper clipping. Two of her siblings were killed in a drug-related shooting. After that, Gumby transferred to Choate Rosemary Hall in Wallingford; a boarding school that her store owning, working-class parents couldn't possibly afford. The fact that Gumby earned a 4.0 GPA at every previous school must have earned her a full ride. The decision to send her out of town was obvious. Her parents didn't want to lose another child; especially one with such a bright future. Achilla imagined her parents making the same decision given a similar situation.

No doubt because she moved so much, Gumby never played for any high school sports programs, but her file was filled with victories in amateur boxing and karate competitions. One season she went undefeated with a 90 percent knockout rate. That explained why she never got arrested for a fight in Waterbury. Achilla imagined that after watching her beat down one hapless opponent, nobody messed with her. Achilla remembered the wide berth that the students gave her at St. Joseph's and Stratford High School. The exultation of a victory often faded to loneliness when everyone was afraid to say the wrong thing to her, but Achilla had her family and Dahntay to keep her company during those years. She wondered if Gumby had anyone she could talk to. Probably not.

Standing six feet tall by the time she transferred to Choate, Gumby had quite a reach in the boxing ring. That reach helped her win three straight NCBA boxing championships for West Point where she graduated at the top of her class. The CIA wasted no time picking her up after she served in the Army. Her file read that she was fluent in Brazilian Portuguese, Spanish, German, Russian, and French. It also called her *lethal* in hand-to-hand combat; citing specific instances in which she ended confrontations with one punch from either hand. The more Achilla read her file, the more it felt like she was reading about a regular human version of herself; the stellar fighting ability, the mastery of multiple languages, the toughness, the grit, the transient loneliness. Achilla grinned at the challenge as she headed out to Waterbury to get to know the city a little better with the CIA's permission. She had only visited there for basketball tournaments as a kid. Now she had to know it as well as any other resident.

After giving herself a tour of the city and its main locations (at night of course), Achilla was familiar enough with Waterbury to pursue the next step of her assignment. Waterbury reminded Achilla of Bridgeport with more hills and a smaller Downtown. The highlight of the entire city was the Brass Mills Center; a shopping mall across the street from I-84. Next to the mall was another shopping center and the Timexpo Museum, and St. Mary's Hospital was just a few blocks away. There was also a UConn Campus within a ten-minute drive. Anything you needed from Waterbury was usually in that area; though there were some shopping centers further away.

When she checked out the local neighborhoods, she learned that Waterbury had an economic disparity that rivaled New Haven's. Its residents ranged from the wealthy who drove fancy cars with one hand while holding their Starbucks coffee in the other, to the poor who drove beat up Hondas that blasted Dipset loud enough to vibrate their black tinted windows. One section of town, the Bunker Hill neighborhood, held beautiful colonial homes with clean-cut lawns and statues in the front yard. Then there were neighborhoods near East Main Street where it wasn't safe to be out at night.

The highlight of the city, and one aspect that brought everyone together, was its basketball culture. Achilla snuck into the YMCA and the North End Rec Center to watch a few pick up games and basketball leagues, and she found herself nodding her head at the talent. Everyone, young or old, could play, and the tournaments often brought out crowds from all over the city. After watching a man in a red t-shirt dunk over a hapless defender who couldn't get out of the way, Achilla laughed at the crowd's hooping and hollering reaction. One group of kids stood up and filed out of the gym as if they had decided the game was over after that play. Achilla followed suit and left, tucking her fitted cap over her face.

After a few more nights of patrolling the city, Achilla noticed that the UConn campus had prostitutes hanging around at four in the morning who would leave before the police pulled in. That area was where she would find her lead to Gumby. If she was involved in sex trafficking, getting to know the sex market in Waterbury was the best way to find her. Achilla noticed that one police officer in particular didn't scare the girls away. He actually picked them up. As she watched his car from an abandoned building across the street, Achilla smirked and massaged her gun. What better way to get inside than to blackmail a corrupt cop into helping her? Her opportunity to meet Gumby had just arrived.

One night, Achilla wore a black sweater with a matching blackout fitted cap and followed the police car from a distance until it pulled over around the corner from the UConn Campus in the parking lot of a closed down bank. She could hear the patrol car shaking from around the corner, and waited until she heard the door open and slam shut. She pulled her brim low over as she turned the corner. As expected, a hazel eyed, tan-skinned girl of average height and weight walked away from the police car as it drove away in the opposite direction. She wore a pink halter-top with a short jean skirt with pink and black sneakers; a little under-dressed considering the brisk fall air that tugged at Achilla's ears. This girl's face told Achilla that she couldn't have been more than nineteen years old, but she possessed a figure like a handcrafted vase. Achilla passed by her with her hands in her pockets at first before turning and clamping her hand over her mouth. The girl tried to scream, but Achilla held her throat and leaped into an alley. She let go of her throat so she could breathe, but pinned her against a building, drew her gun, and waved it in her face. The prostitute took the hint and stopped screaming.

"Who's the cop?" Achilla asked with her brim low over her eyes.

"*No hablo inglés,*" said the prostitute, only it sounded more like *inglaish* at the end.

Achilla knew that accent.

"Nice try," Achilla said. "I believe you mean *eu não falo inglês*. If you're going to pretend to speak Spanish to protect your cop buddy, at least try to hide your Rio accent, *Carioca*."

"No, no, I'm Puerto Rican, I swear!" the prostitute replied until Achilla pointed the gun at her left eye. "OK, I'm Brazilian, but I can speak Spanish too, and people always think I'm Puerto Rican like we all look alike or something. It's really racist, but it doesn't matter, I mean they still pay, so I guess it's--"

"Whatever," Achilla hissed as she pressed the barrel against her throat. "Just answer the damn question before I get angry."

"OK," the prostitute said with her hands up. "His name's Chris. That's all I know."

"How much does he pay you?"

"No money. I give him what he wants, he doesn't bust me."

"Not good enough," Achilla stated. "You have to bring something back to your pimp or you're not on the street anymore and he doesn't get his nightly piece. You arranged something, and if you keep lying to me I'll--"

"OK, fifty dollars," the prostitute sobbed as she pulled the money out of her cleavage and extended it to Achilla. "I mean, it's a discount, but it's something. Here, you can have it."

"I don't want it," Achilla replied. "How often does he see you?"

"He doesn't tell me ahead of time," the prostitute said until Achilla squinted her eyes and pressed the gun against her throat.

"Sorry!" the prostitute whimpered. "Every night. Same spot. Same time."

"Good," Achilla said. "Here's what we're going to do. You're going to meet him tomorrow at your usual spot. You're going to refuse the money--"

"I can't do that--"

"Shut-up," Achilla snapped. "You're going to refuse the money and tell him you're done being a hooker. He'll insist. Take the money. I'll bust him from there."

"You're another cop?" the prostitute asked. "I thought you guys always stuck together."

"Internal affairs," Achilla said. "We eat our own. Give me your name."

"Sandy," she sobbed. "Sandy Carvalho."

"You told the truth that time," Achilla replied with a grin. "I can always tell when you're telling the truth. I can also tell when you're lying. Just keep that in mind from this day forward. Clear?"

"Yes, ma'am."

"Don't call me that," Achilla said. "How old are you?"

"Eighteen."

"Why are you doing this?" Achilla asked.

"My foster parents kicked me out," Sandy said. "I'm too old now. I found a place, but the lady who owns it told me I had to do this to keep my room."

"Really?" Achilla asked with a frown. "Is she Brazilian too? Really tall?"

"Yeah," Sandy replied. "How'd you know that?"

"Nevermind," Achilla said with a wave of her hand. "Her name?"

"Aline Gilberto," Sandy replied. "We all call her Nina, but she doesn't like anyone else calling her that."

Achilla smirked. She didn't need the cop to find Gumby after all. This girl would do just fine. However, the cop could still be useful. Achilla lowered her gun and stepped back with her head down and the brim on her cap low. She stuffed her hands into her pockets as she listened to Sandy's movements. Though she could hardly see her past the brim, Achilla could hear her shivering and sniffling. This girl wasn't hardened by the streets yet. She could be easily manipulated for now; though Achilla pitied the next person who tried to hustle her.

"I'll be back tomorrow at this time exactly," Achilla said. "After that, I will explain the next step."

"Next step?"

"Yeah," Achilla said as she walked away. "You just became my partner."

The next night, Achilla came back to the abandoned building across from the UConn Campus. This time she wore tight jeans, black and green high-heeled shoes, and a bustier. She also wore braided hair and brown contacts and stood outside on the corner like the other prostitutes, making sure to avoid a corner that wasn't already taken. When a white Cadillac drove up to her, she waved it away. A tall tan-skinned male wearing a white tank top stepped out of the car.

"You don't want no trick?" he asked.

"Not you," Achilla replied as she looked past his shoulder at Sandy waiting in her spot. "I don't think you could afford me, honey. Try one of those girls over there."

"Oh, I got money," the man said as he pulled a roll of hundreds out of his pocket. "We doing this."

"I said no."

"Bitch, I said yes."

Achilla held a straight face, but her blood boiled. She took a deep breath before stepping close and wrapping her arms around him. When he leaned in to kiss her, she held his mouth with her right hand. She then pressed one of his ribs with her left thumb until it crunched. The man grunted and grimaced, and she caressed his neck as if they were lovers embracing each other instead of enemies engaged in combat. When he tried to step back, she grabbed his ear and held him in place.

"Never call me that word again," Achilla whispered in his ear with a curled lip. "Behave yourself, or I'll break another one."

The man reached for his waist and Achilla grabbed his wrist just in time to stop him from drawing a gun.

"Tsk, tsk," Achilla sucked her teeth with a pouty face as she snapped his wrist in half, jerking tears out of his eyes. "We can't have that either."

Achilla let go of his ear and used her right hand to press down with her thumb again, crunching a rib on his other side. As he groaned and dropped to one knee, Achilla snatched the gun out of his hand. It was all black and weighed about as much as a gallon of milk. She recognized it as a .44 Magnum Desert Eagle; a powerful weapon for someone to just carry around. She held the gun to his face as he continued to grimace from his injury.

"I'll be keeping your gun," Achilla said as she reached into his pocket and took the roll of cash. "And I'll be taking your money. I also need you to stand up straight for a moment."

She pulled him close and backed into the building behind her. She leaned against the wall and wrapped her leg around his body as she watched Sandy across the street. As far as anyone else was concerned, they were a couple making out on the corner, and no one could see her face. When a police car rolled past them, Achilla pushed the man toward his car. She opened the back door and laid him on the back seat. As he writhed on his leather back seat and groaned, Achilla patted his chest. Hard. The man coughed before he rolled over.

"Well, that was fun," Achilla said as she stepped out of his car. "I guess you could afford me after all."

Achilla left her victim and walked the extra block to the closed down bank parking lot and hid in an alley just a few yards away. As expected, the police car was there shaking and bumping just like last time. Achilla frowned when she noticed the car shaking harder than usual and without any real rhythm to it. As she stepped closer, she heard a scream and bounded toward the car. She looked through the window just in time to see the police officer raise his fist. Achilla ripped the door open and yanked him out by his arm, twisting it around his back as she pinned him to the ground. Sandy stumbled out of the car with a bloody lip and fell on the pavement.

"Sandy, are you OK?" Achilla asked.

"Yeah," Sandy said as she wiped her mouth. "I've been hit worse. I can take it."

"I'm sorry to hear that," Achilla replied before turning to Chris. "You always beat up on girls half your size?"

"I knew you snitched!" Chris snarled as Achilla held his head down by his spiked hair. "I know where you live--"

"That's enough of that," Achilla said as she twisted his arm further with one hand and snatched his holster with the other. "You won't lay a hand on her from this point forward. I'll be taking your badge and your gun."

Chris struggled when she reached for his badge and Achilla smacked his temple. His head shook before he slumped to the ground. She then rolled him over and snatched his badge off of his uniform and grabbed his wallet. Upon searching it, she found his driver's license, Waterbury Police ID, and fifty bucks. Achilla stood up and handed the fifty bucks to Sandy. Sandy swiped it away.

"I'm good," she said as she sat up and leaned against the car.

"You took a beating for me," Achilla said. "It's the least I can do."

"No, I'm done with this shit," Sandy blurted as she wiped her bloody lip. "I'm...I'm just done. There has to be another way. I can't do this anymore."

Achilla lowered her head and looked at Chris' unconscious body. She slid her hand under his back and lifted to check his weight. Achilla estimated that he weighed around two hundred pounds of solid muscle. Judging by her busted lip and black eye, Sandy took quite a pounding. She shouldn't have been able to talk, but here she was sitting on the ground with her arms crossed over her red halter top. Perhaps the streets hardened her more than Achilla anticipated. She raised her eyebrows when Sandy nodded her head toward Chris' body.

"He's not moving," Sandy said. "How'd you do that?"

"Between you and me," Achilla replied with a wink. "I'm pretty strong. If you need someone to back you up, you've got it."

"Thanks," Sandy said with a shrug as if Achilla's words meant nothing.

"I also need something else from you," Achilla sighed as she pulled a pre-paid cell phone out of her cleavage. "I'm going to call back-up for Chris. I need someone to hear my story before it makes the police report. I'm sure you know how that goes."

"I'm not in trouble, am I?" Sandy asked with her hands raised. "I'm serious about quitting. You won't see me out here again."

"Of course you're not," Achilla replied. "That's the part I want to discuss with my backup. Before they get here, I want you to tell me where Nina keeps you and her other girls. Cooperate, and you walk away free."

Sandy looked at her lap. She then looked at Chris. She nodded her head at Achilla and took a deep breath.

"Well she used to keep ten of us," Sandy said. "But after a while, she sends girls down to Brazil, and now there's only me and two other girls. She said I could go down there if I make enough money for her here. She even said she knew some guys who could help me with a legit job or school if I did better than the others. I was kind of looking forward to it. I'm done with this city. I'll go anywhere."

Achilla frowned. Gumby was directly involved in international sex-trafficking now? Perhaps she was entrenched in the criminal element for too long. Agent Jones always told Achilla to be mindful of the temptations of major criminal organizations; money, power, security. Considering how much the CIA pays, it would take a strong will to resist Xerxes' operation; a will that Gumby clearly did not have. Hopefully, that would work in Achilla's favor when they met.

"Where do you live?" Achilla asked. "Look, I know Nina's dangerous; probably more dangerous than Chris, but she's no match for me. I can guarantee you that."

"I believe you," Sandy said with her head low as she gestured toward Chris. "Why don't you just follow me home?"

"Bad idea," Achilla said. "She'll notice and kill you long before I can stop her."

"So what do I do?" Sandy asked with a pleading look in her eyes. "How can I help?"

"Tell me the general area, and I can figure it out from there," Achilla said.

"I mean, she's about three or four blocks from Watertown Ave," Sandy said. "That's what I remember, but I'm not all that good with directions."

"That's all I need," Achilla replied. "Go home."

Sandy stood up and strolled down the street as if she had never been attacked by a police officer twice her size. Achilla still frowned at how easily she recovered from an attack of that magnitude. As she watched her turn the corner, Achilla opened her cell phone and texted Agent Jones for clean-up. From there, she knew he would get a crew to cover up Chris' story that a woman ripped open a locked police car and slapped him unconscious. She doubted anyone would believe that anyway.

Achilla waited until Sandy was out of sight and cut through an alley back to her abandoned building. In there, she changed into her black sweater, sneakers, and looser fitting jeans with black sneakers. She shoved her blackout fitted over her hair before she looked out the window and watched Sandy wipe her nose as she waited on a corner for a red Cadillac Seville to pick her up. As she stepped into the Cadillac, Achilla memorized the license plate number. She then turned away from the window and called Agent Jones.

"I got your text, Achilla," Agent Jones said. "They're on their way."

"I need an address that matches this license plate number," Achilla said before she recited the number to him. "Got it?"

"Pulling it up now."

"Hey, I've got a source who'll need our help when this is done."

"You said that before, Achilla," Agent Jones chuckled. "Did you help those little girls last time?"

"That was contingent on whether I killed their father or not," Achilla replied as she pulled her fitted cap lower. "I didn't. This girl's life may be in danger even after this is over. After I finish this, we need to send her somewhere."

"The CIA isn't a humanitarian organization, Achilla."

"No, but informants can't help you later if they're dead," Achilla snapped. "Can you work with me on this please?"

"Fair enough," Agent Jones said. "Got your address. I'll text it to you. When are you going?"

"Now," Achilla said before hanging up the phone. She purposely misled Sandy so that she wouldn't expose herself and get killed, but she had no intention of leaving her with Gumby any longer. Achilla stood up and stared out the window at the view of Waterbury at night as she waited for her text to arrive. Something about it made her want to punch a wall; the crime, the corruption, all of it. When her phone vibrated, she checked the address. Achilla recognized it from her prior surveillance. Sandy lived on Bunker Hill Avenue a few houses down from Bunker Hill School. Achilla rolled her eyes as she walked down the stairs. Gumby was housing prostitutes a stone's throw from elementary school kids.

As she stepped outside, Achilla watched the sunrise over the UConn campus. The sunlight illuminated the brick road on East Main Street and shimmered off of the glass windows of small stores and barbershops. As much as she disliked Waterbury right now, even this city didn't look half bad with a little light shined on it. Achilla took a deep breath and ran down East Main, and then West Main Street past the Waterbury Green where the sunlight glistened the dew on the grass. Travelling by car would only alert Gumby to her presence and give the neighbors someone to identify, and she could jog there in a matter of minutes without losing her breath. Achilla smirked at the thought of finally facing Gumby as she turned a corner on Grandview Avenue.

When Achilla arrived on Bunker Hill, she spotted Gumby's two-story, white colonial with black shutters. She kept her distance as she listened for any signs of life within the house. It was five in the morning on a Sunday. Most people weren't awake yet, but this house was filled with Brazilian Gospel music that called out *Te adorar, Senhor* over and over so much that Achilla shook her head. How could a whorehouse play songs intended to worship God? Achilla's parents would've vomited.

Achilla kept her head low and her brim over her face as she strolled down the sidewalk as if she were a Waterbury resident just passing through. She stopped and pretended to text on her phone when she heard voices inside. Achilla stared at her phone as she focused until she heard the sound of pots and pans banging around.

"Sandy," a hoarse, but feminine voice called. "*Cozinha isso agora. Preciso você cozinhar pra me.*"

"*Sim, Senhora,*" Achilla heard Sandy say.

"*Você esta consada?*"

"*Consado ,sim.*"

Achilla jolted when she heard a smack.

"Hurry up and cook!" the voice switched to English. "You shouldn't be tired. You didn't make any money last night, so obviously you didn't do shit!"

Achilla clenched her fists as she approached the house. Despite the visible evidence on her face that someone attacked her last night, this woman was beating Sandy again? Achilla had to put a stop to this, and she wasn't asking Agent Jones' permission this time. She walked up the steps to the porch and rang the doorbell. When Sandy opened the door wearing an oversized white t-shirt and faded jeans with a hole in the knee, Achilla held her breath.

Sandy had two black eyes and cotton balls stuffed up her nose. She also had a fresh bruise on her cheek. Whoever hit her cheek packed quite a wallop. Achilla had a feeling that when Sandy said she had been hit harder before, she meant from Gumby. They exchanged glances for a moment before Sandy looked over her shoulder.

"Nina, there's a girl here to see you," Sandy said. "She's the homeless girl I was talking about."

Achilla forced a straight face. Sandy made up a story without telling her first? Did she have any idea how risky that was? A tall woman with skin as dark as Achilla's, but hair twice as frizzy, walked up behind Sandy wearing a navy blue tank top and black yoga pants. She had to be Gumby. Though her lack of make-up or styled hair made her look much different from her college pictures, her height and chiseled arms gave her away. Her hazel eyes also held the same cold stare as Blue Eyes; filled with the kind of relentless intensity that would have frightened anyone else. Achilla could feel them bearing down on her like a cobra preparing to strike, and she removed her hands from her pockets as Gumby stepped outside.

"I'll talk to her out here," Gumby said to Sandy. "Go inside, Sandy."

Sandy lowered her head and closed the door.

"Come on," said Gumby as she turned her back and walked down the porch to a pair of wood chairs. Achilla followed and sat down. Gumby picked her nails and crossed her legs as she stared out into the neighborhood full of two-story colonial homes and condos.

Achilla looked past Gumby's head at the school down the street as she steadied her breathing to calm her pounding heart. Gumby seemed to read Achilla's mind, and she looked in the direction of the school before biting one of her fingernails and spitting over the railing. Achilla leaned back and cross her legs as she read Gumby's body for openings.

"None of my girls go to that school," Gumby said with a hard stare. "I *never* take kids come from that school. They're too young."

"Sounds like you already know why I'm here," Achilla replied.

"Nobody comes here for anything else," Gumby said with her chin raised.

"You sound proud of that," Achilla said with a glare in her eyes. "Maybe a little too proud considering the girl I just saw with bruises on her face. Have you ever thought about getting back in the ring again, and you know, hitting someone who can actually punch back?"

Gumby's eyes flickered for a split second before staring straight out at the street. Apparently, her boxing history wasn't common knowledge anymore.

"Of course, we don't have to go to a ring," Achilla continued without breaking her gaze. "I happen to be someone who can hit back, and I leave a mark when I do it. Why don't you try slapping me?"

Gumby met Achilla's gaze and they stared at each other for a few seconds. Gumby then lowered her eyes, bit one of her finger-nails and spat into the front yard.

"So who sent you?" Gumby asked as if she hadn't heard Achilla's challenge. "Sandy's a stupid girl, but I'm not. Any fool could see that you're not homeless."

Any fool could see that Sandy was lying to Gumby, but Achilla kept that part to herself as she stared out into the street. Sandy was smarter than Achilla gave her credit for. She could apparently play dumb well enough for a former CIA agent to fall for it. Achilla smirked at Gumby as she stared at her. Gumby replied with a nonchalant shrug before biting her nails again.

"You don't talk like a girl who wants to work for me," Gumby sighed. "A hired gun would've shot me by now. Maybe a cop? Or maybe just a nosy do-gooder who wants to play hero?"

"None of that," Achilla said.

"That leaves the CIA," Gumby said as she uncrossed her legs. "Did you come here to tie up your loose ends?"

"Not if I don't have to," Achilla replied. "I just need to know about Xerxes. Tell me that, and I leave."

"You just leave?" Gumby asked. "Really?"

"I also leave with Sandy."

Gumby let out a hoarse, throaty laughter that echoed down the street. It sounded nothing like Ailina's cackle, but the cruelty behind it was just the same. Achilla clenched her teeth and squeezed the arm of her chair so hard that it bent under her grip. Meanwhile, Gumby held her side as she laughed, only stopping to wipe the tears from her eyes. Her expression then immediately switched to a laser-focused glare. Achilla stared back, but she felt the adrenaline pumping through her body. The look in Gumby's eyes revealed just how dangerous she was. An attack was imminent.

"You're such a rookie," Gumby snarled. "I'm insulted that they sent you. I've never even met the man. Didn't you do your home-work before you came here?"

"You expect me to believe that?" Achilla replied while she read Gumby's attack angle.

"I expect you to leave and report that there's nothing here to see," Gumby snapped. "I also expect you to leave empty-handed. Sandy's mine."

She spoke about Sandy the same way Ailina did Achilla when she was a girl; like property. Like a commodity. Achilla grit her teeth as her heartbeat increased.

"Don't make this hard," she said as she uncrossed her legs and turned in her chair to face Gumby. "You won't win, Gumby; not against me."

"You're on my porch and you haven't drawn your weapon," Gumby replied. "And I eat bitches like you for breakfast."

"I suggest you watch your mouth," Achilla growled just before Gumby rushed to her feet. She initiated with a leading right hand.

Achilla deflected with her left hand and propelled herself from her seat with her right. Gumby then threw a left hook that no normal untrained human would have the anticipation to block. In any boxing match, it would have been the knockout punch; perfectly timed and aimed straight for Achilla's jaw.

Fortunately, Gumby had never fought a Nephilim before. Achilla heard the sliding of her feet. She noticed the shift in her balance. Despite the fist in front of her blocking her vision while forcing her to narrow her guard, Achilla knew the hook was coming. Achilla shoved Gumby's right arm down and caught her hook with the same left hand. Gumby frowned as she grunted and pulled to no avail. She swung with her right again, and Achilla pulled her close, slipped the punch, and caught her forearm with her right hand before she could retract it. She then twisted Gumby's arms and sent her spinning to the porch floor in a heap. Gumby hopped to her feet and stared at Achilla.

"I'm being nice right now," Achilla said with a grin on her lips as she held a fighting stance. "Give up, and give me what I need. I won't hurt you unless you force me."

Gumby grunted as she front-kicked at Achilla's midsection. Achilla tightened her abs and let the kick land, and Gumby let out a short cry when her ankle cracked against her body, but she maintained her guard. Achilla stepped forward and feinted with her right hand. When Gumby flinched, Achilla used her left hand to pull her guard down and finger-jabbed her throat just hard enough to make her gag. As Gumby reached up to hold her neck, Achilla delivered a left hook to the ribs. Gumby's hands dropped, and Achilla elbowed her face, snapping her head back. She then leaned her entire torso to Gumby's side, grabbed her lower back, and flipped her onto the wooden porch floor. Gumby gasped and Achilla picked her up by her shirt and set her on her knees. When Gumby tried to turn, she snatched the base of her head and forced her to face front.

"Never underestimate your opponent," Achilla said as she lowered her hand to Gumby's neck. "They sent *me* here for a reason. Now let's talk about Xerxes, hm? How many hookers have you sent his way?"

Gumby didn't move or speak.

"You think this is a joke?" Achilla snarled as she squeezed her neck. "You want to answer my question."

"You won't kill me," Gumby coughed. "You need me alive."

"You'd be surprised at what the human body can survive," Achilla said as she tightened her grip on Gumby's neck. "And you'd be surprised what I can do to you on this porch without anyone else noticing but you and me. For example…"

Achilla leaned forward and wrapped her left arm around her neck. She then ran her right hand down Gumby's back until she found her tailbone. Achilla crouched so far that her cheek rubbed against Gumby's ear. She smiled and squeezed her neck before she pinched her tailbone between her index finger and thumb, covering her mouth as she cried out. Gumby grabbed the railing as Achilla maintained her grip and held her upright.

"To you, that's torture," Achilla whispered as Gumby's tears ran down her forearm. "To your neighbors, the lesbian couple's having a massage session in public."

"OK, I get it," Gumby groaned. "Fifteen."

"Normally torture doesn't work," Achilla said. "The victim will say anything you want to hear to make it stop, but I can always tell when someone's lying. So…"

Achilla squeezed her tailbone again and Gumby went limp as she held her up by her neck.

"Now it looks like we're getting freaky," Achilla said. "Neighbors might complain and tell us to get a room, but I'm an exhibitionist. I'll gladly show the world our love until you give me what I want."

"One hundred," Gumby sobbed.

"That's better," Achilla whispered as she stroked Gumby's hair. "I think things are starting to get serious between us. Now, how do you do it?"

"I don't send them directly to Brazil," Gumby answered. "We have a pipeline. The Connecticut girls fly to Miami first. From there, the Miami connection flies them to Brazil on a private plane. After that, Xerxes decides where they go."

"So how many countries are we talking?" Achilla whispered. "Xerxes doesn't just serve the U.S."

"All of Latin America," Gumby replied. "And the Caribbean. You won't find any major city south of Canada that doesn't have a connection to Xerxes' operation, and he's looking to expand. He'll have the Western Hemisphere under his control within ten years probably."

"That's impossible," Achilla snorted. "How has he managed to dodge the CIA and Feds so long?"

"He catches us early," Gumby said. "For me, he knew a bribe wouldn't work, so he threatened my whole family. When I refused, he started killing my cousins until I complied. He has someone on the inside giving him info on any agent who fucks with him. With the money this man has, he can buy almost anyone's loyalty."

"Is that…right?" Achilla asked as her heart sank into her stomach.

"Yeah, and he moves quick too," Gumby replied. "The fact that you're here means me and my whole family's already dead."

"Didn't the CIA offer you any protection?" Achilla asked as she rubbed the cell phone in her pocket with her now free hand.

"Pffftt!" Gumby spat into her front yard. "Eight cousins dead. What kind of protection is that?"

Achilla flinched at Gumby's words. Eight. Cousins? How easily could he murder Achilla's family? No, that wasn't going to happen to her. The CIA was going to prevent that. Weren't they?

"You're coming with me," Achilla said as she hoisted Gumby off the floor. "You're going to tell my superiors everything you just said as soon as we get to headquarters."

"Fine," Gumby replied. "I'm dead anyway. Might as well talk. If you want the truth, I hate Xerxes. Brazil, the U.S., he's the worst I've seen from either country. Men like him ruin everything."

"You can tell us all of that when we get back," Achilla said. "For now, let's get you the hell out of here and bandage that ankle."

"OK," Gumby said. "Keep me alive, and Sandy's yours."

"Uh, no," Achilla replied as she yanked Gumby's hair and stomped her bad ankle. "How about you leave Sandy alone and you keep this pretty head of hair of yours and the use of your leg!"

"Fine, fine!" Gumby cried out until Achilla released her. "Jesus, where'd they find you?"

"Move," said Achilla as she pushed Gumby toward the steps.

Gumby grimaced as she limped toward the stairs with Achilla behind her. Achilla grinned at her second accomplished mission until her ears perked at a clicking noise from the next house; the kind of click you only hear when someone is loading a firearm. Without giving it any more thought, Achilla let go of Gumby, who immediately turned around. As Gumby raised her fist to strike her, Achilla ducked out of her line of attack. Gumby's punch missed, and Achilla heard the muted squeak of a silenced gunshot.

She looked up just in time to watch Gumby's head burst like a dropped watermelon.

Another bullet whizzed by Achilla's head and through the railing as she dropped to the floor. She rolled over a pile of blood and brain matter before busting through the front door into the house, dropping to the carpet and covering her head. When the shooting stopped, she struggled to steady her breathing as she listened for any movements. She couldn't hear anything over her own heaving, but when she slowed down she only heard water running and plates clanking in the kitchen. Then she looked down and stared at the blood and brain matter on her arms.

Achilla had watched plenty of videos of someone getting shot in the head, but actually witnessing it, and *having it on her* made her world swirl around her ears. Achilla hyperventilated as she felt the warmth that used to heat Gumby's body all over her arms and shirt and watched the blood drip from her hands and fingers onto the off-white carpeted floor like spilled syrup. She let out a slight sob as she wagged her arms, sending blood and brain onto the carpet everywhere, but it never seemed to come off. Achilla looked up toward the kitchen. She was washing this off. Now.

Sandy walked out of the kitchen and crossed the plastic wrap-furnished living room with a plate full of bacon and eggs. She smiled at Achilla before frowning at her. Sandy set the plate down and walked across the living room as Achilla stood up and tried to wipe her arms and hands clean of what remained of Gumby's head.

Why wouldn't it *come off?*

"Hey, what happened?" Sandy asked with a soft, trembling voice as she slowed down and held her hands. "Where's Nina?"

Achilla was about to answer, but she snapped her head to the left when she heard someone sneaking through the backyard with steps that only slightly bent the grass. She then heard another click of a loading gun. Achilla looked at the windows along the side of the house and saw the figure of a tall male behind the blinds before looking at Sandy in front of her. Sandy gasped when she tackled her to the floor out of the line of fire.

"What the--"

"Shhh!" Achilla shushed her. "You're in danger. Is there some-where you can hide?"

"Kitchen," Sandy squealed. "What's going on?"

"Just go!" Achilla hissed as she patted Sandy's shoulder and sent her crawling into the kitchen. Achilla hid behind a couch and watched Sandy crawl behind a cabinet and open a trap door. Achilla would be using that exit next. She drew her new .44 Magnum from last night. It was only half-loaded. She checked her Glock, and it was full. Achilla shut her eyes and listened as she heard steps on the front porch. Whoever was coming wasn't concerned about concealing his presence anymore. This was going to be a shoot-out.

Her first. Shootout.

Achilla had never killed someone before, but she knew it would happen eventually. If she didn't now, she wasn't coming home to her family, and that wasn't an option. She gritted her teeth and closed her eyes as she relaxed her breathing. She then cocked both guns.

"You want a fight?" Achilla muttered as a bead of sweat trickled down her forehead while she pulled her hair back and tucked it under the back of her shirt. "You've got one, motherfucker. You've got one."

Achilla's heart dropped when she heard a rumbling from the staircase and she saw two other girls run downstairs directly in front of her. Why were they here now? Didn't they hear the commotion? Couldn't they stay upstairs until it was over? Achilla looked at them and tried to gesture them back upstairs, but they ignored her. The girls walked into the living room but stopped in front of Achilla as her opponent stepped through the doorway. The tall blonde girl with a nose ring in her left nostril wearing a tank top and jeans looked past Achilla and raised her hands. The other, a redhead with pigtails wearing jean shorts and a tight white t-shirt, sobbed and dropped to the floor with her hands on her head.

"I'm looking for someone," said a male voice with a New York accent speaking from behind Achilla's head. "Black chick wearing a hat. Help me find her, and you'll live."

Achilla knew that was a lie. There was no way that a killer of this caliber would leave behind witnesses. He was going to keep them alive long enough for them to tell on her and then kill them, but not if she stopped him. Achilla shook her head at the girls and raised a finger to her lips. The girls stared at her, and the looks in their eyes made Achilla's hands tremble before she reached for her Magnum.

They were going to sell her out.

Just as both of the girls pointed at Achilla, she turned and shot at the male figure in the doorway. The kick was more than she anticipated and she missed his head, shooting the doorway and sending him rolling away from the door. The two girls screamed and ran up the stairs as Achilla rolled from one couch to another. She heard the man roll behind the opposite end of the couch as he breathed with shallow, labored breaths. Achilla pounded the floor. It had been over a year since she practiced with a .44 Magnum. All of Agent Jones lectures about consistency ran laps in her head until she snapped back to the task at hand. If and when she survived this, she would thank him for the advice.

Achilla survived the first exchange, but if she jumped out now, he was sure to shoot her in the face. She steadied her breathing as she looked into the kitchen. No, that wasn't an option; not with him right across the room. The front door was suicide. The stairs were also a no-go. Even if she jumped out the window he could snipe her from the safety of this house. Achilla clenched her eyes shut as she racked her brain for a solution. If she didn't think of something soon, she was dead. Achilla kept her eyes closed as she struggled to keep her cool. She couldn't die today. Not yet. There had to be a way.

Her eyes snapped open when the thought occurred to her. This man knew nothing about her. He was waiting behind the couch just like she was, most likely thinking of the same escape routes. He had no idea that she was a Nephilim capable of doing things that the average woman could not. Hand-to-hand combat was the best option, but how? How could she close the gap between them? Achilla listened for any sudden movements. He hadn't moved from the couch. He was most likely waiting for her to make the first move so he can shoot her and be done with it. Until then, he was attached to that couch just like she was.

Achilla raised her eyebrows when an idea popped into her head. Yes, he was attached to the couch, wasn't he? She turned and kicked the couch with both legs, crushing him between the couch and the wall with a thud. The man cried out as Achilla pushed harder until he dropped his assault rifle. She then jumped to her feet and darted over the couch, kicked the rifle away, and aimed her Magnum at his ski-masked face. He tried to pull out a knife, but Achilla stomped his wrist and cracked it under her foot. She then lifted him by his bullet-proof vest with one arm and pinned him against the yellow wallpaper. Achilla aimed the gun at his face. One pull of the trigger and this was over.

No. She couldn't kill him yet. Only an inexperienced rookie would do that. She still had an assignment to finish, and this guy just killed her next informant; most likely to silence her. Achilla kept her finger hovering over the trigger, but she calmed down just enough to think of her next set of questions.

"Who sent you to kill me?" Achilla snarled. "Answer truthfully. You've seen what I do to liars."

"I was just following orders--"

"Do not tell me about your orders," Achilla roared as she grabbed one of his testicles and squeezed with her forefinger and thumb as she shoved the gun into his face. "Answer my question, or you'll never have children *if* you walk away alive."

"Blue Eyes," the man screamed. "He said you'd be here next."

Achilla gulped. Blue Eyes was a defense attorney involved in sex-trafficking, and even then tangentially so. How did he know Achilla's location? Gumby didn't lie about Xerxes having people inside, but only Kate and Agent Jones gave Achilla her assignment. Was it them? Achilla's phone vibrated, and she checked the call. It was Agent Jones. She had to call him back. Something was wrong.

Just as Achilla shoved her phone into her pocket, her opponent smacked her gun out of her hand, grabbed her Glock, and pointed it at her head. Achilla ducked before he pulled the trigger, and her cap flew off her head as the gun popped. Achilla grabbed his wrist and exploded back up, breaking his firing arm over her shoulder until the bone protruded from the skin. As he hollered out, Achilla threw him across the room by his broken arm while snatching the gun out of his hand in mid-air. She then shot three rounds into his head, neck, and chest just above his vest before he hit the wall and slumped to the floor.

Achilla stood with the pistol in her hand waiting for her assassin to get up, but he didn't move. He just lay on the floor while his blood leaked onto the carpet. She could no longer hear his breathing, but she heard his heartbeat descending, pumping to a slower tempo with each beat. The sound of his dying heart caught Achilla's attention more than anything else in the house. It nagged at her; taunted her even. The urge to make it stop growled inside of her like a hungry stomach. She raised the gun and aimed at his head. This time, she wouldn't miss. Achilla popped another round through his ski mask, sending more blood leaking onto the carpet. After that, his heart stopped altogether. Her growling sensation settled.

As the man lay motionless on the floor, Achilla dropped to her knees with the pistol in her hand. How did she do that? How did she kill someone so easily and skillfully without a moment's hesitation? In the moments when she feared for her life, Achilla could say that she was defending herself. He tried to kill her. She had to kill him. Simple.

This time was different. He was already dying, but she took it upon herself to speed up the process. Achilla made the *decision* to kill someone. She had been training for this moment for four years but it still made her eyes water as she clenched her fists and stared at the floor. She knew it would happen eventually. It was part of the job. It didn't make her a killer. It was *just part of the job*. That was what she told herself until her phone vibrated. She picked it up knowing it was Agent Jones.

"Achilla, abort the mission!" Agent Jones said. "You need to get back now!"

"Someone tried to kill me," Achilla muttered while staring at the lifeless body in front of her. "I killed him."

"I was afraid of that," Agent Jones replied. "But now that one's found you, more will come. There's a mole, Achilla. That's the only way he could've known you'd be there. You have to get out of there now!"

"I need to find Sandy," Achilla said as she looked around the house.

"Forget Sandy!" barked Agent Jones. "We need *you* alive, Achilla!"

Achilla grabbed the Magnum and sprinted to the trap door. She opened it and found Sandy crouched with her hands over her ears, tears rolling down her cheeks, and snot running from her nose. So it wasn't an exit after all. Achilla sighed and picked her up by her arms and hoisted her over her shoulder. She could feel Sandy shivering and whimpering against her body as she searched the room. The two other girls ran down the steps. The very sight of them made Achilla's body shake. She glared at them and pointed her gun, and they raised their hands and dropped to their knees.

"I should shoot you both," Achilla growled. "You had *no reason* to snitch on me like that! I could've protected you! I *would've* protected you! He would've killed you as soon as he was done! Why would you help him? Why?"

Her finger hovered over the trigger as the two girls sobbed and held their hands on their heads. A stain grew on the crotch of the redhead's jeans and Achilla could smell the pungent stench of urine filling the room. She curled her lip at her. The blonde lowered her head and clasped her hands. She then shook her head and mouthed the word *please* as if she were praying to Achilla, begging for her life. Achilla's eyes zeroed in on her in particular. She should be praying, but not to Achilla; not where her prayer would go unanswered. Achilla's body tensed at the thought of shooting her in the head as she aimed her gun. She was going first. That is until she spoke up.

"*Senhor,*" the blonde sobbed. "*Senhor, por favor!*"

So she wasn't praying to Achilla. She was praying to God Himself. The assassin didn't pray. He tried to kill Achilla, even at the end. This girl was defenseless and asking the Lord for help. Achilla didn't know if God intended on saving her or not, but she relaxed and lowered her firearm.

"You should thank God when you leave, girl," Achilla said. "He just saved you. Run. You have until the count of three."

The girls looked up at her. They then looked at each other.

"Two!" Achilla counted as she aimed her pistol again.

The girls ran out the front door. They were down the street in seconds. Achilla sighed and lowered her gun. Taking a life was getting easier for her than Achilla thought, but not them. It just wasn't their time yet. Achilla patted Sandy's back with her free hand.

"We're leaving," Achilla said. "Close your eyes until I say otherwise. I don't want you to see what happened here, ok?"

"OK," Sandy whimpered.

"Can you drive?"

"Yeah."

"Good because we're stealing a car," Achilla said as she searched the windows. "It's possible that I might get shot on the way out. If that happens, you're on your own."

"Nina's car's in the driveway and she always keeps extra keys in the glove compartment," Sandy blurted. "It's quicker than hotwiring."

"Fine," Achilla said before she spoke into her phone. "I'm taking the girl out of here and taking Nina's car. I know it's broad daylight, but I have no choice."

"Achilla, I gave you an order--"

"I have *no other choice!*" Achilla roared over Agent Jones' voice. "If you don't like it, come pick me up. If you're lucky, you might get here in time to pick up my body! Is that what you want?"

There was silence on the other end of the line.

"I'll text you the address," Agent Jones said. "Just get your ass out of there!"

Achilla hung up the phone and held Sandy tight over her shoulder before she bounded out of the house. She took a sharp turn away from Gumby's body and leaped from the porch to the driveway to a red Cadillac Seville; the most conspicuous car an agent could drive. Achilla set Sandy on the ground and ripped open the passenger side door and the glove compartment before jumping across the car's interior to the driver's side. Achilla flinched when she heard Sandy gasp from outside the car.

"Get in, Sandy," Achilla snapped. "It's dangerous."

"Oh my God!" Sandy shrieked. "What did you do to Nina?"

"It wasn't me, and I can't explain," Achilla said as she grabbed Sandy's hand and pulled her into the car. "For your own good, just get in."

She pulled the car out of the driveway and sped South down Bunker Hill Avenue. She even gunned through traffic lights as she navigated the neighborhood streets. When she reached Downtown, she hopped onto I-84 toward Hartford and put the pedal to the floor. As she weaved through traffic, Achilla noticed Sandy staring at her as she pinned herself against the door as far away from her as possible. Achilla ignored her as she passed another slowpoke.

"You're not a cop," Sandy sobbed. "You didn't arrest anybody. You killed Nina! You're a murderer!"

"Someone else killed Nina," Achilla replied. "Then he tried to kill me, so I killed him."

"Liar!" Sandy cried out. "You're a murderer!"

"I saved your life!" Achilla screamed back. "Now shut up and sit down so I can concentrate!"

Sandy eyed Achilla as she shut her mouth and sat straight in her seat.

"Consider yourself lucky," Achilla said in a deadpan voice. "Your friends saw more than you did. Still, I understand your reaction, but I promise you that I didn't kill Nina."

"They're not my friends," Sandy said through her sniffling. "And what didn't I see?"

"I'll explain later," Achilla said as she passed a tractor trailer. "It looks like I may have to."

"You're not a cop," Sandy replied. "Who are you?"

"Yeah," Achilla said as she focused on the road. "It looks like I might have to explain that too."

When Achilla received the address from Agent Jones, it was in the opposite direction from Hartford. Achilla had to turn around and switch to Route 8 until she arrived in the Lantern Park section of Naugatuck. The text message said to pull across the street from a caged basketball court next to a pond. Achilla found the location and told Sandy to keep her head low. She waited until a black sedan pulled up next to Achilla's car and Agent Jones rolled down the passenger side window. Kate sat on the driver's side. She pointed toward the court before parking in front of the Cadillac.

Achilla stepped out of the car and walked toward the basketball court. She looked down at the dried blood that caked her hands and shuddered before looking straight ahead. Once inside the cage, Achilla stood with trembling fists as she waited for her superiors to walk up. Agent Jones wore a white t-shirt and jeans as he walked with the gait of a tired man who needed to retire. Kate looked like the tireless professional as she walked at a fast pace with her black business suit. When they entered the cage, Kate stood before Achilla with her hands on her hips.

"Report?" Kate asked.

"Gumby got shot right in front of me," Achilla said. "But only because I moved out of the way. I'm pretty sure that I was the target. The killer came for me next, but I got him first. Broken arm, a shot to the chest, one to the neck, two to his head."

"Well done," Kate said. "I'll need your gun back."

"Sure," Achilla said with a frown as she handed Kate her Glock. "I also used this one."

Achilla showed the gun she stole from her suitor last night.

"Desert Eagle," Kate said. "We don't issue those."

"So what?" Achilla asked.

"So that works to our advantage," Kate replied as she reached for the Magnum. "I'll take that too."

"Why don't we figure out who this mole is?" Achilla asked as she pulled her gun back.

"Right now, we need to make sure that nobody knows you were there," Kate said without retracting her hand.

"But somebody does know I was there," Achilla replied through gritted teeth. "That's how I got shot at. Did you miss that part?"

"Kate, just let her keep the damn gun," Agent Jones muttered.

"We have to follow protocol," Kate snapped.

"We have to figure out who tried to kill her," Agent Jones replied. "Whoever sent this guy won't just stop with her. They never do, Kate, you know that, and I warned you--"

"That's why we've taken measures to protect her family," Kate said with narrow eyes before looking at Achilla. "I promise you they're safe."

"He said he was sent by Blue Eyes," Achilla said as she holstered her gun into the back of her jeans. "How'd Blue Eyes know I would be there?"

"He and Gumby were in cahoots," Kate said. "I'm sure they figured it out."

"But they knew *exactly when* I'd be there," Achilla said as she faced Agent Jones. "Only you knew that."

"You think I'm the mole?" Agent Jones asked with his hands raised. "You're mistaken."

"No way," Kate said with a head shake. "Agent Jones' loyalty is beyond reproach. Besides, he's too close to you. He'd have to be a fool, and he's not. Agent Jones, who did you speak to about this case?"

"Nobody else," Agent Jones said. "Either my phone or computer must've been monitored while I looked up the address for her."

"We'll check the tech department first then," Kate said as she stepped toward Achilla. "I still need your gun."

"No," Achilla replied with a hard stare. "You're the one who handed me the assignment in the first place, and I got it *after* blowing my cover in New Haven."

"Achilla, I know you're a bit paranoid right now," Kate said. "Welcome to the business. But we're the good guys."

"We're the only ones you can trust right now," Agent Jones added. "I wish it didn't happen this way, but it did. If we put our heads together, we'll figure it out."

Achilla pulled out her phone and started dialing numbers.

"Who are you calling?" Kate demanded with her hands on her hips. "You're in the middle of a briefing."

"Achilla put the phone down," Agent Jones said. "Come on, now isn't the time for phone calls."

"Samuel?" Achilla asked when the other side picked up. "Samuel, it's Achilla. We haven't spoken in a while, but--"

"Where the hell have you been?" the voice on the other side bellowed.

Achilla didn't like the sound of that. It wasn't the first time that Samuel got angry with her over the phone, but this was different. His voice had the broken hoarseness of someone who just finished weeping. Achilla's insides trembled when she thought about what Gumby said about Xerxes. She closed her eyes and steadied her breathing before she spoke. Perhaps Kate was right. She was probably just being paranoid. The CIA had it covered. They had to.

"Samuel?" Achilla asked as she eyed Kate and stepped back.

"Yeah, it's me," Samuel said. "I've been calling you for hours."

"My phone got shut off," Achilla said as she backed away even further from the agents in front of her. "What's wrong, Samuel? You sound…upset. Did that Trish girl bother you again?"

Achilla froze. Trish. Blue Eyes called his niece Patricia "Trish" over the phone. She might have been the same Trish at Samuel's high school who was always hitting on him. She might have recognized Achilla. No. No, that had to be a coincidence. Achilla wouldn't miss such an obvious detail. She was too smart for that. That was impossible.

"What's Trish got to do with this?" Samuel asked.

"Nothing," Achilla said with the hope that it was true. "Why were you calling me?"

"Oh my God," Samuel moaned. "Oh no, Mom hasn't told you yet."

She had a feeling she knew what would come next, and for the first time in a while, she prayed to God that she was wrong. If the Trish from Blue Eyes' office was the same Trish from Stratford High, then it is possible that she recognized Achilla as Samuel's sister. From there, Blue Eyes would have found out that Achilla was Brendan Johnson's daughter. After Achilla embarrassed him in his own office and stole his business contacts, common sense told Achilla that he would want revenge. What better way for a thug like Blue Eyes to take revenge than to--

"It's Dad, Achilla."

"No," Achilla whimpered as she sank to her knees. "No, Samuel, please don't tell me this."

"They found him in his office when he didn't come home last night--"

"No, no, no--"

"He was shot in the head," Samuel sobbed. "Someone...executed him. The police think it was gang related--"

Upon hearing that sentence, Achilla stared out into the park. Her father was dead?

Executed?

Shot?

Dead?

Achilla ran her hand up to the side of her head and grabbed a handful of hair as her mouth dropped open. Her heart raced and her breathing heaved as her body shook. Agent Jones and Kate looked back and forth at each other, and Agent Jones frowned as he studied her. Kate just stared. Achilla noticed them watching but ignored them in favor of her chest that constricted with each heaving breath.

Her father was murdered?

Executed?

Shot?

In the head?

Dead?

Her father was dead?

Achilla shut her eyes and her chest jolted like lightning just struck her left breast. She clenched her teeth as her knees wobbled and her feet went numb. Though she couldn't see the park anymore, she still felt like it was swirling around her head; the pond, the cage, all of it. The tightness in her chest was too much. Without time to brace herself, she felt her heart bang against her chest so hard that she sucked in her breath. Achilla couldn't exhale. Her heart wouldn't let her. It held her throat with an iron grip as she clutched her sweater. When her heart finally let go, she released a shriek that barreled through her throat, echoed off the pond, and crashed off the steel cage. Agent Jones and Kate cringed and covered their ears at the sound.

Chapter Ten

ACHILLA JOHNSON:20

Brendan Johnson:46

Brendan yawned as he stared at his desk filled with piles of documents. Litigation was never easy, and Brendan took every trial and motion seriously, but this was his most important project yet. After speaking with Tyron Higgins, and multiple Bridgeport residents, he decided to write multiple *habeas corpus* petitions for anyone arrested by Ailina Harris from 1995 through 2003.

Brendan had reason to believe she was torturing black men into signing confessions and forcing others to engage her in sexual relationships in exchange for leniency. He was so consumed with avoiding her for his own safety and for Achilla's sake that he never thought to investigate her police work. Now that Achilla enlisted and Samuel enrolled in college, he didn't have to worry about them, and this kind of brutality was a plague on his city. Brendan took a deep breath as he reread the testimony in front of him. Jared Higgins stated, in his own writing, that Ailina broke his legs because he refused to engage her sexually. She then shoved a gun in his mouth and played Russian roulette until he agreed to sign a confession to an armed robbery he didn't commit. When he tried to take the confession and run, she stomped his spine, paralyzing him.

This was a huge case against Bridgeport PD and one that required the utmost discretion. No one in the firm was allowed to talk about it outside of the office. Even Brendan didn't tell Sam. They couldn't risk any leaks to the press until the time was right. Tipping their hand could result in witness intimidation that they couldn't afford. These men were traumatized and paranoid enough already.

Brendan frowned when he heard a knock and turned from his desk. Tyron stood in his doorway wearing a black suit and red tie. Much like Brendan, corruption inspired him to pursue the law. Now he was Brendan's best law clerk. He came in early and left late. His research was thorough and his memos were flawless. He was the kind of sharp brother Brendan wanted working for him, and with enough time, working next to him as a partner.

"Do you need anything else?" Tyron asked rubbed his hand over his waved hair.

"Not a thing," Brendan said. "My son's supposed to call you, by the way."

"I'll help him any way I can," Tyron replied. "You know I've got you, Mr. Johnson."

"Thank you," Brendan sighed. "But go home. You don't get to work these kinds of hours until you pass the bar and get paid to work them."

Tyron saluted and walked out the door and Brendan returned to his work. How did he end up involved with a woman like Ailina? Achilla was a godsend, but Ailina's past was going to curse him forever. He had to do something about it, and this was a good start.

Brendan jolted when he heard a clattering crash in the office.

"You all right, Tyron?" Brendan asked as he grabbed one of his papers. He frowned when Tyron didn't answer. Brendan stood up and opened his desk drawer, pulling it out his revolver. When he walked to the doorway and heard someone coming, Tyron walked in. Brendan sighed and lowered his weapon.

"You scared the shit out of me," Brendan said with a chuckle as he set his gun down on his desk. "What happened?"

Tyron stared at Brendan and shook his head as tears welled up in his eyes. Then Gabrielli walked in behind him wearing a black trench coat, along with a bald, black man in a hoody and jeans with a pistol pointed at Tyron.

"What's going on here?" Brendan asked as he raised his hands. "You're robbing me now?"

"Why not?" Gabrielli asked. "Your kid robbed me."

Brendan frowned.

"I don't know what you're talking about," Brendan said. "But whatever it is, I doubt Tyron needs to be involved. He can go, right?"

"Sure," Gabrielli said with a shrug. "He can go."

The bald black man shot Tyron in the chest and Brendan jumped before reaching for his gun. A gun popped, and a sharp, burning sensation in his foot made him cry out before the bald man marched over and grabbed Brendan's revolver.

"You won't be using this," he said. "On your knees."

Brendan dropped to his knees as sweat dripped down his face. He kept his hand raised, but the bald man forced him to face the desk.

"What happened, Rob?" Brendan asked.

"Your bitch daughter jacked me up," Gabrielli said. "And what she stole is valuable to some important people, people who would kill to keep it safe. Since I failed to keep it safe, I'm tasked with killing to send a message."

"Why not just have her return it?" Brendan replied.

"You can't *return* information," Gabrielli said. "Once it spreads, it's spread, man. And once the government gets its hands on it…"

"It never goes away," the bald man said.

"I won't lie," Gabrielli said. "I'm enjoying this. You had no business in the same classroom as me, but you had the nerve to refuse my kindness? The less affirmative action babies like you in this profession the better."

"Racist pile of shit," Brendan growled before glaring at the bald man. "And you work with him?"

"I don't like him any more than you do," the bald man said with a shrug. "I'm paid to be here."

Brendan lowered his eyes. A hit man. He always worried that the dangers of his profession would catch up to him. He never imagined another defense attorney hiring a gun to deal with him. He closed his eyes and whispered a prayer for his family.

"Let me know when you're done," Gabrielli said. "I'm Catholic, so I understand."

"Done," Brendan replied. "You won't get away with this."

"Sure I will," Gabrielli said. "Tyron had a beef with some local gangsters. They're already set up for this hit. Well, I'll be going. Just wanted to see your face before the deed was done. Be sure to thank Achilla for getting you killed. Oh, wait. You can't. I guess I'll think her when I kill her next."

"Just please don't hurt her," Brendan called as he listened to Gabrielli's footsteps walking out of the office. "Please!"

Brendan closed his eyes again when he heard the bald man load his gun.

"What's your name?" Brendan asked.

"Sidney."

"You're not from around here, Sidney," Brendan said. "I can tell from that accent of yours. You don't know who we are or what we're about. This is an office for good people."

"I know plenty," Sidney replied.

"Then can you promise not to hurt any more of my employees or my family?" Brendan asked.

"Not really," Sidney said.

"What if I paid you?" Brendan asked. "We can go in my safe right now. If you need more, I can give you a check. Name your price. I'll pay anything to keep my family safe."

"I don't take money from targets," Sidney said. "But you seem like a good guy. I'll do my best unless my hands are tied. Fact is I don't want to kill you, but business is business."

Brendan took a deep, trembling breath.

"What did Achilla steal?" Brendan asked. "If I'm going to die, I might as well know. How can she steal something from across the Atlantic and from who?"

"So that's her cover," Sidney sighed. "I wondered how she kept this from you."

"Kept what?"

"Your daughter's CIA," Sidney said. "She took files from Blue Eyes in the course of her investigation of some powerful people."

Brendan's eyes turned wide. Achilla was lying the whole time? She was a CIA agent? Tears welled up in his eyes before he closed them and let the tears flow down his cheeks. His body trembled as he sobbed.

"Never pictured you to be this scared of death," Sidney said.

"I'm not," Brendan replied with a broken voice. "I'm just so proud. I knew she would make something of herself. I just didn't know how."

Brendan's heart raced when he felt the barrel of the gun rest against the back of his neck. It was still warm from the previous shot. He closed his eyes and took a deep breath. At least at this range, it'll be quick.

"She's going to avenge me," Brendan said with a smile. "God designed that girl for conflict, and you'll regret this. I'll take solace in--"

The gun popped, and everything went black.

Chapter Eleven

ACHILLA JOHNSON: 14

Achilla followed both Brendan and Sam's instructions. Whenever she got angry at someone, she called one of them with the black flip phone that Brendan gave her. After that, they would talk about why she was angry until she calmed down. The only time she did not whip out her cell phone was during her basketball games for Wooster Middle School when it wasn't possible. She learned to ignore the dirty plays the girls from other teams would use or get them back in ways the referees couldn't see.

She was a standout basketball player for Wooster, and she earned a scholarship to play for St. Joseph's High School in Trumbull. Upon receiving the news, Sam jumped for joy and hugged her before giving her a high five and hugging her again. She then took Achilla shopping for new clothes at the Trumbull Mall. When they arrived, Achilla frowned at all of the stores and people walking around. It was as if the entire Fairfield County congregated in this one building filled with bright lights and the combined smell of burgers, fries, and sourdough pretzels.

"You've never been to a mall before, have you?" Sam asked as she shoved her keys in her khaki shorts and hung her brown, leather purse over her red polo t-shirt.

"No," Achilla said.

"Well it's only right that a girl your age takes at least one trip to a shopping mall," Sam sighed. "My girlfriends and I used to go to the mall every weekend."

"You were that rich?" Achilla asked.

"No," Sam chuckled. "No, we didn't buy anything."

"What's the point in that?"

"You...don't think like a girl, do you?" Sam asked. "You're even less girly than I was, and that's saying something."

"What do you mean?" Achilla asked. "I am a girl."

"Right, but you talk like your father did when we were kids," Sam replied. "You're actually sterner than he was come to think of it..."

"I just don't see the point in coming to a shopping mall if you're not going to shop," Achilla said with her hands wide as she looked around the mall. "What's so different about that? I don't understand."

"Do you like boys, Achilla?" Sam asked.

"Do you mean if I find them physically attractive?" Achilla replied.

"OK," Sam said with a nod of her head. "Yeah, let's start there."

"Well, yeah, I do," Achilla said with a shrug. "I'm heterosexual."

Sam sighed loud enough to echo throughout the mall.

"Don't you want boys to like you?" Sam asked. "Don't you want them to look at you and think you're pretty? Does that thought ever cross your mind?"

"No," Achilla said. "Not really."

"So when you see a boy you like, what do you think?" Sam asked.

"I think about screwing him," Achilla blurted.

"Achilla, language."

"Sorry," Achilla replied.

"Don't be," Sam sighed. "I get the feeling Ailina taught you that. You might not understand this now, but boys and girls don't normally treat each other the way you might have seen Ailina treat her men. From what Brendan told me, it can get pretty bad."

"They're not supposed to have sex?" Achilla asked.

"Well, yes, they are," Sam replied as they passed a vendor surrounded by a group of girls no older than Achilla wearing jean skirts, hoop earrings, and gelled hair wrapped in pink bandanas. "But it's best when they love each other. I'm not sure if Ailina loves anyone, really."

"Not even me?" Achilla asked with her head low.

"Now I'm the one who should be sorry," Sam said as she held Achilla's shoulder. "I shouldn't have worded it that way. It's just that a man and a woman should love each other first. Then they should get married. Then they have sex. It's the way God designed us."

"If that's how God designed us, how come my mother never does that?" Achilla asked.

"Because God still gives us a choice to do what we want," Sam replied with her arms wide. "Even if it's the wrong thing, but if we ask Him to forgive us, He will. He loves us that much."

"If God loves me, how come he didn't give me a different mother," Achilla muttered as she stared at her feet. "Instead of one who beat me up all the time?"

"I wish I could answer that, honey," Sam said. "But I'm not God. I can't think for Him. I only know what I've seen and learned so far. One thing I've learned is that a girl at your age should have fun and enjoy being a girl. You really shouldn't be having sex, and Ailina shouldn't have exposed you to so much of it."

"You don't like my mom, do you?" Achilla asked.

"I won't lie to you, Achilla," Sam said. "I don't. I don't like anyone who treats a child the way she treated you. I love children. I don't understand how anyone could abuse one and sleep at night."

Abuse. That word rolled around Achilla's head as she thought about her time in Ailina's house. Achilla never thought of herself as the victim of abuse, but it made sense. It made sense that Ailina didn't love her. Brendan loved her, and even when he was in a bad mood, he didn't treat her like Ailina did. Achilla looked at her black sneakers and shoved her hands in the pockets of her red basketball shorts.

"Well, I do like boys," Achilla replied before looking up at Sam. "How do you get married? Do I just ask him if he wants to get married?"

"No, honey," Sam chuckled. "The man's supposed to do that."

"Why?" Achilla asked. "What if I want to have sex?"

"Wow," Sam sighed and palmed her forehead. "You are a girl, but you think like a lot of the male population. You don't get married to have sex. You get married for love. Your father asked to marry me because he loves me, and I said yes because I love him."

"And then you had sex?" Achilla asked with a grin. "Kind of like you still do now?"

"Achilla that's personal," Sam replied. "I don't feel comfortable speaking about my sex life with you."

"You mean the fact that you and my dad have sex at least twice a week, three times if he has the day off?" Achilla asked.

"How did you--"

"I can hear you," Achilla chuckled as she looked at Sam like she had forgotten her own name. "We live in the same house."

"But your bedroom is on the other side of the house," Sam blurted as she shook her head. "It's impossible for you to hear anything in our room, and we can't hear anything in yours!"

"Maybe you have a hearing problem," Achilla said.

"My hearing is perfect, Achilla--"

"Are you sure?" Achilla asked. "Because it sounds like my hearing's better than yours. For example, two nights ago around eight o'clock at night, you--"

"And that's where the conversation ends," Sam snapped before taking a deep breath. "Achilla, it sounds like you have an advanced familiarity with sex that most girls your age don't have."

"Is that a bad thing?" Achilla asked as she watched a group of boys around her age pass by until Sam tapped her shoulder to keep her attention.

"Well, it either makes everything simple," Sam replied. "Or really complicated."

"How would it get complicated?" Achilla asked as she stared at the group of boys again. "What's complicated about me liking boys?"

"That'll depend on how much the boys like you back," Sam said as they stopped in front of JC Penny. "We're in here. The first thing we'll do is get you some clothes for your school uniform. After that, is there anything you want?"

"Basketball shorts," Achilla said. "And jeans. And sneakers."

"No earrings?" Sam asked. "Or maybe a jean skirt?"

"Ugh!" Achilla scowled and waved her hand.

"You sound like me at your age," Sam quipped as they walked into the store. "Fine, we'll hold off on the girly stuff for another day. I'll just settle for spending the day shopping. Let's get started."

Even after shopping for school uniforms, basketball shorts, jeans, and new sneakers, Achilla thought nothing of Sam's comments about how different she was from other girls. However, after her fourteenth birthday, Achilla started to notice the stark contrast. That difference became clear just before the school year started. St. Joseph's basketball team couldn't legally practice with a coach yet, but the team captain organized workout sessions in the off-season. Her name was Traci Handler, and she was ranked fifth in the state. Achilla first met Traci when she rang the doorbell at the Johnson house. Achilla opened the door to a six-foot-two red-haired, freckled girl who held a stern demeanor until she looked down at Achilla. Then she smiled and handed her a flyer.

"You must be Achilla," Traci said. "You should come to conditioning. We're trying to win the championship this year, and I hear you're really good."

"Thanks," Achilla said with a shrug as she took the flyer. "I'll be there."

The flyer described the workouts they would perform during conditioning: strength-training, running three miles on the track, running suicides, and running up and down the bleachers in the football field. Achilla showed up for the workout and expected a challenge. After the first day, only Achilla and Traci were able to walk to the locker room, and Traci huffed and puffed and held her hands over her head. Achilla frowned at herself after she showered and changed. Deep inside, she knew that she could run at least ten more miles. After a week of conditioning, Achilla decided to try it after practice. She ran home from Trumbull to Stratford. Once she arrived home, Achilla frowned at herself again when she realized that she wasn't even winded. She then dropped to the ground and performed 30 handstand pushups in her backyard. After stretching and showering, Achilla sat in the living room with a bowl of salad as she watched Brendan's collection of Michael Jordan era Chicago Bulls games.

During summer league games, Achilla excelled. Soon, she and Traci started and played the same amount of minutes, but Achilla knew Traci was better. All Achilla knew how to do was score and play defense, but Traci scored, passed, rebounded, and defended better than anyone on the team. After watching Traci for a couple games, Achilla copied her movements. She boxed out more and used her strength to rebound over girls six inches taller than her, and she was learning when to shoot and when to pass. By the end of the summer, Achilla was dribbling the ball on fast breaks and throwing no-look dishes to Traci for lay-ups. Traci and Achilla had become a dynamic duo, and their team went undefeated. When the season started, Achilla was a well-known name around school. For the first time in her life, Achilla had friends. When Achilla asked Sam if she could bring some of her teammates over for dinner, Sam hugged her. Achilla frowned at her father who was standing behind her with a smile on his face. Did such a simple request hold this much importance?

"Of course you can," Brendan said. "And we're proud of you."

"I'll make your favorite," Sam said as she held Achilla by the shoulders. "I hope they like my fried catfish."

"Wait, I thought steak and fries were her favorites," Brendan said with a frown.

"She beat you out a long time ago, Dad," Achilla said, and her parents laughed before hugging her together.

Achilla would stay out late with the team after practice, come home, and do her homework. She sat with the team during lunch, walked with her teammates in between classes, and dressed like the rest of them outside of school; sweatpants, hoody, sneakers. She also wore a pair of sandals with ankle socks after practice just like Traci. The only separation Achilla had from the basketball team was at home with her family. Sometimes, Achilla and Sam would attend Samuel's basketball games at Wooster and cheer him on. Other times, Achilla would sit on the living room couch with a bowl of popcorn and watch NBA games with Brendan; only to end up arguing over who was better between Kobe Bryant and Tracy McGrady. One night when Tracy McGrady faked Kobe Bryant so bad that he fell face-first, Brendan looked at Achilla with a knowing grin on his face. Achilla stormed off to bed as he laughed and pointed at her back.

Unfortunately, St. Joseph's basketball team lost in the first round of states against Kolbe Cathedral from Bridgeport. However, during that game, Achilla couldn't miss. She scored thirty-five points and passed eight assists. Her coach encouraged her to play AAU basketball during the summer so she could get national recognition. Achilla had never received so much praise before. In the hallway at school, kids would nod and smile at her, and she would lower her head and wave. One boy stopped to talk to her one morning before first-period class. He was as tall as Brendan with tan skin, blue eyes and dark, shaggy brown hair that fell past his ears.

"Hey, are you new here?" he asked.

"No," Achilla snorted. "I play for the basketball team. I started varsity all season."

"Oh wait, you're that chick Achilla Johnson, right?" said the boy with a snap of his fingers.

"My name is Achilla Johnson, yeah," Achilla replied before squinting at him. "I don't think I like being called a chick though."

"What should I call you then?" the boy asked.

"Achilla works," Achilla said. "I'm going to class. Excuse me."

"Well, wait a second," the boy said as he flashed a smile. "Aren't you going to let me introduce myself? I'm Stanley Preston. Quarterback."

"Nice to meet you, Stanley," Achilla said as she extended her hand. Stanley's handshake was tight, and he looked into her eyes in a way that made Achilla blush. He then wrapped his arm around her shoulders as they walked down the hallway. Something about the way he held her shoulders made Achilla squirm at first, but she soon relaxed. Achilla's heart pumped out of her chest, and she held her books close.

"I hope you don't mind me walking you to class," Stanley said.

"No, not really," Achilla replied until she stopped in front of her next class. "But my classroom's right here."

"I won't waste any time then," Stanley said. "Let's catch a movie this Friday. I'll pick you up at six."

"Sure," Achilla said as she watched Stanley walk down the hall without waiting for an answer. When Achilla told Sam, she was elated. She asked questions about what Stanley looked like, what he did at school, and if he was nice. She then rushed to the door when Brendan came home and told him the news. He frowned in response.

"You sure you have time to date?" Brendan asked with his arms crossed over his navy blue argyle sweater as he stood in the kitchen doorway. "And who is this Stanley boy? How old is he?"

"I don't know," Achilla said with a smile. "I just want to go."

"Brendan, relax," Sam said. "She's fourteen. Don't you think she's allowed to like boys?"

"I have no problem with her liking boys," Brendan said. "I just think this is moving a little fast. Do you know anything about this boy, Achilla?"

"I know he's hot," Achilla said with a short laugh. "And he's a quarterback."

"Achilla met a quarterback?" Samuel said as he walked into the kitchen wearing sweatpants and no shirt. Achilla frowned at how deep his voice was getting. Any whininess to his tone was completely gone. His body was also more defined than before. Since when did he get in such good shape? Achilla switched her attention to her parents.

"She has a date this Friday," Sam said with a smile.

"How old is he?" Samuel asked with his hands on his hips.

"Why is that a relevant question?" Achilla groaned.

"I don't want you to get taken advantage of by an older boy," Brendan said. "Seniors who target freshmen put a bad taste in my mouth."

"I agree with Dad," Samuel said.

"I agree too," Sam replied with her hands up. "But I think we can trust Achilla. If anything funny goes on, she can call us like she always does. Right, Achilla?"

"Yes, ma'am," Achilla replied. "And thanks."

On the day of the date, Achilla threw on a pair of jeans, white sneakers and a maroon and white St. Joseph's long-sleeved t-shirt. Sam sucked her teeth and promised that she would teach her how to dress up for a date next time. Stanley picked up Achilla at home and met her parents. Something about the way Stanley couldn't look Brendan in the eye made Achilla frown, but she ignored it. Contrary to what her father thought, Achilla assumed that Stanley was an older boy, and she had every intention of taking advantage of him after a few dates. She remembered how Ailina always flirted with her men and copied it throughout the night; holding his hand, caressing his back, constantly playing with her hair when they spoke. After the movie, Achilla walked out with Stanley to his Ford Expedition and held her hand on his lap as he drove. Stanley pulled over in the middle of a dark, wooded area, and Achilla frowned at him.

"Why'd you stop?" Achilla asked.

"You know why," Stanley said as he leaned close. "Why wait?"

Stanley kissed Achilla on the lips. Achilla held his face and kissed him back. Her first kiss made her giggle a little until Stanley started to reach under her shirt. Achilla pushed his arm away. When he tried again, she pushed his arm and shoved his chest.

"What are you doing?" Achilla asked. "Look, I don't want to do this in a truck. Maybe we should hold off on--"

"Come on, you've been hitting on me all night," Stanley said as he crouched over her.

"That's because we're on a date, asshole," Achilla replied. "That doesn't mean we're going all the way right now."

"Yeah, we are," Stanley said as he grabbed Achilla's arm with one hand and lowered her seat with the other. Achilla's heart raced as he pinned her down by her shoulder and moved his hand up her shirt. Her eyes welled up as he reached for her pants. When she reached for the door he grabbed her arm and held it with an even tighter grip than usual.

"Stop!" Achilla cried out.

"Look, just relax," Stanley barked. "You'll like it!"

"I said no!" Achilla screamed. When Stanley dove in to kiss her again, she turned her face and pushed his head away. Achilla then reached for her cell phone. She was calling her father right away. Stanley grabbed her arm and she thrashed about until he pinned her against the seat. Achilla whimpered when he reached under her shirt again and she swiped his arm away as tears leaked down her face.

Stanley grabbed Achilla's throat. Achilla gagged as he pressed her neck against her seat. Achilla then growled and kicked his groin so hard that his backside nearly hit the dashboard. She then punched his left eye and finger-jabbed his throat. Stanley croaked as Achilla opened the door, grabbed his shirt, and threw him out of the car with one arm. Stanley rolled in the grass on the side of the road before stumbling to his feet. He ambled toward the truck and lunged at her, but he was way too slow. Achilla sidestepped and cracked his jaw with a left hook. Stanley crashed on the ground next to the truck, and Achilla lifted him by his shirt and pinned him against the back seat window. He coughed and groaned as she lifted him to his feet. She then grabbed his neck with a slap and squeezed his throat until he gagged and dropped to his knees.

"Motherfucker," Achilla snarled as she grabbed his head and smashed his cheeks. "I told you no!"

Achilla kneed his face and let him drop to the ground in a heap. She then waited for him to get up. He didn't. He just laid face first on the ground without moving an inch. Did she kill him? Achilla wanted to hurt him. She wanted him to pay for touching her like that. She wanted him to know how it felt to get strangled.

She didn't want to murder the guy!

Achilla's knees shook as she backed away from Stanley and

pulled out her cell phone. Brendan was the first number she called. She paced around the front of the truck as she held her phone with a trembling hand.

"What's up, Achilla--"

"He tried to rape me," Achilla said. "He tried to--"

"What?!" Brendan roared. "I'll snap his fucking neck! Is he there or--?"

"Out cold," Achilla blurted as she watched blood seep out of Stanley's nose. "I knocked him out. I think. I haven't checked his pulse yet, but he's on the ground right in front of me."

Brendan took a couple breaths before clearing this throat.

"Check his pulse."

"Sure," Achilla said as she stepped forward and pressed two fingers against his throat; feeling a pulse. "He's fine. Just out cold like I thought."

"Good," Brendan said. "Where are you?"

"I don't know," Achilla sobbed as her hands and knees trembled. "Some random road out in Trumbull. It's dark and there's a bunch of trees. I don't see any houses. Dad, I'm really scared."

"Don't worry," Brendan said. "Everything will be fine. Give me the license plate number. I'll call Trumbull PD, and Sam and I will look for you ourselves. I promise you'll be fine."

"OK."

"Just stay on the phone with me until we find you," Brendan said. "Especially if that punk wakes up."

"He's not moving, Dad," Achilla said. "Like at all."

"I know," Brendan sighed. "I had a feeling he wouldn't be."

Achilla didn't kill Stanley; though his ego might have been a different story. Stanley suffered two black eyes, a broken nose, a broken jaw, a bruised neck, and a fractured testicle. He wouldn't be able to play football or even work out for a while. Stanley's parents tried to sue the Johnsons but backed off when they figured out all of the facts. Were it not for the bruises on Achilla's wrist and neck indicating a struggle, she would have been in serious trouble. Having a reputable defense attorney for a father didn't hurt either.

Unfortunately, Stanley was also a connected kid. His uncle was the mayor of Trumbull, and his father was the CEO of a major business with a headquarters in town. The police refused to charge him, and Achilla had to walk the halls at school the next day knowing that he might come back. After Brendan came home from work one night, Achilla watched him pace their kitchen with a phone in his hand.

"So this boy can do whatever he wants?" Brendan asked as he gripped his black tie. "He can put his hands on *my daughter*, and it's OK? I don't give a….No, it's not because of lack of evidence. You are talking to a defense attorney, and if this boy were my client, I would be pleading down! He is as guilty as they come of assault and battery and the attempted rape of a minor….Bullshit, you cops always bust who you want! I bet if he was black, you'd bury his ass under the jail you no good, racist *pigs!*"

Brendan hung up the phone and threw it into the living room, sending the phone crashing against the wall. He let out a mix between a grunt and a roar as he sat down and covered his head with his hands. Achilla felt a lump in her throat as she watched him. It was the same feeling she had when she watched Samuel cry. Brendan stood up and turned his back on Achilla with his hands on his hips. Achilla never imagined that she would see her father like this. She stood up and hugged him around the waist from behind.

"You tried, Dad," Achilla said. "It's OK."

"If that boy comes near you again," Brendan growled with his fists clenched by his sides. "Call me immediately. If they won't deal with him, I will. Nobody puts their hands on my kids. Nobody. That boy better hope I don't catch him in the street somewhere--"

"It's fine, Dad," Achilla replied with a smile. "But…um…thanks for caring so much."

Things weren't fine, but it wasn't because of any risk to Achilla's safety. Word had spread at school that Achilla beat up Stanley Preston almost ruined his football career. The rumors also made her out to be the aggressor, even though she was half his size and had never been in a fight at school. People cleared a path for her when she walked to class and even some of the basketball players stared at her.

It was that look again.

Fear.

People avoided Achilla in the hallway so much that she ducked into a bathroom stall and cried all through fourth period. That was her first time ever skipping a class. When Achilla approached her teacher to apologize, he handed her the homework assignment and rushed into his classroom. Achilla lowered her head and walked to her next class only to be shunned by the rest of her teachers. Only Traci greeted her after seventh period, but by then Achilla was rushing to the girl's locker room. She changed into her basketball shorts and jogged home like she always did. This time, she ran home faster than usual. When she got home, Achilla overheard Sam on the phone. It didn't take long for her to figure out who she was speaking to. Achilla walked into the living room and watched Sam pace in front of a couch in a purple dress that she bought for herself when they went shopping at JC Penny.

"It's bad enough that you didn't tell me about her," Sam yelled into the receiver. "But now you won't even back her up? The boy tried to rape her, and they're letting him get away with it! Do you understand me? They pulled some strings. Why can't you?..Because we're your family! Are you really going to let this slide?..Oh, that is a pathetic excuse!"

Achilla noticed that Sam did not have a good relationship with her father, Bridgeport Police Chief Gregory Price. He never came over. He never called. Ailina worked for him, yet he never acknowledged Achilla's presence. The more Achilla thought about him, the more she realized he was the male equivalent to Ailina in her eyes. She had grown to dislike him as much as Sam did.

"You are the worst father on the planet!" Sam snarled. "Bye! No, to hell with how you feel because a little girl could've been raped, and you won't do....you won't do shit about it! You don't do shit! You never do shit! *Never!*"

Sam hung up the phone and threw it onto the couch before she sat down and wiped a strand of her hair. She then stood up to leave the living room and stopped when she saw Achilla standing in the kitchen. Achilla also noticed that people had a tendency to be surprised at her presence. It was like Achilla could hear twice as many sounds as her family. Sam sighed and looked at the floor before looking up at Achilla.

"Hey, Achilla," Sam said with a tired look in her eyes. "Sorry, I didn't want you to hear that. How was your day?"

"I want to transfer schools," Achilla said.

"Baby, why?" Sam gasped. "Is it because of Stanley? If anybody needs to leave, it's him and not you."

"Everybody at school avoids me," Achilla said. "They hate me."

"They don't hate you, honey--"

"Don't patronize me," Achilla snapped as a tear rolled down her cheek. "I know what I saw today. They think I'm some sort of monster."

"It'll blow over," Sam said as she approached Achilla and held her by her shoulders. "I promise they'll get over it."

"My teachers won't even look at me," Achilla said. "Even the team acts like I don't exist. I want to change schools!"

"But baby--"

"I WANT TO CHANGE SCHOOLS!" Achilla screamed. "NOW!!"

"OK, OK, shh, honey," Sam said as she held Achilla close. "OK. I'll talk to your father."

"I'm not going back anymore!" Achilla cried out. "I just can't go back!"

"Achilla, you can't skip school," Sam said as she looked her in the eye. "In this house, we don't let people prevent us from doing what we have to do. That's what people like Stanley want. Don't give it to him."

"Yeah," Achilla muttered. "You're right, I won't."

"But I will talk to your father about the transfer," Sam said. "I don't want my daughter in an environment where people stop talking to her after one fight; especially when all she did was defend herself--"

"Wait, daughter?" Achilla asked with a frown.

"Yes, that's what I said."

"You've never called me that before," Achilla replied. "I don't think anyone has except for Dad."

"Well that's going to change," Sam said as she pulled Achilla in for a hug. "As long as you live with us, you're a daughter to me."

"Thanks," Achilla said. "I guess I should you call you Mom, right?"

"If you like," Sam said as she rubbed Achilla's back. "We'll get you through this, Achilla. I promise."

Achilla did as she was told and finished out the school year. She walked with her head held high and ignored the stares in the hallway. She ate lunch by herself and stopped hanging out with the team. She never forgot a single face that changed after her incident with Stanley, and when they tried to talk to her again, she ignored them and kept walking.

On the last day of school, Achilla walked out of St. Joseph's without saying goodbye to anyone. She passed by Stanley and watched him turn his head and walk away with the other football players; on crutches of course. For the first time in her life, Achilla smirked at the thought of someone fearing her. Stanley's skittishness made her laugh to herself as she waited for her new mother to pick her up. She frowned when Traci stood next to her in front of the school wearing the same slacks and blouse that they were required to wear. They stood in silence for ten minutes before Traci extended her hand.

"Good luck," Traci said. "Wherever you go."

"Huh?"

"I'm not stupid, Achilla," Traci said. "If I were you, I'd leave too. These snobbish people can't handle you."

"Why did you stay so long?"

"My mom graduated from here," Traci said. "She won't allow me to transfer unless it's what she considers more prestigious. My family's so snooty. I can't wait to go to college and meet some cool people."

"I'm sorry to hear that."

"And for the record, Stanley's a pig," Traci practically spat her words into the humid June air. "Had I been there when you first met, I would've totally cockblocked. You're not the first girl he's forced himself on, and you won't be the last."

"I don't know," Achilla said with a shrug. "After trying with me, he'll probably need physical therapy just to take a piss. I think the girls at St. Joe's are safe."

"Yeah, but people like him don't learn," Traci said. "I've seen way too many of my friends crying at home thinking they'll change a guy like Stanley. Doesn't happen. Some people are just bad, and they stay that way."

"I think I know what you mean," Achilla said as she thought of Ailina.

"All high school boys aren't like him," Traci said. "I'm sorry you had to go through what you did, but guys like Stanley don't represent them all. You'll see."

"I hope so."

"I know so," Traci replied with a hard look. "If my brother was still around and found out that that asshole tried to hurt a friend of mine, he would've personally kicked his ass."

"Where's your brother now?" Achilla asked.

"Prison," Traci sighed. "He gets out in a few months."

"What for?" Achilla asked.

"Aggravated assault and battery," Traci replied. "I guess beating down someone who tries to date rape your little sister is against the law. My brother went to jail for me. I'll never forget that, even with guys like Stanley walking around."

Achilla stared at Traci with her jaw dropped. Someone tried to rape her too? How common of an occurrence was this? How many victims did Stanley have? Were there more guys like Stanley at St. Joseph's? In high school? The more Achilla thought about it, the more she wanted to find Stanley and finish what she had started. She snapped out of her own thoughts when a black Bentley pulled up to the school.

"This is my ride," Traci said as she gave Achilla a hug and patted her shoulder. "Call me anytime you want to work out. I think you'll be better than me by the time you're a senior."

"Yeah, sure," Achilla said as Traci hopped into the car and rode off. She waited for half an hour as she watched some of the other students mill around the front of the school. Achilla didn't understand why they wanted to hang around so much. School was over. Most importantly, school at St. Joseph's was over for Achilla. When Sam pulled up to the curb, Achilla stepped into the passenger side.

"How was school today?" Sam asked as usual.

"Better," Achilla said with a smile. "I said bye to a friend."

"Oh, good," Sam said as she pulled out of the parking lot. "I'm glad you kept one of your friends, Achilla."

"Yeah," Achilla said as she watched her old high school for the last time. "Turns out we have a lot in common."

Achilla transferred to Stratford High School for her sophomore year. She registered for all AP courses and tried out for the soccer team, basketball team, and tennis team. As expected, each sport came naturally to her, but basketball was her favorite. Something about dribbling a basketball calmed her nerves. On the court, she didn't worry about being superior or everyone hating her. Her teammates were her teammates for the duration. They couldn't abandon her or pretend she didn't exist; not without being reprimanded by the coach. At the same time, there was a competitive spirit to besting her opponent; whether it was the girl in front of her or the entire opposing team. Basketball fed Achilla's desire for acceptance and her hunger to beat the world. She gained no better feeling from any other sport, and Stratford High School's basketball program welcomed her with open arms.

As if she hadn't felt different enough before, Achilla's body was going through more changes. No matter how hard or fast she ran, she never got tired during practice or any of her games. Achilla started running to school in the morning and running home after practice, and every morning before she ran, and every evening when she got home, she skipped down to the basement and performed one hundred handstand pushups.

Achilla noticed in the locker room that her arms and legs were more defined than the other girls, even the seniors. During soccer and basketball games, the opposing teams tried every cheap shot in the book, but none of them even fazed her. For the sake of staying out of trouble, Achilla didn't retaliate, but she was starting to realize that she was physically stronger than every girl she came across. If her incident with Stanley proved anything, she was stronger than the boys too.

While her strength increased, Achilla never grew any more massive than the cheerleaders. She still had slender arms and shoulders and her hips were widening. The boys in school started to check her out, and men on the street would pull over their cars and catcall at her during her jogs home. Since none of them came close enough to touch her, Achilla just ignored them. But she decided if one touched her, he was in for a world of pain.

Achilla's personality started to change as well. She no longer cared about building new relationships. So she made no effort to make female friends and she generally ignored boys in the hallway. She was the opposite of Samuel, who was now the eighth-grade class president at Wooster and always had friends over the house. She turned aggressive on the basketball court, bulling through the lane for layups with the full knowledge that no one could stop her. She also refused her allowance from her parents and opted to pick up a job instead. Achilla worked at Champs in the Trumbull Mall and took the bus to get there. When Sam complained about Achilla not seeing her language tutors, Achilla called them herself and arranged to meet them on the weekends after practice and tipped them extra behind Sam's back.

On one Sunday afternoon, Achilla heard her father walk in the living room while she performed standard military pushups on the floor.

"Achilla, I took my car to the shop today," Brendan said. "You know, because it kept stalling."

"Yeah?" Achilla huffed.

"They found nothing wrong," Brendan said. "I only spoke to you and Sam about it, and Sam knows nothing about mechanics. Did you…fix my car?"

"I gave it a tune-up if that's what you mean," Achilla said in between breaths. "It was supposed to be a surprise. Did you like it?"

"That's not a beginner's car, Achilla," Brendan said. "You can't just tinker around with it, and you especially shouldn't surprise me with anything you do under the hood."

"Well, you heard the mechanics, Pop," Achilla grunted as she started clapping between her pushups. "I fixed it. It was kind of fun actually--"

"Don't do that again without asking first," Brendan said. "I'm not playing, Achilla. That's dangerous. What if something went wrong?"

"Do you really think I'd screw up something that easy?" Achilla replied. "Come on, Dad. Give me a little credit and a little appreciation for--"

"Do you really think you can talk back to me in my house?" Brendan demanded over Achilla's voice. "Stay away from my car without my permission. Period."

"Yes, sir," Achilla groaned as her father walked away.

The Johnson family went to church every Sunday. Samuel dressed up in a shirt and tie every week and always leaned forward during the preacher's sermons. Achilla wore jeans and a t-shirt, and that was only after Brendan berated her when she opted to wear sweatpants one morning. She leaned back into the purple plush church chairs and crossed her arms as the preacher spoke about God's great love and Jesus' sacrifice. During one service, Achilla snorted out loud when the preacher said that all the men in the church needed to protect their women. Everyone within five feet of them glanced at her and swiveled their heads back in front as Samuel lowered his head and covered his face. Brendan and Sam glared at Achilla as they walked to the car after service.

"Achilla, we're not raising you to act up during church," Brendan said as he took off his suit jacket to expose a white shirt, red tie, and red suspenders. "Don't you do that again."

"Yes, Achilla, that was very rude making a noise like that during service," Sam said as she walked next to Achilla in her red blouse and black slacks. "What's gotten into you?"

"He was wrong," Achilla said as she walked with her hands in her pockets.

"No, he wasn't," Samuel muttered.

"Shut-up, Samuel," Achilla snapped. "When's the last time you protected me from anything?"

"Achilla!" Brendan barked. "Don't talk to your brother that way."

Achilla watched Samuel pout and look down the other side of the parking lot as he speed-walked to walk ahead of her. A lump grew in her throat at the thought of hurting his feelings. She grabbed Samuel's arm and pulled him close for a hug. She felt better when he hugged back, but he still couldn't look her in the eye. Achilla forced a smile anyway.

"I'm sorry," Achilla said as she rubbed his head until he smiled back. "Didn't mean it."

"Well, that's a start," Sam said. "We still have to work on your attitude."

"Starting now," Brendan chimed in when they reached the car. "And you're dressing up for church like everyone else--"

"Fine, I'll dress up," Achilla groaned. "For the record, this feels like complete subjugation. Let's just be clear that I'm doing this for you, not for the preacher who thinks I'm too weak to defend myself and need a man to protect me."

"Achilla, why did that bother you so much?" Sam asked.

"There was no man there to stop Stanley," Achilla said with a raised fist. "It was just me and him, and I won."

"So this is about Stanley," Brendan sighed as they stepped into the car and he started the ignition. "I wanted to shield you from that. Lord knows I wanted--"

"And we trusted her to do the right thing," Sam interjected with a frown. "I feel like you're blaming me for this, Brendan."

"He's not," Achilla snarled from the back seat with her head low. "He's blaming himself. He thinks he should've been there to chaperone. Any idiot can see that he's kicking himself for not being the protector the preacher was *just talking about* if you paid attention. You're just too busy forcing your opinion on him to notice how bad he feels knowing that his daughter was almost raped, and he wasn't there to stop it. You should listen more, and let him be a parent too instead of competing with him every time he has something to say.

God, if for once you would just let the man have his own opinion on something--"

"Achilla, that's enough," Brendan said. "Don't talk to your mother that way. You will respect both of us at all times in our house. Understood?"

"OK," Achilla said with a shrug of her shoulders. "OK, fine. I'm just saying, that's all."

"And I think you've said more than enough for today," Brendan replied as Sam looked back and forth between them with her mouth open.

"Is any of that true, Brendan?" Sam asked with a wavering voice. "Now, I know I can be pushy sometimes, but I would never purposely undercut you in front of the kids. I'm sorry if I've ever made you feel that way, I swear I'm not trying to--"

"We can talk later, Sam," Brendan replied with a raised hand. "Let's just go home."

Achilla noticed Samuel staring at her, but she paid more attention to Sam's expression at Brendan. As Brendan drove, he looked straight ahead. They rode in silence for five minutes as Achilla studied her parents. Achilla nodded her head when Sam reached across the aisle and rubbed Brendan's shoulder. Sam gave Brendan a weak smile and held his shoulder for the remainder of the car ride. When they got home, Achilla overheard Sam crying behind their bedroom door.

"How was I supposed to know, Brendan?" Sam sobbed. "I wanted to let her be a teenage girl and date. I didn't know. I'm sorry."

"That wasn't your fault," Brendan said. "Let's just make sure to meet any boys she dates from this point on. I want to meet these boys before they go out with my daughter. That's it."

"So now we're helicopter parents?" Sam asked. "You know how kids turn out when they have smothering parents, Brendan."

"It's not about that," Brendan said. "You said yourself that Achilla needs special attention. That has to include dating. Now that punk got what he deserved, but what about the next time? What if the next guy has a gun in his truck?"

"You're worried she'll get shot on a date?"

"I'm worried that the next person Achilla gets angry at will feel like they need a gun," Brendan said. "If I had a gun when Ailina attacked me...."

Achilla frowned from the top of the steps. Ailina attacked her father? When? Achilla remembered how Ailina beat down all of the other men she brought over; broken jaws, snapped limbs, impaired breathing. When Ailina got angry, no man walked out unscathed. That was why they gave her the cell phone. That was why they were always so worried about whenever Achilla got angry. They thought she was like Ailina. Achilla noticed Samuel watching her from his room but pretended to be oblivious. Achilla was learning to hide the fact that she was more aware of her surroundings than the average person, but when he tried to inch closer, she sighed and shook her head.

"What is it, Samuel?" Achilla asked.

"Why are you listening to them?" Samuel replied with confidence that made Achilla frown.

"You knew I could hear you coming, didn't you?" Achilla asked.

"Yeah."

"Then why bother sneaking around?" Achilla growled. "Why not just come and join me?"

"Because you're weird," Samuel said.

"What do you mean weird?" Achilla replied with a scowl.

"I don't know," Samuel said as he stood ten feet away. "You don't have any friends anymore. You're always out doing something. I don't think you sleep that much and you're really mean sometimes."

"I already apologized for my comment earlier," Achilla said with a pout. "I don't like hurting your feelings, but that service put me in a bad mood."

"Not that," Samuel said. "Everything you do is mean. I used to have bullies at school--"

"Who?" Achilla snapped as she stood up from the steps with clenched fists. "Who's bullying you, Samuel? Tell me his name and I'll fucking--"

"That's what I mean," Samuel said as he stepped back and turned to the side with his hands half raised. "I know those kids picked on me because I'm smart and they're just jealous because the teachers like me. Mom and Dad tell me that all the time and it's true. You're different. You're like....you're like the Blair Witch or something."

"Samuel," Achilla chuckled and shook her head as she stepped forward. "The Blair Witch is a fictional spirit that possessed a man and forced him to make children stand in a corner and listen while he tortured their friends. I get that I've been moody lately, but that's hardly an accurate depiction of my behavior."

"You had me watch while you beat up Marty," Samuel said while he stepped back toward his room. "And that was pretty close to torture."

"Well, that was just to show you what to do," Achilla said with a weak smile. "So you could protect yourself. That's all, Samuel. I'm sorry if I scared you, but I was just trying to help you."

"I'm not as smart as you," Samuel said. "I don't think anyone I know is, not even Mom and Dad. But I know you just lied. You should've seen your face when you were hitting him."

"My face?"

"You were smiling a little," Samuel said as he back toward his room. "You had that same smile after you yelled at Mom in the car today."

"What?" Achilla asked with a frown as Samuel walked to his room. "No, Samuel, there must be a misunderstanding here, I--"

Samuel slammed his door shut. Achilla sighed and stared at the ceiling. Now Samuel was afraid of her too. Achilla hung her head as she walked back to the top of the steps. Brendan and Sam were in the kitchen now. They weren't fighting, but Achilla eavesdropped anyway.

"Do you really think she'll be like Ailina?" Sam asked.

"No," Brendan said. "But something tells me Ailina was trying to make her even worse. I'm her father. It's my job to send her down the right path."

"And I'm your wife," Sam said. "It's my job to help you. I told you I'm down for you one hundred percent, but I wouldn't be a good wife if I didn't tell you I was concerned. She's starting to look like her, Brendan. What do we do?"

"We steer her in the right direction," Brendan said as Achilla got up to walk to her room. "That's all we can do."

Achilla closed her bedroom door without a sound and walked across her room to her window. She had a view of the backyard and the giant oak tree in the middle that was as tall as their house, and she watched a possum climb up the tree and curl in a ball as it sat on top of a branch. She knew that if it was out during the day, it probably had rabies. She stared at the possum until it stared back. The possum yawned and exposed its teeth before going to sleep. Achilla smirked at the thought of grabbing its tail and throwing it across the yard until she thought of what Samuel said earlier. Was she really as bad as the Blair Witch? She shook that thought out of her head and dropped to the floor to bang out another set of pushups.

From that point on, she would keep her strength and intelligence to herself. If she was superior like Ailina always said, Achilla saw no benefit in reminding everyone else. So she decided to tone down her aggression, but Stratford High School didn't make it easy. The kids were different from those at St. Joseph's. At St. Joseph's, you were either on a scholarship, or your parents paid your tuition. Either way, misbehavior and poor performance counted against you. In a public school like Stratford High, the students were required to attend and the teachers were required to teach. Misbehavior cost you nothing but an education; an expense that only the motivated students and teachers would acknowledge. Sometimes students would walk out of class and wander the halls. Fights were a lot more common in between periods and during lunch. After watching two boys duke it out in the cafeteria, Achilla stayed on her guard until the end of the school day hoping that she would never have to defend herself like she did against Stanley. She did not want to ask her parents to pull her out of school again.

Achilla noticed that she was developing a figure; a slender waist with hips that blossomed out from her sides like the head of a rose.

The boys at school stared even more than usual. So did the girls, but their looks were less than friendly. Achilla tried her best to ignore the girls at school, but the boys started to catch her interest. Instead of ignoring the catcalls and whistles, sometimes she would turn around and wink or smile. If she found a boy attractive, she didn't need a catcall. She would stare at him from across the hall before looking him up and down and walking into her next class. Still, she never gave out her phone number or went on any dates. Sometimes the attention was all she wanted, but she started to want more.

Just before winter break, one short, stocky boy with sepia brown skin and shaped up hair, wearing a black and red Michael Jordan throwback Bulls jersey over a gray hoody, approached her while she was opening her locker. Achilla saw him from across the hall and heard him coming, but she didn't walk away. When she turned and faced him, his purposeful walk reminded her of Stanley, but the look in his brown eyes was less intense.

"What's up?" he said with a slight nod to his head.

"Is that all?" Achilla asked. "No licking your lips or '*pssst-pssst!*' to make me feel special? I'm insulted."

"Nah, I figured you had to earn that first," the boy replied with a smirk.

"Oh," Achilla said with a smile as she ran a finger through her hair. "I'll bite. What's your name?"

"Dahntay," the boy replied with a flash of his white teeth. "You?"

"Achilla."

"Like Achilles the warrior," Dahntay said. "It fits. I heard you're killing them out there on that court."

"I've got some game," Achilla replied as she closed her locker and leaned against it with her books against her black Enyce sweater. "You haven't told me what you do yet."

"You didn't ask," Dahntay chuckled. "What do I look like just volunteering that kind of information?"

"All right," Achilla said as she looked down at the floor to hide the smile she couldn't hide. "What do you do?"

"Football," Dahntay said. "I start varsity. Offensive linemen."

"All the work without the glory," Achilla said.

"OK, I see you," Dahntay replied with his hands on his hips. "You know a little football."

"I know a little about a lot of things," Achilla said as she poked Dahntay's chest.

"Oh, is that right?"

"Yeah, it is," Achilla said. "Take me out sometime, and I might show you--"

"Dahntay!"

Achilla rolled her eyes when she saw two girls speed walking down the hallway. One girl had tan skin and curly, dark brown hair. She wore two red hoop earrings, a red hoody, and black jeans with black sneakers. Her friend was tall, dark, with short hair, and she wore a black long sleeved tee shirt and blue jeans. She also wore a lot of rings on her fingers that looked more like weapons than decoration. Dahntay rolled his eyes and leaned against the locker next to Achilla's.

"I'm sorry about this," Dahntay said. "We just broke up."

"Then you have nothing to be sorry for," Achilla said as she watched the two girls approach. The tan one stood in front of Dahntay while the taller girl stepped between him and Achilla. She noticed that the tan girl wore a lot of makeup, but underneath it all her skin was clear and her eyes were a bright hazel. Achilla also noticed her body language. She glared at Dahntay as he rolled his eyes. Something told Achilla that this was a common scenario, so common that it caused their breakup.

"The new chick?" the tan girl asked as she leaned on one leg. "Really? That's how you do me?"

"Look, Monika, it's over," Dahntay said. "I can talk to whoever I want."

"But really?" Monika replied as she pointed at Achilla. "Her? She's fucking hit."

"I don't get it," Achilla said to Dahntay. "Why is she so jealous? I thought you guys broke up."

"We did," Dahntay said. "She's just--"

"Bitch, mind your own business!" Monika snapped with a raised hand. Achilla's hands trembled and she nearly dropped her books. She had never been called that name before. The last man to call Ailina that got kicked across her living room. Sam told Achilla countless stories of fights in high school over that word. The very thought of being called a bitch made Achilla want to break something, and now this girl who didn't even know her was using it in her direction? Achilla's eyes zeroed in on Monika as her friend stood between them with her arms crossed.

"I don't appreciate you calling me that," Achilla said. "I really don't appreciate that--"

"I don't give a fuck what you *appreciate*," Monika replied.

"Go on to class," Monika's friend said with her arms crossed as she lifted a finger to point down the hallway. "We don't need you around here. They've got business to handle."

"I'll leave when she apologizes," Achilla replied as she set her books down.

"So what if I called you a bitch?" Monika demanded. "I'll say it again. Bitch. What?"

"I'm sorry, Achilla," Dahntay said as he moved toward her. Monika blocked his path, crossed her arms, and leaned on one leg. Achilla glared at her past her friend's shoulder. Thoughts of wringing her neck made her knees tremble, but she remembered her promise to her parents. Achilla rubbed the cell phone in her pocket, took a deep breath, and picked up her books. Now would be a good time to call her parents.

"Achilla, just go, all right?" Dahntay said with a wave of his hand. "I don't want you mixed up in this."

"Don't talk to her," Monika screamed. "I'm the only one talking to you right now!"

"Monika, go away!" Dahntay growled. "Why can't you just leave me alone? Just go away, man!"

"I just know you're not picking this new girl over me--"

"OK, I'm leaving," Achilla said with a raised hand. "This is obviously a bad time. See you later, Dahntay."

"See you later?" Monika asked as Achilla turned to walk to class. Achilla hadn't made it ten steps before Monika cut off her path.

Achilla's hands trembled again as she studied Monika's body for openings. Her throat practically screamed for a good punch and her center line was wide open. Achilla closed her eyes, inhaled, and took a step around her.

Monika blocked her path again.

"You're not seeing him again," Monika said while she stood close enough for Achilla to smell the Winterfresh gum on her breath. "You can't see him period--"

"That's enough," Achilla snapped. "You're not my mother, all right? You don't have the authority to tell me who to talk to. Now if you excuse me, I'm going to a class."

"Listen, new bitch--"

"Stop calling me that!" Achilla growled as she dropped her books on the floor. A crowd had already gathered around them in the hallway. "My name is Achilla. You would know that if you bothered to ask."

"I don't give a fuck what your name is," Monika said as she pointed a finger at Achilla's face. "Stay away from Dahntay before you get snuffed! Don't let this pretty fool you. I will fuck you up quick--"

"Do *not* threaten me," Achilla replied with wide eyes that seared into Monika's face. "You need to get out of my face now."

"Or what?" Monika said just before she shoved Achilla's head with her finger. "You won't do shi--"

Achilla smacked Monika's hand away. Monika swung a wide, telegraphed, right punch at Achilla's face. Compared to the fast, straight punches Ailina used to throw without the slightest warning, it was child's play. Achilla ducked and punched Monika in the gut so hard that she dropped to her knees. Monika's friend grabbed her hair from behind, and Achilla elbowed her right side, cracking a rib, before turning and punching her in the jaw. Monika tackled her from behind, and they both fell to the floor. Achilla covered her head as Monika swung with both arms. Her blows felt nothing like the hammering, body-jarring punches Ailina gave her as a child. They were more like mild bee-stings at best. Achilla pushed her arms away before pulling Monika's shirt and head-butting her in the nose, causing blood to leak onto Achilla's sweater. Achilla then raised her hips, wrapped her legs around Monika, and flipped her over, looking up just in time to see her friend reaching for her hair again. Achilla grabbed the friend's left arm and struck her elbow with the heel of her hand with a crack. She then pulled her in by the broken arm and elbowed her right temple. Monika's friend fell on the floor and stayed there. When Monika tried to get up, Achilla swung for her throat, but Monika squirmed at the last minute. She crushed Monika's collarbone instead; making her shriek and hold her chest.

Achilla rose to her feet as Monika moaned and sobbed on the floor. Her friend lay still on the ground without a sound. Ailina had always prepared Achilla to fight at least five people at once by throwing punches and kicks from multiple angles. She was so fast that Achilla felt like there was more than one person. Still, Achilla had never done the real thing before. She frowned as she watched her opponents lie on the school floor staining it with tears and blood. Then a slight grin grew on her face.

"That was…easy," Achilla said to herself before she looked up at the crowd and noticed everyone staring at her. She searched the crowd and found Dahntay still leaning next to her locker. He stared at Achilla with his mouth open, but with a slight smile on the left side. Achilla stepped over Monika and gathered her books.

"Achilla," Dahntay said as he walked past Monika's friend. "How the hell did you--?"

"I have to go to class," Achilla said.

"I'll walk with you," Dahntay replied. "You shouldn't have to walk by yourself. Monika has friends."

"Trying to be my protector?" Achilla asked with a sideways glare. "Do I look like a need saving to you?"

"I mean…not really," Dahntay said. "Not from a fight."

"Then I'm going to class alone," Achilla said as she picked up her books and walked toward the crowd. One look at the nearest person and he cleared a path for her. More fear. This time, Achilla didn't mind it all that much. However, she could hear Dahntay following her. She sighed and turned on her heels to face him. Dahntay stopped a good five feet away with his hands raised.

"I don't want to hit you," Achilla said with a hard stare. "But I'll consider it if you keep following me. I'm not the type to be stalked."

"Look, what you did back there was crazy," Dahntay replied with a smile. "What're you a martial artist or something? Where'd you learn that?"

"Rather not talk about it."

"Well, I could still walk you to class then, right?" Dahntay asked as Achilla turned to walk away. "I mean, it wouldn't kill you to have a friend."

"A friend?"Achilla snorted. "I didn't think we were on the path to a friendship, Dahntay."

"Maybe not, but it doesn't matter," Dahntay said. "I don't care how tough you are. Nobody can do high school by herself. Even Monika had a friend with her, and she's a--"

"A what?"Achilla asked as she turned and glared at Dahntay just before she reached her classroom.

"She's...um...she's not nice," Dahntay stammered.

"Quite the audible there."

"Look, you need me," Dahntay said as Achilla turned toward the classroom door.

"Oh really?" Achilla asked with a cocked eyebrow. "You could barely handle Monika. What you could you offer me that I can't do myself?"

"A witness," Dahntay replied as he looked Achilla in the eye. "It's your word against hers unless I speak up, and I'm good with the Principal. He's my mentor. He'll think anybody else is just talking shit, but he trusts me."

Achilla sighed and looked up at the ceiling. He was right. She needed someone to vouch for her. Otherwise, no one in their right mind would think Achilla was the victim of anything; not after the beat down she just delivered. Her fight with Stanley taught her that. Achilla pulled out her cell phone.

"Phone number," Achilla mumbled.

"Huh?" Dahntay asked as he leaned forward and set his hand

near his ear while holding a grin on his face. "I didn't make that out. What's up?"

"Give me your phone number," Achilla groaned. "I'll get called to the office soon. I'll text you when that happens. Once I'm in the office, I'll make sure to mention your name."

"Bet," Dahntay said as Achilla handed him the phone and he typed in his number. "Yeah, I knew you'd turn around."

"You're trying awfully hard to get next to me," Achilla said with a furrowed brow when he handed her the phone back. "But you're not hitting on me anymore."

"Is now the right time for that?" Dahntay asked.

"I think you're afraid of me and want to stay on my good side," Achilla said, turning to open the classroom door. "If that's the case, don't bother helping me. I don't need a sidekick."

"You make it hard to like you," Dahntay chuckled and shook his head. "But I do."

"Whatever," Achilla replied before walking into class. Her AP Spanish teacher, Mrs. Brown, a blond-haired, green-eyed woman from Argentina, stared at her with her hands on her hips. Achilla stared back before walking to her seat in the front of the class. Mrs. Brown stalked across the classroom in her green blouse and off-white khakis and stood in front of Achilla's desk.

"Achilla," Mrs. Brown said without pronouncing the two l's in Achilla's name. "Would you care to explain to the class why you're late?"

"No," Achilla said before taking a deep breath. "But you're the teacher, so I'll do it. I just beat up two girls at once. I'm expecting a call to the principal's office at any moment."

"*Dios Mio*, "Mrs. Brown gasped before leaning on the desk. "Achilla, are you OK? Are you hurt?"

"Did you not hear the part where I said I beat them up?" Achilla quipped when she heard a knock on the door. Mrs. Brown beckoned for the man on the other side to come in. A six-foot-five, bald brown-skinned police officer with a scar down his left cheek opened the door. Achilla gathered her books and stood up. She could feel every eye in the classroom watching her as she walked toward the officer.

"You Achilla Johnson?" the cop asked.

"Yes, sir."

"Come with me."

As she followed the police officer down the hallway, Achilla texted Dahntay to come to the principal's office. Despite the fact that he was no threat, Achilla studied the openings on the cop's body. A slight limp in his walk told her that she could take out his left knee and run. That scar under his eye could be reopened. Achilla shook those thoughts out of her head when they reached the office. Achilla jolted when she remembered that she never called her father. She whipped out her cell phone again.

"In the office," the cop said.

"Yeah, just let me call my dad first," Achilla said with a wave of her hand.

"No," the cop said. "In the office, now."

"It'll take five seconds," Achilla said as she held the phone to her ear. "I'm not trying to be disrespectful, but I promised to call him whenever something bad happened. I promise it won't take--"

"Office," the cop demanded as he grabbed Achilla's arm. Achilla dropped her phone and pushed the officer in the chest. She gasped when she watched him fly halfway across the hall into a locker. The cop grunted and rose to his feet, but he stopped and stared at her as if he had just realized what happened. Achilla lowered her head and picked up her phone.

"I'll...go to the office now," Achilla said as she walked toward the door. "Sorry about that, but you scared me."

"Yeah," the cop said. "It's...um...it's fine. Just go to the office down the hall."

"You're not going to follow me to make sure?" Achilla asked with a frown. "Isn't that why you're here?"

"I trust you."

"Right," Achilla said with a head nod as she walked into the office. "I get it. Well, thanks for not calling backup I guess."

Achilla walked into the main office and strolled past the secretaries down a hallway. As she walked, she texted Dahntay again to come to the office as soon as he could. Why wasn't he responding? She hoped she wouldn't need him, but she had to be sure. The last office at the end of the hall had a sign that read "Dr. Freeney." Achilla knocked on the door.

"Come in," a deep voice said.

Achilla opened the door and found a white, dirty blonde police officer standing across the room next to a mahogany bookcase. Achilla found the nearest seat and sat down across from a dark-skinned, black man wearing a navy blue suit, a pink tie, and thick-rimmed glasses. For a man with such a deep voice, Achilla found him surprisingly skinny when he stood up and extended his hand. When Achilla shook it, he had a grip that matched his tone.

"I don't believe we've met, Ms. Johnson," Dr. Freeney said. "Though I spoke to your mother when she registered you here. You know, she and I were neighbors growing up."

"I get the feeling that's not going to help me here," Achilla said.

"That is correct," Dr. Freeney replied. "Sam spoke very highly of you, and everything she said was true. But this? I have two girls in the emergency room, and they both say you attacked them out of the blue."

Achilla flinched. She figured Monika would start making up stories, but she hadn't anticipated that they would reach the principal so soon. Judging from the stern look in Dr. Freeney's eyes, he was not inclined to believe anything Achilla said. Dahntay was right. Before she could bring his name up, she had to get her story out in a way that he could believe.

"That's not true," Achilla spoke as each word came to mind. "Monika touched me first. She pushed her finger in my face, I smacked it away, and she tried to punch me. And then this girl grabbed my hair. They jumped me!"

"Can anyone verify that?" Dr. Freeney asked.

"I've already texted Dahntay," Achilla replied.

"There are no phones allowed in this school," Dr. Freeney said with a hard stare. "You should've just given me a name, and I would've called him down--"

Achilla heard another knock on the door.

"Come in," Dr. Freeney called. Dahntay stumbled in and stood behind Achilla's chair. Dr. Freeney frowned and rose to his feet. Achilla lowered her head as Dahntay patted her shoulders. As much as he talked like he was in control, the glare in Dr. Freeney's eyes said different.

"Dahntay, our meeting isn't for another hour," Dr. Freeney said. "What brings you down here?"

"Achilla texted me," Dahntay said. "Is this about the fight--?"

"OK, kids," Dr. Freeney chuckled as he covered his face with his hand. "You can't just blatantly break the rules. Cell phones. Now."

Dahntay and Achilla set their phones on Dr. Freeney's desk. He snatched them and placed them in one of his drawers. As he fumbled with the lock, Achilla noted Dahntay's expression. His jaw was set and he stared straight ahead until he looked down at Achilla. He winked at her and she forced herself to not smile. Dr. Freeney locked the drawer and looked up.

"Right, Dahntay," Dr. Freeney said. "What brings you here?"

"I don't know what's already been said or not," Dahntay replied. "But Monika started the whole thing. She got all jealous when I was talking to her and got in my face. Then she got in Achilla's face, pointing and screaming, and--"

"Slow down," Dr. Freeney said with a raised hand. "Who swung first? "

"Monika," Dahntay said with a shrug.

"And Mya?" Dr. Freeney sighed and shook his head.

"She grabbed her hair," Dahntay replied.

"Sounds like self-defense to me," the cop said. "Might be excessive force though. We've got a broken collarbone, three broken ribs, a broken nose, and something's wrong with one of their kidneys. I've got a hard time believing this girl did all that by herself, but they only point at her. I'll come back when this is straightened out."

"This kind of issue needs time," Dr. Freeney said as he watched the police officer leave, waiting for him to close the door before speaking again. "On my end, I think it's best to send you home for the day. I'll decide a proper discipline later."

"Fine," Achilla said as she rose from her seat.

"And Achilla," Dr. Freeney called to her as she opened the door and let Dahntay out.

"Yes."

"Sam's a good friend of mine," Dr. Freeney said. "I'll do what I can with school, but--"

"Don't risk your job for me, Dr. Freeney," Achilla said.

"What I was going to say is that I have no control over Stratford PD or Monika's parents who might sue the school district and your family," Dr. Freeney said. "And they may not be quiet about it. This isn't the same as…that boy in Trumbull."

"Mom told you?" Achilla asked as she walked back into the office.

"No, but I have an ear to the ground on things," Dr. Freeney replied. "They kept that quiet so as not to sully his reputation or the mayor's. That's how politics works. This is different. Monika doesn't come from a rich family, but her mother is highly involved with the PTA and very combative at meetings, to say the least."

"So she'll pressure the school district to pay the hospital bills," Achilla said with her arms crossed. "If that doesn't work, she'll come for me."

"Your mother said you were smart," Dr. Freeney said. "That's exactly correct."

"You're an easier target than me," Achilla replied. "My father's the best criminal defense attorney around. Why don't you just suspend me to appease her?"

"Wrong."

Achilla whirled around and saw her father standing in the door in his blue suit and sky blue tie. He came? He must have known that something was wrong even without a full conversation. Brendan kissed Achilla's forehead as he walked into the office. He carried his briefcase and set it on a chair before shaking Dr. Freeney's hand. He then sat down and pointed at a chair for Achilla to sit as well. Achilla checked the hallway before she sat down. Dahntay was gone.

"I told him to go to class," Brendan said to Achilla. "He told me everything once I told him I was your father. Seems like a good kid, but this is a legal matter now. He can't be involved."

"OK," Achilla said. "What do we do?"

"Well the suspension is up to Dr. Freeney," Brendan replied. "Though I would advise that he follow the school rules and nothing more; in case Ms. Estevez pushes for an expulsion. She's going to look for someone to pay those hospital bills, Derrick."

"I know," Dr. Freeney said. "If she comes for the district, we may have to settle."

"I believe Sam told you guys to install more video cameras at the last PTA meeting," Brendan said with a slight snarl. "If we had a video of my daughter defending herself, we might not be in this mess. We would all be protected from liability."

"And I believe I told Sam that we have to adhere to a budget," Dr. Freeney replied without a flinch. "Perhaps she should bring her demands to the Board, not me."

Achilla imagined her father watching a video of her flirting with Dahntay and hung her head. That would earn her a good scolding for sure. She then thought of watching herself in action and smirked. She must be awesome to watch on video. Achilla restrained her smile when she noticed her father looking in her direction.

"Unless Achilla has anything else to share," Brendan said before looking at Dr. Freeney. "It looks like you're in a bind, but I can't advise you any further. You should contact the school district's law department. They can counsel you on the next move better than I can."

"I understand," Dr. Freeney said. "I'm going to have to suspend Achilla for about two days. And since I technically sent her home already, today counts. She is scheduled to return bright and early Monday morning."

"Thank you, Dr. Freeney," Achilla said. "That's really nice of you."

"Just promise me that you won't incapacitate any more of my students," Dr. Freeney replied.

"Deal," Achilla said. "Wait, what about my cell phone-"

"I'll pick it up on Monday like any other parent," Brendan said as he opened the door. "I told you to call me, but the rules are the rules."

"Fine," Achilla groaned as she walked out of the office. They rode home in silence until they were within two blocks of the house. Achilla sighed and looked out the window as they passed by the rows of colonial homes in their neighborhood. She then coughed and crossed her arms as she stared at her father. Brendan continued to look straight ahead.

"No scolding?" Achilla asked. "No grounding for three weeks or so? Either today's my lucky day or you're too mad to even speak to me."

"I'm not mad at you, Achilla."

"Then why the silent treatment?" Achilla asked with a slight pout. "You usually ask how my day went or something."

"You had a normal day for a high school girl," Brendan said with a shrug. "You meet a boy, and there's a little friction between you and another girl. Sometimes that results in a fight and sometimes it doesn't."

"They're hurt really bad," Achilla said. "Probably worse than Stanley. The cop said something was wrong with one of their kidneys after I hit her."

"So?"

"Well, I didn't aim for her kidneys,"Achilla said. "The closest I got was one of their ribs. If a rib somehow punctures a kidney, she may have internal bleeding."

"I don't like that your language is so precise when it comes to fighting," Brendan replied. "Ailina really did a number on you, didn't she?"

"It was every day," Achilla said. "When you have to fight that often, you get good at it."

"And she never told you why?" Brendan asked.

"No," Achilla replied. "You and Mom keep asking that. I told you that all she would say was that I was some kind of superior being just like her."

"Are you?"

Achilla frowned. When they pulled the car into the driveway,

Brendan looked at Achilla without an ounce of joviality. Achilla shifted in her seat before looking out the window. She knew the answer. She knew she just beat up two girls and threw a police officer twice her size across a school hallway. But something told her to keep as much of it a secret as possible. The hundreds of hand-stand pushups, the running for miles on end, the balancing school work, athletics, and work on an average of three or four hours of sleep; all of it must be kept secret.

"I don't really know," Achilla muttered. "I can fight, I guess."

"Achilla, I get the feeling that you take after Ailina," Brendan said. "If that's true, you can do a lot more than fight. You can kill a man with your bare hands."

"I wouldn't do that," Achilla replied as she looked at her lap. "I'm not that kind of person."

"Do you know what Ailina did to me when I left her?" Brendan asked.

"No," Achilla said. "You never told me."

"She grabbed my arm like this," Brendan said as he held Achilla's forearm. "And just twisted her wrist. That snapped my forearm in half. But that's not the craziest part."

"What is?" Achilla asked.

"She pulled her own sink out of her bathroom wall and tried to hit me with it," Brendan said. "I never ran so fast in all my days playing basketball."

"I would never do that to you, Dad."

"To me, no," Brendan sighed. "You don't have Ailina's personal-ity. No matter what she said, you're not like her, but you're just as dangerous when confronted. Those girls provoked you, but I doubt they expected you to be as strong as you are any more than Stanley. I didn't expect it from Ailina, and I had known her for years."

"But you didn't do anything to Ailina," Achilla said. "She just attacked you."

"That's why I took you in," Brendan said. "No daughter of mine is living with a monster like that. I'm surprised that she didn't put up more of a fight."

"I haven't seen or heard from her since," Achilla replied as they stepped out of the car. "But if she does pop up, she'll probably try to finish what she started. You're the only man to escape from her unharmed."

"In that case, we'll be ready."

"I'll be ready," Achilla said as she stopped in the middle of the driveway.

"It's not your fight, Achilla," Brendan said. "I'm your father, and it's my job--"

"To protect me, yeah I get it," Achilla snapped. "But you and I both know I'm the only person in the house who can even come close to standing up to her."

"We'll deal with that when it comes," Brendan said as he wrapped his arm around Achilla and led her to the door. "For now, let's focus on the fight at school."

"I'm serious, Dad," Achilla said as she ripped free from her father's arm. "You're not fighting her. I am."

"Achilla, I know you mean well, but you're--"

"If I'm superior like her, then she'll have to get through me before she hurts you again," Achilla snarled before she could stop herself.

"Achilla, calm down--"

"If she comes near any of you," Achilla growled with her fists clenched and tears running out of her eyes. "I'll…I'll kill her!"

Achilla ran away from her father into the house, and the very thought of Ailina hurting her new family, her better family, made her pace around the house. She watched the front door all night and didn't sleep until seven in the morning when her parents left for work. After that, she ran into the basement and started her hand-stand pushups again. She also threw in some shadowboxing and kicks as she recalled all of her fight training. The next time she saw Ailina, she would be ready.

Chapter Twelve

ACHILLA JOHNSON: 20

It wasn't true. There had to be some sort of mistake. Achilla's father wasn't dead. Samuel was lying. He was screwing with her to get back at her for being gone so long…or something. There was no way that Achilla's father just died out of the blue like that. No warning. No farewell. When Achilla came home, she would hug her father, eat his steak and special fries, and watch the game with him. They would argue over who was better between Kobe and Tracy McGrady. Nowadays, Achilla would finally be able to win that argument. He was fine. He was the same man he had always been, and that wouldn't change until he was old and halfway in the grave. Brendan Johnson was alive. He just had to be.

Those reassuring words lasted about five seconds until Achilla's logical brain shut them out. Her father was dead. Samuel wouldn't make this up. He lacked the cruelty. Brendan Johnson was assassinated. Period.

After her logical brain shoved that thought into her consciousness, her emotions took over again. This time, there was no denial. Achilla dropped on all fours as tears jerked from her eyes and her stomach churned. She shrieked again until her throat burned, and she curled into a fetal position in the middle of the basketball court. The thought of Brendan's smiling face, stern eyes, and loving hand no longer welcoming her home sent a ripping sensation through her chest. The thought of those nights watching basketball together made her pull her hair. He was gone, and she would never see him alive again.

Achilla's logical brain kicked in again, but with her emotions working in tandem. All of this training, all of this effort, all of this negotiating, and it was for nothing. Ailina didn't even have to kill Brendan. She wouldn't bother with firearms for a normal human. Some random hired gun was able to get in and shoot him. Where was the security detail that the CIA was talking about? Why didn't they stop this? What happened? Achilla sobbed as tears soaked her face and dripped onto the pavement. She heard Agent Jones and Kate approaching. She ignored them. How could this happen? Where was the mistake made? Was it the mole?

No.

No, they promised a security detail for her family. They promised that if she helped them find and eliminate Ailina, if she risked her life for them, that her family would be safe. Yet while Achilla couldn't even have a one-night stand without the CIA keeping watch, someone was able to break into her father's office and shoot him? There was no detail. They lied.

They all lied.

And now her father was dead.

Agent Jones and Kate tried to grab her arms and help her up. She let them lift her until she was on one knee before she stopped. They must have assumed she was too weak to stand because they kept pulling at her arms. Achilla roared as she rose to her feet and pushed them back, sending them rolling across the pavement in opposite directions. She then stood up straight and stared at them both with wild, bloodshot eyes.

"Achilla?" Samuel said on the phone as Achilla picked it up off the ground. "Achilla, are you all right?"

"I'm coming home," Achilla said on the phone before crushing it in her hand. She then looked back and forth at the two agents she no longer trusted. Agent Jones looked back at her without getting up. Achilla read his body language and he looked lost, waiting for Achilla to speak before he made any conclusions. He wasn't the liar here. When Achilla faced Kate, she was already on one knee with her gun drawn and her eyes set.

She was the one.

This was her fault.

"You promised protection," Achilla growled as she stalked toward her. "My father's dead. Why the fuck is my father dead?!"

"Just calm down, Achilla," Kate huffed as she blinked a bead of sweat out of her left eye. "The mole must have infiltrated the security detail. We'll get him back, but we can't do it if we turn on each other."

"You'll say *anything!*" Achilla snarled with tears running down her cheeks.

"Achilla!" Agent Jones called out. "It's my fault."

"Don't be stupid, Freeman," Kate snapped as Achilla whirled around to face him. "You don't know what she'll do. She's too unstable."

"I should've pushed harder," Agent Jones muttered. "I should've checked more. Had I known--"

"No!" Kate barked before her voice turned soft. "Stop, Freeman. Don't provoke her into attacking you just to save me."

"Achilla, I take responsibility," Agent Jones said with a hand on his chest. "It was my job to keep you informed, and I should've known something was wrong. If you're going to be angry at anyone, be angry at me."

"Freeman, knock it off," Kate cried. "Please!"

"No," Achilla said with a shake of her head. "No, you're too low on the pole to blame. You're not my target."

Achilla turned back around and faced Kate. Her vision blurred around her until Kate and every avenue of attack was all she could see. Kate was her target. She was in charge. She promised protection while keeping even Agent Jones out of the loop. Now it was obvious why. Had Agent Jones known that there was no protection he would have spoken up. He would have told Achilla. He would have apologized up and down and tried to convince her to stay, but he wouldn't have dared hide this from her. Still, Achilla would have left anyway, and Kate knew that. So she withheld information to keep a closer eye on Achilla, and then let her father die.

There was no way in hell she was walking away from that.

"You," Achilla said with a low voice as her eyes dried. "You're a different story."

"Don't be a fool, Achilla," Kate said. "I've studied your kind extensively. Even you couldn't cover this distance without getting shot. Stay right where you are so we can talk this out."

"You think you can stop me with *a pistol?*" Achilla spat as she took a couple steps forward and charged at Kate. Just before Kate could pull the trigger, she zig-zagged with steps ten feet apart and darted to the right toward the cage wall. It felt normal to Achilla, but she knew no regular human could shoot at her accurately when she moved at her top speed. To Kate, she was no more than a blur.

Kate turned around and aimed her gun, but Achilla scaled the cage like she had Velcro attached to her feet. Her eyes were still searching the basketball court when Achilla leaped behind her. When Kate raised her gun to fire, Achilla snatched it from her hand, pulled her arm behind her back, and shoved her face into the pavement but not hard enough to kill her. Not yet. Kate grunted and blew the blood away from her nose as Achilla held her fast.

"You will meet my father and explain yourself *to him!*" Achilla bellowed through her tears as she grabbed a handful of Kate's hair and jerked her head forward to expose the base of her neck. As Kate grimaced, Achilla raised her free hand and straightened her fingers. One good finger stab through the back of the neck should do it. It was a move that she and Agent Jones practiced for quick kills should the need arise. There was no greater need than right now, and it was all she needed to make this woman pay for her father's death. Achilla inhaled to deliver the blow.

"Achilla!" Agent Jones barked and Achilla looked up and saw him aiming a gun at her head. "I can't let you hurt her. Let her go. Now!"

Achilla glared at Agent Jones. How could he take her side?

No, he was doing his job. Kate was in charge. He had to protect her. Achilla knew that she could sever Kate's head, but then Agent Jones would have to shoot her. Judging from the stern but hesitant glare in his eyes, he was willing to do it even if he hated himself after. Achilla dropped Kate's head, stood up and threw her gun in the pond behind the cage. She then searched Kate's clothes, found two more firearms and a knife and threw them into the pond as well, each weapon dropping through the water until Kate was neutered of any ability to hurt Achilla when she turned her back.

"Consider yourself lucky he likes you so much," Achilla said before she spat on the ground by Kate's head and walked toward the cage's exit. "Next time he might not be here to save you."

"Where are you going?" Agent Jones asked. "It's not safe for you to walk around. We need to bring you back to headquarters."

"No protection, no cooperation," Achilla replied over her shoulder. "I'm going home. If someone wants my mother next, they'll have to go through me. Obviously, I can't trust you anymore."

"Achilla, I'm sure there's a way to figure this out," Agent Jones said. "You and I can find the mole. We can find him and make him pay!"

"No!" Achilla roared before pointing a finger at Kate as she struggled to sit up. "Not with her in charge. I'm doing this *my way* before I lose someone else."

"Agent Johnson," Agent Jones commanded. "You will stay. That is an order."

Achilla turned around and saw Agent Jones aiming his gun at her. This time, she knew it had nothing to do with Kate. Achilla was privy to top-secret intel that required protection at all costs. Still, Achilla frowned at the thought that anything she knew was worth killing over. She barely made a connection to Xerxes and wasn't aware of anything that could actually hurt the United States. Or was she? The location of the research center was enough to give an enemy nation a huge advantage. Technically, someone could sneak in and steal Ares' body, but whether that would actually hurt the country remained to be seen. As of this moment, Achilla wasn't sure if anything Agent Jones knew about him was even true or just more lies from Kate.

"Are you going to shoot me, Freeman?" Achilla asked. "Over Ares? Is he worth that much to you? Is he worth more than me after all we've been through?"

"No," Agent Jones replied. "But he is worth that much to the CIA. You're my brightest student, but this isn't personal."

"Interesting language," Achilla said. "You said the CIA but not the U.S. Does the President have any idea about this?"

"He doesn't know much about a lot of what we do," Agent Jones replied. "We don't think he could handle it."

"Vice President?"

"We especially hid this from him," Agent Jones said. "He might handle it a little too well in his favor."

"And how will either of them handle my death?" Achilla asked. "The second a coroner looks at me, I'll be the scientific discovery of the century. The last thing you need is me dead. You need me hidden, and that's exactly why you haven't shot me yet."

"We have people."

"People I suspect might not stay so quiet anymore when they realize you're killing off the Nephilim you were supposed to research," Achilla said. "That is why you recruited me, isn't it? You weren't just going to let me loose against Ailina without learning about my kind, and since you can't pin her down, you have me. Not anymore. I'm done. I'm going home, and if you want to shoot me, go ahead and try. One way or another, I will protect my family."

"Are you suggesting that you'll kill me?" Agent Jones asked. "I'm not like Kate. I know your capabilities and how to counter them. You're nothing compared to Ares and I survived him."

"Yeah," Achilla said as she stepped forward. "You didn't shoot him though, and I have ways to get around a gun that he probably didn't. Will you end up like Kate over there, or will you give me what I want? Let me see my family, Freeman. I don't want to hurt you, but I will."

Agent Jones stared at Achilla for a few moments without lowering his gun. She knew he was calculating the outcome of this situation in his head. He was too smart and too experienced to not analyze every angle in an instant. Achilla stared back until he hung his head and lowered his weapon. Agent Jones was right about one thing. He knew her better than Kate.

From this distance, there was no way Achilla could get to him without taking at least one bullet. They both knew that he could kill her right now to prevent her from leaking government secrets, but Achilla knew he wouldn't. He lacked Kate's coldness, and that was probably why she advanced to a higher rank than him. He wouldn't shoot her in the head. At most he would give her a flesh wound in an effort to slow her down, and Achilla would charge through it and deliver a crushing blow.

Crushing. Not killing.

The truth was Achilla couldn't take Agent Jones' life any more than he could take hers. Their confrontation was pointless. Why bother? A smile grew on Achilla's lips as she watched Agent Jones holster his firearm. He could have kept up a front to prevent her from killing him, but instead, he lowered his only defense. He wasn't just choosing to keep her alive. He was choosing to trust her. A tear leaked from Achilla's eye and she mouthed a thank you to Agent Jones as she waved her hand. Agent Jones nodded his head and waved her off as he turned his back.

Achilla sniffed as she watched him tend to Kate, lifting up her head and inspecting her for any more wounds. Instead of barking orders, she let him stroke her hair. They almost looked like Achilla's parents the way they held each other, but there was no softness to it; like a couple trying to remember how to love each other. Achilla turned her back, walked to the Cadillac and opened the door, wiping her eyes as she started the ignition. Sandy sat up in her seat as Achilla pulled a three-point turn and drove out of the park.

"Are you OK?" Sandy asked. "Was that you screaming like that?"

"Yes."

"Oh," Sandy said as she stared at her lap. "I don't think I've heard anyone scream like that before, and I've heard some--"

"I'm going home to my family," Achilla cut her off. "You're free to go if you please. Just tell me where to leave you."

"I don't have anywhere else to go," Sandy said. "If what you said is true, somebody could still be there waiting to kill me."

"Right," Achilla replied as she turned on to Route 8 South. "You'll have to stay with me then. My mom's awesome. She'll welcome you with open arms."

"What about earlier?" Sandy asked.

"We won't mention that," Achilla sighed. "Here's our story. I'm in the Marines and--"

She stopped when she realized that she was no longer in the CIA. She no longer had to lie about her actions. Besides, no Marine stationed across the ocean arrives home on the same day you call her. Nobody would believe her lie even if she told it. Achilla shook her head as she passed Exit 22. The truth was the only option, even if she hid part of it.

"Nevermind," Achilla said. "I'll handle it."

"Who are you?" Sandy asked. "Can I at least know that?"

"My name's Achilla, and I'm a former CIA agent," Achilla said. "Your landlord was a sex trafficker who was going to send you to Brazil to her boss. I was in the process of linking them together when Nina got assassinated. Now I've just found out that somebody in the same cartel had my father murdered."

"Oh," Sandy muttered. "I'm sorry."

"It's best that you not get too close to me," Achilla continued. "The only reason I'm going to see my family is to protect them. There's no reason for you to get caught up in this."

"If it wasn't for you, I'd still be a hooker," Sandy said. "What other options do I have?"

"I think you made that decision on your own," Achilla replied. "I hardly deserve the credit, and you do have the option of running away right now."

"And be homeless again?" Sandy snorted and shook her head. "Nah, chill."

"Your choice," Achilla replied. "Don't say I didn't warn you."

"Yeah, sure," Sandy said. "I've been warned that I'll have a warm bed and a roof. That's really dangerous."

Achilla sighed one of those impatient sighs you give a child who doesn't see the value in saving their allowance instead of spending it on the first piece of candy she sees. There were other warm beds, and they weren't targets for international criminals. Of course, Sandy couldn't possibly see that right now. She was beaten, frightened, and out of a home. To get her to leave, Sandy needed more incentive. If she were to stay, she at least had to know everything upfront.

"You should also know that I'm not normal," Achilla said. "It's hard to explain, but you might see me do things that might confuse you."

"Like opening a locked car door and knocking out a cop twice your size with a slap?" Sandy replied. "Or grabbing me and jumping into an alley a good twenty feet away?"

"Yeah."

"Or always knowing when someone lies or tells the truth?"

"Right."

"Or pushing two people across a basketball court with one arm each?" Sandy asked. "And then grabbing one of them from behind when she has a gun pointed at you? I saw what happened with your friends."

"Something like that," Achilla said. "And they're not my friends."

"I'm already confused," Sandy replied. "But I could already tell you're not normal. I guess I can get used to it."

Achilla's will to frighten Sandy crashed and burned, but she frowned as she reviewed what she just said. What else did Sandy notice? Taking note of Achilla's abilities and then lying to help her get close to Gumby was no small feat for the average girl. It might be best to keep Sandy close. Leaving her vulnerable to enemy hands now sounded like a really bad idea.

"It's settled," Achilla said as she passed the exit to Ansonia; only fifteen minutes from Stratford. "Just understand one thing."

"Sure."

"If I think for a moment you're going to betray me," Achilla said with a curled lip as she passed a car on the highway, "I will kill you faster than you can explain yourself."

"Right," Sandy said with a weak voice. "I guess I can get used to that too."

As they entered the Town of Stratford, Achilla noticed that Sandy was asleep. As hard as her day was, she forgot that the past two nights were a roller-coaster for Sandy as well: forced into busting a corrupt cop, suffering a beating from that cop, then hiding in a trap door as her madam and her madam's assassin were killed within ten minutes of each other. For someone who lived such a hard life, she slept with so much peace. Even her snores sounded like mild purrs from a kitten. Achilla found herself yearning to protect her the same way she did for Samuel when they first met. She shook her head at herself for threatening to kill her even if her tactical mind told her it was necessary.

When Achilla pulled onto her old street in Stratford, she remembered that her family moved out of the South End years ago. She still drove to the old house, parked across the street and leaned her head against the back of her seat as she watched her old home that was now filled with new residents who probably had no clue what happened in their patched-up driveway. They appeared to be Asian, and they sat at a dinner table by one of the side windows, holding hands as they lowered their heads to pray. Achilla could hear their prayer and remembered how her family said grace before every dinner. Sometimes, after Achilla came home late from basketball practice, she could hear her father pacing in the kitchen praying to God for his family. His prayers weren't as formal as Sam's. They just sounded like a conversation; no different than if he was talking to Achilla or Samuel. Those prayers made her smile as she listened from the top of the stairs. Today, she smiled as she leaned back and watched the orange and red leaves blow across the street. She jolted when she saw flashes of green and heard parrots screech as they weaved around the leaves like they were running from a fire.

The parrots. Achila's father told her that they got loose from the Beardsley Zoo in Bridgeport and multiplied. When her parents weren't home, Achilla would chase them by scaling the tree in their backyard and laughing as they flew away. Unsure of the limits of her abilities, she never jumped from the tree to catch one. Today, she knew she could grab a parrot no problem. She would have liked to capture one and set it in a cage. It would have made a nice gift for her family, and if the noise was too much, she could let it fly away. Now she just watched them weave through the fiery autumn leaves, screeching their freedom proclamation for the South End to hear.

Achilla lost track of time and sat there until twilight cast its dark blue hue over the street. It was usually around now when Brendan came home early from work if he didn't have a trial coming up. Sam would call Achilla and Samuel inside and they showered for dinner. As Achilla grew older, she drove herself home from work, martial arts training, or a basketball tournament and played with her keys as she strolled into the house. She almost always beat Brendan home, but when she didn't, she smiled as they ate dinner in the living room and watched the game. A lump grew in Achilla's throat when she thought of the way he laughed whenever Kobe Bryant missed a shot knowing that he was her favorite player. Her father always had a way of busting her chops like that with just enough tenacity to piss Achilla off but enough love for her to know he meant no harm. She wiped away a tear. That was enough reminiscing. It was time to find her new home. She looked over at Sandy, who was still deep in slumber, before she turned on the ignition and left her old neighborhood.

Achilla remembered the address that Samuel told her for their second house and drove to the new neighborhood filled with massive colonials, perfect paved driveways, and walkways lined with lamps. When she found the house, she pulled over and smiled at the sight of it. The new Johnson house was a white three-story colonial with a three-car garage; both of which had matching red shutters. A regulation basketball hoop with a clear, red-taped, backboard loomed over the driveway; no doubt for Samuel. Achilla nudged Sandy awake, and she groaned and wiped her mouth before she stretched her arms. She looked around with a frown on her face as Achilla unbuckled her seatbelt and jumped when Achilla unlocked the door.

"Problem?" Achilla asked.

"No," Sandy replied. "Just after watching you fight, I didn't think you came from money."

"I don't," Achilla sighed. "My folks got this place after I moved out. My dad hit his peak as a lawyer."

"Your dad's a lawyer?" Sandy asked with a slight chuckle. "You always had money. You just needed more money before you got this house."

"I never thought of it that way," Achilla said, and she meant it. The very thought of coming from money never occurred to her, but it made sense. Brendan was a private defense attorney with a brilliant record and reputation. Sam was a public school teacher with her Masters. Even Ailina was a cop with a decent salary. Achilla had a rough life, rife with abuse, manipulation, confusion, and the constant attempts to mend all of the damage done to her, but at no point had she ever gone hungry.

"I wish my dad was a lawyer," Sandy muttered as she looked down at her lap. "Or even around. I think I met him once. I saw a guy who looked just like me walking around in the mall, and I just knew it. I think he knew it too because he saw me and walked the other way."

"Yeah," Achilla replied with a sharp stare. "Right about now, I wish my dad was alive."

"Sorry!" Sandy gasped. "Oh my God! That was rude of me!"

Achilla remembered how she met her father. The concerned look in his eyes never left her memory. Brendan knew it too. He also knew it on sight. Sandy was probably right. Her father saw her, knew she was his, and ignored her. Unlike Brendan, he ignored the responsibility of taking care of his own.

"No," Achilla sighed. "Don't be sorry. I had my father for nine years after he discovered me. It sounds like yours blew you off, and I couldn't imagine what that must've felt like."

"Yeah, but yours was…" Sandy stopped herself and shuddered. "I can't even say it. I lost the few friends I had the same way. I know how it feels. I shouldn't complain around you. Not now."

"It's cool," Achilla said as she leaned back into her seat. "To be honest, it's hard for me to get used to the fact that he's not going to answer that door. I took that out on you."

"You really loved your dad."

"You sound shocked."

"No," Sandy said with her hands raised. "No, it's just that you seemed so cold before. I never pictured you as the emotional type."

"I don't know what you mean by *emotional*," Achilla replied. "But I'd kill for my family."

"That's emotional," Sandy said with a weak smile. "That's love really."

Achilla pouted a little before stroking her hair. If she loved her family so much, why wasn't she there to stop all of this from happening?

"All right, I'm going to introduce you to my mom," Achilla sighed as she opened the driver's side door. "Just let me talk to her for a bit before you get out."

Achilla stepped out of the car, stretched her arms and legs, and frowned at this neighborhood's new scent. The salty aroma of fried chicken, ground beef, and platanos that used to ride the breeze in her old neighborhood was faint, sterile, and overpowered by the smell of fresh cut grass, mulch, and wet leaves. She noticed a water hose on the side of the house and rushed to it; setting the hose on its highest level and spraying the blood from her hands and shirt. Eventually, her hands returned to their normal color, but the stains on her shirt remained inescapable from her Nephilim eyes. She hoped that her sweater's dark color hid enough of the blood for her mother to not notice but pulled it off and rinsed it anyway. She wrung it out, watching the diluted blood pour onto the green grass before popping it like a rag. Achilla listened for any onlookers as she stood in her gray sports bra but heard nothing. This neighborhood was quiet; perhaps a little too quiet for her liking. There were no heavy bass thumping rap beats or horn blaring, drum banging salsa tunes echoing through the street. There weren't even any cars passing by. It was just houses and driveways. People lived here, but nobody passed through, not unless one of these homes was their destination.

As she pulled her shirt back on, Achilla sighed and looked at the new Johnson house. It was so much bigger than their old house on Stratford's South End. It was also just as silent as the new neighborhood. Achilla bit her lip and stared at her feet. Their old house was never so quiet; not with her father's booming voice echoing through every hallway, the music and mock gunshots of Samuel playing video games in his room, and Sam turning the pages of one of the many essays she had to grade. Now Achilla heard nothing but the breeze passing through her hair and the dripping of the water hose. She reached down and turned the knob until the dripping stopped, instantly regretting it as it left her one less noise to keep her company.

Achilla's heart jumped when she heard movement inside of the Johnson house. It was a shuffling, pounding noise that sent minor tremors through her feet. It was too small to be Samuel and much too large for a mouse. Somebody was walking downstairs to the front door in a hurry. Achilla faced the door when she heard it open. The front light snapped on and a short, middle-aged, brown-skinned woman wearing a blue Duke Blue Devils t-shirt and jeans stood on the steps in her carnation pink slipper socks. She cupped her hands around her mouth.

"Can I help you?" Sam asked. "My water isn't free."

"I think you've helped me plenty before," Achilla said as she stepped into the light. "But, if you need help with the water bill--"

"Oh my God!" Sam screamed as she ran down the steps and embraced Achilla around the waist. Sam's grip was weak but firm like a child holding onto its mother. All those years of fighting and breaking free from strangleholds during training exercises made Achilla forget what a hug felt like. It was warm, non-threatening, and easy to break if it didn't feel so damn good. Achilla hugged back, and Sam grunted and patted her shoulder.

"Baby, that's too tight!" Sam screamed before Achilla let go.

"Sorry," Achilla said as Sam wiped her eyes and stepped back.

"What have they been feeding you in the military?" Sam asked as she rubbed Achilla's arms. "You have grown a foot. Look at how *tight* your body is, girl, it's like you're not even real."

Achilla frowned and looked at her arms. As she looked down at her own body, then at Sam's, Achilla realized just how far along she had come. Before she left the house, Achilla was no taller than Sam. Now Sam had to crane her neck to speak to her. Achilla always knew that her waist and abs were thin but defined and that her arms were lithe and sinewy, but for the first time since leaving home, someone had actually acknowledged her body without commenting on its effectiveness in a fight or in the bedroom. It was a genuine appreciation for her hard work. Such a compliment made a smile creep on her lips.

"Did your eyes change color?" Sam asked with a frown.

"Oh, right," Achilla said before smacking the back of her own head to pop the contacts out into her palm. "No, they're still green. Probably should've taken those out sooner."

"You look so different!" Sam said. "Even with the same eyes you're like an Egyptian Goddess."

"Mom, you always exaggerate," Achilla chuckled. "I miss that."

"No exaggeration," Sam said with her eyes wide. "I never imagined my daughter would turn out this beautiful. Girl, you must be beating those Marines off with a stick."

"Not exactly," Achilla said as she heard the car door open. "Oh, I have a guest. Mom, this is Sandy."

"Oh, you're a lesbian now?" Sam gasped. "Well, I guess that explains a lot. I was prepared for it."

"No, I meant I wasn't rejecting--" Achilla stopped herself and sighed as Sandy approached. "Nevermind. I'm not a lesbian. I just changed subjects. Sandy, meet my mom."

"Hi," Sandy said. "Nice to meet you, Ms..."

"Call me Sam, baby," Sam said as she shook Sandy's hand and then squinted as she examined her face. "What's his name?"

"Huh?" Sandy replied with a frown.

"I know when a man's been beating on his woman," Sam replied with crossed arms. "What's his name? My father's a police chief, you know? I can make sure he's taken care of."

"No, it's nothing like that," Sandy said with a smile. "But thank you."

It was almost exactly like that, but Achilla wasn't going to push it. It would only lead to details that could risk Sam's life if anyone found out that she knew them. Though she smiled and pretended this was a happy reunion, Achilla searched the surrounding trees and houses, listening for any strange noises; any signs that someone could be listening. So far, nothing for miles. Achilla let her body relax. For now, they were safe.

"Told you she was awesome," Achilla said to Sandy as she nudged her with her elbow. "Mom, is Samuel on his way home?"

"Not yet," Sam replied with her hands on her hips. "His plane leaves in a few. Both of you come in. Where's your stuff?"

"Yeah…I want to talk to you about that," Achilla said as they walked into the house. They stepped into a foyer with a glass chandelier and a wood spiral staircase before walking into a kitchen with wood cabinets and an island with a spotless white top. Considering their more modest beginnings, Achilla nodded her head at this new interior. This house even smelled different, lacking the lingering scents of fried catfish and steak fries that used to stick to their old carpet. Now Achilla could smell the fancy cleaning products that filled Mayor Berger's kitchen in New Haven. After a couple more sniffs, Achilla deduced that Sam no longer cleaned her own house. She smiled at the thought that her parents could finally afford a maid.

"You guys were doing well," Achilla said as she looked up at the white ceiling.

"Your father started racking up the not-guilties," Sam sighed as she opened the black refrigerator. "On top of my master teacher salary, we had good money. He was quite the man. He was everything I expected him to be. Sometimes you can just look at a man and see his potential. You just know he'll be good to you, good to your kids, good to everyone. That was Brendan."

"I know," Achilla replied with a smile as she remembered how she thought of her father during her first weeks of living in his house; a man full of righteous anger at the thought of his daughter suffering abuse. As a child, she was so used to Ailina's beatings that she hardly felt anything that didn't break a bone. Brendan and Sam were so different, so loving. Achilla struggled to accept that she deserved so much affection without earning it through her own sweat, tears, and bruises, but it grew on her. Achilla decided to never go back to Ailina and that she was forever in her new family's debt. Her eyes moistened at the thought that her father wouldn't be here for her to repay him. She was sure that she could have made him happy somehow.

"I'm really sorry for your loss," Sandy said to Sam with her head bowed. "Is there anything I can do to help?"

"No, you're my guest, honey," Sam replied. "Where's home for you?"

Achilla and Sandy looked at each other. Here comes the hard part.

"I don't want to complain during your time of grief," Sandy muttered. "With all due respect, I would rather not answer that."

"What does that mean?" Sam asked with a scowl. "Just answer my question."

"She's homeless," Achilla said. "As soon as I find my own place, she'll stay with me."

"Homeless?" Sam said with a frown before holding her hands on her hips. "Find your own place? Were you kicked out of the Marines?"

"No," Achilla sighed. "I was never in the Marines."

"So where were you then?" Sam asked with a sideways stare. "And why did you say you were?"

"For your own safety, there's only so much I can tell you--"

"Now you sound like my father," Sam said before she closed the refrigerator door. "Achilla, give me a straight answer. I lived my whole life with job-related secrets, and I won't have it anymore; especially not now."

"I was in the CIA," Achilla blurted. "I was...I was a spy in training when I left the house, and I met Sandy on my second assignment. Sandy's homeless because of me, and Dad might be dead because of me as well."

The last part slipped. Achilla cringed when Sam jolted, and she scrambled to think of a recovery. None came to mind. There was really no way to reword blaming yourself for your father's death. Achilla pinched her own leg as she watched Sam's demeanor turn numb and still.

"What?" Sam asked with a blank face.

"I don't think this is a good time to tell her that," Sandy whispered.

"Maybe you're right," Achilla said.

"Nope," Sam said with tears in her eyes as she crossed her arms and leaned against the island. "Finish. I want to hear this. Now's...Now is as good a time as any. I can handle it."

Achilla looked away for a split second before staring into her mother's eyes. She looked older, but Sam's demeanor never changed. She still looked Achilla in the eye with the full knowledge that she was in charge despite the fact that Achilla could overpower her at any moment. As much as she wanted to dodge this conversation, Sam's eyes compelled her to tell the truth. Achilla balled up her fists as if she were preparing for a fight that she knew she would lose.

"A man I was investigating is very dangerous," Achilla muttered with a shaking voice. "The CIA promised to keep watch over you guys while I pursued him."

"And?" Sam asked as her face turned slightly red as she pushed off of the island and stood up straight. Achilla's eyes watered as she looked at her mother, standing there with her hands on her hips. Achilla looked away and let out a slight sob, and she sniffed when Sandy placed a hand on her shoulder. Sandy backed away when Sam stepped forward and held Achilla's face in her hands.

"Achilla," Sam said. "You're talking to your mother. Say what you have to say."

"Turns out, he likes to kill family members," Achilla sobbed and heaved. "I'm so sorry, Mom. I didn't know, and I should've."

Achilla dropped to her knees and wrapped her arms around Sam's waist, clutching her jeans as she wept into her shirt. Part of her flushed at the thought of screwing up so bad. Achilla was sure that if she had done more research, she could have found out sooner what Blue Eyes was capable of and how far his connection to

Xerxes could reach. Surely, she could have figured out that Blue Eyes would identify her as the daughter of the man he hated and plot the worst kind of revenge. With all of her intelligence, how could she not see this coming? How could she be so stupid?

"I'm sorry, Mom," Achilla cried out. "It's all my fault! I was sloppy, and I missed details, and-"

"Achilla," Sam sighed. "Oh no, baby…"

"I should've been there," Achilla wailed. "I should've protected him. I'm supposed to keep you all safe and I wasn't there! I'm sorry, Mom! I'm so sorry!"

When Achilla opened her mouth to apologize again, nothing but a blubbering sob passed her lips. She pressed her face into her mother's shirt as her body tensed and tears flowed down her cheeks. She just knew Sam would hate her now. It didn't take a genius CIA agent to know that Achilla was always a burden for her. She was another woman's child living in her house, and not a well behaved one. She beat up kids at school, made inappropriate comments, swore in front of her, and treated church like a boring chore. She was nothing like Samuel, her well-behaved son who actually came out of her womb and did what he was told. Achilla brought trouble to their home over and over, and this had to be the last time. Achilla sobbed some more. As much as she loved Sam as her mother, she wanted nothing more than to run away from her, and she would as soon as she had the strength to let go.

"Achilla, baby," Sam said as she patted Achilla's shoulder. "Get off of your knees. You weren't raised to be there for anyone but God Himself. Get up, honey."

Achilla stood up and wiped her face as if to remove her emotions with her bare hands.

"Mom, I take full responsibility," Achilla stated and raised her chin. "If you never want to see me again, if you want to disown me or kick me out, I'll understand--"

"Achilla, what the hell are you talking about?" Sam yelled. "I'm not *disowning* you. How could you even suggest that? We are a family!"

"But Dad died because of--"

"That is not your fault," Sam snapped with a raised hand.

"Huh?" Achilla said with a frown.

"If this person wasn't doing wrong, you wouldn't have had to investigate, right?" Sam asked with a stomp of her foot. "You did the right thing, and he did the wrong thing. Simple as that, and as for the CIA, they should've been here like they said they would, and they should have protected my husband!"

The way Sam said *my husband* forced a lump in Achilla's throat and she lowered her head to avoid her eyes.

"If I hate *anyone*, it's them," Sam said as tears flowed down her cheeks. "Lord forgive me, but I hate them for letting my husband just *die* like he didn't have a family waiting for him. They were supposed to back you up, but they just didn't care. They just didn't care, that's all."

"Mom," Achilla muttered. "I messed up. I know enough to know that. I'm trained to--"

"What?" Sam cut her off. "Trained to what, Achilla? Be every-where at once? You're not God, Achilla. I don't care how trained you are, nobody can know every detail of *everything*. You needed help, they said they'd help, they didn't and now Brendan's gone! They screwed up, not you."

"I wish it was that simple--"

"It's that simple for me," Sam said as she wiped her eyes. "Brendan was a defense attorney. Before you moved in, we used to get death threats three times a week. Sometimes cops would harass him in the street. We don't fear risk in this house, and from what you've just told me, your father would've been so proud of you."

"You...think so?" Achilla asked.

"I know so," Sam said. "And I don't see any fault here on you. The CIA failed our family, but not you. Ever since you moved into this house, you've done nothing that could ever make us *disown* you."

"You have no idea," Achilla said with a breaking voice. "You have no idea how good it feels to hear that."

"Good," Sam replied. "It's supposed to feel good to come home."

Home. It had been four years since Achilla used that word. She had her apartment. She had her headquarters. She stayed in a hotel room, but she didn't have a home; not since she left home at sixteen. Unfortunately, even her reasons for coming back involved her former job. The word "home" made more tears well up in her eyes before she blinked them back. She couldn't cry anymore. She had to make sure everyone was ok first.

"You should know that I came back to protect you," Achilla said to Sam. "If he got Dad, he might come for you."

"Well, I'm not scared of anybody," Sam said as she reopened the refrigerator and pulled out a Tupperware container filled with pasta. "If he wants some of this, he can bring it. I've got a revolver with his name on it, whoever he is."

"He'll have to come through me first," Achilla replied. "And you're right, I have changed. I'm stronger."

"Glad to hear it," Sam said as she walked to one of the cabinets and grabbed some plates. "Sandy, are you hungry, baby? I've got spaghetti."

"Yes," Sandy said with a smile as she sat at the table. When Sam served leftover spaghetti for dinner, Sandy shoved the spaghetti in her mouth like it was trying to escape. Achilla tried her best to focus on her meal as Sandy cleared her plate in a matter of minutes and Sam served her seconds. Achilla remembered the last time she ate like that. It was the first day she moved in with Brendan and Sam. That day, Achilla ate like a wolf because she had never eaten anything that tasted so good. She had a feeling Sandy ravished her food because she hadn't eaten any in a while.

"Sandy, when's the last time you've eaten some good food?" Sam asked.

"At my old house, I only ate once a day," replied Sandy with her mouth full before she swallowed. "Before that, I had to fight other kids for food. I was always the only girl, so I didn't eat much. When I got older, I learned how to…"

Sandy looked down at her food.

"Sandy, what's wrong?" Sam asked.

"I think I know what she means," Achilla said as she placed a hand on Sandy's shoulder. "Maybe some other time."

"I learned to use my body," Sandy said. "Let's just put it out there. Achilla saved me from a life of…that."

A hush fell over the dinner table as Sandy twirled her fork around a knot of spaghetti and shoved it in her mouth as if it were a plug to stop her from crying. It worked. Sandy's eyes stayed dry as she chewed her food.

"And you'll never go back," Sam said with a firm stare as she grabbed Sandy's wrist. "You'll stay here as long as you want. With Samuel at school and Brendan…not with us, I could use the company anyway in this big old house."

"Thank you so much," Sandy replied with a smile. "How can I repay you?"

"You can start by helping me prepare for this funeral," Sam sighed. "I have so many people to invite. Brendan saved a lot of lives."

As Achilla took another bite of her spaghetti, she noticed slight wrinkles in Sam's face and a hint of gray at the roots of her hair. Her eyes were baggy and red. She was in her mid-forties and looked every bit of it after the death of her husband. Achilla rolled her spaghetti around her fork and watched Sam's trembling hand do the same. Being the strong person she was, she did a great job of hiding it, but Sam couldn't fool a Nephilim. Brendan's death had her on the brink of a breakdown. Achilla's company was necessary for more than just protection, but pointing out her mother's mental state was fruitless. Achilla would play the protector for now and keep her discovery to herself.

"I'll help too," Achilla said before wolfing down a mouthful of spaghetti and swallowing in one gulp. "Besides, I need to be by your side as much as possible. You're not safe."

"Well, I trust your judgment," Sam said. "Did you ever make friends while you were away?"

Achilla thought about Agent Jones for a split second. Then the thought that he might be ordered to eliminate her and her mother made her shake his face out of her mind.

"No," Achilla replied. "Sandy here's the closest I've got to a real friendship."

"At gunpoint," Sandy quipped.

There was a long pause as Sam looked at Achilla and then back at Sandy. Sandy kept her head lowered as she ate more spaghetti. Achilla then covered her mouth as she burst out laughing. Sandy soon joined her, and they giggled like little school girls. Achilla noticed Sam watching them with a blank stare, but she laughed anyway.

"Is that one of those inside jokes you kids use today?" Sam asked.

"No," Achilla gasped as she held her side. "That was true."

"One hundred percent," Sandy added.

"Achilla, you held her up at gunpoint?" Sam asked.

"It's best not to over think it," Achilla replied before patting Sandy's shoulder. "We're good now."

"Yeah, I'm here now, right?" Sandy said with her arms wide.

"What has this world come to?" Sam asked as she stood up from the table. "I have so many questions, but I'm too tired to ask. I'm going to bed. Achilla, help her get set up."

"Yes, ma'am," Achilla giggled.

"And do it without a gun."

"Yes, ma'am," Achilla replied before laughing again. Sam shook her head and walked out of the kitchen as Achilla and Sandy laughed so hard that they leaned forward and rested their heads on the kitchen table. Achilla kept laughing until she noticed that Sandy's head remained on the table without moving. Upon hearing her light snores, Achilla smiled and rubbed her back.

Achilla lifted Sandy into her arms and carried her out of the kitchen as she breathed with the softness of a baby. She found a black leather couch in the living room and set Sandy down there before stretching her arms and laying down on the matching couch across the room. She fell asleep thinking about her father with a smile on her face and a tear running down her cheek. In this room, they would have argued for hours over who was the best basketball player of their era. It was Kobe, of course, but Brendan would have said LeBron just for the sake of argument. That argument reeled through her head before Achilla's snores drowned it out.

When Achilla woke up at four in the morning, she sat up on the couch, scanning the house to get her bearings. She looked across the living room and saw Sandy draped over her couch like an unmade blanket. Achilla swung her legs and sat upright as she let out a small yawn and massaged her neck. Next time, she would sleep in the guest room on an actual bed. She wandered from the living room to the front door in the same clothes she wore for the past two days and frowned as she sniffed her armpits. She was taking a shower soon too.

When she turned the doorknob without a sound and sat on the steps outside, she yawned a little louder and stretched her arms while she stared out at this new neighborhood dressed in early morning blue. It would be quieter if Achilla hadn't developed even sharper hearing over the years. She could make out the snoring in the off-white two-story colonial with blue shutters across the street. The red house to the left with the winding driveway rang with the jingling of keys; someone most likely leaving for an early morning shift. The brick house across the street and two doors down held the gasps and moans of a couple making love. With nothing to distract her, all of these sounds bombarded Achilla as if they were all sleeping, playing with their keys, and having morning sex on the front lawn. Achilla shrugged and wiped the crust from her right eye. At least it wasn't as loud as her old apartment building.

Achilla stood up, inhaled the crisp morning dew and exhaled as she leaned into a handstand and paced the walkway on her index fingers. Normally, she would hide such a feat of strength, but she was too deep in thought to care. She had to figure out her next step. As much as she just wanted to comfort her mother and grieve her father's death, the reality was that her family wasn't safe. Whoever killed Brendan might come back to finish the job; especially if Samuel was flying in. If Achilla wanted to kill a whole family, now would be the time to do it. She could only assume that her enemies had the same idea. She noticed a small white envelope with her name on it in front of her face and she somersaulted to her feet to pick it up. Achilla already knew the author before she sat on the steps and opened it. The letter inside the envelope read:

"I have all the answers to your questions. Meet me at the below address before Brendan's funeral. If you want to keep your family safe, I recommend that they travel with you. Your call."

Achilla sighed and folded the letter before shoving it into her pocket and sitting on the steps. What was Ailina trying to pull? The address in the letter was located in Boston. She was trying to meet out of the state to avoid police, but the Feds and the CIA didn't have such restrictions on their jurisdiction. What was the point in it all? As she pondered what to do next, Achilla pretended not to hear Sandy coming before she opened the door and stepped out.

Sandy sat next to her on the steps and Achilla frowned at her presence. Sandy smelled almost as bad as Achilla, and it took a quiet morning in a sterile neighborhood for her to notice. On the bright side, the bruises on her face were healing, and Achilla bet Sandy could attract as many boys as her if she cleaned up. Achilla patted her shoulder as she stared out at the street.

"You don't sleep either?" Sandy asked.

"About three hours a night," Achilla said with a shrug. "Sometimes I wonder what a long night's sleep actually feels like."

"Me too," Sandy sighed. "I'm so used to being tired all the time."

"That's just it," Achilla chuckled. "I'm not tired. I literally can't sleep any further, even if I wanted to. My body does amazing things, you know? I can jump ten feet in the air. I can punch through concrete and break bones with my fingers. I can see, hear, taste, and smell at a higher level than the vast majority of the human population. But with all that, I can't get a decent, long night's rest. I can't even sleep in on my days off! You know I've never shared a morning with somebody? I'm always awake before they are."

Achilla noticed Sandy staring off into the street.

"I guess everything comes with a trade-off," Achilla sighed as she joined her in staring at the neighborhood. "Not many people can do what I can. I shouldn't complain."

"You're sharing a morning with me," Sandy said.

"Huh?" Achilla blurted as she frowned at her.

"You said you never shared a morning with someone," Sandy said as she smiled at Achilla. "But you're sharing one with me."

"Yeah, I guess you're right," Achilla replied as she looked back out into the street again. She relaxed a little until she noticed Sandy's hand on her lap. Achilla frowned before looking up at Sandy's face coming close to hers with her lips puckered, and she jumped off the steps and landed in the front yard. Sandy flinched and stood up. As she walked toward her, Achilla stepped back.

"What the hell do you think you're doing?" Achilla asked.

"I don't know," Sandy said with a shrug. "I thought you would like it."

"No," Achilla snapped. "I don't. I like men. Didn't you hear me tell my mom I wasn't a lesbian?"

"Well, yeah, but most people don't just tell their parents that stuff right away," Sandy laughed.

"I would," Achilla replied. "And this isn't me."

"You don't have to take it so hard," Sandy muttered as she hung her head. "I just thought I'd repay you for saving my life."

"You're not a hooker anymore, Sandy," Achilla said with her hands on her hips. "You don't have to trade your body for services. God, how could you be so weak?"

"You don't have to be so judgmental," Sandy replied with a frown. "Everybody isn't like you. You've survived doing things your way, and I survived doing things my way. We're different people."

"I couldn't agree more," Achilla quipped. "Hey, I tell you what, I bet the post lady's a female. When she drops off the mail, you can give her a smooch if you want."

Sandy's hands shook as she marched toward Achilla. This time, Achilla didn't back down. Sandy stood under her nose, and her hazel eyes moistened. She never broke eye contact with Achilla, even as a tear rolled down her nose. Achilla stared back without flinching.

"Don't even think about it, Sandy," Achilla said with a low voice. "You would literally last about half a second."

"No," Sandy said with a shake of her head. "As much as I want to, I won't hit you. Unlike you, I don't think hitting is the only way to express myself."

"Or maybe you're too afraid of a fight," Achilla replied. "Maybe you'd just let someone walk all over you and take advantage of you like you always do."

"You could kill me right now, but I'm going to say this anyway," Sandy said.

"And what's that?"

"Fuck you," Sandy said with her middle finger in Achilla's face. "You stuck up....*canhão!*"

"Are we back to your sloppy Portuguese again?" Achilla sneered. "If you want to hurt my feelings, you'll have to come stronger than that, *puta--*"

Sandy let out a mix between a growl and a sob as she slapped Achilla on the cheek. Achilla heard a low crack and Sandy cried out and backed away. Sandy sat on the stoop, nursing her wrist, and Achilla stood in front of her with her hands on her hips. She laughed to herself and shook her head. Sandy knew she couldn't beat her, but she swung anyway? Achilla couldn't help but smile.

"I thought you'd kill me," Sandy said through her sniffling. "What're you all talk?"

"I get the feeling that's what you wanted," Achilla said. "And I'm not giving it to you."

"Oh, so now you're a good Samaritan, huh?"

"No," Achilla replied. "I'm far from good. And maybe I shouldn't throw your past in your face so much. I'm sorry."

"You're...sorry?" Sandy said with a frown before wiping her eyes.

"Yeah," Achilla said as she held Sandy's wrist and examined it. "And the next time you want to hit someone stronger than you, go for the eyes. I'm strong, but my eyes are just as soft as yours, and it's hard to hit what you can't see. Poke out your opponent's eyes, and you'll always be equals."

"Thanks?"

"Now that you've displayed a willingness to fight," Achilla said as she kneeled in front of Sandy. "I think I'll teach you how to defend yourself. There's no reason for you to let people abuse you anymore; not even me."

"You're going to teach me how to beat you?" Sandy asked.

"No," Achilla laughed. "I'm different. My physical capabilities are too advanced, even if you trained for a lifetime, but by the time I'm done with you, men twice your size will be nothing. That much I can guarantee. You down?"

"Yeah," Sandy replied with a smile as she wiped a strand of her hair. "Sure."

"Good," Achilla said with a smile as she massaged Sandy's wrist with her thumb. "I have some things to take care of. After this all blows over, we can start the real training. Until then, I'll teach you here and there. I'm afraid you might need it."

"Is it broken?" Sandy asked as she winced when Achilla's thumb pressed against her wrist.

"Sprained," Achilla replied. "It's actually good that you slapped incorrectly. Had you stiffened your wrist, you might have a worse injury. Hitting someone like me is like hitting a brick wall. Unless you have strength like mine, it won't work. Even knives barely get through my skin without enough force. Against someone like me, you'll need a gun."

"Why are you telling me this?" Sandy asked.

"Because you may have to face someone like me soon," Achilla said. "I haven't told Mom yet, but I have to take a trip to meet my biological mother. With a hit out on anyone close to me, I don't think--"

"Wait, Sam's not your mother?" Sandy blurted. "But you're so close."

"No, she's not," Achilla said. "Not by blood anyway. My biological mother's name is Ailina, and she's just as strong as I am but twice as dangerous. Only I can handle her."

"Why would you want to see her?" Achilla heard Sam say from the front door. Achilla cringed. Yet again, she made the mistake that Agent Jones always warned her about. She didn't focus on her surroundings when it mattered the most. Achilla smiled at Sam.

Sam didn't smile back as she stood in the doorway with her arms crossed over her oversized gray t-shirt.

"I think it's a good decision," Achilla said. "I want to talk to her. There are a lot of things that I need to figure out, and I think she has the answers."

"That woman tried to kill us," Sam replied. "All of us."

"Really?" Achilla asked before walking through their front lawn. When she reached the street, Achilla found a spot on the concrete and stood with her legs shoulder-length apart. She then exhaled hard as she pounded the street with her fist. Achilla's hand punctured the concrete until her arm was ten inches deep into the ground and the street ruptured like broken glass. Achilla pulled her hand out of the concrete and clenched and unclenched her fist. That punch used to make her hands sore. Now it was no different than hitting a mattress. Achilla walked back to her mother with her hands on her hips. She noticed Sandy's jaw-dropped expression, but Sam just glared at her.

"That was about a third of my strength nowadays," Achilla said. "If I throw my body into a proper punch, I can level the trees in your backyard. My kicks are even harder, *much harder*. Ailina was about that strong when we fought. Do you think she couldn't kill us back then if she wanted to?"

"She tried to strangle me," Sam snapped. "And I'm still here."

"And what I'm telling you," Achilla replied with a hard stare, "is that people like me don't have to strangle you. If we want to kill you, we'll just snap the bones in your neck. She wasn't trying to kill you. She was trying to use you to manipulate me into joining her."

"Joining her for what?"

"I don't know," Achilla said. "I suspect that there's a lot more going on with her than we've all been led to believe, and I need to find out."

"And how do you know she won't manipulate you when you see her?" Sam asked.

"I don't know that either," Achilla replied. "But...I would like you to come with me--"

"Hell no, Achilla," Sam snapped.

"Mom, I get it," Achilla said through gritted teeth. "I don't like it either, but if you stay here, the man who killed Dad might kill you when I'm gone."

"He could kill her while you're here too," Sandy mumbled. "Someone killed Nina, right? And you were on the same porch."

Achilla hadn't thought of that. She pinched herself in the leg for missing such an obvious detail. The last man to attack Achilla was a sniper in the next house who was stupid enough to leave his post. Her family was no safer with her here. Achilla turned her back on Sandy and Sam for a moment as she paced the walkway.

"I'm picking up Samuel from the airport," Sam said. "If you want to see Ailina, you can find her yourself, and I pray to God that you'll come back in one piece if you do."

"I can still go with you," Sandy said to Achilla.

"No, stay here," Achilla replied as she shook her head. "Mom needs your help. It's best that I go solo. You make a good point. You're no safer with me here."

"So why go alone?" Sandy asked with a frown.

"If I'm going to protect my family," Achilla said as she looked at the now blue, cloudless sky, "I'll have to meet the threat head-on. No more waiting."

"Take your father's car," Sam said as she turned into the house. "I'll get the keys."

"Thanks, Mom," Achilla said as Sandy stood up from the steps and hugged her around the waist. Her grip was tight but weak and easy to break. It was a hug as good as any. Despite her revulsion earlier, Achilla found herself unable to break free. Sandy then pecked Achilla on the cheek. When Achilla frowned at her, Sandy stepped back.

"Just in case you don't return," Sandy replied with a smile before turning on her heels. Achilla touched her cheek with her hand as she watched her walk into the house with her head low. She had no sexual desire for Sandy, but that kiss made a smile creep on Achilla's lips. She forced that smile down when Sam stepped out and tossed her the keys to the sedan. Achilla snatched them out of the air but walked toward the house.

"I thought you were leaving," Sam said. "Getting cold feet?"

"Mom, please, I haven't bathed in two days," Achilla replied as she ran up the stairs. She hopped in the shower and threw on some clothes that Sam left on the railing outside the bathroom; a pair of jeans, a Duke t-shirt, and an old, blue and white, a pair of sneakers that Achilla used to wear in high school. Achilla ran out of the house without saying goodbye and jogged down the walkway. She unlocked the black sedan in their driveway and slid into its black leather interior. Achilla nodded her head as she started the car.

"I don't deserve any favors from you," Achilla sighed as she backed the car out of the driveway. "But please keep them safe. If you hold them off, I'll come back and deal with all of them myself. "

Achilla pulled out of the driveway and drove down the street. She watched her mother and Sandy standing in the doorway of the house from her rearview mirror before staring straight ahead. From this point on, she had to focus on Ailina. Her heart raced at the thought of seeing those green eyes again. She set her jaw and pushed the gas pedal as she turned the corner.

When she arrived at a dive bar in Downtown Boston, Achilla wrinkled her nose at the stench of beer, popcorn, and buffalo wings. Most of the clientele had tan skin and dark hair, but there were a few black people sitting here and there. They mostly kept to themselves. Achilla noticed a few stares at her Duke shirt, and then looked at one of the television screens. Duke played Boston University in an exhibition just a few days ago, and they were showing a rerun on the television screen. After the crowd cheered when Duke turned the ball over, Achilla decided that this had to be a Boston University bar. Achilla chuckled at herself. And here she was trying not to stick out.

Achilla scanned the polished wood bar as she sat in her seat. Ailina hadn't arrived yet. Achilla noticed as a child that Nephilim had a way of noticing each other's presence. When Ailina showed up, she would know. In the meantime, Achilla was going to watch the game. She raised her hand for the bartender, and a pudgy, bald white male wearing a tight black t-shirt approached.

"What can I do for you?" he said with an accent straight out of Goodwill Hunting.

"Just some cranberry juice is fine," Achilla said. As the bartender brought her the cranberry juice in a medium-sized glass, Achilla watched as they showed Samuel's highlights on the television screen. One clip showed Samuel wearing a dark blue jersey as he dunked one-handed over an unsuspecting center. He screamed and flexed his arms as his teammates shoved him and tapped his head. Achilla smirked and raised a glass to the television. It looked like his training regimen was paying off. When the television returned to the actual game, Achilla felt her neck hairs stand on end, and she controlled her breathing as her heart raced.

Ailina was in the bar.

Without thinking, Achilla reached behind her and grabbed a hand that was headed for her shoulder. She then whirled around and saw Ailina standing before her wearing a black, thigh-length dress and her usual high-heeled black leather boots. Her hair flowed down to her shoulders and her eyes were every bit as cold and intense as ever, but they didn't frighten Achilla anymore. Instead, Achilla found herself smirking at their coldness. After seeing it so often, it was almost comical to her.

When Ailina raised her other hand, Achilla snatched her wrist and held it at her side. Ailina glared at her and she stared back as they engaged in a tug-of-war that no one in the bar noticed but them. Achilla frowned at how easily she held Ailina in place before grinning as she released her. Ailina flinched and massaged her wrist. That confirmed it. There was no telling who would win in hand-to-hand combat, but Achilla had surpassed Ailina in physical strength. Achilla shrugged at her before sitting down and drinking her juice.

"Cranberry juice," Ailina said as she sat next to her. "In a bar. In Boston. You sure are brave."

Achilla frowned at the way Ailina pronounced the word bar. It sounded like a sheep's call.

"Oh what, this?" Ailina asked as she pointed at her mouth. "Yeah, the accent always comes back when I enter the city."

"I almost have pity for you," Achilla quipped. "Now what did you want, Ailina?"

"I know what happened to Brendan," Ailina said. "I'm sorry."

"Says the woman who held him by his throat," Achilla snarled. "Don't even *talk* about my father!"

"You're smart enough to know that I had no intention of killing him," Ailina replied. "All of that was planned. I even waited for you to come home. This was different. This guy wanted your father dead."

"Tell me something new please."

"Fine, I know who did it," Ailina replied. "Roberto--"

"Gabrielli," Achilla sighed as she stood up. "Also known as Blue Eyes. If you're going to waste my time--"

"I can help you get him," Ailina said with a flicker in her eyes. "Is that worth your precious time, Princess?"

"Why the hell would I need your help?" Achilla asked.

"Roberto hides in plain sight," Ailina said. "He's back at work running his law firm as if nothing happened, but if you return to that office, you're dead in a week. He's never seen me before. I'll pose as a police officer and arrest him, and I'll bring him to you. From there, you can do whatever helps you grieve."

"Sounds enticing," Achilla replied as she cracked her knuckles and sat back down. "What's in it for you?"

"I need you to take me to my father," Ailina said. "I know he's alive in there. I just need access to where he's being held."

"Alive is subjective," Achilla replied before taking a sip of her drink and staring down a blonde-haired woman who gave her a nasty look. "He has two bullets in his head. He's most likely in a vegetative state."

"Then let me have his body," Ailina said with a shrug. "How would you feel if someone took Brendan's body and just held on to it?"

Achilla shook any agreement out of her head.

"There's something you're not telling me," Achilla said with a pointed finger as she watched the game. "You must take me for a fool."

"The CIA certainly did," Ailina replied before she leaned closer to Achilla. "How long did it take you to realize that they had no intention of helping your family? You're brilliant but naïve, and they played on your protective nature. They were going to put you in a tank like they did your grandfather, and they want to do the same to me. All they had to do was round us up like cattle."

"Wouldn't they try that if I brought you to Ares?" asked Achilla.

"Perhaps, but we'll be ready," Ailina said with a raised fist. "It'll be on our terms, not theirs."

Achilla took a sip of her drink as she watched Samuel make a three-pointer; his third of the game. She closed her eyes as she sifted the juice in her mouth, savoring the sourness before swallowing it down. She thought about that moment when she found out that her father was murdered. She thought about how Kate didn't bother to console her but insisted on convincing her to stay on their side. Now that she left the CIA, Achilla wouldn't be surprised if Kate tried to torture her family until she turned herself in. Unlike Agent Jones, Kate held no emotional ties to her, and she had the authority to override him. The CIA was about as trustworthy as Ailina, but at least Ailina had a personal interest in keeping her alive. Achilla took another swig of her juice before she turned and faced Ailina.

"If you cross me," Achilla said, "I'll snap your neck."

"Likewise," Ailina replied before standing up and cheering as Boston University scored a basket. Achilla noticed a couple of men with dark hair approaching her as she swayed her hips and clapped her hands. The leering looks they gave her indicated that they weren't strangers in this bar or outside of it. Achilla snorted and shook her head. At least she could take comfort in knowing her standards in men were higher than hers. Ailina raised her finger at her friends before she leaned over to Achilla's ear.

"I have to take care of this," Ailina giggled. "But I'll have Roberto in exactly one week. I'll send you the address beforehand. Be there Saturday at midnight. Sharp."

"Got it," Achilla said.

"We make a good team," Ailina replied with a wink that made Achilla want to punch her eye shut. Ailina grabbed one of the men and kissed him flat on the lips before turning and doing the same with the other, running her hand up his crotch. She then held his hand and walked him out of the bar. Achilla shook her head as she watched the game some more. Despite her ageless appearance, Achilla wondered if those men would ever realize that Ailina was at least forty-five years old. One of the black men from the bar approached and sat next to her wearing a black t-shirt and derby. Achilla looked him up and down, letting her eyes rest on his massive chest. She then took a deep breath and crossed her legs as she fought the urge to take him. Now wasn't the time. When he opened his mouth to speak, Achilla raised her hand.

"Normally I'd welcome this," Achilla said as she stood up. "But I have to take care of something. If I see you again, next time."

"I've heard that before," the guy said. "I look stupid?"

"I don't forget faces," Achilla replied as she caressed his shoulder. "Next time."

Achilla weaved through the crowd. She knew Boston University scored another basket when the bar erupted just as she reached the door. A thunderstorm rolled into the city limits, and Achilla smirked at the sky as it dumped a downpour on her head. As men and women ran inside the bar ducking under their umbrellas and outstretched jackets, Achilla walked through the rain as if she were standing in her own shower. She combed her fingers through her hair as it grew heavy and damp.

The rain always looked different to Achilla. While others had a hard time seeing through it, she found that it provided clarity. Even now it had a way of highlighting Boston's age; like washing away the makeup on a middle-aged woman. Achilla walked through the storm to a parking garage down the street where she kept her father's car. She took her shirt off and wrung it out as she stood outside of the car. When she noticed a man staring at her, she smiled and gave him the finger. The man shook his head and walked away. Achilla then hopped into the car and pulled out of her parking space. If Ailina was on the up and up, Blue Eyes was in for a long, painful death. Achilla gripped the steering wheel and drove out of Boston as the rain washed away her glamour.

Chapter Thirteen

ACHILLA JOHNSON:15

After her suspension, Achilla started piling up her achievements. She made the Connecticut Post Super 15; an article in the newspaper highlighting some of the best basketball players in the state. She averaged twenty points a game and ten assists. Achilla had to focus on tennis in the Spring, but she planned on playing basketball all summer. She also planned on seeing Dahntay a little more. Though she couldn't bring herself to tell him, Achilla couldn't forget how he vouched for her in the office. It also didn't hurt that he stopped by her locker every morning when she came to school. She would greet him, and he would walk her to her class. Achilla was starting to enjoy Dahntay's company. She liked the way he could joke and make her laugh, and whenever she had something smart to say, he always had a comeback. Pretty soon, instead of just walking to her locker, Achilla would stay for a few minutes and talk with Dahntay before hugging him and sending him on his way.

One day, Dahntay didn't stop by her locker. Achilla held her books against her green sweater as she waited for him until the first-period bell rang. She then slammed her locker shut and walked to class in a huff. As she rushed into the classroom late, she spent the entire first period wondering where he was. When she saw Dahntay in the hallway later on, he waved and walked across the hall wearing a blue Elgin Baylor throwback jersey and baggy jeans with white sneakers. Achilla glared at him when he smiled at her.

"What's up, A--"

"Where the hell were you this morning?" Achilla snapped louder than she intended, causing other students to glance at them.

"I was late to school," Dahntay replied with a frown. "Why?"

"You didn't come by my locker," Achilla said with her head lowered. "You didn't say hi."

"I couldn't," Dahntay chuckled. "It's kind of hard to be in two places at once, Achilla."

"Well then call me or something," Achilla demanded. "I was worried."

"About what?"

"I don't know," Achilla said. "Just...never mind. Forget I said anything."

"Look, I got a party at my cousin's house in Bridgeport," Dahntay said. "Why don't you be my date? I mean you're already giving me a hard time like a girlfriend--"

"Don't get ahead of yourself," Achilla said as she turned on her heels and walked down the hall before looking over her shoulder. "But yeah, I'll go to the party. Text me the address."

This time when Achilla told her parents, they both insisted on meeting Dahntay before the day of the party. Dahntay obliged and came over the house to meet Brendan and Sam. He was the opposite of Stanley. He looked Brendan in the eye when he spoke and shook his hand. He also addressed Sam as "ma'am" until she reminded him that she wasn't old. After Dahntay left, Brendan nodded his head with approval.

"I like him," Brendan said as he crossed his arms over his red sweater and watched Dahntay pull out of the driveway in his red Acura. "I knew he was a good kid the second I met him."

"I like him too," Sam said as she held Brendan's arm. Brendan turned and kissed her on the cheek. Sam smiled and lowered her head before walking to the living room and wiping her hands on her jeans before sitting on the couch. Achilla couldn't help but notice how much Brendan and Sam looked at each other for approval. For some reason, the sight of Sam looking back at Brendan with a smile on her face made Achilla smile too.

"Go to the party, Achilla," Brendan said with a wave of his hand as he walked into the kitchen. "I think we can trust you with Dahntay for a night. I'll pick you up from the train station in Stratford by 11 p.m. I'm cooking tonight."

"Cook it up, Big Daddy!" Sam called from the living room to the laughter of Brendan and Achilla alike. "Show me what you're working with!"

It had been a long time since Achilla traveled to Bridgeport. Dahntay's cousin lived just a few blocks from the Trumbull/Bridgeport border. As her father drove her to the house, Achilla watched the street signs turn from green to blue. She noticed that this section of Bridgeport was hilly and wooded with a few colonial-style houses and ranches lining the streets. It was nothing like the high rises Downtown or the smokestacks by I-95. Achilla wondered if her father would have ever found her if she lived in this section of town.

Brendan dropped her off at a yellow colonial ranch with music blaring out of the windows. He kissed her goodbye, and Achilla stepped out of the car wearing a red t-shirt, blue jeans, and white shell-toe sneakers. They were having a warm April, and the humid air stuck to Achilla's skin while the scent of rain filled her nose as she strolled through the even cut grass. When she reached the house and rang the doorbell, she looked through the window and saw kids dancing to reggae music. Dahntay opened the door wearing a black tall tee and baggy black jeans with a black and white Negro Leagues fitted cap. The stench of beer flowed outside as he grabbed her hand to lead her into the house. Achilla ripped her hand free and stepped through the door. Dahntay frowned at her.

"Something wrong?" Dahntay asked

"Yeah, I can walk in myself," Achilla replied.

"Right," Dahntay said with a sideways stare. "I'll leave the rest of the night up to you then. Punch is in the back."

When Dahntay turned to walk away, Achilla grabbed his arm

and jerked him back. Dahntay stumbled and nearly fell on his face. He looked at her with a scowl as Achilla pulled him close by his belt. Achilla grinned back.

"Achilla, are you trying to break my arm?" Dahntay demanded.

"You can take it," Achilla replied as she stood an inch from his face. "Dance with me."

"Later," Dahntay said as he tried to turn away. Achilla held him fast. Despite the fact that he outweighed her by ninety pounds, he couldn't escape her grip. Achilla smirked before she pulled him close and kissed him on the lips. Dahntay stared at her as she led him by the hand into the living room.

"We're dancing now," Achilla said as she snatched Dahntay's cap and placed it on her head while Usher's "Yeah" blasted throughout the house. Achilla had never danced with a boy before. All she knew was what she had seen on music videos and practiced in the mirror, and how she watched Sam dance with Brendan when they thought the kids were asleep. She backed into Dahntay and lowered herself, sliding her hand against his thigh as she came back up. Dahntay grabbed her hand and spun her around before she ground against him again. Achilla and Dahntay danced and kissed for four straight songs until she grabbed his hand and led him to the stairs. At the top of the steps, Achilla pinned Dahntay against the wall and kissed him again.

"Which room?" Achilla asked as she gripped his shirt.

"You sure?" Dahntay replied.

"Which. Room?"

"That one," Dahntay said as he pointed at a brown door behind her. She turned and opened the door that led to a small bedroom with red carpeting and a full-sized bed with a red comforter and white sheets. Without a moment's thought, Achilla grabbed Dahntay's hand and pulled him inside. She then shoved him onto the bed.

"Damn, girl," Dahntay chuckled. "What did I do to deserve this?"

"You're nice to me," Achilla replied as she bit her lip.

"I'm sure a lot of heads are nice to you," Dahntay said as he pulled his shoes off.

"Yeah, but you actually mean it," Achilla said. "I'm ready, and I think you're the right guy."

"Are you sure?"

"No more questions," Achilla replied with a grin as she walked toward the bed. "I said I was ready. That means now."

Sex with Dahntay was not what Achilla expected. It was nice. It was different, but nothing that motivated the screams and moans she used to hear every day coming from Ailina's bedroom. Achilla lay in bed next to Dahntay with her arms crossed. There had to be more to it. She turned over, grabbed her shirt from the floor, and pulled her it over her head.

"You're leaving?" Dahntay asked while she got dressed. "Hey, how was it for you?"

"It was all right," Achilla muttered.

"First time I've heard that."

"You don't have to show off," Achilla said. "It was my first time, not yours. Any mishaps were probably my fault."

"That was your first time?" Dahntay asked as he sat up in bed. "I mean if I knew you were a virgin, I would've gone slower."

"Don't play yourself, Dahntay," Achilla snorted as she tied her shoes. "We both know I was in the driver's seat the whole time."

"What made you do that?" Dahntay asked. "I've never seen a virgin act like that."

"I don't know," Achilla said with a shrug as she walked toward the door. "I just did it."

"Man," Dahntay said with a chuckle. "I have never seen a girl like you."

"I'll take that as a compliment," Achilla replied. "But the truth is I wasn't satisfied. We'll have to practice; if you're up for it I mean."

"Sure, when would--"

"I'll call you when I'm ready again," Achilla replied with a wave of her hand. "Bye."

"Wait, Achilla, I'm supposed to drive you to the train station," Dahntay said as he rushed out of the bed and threw on his pants. "Your pops will kick my ass if he finds out you left by yourself."

"Then he won't find out," Achilla said with a shrug. "I can get there just fine on my own. It's been a while, but I still know my way."

"I can't let you do that--"

"You don't have a choice," Achilla snapped as she stared Dahntay down. "I can do whatever I please. I told you I'm walking, and that's it. Clear?"

"Whoa, OK, Boss Lady," Dahntay said with his hands raised. "Hey that's your choice, but keep in mind that this isn't Stratford. It's Bridgeport. A city. With crime. And it's about ten at night."

"Thanks for the newsflash," Achilla replied as she walked out of the bedroom and trotted down the stairs. Achilla frowned at herself as she walked out the front door. She didn't lie to Dahntay. She had no clue what came over her. For the past hour, all she cared about was hooking up. It was all she cared about the second she left her father's car. Once she got what she wanted, she just left him in the house like an empty can of beer. Achilla felt a tinge of guilt, but it was too late to turn back. She watched the rest of the party dance to Li'l John and walked out the door.

Achilla walked all the way Downtown on her own and made it to the Bridgeport Metro-North Train Station. It looked a lot smaller than when she passed by it as an eleven-year-old, but it was the same old gray contraption it had always been. Achilla crossed the trafficless street and checked the change in her pocket. She had enough for a ride home.

Before she walked into the station, Achilla stopped when she felt the hair on the back of her neck stand on end. Her hands shook and her heart raced when she had the strongest urge to look around for a threat. Something was coming. Achilla stood stock still and pretended to count her money as she scanned the area with her eyes and ears. She shoved her money into her pocket and looked to her left when she heard high-heeled shoes popping on the pavement as they walked toward her.

A tall, olive-skinned brunette wearing a tight black t-shirt, form-fitting jeans, and leather, high-heeled boots approached with one hand in her pocket. Her green eyes glowed in the shadows before she stepped into one of the train station lights. It had been four years, but Achilla would recognize her own mother anywhere. Achilla felt sweat gathering under her armpits when Ailina looked at her and held her hands on her hips like a parent whose child came home too late. No hug. No questions about how she's been after all this time. Ailina's face didn't hold an ounce of concern.

The stark difference between her and the Johnsons couldn't have been any clearer.

"I was wondering when you'd make it out here," Ailina said with a smirk. "You know we always find a way back to our hometown? I was born in Boston, and I can't help visiting every chance I get. I have a theory that we're naturally territorial."

"What?" Achilla asked with a cringe. "Who's territorial?"

"Superior beings like me and you," Ailina said with as she pointed her finger and popped the gum in her mouth. "We're not the same as everyone else, but we have our habits too. My father used to drag me to Philly every summer because that was where he was born. Speaking of my father, man, talk about superior--"

"Why do you keep calling me that?" Achilla asked. "You keep saying I'm superior."

"It's true," Ailina chuckled as she looked up at the night sky. "From what I hear, your strength's coming along pretty good. You really put a number on those girls, and I'm glad you put that pussy Stanley in his place. If any man wants to touch you, he needs your permission."

"That's true with any woman," Achilla said with a shrug. "Or else it's rape. That's a fundamental human right. It doesn't make me superior to anyone."

"Oh, but you should make him beg for the privilege," Ailina said with a flicker in her eyes. "It's so much fun when they beg for it. It's even more fun when they say no at first but can't resist you. But I'm sure you're finding that out already. You smell like sex."

"I....what?" Achilla asked as she sniffed her shirt.

"It's not that strong," Ailina said with a wave of her hand. "Don't worry, your father won't notice. He never did when I was with him. I'm assuming he told you about our break up?"

"You lied about him," Achilla replied. "He's not a selfish man at all. He's a great dad to me and a great husband to--"

"He never communicated with you for eleven years--"

"He didn't know I existed," Achilla snapped before pointing her finger. "And that was because *you* didn't tell him. You know exactly where I am, and you've made no effort to reach out to me for four years! You're the terrible parent here, not him!"

"You're developing your own opinions," Ailina said with a head nod as she paced the sidewalk. "You're thinking critically. I bet even right now your thinking is above most people's heads and far beyond anyone your age. You're what, fifteen? "

"Yeah, so?"

"The mind comes first," Ailina replied. "And it'll only get stronger. You'll watch people interact, and you'll wonder how everyone can be so stupid, but then it'll hit you. They're not stupid. You're just better. You'll notice that you have a photographic memory too. I bet that's how you found your way here after your little house party."

"You're talking crazy--"

"Your body comes a little later," Ailina said with a wide grin. "But you're developing faster than I did. You think you're strong now? Wait about a year, and things will really get interesting. And get a boyfriend soon. Your libido's going to go through the roof, and it's not socially acceptable to have more than one man at your age. You can do what you want once you hit your twenties. It's easier to hide men from each other when you have your own place--"

"That's way too much info," Achilla said as she held her head in her hands. "Why are you telling me this? I'm not like you."

"You're more like me than you think," Ailina replied as she leaned against the train station door. "A lot more. Tell me something, how easy was your first time? I bet you weren't the least bit nervous. I wasn't."

"I'm not discussing my sex life with you!" Achilla said with a scowl.

"I meant the fight," Ailina said with a crazed look in her eyes. "Stanley was your first real opponent and you took him so easily. I bet it was like breathing. My first time was a soccer coach who got a little too friendly. I broke both of his arms and held his balls until he begged for permission to have them back. I've been hooked ever since. Tell me about your fight with Stanley. Wasn't it exhilarating?"

Ailina didn't know about Marty. She most likely only heard about Stanley because the police were somewhat involved. Achilla decided to keep her fight with Marty to herself. The less Ailina knew about her the better. Achilla shook her head and crossed her arms.

"No," Achilla said as she backed away. "I did what I had to do out of fear, not some weird fetish for hurting people. I'm not like you, Ailina. I don't enjoy--"

"We're on a first name basis now?" Ailina asked with a snort. "Brendan put the works on you. I bet he's got you playing nice with his little brat too. Maybe I should go over there and get rid of them so you can come to your senses and--"

"Samuel's not a brat," Achilla snarled. "He's my brother, and you'd better not go near any of them. I won't let you."

Ailina blinked twice before standing up straight. She then threw her head back and laughed into the night air. Her cackle sounded like a train running on frozen tracks. After four years of not having to hear it anymore, it made Achilla's spine shiver. Ailina laughed until she bent over double. When she finished, she stared at Achilla with eyes that froze her feet to the ground.

"It's…it's not a joke," Achilla stammered as she shook her head. "I won't let you hurt my family--"

Achilla grunted from a sharp pain in her gut as her feet left the ground. Ailina had covered the ten feet of space between them before Achilla could react and punched her midsection. After years of fighting her as a child, she had never seen Ailina move that fast or felt her hit that hard. Achilla coughed as tears jerked from her eyes. She fell to her knees, and Ailina picked her up by her shirt and held her against the wall.

"The next time you talk shit to me," Ailina whispered in her ear. "You'd better be able to back it up. Or you could at least stand where the cameras could see you. I would never show my abilities to the entire world. Living in secret is the beauty of being superior. I'm sure you're finding that out too."

Achilla grabbed Ailina's arm, but it was no use. Her legs dangled and her eyes turned bloodshot as Ailina lifted her higher. It was no different than when she was a child. It was as if the gap between them hadn't changed no matter how hard Achilla worked.

Just how strong was Ailina?

"I'm actually holding back right now," Ailina said. "I wouldn't want you to go to the hospital and have your father ask a whole bunch of questions. So why don't we keep this little conversation a secret, hm? You tell anyone, and I'm coming for your family as you call them. And you're right. I know exactly where you are."

Ailina dropped Achilla on the ground. As Achilla struggled to her feet, she saw a small black bag fall on the sidewalk. She looked up at Ailina who still stood in front of her with her hands on her hips. Achilla set her jaw and stood up straight. Ailina smiled and nodded her head.

"Good, you haven't gotten soft," Ailina said. "That's for your fifteenth birthday. Your body's strong enough to take a hit, but you'll need more than physical fitness to meet your true potential. Get out there and fight. Legally. Keep your skills sharp."

"Why...would you help me?" Achilla asked through labored breath as Ailina turned her back and walked away.

"I told you we're the same," Ailina said over her shoulder. "And I always help my own. Go ahead and catch your train. Your father should be at the Stratford stop any minute. He's almost never late to anything. Oh, and I'll be checking your progress."

Achilla walked hunched over to the ticket booth, bought her ticket, and boarded the next train. The pain in her abdomen lessened, but it still throbbed, and when she lifted her t-shirt, she spotted a purple bruise the size of her fist. As she watched the train pass by Bridgeport toward Stratford, Achilla let a tear drop down her face. She promised herself that she would protect her family from Ailina, but now she knew that she couldn't. She opened the bag and found a pair of hand wraps. She would take Ailina's advice and start fighting, but she wouldn't do it for her. She would do it so she could better protect her family. Achilla winced from the pain in her gut as she leaned back into her seat. She closed her eyes for the remaining few minutes until she could hop into her father's car and go home.

Connecticut is one of the few states in the country to have all four seasons in the extreme. The winters are brutal with low temperatures and snow storms dumping up to three feet of snow at a time. The autumns are filled with brisk afternoons and leaves of every color turning the mountain ranges into works of art. The spring always enters with rumbling thunderstorms but always ends with warm air and flowers on trees that were once barren. The spring always reminds you that there is life after a Connecticut winter.

However, the summer in Connecticut is the season where everything truly comes alive. The beaches in Bridgeport, Milford, and New Haven fill up with people wearing two-piece bikinis, baggy swimming trunks, and layers of sunscreen. Festivals like Stratford Day shut down its Main Street for hours with vendors selling everything from hot sauce flavored honey to fried dough. Basketball tournaments like the Rest In Peace Tournament in Bridgeport are in full swing with loud music and the best ballplayers in the state competing for the championship. And after attending every event you can, you can always grab an Italian ice at the local corner store or a scoop of ice cream at Rich's Farm in Oxford. Summer in Connecticut is the best time of the year, and Achilla's summer before her junior year was no different.

Achilla made her mark by playing in girl's leagues all over the state. She had her best games in Hartford, Bridgeport, and New Haven where the competition was fiercest. Soon Achilla started to decorate the living room with her medals and trophies. She also used the money she had saved to take boxing, Muay Thai, Brazilian jiu-jitsu, tai chi, and jeet kune do classes. With the exception of tai chi and jeet kune do, she didn't learn anything new. After a month of combined courses, she was able to take down all of her instructors. Striking was her favorite part of sparring, and she often broke heavy bags when she stayed late at any gym. After breaking her third bag, she decided it was better to work out at home. She bought a heavy bag and installed it herself without telling her parents.

"Achilla!" Brendan called from the basement while Achilla was eating breakfast. Achilla left her bowl of cereal and tip-toed downstairs in her red basketball shorts and gray cut-off shirt. She saw her father standing next to the black heavy bag in his pinstriped black suit and yellow tie, and his eyes glared at her. Achilla lowered her head when she approached.

"When did you put this in?" Brendan asked. "And your mother just told me you're taking five martial arts classes? Who's paying for that?"

"I am," Achilla said. "I saved most of my checks during the school year, and I put in the bag two days ago. You can use it if you want-"

"I don't like people installing things in my house without telling me first," Brendan snapped.

"OK, well I can take it down," Achilla said as she shuffled her feet. "I might have to anyway. I've been running through bags at the gym."

"What do you mean running through bags?"

"I mean...never mind," Achilla sighed as she thought of a way to twist the truth. "I'm not allowed to use the heavy bag at the gym anymore. Apparently, they don't have the right one for me."

Brendan sighed and shook his head.

"Well, maybe this'll raise the property value," Brendan said as he stared at the bag's chain with his hands on his hips. "I suppose there's no harm in keeping it. Sometimes, I wish you'd slow down, Achilla, and realize that the world doesn't revolve around you. You can't just do whatever you want and neglect everyone."

"Who have I neglected?" Achilla asked. "Did I miss something?"

"I'm hosting a barbecue for my firm, remember?" Brendan said. "It's to celebrate our sixteenth anniversary."

"Great," Achilla said with a smile. "When is it?"

"Next week," Brendan replied. "I've been telling you that for weeks, but we've all been talking to your back because you're always out the door. When's the last time you've seen your brother?"

"Oh man," Achilla said. "Maybe a week?"

"He's helping with the guest list," Brendan said. "Reach out to him and tell him who you're inviting."

"Nobody," Achilla said.

"Not Dahntay?" Brendan asked with a frown. "Did you two break up or something?"

"We were never together, Dad," Achilla said. "We're just friends."

"Oh, is that right?" Brendan chuckled with his hands on his hips as he walked past Achilla to the steps. "I've heard that story way too many times before. It never turns out well."

"I'm not leading him on, if that's what you mean--"

"Yeah, sure, Achilla."

"I've made everything perfectly clear," Achilla yelled at her father's back as he walked up the steps. Achilla spotted a full-length mirror against the wall opposite the steps and studied herself in it. Her body was becoming more defined and she had grown to about five-foot-seven. Last Achilla checked she was able to do five hundred handstand pushups and three hundred pull-ups in a superset without stopping. Ailina was right. Achilla was developing an Amazonian figure and strength.

Ailina was right about something else too. Achilla and Dahntay were not officially a couple, but she was at his house at least three times a week and every day since she started her martial arts classes. She repeatedly told Dahntay that he was free to date other people, but she knew he wouldn't. He was too good of a guy, even when Achilla wasn't good to him. One day after Achilla came home from one of her summer league games, Dahntay called her cell phone.

"Hello?"

"Hey, what's up?" Dahntay asked. "Look, I have a weightlifting competition coming up this Friday and--"

"Can't make it," Achilla said before she pulled out her key and opened the front door to her house.

"Oh...OK."

"Yeah, I have three classes on Friday," Achilla said as she walked into the living room and spotted her dad lying on the couch on a rare day off. "Then I have to do my off-season training."

"Right," Dahntay said.

"I'm sure Samuel could make it," Achilla replied. "Want me to ask him?"

"No, I asked you to come," Dahntay snapped. "Why are you blowing me off, man?"

"Don't be a girl, Dahntay," Achilla shot back. "You lift weights every day. What's the big deal?"

"The big deal is I come to your games," Dahntay replied. "I mean, I don't see why you can't make one thing for me, and I don't see how saying that makes me *a girl*. What kind of bullshit is that?"

"Look, that was your choice," Achilla said. "I don't have to go to anything if I don't want to, and I don't want to go, so I'm not going."

"That's fucked up, Achilla," Dahntay said.

"Whatever, bye," Achilla snapped as she hung up the phone. She looked at the ceiling of the living room when she heard her father approaching from behind. When she turned and faced him, he leaned against the doorway wearing a red t-shirt and black basketball shorts that matched Achilla's. He gave Achilla the same stare he always gave her when he disapproved of something. Achilla looked away for a split second before forcing herself to look back.

"Look, I know what you're going to say-"

"Good, then this won't take long," Brendan said. "You know why I like Dahntay so much?"

"Because he's nicer than Stanley?" Achilla asked. "And because he's another brother with family in Bridgeport."

"No," Brendan replied.

"Oh, come on, Dad," Achilla scoffed. "You can't tell me that wasn't at least a factor."

"Nope," Brendan said with a shrug. "But he reminds me of myself when I was younger. Watching how you're treating him right now, you're just like a girlfriend I had a while ago."

"What was she like?" Achilla asked.

"Mean," Brendan said. "Selfish. She always expected me to give to her, but giving anything to me was too much of an inconvenience."

"I remind you of someone like that?" Achilla muttered.

"Yep," Brendan said. "But do you know what about you reminds me of her the most?"

"What?" Achilla asked.

"You have her eyes," Brendan said with a wink before walking past Achilla to the front door. "Yep, you can't miss those Harris eyes."

Achilla's heart sunk to her feet as she watched her father walk out the door. After that conversation, she knew she had to break things off with Dahntay. Achilla refused to be like Ailina and treat a boy like plastic silverware. She had to let him down easy. He deserved better. That was what Achilla told herself as she sulked and ambled upstairs to shower and change.

During her next visit, Achilla woke up in Dahntay's bedroom. He lived right behind Nichols Elementary School, and Achilla could hear the kids playing basketball on the outside court from his bedroom window. She yawned, got dressed in her khaki shorts, thong sandals, and blue t-shirt and strolled down the hall to the kitchen where she followed the scent of smoldering beef. Dahntay stood in blue swimming trunks and no shirt while he grilled burgers on a black mini grill on the white kitchen counter. Achilla rolled her eyes as she stood in the middle of the linoleum floor and crossed her arms. He was actually willing to cook for her.

"Hey," Dahntay said. "You hungry--?"

"Stop," Achilla snapped.

"Stop, what?" Dahntay asked. "I mean, it's cool if you don't want any. That leaves more for me, but you don't know what you're missing."

"Stop being so damn nice to me," Achilla said with her head low. "I'm not that nice to you."

"Achilla, what are you talking about?"

"I use you for sex," Achilla replied. "I don't call you unless I'm horny, and I always refuse to go out with you."

"Sounds like a good arrangement to me," Dahntay said with a shrug.

"Yeah?" Achilla snapped. "Then why do you keep asking me out, and why do you keep cooking for me? You're treating me like a girlfriend, and I don't deserve it. You treat a lot of girls better than they deserve. I bet you were always nice to Monika too."

"I was," Dahntay said. "And then I left her when I realized she was stepping out. The worst part was she had no guilt about it. She just expected me to accept it. I couldn't. I broke it off."

"She sounds like someone I know," Achilla muttered. "Someone I refuse to be. Look, you need to find a girl who's nicer to you. I'm not it. Eat the burgers yourself. I'm going home. I'm not coming back."

"Just like that?" Dahntay asked.

"Just like that," Achilla replied. "I think it's for your own good."

"I don't think you care about that," Dahntay said with a hard stare. "Like you said, you were just using me, right? Maybe you just found somebody else."

"Not yet," Achilla sighed. "And I told you over and over that you could see other people. You just refused to, and I couldn't see someone else knowing that you weren't. It wouldn't have felt right."

"So you're just tired of being my girlfriend then?" Dahntay demanded.

"We're not boyfriend and girlfriend--"

"Achilla, get the hell out of here!"

"I don't understand why you're so angry," Achilla growled. "You don't have to deal with me anymore. You should be happy."

"Maybe because I never saw it as *dealing with you*," Dahntay said. "Man, for somebody so smart, you talk a lot of negative shit about yourself. Anybody ever tell you that?"

"Right, well I'm not putting you through any more crap," Achilla said as she turned her back and walked toward the front door. "We're done. Find someone else. Please."

"If you mean that, then go ahead," Dahntay replied to Achilla's back as she opened the door. "But don't come back around here again."

Achilla walked home. The further she got from Dahntay's house, the larger the lump in her throat grew. She swallowed it and continued to walk until she got home. Samuel was in the driveway shooting on their hoop wearing a white t-shirt and black shorts. Achilla hadn't noticed until now, but he had a growth spurt and was now around Brendan's height and he wielded long, sinewy arms that flexed when he shot a jump shot. When he spotted Achilla, he set the ball down and jogged toward her.

"Hey, Achilla," Samuel said. "Been a while. So look, I need to know who you're bringing to the barbecue."

"Nobody," Achilla said.

"Not Dahntay?" Samuel asked.

"No," Achilla replied with a wavering voice. "We just broke up."

"Oh," Samuel said. "I didn't know he was your boyfriend."

"He wasn't," Achilla said as her eyes welled up. She leaned into Samuel's shoulder and blubbered all over his t-shirt. Samuel held her and patted her back. Achilla didn't know how long she sobbed into her brother's dingy basketball shirt, but she didn't stop until she was out of tears. She then stood up straight and wiped her nose.

"Sorry," Achilla said. "I'm the older one here. I should be stronger."

"I guess it's cool to cry when things hurt, right?" Samuel replied.

"Yeah," Achilla said with a smile. "I guess it is."

"Maybe the barbecue will take your mind off it," Samuel said. "We'll be playing basketball. You can play on my team, even if it's chops."

"It's definitely chops," Achilla replied. "But I'm all right with that."

"Cool," Samuel said as he turned to grab his ball. "Um...look... I don't know how to say this."

"Just spit it out."

"Our grandparents are going to be there," Samuel said. "They don't come over often. They don't get along when they do. Grandpa Price can be--"

"A selfish asshole who cares more about his career than his family?" Achilla asked. "I got that memo a long time ago."

"Yeah," Samuel said. "But Grandma Johnson isn't much better. She has this thing about white women and having kids with them. She gives Dad a hard time about it now that you've moved in with us. I won't repeat the stuff she says."

"Thanks for the heads up, but I'm sure I could've found that out myself," Achilla said. "Why the forewarning?"

"I overheard Mom on the phone with both of them," Samuel said. "Well, not Grandpa Price. They don't talk, but she spoke to Grandma Price about him instead; even though they're divorced. It's weird. Anyway, they don't like you, but they seem to like me. If they give you a hard time, let me know. I'll run interference."

"Thanks," Achilla said with a frown.

"You would do the same for me," Samuel said with a shrug. "What are siblings for, right?"

"Well, you've always been better with people," Achilla sighed.

"You could be good with people too if you tried," Samuel said.

"No," Achilla replied as she shook her head and walked toward the house. "Not like you anyway. You'll always be safer than I am."

Samuel shrugged and shot another jump shot. As expected, he didn't get what Achilla meant. Achilla could already foresee Samuel's future. He was going to be a successful lawyer just like Brendan; maybe even better. He had the natural flair and confidence to draw people to him and make friends. Achilla was convinced that she wasn't designed that way. As she walked into the house, Achilla thought of Ailina and for the first time felt sorry for her. If this was the superiority that she preached about, then she could have it.

Chapter Fourteen

Achilla arrived home with a plan. She decided that she would not tell her mother any details of her conversation with Ailina. Living with a lawyer for over eighteen years must have taught Sam that Achilla had just committed conspiracy to murder, and Achilla couldn't afford her knowing about it. The fewer people in on the conspiracy the better. As she marched up the walkway, Achilla heard "Mas que Nada" blasting from the house. No doubt that was Sandy's influence. Sam was the last person to listen to any contemporary music. Achilla tossed her keys in the air before opening the front door.

Once inside, Achilla saw Sandy dancing with a tall, black man wearing a grey hoody, jeans, and a New York Yankees fitted cap. Sandy held his hands and her feet moved like stones skipping on water while her hips swayed side to side. The man struggled to keep up, but his two-step indicated that he had natural rhythm. Achilla smiled and crossed her arms as she leaned against the doorway. Sandy then pointed behind the man, and he turned around. Achilla flinched when she saw the wide smile that she had known for years.

Before she could stop herself, Achilla bounded across the room and hugged her brother around the ribs.

"Achilla!" Samuel grunted and she let go.

"You've grown so much!" Achilla said. "Oh my God, this is incredible!"

"You look different too," Samuel said with a voice so deep Achilla could hardly recognize it. "Damn how'd you get so cut?"

"You know I work out," Achilla replied with a smile. "I saw your games, you know, and I'm really proud of how well you played against Boston. You were strong, you were aggressive, you were efficient, everything you were supposed to be. Man, you have *really* grown!"

"Thanks," Samuel said. "Yeah, I was serving them out there. Soon as I get back, I'll be serving them again."

"You have more confidence than before," Achilla said with her hands on her hips. "That's good. I'm impressed."

"It's all thanks to you," Samuel replied. "Honestly, the conditioning coaches won't come near me because they don't want to mess anything up. You should seriously be a personal trainer."

"She's going to teach me how to fight," Sandy said as she bounced up and down and held Samuel's arm. "Then I'll be able to beat you up, so you'd better be nice to me."

"Looks like you've met Sandy," Achilla said with a laugh. "Don't mind her. She's a sweetheart."

"I don't know," Samuel said. "She acts like she's the boss of somebody."

"That just means she likes you," Achilla replied with a tap on Samuel's shoulder. "As long as you don't actually do what she says, it's cool."

"Hey!" Sandy said with a frown. "Whose side are you on?"

"My brother's always," Achilla said as she stretched her arms and walked into the kitchen. "Where's Mom?"

"Grocery shopping," Samuel said as he followed behind her. "Look, Mom said you went to see Ailina?"

Achilla should have seen this conversation coming. She stopped and rested her hands on the island. She had to remember how sensitive Samuel could be. She also couldn't tell him what she and Ailina discussed. If Samuel found out that Achilla was planning to murder someone, even their father's killer, he would never forgive her. She was sure of that.

"Yeah," Achilla sighed. "Look, I know that you guys think she wanted to kill you, but--"

"She didn't," Samuel replied. "I know. She told me."

Achilla whirled around and faced Samuel.

"When?" Achilla demanded. "How? *When*?!"

"Senior year," Samuel replied as he sat at the kitchen table. "She told me everything about you and the CIA."

"You should've told me," Achilla said as she pointed her finger at the floor. "She is not to come near you! You should've told me!"

"Didn't want you to get hurt again," Samuel said as he shrugged.

"I can take care of myself!" Achilla yelled.

"All right, well so can I," Samuel snapped. "I'm not some punk little kid anymore, Achilla."

"Neither was Dad!" Achilla replied, causing Samuel and Sandy to lower their heads. "It doesn't matter if you're a *punk* or not! Ailina is too dangerous for trained killers; forget any of you! I'm the only person in this house who can stand up to her! You're not supposed to be alone with her!"

Achilla held her head in her hands as she paced the kitchen. Ailina never once mentioned that she met up with Samuel. She knew that woman was hiding something. What did she say to him? What did she do to him? Ailina's manipulation was limitless. Achilla needed to fix whatever damage she had already done.

"OK," Achilla said as she wiped a strand of hair from her face and stood with her hands on her hips. "OK, I need every detail of that meeting, Samuel. I need to know what she said to you."

"You first," Samuel replied.

"I can't do that," Achilla said. "It's for your own good."

"That's some bullshit," Samuel barked and rose to his feet. "You've been lying to us for years. You owe me at least an even trade."

"Hey, guys," Sandy said as she stood between them. "Why don't we calm down and play some music--"

"I had no choice," Achilla barked back. "I was trying to protect you."

"A lot of good that did," Samuel scoffed. "They played you."

"Never again," Achilla growled. "I will help you as best I can, but it has to be on my terms. I know things that you don't."

"Well let's hear some of those things," Samuel yelled. "Starting with you!"

"Guys, please," Sandy said as she lowered her head and cross her arms. "Stop fighting."

"Who are you, Achilla?" Samuel bellowed. "I know there's a lot more to you than you're showing, and I don't want you hiding from us anymore! We're a family!"

"I'm human just like you," Achilla replied.

"Not from what I've seen," Samuel said. "And neither's Ailina, but at least she doesn't hide it. Hell, she's *proud* of it."

"You talk as if I've committed some crime just by standing here!" Achilla snarled. "Like I'm some freak! God, why does everyone look at me like some zoo animal?"

"I'm talking like you've been lying to us even before you left for the CIA," Samuel replied. "When are you going to be straight with us?"

"It was for your own good!"

"Get the fuck out of here with that bullshit!" Samuel spat.

"It's not bullshit!" Achilla screamed as she smacked her fist into her palm. "I'm trying to protect everybody, but you're too fucking stupid to listen!"

"Stop!" Sandy screeched as she ran across the room and hugged Samuel's side. "Stop fighting, both of you! I'm tired of hearing people fight all the time! Stop it!"

Samuel sighed and patted Sandy's hand. Achilla shook her head and held her hands on her hips. Of course, Sandy was the sensitive one here. Sandy looked at Achilla with tears in her eyes. Achilla looked away before taking a deep breath and steadying her trembling hands.

"All right," Achilla said. "I suppose I can answer your question."

"Yeah, me too," Samuel replied.

"I don't know what our real name is," Achilla sighed as she leaned against the island with her arms crossed. "But the CIA named us Nephilim."

"That's from the Bible," Samuel replied as he sat back down. "Offspring of angels or something, right?"

"Precisely," Achilla said. "We're more like a strain of humans who evolved differently. It's kind of like watching Lebron James play against high schoolers. It's pretty obvious that he doesn't belong there, right? He belonged in the pros even at eighteen years old. Well, that's how I am. Every day, I feel like I don't belong. Only Ailina's on my level."

"Why don't you belong?" Sandy asked with a frown as she stood behind Samuel.

"This part you both know," Achilla said. "My physiology is way above the average human being. Since I don't have any examples to learn from, I tend to surprise myself. Growing up I used to really hurt people, and even now my strength is increasing at a rate that's hard to control; especially when I'm angry."

"Well, isn't Ailina that example?" Samuel asked.

"Not quite," Achilla muttered. "Nephilim are divided into different types. According to the CIA, I'm a brute, or a warrior, something like that. I guess Ailina's more of a tactician. That's what I've gathered so far from the little the CIA's told me."

"She seemed like a warrior to me," Samuel said.

"It's all relative," Achilla replied. "I could easily break her in half, and she knows it. I could feel it when we met."

"Feel what?" Samuel asked as Sandy walked around and held his side.

"Fear," Achilla said with a slight grin. "She fears me."

"A lot of people are probably afraid of you," Sandy added. "But I've never seen fear stop someone from hurting someone else. I mean, if anything fear made someone more likely to do it."

"I agree," Samuel replied. "Achilla, you said yourself she's the brains. If she's so scared of you, why would she talk to you without some sort of scheme in mind?"

"You make a good point," Achilla replied. "But I have a plan of my own."

"And you're not going to share that either," Samuel said with his arms crossed.

"Sorry."

"Achilla…"

"You'll thank me later," Achilla said. "I know it feels patronizing, and maybe it is, but I know what I'm doing. If Mom trusts me, why can't you?"

"Maybe she just knows she can't stop you," Samuel replied.

"All the more reason," Achilla said with a shrug. "You can't stop me either. Might as well do as I say."

"You sound like Nina," Sandy muttered.

"You and I both know why this isn't the same," Achilla stated with a slight glare in her eyes while maintaining a straight face. "We don't have to get into that right now."

Sandy shook her head and walked out of the kitchen.

"What was that about?" Samuel asked.

"Nothing," Achilla sighed. "She's just sensitive. Look I'm pretty sure Mom left a box of some of my old clothes in the guest room upstairs. I'm going to run through it. No offense, but I don't plan on repping Duke during our father's funeral."

"Hold on," Samuel said. "I have a bad feeling about this meeting with Ailina. I need to know more."

"I get that I haven't been forthright with you," Achilla replied with her hand raised. "But seriously, the details of that meeting cannot be shared."

"Not good enough."

"It'll have to be good enough," Achilla snapped. "Why do you keep fighting me on this?"

"Because I'm concerned about you," Samuel replied. "Achilla, you can't make deals with the devil and expect to win."

"Right, more Christianity," Achilla snorted. "Fine, let's play that game. I'm pretty sure God made a deal with the devil in the Book of Job."

"Well I'm pretty sure you're not God," Samuel replied. "And I think it was a bet that He knew he'd win."

"Look, I know what I'm doing, all right?" Achilla said with a wave of her hand as she turned her back. "I expected this kind of nagging from Mom."

"She let you go because she can't stop you," Samuel said. "And neither can I. Just thought I'd let you know that this doesn't look good."

"How about we focus on Dad's funeral," Achilla said as she walked up the stairs. "If you need my help with anything, let me know."

"Yeah, one thing."

"Shoot," Achilla replied from the top of the steps.

"Help me understand you," Samuel said with his hands raised. "Help us understand. You can't be *that* different; even if you're a Nephilim, or whatever it's called."

Achilla sighed and walked back down the steps. She stood under Samuel's nose. He was taller now. He was also at least ten pounds heavier. Still lifting him would be no problem. As frustrated as she was with him right now, throwing him across the street would be pretty easy. Instead, Achilla grabbed Samuel's shirt and pulled him over her shoulder. She then lifted him over her head before twirling him around five times and setting him down. Samuel stumbled and fell to the floor.

"Don't move," Achilla said. "It'll make the nausea worse."

"Why'd you--"

"Notice how different the world looks to you," Achilla said. "See how the house is moving? See how I'm moving with it?"

"Yeah," Samuel replied with a slur to his voice. "Yeah, there's also two of you."

"Imagine a world that looks like this," Achilla said with her arms spread wide. "Imagine a world that changes by the day because your senses keep getting sharper. Imagine that your world is different from everyone else's, and you have no clue why. Stand up."

Samuel rose to his feet and stumbled forward. Achilla ducked under his right arm and held him upright. He was heavier all right, but not heavy enough to pose any challenge for Achilla. She saw no reason to show him, but tossing him in the air would be no different than playing with a newborn baby. For now, she would settle for holding him up.

"See how you almost fell?" Achilla asked. "That's how I feel around people. I'm always worried that I'll lose control and break something valuable or hurt someone innocent. Take all of this and imagine that you're eleven years old. That's how I felt when I came to this house and went to public school. This isn't the cartoons where Goku punches a hole in a car and becomes a hero later. If I expose myself too much, I end up with bullets in my head floating in a tank somewhere-"

Samuel's shaking body and slight chuckle interrupted Achilla's train of thought.

"What's so funny?" Achilla asked. "This is a serious conversation, Samuel."

"Did you just say Goku?" Samuel asked. "As in Dragonball Z? Since when do you watch cartoons?"

"Since I left home," Achilla sighed. "I was so isolated. I needed it to keep me sane."

"But DragonBall Z?" Samuel laughed. "You couldn't watch something with a little depth?"

"Tell me you're not serious," Achilla snapped. "Akira Toriyama is one of the best manga authors of the--"

"You actually know the author?" Samuel snickered.

"Don't laugh at me," Achilla replied with a slight pout. "I'm trying to be serious, and you're making fun of me."

"I can't help it."

"Well then maybe I can't help twirling you like a baton again."

"All right, all right, I'll stop."

Achilla heard Sam's car pull in the driveway. As she listened to her footsteps coming up the walkway, Achilla helped Samuel to the staircase and set him down on the bottom steps. He leaned back and rested his head against the wall and bent his legs to keep his feet on the stairs. Samuel had grown so tall and so strong. Despite the annoyance of having to deal with his questions, Achilla couldn't help but smile at the thought that he asked them. He was no longer a naïve boy; no longer a victim. Achilla kneeled next to him.

"You've grown," Achilla said as she patted his shoulder. "I'm proud of you."

"Thanks," Samuel said. "You've grown too."

"I haven't changed that much," Achilla muttered. "Aside from becoming more dangerous, I'm still the same."

"I disagree," Samuel replied. "You're a lot nicer."

Achilla frowned when their mother stepped into the house and shook her head as she stepped over Samuel up the steps. Achilla was many things, but she knew she wasn't nice. Nice people don't conspire to murder. As she overheard Sam telling her son to get up and help with the groceries, Achilla walked up the staircase to her room. She heard Sam call her name and ignored it as she opened the door and searched through a box of clothes next to the twin sized bed. Inside was a black dress that she used to wear to church. It might be a tad short, but it would have to do until she found something else.

"Achilla!" Sam called.

"Yeah," Achilla replied.

"Help your brother with the groceries!" Sam yelled. "You can punch a hole in the street but you can't carry a few bags?"

Achilla chuckled to herself before turning to walk out the door. She had the strength to do whatever she wanted. She had the means to live on her own. There was literally no reason for Achilla to obey Sam's command, but she walked down the steps, jogged out the door, and grabbed eight grocery bags at once. Maybe Samuel was right. Maybe she was a nicer person. That thought made Achilla smile as Sandy trotted into the foyer and took some of the bags from her. Achilla maintained that smile as she watched Sam and Sandy cook dinner. As she ate a mouth full of salty, juicy fried catfish, Achilla remembered that she was planning to murder Blue Eyes. She also remembered that she conspired with a sociopath who could very easily turn on her whole family. Achilla had to force her smile for the rest of the night before retiring to the guest room. When she heard a knock on the door, she opened it wearing her old basketball shorts and a white tall-tee.

"That's my shirt," Samuel said as he walked in.

"I wouldn't admit to that," Achilla replied as she stretched her arms and sat on her bed. "I always thought it was a nightie."

"And I always told you it was the style," Samuel said.

"You didn't come here to claim your shirt," Achilla asked as Samuel leaned against the wall across from the bed. "What's up?"

"Look, I heard you on the phone," Samuel said. "When I told you about Dad. I'm pretty sure I've never heard someone scream like that, even after a broken leg. You OK?"

"I'm fine," Achilla replied. "I mean, no, I'm not, but I have to be."

"No, you don't," Samuel replied. "None of us do. I wish I knew who it was, man, I'd--"

"Stop!" Achilla barked with a pointed finger. "I won't let you talk like that. You won't be doing anything but mourning our father. Don't even think about it."

"Why not?" Samuel growled. "You think he should just walk away?"

Samuel's eyes burned in a way Achilla often recognized in herself. She looked back and scrambled for a way to extinguish that fire. She didn't need anyone knowing about her plan with Ailina, but she especially didn't need Samuel getting the same ideas.

"I think you have too bright of a future to talk like that," Achilla said before lowering her head. "Not you. Please."

"All right, fine," Samuel said before heading for the door. "I just wanted to check on you. Sandy wants me to try these cookies."

"Wait," said Achilla as she stood up and grabbed Samuel's arm. "I have a question for you."

"What's up?"

"That girl Trish," muttered Achilla. "Have you heard from her? Do you still talk?"

"I haven't spoken to her in months," Samuel said with a shrug.

"What did she do?" Achilla asked as she looked Samuel in the eye.

"I can take care of myself."

"Not my question," Achilla demanded. "What did she do to you? I know she did something. I had a feeling you'd learn about her the hard way just like I had to learn about Stanley."

Samuel looked away for a moment before clearing his throat.

"She said some things," Samuel sighed. "Called me a loser and said my...body was all I was good for. She also called Dad unmanly."

Brendan Johnson? *Unmanly?* Achilla's fists trembled with the desire to go find Trish and ask her to explain those words with a clear, succinct, and toothless plea for mercy. Achilla took a deep breath. She just needed one more question. Her emotions would have to take a back seat to the necessary intel.

"When was this?" Achilla asked with a level voice.

"After the championship game," Samuel said. "After we had sex."

"Oh, so Dad's not a man, and you're just an athlete; an object for her entertainment?" Achilla replied with raised eyebrows as she stepped back and crossed her arms. "And she waited until after sex to say that like you're some walking sex toy? I'll address *that* later."

"Achilla, please don't."

"Nobody talks down to my brother," Achilla snapped with a finger pointed at the floor. "And *nobody* talks shit about my father. I will address her later."

"Fine, just don't catch a case."

"Oh, I won't," Achilla replied. "Has she spoken to you lately? Attempted to call you? Anything?"

"No," said Samuel as he shook his head. "I haven't heard a peep from her."

"OK," sighed Achilla. "Good. A girl like her...."

Before she finished her statement, Achilla remembered how she jumped on Agent Jones and slept with Kelly. There was no love there. No value. She just wanted something and pushed until she got it almost to the point of doing something despicable. Achilla's throat clenched as she thought of someone treating Samuel that way.

"A girl like her," Achilla said, "can't be your girlfriend. She only cares about herself and doesn't give a damn about you unless you give her what she wants. Once your usefulness ends, so does your relationship."

"How do you know that?"

"Because I've been that girl before," Achilla replied, "and I hate it."

Samuel stood in silence as Achilla looked out her window.

"You probably think I'm a hypocrite," Achilla muttered.

"Yep," Samuel said. "A big one."

"Heh," Achilla chuckled and lowered her head. "I have a million excuses, but I won't make them. The truth is I'm not much different from Ailina either."

"I agree about you being a hypocrite," Samuel said. "I don't think you're evil."

"Neither do I," Achilla replied. "But sometimes I wonder."

"Do you at least regret it?"

"Regret what exactly?"

"Being the girl you just described."

"Every day," Achilla breathed with a catch in her voice. "That's another part of being a Nephilim that I haven't mastered yet. Every desire, good or bad, is so *strong*. I can barely control myself. It's kind of like when someone tries to hurt you, Samuel. I have to protect you at all costs. If that means taking risks that nobody else would take, then so be it."

"When you fought Ailina that day," Samuel said, "you couldn't help yourself?"

"No," Achilla replied. "And I couldn't run away either. I had no time for a plan, no time to reason, I just had to fight. I had to fight for you, Dad, and Mom. I just had to...to *fight!*"

Achilla clenched her fists and bit her lip as the memories from that day tightened her muscles. She calmed down just enough to face Samuel and force a smile.

"I think we've spoken about this enough for tonight," Achilla said. "Go on and grab those cookies. I can hear Sandy pulling them out of the oven now, and they smell really good."

"You're not giving me shit about it?" Samuel asked as he half stepped toward the door.

"I think we all deserve a cheat meal right about now," Achilla replied. "Please. Eat whatever you want."

Samuel nodded his head and walked out of the door. Achilla then hopped into a set of handstand pushups to calm her nerves. So Trish never asked around about Achilla; or if she did, she never asked Samuel? That didn't rule out Trish's role in Brendan's murder, but at least Samuel wasn't involved. That would be too much for this family to bear. Achilla finished her thousandth handstand pushup and moved on to body squats before going to bed.

When she woke up the next morning, Achilla threw on her old Stratford High School basketball shorts and a gray t-shirt and tip-toed downstairs. She would normally go for a jog, but after driving all the way to Boston, she wanted to stay as close to home as possible until the time came to deal with Blue Eyes. So she walked out the backdoor into the Johnson's spacious backyard with a wooded area on the far end. She inhaled the scent of tree bark and wet dead leaves from the oak trees that lined the back of the yard before she bent over to tie her shoelaces. She stretched her arms and legs and stared into the woods that were just thick enough to be dark but thin enough that Achilla could see the other side. She estimated at least a hundred yards of vegetation before she broke into another neighborhood. Achilla leaned over into a sprinter's stance before bursting forward.

She crossed the yard in half a second and sprinted twenty yards into the trees before leaping into an oak tree to her left; scaling it with nothing but her feet and momentum before bouncing off the trunk and landing onto another tree. She then skipped through the branches until she reached the far end of the woods. As she stood out and looked into the adjacent neighborhood lined with houses of similar size, she wiped a small bead of sweat from her brow. It wasn't much of a workout, but it would at least keep her level. Fourteen more laps and she would call it a morning for her cardio. Achilla turned her back on the other neighborhood and skipped into the trees again. This time, she would cross cover the entire hundred yards in a shorter time. Achilla counted the seconds as she exhaled so hard with each step that her cheeks puffed out.

An hour later, after fifteen laps of tree-branch jumping and over a thousand one-handed pull-ups per arm on a tree-limb, Achilla showered inside and changed into black sweatpants and a white t-shirt; the same clothes she always wore around the old house. She strolled down the stairs as she heard the jingling of keys in the kitchen. Achilla turned the corner and saw Sam standing by the island wearing jeans and a Columbia University sky-blue sweater under a black jacket. She smiled at Achilla as she tossed the keys in the air.

"Did you get your work out in?" Sam asked.

"Oh, you saw that?" Achilla replied as her cheeks flushed. "I'm not used to people watching me."

"Nope," Sam said as she pecked her on the cheek and walked past her. "I just know you. Come on. Let's go shopping like old times."

"Mom?" Achilla asked as Sam opened the front door.

"If you want to buy jeans and sneakers, it's ok."

"Not my question," Achilla said. "But, I will definitely take you up on that."

"Then what is it?" Sam asked with a frown. "And are you coming or not?"

"Right," Achilla chuckled and shook her head as she followed Sam out the door. With all of her loving, patient, tenderness on the big issues in Achilla's life, she had forgotten how impatient Sam could be with little things. Even compared to CIA agents, she hated the most to be kept waiting. When they entered Sam's silver car, Achilla leaned her head back against the seat. It had been a long time since she rode in this car and it still smelled like a stale lemon air freshener.

"What was your question, honey?" Sam asked.

"Well, did you tell anyone Dad was…um…"

"Murdered?"

"Yeah," Achilla said with a frown. "That."

"No, but it's in the paper and my phone's been ringing off the hook," Sam said. "Why, is it dangerous for me to talk about it or something?"

"No, it's just that…"

"Achilla, you are the last person I expected to pussyfoot with your words," Sam snapped. "Honey, please, spit it out."

"Fine," Achilla snapped back. "Where are your parents? Don't they know that you just lost your husband in a *brutal* murder? God, I mean Chief Price is just the next town over, and I don't know where your mother is, but it doesn't matter. They should be here. Every day. Being your parents."

Sam stared out at the road as she drove down the street and Achilla watched the television poles whiz by.

"Sorry," Achilla said. "I could've worded that better."

"No, you're right," Sam replied with a soft voice. "The truth is, I haven't heard from either of them in over a year, my mother even longer. I wouldn't know if she was dead or alive."

"I shouldn't have reminded you of that," muttered Achilla with her head low.

"Nonsense, Achilla, you think I needed a reminder?" Sam asked before taking a breath. "I just never had good parents. I don't know, maybe their work messed up their heads too much."

"You wouldn't give Ailina that kind of excuse," Achilla replied with her arms crossed. "I don't see why they deserve it."

"It's not about deserving," Sam sighed. "Sometimes it's about forgiveness and understanding. As much as I hate Ailina, Lord forgive me, I have to find a way to understand her too."

"Bullshit!" Achilla spat before covering her mouth.

"This coming from the person who drove out to see her?" Sam asked with a cocked eyebrow.

"I needed information from her," Achilla said. "That's all. It wasn't a loving reunion."

"Yes, but have you ever stopped to think about why Ailina's the way she is?" Sam asked. "She's too dangerous to be around.

Nobody knows that more than us, but have you ever brought your-self to forgive her?"

"I have no intention of forgiving her," Achilla replied. "None. I'm not forgiving anyone who hurts my family."

"Well at least you admit it's a choice," Sam said.

"I do," stated Achilla as she raised her chin. "My choice."

"You're so independent, Achilla," Sam said. "So defiant. Do you always think you have to do everything yourself?"

"Where is this coming from?" Achilla asked as Sam pulled onto the highway.

Sam passed a glance at Achilla before focusing on the road again. Achilla knew that look. She always gave it to her before they had one of their heart to heart talks; specifically, the kind that Achilla was not in the mood for. Achilla covered her face with her hands.

"This is either about God or a boyfriend," Achilla groaned. "Let's just get it over with."

"You know Dahntay's still around," Sam said.

"I knew it!"

"Oh, girl, hush up and hear me out," Sam chuckled. "Now listen, I have a sharp eye for good men. You see I married one, and I introduced Priscilla to one and they got married."

"You want me to *marry* Dahntay?" Achilla moaned as she held her hands on her head. "Mom, I'm twenty-one years old. I can't get married."

"Well, it wouldn't happen right away," Sam replied. "It takes years before you can get there."

"I can't believe we're having this conversation."

"I'm just saying that you should give him a call," Sam said with a smile. "Ask him how he's doing and invite him out to coffee. Maybe later, you guys can have dinner. Then you can invite him over for a family dinner, you know, let him know he's welcome over anytime. Good men are always checking you out to see how good you are, so if you want to keep him, you'll have to work with him a little and meet him halfway. You play games, and he'll walk. Men like Dahntay are always tired of games; especially when they know they deserve better. I've watched a lot of women lose good men over that. Just be straight with him. He'll appreciate it."

"The last thing I need advice about is how to keep a man's attention," Achilla replied. "And for the record, I don't *play games*."

"Then I'll give you some room to work," Sam said with a raised hand. "I won't meddle, but I want to be in the loop. Do you think you'll call him tonight?"

"No," Achilla stated as she crossed her arms and looked out the window. "We broke up. It's over."

"You can try that hard rock act all you want, Achilla," Sam said as she exited the highway. "Maybe you need it from all that spy work, but aside from that, I know better."

"What do you mean you know better?"

"You are no cold-hearted woman," Sam said as she wagged her finger. "I've known a few. You're not one of them."

"I never claimed to be cold-hearted," Achilla replied as they pulled into the parking lot of the Bridgeport Flyer in Milford.

"Sure you do," Sam said as she stopped the car. "Brendan told me about how you used to treat Dahntay; how mean you were to him when he was just trying to treat you right and how long it took for you to be nice to him. That's a claim if I've ever seen one, but I would've never guessed that you were so calloused toward the boy. Just look at the way you cried after you broke up."

"It wouldn't have worked," Achilla muttered. "He deserves better. I told him that before."

"You know, Achilla, it's hard for a man to love you when you don't love yourself," Sam said with a shrug as she opened the car door and Achilla followed her toward the diner. "Next thing you know, every guy *deserves better*, and you'll start pushing them all away. Have you ever thought of that?"

Achilla didn't respond as they walked into the diner and grabbed a booth by the window. She stared out into the parking lot and watched a couple stroll to their car with arms interlocked. She then remembered Dahntay's smile. When she first met him, she thought of him as no more than a loyal lapdog. After a few locker side conversations full of jokes and laughter, she found herself waiting for him every morning at school. He was always there. Always loyal. Something about that thought grew a lump in her throat before she snapped herself back to reality in time to order a large stack of pancakes with bacon.

As she ate in silence, other thoughts popped in her head. She thought about her one-night stands in Hartford. Would any of those men been as loyal as Dahntay had she just given them a shot? Those nights were fun, but she always kicked them out in the morning without so much as a proper goodbye sometimes. They served their purpose, and their further presence was no longer required, but maybe one of them could have been a good guy. Maybe those good guys were now busy being good to other women.

Achilla thought about Blue Eyes and his sham of a marriage. After having three kids, they somehow they managed to avoid making love unless their side pieces were unavailable; which was rare. They didn't even kiss when Blue Eyes came home. If Achilla stuck with Dahntay and even, God forbid, married him, would they end up like that? Would they end up hating each other while pretending to love one another in front of the kids? Achilla shuddered before her plate of pancakes and bacon arrived. The mixed scent of sweet, sugary maple syrup and salty bacon fought for space in her nose as she grabbed a piece of bacon and munched it in half. She moaned when the salty goodness that her CIA diet denied her for so long gripped her tongue. It was a damn good distraction from her concerns, even if it was short-lived.

"Mom," said Achilla as she cut her pancakes.

"Mm-hm," Sam hummed through a mouthful of food.

"How did you do it?" Achilla asked. "How did you stay so happy with Dad?"

"Why wouldn't I be?" Sam replied. "You've seen your father."

"Well, it's just that I've seen marriages that don't work," Achilla said. "One in particular is just bad."

"Well, why'd they get married?" Sam asked before biting a sausage. "Do they love each other?"

"No," Achilla replied. "But I would hope they did at some point."

"Love doesn't just fade, Achilla," Sam chuckled. "Not without something extreme killing it. Otherwise, it wasn't love. Did one of them cheat?"

"Both."

"Well that explains everything," Sam said with a shrug. "They're probably both too selfish to love anyone. They've got the opposite problem from you. They love themselves too much. You're all about everyone else. They're all about me, me, me, and me. Yep, I can tell already. Do they have kids?"

"Three."

"Is he rich?"

"Yeah."

"Her idea," Sam said with a snap of her finger. "I guarantee it. Pop out a few kids and you've got him on the hook. After that, it's cheaper to keep her. "

"That's pretty devious," Achilla replied with a frown.

"Well, she sounds devious," Sam said before pointing her fork. "And he's no better, honey. I can promise you that."

Sam had no idea how right she was. She had no idea that Achilla was talking about the man who was responsible for her husband's death. Achilla shrugged to feign indifference and ate a mouthful of pancakes.

"Are their kids in high school?" Sam asked.

"Yeah, one of them," Achilla said with a slight laugh at Sam's flash of psychic ability. "Why?"

"When the last kid graduates, divorce," Sam said. "The husband'll file for it, and she won't get a dime. Rich people hire PI's and everything."

"Jealousy," Achilla replied. "He does seem like the type."

"No," Sam said with a wave of her hand. "Greed. If she cheats, she doesn't get any money. The kids will, but she won't. Honestly, she doesn't deserve a penny, but I hope he has enough of a heart to look after those kids. What did they do wrong, you know? Depending on how bad she is, he might fight for custody."

"Why would he do that?"

"That depends on what kind of man he is," Sam sighed. "Your

father would've gone to court for you, but she gave you up before that happened. Brendan was trying to save you from abuse. This man you're talking about? The cheater? He might just take the kids to hit her where it hurts. She might do the same thing. You don't know how ugly people can be, Achilla, not unless you've watched them get divorced."

"Yes, I do," Achilla replied. "I've seen people lie, manipulate, and even kill."

"Yeah," Sam said with a nod. "But you haven't seen someone use children as weapons. It's disgusting."

"Mom," Achilla said with a cringe. "You and Dad were so happy. How do you know this stuff?"

Sam took a deep breath before biting her food and looking Achilla in the eye.

"It's an ugly truth that Brendan and I hoped to shield you from," Sam sighed. "It's bad enough that you grew up in such a terrible home. We didn't want you to have a bad adulthood too. We hoped that our marriage would be a good example to you if you decided to settle down with someone. I'm not sure how much good it did now."

Achilla remembered watching her parents interact and how different they were from Ailina. They always kissed each other when Brendan came home. When Samuel and Achilla were old enough, they would sometimes leave the house on dates. Even when they argued, they never spoke ill of each other afterward. The more Achilla thought about it, she never noticed any signs of cheating on any of them; no errant scents of colognes or perfumes, no late nights without an explanation or phone call, nothing. Of course, they weren't perfect. Sam sometimes made decisions without discussing them first; like Achilla's date with Stanley. Brendan had a tendency to entrench himself in his work so much that he missed important stuff; like Achilla and Samuel's basketball games. There were nights when Sam would make a plate for Brendan and it would get cold before Sam marched off to their bedroom. Other times, Brendan would glare at Sam when she punished Samuel without seeking his input. Most times,

Brendan heated up the food and ate it when he got home, and Sam stopped herself and asked Brendan what he thought. They had flaws, but they were trying, and they certainly weren't the Gabriellis. Achilla nodded her head before stuffing down a slice of pancake.

"Can I ask you a really personal question?" Achilla asked.

"Honey, that ship sailed the second you moved in our house and told me you could hear us having sex," Sam said with a weak smile before letting out a laugh. "Oh, I've never been more mortified in my life!"

"In hindsight, that was inappropriate," Achilla replied before looking down at her lap. "I'm sorry for that, and a lot of things I said and did as a kid. It must've been a hassle raising a little carbon copy of Ailina."

"You have never been a carbon copy of *that woman*," Sam snapped with a hard stare. "Now stop that and ask your question before your food gets cold."

"You never cheated on Dad," Achilla said. "And he never cheated on you. I would've noticed. And you're saying that was because you loved him?"

"Absolutely."

"How?" Achilla asked. "How do you just shut it off like that?"

"So that's it," Sam said with a pointed finger.

"What?"

"That's why you won't commit to Dahntay," Sam said. "You think you'll cheat on him."

"I never did in high school," Achilla replied. "And he could barely keep up with me then. I've changed now. It's hard to explain."

"Horniness is never hard to explain," Sam said with a laugh. "Neither is finding other men attractive. What you think my eyes just retract into my skull when a fine man passes by?"

"Then how?"

"Achilla, when you don't love someone all of your needs and desires take priority," Sam said. "Sometimes it's almost impossible to turn down any opportunity that comes your way. But when you love someone, your love dictates your actions. None of those options out there seem worth it, even if they're tempting."

"You've had options?"

"Plenty," Sam said as she waved for the server. "Some of them made more money and worked in safer professions than Brendan, and they had no problem trying to steal me away, but I stayed faithful. I always loved Brendan too much to step out. I just couldn't disrespect him like that. That's how love thinks, Achilla."

"Mom, I'm different," Achilla said. "Everything about me is stronger, even my urges."

"Then it stands to reason that your love will be stronger too," Sam replied before smacking her hand on the table. "You can do it. You just have to give yourself a chance to do it. Now eat. Your. Food."

Achilla smiled and shoved more food into her mouth. As she looked out the window and watched a breeze twist the orange leaves into a whirlwind in the parking lot, she couldn't put her smile down. She had just finished working out this morning in a way that no one for miles thought was possible; let alone could replicate. She knew multiple languages and could learn a new one in a matter of weeks. Still, Sam never ceased to impress her. Achilla's daydream ended when Sam grasped her hand with a firm grip. Achilla frowned at her until she lowered her head.

"Um...Mom?"

"Achilla," Sam said without opening her eyes. "I'm going to pray with you."

"Mom," Achilla groaned.

"Just humor me then," Sam said with a smile. "Can you humor your mother?"

"Fine," Achilla said with a deep breath as she lowered her head and closed her eyes. She expected a long, drawn-out prayer with all of the religious words she heard at church on Sundays as a girl, but there were none. Achilla listened as hard as she could. She heard Sam's heartbeat, her breathing. She heard the diner around her clamoring from dropped plates and scraping forks. She could even hear the wind whistling as it picked up speed between the cars in the parking lot. Still, she heard no words. Sam's prayer was silent until she let go of Achilla's hand. When she snapped her eyes open, she saw tears in her mother's eyes but they wouldn't take the trip down her cheeks. They just settled on her eyelashes until she wiped her eyes, grabbed her fork, and ate the remainder of her food.

"Can I ask what you prayed about?" Achilla asked.

"You," Sam replied without looking up.

"OK," Achilla said with a shaking head and shrug. "Can I ask you what you said then?"

"You can ask," Sam replied. "But I'm not telling. Not this time."

"Why?" Achilla asked.

Sam looked at Achilla with a cocked eyebrow and swallowed her last morsel of pancakes.

"It's for your own good," Sam said with a wink.

Achilla glared at Sam before finishing off her pancakes. Sam's ability to turn her logic against her always made her want to break something. Just like she always did as a child, Achilla would just get over it. Only her parents had that effect on her. Achilla's glare turned into a smile that she couldn't suppress.

"After this, we'll go shopping," Sam sighed. "You need new clothes now that you've grown so tall. So we'll get you some new jeans and sneakers and those baseball caps you like and maybe some sweaters and hoodies."

"I also need a dress," Achilla added.

"What?" Sam asked.

"A dress," Achilla said before chomping down her last piece of bacon. "A black one for Dad's funeral."

"Of course," Sam said. "Well, there is that."

"I also need a red one," Achilla replied. "I like red with those real nice red-bottom shoes. I can pay for all that myself, but I need another woman there to actually watch me try them on. My former boss was terrible at it. I used to have to ask random women to help me out before I left the store looking like a scene from Pretty Woman."

"OK," Sam said with a wide smile. "Yeah, we can do that."

"Sandy doesn't have any clothes either," Achilla said with a shrug. "I sized her up yesterday. She has roughly the same measurements I had in high school. I'll take care of her."

"All right," replied Sam as she nodded her head. "Sounds like a plan. Do you want a manicure too?"

"Ugh!" grunted Achilla before lowering her head. "OK fine. I can do that."

Sam laughed and held her sides before she pulled her wallet out of her purse and raised her hand for the server.

"Oh, you really have grown," Sam said as she took the bill from the server and shoved fifty dollar bill inside. "But you're still Achilla. Let's go. Just last week I saw a red dress in the Milford Mall that's perfect for you. I just hope they have it in your size."

Achilla stood up and followed her out the door. When they stepped outside, her breath flowed from her nostrils like white smoke. Snowflakes sailed through the air and some of them kissed Achilla's nose, causing her to twist her face and blow the melted water away. Sam raised her hands and then zipped up her coat as they walked to the car. Achilla stepped in and leaned her head against the back of the seat again.

"Looks like I'll be buying you a coat," Sam sighed. "I should've known it would get cold early."

Achilla shrugged and dismissively waved her hand as Sam pulled out of the driveway. They had a long enough talk already. She didn't feel like explaining to Sam that she could sit under freezing pond and stand outside in a blizzard without so much as a sneeze. For now, she would just enjoy the time they had together shopping, laughing at old memories, and trying on dresses. Then she would come home and watch with a smile as Sandy cried at the sight of new clothes.

Sam asked Achilla to humor her after all. There was no better way to do that than to pretend to be as normal as possible. She had to care about these things; dresses, shoes, love, marriage. She had to give Sam the comfort of feeling like her daughter was becoming the kind of woman society accepted. She also had to think that her words on forgiveness and understand affected her somehow, instead of only fueling her to find Blue Eyes and torture him for killing her father and taking a good husband away from such an amazing woman. That was a capital offense with Achilla; one that she planned on punishing after she helped Sandy try on her new outfits. When they came home, they watched a misty-eyed Sandy twirl in a brand new pair of jeans and a navy blue sweater before she ran through her entire new wardrobe. Everything Achilla bought for her was a perfect fit.

Chapter Fifteen

ACHILLA JOHNSON:15

The more Achilla watched the barbecue from her bedroom window, the more her prediction about Samuel came true. Wearing jean shorts, a lime green polo, and crisp, white sneakers, Samuel worked the crowd of his parents' co-workers and old friends. Achilla watched her brother's mannerisms; the way he held his hands when he spoke and how he smiled and shook people's hands with a firm grip. He inherited Sam's face, but he was the spitting image of Brendan in every other way. He just knew how to get along with everyone, and he was better at it than the majority of the adults in the yard. Achilla smiled at the thought of Samuel meeting more lawyers and making friends.

It came so naturally to him.

Achilla heard a knock on the door and turned around as Sam walked in wearing a yellow sundress. She leaned against the doorway with her arms crossed and stared at her the way she always did when she was concerned. Achilla had two guesses for what this conversation was about; Dahntay or Achilla sitting in a room by herself. Achilla forced a polite smile and waited for her to start.

"Achilla, why are you sitting by yourself?" Sam asked.

"No reason," Achilla sighed and cracked a smile of relief. "These kinds of functions are more Samuel's thing."

"Ugh, your father too," Sam said as she sat on Achilla's bed. "I can organize one, but I can't stand these kinds of parties. They're so political."

"I agree."

"And look at these men your father does business with," Sam continued. "All some of them care about is making money and having a girlfriend half their age. I don't know how Brendan can stand in the same room with them, but I guess it comes with his profession."

"It's like an opportunity to show off who has the prettiest girl," Achilla said. "How can they just stand there and be someone's trophy like that?"

"Honey, they're paid to be a trophy," Sam chuckled. "Don't be fooled."

"Yeah," Achilla said with a snort. "Probably paid to screw him too."

Achilla hung her head at the words that just left her mouth.

"Sorry," Achilla said. "That was inappropriate."

"Yes, it was," Sam replied. "But you weren't wrong. I don't want you to be like them, Achilla. Sex should be with someone special; someone you love. Now, I would rather you wait until marriage, but I'm no fool. You can tell me anything, and it stays between you and me."

"If you suspect something, why don't you just ask?" Achilla groaned.

"I don't suspect anything," Sam said with her arms crossed. "I just know that you're about to turn sixteen, your first date was trau-matizing, and the second boy you brought over the house suddenly disappears off the face of the Earth. I know it feels like I'm rubbing the past in your face, but I worry about you. I worry that you'll--"

"Be like Ailina?" Achilla muttered.

"No," Sam said. "From what I understand, Ailina would've never brought those boys home. She would've kept them a secret from her parents and each other. I'm more concerned that with a bunch of bad experiences, you'll end up like one of those girls out there."

"Weak and dependent?" Achilla chuckled. "That's not me."

"You're so smart," Sam said. "Brilliant even. But you haven't lived yet. You haven't seen what I've seen, heard what I've heard. Some of those girls are just playing a game, letting the man think he's in control while she's emptying his pockets. Do you know why?"

"Why?"

"Because they think they're superior," Sam said. "They think that all men are dogs who aren't worth anything but the money they make. So they toy with them and take the money. They're some of the most conniving, manipulative people I've ever met, and I can't deal with them. I thank God that I have good friends and a husband who loves me for who I am."

"Sounds like Ailina," Achilla replied. "Only with her, it was sex."

"Well that's no better," Sam said with a hard look. "I could never treat Brendan like some toy. I don't know how anyone can be that selfish."

"You never considered Dad's career?" Achilla asked. "He is a pretty successful lawyer."

"I considered his passion for what he does," Sam said with a smile. "Your father loves criminal defense. He loves the courtroom. He loves wearing a suit. He loves carrying a briefcase. He loves the law. As for his career, when we first met he was a public defender. A broke one."

"That's...really cool," Achilla said. "I don't think I've felt that way about a boy before."

"Honey, you're in high school," Sam said as she stood up and sat next to Achilla on her windowsill. "I wouldn't expect you to find the love of your life yet. The saddest thing is that I can guarantee most of those women down there haven't found him either. They're too jaded and bitter, and ugly inside. I've lost friends who became that woman. I've only kept the ones who didn't. Don't be her. Can you promise me that, Achilla?"

"I can," Achilla replied.

"Good girl," Sam said as she caressed Achilla's hair before standing up. "Aren't you supposed to play basketball with Samuel's friends?"

"Yeah," Achilla said. "But they haven't started yet."

"Well, in the meantime the pool's open," Sam said as she reached behind the doorway. "I was going to give you this for your birthday, but it's about ninety degrees out."

Sam pulled out a baby blue two-piece bathing suit with a yellow sarong and hung it in Achilla's closet. Achilla hopped to her feet and held the bathing suit in front of her face, turning it back and forth. It wasn't until now that Achilla realized she had never worn a bathing suit like this one before. She only wore plain two pieces when she swam laps in the pool at the local YMCA. This suit was stylish. Achilla turned and hugged Sam around the neck.

"Baby, that's too tight," Sam grunted until Achilla let go.

"Sorry," Achilla giggled as Sam massaged her neck. "I've never had one of these before."

"I just didn't understand how a girl so pretty could be so afraid to look good," Sam said. "I'll step out. Try it on."

Sam stepped out while Achilla threw on the bathing suit and sarong. When she knocked on the door, Achilla opened it and posed in the doorway. Sam's eyes turned wide and she stepped back and covered her mouth. She then hugged Achilla and held her out by her shoulders. Achilla couldn't help but smile at the glee in her eyes.

"You look so beautiful, girl," Sam said. "Just make sure you keep the sarong on until you're in the pool. Always cross your legs, and when you get up from a chair, swing both legs at the same time. Kneel to pick things up. Never bend over. It's fine to show a little skin, but this isn't a peep show."

"Got it," Achilla replied.

"And how did you manage to get a stomach like that?" Sam asked as she poked Achilla's abs. "Your six pack looks better than Janet Jackson."

"Mom, stop," Achilla laughed as she shoved her hand away.

"OK, go strut your stuff."

Achilla trotted down the stairs to the front door. Before she could grab the doorknob, Brendan walked in wearing a brown polo and khaki shorts. He stopped and frowned at Achilla. She smiled and posed. When his frown didn't go away, she stopped and slumped her shoulders.

"I'll go change," Achilla muttered.

"You don't have to change," Brendan said with a shrug. "But I thought your mother got you a hat."

"Oh, Jesus, I forgot!" Sam called from upstairs before she ran down the steps. "It's in the bedroom. Be right back."

"You're OK with this?" Achilla asked as Sam ran past her. "I always thought you'd be really protective about it."

"Hey, you're growing up," Brendan said with a shrug.

"Sounds like something Mom would say," Achilla said with a cocked eyebrow.

"Achilla, please," Brendan replied as he chuckled.

Sam interrupted Brendan by shoving a hat over Achilla's head. Achilla ripped it off and looked at it. The hat was yellow like the sarong. Sam held Brendan's arm as she smiled at her. Achilla posed again and both of her parents laughed.

"I think you've made her day," Brendan said to Sam.

"Well, I hope she enjoys it," Sam replied. "Go to the pool, Achilla."

Achilla strolled past her parents to the walkway and noticed a few men staring at her as she passed by. She ignored them and kept walking. When she spotted Samuel talking to one of his friends, she smirked. The opportunity to mess with one of Samuel's freshman buddies was too good to pass up. She held Samuel's shoulder as she smiled at the tan-skinned boy in front of him who wore straight, crew cut hair, and a gray t-shirt and black, knee-length basketball shorts. When Samuel looked at Achilla, the life drained out of his face.

"Hey, Samuel," Achilla said before smiling at the other boy. "Who's your friend?"

"This is Daniel," Samuel muttered. "He was a neighbor until he moved to Bridgeport a few years ago."

"You're awfully tall for a freshman," Achilla said. "But I guess so is my brother."

"Well, I can't speak for Samuel," Daniel said in a Puerto Rican accent. "But I'm no freshman. I'm about to be a sophomore. Hey, I remember you now. You're the girl who beat down Marty way back. You know he was never the same after that."

"Let's skip that, Daniel," Samuel said. "I don't think she needs to hear--"

"No, let me decide that," Achilla told Samuel with a raised hand before turning to Daniel. "What do you mean?"

"Well, he's been in and out of juvie," Daniel said. "He's got a thing for hitting girls."

"I don't think Daniel's trying to blame you," Samuel said with a hard stare at Daniel. "Right, Daniel?"

"No, not at all," Daniel replied with his hands raised. "It's his fault. I mean, he couldn't defend himself so he targets weak girls. Nobody likes that kid. All the boys used to jump him over at Harding High when they found out."

"Good," Achilla said with a head nod before nudging Samuel with her elbow. "See? I can handle it. I'm heading to the pool. It was a pleasure, Daniel."

Achilla turned on her heels and walked to the backyard as another older man with slicked back hair stared at her, and his blonde wife smacked his arm. Once she reached the backyard, Achilla found the pool filled with mostly women in their twenties. A couple looked older in the face, but their bodies were the same; slender and toned with long legs. The men sat in their chairs at the tables nearby playing cards and drinking beer. Achilla made her way toward the pool when she spotted an older brown-skinned man wearing an all-white outfit and brown, wing-tipped shoes approaching her. The second Achilla made out his face, she knew he was Chief Price. Sam clearly inherited her skin tone and facial expression from him, but not his demeanor. His eyes were hard and brown like permafrost and zeroed in on her like she was a suspect for murder.

"You must be Achilla," Chief Price said with a voice even deeper than Dr. Freeney's.

"Yes, sir," Achilla said. "And you are?"

"Gregory Price," Chief Price said. "Police Chief of the Bridgeport Police Department. Samantha's father."

"Interesting," Achilla said.

"Yeah, it's tough work," Chief Price said with a grin and a raised chin as he rubbed his short, salt-and-pepper hair. "But I maintain--"

"No, I meant it was interesting that you mentioned your job before your daughter," Achilla said. "My dad never does that. And how come I'm just now meeting you? Doesn't my biological mother work for you?"

"Ailina's my best detective," Chief Price said. "She does great work for us--"

"OK, so how come it took eleven years for my Dad to know where I was?" Achilla asked with a slight curl of her lip. "You didn't think that was some important information?"

"Well, you must be Achilla!" Achilla heard someone say as he wrapped his arm around her shoulder. Achilla backed away until she saw an older man with nearly black, pockmarked skin and a wide smile wearing jeans and a black polo. His voice gave him away as Grandpa Johnson. Nobody else could give Brendan his distinct voice inflection; a slight southern twang that gave away his Mississippian origins. Achilla couldn't help but smile and hold his arm. Something about him made Achilla want to listen to everything he had to say just like his son.

"Sorry, you don't know me yet," said Grandpa Johnson. "I'm your Grandpa."

"Nice to meet you, Grandpa," Achilla said with a smile. "I can see where Dad gets his smile from."

"Oh don't flatter me now," Grandpa Johnson said. "The boy gets his looks from his mother, but he got his smooth talking from me. That's why he's doing his thing out in that legal field."

"Hustling is more like it," Chief Price said.

"Now, Mr. Price, I have always told you that I am a businessman," Grandpa Johnson replied with a grin. "Name one product I sold that was illegal. Go ahead, I'll wait. Yep, that's what I thought! You see, Achilla, you can't let Mr. Price scare you--"

"It's Chief Price," Chief Price growled.

"Yeah, he likes to remind everybody of his badge," Grandpa Johnson said with a pointed thumb. "Truth is he had to suck up to a lot of white folks to get it, and he has to betray his own daughter to keep it."

"Watch your mouth, Trevor," Chief Price said as he stepped forward. Before she could stop herself, Achilla stepped between them and glared at Chief Price with clenched fists. Even in a bathing suit and sarong, Achilla was sure that she could take him.

"Hey, I got me a bodyguard," Grandpa Johnson cheered. "Well isn't that something!"

"You've always talked too much, Trevor," Chief Price said. "You never respected authority; mine or anyone else's."

"Maybe if you weren't abusing it, I'd respect it a little more," Grandpa Johnson replied. "How many brothers did you help put in jail this past year, huh?"

"The law has to be enforced!" Chief Price replied. "The race of the criminal doesn't matter."

"Hey, for once we agree," Grandpa Johnson chuckled. "Let's start with Detective Harris. I hear she likes to beat brothers down; kind of like my son."

"There was no evidence--"

"Where the hell did he get a broken arm from then?" Grandpa Johnson snapped with an intensity that made Achilla flinch. "Y'all cops always cover for each other, even when they hurt one of your own people--"

"Hey, guys!" Samuel said as he jumped in from the left. "Horseshoe tournament starts in ten minutes. Have you picked your teams?"

Achilla watched Chief Price shrug and walk away. When she looked up at Grandpa Johnson, she saw a smile on his face, but his eyes were just as intense as Chief Price's. Now Achilla had a good idea of where Brendan got his strength and passion for defendants.

Samuel patted Grandpa Johnson's shoulder. Grandpa Johnson shook his hand in return.

"Boy, I'm telling you, don't join the dark side," Grandpa Johnson whispered. "Don't be a Tom like him--"

"Grandpa, what did Dad say about being civil?" Samuel asked. "We all have different points of view."

"There's no different point of view on corruption, son," Grandpa Johnson said. "And that man is corrupt, now, I'm telling you-"

"Grandpa, please," Samuel sighed. "Not at the barbecue."

"His own daughter won't talk to him," Grandpa Johnson hissed as he pointed at Chief Price. "He's only here because it makes him look good--"

"Poppa Johnson, Samuel's right," Sam said as she approached from the right before she kissed him on the cheek. "Not now, OK? Besides, Achilla hasn't gone to the pool yet, and you're holding her up."

"Oh, yeah!" Grandpa Johnson said as he held Achilla's shoulders and rocked her back and forth until she laughed. "My little bodyguard came to my rescue. She stood up to your pops, you know? I stepped in for her and she still backed me up. You're raising a good one here. A strong black woman."

"Well, we're trying our best," Sam said as she held Grandpa Johnson's shoulder and guided him away. "Achilla, I'll discuss that with you later. Go on to the pool."

Achilla nodded her head and walked toward the pool. She threw off her sandals and walked up the steps where she found more women tanning themselves on the deck. Achilla pulled off her sarong and dropped it on one of the chairs. She then stepped into the shallow end of the pool where all of the wives and girlfriends were sitting and chatting. One woman with brown hair and tan skin wearing a pink bathing suit frowned at Achilla.

"Excuse me?" the woman asked. "Are you Brendan's wife?"

"No, I'm--"

"I was told that the pool was for wives only, sweetie," she said as she pointed a French manicured finger toward the yard.

"She's fine, Joan," snapped a blonde woman with blue eyes wearing a purple two-piece standing next to Achilla before turning to Achilla. "I'm Priscilla White. I'm best friends with Brendan's wife. You are?"

"Achilla Johnson," Achilla said. "I'm actually Brendan's daughter."

"See, Joan?" Priscilla said before waving her hands in the air. "You almost insulted the host's daughter and got us kicked out, you *stupida donna*. Sorry about that, Achilla. If it makes you feel better, she's my cousin. I have to put up with her every Thanksgiving and Christmas. She got the good looks, but I got the brains, so I'm the one you should talk to. You can just look at her and ignore what she says like her husband always does."

The other women at the pool laughed except for Joan. She stood with her arms crossed and glared at Achilla. That made Achilla laugh even harder. Achilla noticed that Joan had a large wedding ring, but Priscilla's was larger; almost the size of Achilla's middle knuckle. Priscilla waved her wedding finger back and forth in her face and laughed some more.

"Do you want it?" Priscilla asked. "You can have it."

"I didn't mean to stare," Achilla said. "I've just…never seen a ring like that one."

"My husband designed it," Priscilla sighed with a smile. "He's such a good man."

"Does he buy you a lot of stuff?" Achilla asked. "Is that why you married him?"

"No, you're confusing me with Joan," Priscilla quipped with a pointed thumb. "Not me. Nope. I've got my own catering business and pulled in six figures last year--"

"There's nothing wrong with a man providing for his woman, Priscilla," a red-headed woman piped up. "You always act like you're better."

"I just can't do what you guys do, all right?" Priscilla said with a shrug. "Hey listen, Achilla, I can tell you're like me. You've got that look in your eye. I'm telling you it's possible. You can do it yourself.

If you need proof, look at your mother. We went to college together, you know."

"Really?" Achilla asked.

"Yeah, listen she was there for me during some rough times," Priscilla said. "I told her if she needed anything, she's got it. I even provided the food for this event."

"Nobody cares, Priscilla," Joan called out. "You always brag about what you do."

"Joan couldn't cut it in school, so she married rich," Priscilla whispered in Achilla's ear. "Her man cheats on her every weekend and she lets it slide because she's got nowhere to go. If my man did that, I'm out the door faster than he can say 'baby sorry', but I don't think he would. He's a good one just like your father. Your mother's got great taste in men. She introduced me to my husband, you know? When I first saw him, I just knew I was going to marry him. Oh! He was such a delicious piece of man. Still is."

Achilla giggled and nodded her head. She noticed the other women watching them and suppressed her smile. They all looked so different; some with red hair, blonde hair, black hair. Still, they all held a similar glare when they looked at Achilla. The only woman at the pool who smiled at her was Priscilla.

She was also the only person who could possibly out talk Grandpa Johnson.

"How old are you?" Priscilla asked loud enough for the other women to hear. "And to make that sound less rude, I'll share my age. I'm thirty-seven."

"I turn sixteen next month," Achilla said.

"Holy shit, you're sixteen?" Priscilla gasped and splashed the water with one of her hands.

"Yeah, she's half your age and looks better than you," Joan called.

"If she was half my age, that would make me thirty-two, *stupida*," Priscilla shouted back and rubbed her fingers against the bottom of her chin before turning to Achilla. "See what I mean about brains, honey? Anyway, you must be beating the boys away with a stick."

"Oh, something like that," Achilla said with a sideways glance.

"Hey, Joan!" Priscilla called out. "You better not let her meet your son. He might never come home, and you won't be able to breastfeed him anymore!"

The other women groaned and laughed as Joan stepped out of the pool and stormed off.

"Why are you so mean to her?" Achilla asked as she watched her leave.

"When I needed help, she wasn't there for me," Priscilla said with a shrug. "Your mother was. I'll be honest, I didn't like black people before I met your mother. I was raised to stick to my own, but your mother taught me different. Every single woman at this pool is here because I introduced them to your mother-"

"There you go bragging again," the redhead called out. "Don't talk like you're Jessie Jackson just because--"

"Hey, I'm not done," Priscilla snapped with a pointed finger before turning to Achilla. "She's a real life changer. Your parents are real life-changers. Because of your mother, anything you need, you've got it. I'm already planning to cater both you and Samuel's graduation parties free of charge. I owe your mother that much."

"That's really cool," Achilla said with a smile until she heard basketballs bouncing by the driveway. "I have to go play ball with the guys. Quick question."

"Yeah?"

"The redheaded lady," Achilla said. "Is she your cousin too?"

"Yeah, how'd you know?"

"Family resemblance," Achilla said as she stepped out of the pool. "Nice meeting you, Priscilla."

"Nice meeting you too, sweetheart," Priscilla said as Achilla walked off the deck. "That girl's got a bright future…"

Achilla grabbed a towel and dried herself off. She then threw on her sarong and sandals as she walked across the yard. She made it to the driveway just in time to watch Daniel and Samuel playing on the same team against some older men. Achilla's jaw dropped when she watched Samuel wear a black t-shirt as he dribbled a ball through his dark blue shorts. He had time to change but couldn't tell her that they were starting? He crossed over his opponent and drove the hoop for a layup, and Achilla glared at Samuel until he noticed her. He waved and passed the ball to Daniel before cutting to the hoop, receiving Daniel's pass, and finishing another layup.

"You started without me?" Achilla asked. "Seriously?"

"You were in the pool," Samuel called back as he caught another pass and made a jumper.

"I was trapped in a cougar den," Achilla said with her hands on her hips. "Why couldn't you come get me?"

"Achilla, just play next game," Samuel chuckled.

"Forget it," Achilla said with a wave of her hand as Samuel threw a no-look pass to an older man on his team who subsequently missed a layup. "I'm going in the house."

Achilla had no interest in playing anymore. Besides, she wanted to go inside and tell her mother all the great things Priscilla said about her. Such good news would probably make her smile. As Achilla strolled around the walkway, she heard a commotion inside through one of the windows. When she stopped and listened, it sounded like Sam screaming. Achilla jumped out of her sandals and sprinted in her bare feet to the front door. When she swung the front door open, the commotion inside hit her in the face like a brick wall.

"Get out!" Sam screeched from the kitchen. "Get out of my house!"

"Who the hell do you think you're talking to?" a female voice with a hint of Mississippi replied.

"I'm talking to you!"

"Sam, baby, calm down," Priscilla's voice said in a hushed tone.

"If you want to do something, come on then."

Achilla had just stepped inside when she saw her father run downstairs and bound into the kitchen.

"What's going on?" Brendan asked.

"She needs to get out," Sam said in a crazed voice. "Get her out of here, Brendan!"

"I need to know what happened here," Brendan said. "Look, everybody just calm down for a second."

Achilla tip-toed toward the kitchen door and peeked her head around. Sam stood on one side of the kitchen table with wide, crazed eyes and Priscilla, in her bathing suit, held her back by her shoulders. Brendan stood behind Priscilla, and on the other end of the table stood an old, dark-skinned woman wearing khakis and, a dark green blouse, and white orthopedic shoes. She wore short, grayish black hair that she didn't bother to style, and her jaw moved sideways as she chewed her gum. The old woman stared at Brendan and pointed her finger at Sam.

"Control your wife, Brendan," the woman said. "That's not how a woman's supposed to act at a party."

"Stop, Mom," Brendan said with a hand raised. "Somebody tell me what's going on here."

"That woman is a traitor to her race just like her father," Grandma Johnson said. "That's what's going on in here. I told you not to marry her--"

"Watch your mouth," Sam said as she tried to get around Priscilla. "I don't care if you're old. That doesn't give you the right--"

"No, Sam!" Brendan barked and raised his hand at her. "Mom, you can't say that to my wife--"

"I don't know how you could sit up in here feeding that thing knowing where she comes from," Grandma Johnson said. "I wouldn't give her damn thing. She's not deserving of it."

"She is a child, Loretta!" Sam screamed. "*My child*! You can't talk like that about my children!"

"She's not your child," Grandma Johnson yelled back. "And I didn't work my fingers to the bone so my son can feed the spawn of that white devil cop, you stupid bitch!"

Achilla heard the table and chairs rumble as Sam fought to get around Priscilla. With surprising strength, Priscilla pushed her back toward the wall. Achilla flinched when she reflected on what Grandma Johnson just said. She was talking about her. Achilla felt her muscles tense as she glared at this old lady with a face just like her father's, but with eyes that emitted so much hatred that it was infectious; so much so that Achilla found herself hating her back.

"That's it," Brendan said. "Mom, get out."

"You're kicking out your own mother--"

"That's right!" Sam screamed.

"Sam, let's go," Priscilla said. "Let's go outside, and I'll pour you a drink, yeah?"

"I don't need a drink, Priscilla!" Sam huffed as she ripped her arm free. "I need a new mother-in-law."

"Don't we all," Priscilla replied as she as she held her hands in front of Sam's chest. "But if I were you right now, I'd be getting a drink or six. Let me take you outside. Let me take care of you like you took care of me last time I was this pissed off. Come on, Sam, let's go."

"I'll deal with this," Brendan said. "Sam, go. Priscilla, take her out and tell my Dad to come in here."

"You got it, Big Guy," Priscilla said as she pushed Sam toward the front door. "Let's go, Beautiful. I'm making you my patented Bridgeport Blaster."

"That's not a real drink, Priscilla," Sam said as she walked out the door.

"Well, it's about to be," Priscilla replied. "And you need it."

Achilla hid against the wall as they passed by her out the door. She quietly breathed a sigh of relief when they closed the door behind them. Achilla had never seen Sam that angry before. She was almost as frightening as Ailina. Achilla peeked around the kitchen doorway to watch her father. He stood with his arms crossed facing his mother.

"You heard me, Mom," Brendan said. "You can't stay."

"How come you always take her side?" Grandma Johnson asked.

"Because you always meddle in my life," Brendan growled. "God, even as a kid, you hated every girlfriend I ever brought home."

"It was for your own good," Grandma Johnson said. "Those fast girls always wanted a piece of what we've got. You see I was right about Ailina."

"Making one shot doesn't make you a good shooter," Brendan said. "And one good judgment call doesn't make you right all the time. I'm a man with a family now. You can't walk in here and insult my wife and daughter. It's just not an option."

"How do you know that thing is even yours?" Grandma Johnson snapped. "Ailina was a ho, and a liar, and you know it."

"My daughter has a name," Brendan said. "It's Achilla, and I'm not explaining myself to you. Just go."

Achilla heard the front door open and watched Grandpa Johnson march into the house with Samuel behind him.

"Dad, why'd you bring the boy in here?" Brendan asked. "He doesn't have to see this."

"Never mind that," Grandpa Johnson said. "You want her out of here, she's gone."

"You're taking her side too?" Grandma Johnson asked.

"I sure am," Grandpa Johnson replied.

"Oh, Trevor, you've always been so stupid!"

"Samuel," Brendan said. "Go outside."

"Loretta, we've been married for forty years," Grandpa Johnson said as Samuel jogged out the front door. "If I'm stupid then you're not so bright yourself."

"She can't come back, Dad," Brendan said. "I'm sorry, but this is the last straw."

"Hey, I know it," Grandpa Johnson said. "We tried and it didn't work out. Come on, Loretta."

"I'll never forget this, Trevor!" Grandma Johnson snapped.

"I can live with that," Grandpa Johnson chuckled. "I'm not going to forget having to drag you out of my son's party. I guess I can't take you anywhere."

Achilla stepped into the kitchen doorway just as they were walking out. All three Johnsons stopped moving and stared at her as she stood in the doorway with her fists clenched. Brendan was the first to move forward. He walked past his parents and stood behind Achilla with his hands on her shoulders. He leaned over and kissed Achilla on the forehead. Normally that would make her smile, but she was too busy glaring at Grandma Johnson.

"This is my daughter," Brendan said. "She's quite the spy, but at least now you can meet her. I think you owe her an apology-"

"I've heard enough," Achilla said. "And I'm glad she's never coming back."

"I know you're the devil," Grandma Johnson said as she squinted her eyes at Achilla. "I can tell. You're just like that woman who tried to kill my baby."

"Nonsense, Loretta," Grandpa Johnson said with a wide smile. "She's my bodyguard. She backed me up a little while ago."

"I'm so sick of you, Trevor!" Grandma Johnson snapped. "How can you be so *stupid*?"

"Please, get her out of here, Dad," Brendan said as he guided Achilla out of the doorway.

Achilla watched as her grandparents and Samuel walked toward the front door. Every time she looked at Grandma Johnson, Achilla's hands trembled. She couldn't take her eyes off of her until her father tapped her shoulder. He then pulled her in and hugged her. Achilla watched the door as Brendan held her head against his chest.

"I'm sorry you had to hear that," Brendan said. "It's not something a kid wants to hear from her grandmother. She's been through a lot and she's stuck in her ways, but I want you to know that we all love you. You're family no matter what she says."

"Is Mom OK?" Achilla asked. "She was really mad."

"Yeah," Brendan sighed. "She'll be fine. She's always had a temper."

"I never noticed," Achilla replied. "Even when she gets mad at me, she never seems that bad."

"Sam doesn't like to talk about it," Brendan said. "But we're the only family she has me, you, Samuel, my dad. Even Priscilla's the closest thing she has to a sister. Her own parents are less than supportive. She tends to direct her anger at them and anyone who reminds her of them."

"Why?" Achilla asked.

"I think it's best for Sam to tell you that herself," Brendan replied. "In the meantime, I'm more concerned about you. Will you be OK?"

"Yeah, I'm fine," Achilla sighed.

After the barbecue, Achilla showered and changed into black basketball shorts and an old green t-shirt. Around midnight, she walked downstairs to grab some water when she found Sam sitting by herself in the kitchen with a glass and bottle of wine. Achilla had never seen her drink a drop of alcohol before. Perhaps Priscilla was right about her needing a drink. When Sam saw Achilla she shrugged and sipped her glass.

"Is that the 'Bridgeport Blaster'?" Achilla asked as she made mock quotes with her fingers.

"No," Sam replied with a smirk. "That was her fancy word for vodka and sprite with a lemon."

"Oh," Achilla said. "I was closer than I thought."

"Brendan told me he spoke to you," Sam said. "I'm sorry you had to see me like that. I wanted you to meet your family, and I hoped they could get along for five minutes."

"Not your fault," Achilla said as she opened the refrigerator. "We all have free will, right? Isn't that what they say in church?"

"Yeah," Sam replied with a smile. "I thought you didn't like church."

"I don't," Achilla said as she sat at the table. "But if you want me to go, I'll go, and if I'm going to be there, I might as well listen."

"I'm sorry about my father," Sam said. "And I'm sorry my mother didn't even show up. She's been more distant than him."

"Why are they like that?" Achilla asked.

"I come from a family of cops," Sam said with a weak smile. "Marrying a defense attorney wasn't in their plans for me; neither was being a teacher. Everyone else wanted me to make money like Priscilla does. Maybe one day I'll start my own business when I retire, but I love teaching. I love kids. I love my husband, and I love my family. I'm happy with my life. When you find what you love, don't let it go, Achilla; not for all the money in the world and not for your parents."

"Can I ask why Priscilla likes you so much?" Achilla asked before taking a swig of her water. "She said she didn't like black people before she met you."

"Oh, God," Sam said as she rolled her eyes. "Why does she still tell people that? She grew up sheltered into thinking that all black people were stupid and lazy. Then one day, I out debated her in our religion class at Columbia. She was so shocked at how smart I was at first but we became friends. Of course, her family didn't approve of me, and they flipped their lid when they met her now husband; who I'm sure Priscilla talks about all the time. She's been obsessed with him for thirteen years."

"Why wouldn't her parents like that?" Achilla asked with a smile.

"You and all these questions," Sam chuckled before sipping her wine. "Her family's very stuck in their ways, but she's working on them. Her parents are worse than mine; especially when she got married. They refused to go to the wedding."

"Is her husband black too?" Achilla replied.

"You're catching on."

"Ailina never told me that race mattered so much," Achilla said as she shook her head. "I feel like I've been walking around blind."

"That's because you have, honey," Sam replied as she reached across the table and squeezed Achilla's hand. "And it's our job to open those eyes a little bit at a time until you're ready to face the world on your own. That's what parents do."

"Thanks, Mom," Achilla said with a smile. "You know, Priscilla said that you and Dad are life-changers."

"Oh, well that was nice of her," Sam said as she chugged her last bit of wine and set her glass down with a slight clank that shook the bottle. She then grabbed the bottle and set it in the refrigerator. As she watched her grab some leftover food, Achilla couldn't figure out why race mattered so much. It mattered so much that it divided Brendan and Sam's families despite the fact that they were all black. Yet at the same time, it mattered so little to people like Sam and Priscilla that they could be best friends. With all of the history books she had read and all the news she followed, Achilla found no justifiable reason for the racial prejudice she witnessed today. All it did was tear up families. Achilla shook her head as she sat at the kitchen table.

"You look upset," Sam said as she bit a hot dog. "Want to talk about it?"

"I get it, but I don't get it," Achilla said. "This whole race thing still confuses me sometimes. Would Grandma Johnson hate Ailina any less if she was black?"

"I don't know," Sam replied. "But I know this. Black or white, if someone comes at my husband or my family with bathroom sinks or whatever, she's getting hurt. I can promise you that."

"Even Ailina?" Achilla asked as Sam walked toward the kitchen doorway.

"Especially Ailina," Sam said over her shoulder. "Somebody has to stand up to her. It might as well be me."

Achilla sat in the kitchen by herself for a while until she stood up and looked at the window into the backyard. It was pitch black. If she were standing out there right now, in the dark, nobody would know her skin color. Nobody would know what race she was, and she wouldn't know anyone else's race either. They would all look the same. As Achilla stared at her brown hands, she wondered if she should have ever stopped living in the dark.

Then she thought of her mother and Priscilla and shook those thoughts out of her head. She thought about Ailina as well. No matter what race Ailina was, she would always be evil. Priscilla had the same skin tone as her, but she was one of the nicest people she had ever met. Achilla clenched her fists as she stared out into the backyard. Living in the dark wouldn't solve anything, and she had a feeling that it was exactly what Ailina wanted. Achilla left the lights on as she left the kitchen, walked upstairs, and went to bed; vowing to wake up and never wish to live in the darkness ever again.

Chapter Sixteen

ACHILLA JOHNSON:20

Achilla lay awake in bed at three in the morning with her eyes shut, listening for any sudden movements. Her neck hairs stood on end as she felt the presence of an intruder. Her blinds were shut, and even if she opened her eyes, she knew she could not see, but Achilla smelled the scent soap and water coming from her doorway. It was the kind of soap that nobody in the Johnson house used, so it wasn't Samuel or Sam checking up on her. Sandy would have made her presence known by now. No, the scent at the door didn't belong in this house. That was certain.

However, the scent was familiar. It was the brand of soap Achilla bathed with as a child, flowery with a hint of honey, and it reminded Achilla of those nights when she felt like she was fighting for her life against a cruel, unbeatable opponent. That very thought made Achilla clench her fist under her bedsheets. Whoever stood in this doorway, certainly picked the wrong brand of soap today. Achilla grabbed her gun from under her pillow, rolled into a firing stance, and aimed for the door. She couldn't see a damn thing, but she knew her visitor was standing there. Achilla caught her breath and shook her head as she remembered who else would bathe with that same brand of soap and break into the Johnson house on the same night.

"What is it, Ailina?" Achilla asked. "You should make your presence known next time. If you didn't use the same hygiene products for the past twenty years, I would've shot you by now."

"Your senses have developed faster than I anticipated," Ailina said with a tone so low that Achilla knew only she could hear it. "I just walked into this room. It used to take you forever."

"Cut the assessment, and just tell me what you came for," Achilla replied as she mimicked Ailina's volume level.

"You can put the gun down now," Ailina said.

"Answer my question first," Achilla snapped. "I haven't shot you yet. Your next words may or may not change that."

"I have Blue Eyes," Ailina said with such a giddy tone that it made Achilla's stomach turn. Achilla sighed and lowered her weapon as she rose to her feet wearing nothing but the brand new underwear Sam bought her. She should've known Ailina would do things her way. Reliability wasn't her strong point.

"You said a week," Achilla snapped. "Doing things too early can screw up a mission."

"So can a lack of flexibility," Ailina said. "Anyway, Blue Eyes decided to take a trip to Miami. An interesting time to take a vacation when your classmate has been brutally murdered. If I was still an officer, he would've been my prime suspect. Anyway, I had to snatch him up earlier than expected. It was out of my control, what can I say?"

"Jesus, fine," Achilla groaned. "Where is he?"

"His flight would've left by now," Ailina replied. "So I had to make sure nobody saw him in the state. I drove him back up to Boston. Give me a ride, and I'll show you."

Achilla frowned.

"You look displeased," Ailina said. "Which isn't much different from how you usually look."

"Only when I see you," Achilla replied while wondering how the hell Ailina could see her in the dark. "Can't you drive yourself?"

"It would look suspicious."

"Vague answer," Achilla said. "And you and I in the same car looks suspicious; especially for the CIA who is most likely watching my every move. They probably saw our meeting in Boston last time."

"Yes, but if you and I are in the same car, then they can use that to their advantage," Ailina replied. "Hypothetically, they could convince you to kill me. They won't bother us. Trust me."

"Everything about this sounds funny," Achilla said as she shook her head. "How can I trust you?"

"You don't have to," Ailina chuckled. "That's your choice, but you should keep in mind that I haven't harmed you or your family; despite the fact that I know you can't see me yet."

Ailina was right. All Achilla could see was black. Still, night vision was most likely a Nephilim trait. She just had to figure out how to use it. Achilla focused her eyes until she could barely make out a black figure leaning in the doorway. The figure stood up straight, but that was all Achilla could make out.

"That's better," Ailina said. "Your eyes just glowed a little there. The first time you develop night vision your pupils will glow in the dark, but once you use it all the time, they'll go back to normal. There's no rush. It took me a while to develop it. For now, you'll have to rely on your other senses. You'll do just fine."

Achilla remembered Ailina's glowing eyes four years ago. Now they didn't glow at all. It took Ailina that long to perfect her night vision? If Achilla was seeing in the dark now, she was light years ahead of her. Agent Jones didn't lie. Achilla was developing at a much faster rate. Since she knew Ailina could see her, Achilla suppressed her grin as she stood up and stretched her arms before bending over and touching her toes. She then opened her night-stand and pulled out a black t-shirt.

"So when are we making this trip?" Achilla asked while pulling her shirt over her head and pushing her legs into a pair of gray sweatpants that she left on the floor.

"Now," Ailina said as she strolled across the bedroom to Achilla's window. "Are you able to withstand a drop from this window?"

"I can withstand a drop from five stories," Achilla replied while tying her black sneakers. "A jump from this window is child's play."

"So that's a yes," Ailina snapped. "I need you to answer my questions instead of bragging."

"I'm sure I get that honest from you."

"*Get that honest?*" Ailina said as she opened the blinds and then the window, letting a blast of cold air bully the warmth out of the room. "You've been hanging around Samantha too much."

"I like it," Achilla replied. "And I prefer taking after her over you."

"We can discuss your hatred of me in the car," Ailina sighed. "For now, let's move."

Achilla snatched her car keys from the nightstand and heard Ailina jump through the window. Achilla followed and leaped head-first into the frigid night air that rushed past her face as she descended. She somersaulted and landed on the balls of her feet on the grass and muddy soil before bounding to her right toward the driveway. The stars peaked out of the cloud cover, and she could see Ailina standing by her car wearing a navy blue sweatshirt and dark blue jeans. Achilla strolled to the driver's side, unlocked the doors and stepped in. As Ailina buckled her seatbelt, Achilla started the car.

"My folks might hear this car start," Achilla said.

"No, the Prices are all heavy sleepers," Ailina said. "I've broken into their bedrooms more times than I can count."

"Why?"

"You won't believe this," Ailina said as Achilla backed out of the driveway. "But it was to protect them."

Achilla cocked her eyebrow at Ailina like she told a bad joke.

"If your family dies, I lose my leverage," Ailina sighed. "And when I noticed the CIA wasn't protecting them, I thought that they would stage a hit and blame me."

"Hm," hummed Achilla as she drove down the street. "I actually believe that."

"It's not in my best interest to lie to you," Ailina said. "I need your help."

"Well don't expect any more after this is over," Achilla replied. "You can have Ares' body and burn it for all I care, but don't come near my family again. That includes Samuel. I heard about your little visit, and I don't appreciate you talking to him."

"Ares is your family too," Ailina chuckled. "You take after him a lot."

"Like you?" Achilla scoffed. "Yeah, no thanks. We're blood, but we're not family."

"I don't understand why you hate me so much--"

"Really?" Achilla snapped. "How about beating the shit out of me my entire life, and then when I finally meet someone who cares about me, someone who's *nice* to me, you strangle them until they're unconscious! I wouldn't have bothered with the CIA if I didn't think it would help me protect them from *you*."

"So I'm the problem here?" asked Ailina with a frown.

"Yes!" Achilla screamed. "You're everyone's problem! If you didn't get Blue Eyes for me, I wouldn't bother with you!"

When Achilla boarded the Merritt Parkway, Ailina sighed and crossed her arms as she looked out the window. Achilla scowled. Was this woman seriously hurt? Was she actually upset by Achilla's words after all she had done? Achilla stared out at the highway as they rode in silence for half an hour.

"My methods may have been harsh," Ailina said with her arms still crossed over her chest. "Perhaps to the point of turning you against me. But I was trying to show you a harsh reality."

"Don't try to convince me that you were doing me a favor," Achilla snarled. "You're selfish and evil. Plain and simple."

"You're still a child," Ailina snapped back. "Judging someone's character with blanket, unquantifiable terms like that is the calling card of naiveté, Achilla. I thought I raised you better than that."

"So is trusting someone like you," Achilla replied. "And you didn't *raise* anyone. Don't kid yourself."

"You think the CIA only met with you?" Ailina asked. "They only contacted you because they couldn't use me. They backed Chief Price into a corner and forced him into playing surrogate father when my real father got shot and tried to mold me into some kind of tool. Sound familiar?"

Achilla stared out the window. She refused to admit the similarity between Chief Price and Agent Jones. Still, Ailina had a talent for twisting circumstances in a way that fit her agenda. Achilla remembered the things she would say about her father; how she made him out to be this selfish, deadbeat dad who left her to raise a child on her own. It was precise. It was detailed. It was convincing.

It was also one hundred percent false.

Still, with the CIA betraying Achilla's trust, this story was very plausible; even coming from her. Achilla had no clue how her father died. She didn't know if the CIA let someone in or never guarded him at all. At this point, trusting Ailina might actually be the better option. Achilla clenched her teeth as she pushed a little harder on the gas pedal and exited Route 8 to board I-84.

"I'll take your silence as a yes," Ailina said. "Look, once people find out who we are, they change. They fear us, and human history shows that we kill what we fear. With all that Black History Samantha kept showing you, you should know that."

"You're not black, Ailina," Achilla quipped.

"Yeah, I noticed," Ailina replied. "But they apply the same principals to us. Keep the mind weak and the body strong. Use them for your purposes and then exterminate them. I bet they never told you that Ares was a police officer. They never told you that he served Boston and Bridgeport for fifteen years."

"Didn't he kill your mother?" Achilla asked.

"Achilla, wake up and stop listening to their stories," Ailina barked as she clapped her hands. "The CIA posed as police officers and shot her. Chief Price wasn't part of it, but at that point, my father couldn't tell who was friend or foe. He attacked him just the same, got shot, and here we are. There's a lot more to the world than what the CIA tells you, Achilla. A lot more."

"Why should I believe you?" Achilla asked.

"Because you can tell when someone's lying," Ailina said. "Just like I can. I haven't lied yet, have I?"

"No," Achilla muttered. "No, you haven't."

"When will you wake up?" Ailina asked as she uncrossed her arms and glared at her. "Your family, as you call them, may be an exception, but you don't have friends; not without hiding who you are. We don't get that kind of privilege."

"Maybe I can change that."

Ailina stared at her for a few seconds. She then shook the windows with a raucous cackle. It was the same cackle that used to make Achilla's spine shiver. Now she just blinked back tears. Achilla forced herself to focus on the road as Ailina laughed at her.

"You don't really believe that," Ailina snickered. "You don't *honestly* believe that you can change human nature on your own."

"Nope," Achilla sighed. "But I think that if I can show people that I'm not here to hurt them, they won't fear me so much."

"Well isn't that sweet," Ailina said with a sneer. "Are you going to do that before or after you murder Blue Eyes?"

"Blue Eyes is different," Achilla replied with a set jaw as they reached the Hartford city limits. "He killed my father. He can't live."

"Yes, and you have the power to determine whether he lives or dies," Ailina said with a low voice. "You don't think that's something to fear? Why do you think I bothered teaching you everything I know? You're a target whether you like it or not, and whether you like me or not, you can't deny that I equipped you with the tools to defend yourself. I refuse to let my child be someone's *victim*! If you hate me for that, so be it. You can hate me for the rest of your long, natural life."

Achilla stared straight ahead as they left Hartford and passed through another wooded section of Connecticut. Ailina sounded so much like Chief Price that it made her heart sink.

If you hate me for that, so be it.

Achilla felt the same way about Samuel. They rode in silence again for over an hour until they reached the Boston city limits. Ailina leaned back in the seat and clasped her hands behind her head as she instructed Achilla on where to go. When they reached an area with three-story condominiums and brick apartment buildings, Achilla frowned. She nearly ducked her head when police cars passed by with blaring sirens.

"This is not the Boston I'm familiar with," Achilla said.

"It's Mattapan," Ailina said. "Where I grew up before I moved to Bridgeport and where I returned after the CIA took my father. I came back to Bridgeport as soon as I could, but I couldn't find him. I contemplated bringing you back when you were born."

"Why?" Achilla asked as they passed a street corner with police tape surrounding a body covered with a white sheet. "Don't they call this section Murderpan?"

"Not a fair characterization," Ailina said with a raised finger. "Mattapan has plenty of good parts to it; law-abiding lawyers, doctors, bankers, everything. Not too long ago, I dated a garbage man out here. Good guy he was."

"How long did it take you to kill him?" Achilla asked.

"About a year," Ailina sighed before adopting a mock southern accent. "He wanted to move away, and I couldn't bear to see him with someone else."

"You make me fucking sick," Achilla spat.

"Be that as it may, my point still stands," Ailina said. "Mattapan has plenty of good qualities. You would've liked it."

"Is this one of those good parts?" Achilla asked.

"Not really."

"Then why raise me here?"

"It would've been easier for you to blend in," stated Ailina as she looked out the window. "Had you beat down that football player from St. Joes around here, no one would've noticed but the locals. It would've been safer for you to make mistakes here while you learned how to blend in and control yourself. Chaotic environments are perfect training grounds."

Ailina was half right. Her training with Agent Jones proved that chaotic, wild places were the perfect environments for Achilla to train. In the forests and mountains, she could be herself and no one would notice. Society never disturbed her, and she never disturbed it. A city was different. Everything about her movements in urban centers required subtlety and misdirection and swift, deadly efficiency in a conflict. A city was never the proper arena to make mistakes; not when hurting the wrong person can destroy its way of life. Achilla learned that from her encounter with Stanley and his enablers. She also learned the hard way with Blue Eyes.

"That's not exactly how America works," Achilla told Ailina. "If Stanley died here, the police would've rushed the neighborhood in five seconds; probably shooting a few black men in the process. But if Stanley killed me, well, they might stop and grab some coffee and doughnuts first."

"Typical black person's skewed, cynical view of the police," Ailina chuckled.

"Typical white woman's naïve trust in them," Achilla shot back.

"Naïve trust?" Ailina chortled. "You are aware that I'm a former police officer."

"So what?" Achilla snapped. "You're just as much a corrupt piece of shit as anyone else."

Those words came out like a bowel movement after waiting three hours for a rest stop. Ailina glowered at Achilla. Had she spoken to her that way five years ago, it would have resulted in a terrible beating. She broke Achilla's bones for less. Now she held back; no doubt out of self-preservation. Good. Achilla waited for the day when she could give her a piece of her mind without fearing for her life.

"Wow, that felt pretty good," Achilla said with a grin. "Oh, did I hurt your feelings?"

"Just pull over here."

Achilla parked next to a condemned, three-story brick building. As they stepped out of the car, a group of five, brown-skinned men wearing baggy jeans, white tees, and bright green Boston Celtics fitted caps cut off their path to the house. Ailina stared at them for a few seconds before they parted and let her through. Achilla followed and they cut her off. She glared at the tallest man in front of her, but he stared back.

"Let her through," Ailina replied from behind them. "She's my daughter."

"Didn't know you liked the brothers, Ailina," one voice chimed in.

"Yeah," Ailina nodded. "I do. Now let my girl through."

As the group parted, Achilla passed through them and couldn't help but remember the gang of boys she beat up in Bridgeport who wore identical white t-shirts. She could have taken these guys just the same. Still, now wasn't the time. She had to focus on Blue Eyes. Achilla followed Ailina up the walkway to the front door of the house.

"You're popular," Achilla said as Ailina pulled a key out of her back pocket and unlocked the door.

"Those guys are like my godkids," Ailina said. "Their mother was my neighbor growing up."

"Where's she?"

"Dead," Ailina replied with a deadpan voice. "Because of them. Look, we don't survive bullets. Don't talk to those guys without me. Understood?"

"Got it," Achilla said as they entered the dark house. Achilla used her senses as Ailina instructed and followed the sound of her footsteps to a staircase. The rank smell of rotting wood, urine, and squirrel droppings wrinkled Achilla's nose as she walked up the wooden stairs. Once upstairs, Achilla saw a light shining out of a room to the left. Ailina stalked down the hallway and into the room, and Achilla followed as the wood floor creaked under her sneakers. In the room, Achilla saw the back of a navy blue-suited man with oily, shaggy hair sitting in a chair. His wrists were tied behind the back of the chair with handcuffs, and his feet were strapped into the chair's legs with plastic ties.

"How's it going, Roberto?" Ailina said as she walked across the room and caressed his shoulder before she yanked his hair. "I've brought you a visitor."

Ailina turned him around, and Achilla saw his blue eyes stare back at her with a cold intensity that matched Ailina's. His face turned red as he glared at her. No wonder Brendan disliked him so much. Achilla could look at him and read the disdain he had for her. He didn't hold the stare of a victim looking for revenge. It was the look of a king betrayed by the peasants. Even when he was tied up he thought he was above her. As Achilla stepped forward, he spat on the floor and just missed her feet.

"Whoa, he's still got some life in him," Ailina chuckled before twisting Blue Eyes' ear. "But we'll take care of that."

"Fuck you both!" Blue Eyes barked. "I know people! Your families! Your friends! All dead! My people will take care of them! You just started a war with the wrong guy!"

"And where are those people now?" Ailina asked. "You know, Brendan was the father of my child. I would've killed you myself, but I think his daughter would enjoy it a little bit more."

"Before I do that," Achilla said as she stepped over the glob of saliva on the wood floor. "I need to know how you figured out my identity. Was it Trish? Don't lie. I can tell when you lie."

"A bird told me," Blue Eyes replied with a grin.

Ailina yanked his ear off, sending a waterfall of blood onto the floor. Blue Eyes screamed out as blood leaked down the side of his head. He hyperventilated until Ailina kicked his chair out from under him and sent the back of his head bouncing off of the floor. As crimson blood continued to leak out of his head and soak the floor, Ailina stepped around to his remaining ear. Achilla stared at her and she smirked back.

"Sorry," Ailina said with a shrug before tossing the ear across the room. "He just irritates me. I couldn't control myself."

"The less blood on my hands the better," Achilla said as she kneeled next to Blue Eyes' remaining ear. "Answer my question, Blue Eyes, while you can still hear me."

"I'm going to die anyway," Blue Eyes huffed. "Why should I?"

"Answer it, or you'll die slow," Achilla replied as she ran her hand down his chest, moving toward his right side. "You'd be surprised at what I can do to someone without killing him. I'll start with your ribs--"

"Yes," Blue Eyes cried out. "She thought we had an affair and said she knew you from a yearbook. From there, I used a connection in the CIA to do the rest. Well, actually Xerxes did."

"I have good news for you," Achilla said as she cracked her

knuckles. "Based on that, I won't kill Trish. A severe beating might still be in order for her if you don't tell me how to find Xerxes."

"Look, I don't know," Blue Eyes replied. "All I know is that his people send girls to Miami from Connecticut. I haven't met him myself, but whenever I take care of his guys, he pays extra."

"He's telling the truth," Ailina chimed in. "I tried getting info out of him so I could give it to you in exchange for Ares' location. That's all he knows."

"I'll have to take a trip to Miami at some point then," Achilla said to Ailina before turning to Blue Eyes. "Now, how am I going to deal with you? I'm a woman of my word. I'll be quick--"

"Just get it over with," Blue Eyes replied with a cold stare.

"But I never said how quick," Achilla said as she reached for one of his ribs. "Your stomach is pudgy. Breaking your ribs should take about thirty seconds."

"No--"

Achilla squeezed his side and snapped a couple ribs with a crunch. Blue Eyes cried out, but Achilla could still hear Ailina giggling in the background. Achilla frowned and stood over Blue Eyes with her hands on her hips as he breathed heavy and fast. She looked at Ailina who covered her mouth and laughed before nodding her head toward Blue Eyes, the *do it again* look on her face goading Achilla to continue. Achilla shook her head.

"No," Achilla said. "No ribs. That's a better injury for someone who'll live. I'll need something much worse."

"And you said I was evil," Ailina chuckled as she stepped back with her arms crossed. "I was fine with just the ribs. It was pretty funny actually."

"He killed my father," Achilla snarled as she stepped over Blue Eyes and stood with his torso between her legs. "*Not yours!*"

"Hey it's your world, kid," Ailina said as her Boston accent kicked in. "Don't let me stop you."

"I bet," Blue Eyes said through shortness of breath. "I bet your father'd be really proud."

"What?" Achilla demanded.

"He was always such a goodie-two-shoes," Blue Eyes huffed.

"He never wanted to get his hands dirty, even if it might've made him a little more money and a lot more connections. It was so pathetic I couldn't stand it, but at least he was consistent. He married a woman like that. His boy's like that too, but you? No. There's no way in hell he'd be proud of you, even if he was alive."

"You know that for a fact?" Achilla asked.

"Achilla, don't," Ailina called from behind. "He gets off on getting in people's heads--"

"Yeah," Blue Eyes half-coughed half-laughed his statement as if Ailina weren't there. "I do. Why do you think I made sure my girls didn't date anybody darker than a paper bag? Nobody, I mean nobody, wants their kids too close to their clients. You would've driven him to an early grave. You should be grateful that I put him out of his misery before he saw you like this."

"That's enough!" Ailina snapped as Achilla lowered her head. "Don't listen to him, Achilla. He's just trying to play on your guilt so you won't go through with it. Kill him now before he twists you around."

"Like I said, I'm already dead," Blue Eyes coughed as Achilla clenched her trembling hands and bit her lip. "But at least I can take some solace in knowing it took a couple of freaks of nature like you to do it. The best part is, you're Brendan's kid. Who'd've thought with his little Martin Luther King shtick, that he was raising just another *moolie* murdering thug he'd have to defend in court for half the price he would get if he gave less a shit about his morals and more about providing for the good kid in his house. What an uppity fucking moron that guy was."

"Achilla!" Ailina barked. "Shut him up! Now! What the hell are you doing?"

"Yeah uppity's the word," Blue Eyes continued. "I hated that porch monkey with a passion because he thought he was better than he was; always raising his hand in class and running for student office and speaking and organizing shit he had no business getting involved in. He must've thought he could make up for being a *moolie* by putting up some front, but I know your kind too well to fall for it. I just couldn't prove it until now. Looking at you, I see the proof.

You're all alike, and Brendan was the worst because he thought he was better. Monkeys can't help being criminals, even when they dance and sing like your father did."

"OK, *no!*" Ailina snarled as she stepped forward. "You've said enough! You'll deal with me now you piece of sh--"

"No," Achilla said as she shoved Ailina back until she nearly stumbled into the wall. Ailina gathered herself and stepped in front of her with reddened, wide eyes.

"How dare you," Ailina growled.

"He's mine, Ailina," Achilla replied. "You've done your part. Now stay out of it."

"Why haven't you done it, then?" Ailina demanded.

"I had to make sure."

"Make sure of what?" Ailina asked as she pointed at Blue Eyes. "He already killed Brendan, and he didn't even have the balls to do it himself. He had someone else shoot him from behind. He's nothing but a coward who doesn't deserve to live *a second longer!*"

"I'm not explaining myself any further," Achilla stated with a straight face as she looked Ailina in the eye. "He's mine, and I'll deal with him any way I want. If you don't like it, you can leave. Get in my way, and you're next."

"Oh, is that right?" Ailina asked with a flicker in her eyes.

"Yeah," Achilla replied to Ailina before shouldering past her and facing Blue Eyes. "Your time's up. If you spent that time praying instead of running your mouth, I might've gone easy on you. Too late now."

"Gone easy?" Blue Eyes snickered. "I can't wait until my people find you, especially Xerxes. You don't know who you're dealing with. That guy's *everywhere*, and if he doesn't like you, you'll wish you were never born. He's going to have a picnic stringing up the rest of your coon family, you black bi--"

Achilla snatched Blue Eyes' throat, and he gagged as she held him suspended in the air. Blue Eyes' limbs trembled in his chair as he dangled in Achilla's fingers. Achilla squeezed even tighter until she saw his face turn purple and his eyes turn bloodshot. She could feel his breath leaving his neck inch by inch and tightened her grip.

"Strangulation," Ailina said from behind. "An oldie but a goodie. You hang him in the air like that and you might as well slip a noose around his neck. Considering his thing against black people, it's pretty fitting."

"Oh, he'll get much worse than that," Achilla said as she released his throat, let him drop, and kicked through the chair into his groin. Blue Eyes wailed as tears jerked from his eyes, and he fell to the floor in a pile of wood. Achilla lifted him by his throat again and kicked his groin as blood stained the crotch of his suit pants and dripped out to his shoes. Blue Eyes' mouth gaped open but no sound came. He cried with his tears and the snot running out of his nostrils, but not his voice.

"Jesus Christmas!" Ailina said before she threw her head back and laughed. "You literally break his balls, but you choke him so he can't even scream? Remind me not to piss you off."

Achilla snarled and choke-slammed his head through the floor with a crash. She then lifted his head and raised her foot to crush his face. She lowered it when Blue Eyes could no longer look at her. The defiant stare he once held was gone and his eyes were closed. His oily, disheveled hair, his weathered face with slight wrinkles, and the bags under his eyes all looked like a hardworking lawyer just like Achilla's father.

She shook that thought of her head. No, this man was nothing like her father. Brendan was stern but kind and caring and would do his damnedest to do right by everyone; especially his family. He didn't deserve his death. He didn't deserve to get shot in his own office, and Sam didn't deserve to find out that he would never come home. Blue Eyes deserved this punishment. He no longer deserved to live. Achilla roared and stomped his neck through the floor. When he didn't move, Achilla kicked his lifeless body across the room. She was about to stomp him again when Ailina blocked her path. Achilla glared at her, but she shook her head.

"Lesson one about murder," Ailina said with her hands up. "You never hit more than you have to. It only leaves more evidence for the authorities. This building gets demolished tomorrow. Those boys outside burn the body, the city demolishes the building, and we move on. At most, it'll be another unsolved murder in a major city that'll make the nightly news and go away with the Celtics game. He's dead. You're done. Got it?"

"Fine," Achilla said as she stomped out of the room. When they left the house, the same men were waiting outside. Achilla didn't wait for Ailina this time when she shoved through them until one grabbed her arm. Achilla grabbed his shirt and threw him over her shoulder into the chain link fence. Another man pulled out a gun, and Achilla kicked his wrist before snatching the gun out of the air and cracking his jaw with an elbow. He hadn't even hit the ground before Achilla whirled on her next opponent with the pistol aimed between his eyes, but Ailina stood in her path.

"Easy," Ailina said as she raised her hands. "Stand down, fellas. She's not in a good place right now."

"That costs extra, Ailina," the tall man said. "I didn't plan on sending my people to the ER."

"Yeah, I know," Ailina said as she dug a couple rolls of hundreds out of her pockets and handed them to him. "Here. Have fun. Let's go, Achilla."

Achilla turned on her heels and marched to her car. She noticed a couple pushing a baby in a pink stroller. The father, a man wearing a gray polo shirt and baggy jeans, held the mother back with his arm; stopping the baby just as Achilla stormed past them and stepped into her car. She didn't wait for Ailina before starting the ignition. Ailina rushed into the passenger side and had barely closed the door when Achilla pulled off the sidewalk.

"Hey, slow down," Ailina snapped. "I still need you to make good on your end of the deal."

"I know," Achilla said as she drove through Mattapan. "I have a funeral to attend tomorrow. After that, we get Ares."

"How can I trust you?" Ailina asked.

"You can tell when someone's lying, can't you?" Achilla asked as she drove through a stop-sign.

"Yeah, I can," Ailina said as she leaned back in her seat and shielded her face from the rising sun that gleamed through Achilla's window. "And you haven't told a lie all day."

It was done. Achilla had avenged her father's death by killing the man directly responsible. Still, her hand gripped the steering wheel until she had to stop herself from damaging it. She wasn't satisfied. There were more people behind this; more people who worked for this Xerxes. Shouldn't they all pay the price too? Achilla calmed her nerves as she rode down I-84, but her bones yearned for more. More people had to pay. More people would pay. She just had to figure out who and how. Until then, she had a funeral to prepare for. Achilla dropped Ailina off at a train station in Waterbury and they stood out front as people passed by listening to headphones and carrying their bags from the mall.

"We rendezvous after the funeral," Achilla said. "Give me a day to grieve."

"Whatever you need," Ailina replied as she turned her back to the train station.

"Wait!" Achilla blurted as she stepped forward.

"Hm?" Ailina hummed as she looked over her shoulder. "What is it?"

"Well," Achilla murmured. "I mean, aren't you at least going to be there? You said something earlier about Dad being the father of your child, and you got pretty pissed off at the stuff he said about him. That was a little sentimental. Look, I don't like you and you don't like me, but--"

"No," Ailina replied with a curt tone as she turned her back. "I felt nothing for him. He was a means to an end. I won't be mourning his death."

Achilla stared at Ailina's back as she fought back the really, really, stupid tears in her eyes and the lump in her throat.

"However," Ailina sighed. "I understand how attached you were to him. So, I'll wait until you're done."

"OK."

"Please tell me you're not about to cry like some weakling," Ailina said.

"You're lying," Achilla said with a flat tone as she won the battle with her tears.

"I needed a child, Achilla," said Ailina while turning to face her.

"Brendan provided one. You. I didn't lie about that. He was a means to an end."

"No, that part's true," Achilla replied. "But you lied when you said you felt nothing for him. My instincts are sharper than you give me credit for."

"I don't need this," said Ailina as she walked away until Achilla grabbed her shoulder and held her in place.

"I don't know if you're capable of love," Achilla said with a soft voice, "or even know what it is, but you attacked my father when he broke up with you. I did the math. You were already pregnant by then. If all you needed was a child, then his role was complete. So why did you care so much whether he came or went?"

"I like to decide when it's over instead of letting the man-"

"He was more than just *the man* to you," Achilla snapped. "You were obsessed with him. You think I forgot all those nights watching you get yourself drunk over him leaving you?"

"I was not--"

"And I saw how mad you got at Blue Eyes," Achilla kept going. "You were insulted. You were insulted just like I was because he disrespected my father. He disrespected the man you love and--"

"Just shut up and go to your funeral!" Ailina snarled before she smacked Achilla's arm away and marched away.

"I'm not done talking to you," Achilla commanded as she grabbed Ailina's shoulder again. Ailina whirled around and swung a right hand at her face. It was a punch that would have broken her nose during her childhood, but Achilla slipped it, ducked inside, and snatched Ailina into a full nelson. She slid her ankle between Ailina's legs in case she decided to kick, and Ailina growled as she struggled. Passersby in the stared at them but kept walking just as Achilla wanted. Still, she could feel the concrete cracking under her feet as they struggled.

"Let me go, Achilla!" Ailina snarled as she reached for Achilla's hair. Achilla leaned back and tightened her grip by pushing her hands down at the base of Ailina's head.

"You loved my father, didn't you?" Achilla grunted. "With all of that tough talk, you loved him."

"No!" Ailina growled.

"You didn't need to help me kill Blue Eyes," Achilla replied as the concrete block beneath them cracked between their legs. "You wanted him dead as much as I did because he killed the man you always loved. Admit it, dammit! You loved Brendan Johnson! You loved my father!"

Achilla let go and pushed Ailina forward. Ailina stumbled for a bit before turning to face her with eyes that flickered even in broad daylight. Her body shook, and her hands balled into fists, but she did nothing. Ailina took a deep breath before wiping her hair from her face. She then turned her back on Achilla.

"You've gotten strong," Ailina said. "I'll give you that, but I won't be joining you when you mourn Brendan's corpse. He won't even be there to see it. I just don't see the purpose."

Achilla frowned as she watched Ailina march into the train station. She then hopped into her car and drove out of Waterbury. Did Ailina have feelings for Brendan? Achilla still couldn't fight the fact that she knew Ailina was lying about not caring, but it didn't matter now. Brendan was gone, and even if he were alive, he wanted nothing to do with her. It was over between them long before Brendan's death. There was no chance that her biological parents could get along; especially if one of them held the other by his throat. Perhaps Ailina was right. Part of Achilla still thought like a child.

When Achilla arrived home and walked up the walkway toward the house, she looked at her hands. She had just taken a life, and for the first time, she was the aggressor. She had just committed first-degree murder, but her hands looked so clean. By looking at her hands, one would never know that they had just finished torturing and strangling someone to death. She opened the front door and saw Sam, Samuel, and Sandy standing in the foyer. Sam wore her bright red robe and carnation slippers. Samuel stood in a white t-shirt and knee-length black basketball shorts. Sandy wore a sky blue Columbia University t-shirt that she must have borrowed from Sam. Their clothes were nothing out of the ordinary, but their faces struck Achilla the most. Their expressions bombarded her with questions. Where was she? When did she leave? Why did she leave? Did she go see Ailina again? Achilla sighed and faced them with her hands on her hips.

"I know what's coming next," Achilla said. "And--"

"Save it," Sam said with a raised hand. "I'm not going to ask you anything. You're not going to tell us anyway, and quite frankly, I'm done worrying about you."

"OK," Achilla replied with a frown. "I'm...sorry."

"Don't be," Sam said. "I know you saw Ailina again. I don't know why, and I know it's nothing good, but you're a woman now. I can't tell you what to do. All I can do is pray for you."

Achilla watched Sam turn her back and walk into the kitchen. She could tell by her brother's hard stare that he shared her sentiment. They'll be praying for her, but they'll also be praying for the strength to forgive her. Sandy's expression was different. It was less angry and more knowing, and it made her shift her feet. Achilla walked up the steps to the guest room where she was going to shower and change before eating an awkward breakfast with her family. As she sat on her bed and pulled up her shirt, she heard someone stand in the doorway. She pulled her shirt down and looked over her shoulder to see Sandy standing there with her arms crossed.

"What's up, Sandy?" Achilla asked.

"You have blood on your shoes," Sandy said as she pointed at Achilla's sneakers. "It's kind of hard to see when you're wearing black sneakers, but when you've seen it before, you know it. That's blood, and since you don't look hurt, I don't think it's yours."

"Really?" Achilla asked without looking down. "Oh no, it must be--"

"Don't bother lying," Sandy snapped. "You killed someone."

"Sandy, I--"

"I grew up rough too," Sandy whispered as she looked around before continuing. "I know a murderer when I see one. How could you bring this on your family? They don't deserve it."

"I don't have time for your sensitivity, Sandy," Achilla muttered. "Now leave me alone so I can--"

"Change?" Sandy asked. "Or get rid of the evidence?"

"You don't know what you're talking about."

"You're not even denying it," Sandy hissed as her voice raised its pitch. "Did you kill Nina too?"

"No," Achilla replied. "I told you what happened then, and I would rather not have this conversation. We're done talking about it."

"What makes you think you can decide everything?" Sandy asked. "You think just because you have some weird super strength that you're better than everyone else, but you're not. You can't kill people any more than I can. It's not right!"

"Sandy," Achilla growled as she gave her a sideways glare. "I have had a very long morning, and I would like to be left alone. Leave. Me. Alone."

"Where were you?" Sandy asked. "And who was it? That's all I need to know--"

"That's enough," Sam said from behind Sandy as she patted her shoulder. "Go on and make breakfast, Sandy. I taught you how to make my special blueberry pancakes. Let me see you do it on your own, all right?"

Sandy stared at Sam with the same knowing look she gave Achilla.

"Go on, Sandy," Sam said with a smile. "I'll talk to her. I'm her mother."

Sandy turned and trotted down the stairs, and Achilla ripped off her shirt and stared out the window. When she heard Sam walk behind her, she clenched her fist. Her urge to fight hadn't left her since her visit to Mattapan, and Sandy had only made things worse. Achilla bit her lip to prevent from swinging at her mother when she touched her shoulder. Sam's hand recoiled.

"Honey, you are hard as a rock," Sam said.

"Sorry, it's been a while since I've had a massage."

"I don't appreciate sarcasm, and you know that," Sam replied. "The truth is you're even more tense than usual. You've always had this me against the world mentality, but even this is strange."

"What can I say?" Achilla said with a shrug without turning around. "I'm a strange girl."

"Achilla, you will face me when I'm speaking to you," Sam said in a low, steady voice. "I am still your mother, and you are standing in my house."

Achilla sighed and turned around. Sam had changed into one of Brendan's black and red Fairfield University Stags t-shirts with a side view of a deer's head in the center. The more Achilla looked at it, the more it reminded her of Brendan and how at one point, she considered applying to Fairfield just because he went there. She thought it would have made him proud to play for their basketball team. Now she stood in the guest room of her parents' new house with the blood of a dead man caking on her black sneakers. Achilla lowered her head and stared at her feet until Sam held her by her shoulders and looked her in the eye.

"You don't have to tell me anything," Sam said. "But I heard that whole conversation with Sandy."

"I know," Achilla murmured. "I heard you coming. I can hear everything in this house."

"Good, then you understand why I won't pressure you," Sam replied as she patted Achilla's left shoulder. "I have no clue what kind of life you've had to live over the past few years, but if it's anything like my father's, I want no part of it. I know why you're here, but I don't want a repeat of what it was like to live in a house full of secrets."

"Mom, if I have my way, you never will," Achilla said. "I can promise you that. I just…I just can't tell you everything right now. There are a lot of things I have to do that you can't know."

"You have more control over your life than you think," Sam replied. "We all do. There's always a choice. Always."

"Mom," Achilla started to sob. "I wish I could explain to you why that's not always true."

"Stop," Sam snapped with her hand raised. "Stop talking like that. No matter what happens, no matter what anyone tells you, you have a choice. It may not be easy, but nothing can prevent you from having the life you want. Nothing can stop you. All right?"

"Yes, ma'am."

"You may not believe it," Sam said. "But God has always had a plan for you. He'll reveal it in good time."

"I don't deserve your God, Mom," Achilla heaved.

"Neither do I," Sam replied. "But nothing you say or do is too ugly for Him. Trust me. I want you to think about that. Then I want you to freshen up before breakfast. You stink."

As Sam rubbed her arms, Achilla laughed a little. She stopped laughing when she realized that she smelled fine. It was the stench of the abandoned house and Blue Eyes' adrenaline drenched body odor and blood that stuck to her clothing. The scent was so strong that even a regular human could pick it up. She relaxed at the realization that Sam had no clue what a fight to the death smelled like. She raised her head and forced a smile.

"Your father and I promised to always love you," Sam said as she smiled back. "I'm keeping that promise. See you downstairs."

Achilla nodded her head as Sam turned to leave the room. She then walked across the guest room and closed the window that she left open just a few hours ago when she snuck out to avenge her father's murder. The image of the tired look on Blue Eyes' face before she stomped his throat racked her brain like a migraine, and Achilla held her head in her hands as she sat on her bed. She killed a man this morning, but that wasn't what bothered her the most. As Achilla replayed the killing in her head, she watched herself torture and kill a man with so much *ease* that it made her nauseous. She remembered the rage in her eyes while she kicked him. She remembered that Ailina had to stop her from ripping his body apart. Ailina, the sociopathic, sadistic, abusive mother, *had to restrain her*.

That was it. She didn't care what Sam said about God. If God was real, and He was so *good*, He wouldn't allow someone like Achilla to walk the earth. She didn't deserve to live any more than Blue Eyes. Achilla reached under her pillow and pulled out her .44 Magnum. She faced the window as she held the gun to her head with a trembling hand. With one click, there would be one less murderer walking the earth. The CIA couldn't use her anymore. Ailina couldn't use her anymore. Her family would have nothing to fear. Her death could solve everyone's problems. Tears leaked down Achilla's cheeks as her finger hovered around the trigger.

"Hey Achilla, how do you want your eggs?" Sam asked from behind Achilla's back until she gasped. Achilla cringed at herself. She forgot to listen for anyone coming, but it was too late anyway. No one could stop her now. One click of the trigger and she wouldn't hurt anyone else.

"Achilla," Sam said in a low voice. "Baby, what's wrong? Whatever it is, we can work it out."

Achilla whimpered and heaved as her finger hovered over the trigger. She wanted to tell her, but she knew she couldn't. Sam couldn't know that the daughter she raised and loved was a murderer. She couldn't be forced to testify in court on her behalf, or against her, if and when the FBI found out. It was bad enough that Achilla's father was dead. She couldn't live with ruining her mother's life.

"Baby, please," Sam said with a shaking voice. "Please don't. I don't know what Ailina said to you, but whatever it is, it's *not true!* OK, Achilla? It's not true. She's lying. She's lying, Achilla. She *always lies.* Your father would always say that. He called her a machine. Just stick a quarter in her and out comes a lie."

Achilla set her jaw and took a deep breath. She was a murderer. She didn't deserve to live. Sam deserved a better daughter. Samuel deserved a better sister. Achilla was putting an end to this now.

"Lord, please," Sam wailed as Achilla heard her drop to her knees. "Please, God, not her too. Please...please don't let her do this. Don't....Please don't take my daughter away! I'll...I'll do anything!"

Achilla shook her head. No prayer was going to stop this. This wasn't God's decision. It was hers. For the first time in a while, Achilla knew that she held the keys to her own life; not Ailina and not the CIA. Not even the Good Lord Himself. This was her call and she made it. Achilla clenched her teeth, closed her eyes, and pulled the trigger.

She flinched when she heard Sam scream. She then frowned and looked at the gun. In her emotional state, Achilla didn't bother to check the weight. Upon bouncing the .44 Magnum up and down in her hand, she realized what should have been obvious.

She was out of bullets.

No.

Somebody took her bullets.

Achilla turned around and looked at her mother's tear-soaked face. Sam rushed across the room and hugged her around the waist. She stood with a dazed expression as her mother sobbed into her breasts and thanked Jesus over and over. Achilla dropped the gun on the floor and hugged her back as Samuel and Sandy rushed into the room. Samuel looked at Achilla then at the gun on the floor and his jaw dropped. Sandy burst into tears and darted across the room as Sam cried so loud that it echoed around the house. Achilla still held her dazed look as Samuel ambled across the room and embraced them with arms long enough to cover them all. As her family wept, Achilla stared out of her door.

Only a person with a working knowledge of firearms would know how to completely disarm a .44 Magnum Desert Eagle. Nobody in this family had that knowledge. The only person who entered Achilla's room within the last few hours with that kind of training was Ailina. However, Ailina hadn't made it past her doorway before she woke up. Achilla would've noticed if she reached under her pillow while she was sleeping. Was it really a miracle? Did God save her life?

No, there was one person left whom Achilla hadn't considered.

"God is so good!" Sam cried out as she clutched Achilla's back. "Thank you, Jesus!"

"Sandy," Achilla said.

"Yeah?" Sandy asked as she wiped tears from her face.

"Did you unload my gun?" Achilla asked as she stared out into the hallway.

"Yeah," Sandy said. "When you threatened me, I got scared. So I waited until you weren't home."

"Thanks," Achilla said. "How did you know how to do that?"

"I watched Nina."

Achilla laughed and shook her head. One thing Achilla remembered from church growing up was how miracles work. They're seldom magical events where someone's leg grows back or they rise back from the dead. Miracles were usually a chain of events with links that tighten at just the right time to stop the terrible from happening. It only made sense that Sandy would know how to unload a gun. She worked for a former CIA agent who most likely planned on teaching her how to protect her business. With all of her genius intelligence, Achilla couldn't believe that she didn't see it coming. A smile crept onto her lips as she looked up from her family.

"Well played," Achilla said to the ceiling.

"What?" Sandy asked.

"Nothing," Achilla replied before she hugged Sandy and Sam, taking care to keep her embrace as gentle as possible. "And I promise I'll never do that again."

Chapter Seventeen

ACHILLA JOHNSON:16

Achilla's sixteenth birthday marked her most drastic change. She woke up at four in the morning, threw on a black t-shirt, shorts, and sneakers, and did her usual routine: ran twenty miles, ran back, performed hundreds of handstand pushups and body squats, and did thousands of crunches in their basement. She could now hold a fifteen-minute plank as well. Though she worked hard in her boxing class, Achilla realized that if she punched her hardest during sparring matches, she would knock out her opponents. She saved her true punching power on the heavy bag at home. As she predicted, she had already broken the chain on her first bag. So she installed a new one with double chains and a cinder block holding it from the bottom. This morning, Achilla stood in her boxing stance and threw her weight into a left hook with perfect form and proper snap.

Achilla gasped when a small hole burst into the bag and sand poured onto the floor. She then jumped back when the chains snapped and the bag dropped with a slam. She stared at her fist, then at the bag. Normally when she hit too hard, the bag swung loose and snapped the chain. This time, the force of her punch destroyed the bag from the inside-out. Also, the bag felt light. It was the heaviest bag she could find, but it felt no different than hitting a pillow.

She decided to test her strength and stepped out the front door, breathing in the morning air. The sky was dark blue, and the mockingbirds sang their morning mix as she strolled through the front yard until she reached the street. Achilla looked both ways to check for cars or spectators, and she saw and heard no one around. She then stared down at the street in between her black sneakers. After staring at the ground for five minutes, she exhaled as she punched the pavement with a thud that echoed and bounced around the neighborhood. At first, she grimaced and held her throbbing right hand. Upon further inspection, her hand was fine aside from slight swelling in the middle knuckle.

Achilla covered her mouth when she looked at the pavement. Cracks spread from the spot she punched until they created a circular spider-web shape that was at least a foot and a half in diameter. She shook her hand and walked back to her home with a wide-eyed smile. She would soon have the power to punch through concrete.

Ailina had better watch out.

Achilla finished her workout, showered, and changed into a white t-shirt and black sweatpants. She then trotted down the stairs in her ankle socks and sandals, jogged into the living room, and hopped the couch with a giddy grin on her face. She turned on the television and shifted on the couch as she searched for an ideal posture for pretending to be an unsuspecting victim. Achilla's family had no clue, but she knew they were going to throw her a surprise birthday party. Her superb hearing didn't allow for any of them to discuss things without her knowledge, but she loved the fact that they tried. In return, she would humor them. They deserved as much.

She changed the channel to ESPN when she heard her brother creeping down the steps. She suppressed a giggle when she heard her parents step out of their bedroom. None of them said a word. A house with a deep-voiced defense attorney, a son who takes after him, and a teacher who talks as much as he does was silent first thing in the morning? Achilla chuckled and shook her head. Even if she had no clue what they were doing, she would have figured it out within five minutes.

"Achilla!" Brendan bellowed. "We need you in the kitchen. There's something we need to talk about as a family."

This was the part where Achilla was supposed to look scared. Achilla stood up with as convincing a frown on her face as she could muster and ambled into the kitchen. Brendan stood in his customary black hoody and sweatpants as he held his hands on his hips. Achilla noticed Sam was standing behind Brendan. She also heard a shifting movement in the hallway by the staircase. Samuel was hiding. This was better planned than Achilla thought.

"Achilla," Brendan sighed. "We've decided that it's about time that we--"

"Wished you a HAPPY BIRTHDAY!" Sam screamed as she jumped out from behind Brendan carrying a thin white box in her hands. She also wore a t-shirt that said "Happy Sweet Sixteen Achilla Johnson!" in pink and blue spray-painted, cursive letters. Achilla frowned for real this time. She didn't recall hearing them talk about t-shirts. Brendan ripped off his hoody and revealed a matching shirt. Achilla covered her mouth with her right hand as a lump grew in her throat. She didn't even notice Samuel sneaking up on her until he jumped into the kitchen wearing the same shirt while holding three red, gift-wrapped boxes.

"HAPPY BIRTHDAY!" they all yelled in unison.

"Thank you," Achilla managed to utter as her family hugged her around the shoulders.

"It's not every day my girl turns sixteen," Sam said with a smile. "We wanted to make it special."

"I...." Achilla stammered. "The t-shirts....I..."

"We discussed that out of the house," Brendan said. "Samuel's idea. Apparently, you can hear everything or something like that. We wanted this to be a real surprise."

"Samuel, you jerk," Achilla laughed as she grabbed Samuel's head and pulled him in for a headlock. "You tricked me!"

"I had to!" Samuel replied. "Hey look, you can't strangle me before we do presents, all right?"

The birthday cake was dark chocolate with vanilla ice cream layers, and her name was written strawberry frosting at the top. Achilla sat at the kitchen table and wiped her tears as she watched her mother light the candles. When they asked her to blow them out, Achilla blew with all of her might; ripping some of the candles across the kitchen. Achilla looked up at her family and they were all smiles, despite the spattered ice cream and frosting all over the floor. Achilla noticed that they always smiled at her, no matter what she did. Achilla laughed and wiped her hair away as Brendan handed her a knife and she cut the first slice.

Achilla was pleased with her presents. Sam got her a multi-language dictionary. Brendan brought her a DVD of an entire UConn Women's basketball series with Diana Taurasi; Achilla's favorite woman ball player. Samuel gave her a new pair of boxing gloves. Finally, Achilla got a gift from both Mom and Dad; a thin, black-banded, white-faced, watch. Achilla smiled and hugged them all before running off to work wearing her new watch. As she stocked shelves with sneakers and helped customers find the right pair of running shoes, Achilla held a smile for her entire shift.

After a great day at work, she closed that night and took the bus home. Achilla normally rode all the way to her stop by the Stratford Library; which was about a fifteen-minute walk from the house. However, tonight the bus broke down in Bridgeport. Achilla walked off the bus behind the grumbling passengers in the usual Champs uniform: a black t-shirt and black and white windbreaker pants with black shell toe sneakers. She called Brendan and stared at one of the downtown high rises before he picked up.

"Hey Dad, are you at work?" Achilla asked. "My bus broke down. I'm in Bridgeport by the train station."

"You caught me in the middle of this deposition," Brendan replied. "I really can't get away, but your mother's close. I'll call her right now."

"OK, well can you tell her to meet me at the Stratford stop?" Achilla said. "I can take the train from here."

"I don't like you outside in Bridgeport this late," Brendan said. "You know it's dangerous out there."

"I know, but the train's right down the street," Achilla replied. "Besides nothing's open, so I'll just be a sitting duck out here. I can be in Stratford by ten."

"Works for me," Brendan said before he yawned. "Call me when you reach the train."

"Yeah, sure," Achilla sighed. "I'm moving now. Bye."

Achilla strolled down Water Street toward the train station. She could always run home, but the urge to keep her abilities a secret made her walk to the train. Despite her disdain for Ailina, she found herself obeying her advice almost as much as Brendan or Sam. It was like she was trained to listen to her voice no matter how many times she had lied to her before. Still, it was a nice summer night. A view of Bridgeport from the train couldn't hurt. The view of the water was even better. It would be a perfect way to end her awesome birthday. Achilla smiled and held her head high as she walked with a bounce in her step.

Achilla stopped bouncing when the hair on the back of her neck stood on end. Was Ailina nearby again? No, this was different. Somebody was watching her, but she didn't hear the popping of Ailina's leather boots. Achilla kept walking but watched and listened for any sudden changes in her environment. She stopped when a tall, black male wearing a white t-shirt, dark jeans, black Timberland boots, and a black ski mask jumped out in front of her from an alley. Achilla turned to walk the other way and saw four other men in ski masks walking toward her about thirty feet away. She turned around again when she heard the first man step toward her.

"What do you want?" Achilla asked. "Money? Look, I'll give you the cash that I have."

Achilla dug into her pockets and threw out a twenty dollar bill. The man picked it up, stuffed it in his pocket, and continued to walk toward her. By now the other men were within striking distance, and Achilla could hear their breathing from behind. They were all around the same height with different skin tones on their arms; only the pale one was shorter than the rest. They also all wore white t-shirts and black Timberland boots. The first man pointed at Achilla's watch. Achilla shook her head until he pulled out a knife and flicked out the blade. Brendan always told her that if someone stuck her up, just give them what they want and tell the police later. Achilla could hardly hold back her tears as she pulled the watch off and extended it.

"Just take the damn thing," Achilla said with a catch in her voice. "And go--"

Someone grabbed her neck from behind, and she spun around and elbowed him in the head, sending him to the ground in a heap as the four other men jumped toward her. The man with the knife was first. Achilla dodged his knife thrust, knelt down, pulled his arm over her shoulder and snapped it. He cried out before she tossed him over her shoulder into a parked car. She then side kicked the closest guy into one of the cement buildings. She heard his bones crack as he slammed against the building and dropped to the sidewalk. The other two stood with their hands raised as Achilla stalked toward them. One of them pulled out his own knife, but he was too late. Before he could use it, Achilla crushed his nose with a right straight punch that sent him flying ten feet and rolling on the pavement. When the pale man tried to run, Achilla grabbed the back of his shirt and pulled him into a choke hold.

"You like to jump unsuspecting girls?" Achilla snarled in his ear as his face turned reddish purple. "You like to take their shit? You know I got this watch from my family for my Sweet Sixteen. And you want to just take it? Is that what you like to do, huh? Is that what you punks like?!"

Achilla squeezed his neck a little tighter. She could feel the air leaving his body and not coming back. She squeezed a little more. Now his movements were slowing down. He was losing consciousness. Just a little bit more, and he would never rob anyone else again. When his knees gave out, Achilla thought of today's birthday party. She thought of her family, and how they threw her a surprise birthday party. She thought of the frightened look they had during her first year at their house and Sam's smile during the barbecue when Achilla wore her new bathing suit. She thought about Samuel and the fear on his face when she beat up Marty in front of her.

She thought about Grandma Johnson calling her the devil.

Achilla let go of the pale man and let him drop to the ground. She then backed away from him and leaned against a car. Had she really almost killed someone? She looked around at the five men she had just beaten up. None of them were moving. Achilla walked around and checked their pulse's one-by-one. They were all alive. She let out a sigh and held her hands on her hips. She had to be more careful or the next person she fought might not survive. When the pale man rose to his feet, Achilla lunged at him and grabbed him by his shirt.

"Please, don't hurt me," he squealed as she pinned him to the nearest building.

"Hurt you?" Achilla asked with a scowl. "You're lucky I didn't kill you. What are you guys a gang or something?"

When he didn't answer, Achilla tossed him in the air before punching his gut and letting him drop to the sidewalk. She then picked him up by his throat. His neck was sweating through the mask, and he coughed until Achilla clamped her hand over his mouth. She then grabbed his hair through the mask and yanked it until he cried out under her hand. Tears leaked from his face down her wrist as she pulled his head back.

"I'm not going to ask you again," Achilla growled with a wide-eyed glare. "Show me your teeth when you're ready to talk."

Achilla removed her hand from his mouth and held his neck. Even his lips trembled as he bared his teeth. She let go of his hair, and he dropped to his knees. Achilla then pushed him onto his back and stood over him. This time, he didn't run. Achilla held her foot on his knee just in case he got any ideas.

"No gang," the man said with a shaky tone. "We just like to play knockout and stuff."

"You lost," Achilla replied before frowning at his voice. "I know you from somewhere."

"No way," he said until Achilla ripped off his mask. A pudgy face with blue eyes and a pointed nose stared back at her. Achilla scowled. She knew that face anywhere. The redness, the tears, and the heavy breathing all fit. It was Marty; the same Marty whom Achilla beat to a pulp for picking on Samuel when they were kids.

"Marty?" Achilla asked. "Are you kidding?"

"Look, Achilla, I--"

"You knew it was me?" Achilla snapped as she grabbed Marty's shirt and pulled him off the ground. "You recognized me, and you still tried to jump me? This isn't some game! You tried to get back at me!"

"No, it's not like--"

Achilla punched Marty in the mouth and let him slump to the ground. She watched blood leak out of his fingers as he held his hand over his mouth and groaned just like old times. As he rolled on the ground, Achilla stopped him with her foot. She then picked up a couple of teeth from the sidewalk and threw them at his belly before pulling him close by his shirt.

"Tell anyone, and I'll find you, Marty," Achilla said as she pointed her finger at his face. "I'll find you, and I'll...."

Achilla took a deep breath and turned to walk toward the train station, leaving Marty and his friends on the sidewalk. She didn't know what bothered her more; the fact that she almost threatened to kill Marty, or that she knew she could back it up. Achilla stared at her hands. Aside from the swelling from this morning, they had minimal damage, and she felt no pain. Worse, she felt no guilt or fear; even knowing that she severely injured five people and left them in the street. Self-defense or not, Achilla knew that the chance to fight made her heart race. She caught herself smiling at her victory. Achilla shook those thoughts of her head. Right about now, there was nothing she would enjoy more than going home.

After she bought her ticket at a kiosk and waited outside on the wooden platform for her train, Achilla contemplated how she would explain herself to her parents. She decided not to. The less her family knew about her ability to kill, the better off they were. Achilla didn't want them making any connections to her contact with Ailina; connections that could cost them their lives. She caught the next train and made the Stratford stop by 10:15 pm. Achilla hid her hands under her shirt as she sat in her mother's silver sedan. Sam sighed as she stopped at a red light.

"Achilla, why didn't you call your father?" Sam asked. "We were worried sick."

"Oh," Achilla said as she pulled out her cellphone and noticed six missed calls. "I'm sorry."

"It's fine, but you know how we worry."

"I understand," Achilla groaned. "It won't happen again."

"Well anyway, I hope you enjoyed your birthday," Sam said as the light turned green and shined on the long red Fairfield University t-shirt that she must have borrowed from Brendan. "I'm sorry you had to work."

"I made money," Achilla replied with a shrug. "I can live with that."

"You get that honest from Brendan," Sam said with a slight chuckle. "That's that Johnson work ethic."

"Thanks," Achilla said with a smile. "I'll take that as a compliment."

"So listen, we don't like you out so late," Sam replied. "Your father thinks it's about time we got you a car, and I agree."

"Really?" Achilla asked with a frown. "You didn't argue with him about it?"

"Yes, really," Sam replied before pointing at Achilla. "And don't get smart. You're out and about a lot, and Lord knows what can happen."

"Yeah," Achilla said as she looked out the window. "So, about that--"

"Besides, we might need you to pick up Samuel now that you guys go to the same school in the fall," Sam continued. "It's a win-win for everyone. Let's pick out a car this weekend."

"Cool," Achilla sighed as she leaned her head back against the seat.

"I have to stop at the store before it closes," Sam said as she drove past their street. "I'm sorry, Achilla. Were you saying something earlier?"

"Nope," Achilla replied as she looked out the window. "Nothing important."

When they arrived home, Achilla gasped and rushed out of the car. She forgot to clean up her heavy bag from this morning. Sam grabbed her shoulder before she got too far. Achilla looked at her, and she handed Achilla a couple bags of groceries. Achilla rolled her eyes and carried them into the house.

"Hey, what's the rush?" Sam asked as Achilla set the bags on the kitchen table and ran toward the basement door. "No girl talk tonight?"

"I left a huge mess downstairs," Achilla said as Sam walked into the kitchen. "Dad's mad enough about the punching bag. If he sees a pile of sand, he'll flip out, and I'll never be allowed to have one. I have to clean it up."

"Shovel's behind the door," Sam said with a pointed finger and cocked an eyebrow. "You're lucky your father's been at work all day and night preparing for this trial."

"I know," Achilla groaned as she opened the basement door and grabbed one of their snow shovels. She rushed downstairs, skipping every other step with the shovel over her shoulder. Once Achilla reached the bottom of the steps, she flipped the lights on. What she saw in the basement made her drop the shovel. Achilla walked into the basement with her jaw dropped as she looked at a brand new, black heavy bag with gold and white numbered strike-points on it. Achilla pushed the bag with her hand and noticed that it was the heaviest bag she had ever felt. It must have been a surprise birthday present. Achilla stood in front of the bag with a giddy smile on her face as she heard Sam walk down the stairs. She squealed and jumped up and down. This day just couldn't get any better.

"Hm, that's fancy," Sam said with her hands on her hips. "Did Brendan buy that for you?"

Achilla stopped jumping and frowned. Brendan and Sam never bought gifts for her without speaking to each other first. So who set bought this bag and installed it? Achilla's throat dried up as she walked around the bag. There was a piece of paper taped to it. Achilla ripped it off and folded it before shoving it in her pocket.

"Achilla, I asked you a question," Sam said with a stern voice. "How did this bag get in here? Never mind, I'll just ask your father--"

"I bought it," Achilla blurted.

"But you just said--"

"I forgot," Achilla said with a weak smile. "It's been a long day, Mom. I must've made the mess last night and cleaned it."

"Girl, you have been losing your mind," Sam said as she walked upstairs. "Maybe you need to drop some of those commitments you have. I'd hate to see you forget a homework assignment like that."

Achilla waited for her mother to close the basement door shut before she reached into her pocket for the paper. She then held the folded paper in her hands as if it would explode upon opening. As Achilla opened the paper, her hands shook and tears welled up in her eyes. She swallowed hard as she read the note. It read:

"You've progressed nicely. Here's a new bag for all of your hard work. You'll find it much more durable than the others. I designed it just for you.

:) :) :) Happy birthday! :) :) :)

p.s. Tell Sam that she shouldn't blast music in her headphones while she vacuums. It's really bad for her ears and makes it difficult to hear an intruder. We don't want her to get hurt, right?"

Achilla crumpled the note in her hands. She then growled to herself as she ripped the paper into small pieces and dumped them in a trash can by the staircase. Now Achilla looked at the bag with a scowl. This was not a gift from her father. It was a threat from Ailina. It was also the worst kind of threat to Achilla's family; the kind that only she could see. Achilla shut off the lights in the basement and walked upstairs. The next time she saw Ailina, she would respond in kind.

By the time her junior year started, Achilla got her license after a month of driving school and a black sedan as her parents promised. Per her father's orders, she was required to keep it clean or she couldn't drive it. Brendan told Achilla to expect random inspections of her car's interior. He also told her to take it to a mechanic before tinkering with it on her own, but after watching her work around a car, he changed his mind. Achilla enjoyed her first car and her school parking space, courtesy of being a star basketball player. What she didn't enjoy was her new startling revelation.

Her brother had no concept of time.

Aside from family outings, Achilla never had to travel anywhere with Samuel before, but now that she could drive, it was her job to take him to school. Up until now, Achilla never noticed how long it took the boy to dress himself, and his slow pace made her grind her teeth. It was September and Samuel's first day in high school. Today, of all days, he managed to run behind.

"Samuel, hurry up," Achilla called as she tossed her car keys between her hands. She wore a navy blue cutoff shirt and black basketball shorts as she leaned against the front door and looked out one of their windows. A morning fog that enveloped the street started to clear out with the morning sunrise, and Achilla sighed and stroked her ponytail as she turned her attention to the staircase that Samuel should have walked down by now. She crossed her arms, tapped her foot, and checked her watch as she listened to his fumbling around in his bedroom.

"Samuel!" Achilla barked with a Brendan-like tone of voice. "We're running late."

"No, we're not," Samuel said as he walked down the steps in a sky blue t-shirt and black basketball shorts. "We have two and half hours."

"We have practice in the morning," Achilla replied with her hands on her hips as she squinted her eyes at him. "Or did you forget about that, Samuel? Where is your change of clothes?"

Samuel cringed and ran back up the steps. Achilla decided to take care of Samuel's conditioning and skills training before he tried out for the basketball team. That meant waking up early and practicing with her. He was expected to run three miles, thirty bleachers, and perform as many pushups as he could in two minutes. He was then expected to shoot twenty jump-shots from five different spots on the floor and make twenty layups with each hand. That was the warm-up. After that, they would run suicides, do defensive slides across the court with weighted bricks each hand, and commence ball handling and shooting drills. Samuel then had to make ten free throws in a row and run a sprint for every free throw he missed. It was nothing for Achilla, but she knew it would be hell for him. She wanted Samuel to start varsity during his freshman year. The Johnson household deserved nothing less. Achilla glared at Samuel as he ran out the door with his gym bag. He was running a few extra bleachers for making her wait.

He didn't realize it yet, but Samuel had lots of potential. Despite Achilla's superior athleticism, Samuel had far greater natural talent on the offensive end. He was a natural ball handler with great court vision, and he could get to the hoop better than anyone with his knack for finding holes in the defense and creating space for himself. He was a Division I guard in the making. He just needed to be pushed. So Achilla pushed him that morning until he vomited in a trash can. Samuel wiped his mouth with his t-shirt and held his hands over his head as he walked toward the gymnasium doors.

"Where the hell do you think you're going?" Achilla asked with her hands on her hips. "We're not done."

"I'm done," Samuel huffed. "I can barely walk. I'm exhausted."

Achilla sprinted across the room so fast that Samuel flinched when she blocked his path to the door. Samuel stepped back, but Achilla grabbed him by his shirt and pinned him against the gymnasium wall. He tried to break free, but Achilla knew she was too strong for him. She would never hurt him, but she wasn't going to let him go.

"You don't know what exhausted even means," Achilla snarled as she pulled him close. "You can barely walk? You made to that door just fine. You didn't have to crawl! No...no, you're not exhausted. You're breathing heavy. You're in pain. You're nauseous, but you're not exhausted. And since you don't know what exhausted means, I will decide when you're exhausted. Get out there and run those damn sprints or you'll have to deal with me!"

Achilla shoved Samuel onto the court. Samuel looked back at her with tears in her eyes, and Achilla crossed her arms and nodded toward the court. He then turned around and sprinted. When they finished with practice, Samuel laid in the middle of the gym floor in a pool of sweat, and Achilla smirked and helped him up. Samuel's knees wobbled, but Achilla ducked under his armpit and helped him walk. It was a lot easier to do that now that he was taller than she was.

"Why'd you do that earlier?" Samuel asked as Achilla walked him toward the boys' locker room. "That whole speech."

"You have a lot of potential, Samuel," Achilla replied just as they reached the locker room doorway. "You don't see it, but I do. I'll be damned if I watch you mess it up on purpose. Get dressed. I'll wait outside."

Achilla showered and changed into the clothes she packed for school; a plain gray t-shirt, a pair of blue jeans, red and black sneakers, and a matching black-out Chicago Bulls fitted cap with the tag on the brim; letting her jet black hair flow down her back. She stood in the hallway, leaning against the wall by the gym doors as other students passed by. Achilla lowered her head and picked her nails when a couple girls stared at her. As usual, the haters were in full effect. Achilla never understood why girls in school hated her so much, but at least they all knew better than to fight her. Monika most likely spread the word on making that mistake.

She stood up when she saw Samuel step out of the gym wearing khakis, black shell-toe sneakers, and a black t-shirt. Somehow, Samuel's clothes seemed just professional enough to impress the teachers but cool enough to blend in with high schoolers. Samuel stood in front of Achilla with his hands on his hips and smiled. Just earlier, he had to be helped off of the court. Now he was smiling? Achilla needed no more evidence that Samuel was a top-level athlete.

"Good practice, Samuel," Achilla said. "Keep that up, and you'll be a star. When's your next class?"

"AP English," Samuel said. "Mr. Jensen."

"Good," Achilla replied. "English is easy. Knowing you, it's probably your strength."

"Do you really think I'm that smart?" Samuel asked.

"Yes," Achilla replied with a snort. "Look, you're like Dad. You know how to talk to people and that probably translates into your writing assignments. You'll do fine. You're going to make lots of friends too. High school's built for kids like you."

"Thanks," Samuel said. "So which way is room 210?"

"I forget,"Achilla said with a shrug as she walked away. "Go find it."

Achilla suppressed her smile as she watched Samuel roll his eyes and speed walk down the hallway. Every time she looked at Samuel she saw all of the positive qualities that she did not possess. With all of her intelligence, Achilla had to make a conscious effort to not say the wrong thing and offend someone by pointing out their character flaws or inefficiency at completing a task. To Achilla, it was just an observation. To anyone else, it was an unsolicited criticism. Samuel always knew when to speak up and when to shut up. The same way Achilla could fight her way through five men jumping her in Downtown Bridgeport, Samuel probably could have convinced them to change their ways and join the local chapter of Habitat for Humanity. He just had a gift; a quality that Achilla couldn't see in any other kids at Stratford High School. She decided that she was going to make sure he used it to the best of his ability.

As expected, it didn't take long for Samuel to blossom. Within two months he was able to finish his morning workouts without collapsing. He was also the most popular freshman in school. Whenever Samuel rode in Achilla's car to school or the mall, his cell phone was constantly vibrating, and it was usually a girl's phone number. One day, Achilla decided to reward Samuel's hard work by taking him to the Trumbull Mall. There was an FYE on the bottom floor that was selling a video game Samuel was dying to try. As they pulled into the parking lot, Achilla heard Samuel's phone vibrate. He rushed to pick it up, and Achilla grabbed his wrist with her free hand.

"No," Achilla said. "Let her wait."

"But this girl--"

"Let her wait," Achilla cut him off with a pointed finger at his phone. "Girls like guys who have things to do. Nobody wants a guy with no life."

"OK," Samuel said. "I see your point there. Play it cool."

"Are you a virgin, Samuel?" Achilla asked.

"Uh...I mean--"

"That's a yes," Achilla quipped. "Look, you'll stay a virgin for a long time if you jump at every girl's call. Chill out and give her a chance to want you too."

"That's not what Mom says."

"Mom's married," Achilla sighed as she searched for a parking space. "Married people are different. They're comfortable with each other. No need for games. Mom's been married for over fourteen years now. She doesn't know anything else anymore. But if you notice, Mom loves Dad and he works his ass off. He doesn't call her right away because he's busy. Dad's a man who's doing something with his life. Don't you want to be like Dad?"

"No," Samuel said. "I want to be myself."

"Good," Achilla replied with a grin. "That's an even better answer than I wanted."

"So when do I call?" Samuel asked.

"Don't know," Achilla said with a shrug. "Whenever you feel like it. You shouldn't feel compelled to call someone. Just call her whenever it suits you."

"I thought you weren't good with people," Samuel said. "Where'd you learn that?"

"Experience," Achilla said. That statement was only half-true. She grew up watching Ailina do the same thing to her men. They usually ended up calling every day. Achilla nodded her head when Samuel let his phone ring. A voicemail indicator popped up on the screen and he tucked it in his pocket.

"That's good, Samuel," Achilla said as she pulled into a space on the far end of the parking lot. She was about to unlock the doors and step out when she noticed a black car pull behind them. It looked like the cop cars that detectives drove; plain with the small siren light on the windshield. Achilla's heart pumped through her t-shirt when she noticed a woman in the driver's seat. She gasped when the woman looked up with a pair of glowing green eyes.

When Samuel unbuckled his seat beat, Achilla grabbed his red button-up shirt and held him against his seat.

"What the hell--"

"Quiet!" Achilla hissed as she watched Ailina step out of the car wearing black slacks, a gray button-down shirt, and suspenders. "Stay in the car at all times no matter what you hear or see. Got it?"

"What are you--?"

"Don't argue, *don't even talk*, just do as I say," Achilla said before giving Samuel a pleading look. "Please!"

Samuel nodded his head and Achilla checked her rearview. There was no avoiding her. If they drove off, she would just follow them home. Achilla had to deal with this now, and her hands trembled when she stepped out of the car. She rubbed out her hands on her red t t-shirt and faced Ailina as she approached wearing her usual high-heeled boots. Ailina smacked her gum as she stood with her hands on her hips. She then pulled the pencil out of the bun in her hair and pulled a notebook out of her back pocket. Achilla frowned when she started writing. Ailina smirked when Achilla stepped away from the car.

"Don't mind me," Ailina said before pointing at the car with her pen. "Your taillight's out, that's all."

"No, it's not," Achilla replied. "So what're you writing there?"

"Your license plate number," Ailina said just before she finished writing and shoved the notepad in her back pocket. "I wish you'd've told me that you got a new car. Who's the passenger?"

"A friend," Achilla said with a wink. "A boyfriend actually, just like you wanted. You mind giving us some alone time--"

"Yeah, don't bullshit me," Ailina snapped. "I know that's Price's grandson, and I know you've become his chauffeur. When are you going to stop lowering yourself, and realize who you are?"

"You have a strange way of talking about normal relationships," Achilla replied with a sideways stare before letting out a grin. "Do I detect some jealousy?"

"No, but does he know how dangerous it is to be in close quarters with you?" Ailina asked. "You might knock out his teeth, break his jaw, shatter four of his ribs, and, my personal favorite, dislocate two disks out of his back. I believe that's what you did to those five guys in Bridgeport this summer. Do you know how hard you have to hit someone to knock two of their disks out? I'd be impressed if I didn't have to bend over backwards to cover it up--"

"Don't want to talk about that," Achilla said. "Am I under arrest? If so, I need to call my Dad. He's my attorney. Or maybe you can talk to him since you enjoy breaking into my house."

"Nope," Ailina replied. "I just thought I'd find you and congratulate you in person this time. Your body is maturing. Of course, you're not done just yet. In a couple years your strength will surprise you. It'll get harder to hide, but you'll learn how just like I did."

"Why are you telling me this?" Achilla asked. "If I didn't know any better, I'd think you were trying to help me like a good mother should."

"I told you before that I help my own."

"So what does that mean?" Achilla asked. "What are we?"

"We're superior--"

"Beings, yeah you said that before," Achilla snapped with a raised hand. "You'll have to explain more than that. Otherwise, you just sound like a sociopath with a God complex; which might still be true."

Ailina blinked twice at her before crossing her arms and sighing like a frustrated teacher. Achilla kept her eyes trained on her, but she listened for any movements in the car. She really hoped Samuel wasn't stupid enough to get out. There was no telling what Ailina might do to him if he did. Achilla shifted her stance a little closer to the car as Ailina opened her mouth to speak.

"Well, we're human," Ailina said. "For lack of a better word anyway. But we're advanced humans; we're smarter, faster, and stronger."

"That's vague at best," Achilla said with a frown. "Care to elaborate?"

"Think of Hercules," Ailina replied. "Or, since you like to go to church, Samson. People who were regarded as so great that they were called either sons of deities, angels fallen from heaven, or even regular people blessed by God somehow were most likely like you and me. The truth is we're just the next step in the food chain and nothing more."

"Then how come there aren't more of us?" Achilla asked before holding her hands on her hips. "Assuming anything you just said isn't complete bullshit."

"Watch your language," Ailina said as her eyes turned into green orbs of ice. "You should give your mother a little more respect."

"I think mother is a little strong," Achilla replied. "Egg donor's more like it--"

Ailina closed their gap and pinned her against the car by her shirt. Achilla smacked her arms down and swung at her face, but Ailina slipped her punch, grabbed her wrist, and turned her around. She twisted Achilla's arm behind her back and clamped her hand over her mouth. When Achilla tried to bite one of her fingers, she rolled her hand until it pressed against her nose. Tears rolled down Achilla's face as she gasped from the ripping sensation in her nostrils.

"You put up a fight this time," Ailina whispered in Achilla's ear as she tightened her grip on her arm. "But it's nowhere near good enough. Of course, I have to go easy on you because we're in public. Try that in the privacy of an abandoned building, and I might've slammed you through the floor. By the way, little Samuel's watching. Should I introduce myself?"

Achilla tried to break free, but Ailina twisted her arm further and used her right leg to spread Achilla's feet. She then pressed harder against her nose until the bridge crunched. Achilla sobbed when she could taste blood in her mouth. Her nose and shoulder screeched for mercy, but all she could think about was Samuel. More tears leaked out of her eyes at the thought of him running into Ailina. Achilla had to think of something quick before Ailina decided it would be more fun to torture her brother instead.

"Yeah, I think I'll meet him," Ailina snarled in Achilla's ear. "It would only be proper for your brother to know who I am. After all, I'm your *egg donor*, as you put it. If it wasn't for me, you wouldn't be here, right? If it wasn't for me, *you wouldn't be alive*, right? Isn't that true, Achilla? I did *give you life*, didn't I? Maybe he'd appreciate that more than you do, you ungrateful bitch!"

Achilla slipped her foot around Ailina's and stomped down toward her toe. Ailina moved her foot, leaving her off balance for a split second. Achilla turned into the twist in her arm and punched Ailina in the gut with her free hand. It was no different than punching the concrete. Achilla's hand throbbed as she ripped her other arm free and swung a right straight for Ailina's throat. Ailina blocked with her forearm and reached for her neck. Achilla slipped her reach and jumped back to the driver's side door of the car. She stood in a fighting stance as she waited for Ailina's next move.

Ailina stared at her with crazed, unflinching eyes as she rubbed her stomach and cracked her neck. She then laughed that awful laughter that made Achilla's knees tremble. Achilla flexed her jaw and set her feet. No more fear this time, not with her little brother in the car. Ailina finished laughing and clapped her hands the same way adults would applaud a child after she sang her favorite Barney song.

"Well done, Achilla," Ailina said as she backed away toward her vehicle. "I'll let you go this time. I think it'll be more fun to know how much you'll have to explain to our audience."

Achilla watched her walk to her car, and didn't move until she started it and drove out of the parking lot. She looked into the Honda and saw Samuel slouching in his seat. He was hiding the best way a tall, lanky fourteen-year-old could. Achilla leaned against the car and stared at the sky as she let out a whimper. Had Ailina decided to keep fighting, she could have taken Samuel away. Achilla had a long way to go. She wiped her eyes and checked her nose for more blood. It was leaking like a faucet and staining her t-shirt and brand new blue jeans. Achilla knocked on the driver's side window and gave Samuel a thumbs-up before beckoning for him to come outside. She heard the passenger side door slam and saw Samuel run around the car to her side.

"What just happened?" Samuel asked.

"Listen carefully," Achilla said as she opened the driver's side door and popped the trunk. "There's a white towel in the trunk. Get it for me."

Samuel did as he was told and Achilla wiped her nose and pressed the towel against it.

"I think you need to go to the hospital," Samuel said.

"I'm fine," Achilla replied. "And I'm not going to the hospital. I recommend you turn around for this part."

Samuel turned his back, and Achilla braced herself for what she had to do next. She grabbed her nose and realigned it with a crack. Achilla then stuffed some of the towel into her nostrils. She held the towel and leaned against the car as she watched the parking lot. Ailina never returned or circled back. She was gone for real. For now.

"You're fine now," Achilla said with a nasal pitch. "Sorry. I didn't want you to see that."

"I've seen a broken nose before," Samuel replied. "I've broken my nose in basketball games."

"I meant the fight," Achilla muttered as she looked at her feet. "I barely escaped."

"Who was that lady?" Samuel asked. "She moved as fast as you do. And what was up with that laugh? I mean, that just didn't sound right."

"Lady's a strong word," Achilla said. "And she's faster than I am. But you're right about the rest. She's my biological mother. We don't always get along."

"Runs in the family," Samuel said. "Dad doesn't like his mom all that much."

"Yeah," Achilla replied with a frown. "I wish that was a good comparison. Do you think you can remember her face?"

"I mean, yeah," Samuel said. "How can I forget after that?"

"Good," Achilla said. "If you ever see her anywhere, run into the nearest crowded place you can find. She doesn't like crowds or cameras. And don't tell Mom or Dad about this."

"OK," Samuel replied with a head nod. "Won't tell Mom or Dad."

"I don't like the way you said that," Achilla said with a squint. "How about you promise not to tell anyone, hm?"

"I promise."

"All right," Achilla sighed. "And I'm glad you're OK."

"Are *you* OK?" Samuel asked. "That was crazy."

"Yep," Achilla said as she flexed and rotated her shoulder. "Physically at least. As soon as the bleeding stops, I'm driving you home. Cool?"

"Cool," Samuel said. "And thanks."

"For what?" Achilla asked with a frown. "I didn't win."

"For protecting me," Samuel said. "I'll have to return the favor."

Achilla's heart jumped out of her chest upon hearing those words. She glared at Samuel as he stood there with his hands on his hips like what he had just said wasn't a death wish. Achilla reached over to Samuel and pulled him close by his shirt. Her eyes drilled into his as she held the towel with her other hand. Samuel stared back with wide eyes.

"No, you won't," Achilla said with a slight catch in her voice. "I will deal with her, not you!"

"OK, I got you-"

"I won't let her hurt you," Achilla growled. "And I won't allow you to come near her. Promise me that the next time you see her, you'll do exactly what I just said."

"Fine, Achilla--"

"No!" Achilla yelled. "I said promise! Fucking say it!"

"All right, I promise to do what you say," Samuel screamed with his hands raised. "You're hurting my neck, Achilla, calm down!"

"Thank you," Achilla said as she let go of Samuel's shirt and stared at the dusk sunset. "Never scare me like that again."

"That's how you look when you're scared?" Samuel asked as he fixed his shirt.

"Yeah, it is," Achilla replied as she checked her now dry nose. "You don't like it, don't say stupid shit like that."

"Fine, you made your point."

"Bleeding's stopped," Achilla said as she sniffed and wiped her nose before pointing at the car. "Get in."

"Yeah, all right," Samuel muttered. Achilla climbed into the driver's side seat and watched Samuel amble into the car. She swallowed the lump in her throat as she fumbled with her keys. She gave Samuel a weak smile when she noticed he was looking out the window. It didn't take a superior being to figure out that she had frightened and upset him. Again. Achilla lowered her head before reaching across the car and rubbing Samuel's hair.

"Hey," Achilla said. "I'm sorry I did that."

"But…"

"But nothing," Achilla replied. "I'm just sorry. If I made justifications, it wouldn't be a real apology."

"Yeah, I was wondering when you would learn that," Samuel said as he turned and faced her. "So what are you going to do about her?"

"I don't know yet," Achilla said as she started the car. "But I know I'll think of something. Just leave her to me."

Chapter Eighteen

ACHILLA JOHNSON:20

Achilla wore a black dress as she sat in the front row of the sanctuary of an old Baptist church in Bridgeport with two levels of seating, an organ on the stage, and wooden pews. Achilla had never seen it before, but according to Sam it was the church where his parents took him every Sunday as a boy, and in his will he required his funeral be held there. He left a third of all of his assets to Sam, Samuel, and Achilla each. The rest, was up to Sam: the funeral arrangements, their house, everything. When a lawyer friend of Brendan's read the part of the will that called Sam his *guardian angel with whom all could be trusted*, Sam wept until Samuel carried her out the door. She never cried again until the day of the funeral. As Brendan's guardian angel, she honored his wish and ran everything with precision.

Sam decided to cremate Brendan's body and keep the urn. So at the funeral service, all they had was a picture of Brendan posing in a courtroom wearing a navy blue suit and matching tie. His smile was radiant as always, but his eyes shone with the fire and passion of a defense attorney who won over half of his cases. Achilla crossed her black stocking covered legs as she looked around the sanctuary.

It was filled with so many coworkers, classmates, and former clients that some of them had to stand along the walls. Achilla smiled at the fact that her father was known and loved by so many people.

She never got to say goodbye. After Brendan took her in and loved her in a way she never thought was possible, Achilla couldn't imagine a day when he wasn't just a phone call away. Now he was gone, and she never got to see his last moments. She couldn't share a meal with him or talk about life with him again. In a world where people met her with fear and hatred, Achilla only felt like she could be herself around her father. He always said that she would be his *baby girl*. Now he was gone. As much as she fought them, the tears won their freedom and rolled down her face.

Why did the CIA lie? Why was there no security detail there to protect him? Had Achilla known the truth, she would have never left home. She would have stayed behind and protected her family. Achilla read the obituary. She read the story in the papers. Her father was shot twice in the back of the head. The reporter didn't write it, but Achilla knew what happened. Whoever did this walked behind him and executed him from close range. Achilla would have never let someone get that close with a firearm. She would have spotted the weapon, disarmed him, and force-fed the offender her fist. That was what angered Achilla the most. This wasn't an elaborate scheme. This wasn't a challenging opponent like Ailina. It was a simple walk-in-the-room-and-shoot-the-guy hit. Achilla could have eliminated such an easy threat in less than three seconds. She clenched her eyes shut and cringed as more tears dripped from her face into her lap. Had she just been there, none of this would've happened. She would've saved him *easily*.

Achilla snapped out of her thoughts when Sam let out a whimper as the organ chimed throughout the church. Achilla held her hand as she blotted her tears with a tissue. The service was short, but she wept the whole way through. Achilla regretted pulling a gun on herself. How could she put her mother through that now of all times? She shook her head just as the service ended and everyone rose to their feet. Samuel, wearing a black suit and tie, walked their mother down the aisle as Achilla trailed behind; trying her best to ignore all of the eyes in the room watching them. The way some people in the room stared at her made Achilla look at her hands. She knew they had no knowledge of her killing Blue Eyes, but their eyes still shot her with lasers of guilt. No doubt some of them knew her past and the Harris blood that ran through her veins, and they judged her, even now. If Achilla could spit on them, she would. Maybe after her father's funeral.

As she followed her brother and mother, Achilla spotted Chief Price in the crowd wearing his full military bearing. His hair was gray, but he generally looked the same. It took Achilla a moment to register that he was alone. She would never bring it up to Sam, but she now realized that her relationship with her mother was even worse than with Chief Price. She also saw Principal Freeney wearing the same uniform as Chief Price but with fewer badges and pins. She would've never guessed that he was a Marine. She noticed Dahntay sitting near the back wearing a black suit and black tie that fit snug around his muscular shoulders. Leave it to Dahntay to always be there. He always showed up for Achilla when she needed someone the most. Achilla smiled and lowered her head as she passed by him.

When the reception downstairs started, Achilla sat at her family's table with a plate full of fried chicken, spaghetti, and coleslaw; food she normally loved but tasted dull and soggy now. She watched as Chief Price left his seat two tables down(he couldn't even sit with his daughter?) and walked toward the bathroom near the back. Achilla stood up to follow him when she saw Dahntay walking her way. She sighed and wiped a strand of her hair before facing him. He hugged her and she wrapped her arms around his massive back and squeezed. She placed Dahntay at around 230 pounds give or take. She gripped him a little harder and rubbed her fingernails on his triceps until he patted her shoulder for freedom. Achilla lowered her head at the thought of letting him go. Sometimes her strength really did get in her way.

"Man, this might sound funny," Dahntay said. "But you feel even stronger than before. You hit the weights more than usual or something?"

"Not exactly," Achilla said with a sideways glance before squeezing his arm. "So, um, how've you been?"

"Good," Dahntay replied. "I just got a new job."

"Great!" Achilla said with a smile as she held her hands on her hips. "Good for you!"

"Yeah, now I'm at Sikorsky in Stratford," Dahntay sighed. "It's hard work, but the pay's not bad. Look, I'm sorry for your loss. I always liked your pops."

"What wasn't there to like?" Achilla asked. "He saved my life."

"You always said that," Dahntay replied. "One of these days, you've got to tell me how."

"Maybe one day I will," Achilla said as she smiled wide and poked his shoulder. "Look, sorry, but I have to take a leak. I'll be right back."

"*Take a leak?*"

"Yeah," Achilla replied with a frown. "Is that a problem?"

"You haven't changed one bit," Dahntay said. "I'll wait."

"Awesome," Achilla said as she turned on her heels and walked across the room. She waited for a couple men to walk out of the door before she snuck into the men's room and saw Chief Price standing in the mirror adjusting his shirt. Before he could turn and address her, Achilla darted across the floor, grabbed him by his suit and carried him into a bathroom stall. She pinned him with one arm against the wall just behind the toilet and glared at him. He didn't show any signs of shock or fear almost as if he knew she would find him. Achilla gripped his shirt as tears welled up in her eyes.

"Achilla--"

"You know what bugs me the most isn't that things didn't turn out like you said," Achilla hissed. "Though as you can see, you were very, very, *wrong.*"

"Achilla, listen--"

"But you haven't visited your daughter *once*," Achilla snarled. "Her husband is dead. Dead! Murdered. *Your daughter* had to come home from work and wait all night to find out that her husband was *shot in the head* and would never come back. Knowing that, you don't come to see her. You don't pay your respects. You don't offer to help with anything. You only come to the funeral and then you don't even sit with her. You haven't changed one bit."

"What do you want from me?" Chief Price asked.

"I want you to be a man and support your daughter," Achilla replied. "And about the CIA, they lied. There was no detail. They can't walk away from this. If it wasn't for your daughter, you wouldn't either."

"You think you can take the CIA alone?" Chief Price scoffed. "I'm sure you're good, but not that good."

"Watch me," Achilla said. "And let your buddies know I'm coming for them."

Achilla kicked the bathroom stall door open and dropped Chief Price to the floor. She then walked out of the bathroom. When an old man frowned at her, she shrugged and pointed at the long line of women in front of the ladies' room. He shrugged back and walked into the bathroom. Achilla adjusted her dress and walked back into the reception room where Dahntay was waiting with a couple glasses of wine. He tried to hand her one and she waved it away.

"Alcohol's for the weak," Achilla said with a harsher tone than she intended. "I mean…no offense."

"You would say that," Dahntay replied. "And none taken. What're you up to?"

"I just quit my job," Achilla sighed as her smile returned. "Somehow I managed to land a gig with the Central Intelligence Agency."

"You quit *that?*" Dahntay asked with wide eyes. "Are you crazy?"

"I hated it," Achilla replied with a shake of her head. "Not worth the stress."

"What did you do?" Dahntay asked.

"Classified," Achilla replied with a shrug as she picked her nails. "That's the main reason it was so stressful."

"Hey, I feel you."

Achilla glanced over Dahntay's shoulder and spotted a girl with red hair wearing a black dress and black and green high-heeled shoes; the kind that only the wealthy could afford. The girl looked just like Patricia from Blue Eyes' firm. She confirmed her identity by approaching Samuel and placing a hand on his shoulder. Samuel patted her hand and smiled at her before she moved her hand down and rubbed his back. Achilla clenched her fist and took a breath before smiling at Dahntay.

"Who's that girl?" Achilla asked.

"That's Trish O'Brien," Dahntay said. "Yeah, I think her uncle's some big-time attorney."

"Introduce me," Achilla said as she hooked Dahntay's arm.

"I don't know her that well," Dahntay replied.

"Introduce me anyway," Achilla pressed.

"Bossy as always," Dahntay sighed as they walked toward Samuel and Trish. When Trish looked up at Achilla, she took a step back before smiling at her. She didn't know it, but she gave herself away. Achilla grinned as she forced eye contact with her.

"How are you guys?" Dahntay said as he shook Samuel's and Trish's hands. "Trish, have you met Samuel's sister?"

"We've met," Trish replied.

"Achilla," Dahntay said with a frown. "Why'd you--"

"I didn't know you were the Trish my brother knew," Achilla said. "He's told me a lot about you."

"Achilla, not now," Samuel said in a low voice.

"Well, I hope he said good things," Trish said with the awkward laugh of a thief caught running from the store.

"Something like that," Achilla replied as she eyeballed her. "So Trish, how's your uncle?"

"Wait, you know Trish's uncle?" Samuel asked Achilla. "How'd you meet Mr. Gabrielli?"

"It was a business meeting," Achilla answered with a slight grin.

"Oh, OK," Samuel said with a look that wondered what the hell kind of business Achilla could have had with a defense attorney; particularly one their father hated. Achilla avoided Samuel's eyes as they trained on her. She had to focus on the enemy in front of her.

"I'm sorry, Trish, continue," Achilla said.

"Um...he's busy," Trish said with a sideways glance before

staring back at Achilla. "He's out of town on business. He actually wanted me to extend his condolences to your mother."

"Did he?" Achilla asked with a frown. "That's interesting."

"What's so *interesting* about that?" Samuel retorted as he shot Achilla a hard look.

"You would think he'd ask his wife to do that," Achilla said.

"She's out of town too," Trish replied with a glare at Achilla. "She and the kids are staying with her mother for a bit. I'm sure you can understand why."

Achilla lowered her eyes for a split second. Trish was still under the impression that she and Blue Eyes had an affair. Logically that meant that he and his wife were on the rocks. Without knowledge of Blue Eyes' involvement in Brendan's murder, Trish couldn't possibly piece together the truth. Once his hitman didn't report back, he skipped town and sent his family away for their own safety. Even in his last days, he followed the rules and never involved his family in his affairs. Achilla shuddered at the fact that she could actually relate to him.

"Why is she staying with her mother?" Samuel asked as he looked back and forth at Achilla and Trish. "Did I miss something?"

"My grandmother's not well," Trish said, a statement Achilla knew was a lie. "And we both know how lawyers work. Uncle Rob had to travel and couldn't be there."

"I understand," Samuel said with a nod of his head. "Well, I'm glad you came, Trish."

"No problem," Trish replied with a smile as she caressed his shoulder. "It's always good to have a friend at a time like this."

"Yeah," Samuel sighed.

"And yet they're so hard to come by," Achilla quipped, causing Trish to stare at her.

"See you later, Trish," Samuel said with a glare at Achilla.

"We'll meet again," Achilla said as Trish walked off.

"What was that about?" Dahntay asked.

"I just wanted to say hi to her," Achilla replied with a shrug as she watched Trish speedwalk across the room. "Why was she so skittish?"

"You intimidate people," Samuel said. "Especially other girls. Dad always told you to have a friendlier face. And better manners. I think now of all times we can all be cordial."

"Was that was she was doing?" Achilla asked with a cocked eyebrow. "It didn't look like she was being *cordial* with you, Samuel."

"Think what you want, but you know I'm right," Samuel replied. "Cut it out. This is Dad's *funeral*."

"I know," Achilla muttered. "I'll work on it. It's the least I can do for him now."

"You never intimidated me," Dahntay said with a frown as he faced Achilla and crossed his arms. "And I've never seen you scare anybody unless they did something. Under what circumstances did you two meet?"

"Let's not talk about that," Achilla said as she hooked her arm under Dahntay's again and turned him away from Samuel. "Have you given your condolences to my mother?"

"No, not yet."

"Let's go," Achilla said as she pulled Dahntay toward Sam who was sitting on the other side of the table in a black dress. Sam smiled as two women in black dresses hugged her and walked away. She then turned to Achilla and Dahntay and frowned. She held her hands on her hips just as they reached her. Achilla smiled but Sam did not smile back.

"Achilla, I think the man can walk for himself," Sam said with a stern look as she gestured for them to separate. Achilla let Dahntay go and he hugged Sam. It wasn't until then that Achilla realized that Sam never held Brendan the way she was holding Dahntay. When they walked together, they just never left each other's sides. Achilla hung her head when she thought about the way Ailina used to grab her men and yank them everywhere she wanted them to go. From that point forward, Achilla wouldn't pull Dahntay around anymore.

"I'm sorry," Dahntay said to Sam. "Your husband was a great man."

"Thank you, Dahntay," Sam replied. "And you look like you're doing well for yourself. How are your folks?"

"They're good."

As Sam and Dahntay spoke, Achilla's eyes continued to search for Trish. Her mouth watered at the thought of frightening her again. Despite the fact that she almost killed herself over it, Achilla had the strongest desire to finish what she started in Mattapan, starting with Blue Eyes' niece; the little snitch who ratted her out and got her father killed. Achilla's fists clenched and her knees trembled as she searched the room. She snapped back to reality when she felt a tap on her shoulder. She turned and saw a tall blonde woman wearing a black dress and gold hoop earrings with black and gold shoes. Only Priscilla would turn a funeral into a fashion show. Achilla smiled until Priscilla hugged her around the arms.

"Oh my God!" Priscilla gasped. "Look how much you've grown! You look like a real woman now!"

"Thanks?" Achilla replied with a snort. "I wasn't real before?"

"Don't get smart, honey, it's not becoming," Priscilla replied with a wave of her hand. "Sam told me you got into Loomis Chaffee. Great school. But why the Marines, Achilla? Someone as smart as you didn't want to go to college?"

"I love to fight," Achilla said with a shrug. "Plus, I got another job later, so--"

"Is that my bodyguard?"

Achilla whirled around and saw Grandpa Johnson walking with the slow gate of an old man with sore joints. He leaned onto a wooden cane and his face and frame appeared frail and thin inside of his black suit and black tie. Grandma Johnson walked alongside him. Her appearance hadn't changed much. Her skin was still dark and ashen, but her hair was so white that it made her black dress look even darker than Achilla's. They almost leaned on each other for balance as they approached.

"Grandpa!" Achilla squealed as she hugged Grandpa Johnson, taking extra care not to squeeze him. When he didn't squirm, she knew she got it right. When she turned and faced Grandma Johnson, she held back. They stared at each other for a few seconds until Sam stood between them. Sam glared at Achilla, then at Grandma Johnson.

"You lost a son," Sam said to Grandma Johnson before turning to Achilla. "You lost your father. I lost a husband. I think the least we can do today is get along."

"I can do better than that," Grandma Johnson sighed as she extended her shaky hand to Achilla. "I apologize to you."

Achilla flinched and backed up.

"Yeah, I said it," Grandma Johnson said. "You were a child. I had no business calling you a devil. I'm sure my son raised you right, and from what I hear you're out there making him proud. I suppose I could be proud of you too."

Achilla's mouth trembled as she stared at her hand.

"You don't have to accept it now," Grandma Johnson said. "If I were you, I probably wouldn't--"

"Today she does," Sam said before looking at Achilla. "Achilla, take her hand."

Achilla pumped Grandma Johnsons' hand before storming off.

"Achilla!" Sam shouted from behind her. "Oh, Lord, I'm sorry, Loretta..."

Achilla speed-walked to the woman's restroom and ran into a stall, slamming the door shut so hard that the lock flew off. She hyperventilated as she held her head in her hands. No matter how much Sam reassured her, Achilla couldn't take the hypocrisy of shaking that woman's hand. If Achilla wasn't the devil, then she was damn close. She fought the tears in her eyes and wrangled her breathing to a controllable pace as she stared at her face in the toilet water. She had to keep her composure. She had to go back out there. Just not yet. Achilla jumped when she heard someone walk into the bathroom.

"Achilla, where are you?" Sam asked. "Look, I saw you come in here. Baby, what's wrong?"

She always cared. No matter what Achilla did, no matter what she put Sam through, she was always there. Caring. Why did she care so damn much? Why couldn't she just leave her alone? Achilla growled and punched a hole in the wall behind the toilet before swinging the stall door open.

"Achilla, calm down," Sam said with her hands raised. "I know it's hard for you to forgive her, but--"

"I don't give a-a care about her," Achilla snapped.

"Then what's--"

"I don't deserve it," Achilla said.

"This again?" Sam asked with her hands on her hips again.

"You don't understand," Achilla said. "You'll never understand what I've done. What I've had to do. What I've *enjoyed* doing. You'll never get it, Mom. You're too *good* to get it."

"Achilla, what are you talking about?" Sam replied.

"Nothing about my life would make Dad proud," Achilla said. "If he saw me right now, he'd be ashamed--"

Achilla flinched when Sam slapped her on the cheek. It didn't hurt, but Achilla held her cheek anyway. Sam's eyes cringed but she maintained her stare. That slap must have hurt her hand, but she powered through it. In the face of such strength, Achilla's normal urge to strike back dwindled.

"No," Sam growled with her finger in Achilla's face. "You will not talk like that. Not now. Not ever. You will not dishonor your father like that in front of me! You don't know how much he sacrificed for you. You don't know how much he loved you. You were always his little girl. You should've seen his face when you left us."

"His...face?"

"He was so proud," Sam said with a hard stare. "He was so proud of how strong you were. While everyone else was *so afraid* of you, he was proud, Achilla. You have no business assuming anything less."

Achilla hung her head and walked to the mirror. When she looked up, she saw her mother standing next to her. The difference between them was staggering. Achilla stood head and shoulders taller. Her hair was as black as her dress. Her green eyes shined so bright that Achilla thought they might crack the glass. Her arms looked like thin steel cables wrapped in brown cloth. Standing next to her mother, Achilla couldn't help but notice her youth and beauty. She ran her hand across her face and Sam chuckled as she wiped her eyes.

"Have you ever looked at yourself before?" Sam asked with her hands on her hips. "You look shocked."

"Of course I have," Achilla replied.

"Then why are you just now realizing what you look like?" Sam asked. "I told you. You look like a goddess. Your father would be the happiest man in town if he saw you now. That, and he'd be the most protective and paranoid. You know how men are about their little girls."

"Yeah," Achilla said with a short laugh.

"How many times do I have to remind you?" Sam asked. "You're a woman now, Achilla. I can't keep having to give you the confidence in yourself that you should already have. From this point on, you need to believe in yourself. I can't do it for you anymore."

Achilla stared at herself some more. Sam patted her shoulder.

"I'm going back out," Sam said as she pointed at the door with her thumb. "I'm going to tell your guilt-ridden Grandma that you don't hate her anymore, and then I'm saying goodbye to my guests. Take all the time you need. I'll be back to get you."

"Sure," Achilla replied as Sam walked out of the bathroom. She cracked her knuckles and glared at her reflection. She watched her pupils dilate as her eyes lit up with a fire that engulfed the entire room. So this was what everyone saw? No wonder they were afraid. Achilla smirked at herself until she heard the bathroom door open again. Achilla turned to face the door and saw Trish stop in her tracks. When she turned to leave, Achilla darted across the room and blocked her path to the door, and her speed made her flinch.

"Don't leave yet," Achilla said as she stalked toward her. "I just want to talk."

"What do you want?" Trish asked while stepping back. "I don't want any trouble."

"I know what you think of me," Achilla said. "I assure you nothing happened between me and your uncle that day, nothing sexual anyway."

"Yeah, right," Trish replied. "Then why was your hair all messed up and your blouse unbuttoned?"

"A ruse," Achilla said. "One that clearly backfired for reasons I can't explain."

"Why would you pretend to sleep with a married man?" Trish asked.

"Like I said, I can't explain," Achilla replied. "You're from Daniela's side of the family, right?"

"Yeah, so what?"

"Is your father rich too?"

"Yeah," Trish said as she stepped back again.

"That explains why you're here," Achilla said. "When Samuel spoke about you, I didn't get the impression that you cared enough about him to help him mourn. You might have him fooled, but not me."

"What are you--"

"This is a funeral," Achilla said with her hands on her hips. "I know your real intentions with my brother, and I've got to tell you. It takes balls to come here when he's mourning his father. You are seriously low class."

"I don't know what you're talking about," Trish replied. "But I really like Samuel, and--"

"Cut that bullshit out," Achilla snarled. "It won't work with me."

"Did you just swear?" Trish hissed. "In a *church*?"

"I think God'll get over my language," Achilla said with a shrug. "Especially when he knows I'm protecting my brother from evil."

"I'm not *evil*," Trish demanded with a hand on her chest. "I don't know what Samuel told you, but despite some of our differences, I really care about him."

"You'll say anything," Achilla snarled. "But I'm not buying it. I know your type. It runs in your family."

"I'm not any *type*, all right?" Trish said with her hands raised. "So don't judge me without even knowing me."

"Yes, you are," Achilla snapped as she grabbed Trish by her dress and pinned her against the bathroom wall by the door. "And I know you real well. You came here because you know my brother stands to inherit something from my father's death. You know he has the potential to play professional basketball overseas if not the NBA. That means you know he's a cash cow. You also know my brother's just vulnerable enough to let you back in despite the *horrible* things you said to him."

"What horrible things?"

"Calling my father *unmanly?*"Achilla growled as tears welled up in her eyes. "Telling my brother that his body is *all he's good for?* You talk like that to *my family*, and then you have the nerve to come around here? I should stomp you right now, but I won't do it. Consider yourself lucky that we met here and not in the street."

"OK, we had an argument, but Samuel's a nice guy," Trish stammered. "He's great, and you're lucky to have a brother like him. I just want to make things right, you know? I figured being here when he needs someone would be a good start."

"Well, we agree on one thing," Achilla said. "Samuel's a nice guy all right. I'm not nice. I won't let you hurt my brother anymore even if that means I have to hurt you."

"I swear I would never--"

"Do not speak without my permission!" Achilla barked as she shoved her face into Trish's. "Let me make this clear. After today, you will stay away from my brother at all costs. Do you understand? You can speak now."

"I'm sorry--"

"I didn't ask for an apology that you and I both know you don't mean," Achilla snarled with a wild-eyed glare as she yanked Trish's hair back, jerking tears from her eyes. "You don't get it, do you? My family is the only good thing that I have left, and I just lost a very important part of it. I will not let you ruin another. I won't let you hurt my brother. I won't! One of us will die first!"

Trish lowered her eyes as tears rolled down her cheeks.

"I do mean it," Trish sobbed. "I'm sorry for what I said. It was wrong, and he didn't deserve it. I just--"

"Shut-up!" Achilla barked. "I didn't say you could talk. Now if I find out that you are within half a mile of my brother, I will *murder* you. "

Achilla punched a dent in the wall next to Trish's ear. When Trish cried out, covered her head and tried to run, Achilla yanked her hair again and pinned her against the wall. She then wrapped her hand around her neck. Trish whimpered and sniffed as Achilla squeezed just tight enough to let her know that she wasn't going anywhere without Achilla's consent. Achilla turned Trish's head and stared into her eyes.

"No one will be able to stop me from getting to you," Achilla whispered without breaking eye contact. "If I find out that you even give my brother a passing nod in the street, nothing will stop me. You see that wall? It's a lot harder than your face, and your body is a lot easier to hide. I could crush you like a potato chip. Test me if you think I'm joking. Test me!"

Trish stared with a blank expression as she breathed so hard her shoulders shrugged.

"You will stay away from my brother," Achilla said. " Do you understand? Speak and answer the question directly."

"Yes," Trish whispered with a dead look in her eyes as the tears stopped flowing. "Yes, I understand."

"If I see you again, nobody else will," Achilla said. "Do you understand that? Speak."

"Yes," Trish replied with an almost robotic tone.

"You leave now,"Achilla said as she shoved her toward the door. "And don't come back. Ever. In your life."

Trish fell on the floor and lay there for a few seconds. Achilla had half a mind to check if she was alive, but she could hear her breathing just fine. She just lay still on the floor like she was playing possum and hoping Achilla would leave her alone, but Achilla wasn't going anywhere. She wasn't going to sit back and watch while her brother ended up in a marriage like the Gabrielli family; devoid of the love and care that their parents showed each other and their children. She wasn't going to watch Samuel turn into a man like Blue Eyes; all about money and appearances. She for damn sure wasn't going to let him get involved with a carbon copy of Daniela. She had to protect her brother from that life, and she would not rest until Trish was nothing more than a distant memory to him. So she stood there and waited for Trish to leave. Trish rose to her feet with her head low and her arms at her sides. She avoided Achilla's gaze as a single tear dripped down her chin and fell on the floor. Achilla set her jaw and pointed at the door. Without looking up, Trish opened the door and ambled out.

Achilla took a deep breath and walked back to the bathroom mirror. She fixed her hair before turning her back on her reflection and leaning against the sink. She sighed and stared at the ceiling. With everything that occurred over the past year, it was hard for Achilla to accept that her father was gone, but she avenged him. Still, the fight wasn't over. The CIA was next on her list. This time, she would have a plan, not Ailina.

"I don't think you'll like how I do things," Achilla said to the ceiling. "But with all due respect, I don't care. You watched my father die, and even now you're letting the people involved go unpunished. If you don't want to take care of it, I will. Nobody walks away from this."

Achilla felt the midday sun bearing down on her through the ceiling, telling her that her way was wrong, telling her not to kill. She clenched her fist and hung her head. She knew it was wrong to kill. She knew it was wrong to hurt people. Yet the memory of her day with Blue Eyes made her heart thump through her chest. After committing murder, she knew her life would never be the same, but she could at least make sure that anyone who might come after her family never got the chance.

After she took a deep breath, Achilla turned on the faucet and washed her hands. Facing the CIA was unavoidable at this point. So was fighting Xerxes, and with both of her opponents, winning was the only option. Achilla nodded her head at her own reflection before walking out of the bathroom. From there, she went home with her family knowing that she may never see them again after today. She ate dinner and laugh with everyone about the fond memories of her father. She asked Sandy how her day went. Since she was not a member of the family, Sandy refused to attend the funeral. To her, it would have been disrespectful to go. Still, she baked brownies for the family after dinner and laughed with them just the same. Sandy fit right in with the Johnsons. Perhaps the next time they had something important, she wouldn't feel so bad about attending. Achilla just hoped it wasn't another funeral.

After everyone else had gone to sleep, Achilla lay awake in her bed. She knew that after tomorrow, her life would never be the same. She might never come back to Stratford again. She grabbed her cellphone from the nightstand and called the number that Dahntay gave her after the funeral. It rang twice.

"What's up?" Dahntay answered as Achilla swung her legs out of bed.

"I want to see you," Achilla said. "Now."

"Achilla," Dahntay chuckled. "Is this what I think it is?"

"Yep," Achilla replied. "Is that going to be a problem?"

"Nope," Dahntay said. "Cool with me."

Achilla changed into a pair of jeans and a white t-shirt under a gray hoody. She then took her father's car and drove down to the Quality Inn on the other side of town. Dahntay waited for her there wearing sweatpants and an orange Cornell long-sleeved tee. Something about this hotel screamed midnight hook-up, and that was exactly why Achilla invited him. She led him inside and checked a room on the second floor. Once they reached the door, Achilla wasted no time jumping on Dahntay and wrapping her legs around him.

Afterward, Achilla sat at the foot of the bed and tied her sneakers as Dahntay did the same on the other side. She missed watching him get dressed. Lately, she saw sex as a sort of conquest; the idea that she could get a man to lie down with her whenever she wanted gave her a rush. This time was different. She needed to see Dahntay only, and it wasn't any more ambitious than that. Achilla stood up and grabbed the back of Dahntay's head, shaking it like a bobblehead doll. She giggled when he swiped her hand away.

"Come on," Achilla said. "I want to talk to you outside."

After checking out of the hotel, they held hands as they walked out into the parking lot. They leaned against Dahntay's red Volvo and looked up at the night sky filled with stars. The breeze carried the slight stench of low tide that Achilla missed after living in Hartford for so long. She closed her eyes and soaked in the sounds of water lapping against the beach down the road until she focused on

Dahntay. She turned and kissed him on the lips before patting his chest.

"If you wanted more of that, we could've stayed inside," Dahntay said.

"I do, but I can't," Achilla replied. "I have something important to do, and that's kind of what I want to talk to you about."

"What's up?" Dahntay asked.

"I need your secrecy on this," Achilla said as she stared out at the empty road.

"You know you can tell me anything."

"Yeah," Achilla replied with a smile. "I do."

"So what is it?" Dahntay asked.

"Dahntay, I told you that I got a job with the CIA," Achilla replied. "What I didn't tell you was that I was an agent and--"

"No shit!" Dahntay said before he smiled wide. "Man, that is *crazy*! You're a spy?"

"Dahntay," Achilla snapped. "I wasn't done!"

"Sorry," Dahntay laughed. "Hey, I got a little excited."

"You know I hate when you do that," said Achilla as her sharp voice took a whiny tone. "I'm trying to tell you something and you just cut me off."

"I know, I know," Dahntay replied with a slight chuckle. "Go ahead."

"Thank you," Achilla said before clearing her throat. "The CIA recruited me because I have some special abilities; abilities that I don't usually show to anyone."

"Abilities?" Dahntay asked. "You mean how you can fight, right? Because I've never seen anything like that."

"That was nothing," Achilla said as she craned her neck to the night sky. "I'm strong enough to flip your car over if I wanted to."

"OK, Achilla, you need to stop messing around," Dahntay laughed. "You can't lift a car."

Achilla kneeled and reached under the Dahntay's car with one hand. Once she had a good grip, she stood just high enough for the car to lean to one side. Dahntay jumped back as Achilla set the car back down and he stared at her with wide eyes.

"The fuck?" Dahntay blurted.

"Only the CIA and my family knows," Achilla said. "The only other people who know how strong I am are either dead or too afraid to talk. I need you to understand that I've been used as a weapon for so long that I don't really know how to be anything else. We have no future."

"Why would you say that?" asked Dahntay.

Dahntay's question bounced around Achilla's brain, jarring loose the memories of their high school relationship. Achilla never forgot Dahntay after all this time. She could literally take home any man she wanted. Any room she entered was full of potential suitors, or even just hook-ups. Still, Dahntay's smile remained etched in her psyche. Achilla fought the smile that crept on her lips before she turned and kissed Dahntay again. She looked into his eyes and caressed his face as she spoke.

"Because I love you," Achilla replied with a crack in her voice.

"You…do?" Dahntay asked.

"Yeah," Achilla said.

"Achilla, I love you too," Dahntay replied. "Look, I'm not going to lie. I've played the field like anybody else, but you're the one I always think about."

"Same," said Achilla. "But I want you to be happy."

"OK, then let's find a way to make it work," Dahntay said. "I won't tell anybody about the whole lifting cars thing, and if you're back in Stratford, then we could figure out the rest."

"Oh, you're just like Mom," Achilla replied with a misty-eyed smile. "You're so good. You just think that everything will work out."

"You talk like that's a bad thing," Dahntay said with a frown. "I believe in us. I think we can do it."

"You're too good," Achilla said as she stood up from the car. "I can't be around you. I'll just ruin you."

"Here you go with that negative talk," Dahntay replied as he held Achilla's arms. "Achilla, nobody's perfect. You've got, I don't know, super-strength or something, which last I checked, isn't really a bad thing."

"The strength isn't the issue," Achilla muttered. "It's what I've done with it."

"I get it," Dahntay replied with his hands raised. "If you were in the CIA, you've probably killed somebody, right?"

Tears flooded Achilla's eyes as she nodded her head.

"Right, well, look, I purposely went for someone's knees during a game," Dahntay said. "He was an asshole, but you know, it's still dirty, and it could've ruined his future in football. I'm not perfect is what I'm saying, so you don't have to be perfect either."

"Dahntay, that's an absurd comparison to murder," Achilla snarled as she lowered her head from his eyes. "Sometimes I wonder if your head is on straight when you say shit like that."

"I could say the same about you," Dahntay replied as he lifted Achilla's chin with his finger and kissed her on the lips. "Crazy attracts crazy, right? Maybe you need someone as crazy as you are."

"No," Achilla said as she shook her head. "No, this isn't right. It's not fair to you."

"Let me decide what's fair for me," Dahntay said. "Look, if anything goes down, you can consider me warned, all right?"

Achilla sniffed and wiped her face as she looked at Dahntay. He always said the right things when she needed to hear it most. He was always there for her. The more Achilla stared at Dahntay's dark brown eyes, the more she was convinced that he was more than she deserved. He was a good kid when they met; a little foolish at times but he never did her wrong. He was so good that she had no clue what to do with him. Now he was a good man just like Sam said. Knowing that her past was possibly ugly beyond his wildest dreams, he still stuck by her. He saw the good in her, but he was still a fool. He was picturing a level of goodness that Achilla knew died with Blue Eyes in that abandoned building in Boston. Achilla didn't deserve a man like Dahntay, and he for damn sure didn't deserve to be burdened with her. As much as her heart slowed at the thought of leaving, her brain demanded it. Achilla kissed Dahntay again as she gripped his shirt tighter than she probably should have.

"Dahntay," Achilla breathed after releasing his lips.

"Yeah?"

"Remember when I told you that my dad saved my life?"

"Yep."

"He saved me from myself," Achilla said. "And now that he's gone, there's no one left to save me."

"Achilla, what the hell are you talking about?" Dahntay asked. "I mean, you've still got your mother and brother. You've got me. Whatever it is, we can get through it."

"But I can save everybody," Achilla replied with a weak smile as if she hadn't heard him. "You, Mom, Samuel, Sandy, everybody. After tomorrow, you'll all be safe."

"Save us from what?" Dahntay asked with a frown. "Achilla, you're not making any sense."

"From me," Achilla said just before she kissed Dahntay again. She ran her hands across his waved hair and wrapped her leg around him as she held his lips. This night was all she needed. She needed to feel him inside her one last time. She needed to kiss him goodbye under a night sky like when they were kids, but this was different. She wasn't a teenage girl. She was a woman now; a woman who knew men well but still yearned for him. She knew she had to wean herself from thinking of him, but one last lip lock wouldn't hurt. It would hold her for a while at least.

She held the kiss and he kissed back, wrapping his arms around her and lowering his hands to her bottom; the part of her body that he always complimented the most. Achilla felt his lips smile a little as he gave it a squeeze. She reached around and returned the favor. They stood intertwined against his sedan as Achilla freed one hand and caressed the side of his face before she bit his lip. This was the tail end of the kiss. The ending of their last embrace. She held his bottom lip in her teeth before giving him one last smooch and removing her hand from his cheek.

Achilla popped Dahntay with a short punch to the temple that rattled his head, dropping him into her arms with a dead weight that would have bowled over a normal woman. Compared to the punches she delivered to her enemies, it wasn't particularly hard. Years of fighting and studying the world's martial arts taught Achilla that it wasn't the hardest punch that knocked you out. It was the deceptive blow, the kind that required misdirection to set up before it stirred your brain like a strong mixed drink. Achilla would never have to hit Dahntay hard; not when he was too innocent to anticipate her attack. She held him with one arm and opened the passenger side door before lifting his legs and setting him in the chair. The door locked after she closed it.

"I'm sorry," Achilla muttered through the window to Dahntay's unconscious face. "You'll probably think there were a thousand ways to do that, but this was the best one. I want your forgiveness, but it's probably best that I don't have it. Live your life, Dahntay. You deserve so much better. Move on from me, OK?"

Achilla wiped her hand across the glass as she stared at him. He looked so peaceful, and she could hear his breathing and heartbeat slowing down as his body readjusted after their make-out session. She bit her lip as she scratched the window with her nails.

"I love you," Achilla whispered. "Goodbye."

As she walked to her father's car, Achilla sighed and looked up at the night sky. By the time Dahntay woke up, Achilla would be gone. It would then dawn on him that she gave him a concussion. After that, he would hate her and never want to speak to her again. At least, that was what Achilla hoped would happen. Otherwise, he might go looking. Knowing Achilla, she would probably let him find her. She wiped her eyes and stepped into her father's car, but she looked at Dahntay for one last time before she pulled out of the parking lot and went home. She had just enough time to get a few hours of sleep before her next mission, and she needed her rest.

Chapter Nineteen

ACHILLA JOHNSON:16

Achilla wore a black hoody and gray sweatpants with black sneakers as she leaned across two seats in the back of the bleachers in the Sterling House Community Center on Stratford's Main Street. She popped her spearmint gum as she watched Samuel's first fall league game. It had been three weeks since Achilla's run-in with Ailina, and three weeks since she told her parents that she broke her nose during a sparring match. By now her nose had recovered, but her mind hadn't. Ailina was getting too close to her family. It was only a matter of time before she would strike, no matter what promise she made. How could she stop the only person in Fairfield County who was stronger than she was? Achilla sighed as she searched her brain for answers.

If there was any bright side to this month, it was Samuel's performance on the court. By the fourth quarter, Samuel had already scored twenty points by making layups, free-throws, and all four of his three-pointers. His movements were fluid. His defense was sound. His passing was excellent. He just needed to get stronger, but that would come with time. Achilla smirked as she watched Samuel catch the ball on a fast break with a defender in front of him. She knew what would happen next, and she sat up in her seat. Samuel dribbled the ball once and his white and red sneakers squeaked against the polished wood floor as he spun around his defender like a red blur; causing the crowd to "oooh" and "aaah" and cheer. He then smacked the backboard on his layup before jogging down the court. That was a move that he had practiced for hours before school and in their driveway when they came home. It never worked on Achilla, but she knew that was only because she was stronger and faster than the average professional athlete. Achilla was confident that no high school boy in their conference could stay in front of Samuel, and tonight he was confirming her theory.

After Samuel's game, Achilla drove him to Duchess Diner on Stratford Avenue. As a reward for his twenty-five point game, she treated him to a bacon double-cheeseburger with fries. Since she had been monitoring his diet for over two months, Achilla figured he would be elated. She smiled as Samuel wolfed down his food and guzzled his cup of soda that he nearly spilled on his gray hoody. She noticed Samuel's frown when she ordered two plates of salad for herself.

"You eat that much salad?" Samuel asked.

"Yeah, my metabolism's pretty high," Achilla replied. "I'm surprised you never noticed before. I guess it's because I'm not home much."

"How come Mom and Dad don't bother you about that?" Samuel asked. "They always try to make sure I'm home and focused on my work."

"They'll lay off when you prove yourself," Achilla replied before pinching Samuel's left cheek and pouting at him. "Besides, you're the little baby."

"I've still been thinking about what's her name," Samuel said as he swiped Achilla's hand away. "Ashley?"

"Ailina."

"Right, her," Samuel said with a wave of her hand. "Was that a cop car she was driving?"

"Why do you ask?" Achilla replied with a glare.

"I was…just wondering--"

"If you're thinking about telling your grandfather, forget it," Achilla snapped. "He won't do anything. Don't investigate any further. If you see her face--"

"Run, yeah I heard you," Samuel replied. "You don't have to boss me around all the time. I'm just trying to figure out what we can do."

"*We* won't do anything," Achilla said. "I'll take care of Ailina. And maybe you don't like my approach, but I'm trying to protect you. You don't know how dangerous she is. Let me focus on her. You focus on school."

"What about you?" Samuel asked. "You're in school too. You're taking AP classes and playing three sports a year. Don't you think you should focus too?"

"I can do all of that in my sleep," Achilla replied with a wave of her hand. "Besides, Ailina's always been my problem. I don't want her to be yours."

"Achilla, I'm smart too," Samuel said. "I'm smart enough to know you're hiding something. I mean, why would she attack me in the first place? And why can't Mom and Dad know about it? They're our parents."

"I admit there's a lot you don't know," Achilla replied with a shrug. "There's a lot you don't know about me."

"Why?" Samuel asked with a scowl. "I thought you were my sister--"

"Because I never had a childhood," Achilla snapped. "I never went to kindergarten. I never watched Saturday morning cartoons. I never had normal parents until I moved in with you. As much as I hate Ailina, I can't change the fact that we're blood, and we'll always be connected. You have a choice that I don't have. You don't have to cross paths with her, so don't."

Achilla caught her breath and shoved a forkful of salad into her mouth. She looked up when she noticed Samuel staring at his food. Achilla pinched herself in the leg. No matter how smart and driven he became, Samuel would always be a sensitive boy. He might even grow up to be a sensitive man. She had to be aware that he might take things harder than she would. Achilla sighed and scratched her head as she thought of the next thing to say.

"Look, I'm sorry, but it sounded like you needed me to be honest," Achilla said.

"I don't need an apology," Samuel said with a shake of his head. "You don't have to coddle me. And no, you're not being honest."

"I didn't lie to you, Samuel," Achilla replied.

"You're lying to yourself though," Samuel said. "I'm a kid. I can't even drive yet, and I can see it's not that simple. We lost that choice the second you moved in with us."

"Samuel, that's not true," Achilla replied. "I don't want you involved--"

"Look, Dad must know how strong she is," Samuel said. "He was screwing her, and that's why you're here, right?"

"Samuel!" Achilla hissed as she looked around the restaurant.

"He had to know the risks before he took you in, but he did it anyway," Samuel continued with a shrug before he bit into his burger. "That's all I'm saying."

"You're blaming Dad?" Achilla asked with her arms crossed. "You're seriously blaming him?"

"No," Samuel snapped. "He brought you in to protect you from her, but the second the time comes for him to protect you, you hide it from him. I'm blaming you."

"You're absolutely right about everything but one simple fact," Achilla replied as she pointed down at the table. "Even Dad doesn't know the full extent of how dangerous she is. He caught a glimpse, but--"

"You think he doesn't know that?" Samuel asked. "Look, I get that you're some super genius, but give the rest of us regular people some credit. We're family, Achilla. If you go down, we all go down. We don't need another Jesus to die for us."

"Samuel," Achilla said as she leaned forward and glared at him. "Don't tell Mom and Dad. If you do, everything will get worse."

"Things got worse the second she attacked you in that parking lot," Samuel replied. "Come on, Achilla. What's to stop her from knocking down our door right now? We need to take protective measures for our safety and to protect us from liability in case something goes down. Now if we can get something on the record or some kind of document proving how dangerous she is, then we can--"

"Wait, a second," Achilla replied as she rose from her seat. "You sound like Dad."

"Well, thanks, I--"

"Too much like Dad," Achilla snapped. "You already told him!"

"Achilla, I had to," Samuel replied. "She could've really hurt you before, I mean, I can't just watch--"

"You idiot!" Achilla shrieked as she held her hands on her head. "You promised!"

"You would do the same thing--"

"Shit, shit, shit!" Achilla screamed and stomped the floor as the other guests stared at her. She pulled at her hair while she paced the diner. How long would it take before Ailina found out? How soon could she get to their house? What was Achilla going to do? She wasn't ready to face her yet. It was too late to worry about that now. Whether she was ready or not, she had to try. If she didn't, her whole family was dead anyway. A tall, tan-skinned male manager wearing a black collared shirt and black slacks approached and tapped her shoulder.

"Miss, is everything, all right?" he asked. "Was the food-"

"We need to go," Achilla said as she shoved the manager out of the way and grabbed Samuel by his shirt. "Get up!"

"Hey, you guys haven't paid--"

"Achilla, we have to pay--"

"Oh God, here!" Achilla said as she pulled a fifty dollar bill out of her pocket and shoved it in the manager's hand. She then pulled Samuel and dragged him out of the door and down the steps to their car. She pinned Samuel against the car with one arm while she opened the driver's side door. Samuel squirmed and she let go, but she still leaned forward against the car. Samuel crossed his arms and looked away when she looked him in the eye.

"When did you tell Dad?" Achilla asked with a hard stare. "Answer quick, we don't have much time!"

"This morning."

"Time, Samuel!"

"About eight?" Samuel replied with a shrug. "In the middle of first period."

"And what did he say?" Achilla demanded. "Tell me everything you remember."

"He said he'd file a restraining order to start," Samuel muttered. "I'm not sure what else he's planning."

"There's no way he did that without her finding out," Achilla said as she opened the door. "I'm taking you home now."

Achilla hopped in the driver's side and started the ignition. She pulled out just as Samuel closed the back driver's side door and sat behind her. As she sped out of the parking lot, Achilla prayed to God that she would make it home before Ailina found out about the restraining order. Common sense told her that was impossible. She then prayed that she could stop Ailina from killing her parents.

"Samuel, I need you to know something," Achilla said. "Whatever happens from this point on, I love you."

"I love you too," Samuel replied. "But why are you talking like that? Look, if Dad files the restraining order--"

"Ailina doesn't *follow the law*, OK?" Achilla said with a scowl as she ran a red light and dodged a pick-up truck. "Just be ready for anything."

Achilla's heart raced as she turned onto their street. Her palms were so sweaty that she had to grip the steering wheel extra tight to maintain control and straighten it out. She slowed the car down as they neared the house. Achilla saw her parents' cars, but no cop car. Achilla breathed a sigh of relief. At least now she could have time to get ready, but they had to move fast. Achilla was about to pull in the driveway when the hair on the back of her neck stood on end and her heart pumped out of her shirt.

Was Ailina here?

Achilla searched the street. She was hard to see in the dark, but Achilla spotted a woman walking down the sidewalk toward the house wearing black jeans, a black sweater, and a black winter cap. She also wore black gloves. Achilla turned her lights off and watched until the woman turned into their driveway. It was Ailina, and she wasn't wasting any time.

"Oh God, no!" Achilla gasped as she shifted the car in drive and gunned the engine.

"Achilla!" Samuel screamed in the back as the car launched forward. "No, Achilla!"

Achilla drove straight to Ailina's back. Ailina turned and pulled out a gun, but Achilla slammed the car into her hip with a thump just as the gun popped into the sky; sending Ailina flying twenty feet into the driveway. Achilla jumped out of the car and sprinted toward Ailina as she reached for her gun. She jumped over Ailina's head and kicked the gun into the dark backyard. Before she could turn and kick Ailina's face, Ailina grabbed her ankle and pulled her to the ground, sending her to the pavement head first. Achilla then felt two sharp blows to the back of her head that cracked the ground under her face. After that, Achilla felt a tug on her legs before she flew into the backyard. Her back slammed against the oak tree, and it cracked and toppled over; crashing to the ground. Achilla rolled across the trunk and into leaves that landed on the grass, and she lay in the dark for a few seconds as her head spun. The Autumn-chilled leaves and grass felt like sprinkled ice water on her face as Achilla rolled off of the tree trunk and felt the scattered bark strewn across the grass to get her bearings. She rubbed her nose and spat out a tooth as she tasted the iron flavor of blood leaking into her mouth. When she tried to get up, a sharp pain shot up her back and held her in place. Achilla grimaced but turned her head and watched Ailina walk toward the house. If she made it inside, she could kill Achilla's parents before they even realized she was there.

Achilla gritted her teeth and rose to her feet. Her back screeched with each step, but Achilla charged across a hundred feet of grass in just a few seconds and stood in front of Ailina just before she reached the front door. She swung a punch that Ailina slipped before grabbing her arm and flipping her onto the walkway. Achilla cried out from the crescendo of lightning bolts running through her back, but she hopped up and shoulder-rammed Ailina's midsection into the house.

"The hell are you doing?" Ailina snarled as she yanked Achilla's hair. Achilla ignored her and lifted her overhead; leaning back into a suplex that rammed Ailina's head into the walkway. Achilla turned and straddled Ailina, and she grabbed her shirt as she swung a punch at her throat. Ailina smacked the punch away with her left hand, wrapped her right arm past Achilla's right shoulder, and flipped Achilla over. She then pinned Achilla to the ground by her shoulder before swinging for her head. Achilla slipped her fist, as she punched a hole in the ground next to her ear, grabbed Ailina's arms, and wrapped her legs around her waist. If she couldn't land a punch on her, she would just have to hold her in place until her family could escape. Achilla watched as Samuel stepped out of the car, but Ailina grabbed her attention when she snatched a handful of Achilla's hair again.

"You're making it very hard not to kill you," Ailina said with eyes that glowed in the dark. "We had a deal. You don't talk, I don't bother your family."

"No!" Achilla screamed as she grimaced from Ailina's nails digging into her scalp. "Leave them alone!"

"I'm still toying with you," Ailina replied while Achilla held her arms fast and squeezed her ribs with her thighs. "You're still not strong enough."

Ailina let go of her hair, ripped her arms free, and snatched Achilla's throat with both hands. Achilla bared her teeth as she grabbed Ailina's forearms and continued to squeeze her thighs until she felt Ailina's ribs starting to bend. Whether Ailina admitted it or not, Achilla knew she could hurt her just enough for her family to get away. She looked to her right when she heard the front door open and saw Brendan standing in the doorway. If she could talk, she would have told him to run. As if he read her mind, Brendan ran back in the house.

"Your father's running away just like last time," Ailina grunted with a sneer. "He's still a pussy."

Ailina's pupils dilated to the size of quarters as she squeezed tighter around Achilla's throat. Achilla's peripheral vision faded as she squeezed her thighs and felt a couple ribs bend from the pressure. Ailina winced but didn't let go. Achilla's vision nearly faded to black when Ailina suddenly let go and leaped toward the house. Achilla rolled over and held her throat. During all of the years she spent sparring with her, she never felt a grip quite like that. Achilla grimaced before she looked up to see Ailina holding Brendan over her head by his neck with one hand and holding a revolver with the other. Ailina held the gun by its barrel and squeezed it into a ball before dropping it on the ground.

"I can't have you using that," Ailina chuckled. "Lucky for me, you're not a very quick shooter, Brendan. I knew fucking a lawyer would come in handy somehow--"

"Brendan!" Sam screamed as she lunged at Ailina from inside the house. Ailina snatched her up by her throat and held her overhead as well. Achilla rose to her feet as her vision returned to normal. She took a step forward, but her legs wobbled and her spine vibrated causing Achilla to drop to one knee. Tears leaked down her eyes as she tried to yell for her help, but her throat wouldn't cooperate. All she could do was amble forward and watch as Ailina held her parents by their necks. Achilla could hear them both gurgling from the pressure around their throats. It was almost over, and if she didn't think of something quick, she would have to watch her parents die in front of her.

Achilla gritted her teeth and forced her legs to run until she charged Ailina's midsection and pinned her against the house again. She wrapped her arms around Ailina, but this time she didn't body slam her. Achilla clenched her eyes shut as she bear-hugged her until she heard her ribs pop. Ailina shrieked and let go of Achilla's parents, dropping them in front of the door. She then punched the back of Achilla's head until Achilla let go and dropped to her knees. Achilla fought through the pain in her head and headbutt Ailina's chin so hard that her feet left the ground. Achilla caught one of Ailina's legs and threw her off the top of the steps, and Ailina landed on her back and hopped to her feet just in time for Achilla to leap off the steps and clothesline her across the neck, sending her back to the ground. Achilla kneeled over Ailina and snarled as she punched her face. She then turned Ailina around and bashed her head into the walkway. After that, she punched the back of Ailina's head as the walkway cracked under her blows.

"You think you can come around here and hurt *my family*?"Achilla roared as she pounded Ailina's head. "I'll fucking kill you--"

Ailina whirled around, grabbed Achilla's wrist, and stared back at her with a bloody smile. Achilla flinched at Ailina's face. She only had a minor cut under her eye. Anyone else would have been unrecognizable. What the hell was her skin made of? Achilla struggled to break free, but Ailina held her fast with one arm as she grinned at her. After all of that, she still had this much strength? Achilla's heart pumped as her mind scrambled for her next move.

"That's it," Ailina hissed as Achilla grunted and pulled to no avail. "Yes, you're learning to kill! I love it! I can see *murder* in your eyes! That's good! That's really good!"

Achilla rose to her feet and pulled, but it was no use. Ailina just grinned at her as she lay on her back and held Achilla's wrist with one hand. When Achilla raised her other arm to swing a punch Ailina snapped her wrist with a flick of her hand. Achilla cried out from the fire burning in her forearm and dropped to both knees as Ailina stood over her. When Achilla tried to stand, Ailina kneed her in the gut, knocking the air out of her mouth. She then grabbed her by her hoody and flung her into the front yard; sending her rolling across the grass. Achilla hopped up to charge again, but Ailina stood in front of her before she could take a step. Achilla flinched before she swung for her head, and Ailina ducked.

Before Achilla could throw another, she grunted when she felt a chop to her broken arm. Achilla turned and saw Ailina over her shoulder. By the time she finished turning, Ailina stood at her left side and delivered a punch to her gut that knocked her off her feet before grabbing her shirt, twirling her overhead, and slamming her into the grass with a thud. Ailina snatched her throat and lifted her up. Achilla grabbed Ailina's forearm with her good hand, but it dropped as her vision faded even faster than last time. Somehow, Ailina's grip was even stronger than before.

"Not bad, Achilla," Ailina said as Achilla gagged. "You have the will, but your body hasn't caught up yet. Still, I am impressed. You have proven yourself."

Ailina maintained her grip as she eased Achilla into the crater her body made in the front lawn. Achilla's back throbbed, her throat felt like a crushed soda can, and her right arm buzzed like a hundred bees were stinging it at once. With all of her training, with all of her increased strength, Achilla still felt no different now than when she was a little girl fighting for her life in Ailina's basement. After a few minutes, Ailina let go of Achilla's throat, and she gasped for air as she rolled onto her stomach. She gasped again when Ailina drove her knee into Achilla's back and grabbed the top of her head.

"Don't worry, I won't kill you," Ailina whispered into her ear as she squeezed her scalp. "You're too valuable. But we need to work on this attachment to inferior beings. I'm worried that you might actually think you're one of them. I think I'll just kill them. How does that sound?"

Ailina turned Achilla around and punched her temple, and Achilla's world hazed and her vision doubled as she slumped to the ground. She watched Ailina walk around to her right leg, but her body refused to move. When she grabbed Achilla's leg, she lifted it by the ankle, rolled up her pant leg, and ran her hand up her shin to her knee with a soft caressing touch. It almost felt like one of the massages Dahntay used to give her after her basketball games. Achilla continued to watch through her dazed state as Ailina smiled at her. That smile made Achilla frown. Her smile was unlike anything Achilla had ever seen from her. It was nice, even gentle. Achilla lay back with a blank face as Ailina caressed her thigh and moved down toward her kneecap.

Then her leg cracked as Ailina snapped it at the knee.

Achilla shrieked as her right leg smoldered. Ailina shushed her and patted her head as she wailed. She then turned her back to walk toward Achilla's parents. Achilla snarled, grabbed her ankle, and tried to pull her back. Ailina replied with a stomp on her forearm; crushing it under her heel and sending Achilla's head reeling. She then turned her back on Achilla and walked toward Brendan and Sam who were still lying in the doorway.

"Hey," Achilla called as she crawled with one arm. "Where the hell do you think you're going?"

"I admire your tenacity," Ailina said as she looked over her shoulder. "I'm so proud I could shed a tear."

"Don't go near them!" Achilla growled through her teeth. "Your fight's with *me*! I can still fuck you up--"

"That's a nice sentiment, but we both know it's over, Achilla," Ailina said with her arms wide. "I've completely immobilized you. All you can do is watch. "

Achilla's heart dropped to her stomach as she watched Ailina walk toward Brendan and Sam. Brendan laid his body across Sam as Ailina came closer. Achilla still crawled forward, but she knew she could never get there in time. Her parents were as good as dead. Achilla's vision blurred from the tears welling up in her eyes as she kept crawling.

"Mom," Achilla whispered through her thrashed throat as she scratched the earth. "Dad...I'm...I'm sorry!"

Ailina stopped when a figure ran out of the house and stood in front of Brendan and Sam. Achilla blinked her tears away and saw Samuel standing in the doorway brandishing a kitchen knife. Achilla shook her head and crawled forward.

Not him too.

Achilla cringed when Ailina threw her head back and cackled.

"No," Achilla sobbed as she crawled forward. "No, Samuel, run."

"I didn't come here to kill you, boy," Ailina said. "Move aside."

"No!" Samuel barked as he brandished the knife.

"Look at my daughter," Ailina said. "She's at least four times stronger than all of you, and I turned her into a cripple. Dealing with you would be so easy--"

"I don't give a fuck!" Samuel snarled. "I'm not letting you do this!"

"What do you mean *let*?" Ailina replied with a snort. "You don't actually think you can stop me, do you?"

"You can't kill my family!" Samuel screamed with wide eyes and sweat running down his face.

"Samuel, run!" Achilla croaked. "I told you to run! Just go! Please!"

"No," Samuel said as he glared at Ailina. "She doesn't scare me! She's just a bully!"

"Step aside, boy," Ailina said. "Or I just might kill you for shits and giggles."

"Try it then!" Samuel roared. "If you want to do something, let's do it!"

Ailina stood with her hands on her hips. She then chuckled and shook her head. Achilla hyperventilated as she tried to get close enough to Ailina to grab her leg. She scratched at the dirt as she crawled closer. She was only ten feet away. Just a little closer and she could distract her. Just a little closer and her family could escape. If it cost her life, so be it. Achilla gritted her teeth as she clawed at the ground beneath her. Her eyes turned bloodshot as she reached for Ailina's ankle.

Just a little more and she had her.

"I'm done," Ailina said with a raised hand. "I won't kill you."

Achilla frowned and dropped her hand. Samuel flinched but still held the knife. Even Brendan furrowed his brow before holding Sam in his arms. Beads of sweat dripped down Achilla's face as she struggled to look up at Ailina. Ailina looked at her and smirked before facing Samuel.

"Look at you," Ailina said with a softer voice. "You know you have no chance of survival, but you still stand firm. You look death in the eye without fear. I've met grown men who can't do that."

"Men...like Jared Higgins?" Brendan asked before coughing.

"I was actually referring to you," Ailina said. "Looks like your son has bigger balls than you do, but I guess that's not surprising."

Ailina turned on her heels and walked toward the driveway. She winced and rubbed her ribs as she leaned against the car. It was the first time Ailina showed any substantial sign of pain the whole night.

Achilla stared at the ground. Now she understood what Ailina meant when she talked about being superior. Any normal person would have died from Achilla's assault, but not Ailina. Instead, Ailina was uncomfortable at most. Tonight proved that Achilla never had a chance. She looked at Samuel and saw him still holding the knife. Achilla couldn't shake the thought that she should be protecting him, not the other way around. The flush of embarrassment flooded her face as she gazed at the grass

"You're going to be a strong man," Ailina said as she pointed at Samuel. "Oh yeah, I see it now. You've got potential. Killing you would be a travesty, and that kind of takes the fun out of it. I won't hurt your family, boy--"

"Samuel," Samuel barked as Ailina turned to walk away.

"What?" Ailina asked as she looked over her shoulder.

"My name's Samuel," Samuel said as he loosened his posture without letting go of the knife. "And don't come back."

"Such boldness," Ailina replied with a smile and a slight giggle as she faced Samuel and flicked her hair. "I expected that from Achilla, but from you? I'm impressed. We'll meet again, Samuel, when you're a little older. I think someday we'll be friends."

"No," Samuel said. "We won't."

"That's what they all say," Ailina said as she bit her lip before she turned her back. "I'm leaving for now. You should help your family. They need medical attention."

Ailina strolled down the driveway without giving Achilla a passing glance. Achilla glared at her back. If she thought Achilla would let her just walk away, she had another think coming. Achilla tried to rise to her feet, but she dropped when her broken leg gave way under her weight. When she looked up, Ailina was gone.

Just like that, she disappeared.

It was just like those days when she left Achilla in the middle of her basement lying in a pool of her own sweat, covered in cuts and bruises, and curled in a ball like a crumpled piece of paper. The same tears she felt back then welled up in Achilla's eyes as she gritted her teeth and pulled a handful of grass out of the ground.

"Dammit!" Achilla screamed. As much as she talked about

protecting her family, she was useless when it mattered. She rested her forehead on the ground as she heard Samuel ask their parents if they were OK. She then rolled onto her back and groaned when the adrenaline rush faded and the real pain in her back, legs, arms and face set in. Achilla turned her head when Samuel rushed to her side and tried to set her up. Achilla shrieked and pushed him away with her elbow. Samuel raised his hands but stayed by her side.

"Don't move me!" Achilla cried out. "Oh God, please don't!"

"Sorry," Samuel said. "Are you OK?"

"Fabulous," Achilla replied. "How are Mom and Dad?"

"They're fine for now," Samuel said. "But their necks look bruised. I called 911 while you two were fighting. You weren't kidding about Ailina. How did you survive that?"

"Samuel, Ailina and I aren't…normal," Achilla said as her voice started to slur. "You weren't supposed to see that and live. I forced her hand a little, but you…saved…"

"Good, the ambulance is here," Samuel said as Achilla fell into a haze again. Ailina's punch must have given her a concussion. After a few seconds, she could see bright lights but heard no sirens. She also couldn't hear the brown-haired, blue-eyed, EMT when he kneeled next to her and spoke to her as he placed an oxygen mask over her mouth. She watched Samuel run over to their parents as the other EMTs rolled them toward two other ambulances. Three other EMT's brought a stretcher and lifted her onto it. As her vision faded out, the last thing Achilla saw was Samuel running back toward her as the EMTs wheeled her toward an ambulance. Samuel stood by her before they carried her inside. Achilla reached out to her brother before everything went dark.

Achilla woke up wearing a white gown under white bed sheets. She tried to sit up in bed and noticed that her right arm, right leg, and left hand were cast. Her back throbbed but it was nowhere near as bad as before. Achilla rolled over on her side and saw Samuel sitting on a chair with his chin tucked into his chest, his eyes closed and his arms crossed. A trail of drool leaked onto his black-t-shirt from his lower lip. Achilla checked the time on the 24-inch television across the room. It was four in the morning, and at least eight hours had passed since Ailina's attack.

"Samuel," Achilla croaked through her dry throat, and Samuel jumped awake, wiping his mouth and rinsing his hands in the sink to Achilla's left.

"You're awake," Samuel said as he rushed to Achilla's side. "Good. We're at St. Vincent's. The doctor said you'd be OK after the back surgery, but he said it was the hardest surgery he's ever performed. Something about your skin being really tough. I don't know, it was weird."

"Where are Mom and Dad?" Achilla asked as Samuel grabbed a cup of water with a straw and set it to her lips.

"They're fine too," Samuel replied as Achilla guzzled the luke-warm water that massaged her throat. "They both had slightly collapsed tracheas. The doctor said if their attacker kept squeezing they would be dead. You saved them, Achilla."

"No, you did," Achilla sighed and leaned back in her bed. "You were so brave."

"It was the least I could do," Samuel said with a shrug. "I told you I'd return the favor."

"Thanks," Achilla said with a smile before glaring at him. "But if you scare me like that again, I'll kill knock you out! Are you crazy? You could've been killed!"

"Yeah, your personality's back to normal," Samuel said with a chuckle as Achilla got back up for another round of water. "How do you feel?"

"If I didn't know any better," Achilla replied in between sips, "I'd think I was the one who got hit by the car, not Ailina. I underes-timated her."

"About that," Samuel said as Achilla pushed the cup away with the back of her hand. "I saw you hit her with a car at like forty miles an hour, and then she got up and threw you into tree, and then I'm pretty sure she punched your head so hard that it made a pothole in our driveway, but you punched her so hard that made a hole in the walkway--"

"It's hard to explain," said Achilla with a shake of her head. "Just think of me as Wonder Woman or something."

"I knew something was different about you when you first came to our house," Samuel replied. "The way you beat up Marty wasn't normal. It was like I was watching a grown-up abusing a kid."

"You were," Achilla stated as she watched the nurses walk around the emergency room in their navy blue scrubs and then turned to Samuel. "I told you I never had a childhood. You can thank Ailina for that. She practically raised me to be a fighting machine. Speaking of Ailina--"

"That's where I come in."

Achilla's head snapped toward the deep voice and saw Chief Price standing in the doorway wearing a gray t-shirt and jeans; the first time Achilla ever saw him not wearing a uniform. He closed the slide door behind him and stood with his hands behind his back as if he were still wearing all of his badges. Achilla glared at him at first until she smelled the stench of pollen filling the sterile hospital room and crinkling her nose. She noticed a bouquet of pink flowers in his left hand with a card on top. Achilla busted out laughing and pointed at the flowers with her casted hand. Samuel frowned and tapped her shoulder.

"Hey look, Samuel," Achilla quipped. "He's pretending to be a grandfather, but if he really cared about us he'd know that I can't stand flowers. God, they smell!"

"You're welcome," Chief Price said as he set the flowers on the counter. "Samuel, how are you?"

"Doing well, Chief," Samuel said with a voice that reeked of forced formality.

"Well, it's good to know you're OK," Chief Price replied. "I'd like to speak with your sister alone. There are other guests in the lobby who need an explanation on Achilla's status, namely Trevor. He refuses to listen to me."

"Chief Price, with all due respect--"

"Go, Samuel," Achilla said. "Grandpa Johnson's going to cause drama out there. You know that man can't stop talking."

Samuel nodded his head and walked past Chief Price before he opened the slide door. He looked back at Achilla and she nodded at him before he walked out and closed the door. Achilla watched as Chief Price paced the hospital room. His face was stone straight, but a bead of sweat leaked down his forehead. When he finally faced Achilla, his eyes avoided hers. Achilla frowned.

"Are you...nervous?" Achilla asked with a slight snicker.

"Guilt-ridden is more like it," Chief Price replied. "And embarrassed. I had no idea that things would end up this way."

"You always knew that I was Dad's kid," Achilla said. "You had to know."

"That's correct."

"Then why?" Achilla asked. "Why didn't you tell my Dad sooner? And why didn't you do something about Ailina? She's a threat to everyone she comes across, and you can't just let her walk the streets, let alone have a badge and a gun."

"I know," Chief Price said. "And I wasn't supposed to tell you this, but the recent developments have forced our hand."

"Our?" Achilla asked with a sideways glance. "What's going on?"

"I work closely with the CIA," Chief Price said. "It's not official BPD business, but we've been monitoring Ailina since she was a little girl."

"The CIA?" Achilla asked as she mouthed the letters like they were large morsels of food.

"Yes," Chief Price said. "They have reason to believe that Ailina is capable of murdering hundreds of people if she is not contained. Bridgeport Police seemed to be working for her as a positive outlet, but she became increasingly unstable. As she moved up in the ranks, we received reports of police brutality that only got worse as the years went on. Suspensions didn't even faze her. I got more concerned when all of the complaints stopped."

"She figured out how to beat her victims into silence," Achilla replied. "I've seen how she treats her lovers. I couldn't imagine what she does to a suspect."

"When she got pregnant, things got worse," Chief Price continued. "Even while on maternity leave, neighbors complained about screams coming from her house. Your father was one of many targets. Compared to her other men, he got off pretty lucky."

"Knowing that, what took you so long to get me out of there?" Achilla asked before raising her casted arm. "She's not exactly kid-friendly."

"At this point, you have a right to know," Chief Price said before clearing his throat. "We needed more information about her intentions; what her next move would be once she had a child. Now we suspect that she trained you at an early age to be her accomplice. I used Brendan's discovery as an opening to separate you two. Once Brendan started sending a private investigator over to your house, and she caught him, we knew it was only a matter of time before Ailina's abilities were exposed."

"So what?" Achilla asked with a shrug.

"When you put someone of…your kind out in the open, it gets dangerous," Chief Price replied as he looked away. "It's like hiding a wolf in your basement and then unleashing her at a cocktail party. Too much exposure too soon, and she's snarling and biting everyone until they leave her alone. We wanted to minimize the damage she could cause, especially if she had you on her side. Her secretive nature worked in our favor, but now that she's willing to engage you in a residential neighborhood, we'll have to change strategies."

"Once you heard about my fight at the basketball game you knew you had to separate us," Achilla replied with a head nod. "That wasn't in my best interest at all."

"Yes, it was," Chief Price said. "You and everyone else. We thought we nipped things in the bud, but Ailina's very adept at manipulation and brainwashing. She apparently raised you to be a powerful ally, so much so that you maintained your fighting abilities even in her absence."

"I'm not her ally," Achilla snapped. "She maimed me and tried to kill everyone I love."

"That was an attempt to get you back on her side," Chief Price said. "It was essentially my tactic in reverse. I'm not sure why she didn't kill them, but I'm glad she didn't."

"Samuel stood up to her," Achilla replied. "She said it would be a travesty to kill him."

"Ailina especially sees men as tools," Chief Price said with his arms crossed. "She saw something in Samuel that she could use. I'm afraid she's just saving him for later."

"Not on my watch," Achilla snapped. "I'll kill her first."

"Which leads to why I'm here," Chief Price said as he extended his arms. "If I understand correctly, you can speak four languages?"

"Five," Achilla said. "I just got pretty good at Farsi, but I haven't had much chance to practice it in real life."

"You're more than proficient in five martial arts," Chief Price continued as he paced the room. "And you possess a body that no one has been able to explain. Your doctor is apparently a comic book nerd. He compared your skin to Aquaman."

"He is a nerd," Achilla said slight frown. "I'm not sure how to take that."

"It means that pretty soon your skin will be tougher than the tires on an eighteen wheeler," Chief Price replied. "We had the same issue with Ailina's father, Ares, your grandfather."

"What happened to him?" Achilla asked. "He's probably the only person Ailina has anything positive to say about."

"I shot him in the head," Chief Price replied before pointing at his knee. "That was just before he'd crushed my legs with my own squad car and took me off the streets for good. I can walk, but thanks to him, chasing criminals is wishful thinking for me."

Achilla frowned at the thought of someone lifting a car and throwing it like Superman in the cartoons.

"Wow," Achilla said. "That's impressive."

"He was…a monster," Greg Price breathed as he shook his head and shuddered. "It was like fighting the devil himself. Nothing worked until I got close enough to shoot him at point-blank range. We couldn't afford another Ares running around, so we tried to contain Ailina at an early age and divorce her from his ideologies. You've seen the results."

"Yeah, a sociopath with a badge," Achilla said. "How do you justify giving her a gun?"

"When man had to compete with wolves, we knew we couldn't kill them," Chief Price said as he paced the room. "So we domesticated them and made them our friends, but sometimes a wolf stays a wolf no matter what you try. In that case, you need a trained wolf to catch that wolf."

"Aside from the fact that you rely on Denzel Washington for your analogies," Achilla quipped, "it sounds like you tried to use her and it didn't work."

"That's not entirely wrong," Chief Price replied. "It's also why I'm here."

"You want me to be a Bridgeport cop now," Achilla snorted. "If it means working for you, no thanks."

"No," Chief Price chuckled and shook his head. "No, your talents don't belong on a local police force. You have the potential to be something far greater to your country. The CIA wants you."

Achilla flinched and shifted in her bed. The CIA wanted her to join? Achilla didn't know that the CIA recruited people like this. The smile on Chief Price's face told her that he was telling the truth. Achilla took a deep breath before looking up at him.

"I'm…I'm only sixteen," Achilla stammered. "I mean, I just started driving a few months ago. I don't even have a high school diploma yet. How am I qualified to be a…a spy?"

"Well, you're a genius," Chief Price replied with a smile. "And degrees aren't everything. I'm sure they can make exceptions for someone with your potential."

"Or potential risk," Achilla replied. "You're all scared that I'll end up like Ailina."

"No," Chief Price said. "I can't speak for the CIA, but I'm more concerned about whose side you're on. Whether you end up like Ailina cannot be controlled."

Achilla frowned and pouted. That was a sharp contrast to Achilla's meeting with her parents when they gave her that flip phone.

"You don't have any faith in me," Achilla muttered as she shook her head. "You're nothing like my parents."

"In return for your service they promise twenty-four-hour

protection for your family," Chief Price said as if Achilla never made that comment, "in case Ailina changes her mind and decides to attack again. She's strong but she's not invincible, and she's nothing compared to Ares. With enough men and enough bullets, she can be neutralized in the event that she threatens your family."

"I think they're your family too," Achilla said with a squint. "And where is Ailina?"

"We don't know," Chief Price sighed and shook his head. "She disappeared after your fight. As the best detective in the state, she has intimate knowledge of how to evade law enforcement. Unfortunately, that was a risk we were willing to take when I convinced her to join the police academy."

"And now the CIA wants me to hunt her down," Achilla said with a smirk. "They want me to clean up their mess."

"That will be one of your assignments, but I doubt that will be all," Chief Price said.

"They just want to hold onto me until the time comes," Achilla replied. "So what am I the trump card or something?"

"They're desperate, Achilla," Chief Price said. "Giving a minor this level of government clearance is unheard of. They'll allow you to communicate with your family under the condition that you don't utter a word about your CIA affiliation."

"And they promise round the clock protection?" Achilla asked. "If anything happens to them--"

"Yes," Chief Price said. "I know we don't see eye to eye on everything, but I recommend that you take it."

"You don't have to sell it," Achilla said. "I'll take it. All I care about is my family. We can figure out the rest."

"Good," Chief Price replied. "Your parents will be receiving letters from a prestigious boarding school out by Hartford called Loomis Chaffee. We've made arrangements for you to stay there as your home base. While you attend school there, they'll send you assignments. As far as anyone up there is concerned, you're just a gifted kid. Got it?"

"I can handle that," Achilla said as Chief Price turned to leave. "By the way, what do you get out of this?"

"I get to rest easy knowing that my daughter is safe," Chief Price said as he faced Achilla with eyes that looked like they hadn't slept in years. "Even if she hates me for the rest of my life, it's worth it."

"Why do I not buy that?" Achilla replied.

"You don't have to," Chief Price said. "But you'll start to understand all too well. You'll find out that the world is an ugly place, Achilla. When you do, you'll do whatever you must to protect your family."

Achilla frowned at Chief Price as he walked out of her room with the slow gait of a tired old man. She then stared at the white ceiling and cracked a smile. She would be working for the CIA. Her parents would be safe. Things were looking up. Achilla laughed when she heard Grandpa Johnson, Samuel, and Priscilla walking toward the room and making a commotion as usual. She looked down and watched Samuel stand between them with his hands raised. Achilla's smile softened when she saw a shorter, muscular boy with shaped-up hair wearing a black bubble coat, dark blue jeans, and black Tims with the tag wrapped around the laces walking behind them. Samuel must have told Dahntay where to find her.

"And I just think it's ridiculous that it took so long," Priscilla said as she opened the door wearing a red blouse, jeans, and red high-heeled shoes. "Oh, my God, Achilla, you poor baby! Samuel told us everything about your car accident!"

Achilla passed a glance at Samuel as Priscilla rushed around the bed and hugged her around the neck. Samuel lied? Samuel never lied, but then again he did tell their parents about Ailina without Achilla's knowledge. Achilla was starting to wonder if Samuel was wilier than she anticipated. She would worry about that later.

"Honey, how did you manage to survive knocking down an oak tree?" Priscilla asked as she played with her gold-hooped earrings. "Boy, you Johnsons are durable, let me tell you! Can't drive though."

"The girl drives just fine," Grandpa Johnson said as he hiked up his jeans and walked across the room with his chest poked out in his blue button-down shirt. "She drives like her Grandpa. There must've been a problem with the car. Now your father tells me that you like to fix it yourself, but you need a mechanic there with you. Luckily, I'm such a man. I can help you make sure this never happens again, but I hope you learned your lesson. You can't be my bodyguard when you're hurt."

"Yes, Grandpa," Achilla said as she struggled to withhold her laughter. "I'll definitely be more careful. You'll be the first person I call."

"OK, everybody out," Samuel said as he pushed Grandpa Johnson and Priscilla toward the door. "She needs some space."

"That means she needs to be alone with her boyfriend," Priscilla said to Grandpa Johnson as she winked and nudged his side.

"Hey, I know it," Grandpa Johnson chuckled. "They're at that age of fraternization."

"Oh, he's just so cute," Priscilla said as she pinched Dahntay's cheeks and turned to Grandpa Johnson. "He reminds me of my husband. Oh, I could just eat him up. Couldn't you eat him up?"

"Now that I don't know about," Grandpa Johnson replied. "Y'all I-talian women sure like to eat."

"It's pronounced *Ita*lian, old man," Priscilla said with a pointed finger as they walked out the door. "And look who's talking. My husband's as dark as you and eats like a mustang after its first race. Our food bill is insane. Boy, you know, if he wasn't so damn sexy....."

Dahntay sighed as he closed the slide door behind them. He then turned and smiled at Achilla as he held a plate covered in aluminum foil in his hand. Achilla laughed when he raised the plate in front of his face like a cartoon butler. She laughed even harder when he sidestepped across the room before laying it on the counter. Dahntay performed a turn and then bowed before his one girl audience.

"Stop that and get over here!" Achilla said with a grin as she stretched her arms.

Dahntay walked across the room, set the plate down by the sink, and tried to kiss Achilla on the cheek. Achilla turned her head and kissed his lips. It was just like old times. The gentleness of his lips never faded. Dahntay was always gentle with her. Taking a beating from Ailina made her appreciate that all the more.

"What's up?" Achilla said.

"What's up?" Dahntay replied.

"I know you want me in this sexy gown," Achilla said. "But it'll have to wait. I can't even feed myself right now."

"That's why I brought this," Dahntay said when he reached over his shoulder and grabbed the plate. "Fried catfish with string beans with my mother's regards, and I brought a few plastic forks."

"My favorite," Achilla squealed before cocking her eyebrow at Dahntay. "I don't know if it's better than my mom's though."

"Here you go competing with everything I say again," Dahntay chuckled. "You hungry?"

"Hungry enough for a cute boy to feed me?" Achilla asked. "Absolutely."

Dahntay fed Achilla her plate one forkful at a time. He then held her drinking cup as she guzzled her water. Sometimes, he made her laugh so hard that she spit the water out on herself. He would then wipe her mouth with a napkin and try again. After she finished eating Dahntay grabbed the remote control.

"Anything you want to watch?" Dahntay asked as he leaned forward on her railing. "This is your morning."

"What day is it?" Achilla asked.

"Saturday."

"In that case," Achilla said with a raised chin and a British accent. "I have a request."

"Shoot," Dahntay said.

"Cartoons," Achilla replied as she rested her head on Dahntay's forearm. "I'm definitely in the mood for some Saturday morning cartoons."

Chapter Twenty

ACHILLA JOHNSON:20

Achilla hopped out of bed at four a.m. She stretched and banged out a couple hundred handstand pushups before getting dressed in a bright red t-shirt and blue jeans with a pair of her old red and white basketball sneakers. It was conspicuous, but that was her intent. Achilla had no reason to sneak into the CIA when she knew they were waiting for her. She texted Ailina to meet her at the Waterbury train station. From there, they would use public transit to Hartford. As nice as it sounded to have a getaway car, a train was a lot less likely to get pulled over during a high-speed chase and didn't lend itself to shooting someone without the public noticing. Achilla grabbed her .44 Magnum and shoved it into the back of her pants. It was still empty, but she figured she could steal some ammunition on the way if need be. She walked out of her room and tip-toed down the stairs before opening the front door. There was no need to sneak out the window this time. Achilla had a feeling that her family no longer had any intention of monitoring her whereabouts.

She shut the door when she heard footsteps behind her, turned, and saw Sandy standing in the foyer wearing nothing but one of Samuel's black and blue "Blue Devils" t-shirts that flowed just above her knees as she held her hands behind her back. Achilla could smell Samuel's cologne on her from where she was standing, along with his distinct scent. She wanted to slap her forehead. Had she known Sandy and Samuel would end up hooking up so soon, she would've demanded that Sandy get tested first. She also might have informed Samuel that she used to be a prostitute. Sandy frowned as if she knew what Achilla was thinking.

"We didn't do anything," Sandy said. "Well, we kissed, but I needed a shirt. Sam's doing laundry and--"

"The best lies have a hint of truth to them," Achilla replied. "But they don't work when there's evidence to the contrary. You smell like Samuel."

"Well, I am wearing his shirt," Sandy said with a slight chuckle and roll of her eyes as she shuffled her feet. "So obviously I'm going to smell like him, right?"

"You also smell like sex," Achilla replied. "Both male and female genital secretions have a pretty strong scent; especially when they're mixed together with latex. The average person might not notice in this open space, but with me, you might as well put it in a bottle and spray it around the house. I wasn't going to mention that until you decided to keep lying."

Sandy hung her head.

"As long as he didn't pay you, I don't care," Achilla said with a raised hand. "You are clean, right?"

"You're so cruel," Sandy muttered. "Why would you ask me that?"

"My brother has a bright future," Achilla replied.

"And I don't?" Sandy asked with a low expression. "Am I just a worthless *jump-off* to you?"

"I didn't say that," Achilla sighed. "But if you give him an STD, your future remains the same while his changes. It's not really fair."

"I don't have any STDs," Sandy growled. "Nina made us get tested every week. She said a girl with bumps was a defective product."

"And you think I'm cruel?" Achilla asked with a cocked eyebrow.

"At least I don't treat you like merchandise. Look, I have to go take care of something."

"You'll need your bullets, right?" Sandy asked.

Achilla frowned as Sandy walked into the kitchen without waiting for an answer. She returned with a handful of .44 caliber rounds. She grabbed Achilla's hand, placed the rounds in her palm, and closed her fingers around them. Her grip was tight but gentle. Sandy then looked at Achilla with hazel eyes that pleaded for her to be careful. Something about Sandy's eyes made Achilla look away for a split second. It was the same look Sam used to always give Brendan before a big trial. Now Achilla understood why Sandy was lying. She was feigning a faithfulness to her that wasn't required.

"I swore you'd find them," Sandy said with a smile. "I guess I'm better at hiding things than I thought."

"I didn't look," Achilla replied. "I kind of had a funeral to go to."

"Are you coming back?" Sandy asked as she squeezed Achilla's hand. "You said you'd teach me how to fight."

"I have every intention of coming back," Achilla replied. "But I can't confidently promise it."

"Why not?" Sandy asked as she gripped Achilla's hand even tighter.

"Because it may not be to your benefit," Achilla said as she pulled herself free.

"So you're just going to leave?" Sandy asked with a crack in her voice.

"I didn't say that," Achilla snapped. "I said I wouldn't come back *here*, and even that's a maybe. I'm many things, but a liar isn't one of them; not if I don't have to be."

"We both know that's not true," Sandy replied. "If you told the truth from the start, I wouldn't be here, but it's turned out all right. I like it here. So I forgive you."

"I don't recall asking for your forgiveness."

"If you have to ask it doesn't really count," Sandy said with a weak smile. "That's what Sam says."

"How'd that come up?" Achilla asked with her arms crossed.

"When I asked what she wanted to do about the guy who murdered your dad," Sandy replied.

Achilla's insides twisted in a knot. Was Sam willing to forgive Brendan's killer without any retribution? No jail time? No physical punishment? Not even a confession and letter of apology? How could she do that? Achilla swallowed a lump in her throat as she thought about how much resolve that must have taken.

"Hold on," Achilla said with a sideways look. "What did you suggest she *do about him*?"

"I know some bad guys up in Waterbury," Sandy said with a shrug that made Achilla glare at her. "Throw them a little cash and they can find whoever you need. It'll never get back to you, and I told her that, but she didn't want to. I mean, I guess I can't blame her."

"Sandy," Achilla said with a low voice.

"Yeah?"

"If I hear you talk like that ever again, I'll kill you myself," Achilla snarled with her fists clenched. "Don't *ever* do that again. Don't ever bring that kind of violence to my mother's house. How dare you!"

Sandy backed away and hung her head again.

"What's the difference?" Sandy mumbled. "You bring violence everywhere you go. You're such a hypocrite."

"Only to those who don't get it," Achilla replied as she turned her back. "And I don't expect you to. For your own good I haven't given you all of the information, so I guess that's my fault. "

"Aren't you going to tell Sam?" Sandy asked. "Or Samuel?"

"I'll cross that bridge when I get to it," Achilla replied with a wave of her hand.

"That's selfish," Sandy muttered.

"It really isn't," Achilla said as she opened the door. "Thanks for the bullets."

"How many?" Sandy asked as she speed walked to Achilla's side.

"I count about ten," Achilla replied with a shrug.

"You know I mean the people," Sandy snapped as she shut the door. "How many people are you going to murder today?"

Achilla stared at Sandy and she glared back with her arms crossed. Sandy was changing into a stronger person; no doubt through Sam's influence. She even cocked her eyebrow at Achilla the way Sam always did. Achilla chuckled and shook her head. She then hugged Sandy around the neck.

"I've changed my mind," Achilla said to Sandy as she stood with her mouth open. "I'm coming back no matter what."

"OK," Sandy replied as she wiped a strand of her hair and waved. "Bye."

Achilla walked out of the door and speed-walked to her car. Sandy was smart. She had the natural perception skills to be a good police officer one day, but she was emotional. The slightest soft touch and she believed anything Achilla said. As much as she hated it, Achilla had to use that to make her stop worrying. Perceptive worrywarts always find a way to follow you; a lesson Achilla learned from Sam. Achilla's cell phone vibrated and she received a text from Ailina. She was waiting at the rendezvous point. Achilla hopped into her father's car and high-tailed it down the street. As usual, Ailina was too early.

When Achilla arrived at the Waterbury train station, she spotted Ailina wearing a lime green t-shirt and blue jeans with green sneakers that looked like they could glow in the dark. Apparently, she had the same thought process about bright clothing. Ailina glowered at her with her hands on her hips. Achilla smirked and walked past her into the station.

"Mind telling me what took so long?" Ailina asked.

"Timing is everything," Achilla replied as she bought a ticket at a kiosk. "Trust my judgment on this one."

"I don't like to be kept waiting," Ailina replied with a slight flicker in her eyes.

"That was your fault," Achilla said. "You seem to expect me to move at your speed, but I'm the one with CIA experience and the knowledge of the Hartford office. We'll do things my way today."

"Fine," Ailina said. "As you wish, Princess."

"Cut the spoiled brat routine and come on."

They took a train up to Hartford and walked a few blocks before they arrived at the old CIA parking garage. Achilla spotted a few lookouts in the restaurant across the street and on a bench ahead of them. She also knew there were at least three snipers in the surrounding buildings. Still, nobody shot them. If the CIA planned on killing her, they wanted it done inside the building away from the public eye. Achilla took a deep breath as the morning sun beat down on her face. Hartford in the summer was like one big skillet set on top of a stove burning on high all day.

"They're watching us," Achilla said at a volume that she knew only the two of them could hear. "But they haven't stopped us from getting this close to the door. The majority of their defense is inside."

"Letting us walk into a trap?" Ailina asked as she looked around.

"Pretty much," Achilla replied as she opened the door and walked inside. "Our target is inside of an underground facility within the garage that can only be accessed by the backdoor in the elevator. They're most likely waiting for us there. "

"Knowing that, what do we do?" Ailina said as Achilla approached the elevator and pressed the button. The door opened and they stepped in.

"There's no point in trying to sneak in," Achilla said. "So we'll bust in. Follow my lead if you can keep up."

"You know I can," Ailina replied with a smirk. "I'm the one who taught *you* how to fight, remember?"

"You didn't teach me everything," Achilla said. "Let's go."

The elevator descended to the basement and stopped. Instead of waiting for the doors to open, Achilla kicked the back door, sending it flying into the hallway and crashing into a group of men waiting in front of them. Achilla stomped the door, and the people under it, and clomped one of her opponent's wrists that held an AK-47. Achilla snatched the gun and sprinted down the hall. She overheard footsteps approaching from the front and ducked into an adjacent room, but she frowned when she noticed that Ailina didn't follow. Where was she?

Achilla then heard the rattling of an AK-47 firing and men and women screaming for thirty seconds. Before she could turn and see what happened, Ailina popped into the room with an identical gun.

"Why are you waiting here?" Ailina hissed. "We have weapons."

"Did you shoot all of those people?" Achilla replied as she set her gun down. "Did you shoot to kill?"

"Well, yeah, Achilla--"

Achilla snatched the gun out of Ailina's hands and tripped her feet until she backpedaled into the wall. She then pinned her against the wall by her throat with her free hand and squeezed the barrel of the gun shut with the other before dropping it on the floor. As Achilla pulled a knife out of her back pocket and pointed it up her nose, Ailina raised her hands but grinned at her as if she were entertained by her strength. Achilla set her jaw and caressed the rim of Ailina's nostrils with the blade to show her lack of humor on the subject. Ailina's grin persisted.

"Kill anyone else, and you will join them," Achilla said. "No unnecessary casualties."

"Oh, you're so soft," Ailina spat. "Just let me have a little fun, huh?"

"I told you we're doing this my way," Achilla growled. "No. Unnecessary. Casualties. Period."

"Where was this pity for Blue Eyes?" Ailina replied with a sneer.

"In my father's grave," Achilla said. "These people are just following orders. We will disable them. Break their arms and pull out their eyes if you have to, but don't kill them unless it's absolutely necessary. That's my plan. Cooperate."

"Fine," Ailina said with a shrug. "Have it your way."

"Follow my lead," Achilla replied before leaning against the wall next to the door. She listened for any footsteps, even the kind she could hear when someone attempted to be quiet, but she heard nothing. Achilla frowned again. Not much resistance. Ailina couldn't have shot more than nine agents so where were the rest? Achilla drew her gun and stepped into the hallway. She signaled for Ailina to follow and sprinted down the hall. When she reached the old interrogation room, Achilla turned the corner and found three men wearing all black standing by the window. Just as they drew their guns, Achilla rolled on the floor and shot their knees before rising to her feet and side-kicking one man across the room. She then turned and punched the other in the face before grabbing the man in the middle and elbowing him in the gut. She used the unconscious man's body as a shield and rammed into the window, pushed herself free from his body in mid-air, and somersaulting to the floor, and landing on her feet while catching him in her arms. She set the man on the floor and checked his pulse. He was alive but in for a very painful few weeks.

Achilla's ears twitched and she gripped her .44 Magnum. Someone was waiting for her in this room. When she felt a presence behind her, she whirled around with her firearm aimed at eye level. She saw Agent Kate wearing a black t-shirt, jeans, and boots with a .22 Glock pointed at her face. She still had a scar on her cheek from their last encounter.

"You noticed me," Kate said with a smirk. "It's about damn time you started doing what Freeman taught you."

"Don't stand in my way, Kate," Achilla replied. "Nobody'll stop me this time."

"Where's Ailina?" Kate said. "I know she came with you. I evacuated the facility just in case."

"Lagging behind," Achilla said before looking at the floor for a split second. "For some reason."

"Not exactly the best teamwork," Kate replied. "Looks like she sent you in here to get shot so she could grab Ares and run. That woman tried to kill your family. How could you let her manipulate you this badly?"

"I could say the same about you," Achilla replied as she kept her gun level.

"I told you it was a mole," Kate said through her teeth. "We work in intelligence, Achilla. Almost nothing goes according to plan. There was supposed to be a detail there."

"Why should I believe you?" Achilla demanded.

"You don't have to," Kate snapped. "But neither of us has any control over reality. Things happen whether we believe they can happen or not. I couldn't believe people like you existed until I saw Ares lift a police cruiser over his head."

"You'll say anything," Achilla replied. "When I found out my father died, you didn't even flinch."

"That happens when you've watched people die for most of your life," Kate said. "I'm hardened, but I'm no traitor to my country or my comrades."

"Not buying it," Achilla snapped.

"Achilla!"

Achilla glanced to her left without lowering her gun. The figure to her left had the height, build, and gait of Agent Jones. Achilla returned her focus to Kate who hadn't lowered her gun either. However, Kate's slight change in disposition told Achilla everything. As hardened as Kate said she was, her eyes softened for a split second at Agent Jones' voice.

"You brought him here to soften me up?" Achilla asked before sneering. "Or did you tell him to stay away *because you care?*"

"Neither," Kate growled with a ferocity that told Achilla that her second accusation was dead on. "I specifically ordered him to stay away because I question his ability to be impartial. He should've shot you before."

"Achilla, don't do it," Agent Jones said. "Look, it's my fault that your father died, but freeing Ares is a mistake."

"Freeing?" Achilla asked with a scowl. "He has two bullets in his head. Ailina just said she wanted his body."

"So smart, but so naïve," Kate said.

"Ares is more than just alive in that tank," Agent Jones said. "His brain functions are normal. The second we drain out the fluid, he'll regain consciousness. We had to keep him that way for research purposes. We needed to find out about Nephilim cell regeneration. He shouldn't have survived that gunshot. It's imperative that we find out why."

Kate frowned at Agent Jones.

"Don't look at me that way, Kate," Agent Jones snapped. "Did you really think you could hide what you were doing in here from me?"

"What have you found out so far?" Achilla asked without taking her eyes off of Kate. "Or maybe I should ask you, Kate. Answer now. You don't want me to force it out of you."

"That's classified information," Kate replied before narrowing her eyes. "And you're welcome to try. You won't get me with the same trick twice. We've discovered ways to defend ourselves against Nephilim, and I'd be happy to test my theories on you--"

Before Achilla could reply, Ailina flew down from the window and landed behind Kate. Kate turned but Ailina grabbed both of her arms and snapped them in half like she was popping a towel before snatching her gun and elbowing her face. Kate flew into Achilla's arms like a wet rag, and her obliterated nose leaked down blood her chin. Achilla checked her pulse. She was alive but out cold. Achilla glared at Ailina as she walked toward the tank. She then heard a click and saw Agent Jones standing in a white t-shirt and black bulletproof vest as he aimed his pistol at Ailina.

"Are you going to shoot me, Freeman?" Ailina asked with a grin.

"You know him?" Achilla asked.

"We met the night we took her father," Agent Jones said.

"They always had you playing babysitter," Ailina cackled. "I should've known they'd assign you to her too."

"Ailina, I can't let you any closer to the tank," Agent Jones shouted. "You can't take advantage of me like you just did your daughter."

"Oh, like you?" Ailina replied with her hands on her hips. "How long were you going to keep her in the dark about my father?"

"What the hell is going on?" Achilla screamed. "Can someone clue me in, please?"

"Achilla, if she opens that tank, the whole country is in danger," Agent Jones said. "Maybe the world. You have to believe me."

"If I don't open this tank, we could go extinct," Ailina replied. "You know I'm not lying."

"She's not lying, but she's omitting the truth," Agent Jones yelled. "Who better to play a Nephilim than one of her own kind?"

"What are you two talking about?" Achilla demanded.

"Stay away from the tank, Ailina," Agent Jones barked. "Even you can't dodge bullets!"

"Neither can you," Ailina said as she darted behind Achilla, pulled Kate's gun, and fired past Achilla's shoulder, shooting Agent Jones twice in the chest just above his vest. Achilla gasped and ran to his side as he fell to the floor. She checked his pulse. Ailina was good on her word. He had no signs of imminent death. Still, he lay on the floor with blood staining his shirt.

Ailina was on top of them before Achilla could stop her, and she stomped Agent Jones' forearm in half. She then snatched the gun out of his hand and grabbed his throat. Achilla yanked Ailina's arm and shoulder tossed her, but she twisted to her feet and swung a backhand at Achilla's head. Achilla blocked with her left arm and grabbed Ailina's wrist before swinging a punch over Ailina's shoulder. Ailina slipped left and swung a right punch.

This was the punch that always tagged Achilla as a little girl, but not this time. Achilla released Ailina's wrist, ducked just under her arm and returned a left hook that was just slow enough for Ailina to see but too fast to duck. Ailina blocked with her right arm and threw a left jab at Achilla's nose. Achilla smirked as she watched Ailina's fist lunge toward her face. A punch that she could never see four years ago now looked so slow that her next counter was obvious. Achilla blocked with her right elbow and whipped a right backhand into Ailina's face before delivering a short hook to Ailina's temple. Ailina grunted and flinched before reaching for Achilla's shirt. Achilla side-stepped to the right, planted her right foot, and rolled her right shoulder as she slammed her fist into Ailina's jaw; sending her stumbling across the room until she planted her feet with a grinding halt.

"No!" Achilla barked as she shook her head. "Not him!"

Ailina's knees trembled as she rubbed her jaw. She glared at Achilla for a moment, and Achilla stared back as she held her stance. Ailina then grinned and grunted as she cracked her neck and shrugged her shoulders. Achilla frowned. She always pictured that punch knocking her out, but she held her ground. Yet again, she underestimated the reserves of Ailina's strength. No matter. Judging from her wobbly legs, three or four blows would do the job should Ailina continue her assault.

"Not bad," Ailina said with a smirk. "I don't think I taught you that one."

"Anchor punch," Achilla replied. "Muhammad Ali."

"Ah, of course," Ailina sighed. "You would take pointers from that babbling fool as if he's ever fought a real opponent."

"It worked on you," Achilla quipped. "Come any closer, and you'll see what else I've learned."

"And that block and backhand," Ailina hummed as she massaged her fist. "I think I broke a knuckle. Impressive."

"52 blocks," Achilla replied. "A perfect defense for a striker like you."

"You've done your homework," Ailina said.

"That's right," Achilla snapped. "And if you think it's going to end like last time, I've got something for you. Try me."

Ailina stared at Achilla with ice cubes for eyes. Achilla looked right back. She wasn't losing this time. Achilla centered herself and prepared for their next exchange until Ailina relaxed her posture, turned her back, and walked toward Ares' tank. Achilla flinched. Normally it took less than that to get a fight out of her. Why would she back down?

"You OK, Agent Jones?" Achilla asked as she watched Ailina work with the controls.

"I'm fine," Agent Jones said before pointing at Ailina. "Stop her!"

"Why should I?" Achilla asked. "Everything she told me about Ares is true."

"Ares is a terrorist," Agent Jones replied. "We infiltrated his home because he planned on assassinating the Governor, and Rosa's call gave the police an excuse to get involved. Given his abilities, it was only a matter of time before the president was next. We had to stop him, so we did."

"Who killed Rosa?" Achilla asked.

"All of us did," Agent Jones said. "We used her as an informant in exchange for Ailina's safety. Once Ares figured it out, he mutilated her."

"Ailina's mother died for her?" Achilla murmured as she watched Ailina work the controls. "But she didn't mention it?"

"Now do you see what we were so afraid of?" Agent Jones asked. "Yes, we were using you. Yes, we should've been more straight with you, and if you hate us that's fine. But for the good of all the innocent Americans out there, don't let her do this!"

"Why should I help people who'll only hate me later?" Achilla asked. "You said yourself that we could go extinct. I wonder why that is."

"Don't be stupid, Achilla!" Agent Jones snapped. "There are ways to prevent that. What the hell do you think we've been researching this entire time? If we wanted all Nephilim, I would've shot you long before I had a chance to get to know you. We're trying to learn more so we can *coexist*."

"You sound like Kate," Achilla replied. "Why should I believe someone who didn't protect my father like they promised?"

"Fine," Agent Jones said. "Don't trust me. Don't trust anyone in the CIA. You're justified. But here's a better question. Why would you help someone who just used you as a human shield? She's playing you, Achilla! God, how can you not see that?"

Achilla's heart double pumped as she replayed the whole scenario in her head. Agent Jones could never shoot Achilla if he didn't have to, and Ailina knew that. Or did she? Why would she take that kind of risk with her own daughter? Even with that whole speech about equipping her to survive, Ailina was willing to sacrifice her to achieve her goal. There was no motherly love in her heart. There never was. Achilla bit her lip and clenched her fists.

How could she be so stupid?

Achilla watched Ailina press a few buttons. Soon after, the fluid in Ares's tank drained until it was just above his head. Achilla stalked behind Ailina and pointed her gun at her head. This was Achilla's mistake, and she was going to rectify it. Achilla set her jaw as she steadied her firearm.

"Normally, that may be a wise decision," Ailina said without turning to face her. "But I wonder if you could live with it."

"Killing you wouldn't be all that hard,"Achilla replied. "You're no mother of mine."

"How about a child?" Ailina asked.

Achilla flinched and nearly lowered her gun.

"Yeah," Ailina said. "Why do you think I needed you to do all the hard work getting in here? I have to protect the next generation."

"Those guys at the bar?" Achilla replied.

"What do you take me for?" Ailina chuckled as the fluid drained to Ares' waist. "They weren't nearly good enough specimens to breed with me. Your brother on the other hand--"

"What?" Achilla snarled as her finger hovered around the trigger.

"He never told you," Ailina sighed as she shook her head. "I'm not surprised. He's real protective. In his defense, he has no clue that I'm pregnant. I usually don't tell the men, you know. They're not properly suited to raise my children. You've proven that. So now I'll start over and do it right by myself."

Achilla's eyes turned cranberry red as she aimed for the back of Ailina's neck. If she touched Samuel, maybe it would be better to shoot her in the throat and let her think about it before she died.

"If you're going to shoot, go ahead," Ailina said with a shrug. "Once my father's free, he can repopulate at a much faster rate than I can. My role is complete."

"My father," Achilla said. "Samuel. You just used them to *repopulate*? But what about before at the station? I could've sworn that you lied about not having feelings for my father. I could've sworn--"

"I never lost sight of my goal to preserve our people," Ailina replied as she turned with her arms crossed. "My personal feelings were irrelevant. I owed my father that much after Rosa betrayed him. She failed to understand the importance of our survival. I didn't."

"You said the CIA shot her," Achilla said.

"They did," Ailina replied with a shrug. "She just happened to already be dead. I never lied to you. I just left out the facts that would only distract you from your purpose."

Achilla's jaw-dropped at her own utter naiveté. Every word Ailina told her, every "truth" that she explained, it was all designed to manipulate her. Ailina stayed away from Achilla for all these years because they both knew that she could no longer kill her in a fight. However, while Achilla was mourning for her father, Ailina knew she would be vulnerable. So she used Achilla's newfound strength to her advantage.

Achilla was the perfect sucker, and just like a sucker, she didn't realize until it was too late.

"Now that he's free," Ailina said with crossed arms and a thumb under her chin, "it'll be easier to protect the fetus until it's born. What should I name it? What do you think of Apollo for a boy? Athena for a girl?"

"You...toyed with me," Achilla replied with a wavering voice. "You never meant any of it. Not a word."

"Did you expect anything less?" Ailina asked before turning around to face the tank. "Come on, even you figured out that I pretended to try to kill your parents to get you on my side. Looks like it worked."

"No," Achilla replied as she shook her head. "I'll never join you."

"You don't have a choice," Ailina snapped as she looked over her shoulder with a crazed look in her eyes. "No one else can take you in now. The CIA will hunt you down like a dog, and Xerxes will do the same. It's all a matter of who gets to you first. You're as good as dead without us."

"You've been planning this for weeks," Achilla said, her voice barely a whisper.

Ailina cackled so loud that her laughter reverberated off of the walls. She never changed. She never cared. She was the same sociopath that she always was. How could Achilla lose sight of that?

"I've been planning this for years," Ailina announced. "You were born to help me release my father out of this tank, and help us take our rightful place. I told Brendan that you would always belong to me. My only regret is that he isn't alive to see this. Oh, I would've loved to see the look on his self-righteous face."

Achilla flinched as tears streamed down Ailina's face. Though her face showed no signs of distress, the tears fell from her eyes like a melting iceberg. Achilla was wrong. Ailina didn't love Brendan. She loved herself and hated the fact that someone else didn't. She was everything Sam described at the Bridgeport Flyer. No, she was worse.

Ailina's next words came as no surprise.

"It serves him right for leaving me," Ailina growled as she faced Achilla again. "I was the best thing he'd ever had. The best! I gave him everything that no other woman could, and then *all of a sudden*, he just left me because I wasn't some perfect little angel. He had no objection when I gave him my body, but the second I do something he doesn't like, he just leaves me!"

Achilla stepped back as Ailina bared her teeth and her eyes bulged and glowed like fluorescent bulbs. Her face was so contorted with anger that all of her superficial beauty was gone. All Achilla could see was a monster with dinner plate pupils and disheveled hair. Was this what Brendan saw the day he broke up with her?

No wonder he ran away.

"No more!" Ailina roared as she pointed at Achilla. "You won't escape either! One way or another, you will return to me and do what you were born to do. If I have to turn all of your little *humans* against you for you to come to your senses, then so be it. Oh, and despite what you like to think, *I am your mother!*"

Achilla lowered her gun as she watched the fluid in Ares' tank drain down to his feet. What had she done? How could she let her emotions dictate her decisions and convince her that anything about Ailina had changed? If Ares was anywhere near as bad as Agent Jones said, Achilla was single-handedly responsible for the deaths of hundreds, maybe thousands of people. She watched as his muscular frame collapsed and leaned against the glass. It wasn't too late. Achilla could still stop them. She raised her gun and aimed for Ares' head, but Ailina jumped onto the platform and spread her arms.

"You'll have to shoot me," Ailina hissed with the same wild look in her eyes. "And my baby. Got it in you?"

"How do I know you even have a baby?" Achilla asked.

"You and I both know I'm not lying to you," Ailina replied. "But be my guest. Shoot me."

Achilla's finger hovered around the trigger like a hummingbird on a flower. All she had to do was pull and this would be over. No more games. No more murders. No terrorist threats. Achilla could end this right here, right now.

Still, an innocent child who knew nothing, planned nothing, did nothing, would die. If it was Samuel's child, then Achilla would be guilty of murdering a member of her own family; a blameless member. Achilla's hand trembled as she zeroed in on Ailina's wide-eyed, predatory staring face. It would be worth it to rid the world of this monster and her father. The children would just be collateral damage. Samuel, Sam, Sandy, they would all understand. Even better, they wouldn't have to know. Samuel had no clue that Ailina was pregnant and would never find out if she just killed her right here and now and then killed Ares before he knew what hit him.

Achilla set her jaw and steadied her aim at Ailina's forehead. Her finger inched toward the trigger. Now was the time to kill Ailina. Now was the time to save everyone. She had to eliminate the threat. A growling desire from the pit of her stomach roared for Ailina's head.

She had to kill Ailina.

NOW!

The trigger finger moved on its own but stopped when Brendan's face barged into Achilla's thoughts with the worried, furrowed brow expression he wore when he first met Achilla at her basketball game. She could tell by the way he challenged Ailina that he wouldn't rest until his daughter was safe, despite knowing her for five minutes. When she first showed up on his doorstep, Sam welcomed her with open arms, smiled at her, fed her, knowing that she was the child of a woman who threatened her husband's life. Achilla remembered her first time watching television with her father. He offered her half of his food when he heard her stomach rumble from her insatiable appetite, even though she already ate dinner and he just got home from a long day at work. Achilla's throat tightened that night as she devoured the rest of his steak, and it tightened now when she remembered the smile on Brendan's face as he laughed at her eating habits and then taught her how to properly cut small pieces with a steak knife.

No. Achilla couldn't do it.

Brendan went eleven years without knowing she existed and then immediately fought for the right to take her in. He could have left her with Ailina and let her grow up to be as evil as her, but he didn't. Samuel deserved the same chance, and so did his child. That was what Achilla's heart told her over and over as she lowered her gun and held it at her side, and her gut told her that Ailina knew this would happen. She knew Achilla could never kill a child. Her pregnancy wasn't just about repopulation. It was her trump card in case Achilla turned on her, and it worked. Agent Jones' intel on Ailina was spot on. She was smarter than Achilla, and now was the absolute worst time to realize it.

"I hate you," Achilla snarled at Ailina with her head low.

"You hate yourself," Ailina snapped before pointing her finger. "You hate that you're just like me *except when it counts*."

"I'm nothing like you," Achilla muttered.

"Yes, you are," Ailina said. "You just let them tame you. I never made that mistake, and I never will."

Ailina turned and punched through the glass, letting Ares' body fall out into her arms. She swung his arm over her shoulder and leaped off of the platform over Achilla's head. When she landed, Ares coughed until Ailina eased him onto the floor. He then vomited clearish pink bile before he hacked some more. Ailina rubbed his head as he lay face down on his forearms.

"It'll take a while for him to regain his strength," Ailina said. "But he's alive and well. I thank you, Achilla. You were good on your word. But since the deal's finished…"

Ailina stood up and shot Agent Jones between the eyes, and his lifeless body slumped to the floor without another movement. Achilla dropped to her knees as she stared at Agent Jones; the one man in the

CIA she could trust. Now, just like her father, Achilla failed to protect him. She dropped her gun and clenched her eyes shut as her fists trembled. How could she let Ailina do this to her? With all of her training, intelligence, and newfound strength, she should have been able to stay above her manipulation. Instead, she was Ailina's sucker just like always, and yet another person close to her paid the price. Achilla turned her head and watched Ailina lift Ares off the floor and pat his face.

"*Bampás*," Ailina whispered with a giddy smile. "It's me, Ailina. You're going to be ok. I saved you, *Bampás*."

I saved you. Those words grabbed Achilla's intestines and squeezed with a vice grip. Even Ailina knew how to protect her own, and here Achilla was sitting on the ground like a defenseless child with no answers, no plan. Though she wanted to cry, Achilla no longer had any tears left. She just stared out with a numb expression on her face.

"Take good care of that baby," Achilla said to Ailina as she looked back at Agent Jones. "As soon as it's born, I'll kill you and Ares before you can fuck up its life like you did mine."

"A traitor to her own race," Ailina replied as she lifted Ares over her shoulder. "So be it. Just know that by the time you find me, my father will be stronger than both of us combined. You'll have a lot more to deal with than you think."

Both of them combined? Achilla's eyes widened as she stared at the floor. How was that even possible? Achilla assumed Ares was strong, maybe even stronger than her, but this kind of opponent sounded impossible to beat. She clenched her fists at the thought of what she had just done. Achilla helped her most powerful enemy release someone who was even stronger and probably just as ruthless.

"By then it'll be too late for you to come back," Ailina said. "He's not as gentle as I am, but I'm merciful. I'll give you time to come to your senses and realize your calling. Find me when you're ready to come back or when you're ready to die. It's up to you, Achilla. It always has been."

Ailina jumped back up to the window and disappeared, leaving

Achilla by herself in the lab just a few feet from a dead CIA agent and his unconscious boss. Her trained mind told her this was life in prison waiting to happen. She couldn't stay. Achilla sighed, walked toward Agent Jones' body and lifted him in her arms before she jumped up to the window. She looked over her shoulder at Agent Kate and spat on the floor. She didn't care much for her, but at least Agent Jones deserved better than lying in the middle of the floor like a poisoned roach.

Achilla set Agent Jones' body in one of the chairs when she noticed a rectangular object in his back pocket. She dug into his back pocket and found the same flash drive that she took from Blue Eyes. She nodded her head. There was no way that he carried such valuable intel on his person by accident. He knew he would die today, and he knew Achilla would need to find all of Xerxes' people. She smiled and carried his body into the hallway. Achilla was giving Agent Jones the burial he deserved.

When she saw a group of CIA agents standing in front of her with their weapons drawn, she stopped in her tracks. They were the same agents that Achilla disabled earlier by the elevator. There was no way that she could avoid this many guns in such a tight space. Judging from the hard looks radiating from their eyes, they had no intention of returning her mercy. Achilla sighed and shook her head. Of course. This explained why Ailina spared the agents Achilla attacked and killed the rest. She was setting her up as a target for the CIA, and there were just enough agents in front of her to hit the mark. Was there anything that woman didn't think of? Achilla hoped that her family would fare better than she did as she closed her eyes and prepared herself for death.

"Wait!" a familiar voice screamed. "I know this woman!"

Achilla's eyes snapped open and she saw Agent Bryant approaching the front of the crowd wearing a black bulletproof vest over a gray t-shirt with an AK-47 in his hand. He glared at Achilla, but she could see the pain in his eyes. He was willing to kill her, but he didn't want to. Achilla nearly smiled at his familiar expression until he raised his gun.

"Agent Johnson," Agent Bryant called out. "Why are you carrying Agent Jones' body?"

"He's dead," Achilla replied. "My accomplice killed him against my wishes."

"And what wishes were those?" Agent Bryant asked. "Talk fast."

"I kept you all alive for a reason," Achilla said. "I didn't want any casualties. I just wanted to grab Ares and get out of here, but Ailina had other plans. For that, I am truly sorry. Now she's escaped with Ares. They are both extremely dangerous. Only I can stop them. Before I do that, I need one of you to take Agent Freeman Jones' body. He deserves a proper burial."

All of the agents stared at her until Agent Bryant raised his hand. The crowd lowered its weapons. Agent Jones handed a female agent his gun and stepped forward. When she grabbed his arm and shook her head with a pleading look in her eyes, Achilla allowed herself a weak smile. It looked like he found someone who loved him. Agent Bryant patted her hand and nodded his head. When she let go, he approached Achilla with his arms extended.

"I'll take him, Achilla," Agent Bryant said. "He was my mentor."

"Mine too," Achilla replied. "And I failed him. Please. Take him. I don't deserve to carry his body any further."

Achilla handed Agent Jones to Agent Bryant, and he carried him back to the crowd.

"Within the next few days, you'll most likely receive orders to capture or even kill me," Achilla shouted. "I hold no ill will against any of you, but please understand that I have a personal mission to complete. Tell your superiors that I will deal with Ailina, Ares, and Xerxes. It's unsafe to stand in my way."

Achilla walked toward the crowd and they drew their weapons. She walked anyway until she was within attack range. One way or another, Achilla was leaving this hallway. She readied herself to charge through the crowd until Agent Bryant raised his hand. On his signal, they all lowered their guns and parted ways for her. At that moment, it became apparent to Achilla that Agent Bryant was more than Agent

Jones' student. He was his best pupil. As she passed through the group of agents, Achilla had a feeling that she would see him again. Unfortunately, it wouldn't be as coworkers, or lovers, anymore.

As she wandered through Hartford and caught the train, Achilla wondered how far Ailina escaped. By now, she was probably in a stolen car and well on her way to Boston. Achilla would not follow. There was no point in any further contact with Ailina unless it was to destroy her. As long as she had an innocent life inside of her, that was not an option. Besides, Achilla had a couple promises to keep. The first one she could keep right now.

Once she arrived in Downtown Waterbury, Achilla drove her father's car home. As she sat in her mother's driveway, Achilla stared out at the backyard that shined under the afternoon sun. It amazed her that she could leave the war zone inside that CIA building and find such peace and tranquility at the Johnson house. Achilla leaned back into the car seat and fell asleep. When she heard someone approaching the window, she jumped awake to find Sandy standing in the driveway. The sun was setting and the dusk haze fell on Sandy's curly hair like orange highlights. It wasn't often that Achilla nodded off like that. Achilla opened the door and stepped out of the car.

"I'm back," Achilla said with a crooked smile. "As promised."

"How many?" Sandy asked with her arms crossed.

"None," Achilla said. "But their deaths are still my fault."

"What are you going to do?"

"Leave as soon as possible," Achilla replied. "It's no longer safe for me to stick around you guys. I'm the target now, and if I hope to survive, I'll have to strike first."

"OK," Sandy said. "Then I'll come with you."

"Too dangerous."

"Hello, former hooker?" Sandy said as she pointed at herself. "I can handle dangerous."

"Every one of my enemies will be trained killers," Achilla snapped. "I'll never stay in the same spot for more than a few months if that. Until my job is done, I'll be dodging bullets every day and sleeping with one eye open. I'm built for that life. I don't know if you are."

"You promised to teach me," Sandy said. "Besides, nobody survives a life like that on their own. You need a partner."

"My entire life will be dedicated to killing everyone who had a hand in my father's death," Achilla said. "Do you think you can handle that? Do you really think that you can live your life that way?"

"Yep," Sandy replied without so much as a blink.

"Look, you have opportunities here," Achilla snapped at Sandy's quick response. "Mom's connected, and it looks like you and Samuel have a thing for each other. You have a chance to live a normal life."

"You. Promised," Sandy demanded.

"Fine," Achilla snarled. "You want to learn something?"

Achilla pulled out her .44 Magnum and aimed it at Sandy's face. Sandy stepped back and raised her hands.

"It's not enough to learn how to fight," Achilla said as she walked toward her. "You have to *want* to fight. You have to want to win more than you want to survive. You have to face death and fear it, but fight anyway."

Sandy continued to back up with her hands raised.

"Everyone I will face can do that," Achilla continued. "But you can't because you're a normal, good person. You don't have to live the life that I do, so don't. I'm telling you to stay away from me from this point forward--"

Sandy interrupted Achilla as she rushed past her gun and hugged her around the waist. Achilla stood with a blank face and her gun aimed at nothing but her mother's house. Sandy held her waist tight, and her embrace was warm; so warm that Achilla lowered her gun. Sandy hugged her even tighter until Achilla pushed her away with her other arm, using more strength than she normally would with a friend. Sandy stumbled until she bumped into the side of the house, and she cringed as she kneeled and rubbed her back.

"What do you think you're doing?" Achilla demanded.

"Doesn't that count?" Sandy asked. "You could've shot me."

"Yes,"Achilla replied. "It does, but--"

"Then I'm coming with you."

"I can't let you do that," Achilla said.

"Why not?"

"Because I don't want you to die," Achilla said. "Not you, not Mom, not Samuel. I want you to live your lives and be successful. You're really smart, Sandy. You can do it."

"Fine, then stay with us," Sandy replied. "You can do it too. Someone like you could be good at anything."

"Not yet," Achilla replied as she walked past Sandy toward the front door. "There's a whole other world out there that you know nothing about, and if I don't do something, it'll kick your door in and murder you all in cold blood. I won't let that happen."

Achilla opened the door just as she finished her sentence and saw an empty foyer. She half expected her mother and brother to be home. She frowned and looked around the house, stopping in the living room. Nobody was there. Had they been gone all day?

"Sam drove Samuel to the airport," Sandy said from behind Achilla. "When you disappeared this morning, they knew you were going to see Ailina. Your mom loves you a lot, but she's done waiting up for you. I don't blame her."

"Neither do I," Achilla sighed. "It's better that way anyway."

"You're lying."

"I wouldn't lie to you if I didn't have to."

"You'll lie to yourself," Sandy said as Achilla walked past her into the foyer and jogged up the steps. "You do that a lot."

Achilla marched into the guest bedroom and threw all of her clothes into a black gym bag. She then grabbed a pen and paper and wrote something down before she jogged down the stairs. She had to escape before her mother returned. Seeing her face would only make it harder to leave. Achilla rolled her eyes when Sandy blocked the door.

"I'm coming with you," Sandy said with a hard stare. "Or you're not leaving. Your choice."

"I admire your determination," Achilla replied. "But if you really want to learn to fight with me…"

Achilla dropped her bag, darted across the room and kneed Sandy in the gut before the bag hit the floor. Sandy grunted before she collapsed. Now Sandy looked like she took a nap in the middle of the foyer. Her abdomen would be bruised for a while, and she might have a few broken ribs, but she would recover just fine. Achilla picked up her bag and opened the front door, leaving Sandy on the floor.

"Figure out how I did that," Achilla said. "After that, maybe you can be my partner. Until then, stay here and live your new life."

Achilla shut the door behind her and tossed Brendan's keys in the air as she strolled to his car. When she was a teenager, Brendan once promised that she could have his car, or something similar, when she graduated from college. Achilla had no intention of taking this car anywhere but to New Haven Tweed Airport where her family would eventually find it. They would never find her though. Chief Price told Achilla years ago that the world was an ugly place and that he had to protect his daughter from it, even if she hated him. He was right. Now Achilla was going to spend the rest of her life getting her hands dirty, bloody even, to clean it up. She leaned against the car and stared out at the tranquil suburban neighborhood for the last time. She then pulled out of her family's driveway and drove out of Stratford.

Within a couple hours, she would board a plane(illegally), but she had another promise to fulfill. She wasted no time driving to Woodbridge to Blue Eyes' old street. When she arrived at his house, she saw a moving truck out front. Achilla parked a hundred feet from the truck and opened her gym bag to grab a gray hoody that she slipped over her head. She then untied her ponytail and straightened her hair out to her shoulders. Though she kept her Magnum in the back of her pants just in case, protecting her hair was not necessary. She didn't come here for a fight.

Achilla reached into the bag and pulled out an envelope before stuffing it in her front hoody pocket. She then stepped out of the car as she watched a brown-skinned man carry a desk into the truck. His chest was almost as wide as Achilla's shoulders and it stretched his black t-shirt. Achilla recognized him by his chest and his short, spiky black hair. He was Juan, Daniela's personal trainer. As Achilla approached, he stopped and stared at her before wiping his hands on his jeans.

"Can I help you, Miss?" he asked.

"I need to speak with Daniela," Achilla replied. "It's urgent."

"Your name?"

"Just tell her I know Blue Eyes."

"Who's that?" he asked with narrow eyes.

"She knows who it is," Achilla said with a hard stare. "Please don't make this difficult."

A flicker of defiance flashed in his eyes before he nodded his head and turned his back. Achilla overheard his conversation with Daniela inside the house. When he mentioned Blue Eyes, her tone changed; dark and knowing. Of course, Juan didn't notice. Achilla could tell by looking at him that he was too good to notice something like that; too naïve of the world's criminal element. Daniela was probably the first married woman he had ever slept with and no doubt by her seduction. Achilla's ear twitched when she heard the front door slam shut and saw Daniela step out wearing gray yoga pants and a hot pink t-shirt. She pulled her hair into a ponytail as she walked down the walkway in her pink and green sneakers.

"Juan said you knew Blue Eyes," Daniela said with burning eyes. "The people who called my ex-husband that name weren't allowed to come by this house. How dare you come around here now?"

"It's not what you think, Daniela," Achilla replied.

"Yeah, what do you want?" Daniela snapped. "Money? I don't know what Roberto owes you, but he didn't leave any to me."

"Was that because he found out about Juan?" Achilla asked before she watched Daniela's face jolt and then compose herself.

"Something like that," Daniela replied as she popped her gum. "I don't know why. He didn't hide the fact that he had plenty of you around. Oh, and I swear to God, if you're claiming that you had one of his kids or something, you are barking up the wrong tree, sister!"

"I'm not one of his girlfriends," Achilla said with a deadpan voice.

"Who are you then?" Daniela demanded with her arms crossed. "Roberto wasn't exactly chummy with black people unless he was screwing them one way or another."

"Sounds like you and Puerto Ricans," Achilla replied as she nodded toward the house.

"That's just..." gasped Daniela with a shaking head. "That's not true."

"Sure thing, Daniela," Achilla said. "And to answer your question, my name is Achilla."

"Oh!" Daniela gasped as her face turned beet red. "My niece told me about you stopping by Roberto's office, and you have some nerve--"

"A ruse," Achilla said with a wave of her hand. "I promise you there was nothing sexual happened. She had to think we had an affair. It was better than the alternative."

"Being?"

"I was CIA at the time," Achilla replied. "There on a classified matter."

"Why would you share that with me?" Daniela asked. "Aren't you guys supposed to keep that stuff a secret?"

"Because I have some incentive for you to keep it a secret," Achilla said as she stepped forward. "I understand that all of your daughters go to Hopkins."

"Yeah, so what?" Daniela asked with a shrug that was an obvious attempt to hide her shock at someone knowing where her children attended school. "It's a good school."

"A lot of Blue Eyes' buddies have kids at Hopkins," Achilla said. "It's too close. Judging by your moving truck, it looks like you want to escape and start over."

"I didn't get the house," Daniela said with her thumb pointed at the home. " So Juan and I are moving in together."

"Has Esther pointed out your hypocrisy yet?"

"Look, I made mistakes," Daniela snapped. "All right? I married a rich man, had his kids, and did whatever he said. There, I admit it. Until I met Juan, I thought that was what you were supposed to do. And what do you care anyway, huh?"

Achilla stared at Daniela until she wiped stray strand from her forehead and looked away.

"I believe you this time," Achilla said as she reached into her hoody pocket. "I'm just not sure if Esther will be as forgiving as you'd like."

"She'll come around," Daniela replied while avoiding eye contact. "They all will. They'll understand that people can change and that their mother isn't perfect. Nobody is. Nobody has to be either."

"And by not perfect, you mean cheating on their father and moving them in with the man you cheated with?" Achilla asked. "Quite the stellar example you've set."

"Look, this is none of your business," Daniella hissed. "Who are you to look down on me, huh? Who the hell are you?"

"I'm someone who watched your daughter go from a happy little girl to a bitter, angry one," Achilla snapped. "Call me concerned. I don't really care who you sleep with, but if it hurts innocent children, then that's a problem."

"You think I'm the bad parent?" Daniela asked with a head nod and curled lip. "Is that it? Let me tell you something. Roberto hit my girls every time they did something he didn't like."

"And you sat back and watched it happen," Achilla replied with a raised chin.

"What was I supposed to do?" Daniela almost screamed. "What, call the police? Sorry, that's not how things work out here, not with Roberto as a husband. The man got away with everything."

"Not your daughter," Achilla snarled with her fists clenched. "He can't get away with that. If anyone touches my family…"

Achilla stopped herself and lowered her head. She had to get a hold of herself. The purpose of this visit wasn't to argue or judge. Of course, Daniela didn't know that. She crossed her arms and lowered her head before she spoke.

"You should hear what some of my *former* girlfriends do to their children," Daniela continued. "It's sick. They're all sick, but they all look so *perfect*, and I'm tired of how fake it is. I'm not claiming to be perfect, but I'm better than them. At least Juan doesn't judge me like they do. He doesn't care about where I went to school or what dress or make-up I'm wearing. He loves me more for me."

"Is that right?" Achilla asked.

"Yeah, it is," Daniela snapped. "And for your information, the girls love him, and he loves them. Even Esther's warming up to him, especially after he encouraged her to dye her hair black again. It's me they hate. They don't even know I had an affair. They just hate that I moved on so quick."

"They're still young, but they're smart," Achilla replied. "Give them a couple of years and they'll piece it together. What then?"

"I don't know," Daniela sighed. "I just don't know yet, all right?"

"Well, I wish you luck," Achilla said as she handed Daniela the envelope. "I get the feeling you'll need it. In the meantime, it might be best to send Esther away for a bit."

"What's this?" Daniela asked as she tapped the envelope in her hand.

"A little assistance," Achilla replied. "There's a stellar recommendation in there from someone who graduated first in her class at Loomis Chaffee and joined the Marines."

"Who's that?" Daniela demanded with a cocked eyebrow. "Doesn't sound like anyone I know."

"Me," Achilla said. "I'd offer money, but I need to save my cash. Besides, with her grades, she'll get a free ride."

"You're that sure?" Daniela asked. "How do you know?"

"Esther's level of brilliance is rare in regular society," Achilla sighed. "But it's common in my former line of work, and I can recognize it easily. Your daughter has the potential to be great at whatever she puts her mind to. You just need to get her away from these distractions. Your husband's death, your boyfriend, New Haven, all of it. If you don't get her out of here now, her life might go off track."

Daniela hung her head before looking up at the sky. Achilla held her hands on her hips as a breeze passed between them, fighting the urge to tell Daniela how much her daughter reminded her of herself. As the image of Esther's boiling eyes filled with repressed rebellion passed through her mind, it reminded her so much of what it felt like to live with Ailina: always on edge, always pressured, always pushed into being something without a choice. Just like Achilla, Esther needed to escape. She needed to leave her mother's house. Achilla raised her eyebrows when Daniela looked at her again.

"Loomis Chaffee?" Daniel asked with a frown. "Up by Hartford? That's pretty far."

"It's the perfect school for her," Achilla said. "They have rigorous academics and they require that you play three sports. Esther has a talent for basketball."

"Yeah, she's the real athlete of the family," Daniela quipped as she pointed at the house with her thumb. "The others aren't all that great. She gets that from me, you know. I was All-State cross country. Roberto couldn't run a mile if a dog was chasing him."

"Ah," said Achilla as she grinned and nodded her head. "That explains Juan."

"Yeah," Daniela said with a smile as she stroked her hair. "I won't lie about that."

Achilla tried to keep a straight face. She really did. But the image of Blue Eyes actually running anywhere forced a guffaw through her lips. Daniela's shoulders shook until she let out a giggle that turned into a cackle. They shared a laugh until Daniela stopped and furrowed her brow at her.

"Something wrong?" Achilla asked.

"Yeah, why'd you do this?" Daniela replied. "What's in it for you?"

"I'm going to disappear for a while," Achilla replied. "I didn't want to do that before fulfilling a promise to myself."

"What promise was that?"

Achilla's training told her to dodge this question. It told her that it would compromise national security and maybe her loved ones. The look on Daniela's face told her different. It lacked the coldness of someone who could kill your whole family and write it off as the expense of doing business. Daniela married a crooked thug for a lawyer, but she wasn't one herself. The regular humans of the CIA couldn't possibly read her well enough to take this risk. A Nephilim on the other hand...

"I promised that if I ever killed Blue Eyes, that I would take care of his daughters," Achilla said without breaking eye contact. Daniela stared back without so much as a flinch. Her eyes filled with tears as she stared at Achilla, but there was no anger. There was no fire that could only be quenched by revenge. Instead, a single tear rolled down her cheek as she nodded her head.

"OK," Daniela said with a cracked voice. "Yeah, um...I'll be sure to give this to Esther. What do I tell her? The girl never stops asking questions."

"Tell her that she has an opportunity to start over," Achilla replied.

"Sure, I can do that."

"Where are you guys moving?"

"Shelton," Daniela said with a weak smile as tears leaked down her cheeks. "It's a nice town, and it works for both of us. I'm...I'm going back to school, you know. I'm a good cook, and there's a culinary program in the area. Juan and I, we're going to start a business together. Fitness and wellness kind of thing. It's all above board, I promise, and I promise not to tell--"

"I didn't come here to kill you," Achilla sighed. "Relax. You're not on my list of targets."

"All right," Daniela replied with a shaky voice. "It's just that, we can all start over, you know, and--"

"I hope it works out for you," Achilla said as she turned her back. "You should know that I had no intention of killing Blue Eyes; not until he sent someone to shoot my father. I'm not a hired gun. I'm a daughter who lost her dad. I hope that gives you some closure."

"Yeah," Daniela said with a wavering voice as she sniffed. "Who was your father?"

"Brendan Johnson," Achilla replied.

"Oh, no," Daniela gasped as she covered her mouth. "Oh my God, my husband did that?"

"Yes," Achilla said with a flat tone.

"Brendan was a good man," Daniela said. "Rober-I mean Blue Eyes was always so jealous of him. He would never admit it, but he kind of hated him."

"I know," Achilla sighed.

"I'm sorry," Daniela said in an almost whisper. "I didn't think he'd take it that far. I turned a blind eye to a lot of things, but if I knew he'd have someone murdered--"

"It's not your fault," Achilla said as she looked over her shoulder and forced a smile. "Just make sure Esther gets that letter. After that, you'll never see me again."

"I will," Daniela replied. "And thanks."

"For what?"

"For not killing me and my girls too," Daniela said. "He took your father away. The crowd he hung out with would've wiped us out if he did that to one of them."

Achilla stared at Daniela for a few moments as a lump grew in her throat. Knowing that she killed her husband, this woman was thanking her? An expression of gratitude was the last thing Achilla expected to hear.

"Just...give Esther the damn letter," Achilla said with a crack in her voice before turning her head. She walked to her car as she listened to Daniela stepping up the walkway. As she hopped into the driver's side, she watched Daniela hand a short black-haired girl an envelope before hugging her around the neck. Esther hugged back, albeit only for a second. As expected, she was holding a grudge, but she still loved her mother. Some time away from home to be herself would help her heal. Achilla just hoped it would work out better for Esther than it did for her. Since she didn't have a sociopathic Nephilim for a mother, her chances were pretty good. Now that she had fulfilled her promises, Achilla had a mission to complete. She pulled out her Magnum and caressed it like a new pet before placing it in her bag.

"Always a choice," Achilla said to the sky as she started the ignition. "Well, I've made my choice. If you don't like it, stop me."

After Achilla took a flight out of Tweed and arrived in D.C., she bought a laptop and inserted the flash drive she got from Agent

Jones. After sifting through all of Blue Eyes' former clients, she formulated a plan of attack. She would hit each city, find its head trafficker and assassinate him. No, she would do more than that. She would mutilate him to send a message to Xerxes and the rest of his operation. Someone was willing to do more than the Feds, more than the CIA, and that someone had no jurisdiction or laws to follow. As long as they continued to kidnap and traffic children, that someone would keep them up at night.

Her next destination was the closest major trafficking city; Philadelphia, Pennsylvania. It would be there where she would find her first of many targets. Xerxes, the CIA, Ailina, Ares, none of them would know what was coming to them. A grin crept onto her lips and a wild glow lit her eyes as Achilla carried her bags through the terminal. Victory was within her grasp. So was revenge.

Chapter Twenty-One

ACHILLA JOHNSON:16

Over the next two months, Achilla learned how fast her body could heal. The muscles in her leg, arms, and hand regenerated themselves at a faster rate than the doctors had ever seen. Achilla was walking without crutches by the November, and she was punching the bag in their basement at three-quarters strength by the end of December.

Achilla also received letters from Loomis Chaffee in the mail. When she showed them to Sam, she hugged Achilla, jumped up and down, and clapped her hands. Achilla hated that a lie brought her such happiness, but at least their family would be safe. She took comfort in that thought when she told everyone that she had a scholarship to Loomis Chaffee. Lying to Samuel hurt most of all, but something told her that he knew the truth. His perception and intelligence never ceased to surprise her.

She only played in the second half of the season, but Achilla had her best game against Naugatuck High School in the first round of states. They still lost. After her game, she made no attempt to hide the fact that Dahntay was driving her home. She kissed him in front of the team and waved as she hopped into his gray car. When people asked, Achilla called him her boyfriend. Even though she knew it was short-lived, she figured he deserved that much. Besides, once Achilla left home, she probably wouldn't have another boyfriend for a long time. She did some research on life as a CIA agent. It didn't lend itself to long-term relationships.

Achilla made it a point to visit old friends before she left. She visited Traci when she came home from UCLA in May and met her brother; a monstrous red-headed man with a scar down his left eye. As intimidating as he looked, he was so kind and loving toward Traci that it made Achilla smile just watching them interact. Traci told Achilla that she was going to get more playing time for UCLA next season and that she should expect to see her on television. She showed Achilla all the pictures she had with her new teammates, and she described each one. None of them came from a wealthy family.

When Achilla walked out of Stratford High School for the last time, she wore her red and gold letter jacket. Since it was around eighty degrees outside, she wasted no time taking it off as soon as she got to the car, exposing her black t-shirt, jeans, and black and white sneakers. As she stuffed her backpack and gym bag in the back seat, Achilla heard someone walking behind her. Samuel took the bus with a new girlfriend, and Dahntay was out with the other football players. Achilla turned around and saw Monika standing in front of her wearing a pink t-shirt and black skirt with white shell-toe Adidas. Her normally hostile demeanor faded when Achilla looked her in the eye.

"How's Dahntay?" Monika asked. "I hear you guys are official now."

"I'm not inclined to answer that," Achilla said as she crossed her arms. "Why don't you let me worry about how Dahntay's doing?"

"Yeah, I got it," Monika said as she hung her head. "Look, I was mean to you, and that was grimy as hell since you were--"

"And I broke your collarbone," Achilla replied. "Let's just call it even and move on."

"Yeah…"

"There's something you want to tell me," Achilla said with a squint. "But whatever it is, it makes you uncomfortable."

"You can tell, huh?"

"Yep."

"Um…look," Monika said as she opened her pink backpack. "Some weird lady gave me this note to give you. I didn't want to do it at first, but she knew everything about you. She knew everything about me and my parents too--"

"Did she look like a tall, white version of me?" Achilla asked with her hands on her hips.

"Yeah," Monika said as she shuddered and crossed her arms. "But she gave me the creeps because she wouldn't stop staring at me. I mean, it was like she couldn't even blink. I've been having nightmares after talking to her."

"Give it here," Achilla said with an outstretched hand. "She's a relative who's not allowed to come near me. The next time you see her, run. You're having nightmares for a reason."

"Damn, your life's really rough," Monika said as she handed her an envelope. "No wonder you could bang like that."

"I need to be alone to read this," Achilla said with a cocked eyebrow. Monika nodded her head and walked away. Achilla then looked around for any onlookers. Just to be safe, she stepped into her car before opening the envelope. She took a deep breath as she unfolded the paper and found a letter. It read:

"Congratulations on the new school. You're progressing nicely. We will meet again."

Achilla smirked and threw the letter on the front passenger side seat. Ailina was somehow evading the police while checking her mail. The second Achilla moved away, she would no longer be able to do that. Achilla started her car so she could drive home to pack, but first, she pulled out her cell phone and called Dahntay. Today was her last day in Stratford, and she had to see him before she left.

When Achilla arrived at Dahntay's house, he was waiting on his porch wearing baggy jeans, black and red sneakers, and a throwback black and red-striped Michael Jordan jersey over a black t-shirt. He held a bag of peanuts and popped one in his mouth as

Achilla parked in front of his lawn and checked her hair in the rear-view mirror. When she stepped out of the car, she knew what happened next. It was obvious. Dahntay was staying in Stratford. She was moving to Windsor over an hour away. As much as the thought of holding onto him made her heart flutter, she knew it would be wrong, and as much as the thought of breaking his heart made her stomach turn, she knew it would be wrong to hold him.

She knew she had to break up with him.

Achilla gave Dahntay a forced smile as she walked up to his walkway.

"Hey," Achilla said as she climbed his steps with her hands in her pockets.

"Sup," Dahntay replied as he popped another peanut in his mouth and forced eye contact.

"It looks like you know what I'm going to say," Achilla said with a slight catch in her voice. "Your...um...your eyes are dry, but you're swallowing a lot. You're preventing yourself from crying."

"I could say the same to you," Dahntay said. "I think I'm a little better at it though."

"It's not really a competition," Achilla replied

"Now you are the last person I expected to say that," Dahntay said with a chuckle.

"So...um...I came to see you before I left," Achilla said with a smile.

"I appreciate that," Dahntay said as he stepped forward and kissed Achilla on the lips. Achilla gripped his shirt and held the kiss until she pulled away and wiped a tear from her cheek. Dahntay's eyes were red but no tears fell. Unlike Samuel, Dahntay was much better at hiding his emotions. Achilla noticed that most boys were, but Dahntay was especially good at it.

"Hey, just let me know when you get home safe," Dahntay said as he rubbed Achilla's arms.

"What are you talking about?" Achilla asked before grabbing Dahntay's hand and walking toward the front door of the house. "We're not done yet."

"I thought we just said goodbye," Dahntay replied.

"We started," Achilla said as she led him into the house. "Now we're going to finish. Did you really think I'd leave you without a good memory of me?"

"Nah, I wouldn't dare."

"All right then," Achilla replied with a smile as she let the door slam behind her and led Dahntay up his wooden staircase. "Pick up the pace. I've been waiting for this all day."

"Always the boss," Dahntay said as he skipped the stairs and picked up Achilla in his arms. "Not today though."

Achilla frowned and then giggled as Dahntay carried her to his room. Afterward, Dahntay lay asleep as she sat at the foot of his bed and slipped her t-shirt over her head. When Dahntay jumped awake, Achilla rested her finger on his lips before kissing him. Achilla smiled and kissed him again as she leaned onto his chest. Achilla would rather lie on Dahntay's chest, but she knew she had to go. She knew she couldn't hold onto him forever.

"You were good," Achilla whispered as she caressed his chest with her finger. "You're always good. Now we can say goodbye."

"Goodbye," Dahntay said.

"Goodbye," Achilla said before she stood up and speed walked out of the house. She didn't want Dahntay's last memory of her to be one of her crying her eyes out. She leaped down the flight of steps and bounded out the door. She hopped in her car and drove the ten-minute ride home, and she made it to the door just in time for Sam to open it wearing a full-length black dress. Sam shook her head as she stood in the doorway.

"We need to talk about this," Sam said as she pointed at Achilla's shirt. "We can't be matching every time we leave the house. I love you to death, girl, but come on--oh! Oh, baby, what's wrong?"

"I just broke up with...Dahntay," Achilla said with tears streaming down her face that she didn't notice until Sam wiped them away. "I was hoping to be alone."

"No, baby," Sam said. "You shouldn't be alone."

"I don't...want," Achilla stammered as her chest heaved. "I don't want people to...see me like this."

"Well, I'm not people, honey," Sam replied as she hugged

Achilla and rested her head on her shoulder. "I'm your mother, now come here. It's going to be OK."

Achilla leaned onto her mother's shoulder and wailed until she soaked her shirt. Sam shushed her as she stroked her hair; a sensation that made Achilla grip her even tighter. Sam tapped her shoulder and Achilla let go. Sam held her by her shoulders and wiped her face. Achilla smiled until she saw Brendan walk into the doorway in a white shirt and red tie.

"What's wrong?" Brendan asked.

"She had to break up with Dahntay," Sam said. "She was a little embarrassed about being upset, but I think she'll be fine--"

Achilla wrapped her arms around Brendan and cried into his chest. Brendan slowly wrapped his arms around her shoulders and held her tight. He rubbed her back as she cried until hiccups bounced in her throat. She then let go on her own and looked at her feet as her eyes continued to leak.

"I'm sorry," Achilla said with a wavering voice. "That was weak."

"Don't be," Brendan replied with his hands on his hips. "You have a right to cry like everyone else."

"That's right," Sam said as she rubbed Achilla's shoulder. "Love is hard, Achilla, and Dahntay was a good boy."

"He was," Achilla said.

"You did what you had to," Brendan said. "We all have to make sacrifices. That's what growing up is all about, but that doesn't mean you have to like it. Nothing wrong with showing a little emotion, right?"

"Right," Achilla replied as she wiped her eyes.

"It's not easy right now," Brendan sighed as he rested his hand on Achilla's shoulder. "But, in the end, you made the right call. I'm proud of you."

"Thanks," Achilla muttered. "I think I'm better now."

"If you need anything else, let us know, OK?" Sam asked with a smile. "We're home all day."

"Yeah," Achilla said as she walked past them toward the house.

"Hey, it's our last night before you leave," Brendan said as he held Achilla's shoulder. "Why don't we all go out to dinner? Anywhere you want to go. Money is no option."

"I think that's a great idea," Sam said as she tapped Achilla's other shoulder. "What do you say, Achilla? Let's take your mind off of it."

"Sure," Achilla muttered as she stepped back onto the stoop. "I'll wait out here."

"I'll get my wallet," Brendan replied as he stepped into the house. "I'll grab Samuel too."

"See?" Sam said as she rubbed Achilla's back. "It's going to be fine. Let's celebrate your achievement. Not every kid gets into Loomis Chaffee. This is a big deal. You should be proud of yourself."

"Yeah," Achilla said as she forced a smile. "Yeah, thanks, Mom."

The Johnsons went out to a fancy Italian restaurant in Fairfield. Eventually, Achilla was able to laugh and enjoy herself, but Dahntay never left her mind. Even when she came back home, she thought about him. She also thought about the family she was leaving and the danger they would be in with Ailina walking around. She was sure that she made the right decision to join the CIA, but walking away from so many great people wasn't easy. Like her father said, sacrifices had to be made.

Achilla cried herself to sleep, but she woke up the next morning with her mind made up and banged out her usual set of handstand pushups next to her bed. She packed her bags and waited outside in her typical attire; a gray t-shirt and red basketball shorts with white ankle socks and sandals. Chief Price arrived in his SUV at six in the morning. When she showed him the letter, he shook his head.

"Checking someone's mail is one of the easiest ways to get caught," he said as he stood on the walkway. "She's mocking us. Once the agents are in place, that all stops."

"I hope so," Achilla said as she wiped a bug away and looked out the front lawn covered in morning dew. The walkway and driveway had been repaired, and Achilla's parents planted a new tree in the backyard. Achilla sighed and clapped her hands as she walked toward the house. Her bags were inside along with her family who all got up early to say goodbye.

"Make your goodbyes quick," Chief Price said. "We have to get you settled."

"You could come inside," Achilla replied while looking over her shoulder. "This is your daughter's house."

"She's not ready to talk yet," said Chief Price with a sideways look. "I tried last night."

"She'll never be *ready*," Achilla said with rolling eyes as she opened the door. "You'll just have to keep trying. Try pretending that she's your daughter and she's worth the effort. That approach worked wonders for my Dad."

Achilla walked into the house and found Brendan and Sam standing in the kitchen. Samuel came downstairs. They all wore red t-shirts designed by a friend of Grandpa Johnson's that read in gold lettering: "Good luck to Achilla the Bodyguard." Achilla laughed every time she saw the shirts. She then jogged into the kitchen and hugged her parents. She felt Sam's body shake as she wept into her shoulder. Brendan smiled and kissed Achilla's forehead as a tear leaked down his cheek.

"We'll miss you," Brendan said. "If you need anything, anything at all, you call me."

"I will," Achilla said with a smile. "Thanks for everything. You guys saved my life."

"I think you saved ours," Brendan chuckled.

"Oh, trust me, I was returning the favor," Achilla replied. "I'm still indebted to you."

"Where's Dahntay?" Samuel asked.

"I saw him off last night," Achilla said with a grin. "Vigorously. He's probably still asleep--"

"Achilla, that's inappropriate," Sam said as she wiped her eyes.

"OK, I think I've earned a little slack," Achilla replied with her hands on her hips.

"Achilla, respect your mother," Brendan said with his arms crossed.

"I rescue you guys from impending death, and I still get scolded for my language?" Achilla cried out with her hands in the air. "I can't get a break!"

"That's right," Sam said with a sniff. "That's because we'll always be your parents, Achilla. You'll always be my daughter."

"And you'll always be my baby girl," Brendan said. "It's so good watching you grow up."

Achilla hugged her parents before turning to face Samuel. This time, he didn't wail like a little baby. He smiled and extended his arms. Achilla hugged Samuel around the neck. She smiled back as she rubbed his head.

"You take care of them," Achilla said. "I think you proved that you can. I'm counting on you."

"I will," Samuel replied. "What're siblings for, right?"

"What're siblings for?" Achilla replied before turning to leave.

"Achilla!" Sam called just as she reached the door.

"Yeah?"Achilla replied as she opened the door.

"Tell my father that the next time he comes over here he'd better come inside," Sam demanded. "Please."

"I will," Achilla said with a smile. "Goodbye."

"Well, you'll be back for summer vacation right?" Brendan asked. "Don't look too upset."

No, she wouldn't. Achilla knew that the CIA wouldn't allow a full summer vacation away from her home base. Still, she had to maintain appearances. Achilla struggled to hold back the waterfall of tears welling up in her eyes as she nodded her head and waved before closing the door. She composed herself just long enough to keep her chin raised as she approached Chief Price.

"Did you hear your daughter?" Achilla asked.

"Yes," Chief Price said. "You know, Achilla, there's no shame in crying."

"Yeah,"Achilla replied with a slight crack in her voice as she swallowed the lump in her throat. "You first."

"I can respect that," Chief Price replied as they stepped into the SUV and he started the ignition. "This may not mean much coming from me, but I hope this works out. If Ailina's as dangerous as they say, you may be our last hope."

Achilla watched the house as Chief Price pulled out of the driveway. Her family stepped out front and waved just as they reached the street. Achilla smiled and waved back. She smiled knowing that it would be the last time she saw them for the next few years; maybe even longer. She smiled knowing that she did what was necessary to keep them safe.

"I won't lie to you, Achilla," Chief Price said as they drove down the street. "This is a tall task; the tallest of tasks. It'll take years of hard work, and all of it will be thankless. You'll spend most of your life hiding in plain sight and jumping into high-risk situations that even I would avoid. Do you think you're up to it?"

Achilla sighed as she looked up at the wispy cirrus clouds in the blue sky. She watched the colonial style houses and wooden telephone, the green stop signs and streetlights that she used to call home, and the corner stores with their managers unlocking their doors to start the day, all whip by. Achilla set her jaw when she thought about how amongst all of this normalcy, in the midst of this suburban Connecticut town full of working class and white-collar alike, an enemy was hiding. The hair on the back of Achilla's neck stood on end as she closed her eyes and imagined Ailina's green-eyed gaze bearing down her family. She clenched her fist until her nails cut her palms.

"Yeah," Achilla said as she reached into the glove compartment for a handful of tissues and dabbed the blood in her hands. "I'm up to it. I'm more than up to it."

"What makes you so sure?" Chief Price asked.

"I'm a Johnson, Chief," Achilla said as she glared out the window, imagining that Ailina was right outside the car staring back at her. "An inferior specimen like Ailina wouldn't stand a chance."

Chapter Twenty-Two

ACHILLA JOHNSON:20
Samuel Johnson:18

Samuel Johnson was a beast. As a McDonald's High School All-American, he averaged 36 points, 6 assists, and 5 rebounds per game during his senior season for Stratford High School. Despite often being the thinnest guy on the court, he was usually the strongest and the most explosive player; so much so that people would leave work early just to watch him dunk during the pre-game warm-ups. During the game, Samuel would use his strength and vertical leap to catch his opponents off-guard with thundering dunks through the lane. He especially had a taste for dunking on opponents larger than him Of course, Samuel's athletic marvels were no surprise to his family. He inherited his deceptive strength from his father. Samuel also had the state's smartest personal trainer in Achilla.

Moving away to Loomis Chaffee did not prevent Achilla from helping Samuel with his training. She emailed his meals and workouts and scolded him by text if he didn't follow her regimen; sometimes threatening to "come down there and force feed" him a healthy diet. With Achilla's knowledge of nutrition and fitness,

Samuel grew stronger, faster, and more explosive while gaining minimal weight. As a result, every crowd that watched Samuel play would gasp whenever he rattled the hoop with a dunk. He soon gained a reputation as the strongest dunker in the SWC conference.

Samuel owed Achilla a debt of gratitude for her constant training and advice. So the day before her graduation ceremony, he took Achilla to a diner in Hartford. He was a junior at the time, and he had just started driving himself to his new job at the Champs in the Trumbull Mall. He used his newfound money to cover Achilla's four plates of salad. Samuel ordered a burger and fries, and much to his amazement, Achilla didn't chastise him.

After not seeing her in person for over two years(she said sports and extra-curricular required her to stay on campus), Samuel noticed a change in Achilla. She always looked old for her age and spoke with even more maturity, but as he sat across from her at this white table piled with bowls of green lettuce and plump red tomatoes, he almost felt like he was hanging out with one of his teachers. Achilla spoke with perfect grammar, only occasionally switching to colloquialisms in a way that made Samuel feel like she was dumbing herself down for him. Her jet black hair fell straight down her back, lying against her maroon t-shirt like an ironed towel. Her green eyes were more intense, something that Samuel didn't think was possible, and though she looked at Samuel when they spoke, she had a tendency to look around the room for half a second before taking a bite of her food. Samuel noticed an elderly couple staring at her from behind, but Achilla raised her hand to keep his attention.

"Don't mind them," Achilla said.

"Why would two random people just stare at you like that?" Samuel asked.

"Ten."

"Huh?"

"Ten people stared at me when I walked in," Achilla said before taking a bite of her salad and dabbing her mouth with a napkin. "The two you're noticing haven't stopped or bothered to hide it. The other eight are eating their food and pretending not to notice we're here."

"OK, care to answer the why part?" Samuel asked.

"You're so unassuming," Achilla said with a smile as she shook her head. "You really do admire me, don't you?"

"Well, yeah," Samuel said. "Because of you, people say I'm going to be the best player in the state next season. Maybe even New England."

"Samuel," Achilla said with a chuckle. "That's why they're staring. We look nothing alike, so I'm assuming they think I'm your girlfriend."

"Oh."

"Yeah," Achilla said with a head nod. "You're the star here, not me."

"I guess," Samuel replied with a shrug. "All I do is play ball. You're the Marine."

Achilla covered her mouth as she let out a short giggle; the kind that hadn't changed since they were kids playing basketball in their driveway on long summer afternoons or bundling up in front of the television watching cartoons when Connecticut's brutal blizzards gave them a snow day. Samuel remembered that laugh during snowball fights outside when Achilla would belt him with snowballs by throwing them over the roof of their house.

"I'm actually glad that I have to explain this," Achilla said with a smile. "It means you're humble. Just so you know, you'll notice more of this later."

"More of what?" Samuel asked.

"Fame," said Achilla before biting into her food. "Your level of talent makes you a household name pretty quickly. Just watch."

Achilla's undying faith in Samuel was well placed, and during his senior season, Samuel watched her words come true. Soon college recruiters flooded the stands whenever Samuel played, and he received letters from Kentucky, Duke, and Kansas to name a few. When restaurant owners in Stratford recognized Samuel, he ate for free. Teachers, counselors, nurses, police officers, you name it; they all pulled over their cars and thanked Samuel for his game last night and asked him if he would do it again next time. The answer was always yes. Samuel answered head nods, salutes, and waves from random people when he walked through the Trumbull Mall with his team wearing his letter jacket. Everywhere he went, someone knew his name.

Samuel was also the object of many crushes. Girls at school bumped him in the hallway and "accidentally" leaned into his chest before apologizing, caressing his chest again, and giggling as they speed-walked to class. Girls at away games waited outside of his locker room and grabbed his butt as they slipped their phone numbers into his pockets. On the off chance that he had time for a date, other girls would literally show up and interfere until he demanded that they leave him alone, or his date gave up and walked away; sometimes both. Some girls pestered him every day until he blocked their phone numbers and Facebook profiles.

Even when the Johnsons moved to a wealthier section of Stratford, some of the girls found his home and came over unannounced. The Johnson property had a cement walkway that led to a driveway with enough space for Samuel to shoot around on his brand-new regulation hoop, a three-car garage, and a spacious front and back-yard with some woods on the edge of the property line; and Samuel found a high school girl hiding in every corner. One day, Samuel looked up from a curly-haired brunette lying on the living room couch and found his father Brendan, standing in the doorway with his arms crossed over his navy blue suit. Samuel removed his hands from her belt and raised them like he was under arrest. Brendan averted his eyes as the girl rushed to cover herself with the green sweater she left on the off-white carpet. Samuel's heart pumped out of his chest as he scrambled to think of an excuse while she rolled off of the couch and ducked her head like she was evading enemy fire. She was the fifth girl to visit this couch, but the first one his father had actually met. Samuel breathed a short sigh of relief that his mother was still at parent-teacher conferences.

"I know, son," Brendan said with a raised hand as the brunette ran past him to the door. "I also know she's not the only one. Not for a kid like you."

"Am I in trouble?" Samuel asked.

"For what?" Brendan chuckled.

"Mom would be pretty upset."

"I'm not your mother," Brendan replied as he stepped into the living room. "And your mother doesn't know what it's like to be a high school boy with girls knocking down his door."

"So now what?" Samuel asked with a frown.

"So this stays between us," Brendan sighed as he patted his shoulder. "This isn't a moment for punishment, but I do have some advice. Be careful, son. You might be having fun, but some of these girls take this thing real serious."

"Didn't seem serious," Samuel quipped. "I met her three days ago, and she popped up here looking to smash."

"She found your address in three days?" Brendan asked with a cocked eyebrow. "Son, we need to help you with following your gut because that sounds plenty serious to me."

"OK," Samuel said. "What do you mean?"

"First, don't do that anymore," Brendan said with a thumb toward the door. "Girls who pop up at your house out of nowhere are not the ones you screw with. Be honest. Were the girls who kept calling until you blocked their numbers the same ones pulling that kind of crap?"

"Well…yeah," said Samuel as he scratched his head.

"OK then," Brendan replied. "And don't be like me. I used to fool around with everything that moved until I screwed somebody's girlfriend over on the West End and almost got shot. Learn something about them first."

"Got it."

"And use protection," Brendan said with a wave of his hand as he turned his back. "No diseases. No babies."

"Yes, sir."

"Oh, and one more thing," Brendan called as Samuel readjusted the pillows on the couch.

"Yes?" Samuel answered with raised eyebrows.

"Be real careful about parties or alcohol," Brendan said. "It's rape if she's drunk. It's wrong and against the law. Period. I didn't raise you to take advantage of women like that punk, Stanley."

"Right," Samuel replied as he remembered the night Achilla

came home crying and hugging their parents after Stanley attempted to rape her. Fortunately, Achilla was not a normal girl. After a few days, Achilla transformed from being afraid for her safety to worrying if the damage she had done to her attacker would land her in prison. Thanks to Brendan, it didn't, and Stanley's football career never recovered. Last Samuel heard, he applied to the University of Chicago probably with the sole purpose of avoiding Achilla. Samuel hoped he lived the rest of his days in fear.

"I won't be like him," Samuel said with a hard stare. "He disgusts me."

"And if she lies about *anything*, don't do it," Brendan continued. "Anything. Understand? I don't care what it is. It could be the time she got up this morning. Just get up and walk out. I don't care if she's ready for whatever. If you catch her in a lie, any lie, leave."

"Why?" Samuel asked. "It's not like she's my girlfriend, right? I don't have to trust her if that's all we're doing."

Brendan stared at Samuel until he looked away. He then stepped back into the foyer and pointed at the couch. Samuel sat down and Brendan lounged on the other end as he unbuckled his silver and black-faced watch. He had a habit of doing that when he came home. Samuel wondered if the watch was too heavy for his wrist.

"Son," Brendan sighed. "As a man, and especially as a black man, you need to understand what I just said to you."

"Why?"

"Because you have no idea what a dishonest woman could do to you," Brendan said. "All it takes is one lie and enough evidence to convince a judge, and your hoop dreams are over. I know this from experience, son. I don't want you to end up like some of my clients."

"I understand," Samuel replied with a head nod. "I'll do my best."

"Good," Brendan said with a slight smile. "I hope you find someone good, Samuel. Someone who's on your side like your mother's always on mine. And I hope you find her a lot sooner than I did."

"Is this about *her*?" Samuel asked. They both knew he was referring to Ailina Harris; the Bridgeport Cop turned freak of nature who attacked them four years ago. Samuel hadn't seen her since, but her glowing green eyes still haunted him in his sleep on occasion. He was convinced that if Achilla didn't step in when she did, they would all be dead, but watching them fight made his jaw drop. Achilla kept her at bay, but she didn't disable her, and if she couldn't, none of them could. If she ever came back without Achilla around, they were done for unless God Himself intervened. So sometimes, saying her name was too frightening.

Her was enough.

"Yes," Brendan said. "The only good thing about *her* is the fact that we have Achilla in our family now. But she's not the only manipulator in the world. They start early, son. Just be careful. That's all I want."

"Got it, Dad."

"All I want is for you two to be happy and successful," Brendan replied. "I want that more than all the high profile cases and money in the world."

"Thanks," Samuel replied with a smile. "I won't disappoint."

Per his father's advice, Samuel slowed down. He no longer took unannounced visits, and if he liked a girl, he would take her on a date first before they did anything. His mother Sam became a gate-keeper for the girls he dated. She made it a point to find out everything she could about every girl who came Samuel's way, and they often didn't measure up. The Johnson house protected its son at all costs. Diseases, babies, and even unsavory rumors were to be preempted by screening every girl who crossed paths with him until word spread around Stratford High School that the turnover rate for being Samuel's girlfriend was very high. Samuel didn't mind. He needed more time to work on his post game anyway. That was the next addition to his repertoire, and until he mastered the Dream Shake, the girls could wait for a while.

On a mild, March Saturday afternoon, Samuel decided to practice those post moves. He threw on a gray t-shirt and black basketball shorts that hung past his knees and followed his usual warm-up routine of twenty shots per spot before making thirty free-throws. Then he would practice hook shots and pump-fakes. Before he finished his first set, a lollipop blue sports car pulled into the driveway. Samuel sighed and tossed the ball between his hands.

It was Trish O'Brien and the last person he wanted to see today.

Trish was a red-haired, freckle-faced girl from his psychology class who was pretty popular at Stratford High as the captain of the tennis team and the soccer team. Though both teams were not particularly good (they tanked after Achilla graduated), Trish's individual accolades and her 4.0 GPA were enough to garner attention from Ivy League schools and sports programs. The fact that she was the offspring of two Yale alumni didn't hurt either. Trish's father was a doctor, and her mother was a physician assistant. She came from money and she often thought it could buy her anything, including Samuel. The last time they spoke, she insisted on giving him her phone number and offered to buy his lunch at school. Samuel took her phone number but refused the food three times until she walked away in a huff. Now, like many others, she found out where he lived and decided to drop by for a visit.

Samuel made another jump-shot and jogged to pick up the ball as Trish parked just far enough to avoid any loose rebounds. He shook his head as Trish stepped out and sauntered toward him wearing a white blouse, black knee-length skirt, and shiny black Mary Janes from a French designer whose name Samuel couldn't pronounce; not that he particularly cared to learn it. Though he noticed her pale but defined calves accentuated by her high-heeled shoes, that wasn't her most alluring attribute. It was the fact that her blue eyes always met his before she spoke. Trish always approached him with the sort of confidence that baffled Samuel considering how often he rejected her advances. He might have found her attractive if she wasn't, well, Trish.

"Hi, Samuel," Trish said with her chin raised. "How are you?"

"What's up, Trish?" Samuel asked before turning and shooting another jumper.

"I just thought I'd ask why you didn't call me last night," Trish asked with her arms crossed as Samuel dribbled through his legs. "I was waiting for your call, you know."

"I was busy," Samuel replied with a shrug.

"I offered to take you shopping," Trish said. "All you had to do was tell me when you were free to go, and I would've bought you a new pair of sneakers. You'll need that for off-season training, right? I noticed a great pair that would've been perfect. You would've been pleased."

"That's really not necessary," Samuel said with a chuckle as he dribbled his ball behind his back. "I mean, to be honest, it's a little weird of you to just offer to buy me stuff out of nowhere."

"I don't think it's weird at all," Trish replied. "It's a nice gesture."

"Yeah," said Samuel as he low dribbled the basketball with his finger-tips. "I don't need you to be that nice. I mean, I didn't ask for it."

"Well, I think you need someone like me," Trish said as she paced the driveway with her chin in the air. "Someone who can do those kinds of things for you without you having to ask."

"And by that, you mean regardless of whether I say no?" Samuel muttered.

"I'm persistent," replied Trish with a shrug and a pearly white smile. "So sue me. There's nothing wrong with showing how much you like someone, right?"

"Maybe," Samuel said before throwing up a sky hook that bounced off the backboard and through the net. "But I don't see how that involves you taking me shopping for shoes you picked. I mean, it's not required. You're not even my girlfriend."

"That could change," Trish replied with a grin. "And it comes with a lot of benefits."

"Haven't had much trouble getting those benefits on my own," Samuel said.

"Not all of them," Trish said while she pointed at her car. "My Dad treats my boyfriends really well. My ex got season tickets to the Knicks."

"Didn't he give you those tickets back after he broke up with you?" Samuel quipped.

"He was very stupid," Trish snapped before taking a deep

breath and wiping a strand of her hair. "You're not stupid. You should have them instead. You deserve them."

"That's cool, but I'm not a Knicks fan," Samuel said before he laughed. "Not that I don't appreciate re-gifting."

"You know what I mean," Trish said with a roll of her eyes. "It can be any team you want. Maybe the Celtics?"

"I'm actually a Lakers fan."

"Oh, well I'm sure we can figure out when they're in town--"

"Trish, I can't focus on a relationship right now," Samuel sighed as he dribbled the ball through his legs and whipped out a crossover before finger-rolling the ball into the hoop. "I've got too much going on. Didn't we talk about this already?"

"I'd like to talk about it again," Trish said with a soft voice, but a not so friendly stare. "When is your birthday, Samuel?"

"None of your business if you're trying to buy me something--"

"Samuel!" Sam called as she walked out of their house wearing her typical sky blue t-shirt and jeans. She stood with her hands on her hips as she stared back and forth at Samuel and Trish. With his skyrocketing success in the courtroom, Brendan now spent the majority of his time at the office, even on the weekends. Thus, Sam was in charge of most of the day-to-day tasks around the house.

This made her gatekeeping role especially easy.

"Samuel, does your friend need something to drink?" Sam asked.

That was their code phrase for *is she welcome?*

"Nope," Samuel said as Trish frowned at him.

"All right, well I need you in here to change these light bulbs," Sam said as she turned her back to walk in the house. That was Samuel's escape route. He waved at Trish and jogged into the house, leaving her standing in the driveway. When Samuel came inside, he and his mother laughed as they watched Trish drive away. Another one bites the dust.

"Hey, I don't know, Samuel," Sam said with a nudge of her elbow as they walked into the kitchen with brown marble counter-tops and an island. "You could've at least gotten some season tickets out of it."

"No way, Mom," Samuel replied. "She'll never leave me alone then."

"So have you decided on a school yet?" Sam asked.

"No," Samuel groaned.

"Cutting it close there, Samuel," Sam replied with a cocked eyebrow. "You need to make a decision so we can help you prepare."

"I know," Samuel said. "I'll decide. Soon."

"Good," said Sam. "Just know that we'll support you with any school you choose. We're all in this together."

Samuel hated to admit it, but he was frightened of college basketball. The opportunity to compete against top-level basketball players excited him, but the big stage seemed so overwhelming. It wasn't that Samuel had a problem with people. He was the Senior Class President, captain of the debate team, and a regular volunteer at church. Still, the big stage brought so much pressure that it kept Samuel up at night. His insomnia got worse before the state championship game at Mohegan Sun. Stratford High was scheduled to play against Crosby; a public school in Waterbury with a starting line-up of DI prospects. Samuel played against them before in AAU tournaments and leagues around Bridgeport, Hartford, Waterbury, New Haven, Boston, and New York City. He knew he could take them, but he still couldn't sleep.

He called Achilla at around two in the morning and she picked up after four rings. Since she decided to enlist in the Marines, an odd choice to everyone who had never seen her fight before, she was deployed in Iraq. Still, she told Samuel that he could literally call her anytime. Her answer made Samuel regret accepting her invitation.

"What is it, Samuel?" Achilla snapped. "I'm busy."

"At two?" Samuel asked. "What do they have you do in the Marines? Shouldn't you be asleep? I mean I was expecting to leave a voicemail-"

"It's not that early over here, Samuel."

"Oh, so were you at work or something--"

"God, what do you think I was doing?" Achilla hissed while

Samuel heard shuffling in the background. "I had a guy over, and now he's leaving. You know I always pick up when you call."

"Oh, sorry--"

"Don't sweat it," Achilla sighed. "I told you to call me at any time. I shouldn't get mad at you when you actually do it. You're nervous about your game. I can hear it in your voice."

"I'll be all right," Samuel muttered as he lay down in bed.

"Just remember how great you are," Achilla said. "Know that, and nobody can take you. You have it. You've worked too hard not to."

"What about you?" Samuel asked.

"What do you mean?"

"Well, aren't you nervous?" Samuel asked. "You've been deployed."

"If you think the Marines are a challenge for me, you're bugging," Achilla said. "I'm just here because they'll let me fight."

"Do they know about you?" Samuel asked. He noticed a long time ago that Achilla liked to keep her abilities under wraps; especially her super strength. He wondered how well she could hide something like that while serving in the armed forces. If her battle with Ailina proved anything, it was that emergencies tended to draw out her true nature. A warzone would provide plenty of opportunities for Achilla to become a hero and overnight sensation; the exact opposite of what Achilla wanted.

"No, and I'd like to keep it that way," Achilla replied with a rushed tone. "I have to go."

"Night, Sis."

"Hey wait, quick question," Achilla said. "While you're awake. Has that girl Trish come around lately?"

"Yeah, but--"

"Stay away from her," Achilla said with a curt tone. "She sounds like Ailina."

Achilla was the only Johnson who had zero problems uttering Ailina's name, but she always spat it out like a mouthful of spoiled milk.

"Achilla," Samuel groaned and wiped his face before turning on his side. "She's pretty aggressive, and maybe a little shallow, but I wouldn't compare her to *her*. Come on, don't exaggerate."

"She might be less extreme," Achilla said. "But I know the mentality when I hear it. Come on, she's always trying to buy you stuff. She keeps saying you need her. She thinks she's better than you, Samuel, and she's trying to make you dependent on her so she can use you and drop you. Didn't you say there was a cute girl in your Trig class?"

"Yeah, she's straight," Samuel replied with a shrug. "I guess she's kind of nice."

"Nice is good," Achilla said. "I like nice. Talk to the nice one."

"I think it's my choice, Achilla."

"Yes, it is," Achilla replied with a smile that Samuel could hear through the receiver. "OK, I'm going for real now. You're going to destroy them tomorrow. Remember that and get some sleep."

Stratford High School won the state championship with an undefeated record. Samuel was the MVP of the entire tournament, and he scored 40 points in the championship game; mostly through dunks and layups. Samuel's teammates carried him toward the locker room, but he commanded to be let down. He then grabbed their coach, and they carried him instead. After he showered and changed into a gray hoody and jeans in the locker room, a reporter for News Channel 12 approached him for an interview.

"Rich Feinstein reporting live," he said as he shoved a microphone in Samuel's face. "Samuel, you scored 40 points on 15 of 25 from the field and sank 10 straight free-throws. How did you do it?"

"Well first I want to thank God," Samuel said. "And then I want to thank my family for supporting me. Without them, none of this is possible. To answer your question, I mean, I just went out there and played and took what the defense gave me. You know, Crosby played excellent defense and pushed me off the perimeter, so I took it to the hoop and showed that I could handle the physical play."

"Samuel, you have recruiters from all over the country knocking down your door," Feinstein said. "Have you made a decision yet?"

"Not yet," Samuel replied. "When I do, I'll let you know."

"Thanks, Samuel," Feinstein said. "You have a great future, and good luck to you."

"Thanks," Samuel said as he walked away toward his parents on the other end of the court. His father wore a black hoody with jeans and black and white sneakers; his typical basketball game attire. His mother came straight from school and wore a tan blouse with green slacks with green shoes. No matter how much older they looked, no matter how much Samuel had grown, his parents were always the same. Samuel hugged them both and Brendan rubbed his head.

"Great game, son," Brendan said. "Great game!"

"You were wonderful out there," Sam said.

"Thanks," Samuel said. "You guys can thank Achilla for that. She worked me so hard."

"And it paid off," Brendan replied.

"I shouldn't be surprised," Sam said with a frown. "And here I was worried that her standards would be too high."

"That's the thing," Samuel chuckled. "She always tailored everything to me. It was perfect."

"Sounds like Achilla to me," Brendan said. "Look, we're going to head home. You go party with your team."

"Just call us and let us know where you are," Sam said. "Have fun!"

Samuel did just that. He drove his blue sedan down to the South End of Stratford where Brian, the senior point guard, was throwing a party. Samuel didn't drink (Achilla and his parents would kill him if he did), but the rest of the team guzzled beer the entire night. As Samuel sat on a red couch with a bottle of water in his hand, he spotted Trish sauntering across the room wearing a burgundy and black plaid shirt and khaki shorts that hugged her porcelain thighs. She sat next to him and crossed her legs so that her sandaled foot tapped his knee, and she played with her hair as she smiled at him. Samuel sighed and leaned back. Normally, he would avoid her, but tonight was a celebration. Seeming to have read his mind, Trish leaned over and kissed Samuel on the mouth. She then grabbed his hand and led him an empty bedroom in the back of the house.

After they finished, Samuel lay in a bed with black bed sheets and looked at the red-haired girl next to him. She slept on her side with her hair over her face and her arm across Samuel's chest. This was the same girl who just the other day, Samuel thought was too crazy to meet his mother. Now he was lying in bed with her wondering how he can get away. Samuel stared at the ceiling as a tinge of guilt gathered in his throat. This girl, no matter how rich and snooty she might have been, was still another person. She at least deserved his honesty. Samuel nudged her awake and she grinned and scratched his chest.

"Hey," Trish said as she bit her lip.

"Hey," Samuel replied. "Look, I don't want to lead you on. I know you wanted a relationship, but I can't give you that. I'm sorry I waited until after sex to--"

"No biggie," Trish said as she stretched her arms and legs under the bed sheets.

"What?"

"Look, I only offered to be your girlfriend because everyone kept telling me how much of a good boy you were," Trish said. "That and your mom's like super protective. This was really all I wanted, and I didn't think you would do it without a date first. Everyone says that all guys care about is sex, but that's not true. Guys like you have to feel all special first, and I get that. My ex was the same way, but you're way hotter. You know, I have to admit this was definitely worth the effort--"

"Wait," Samuel replied with a frown. "So you don't actually like me?"

"I like your body," Trish said with a smile as she caressed his chest. "But you're not exactly the guy I would *date* date. Think about it. What's your plan? Have you even picked your school yet?"

"No," Samuel said.

"I'm going to Yale," Trish replied. "And I'm going to major in pre-med. After that, I'm going to Johns Hopkins for med school so I can become a neurosurgeon. Are you going to play basketball your whole life? Let me tell you, the NBA isn't exactly the easiest or most sustainable job to land. It's a good dream and all, but that's usually all it is."

Samuel frowned. As much as he enjoyed basketball, and intended to use it to pay for his education, he hadn't thought about going pro. He dreamed of wearing a suit and carrying a briefcase to his next trial while answering reporters and guiding his client to his car just like his father. He wanted people to depend on him like they did Brendan, calling him in the middle of the night to save them from unfair prosecution. He wanted to be the reason the wrongfully accused never lost their freedom, not under his watch anyway. Samuel always wanted to be a defense attorney. He watched the NBA on television, but he never imagined himself playing in it.

"I'm going to be a lawyer like my dad," Samuel said. "Better than my dad."

"Oh right, you're Brendan Johnson's kid," Trish said with a head nod. "I guess that stands for something. I hear your father's a real bleeding heart though. He turns down clients who can offer him more money so he can *help those who need it*. I guess it's worked out for you, but he's not exactly the manliest guy around--"

Samuel shoved Trish's arm away and turned his back on her to grab his pants.

"You're mad at me?" Trish asked as she sat up. "Come on, five minutes ago you were about to give me the 'it's just sex' speech. If guys can do it, why can't I?"

"You think I care about that?" Samuel snapped.

"Then what's the problem, Samuel?" Trish asked. "Jesus, boys are so sensitive nowadays."

"*Nobody* talks shit about my father in front of me," Samuel growled as he pointed his finger at Trish's face. "If you were a dude, we'd be banging out right now."

"Oh bullshit, like you've ever had to fight someone," Trish replied with a sneer as she pushed his hand away and covered herself with the sheets as she reached for her shirt. "You always had your butch sister protecting you. Everyone knows that."

"You don't know what you're talking about!" Samuel snapped as he pulled up his jeans and threw his t-shirt over his head. "And for your information, my father's a great man. He's been my hero my whole life."

"Well if he's your example, I'm glad we did this now," said Trish as she buttoned her shirt and pointed at her breasts. "Later on I won't have time to waste all this on some mediocre lawyer, and besides, I have a reputation to uphold. If anyone finds out about us, I can just tell them I was young and dumb or something, or that I had a thing for black guys in high school."

"What?" asked Samuel with a curled lip. "Man, how do you sleep at night--?"

"I sleep just fine," Trish cut Sam off with fire in her eyes. "And you'd better wake up! Girls don't like guys with no future, and I don't think you have one. You probably won't make it pro, and you can forget being a lawyer who makes any money. I hate to break it to you, sweety, but outside of some good bone, you're pretty pathetic."

"Shut the hell up!" Samuel fired back.

"Aw, did I upset you?" Trish replied with a sideways grin. "Is the big strong ball player going to cry like a little bitch? Well, newsflash, your cock's probably all you're good for, and every girl knows it.

"Man, everybody's not like you, Trish," Samuel said. "Everybody isn't--"

"Yes, they are," Trish said. "They're just too nice to tell you. I've heard about the girls you hooked up with. I know their boyfriends too. They're the ones who get to meet the parents and go to prom because they're actually worth something. You are literally a fun ride with like zero relationship potential."

"No," muttered Samuel as he shook his head. "No, you're wrong. Watch me. I'll change lives just like my dad did; more than he did. And when I do, you'll regret everything you just said."

"Oh, God another bleeding heart!" groaned Trish as she covered her face with her hands and shook her head. "I am *so* glad we used a condom. You're such a loser!"

"To hell with you, Trish," Samuel said as he walked out the door. "I bet this is why your last boyfriend dumped you!"

"No *to hell with you*, asshole!" Trish snarled at his back. "You and your beta male for a father!"

Samuel rushed out of the party without saying goodbye to his teammates and hopped into his car. As tears welled up in his eyes, Samuel pounded his steering wheel. Why was he crying over her? How could her words cut so deep? Samuel wiped his eyes and started his car. Trish didn't know anything. She didn't know about the night he stood up to Ailina and was ready to die for his family. All she knew was that he was an athlete, and that was all she ever bothered to see. He was nothing more than a tool to her. What about the rest of those girls? Was he just an object to them too? Did they just *have a thing for black guys in high school*?

Samuel shook his head as he pulled out of the driveway and drove slow down the street. No, Trish was lying. Maybe some people thought like her, but not all and certainly not most. The more Samuel thought about it, the more he realized just how different from everyone else Trish was. The other girls who came to his house to hook up were upfront about it, but Trish pretended to want a relationship just to have his body. When that didn't work, she waited until his defenses were down and used a different angle. Samuel was sure that Trish enjoyed manipulating him as much as she enjoyed the sex itself, and the moment he showed a sliver of dignity she went out of her way to cut him down. He told himself that he would never speak to Trish ever again.

Samuel was halfway home when blue and red lights flashed behind him. So he rolled his eyes and pulled over. As his father had taught him, he cracked his window and placed both hands on the steering wheel. He closed his eyes and rehearsed the polite tone he would use when he requested to go home. Brendan had a knack for foiling corrupt police officers in court, and he always taught Samuel to never give a cop an excuse to mistreat him. As a black male, he had to be extra vigilant, and if anything funny happened, he should tell Brendan everything down to the minute detail. Samuel took a deep breath and calmed his nerves for the oncoming conversation.

He frowned when he noticed a statuesque female figure with back-length hair approaching in his rearview mirror, but he couldn't make out who she was with the lights flashing behind her. Still, her height and gait made his heart race. When the officer approached next to his car, she shined a flashlight in his face and beckoned with her hand for him to lower the window. Samuel maintained a straight face as he pressed the button and watched the glass descend. The flashlight shined so bright that he had to force himself to look forward. Once the window lowered, the officer leaned in, and he could smell the mint gum in her breath. Samuel's heart pumped even harder. Brendan told him that the police weren't supposed to do that. Already, this cop's conduct was suspicious, and Samuel planned on telling his father.

What he heard next made his heart jump out of his chest.

"Why hello there, Samuel," said an all too familiar female voice that sounded like a cat purring with a slight Boston accent. "My you've grown."

Samuel's head snapped to his left and he saw Ailina's green eyes staring back at him inches away from his face. He tried to jump to the other side of the car, but his seatbelt held him in place. He unbuckled and reached for the passenger side door. Ailina grabbed his hoody and slammed him back into his seat, and he grabbed her forearm to break free.

It was like prying open the jaws of a crocodile.

Ailina giggled at his struggle as she waved the flashlight in his face before dropping it inside the car.

"Brendan taught you well," Ailina said as she stiff-armed Samuel against his seat. "Had the officer I killed pulled you over instead of me, you might be home free by now. He was a pretty straight-laced cop. Now me? I wouldn't let you go until I was done with you."

"Look, just leave me alone--"

"Aww, now he's scared," Ailina cooed with a pout on her face. "What happened to the boldness I saw a few years ago? I liked that."

"Get the fuck off of me!" Samuel growled. "Did you like that?"

"As a matter of fact, I did," Ailina replied as she pushed Samuel to the other side of the car, slamming his head into the corner of the passenger's side window. Ailina then reached through the window and unlocked the door before sitting in the driver's seat. Samuel reached for his keys, but she snatched his wrist and shook the car when she pinned him back. He then opened the passenger side door and dove for the street. Ailina grabbed his hood and yanked him back in before he touched the ground. Samuel gasped at first, but then he roared and kicked at her face. Ailina grabbed his leg and flipped him upside down until his face was under the glove compartment. While the blood rushed to his head, Samuel's mind scrambled to think of another way to escape.

"If you have half a brain, you're probably wondering why I've bothered to keep you alive," Ailina said as she started the car. "Two reasons. First, I find your boldness irresistible. Second, we need to talk."

Suddenly Trish didn't seem so bad, but Achilla would've been much better. If he could get a hold of her, it might not save his life, but at least he'll be avenged. Samuel dug his cell phone out of his pocket. He groaned when Ailina grabbed his wrist and snatched the phone away.

"You won't be calling Achilla," Ailina said. "Not yet. And you'll find out soon enough why that is. Don't worry. I'm good on my word. I won't kill you or your family."

"I don't believe a word of that," Samuel replied.

"If I wanted to kill you, Brendan, or Samantha, you'd all be dead," Ailina snapped. "And that's a huge problem that I want to talk to you about."

Ailina pulled into the Quality Inn, a nondescript hotel that Samuel always passed by but never stayed in. She reserved a room and nearly dragged Samuel to the elevator. Once they reached the third floor, she swiped her card key and then pulled Samuel inside. He grunted when Ailina tossed him onto a bed with a red comforter over white sheets. Before he could sit up, she pinned him down by his shoulders and straddled him. He grunted and struggled with her until her green eyes glared at him and held him in place.

"Look," Samuel said as his eyes refused to look away from Ailina's gaze. "I'm not--"

"Oh, you will," Aiilna said with a grin as she unbuckled his belt and ripped it off of his jeans. "It's too late now. I paid for this room. We're doing this."

"No!"

"I've been waiting for you to mature, Samuel," Ailina breathed with dilated pupils the size of quarters. "You've grown strong enough for me, and I'm ready. The time for us is now, Samuel! No more waiting!"

"Help, somebody--!" Samuel screamed until Ailina clamped her hand over his mouth and shushed him.

"You scared, baby?" Ailina cooed into his ear before releasing his mouth. "You're a man now. This is what you're supposed to do. Now we can do this the easy way, or the hard way. Your call."

"No!" Samuel growled as he sat up, only to get slammed down by Ailina's forearm to his chest.

"Not an option, Samuel," Ailina said with a sing-song tone. "But I love that you tried. You're a good challenge, and that really turns me on. Aren't you excited?"

"No!" Samuel snarled as he pushed against Ailina's arm. "I'm not doing--"

Ailina interrupted Samuel with a kiss on the lips. She used lots of tongue and a bite to his lower lip at the tail end, but something about it was different. He squirmed like a child forced to drink his first shot of whiskey. Ailina slammed him against the bed and held his throat. As she glared at him with glowing green eyes, Samuel found himself unable to look away or even move.

"I don't care if you want to or not," Ailina said with a low voice. "We're doing this. The more you resist, the more it'll hurt, or did you forget what I did to your half-sister?"

Samuel didn't forget. He remembered watching Achilla fly into a tree. He remembered Ailina snapping her leg like a twig. He remembered the potholes in the driveway from their altercation. Samuel knew he stood no chance against Ailina in a fight.

So like a trapped rat, he relaxed and lay flat on the bed. He then looked away from Ailina as she pulled his shirt over his head and scratched his chest before pulling off his boxers with her teeth. The next forty-five minutes were nothing like anything Samuel had experienced with any high school girl. Sex with Ailina was like a drug injected into you without consent. He found himself paralyzed to the bed for the rest of the night as Ailina had her way with him. By the time she was done, Samuel couldn't tell if he was asleep or awake anymore.

He just lay there.

Numb.

The following morning, Samuel woke up from his deepest sleep in months. He wiped his eyes and looked around the still, quiet room as he tried to piece together what happened last night. Did he actually have sex with Ailina, or was that just a weird dream? If it was a weird dream, why was he in the hotel room? Samuel realized that he still couldn't feel his feet. When he looked down at his legs, he saw Ailina at the foot of the bed pulling down a black t-shirt. When she bent over to tie her shoes, Samuel noticed the upper crack of her toned rear peeking out from her dark blue jeans. Samuel pulled himself upright with his arms, dragging his feet as far away from Ailina as possible.

"Relax," Ailina said with a wave of her hand without turning around. "You're in no danger. I just thought I'd let you sleep. My men always need a lot of rest after their first time with me; though I usually don't use a hotel room. They're pretty impersonal, but our circumstances left me no other choice."

My men? Impersonal? He did have sex with Ailina! Samuel held his head in his hands as he put the pieces together.

"I just had sex with a woman who tried to kill my parents!" Samuel groaned with a catch in his voice. "Aww, dammit!"

"You couldn't help yourself," Ailina said as she rose to her feet and stretched her arms before scratching under her left breast. "The females of my kind have higher levels of testosterone than any regular man. I'm not exactly in my best years, but I was more than enough for you. Seduction's kind of my specialty."

"You threatened to kill me!" Samuel replied.

"You would've done it anyway," Ailina sighed with a shrug of her shoulders. "Brendan was the only man to avoid me of his own free will, and that was because I tried to crush him with a sink. Fear always trumps arousal, unfortunately."

"Why would you do that?" Samuel asked. "A sink? Are you crazy?"

"I was pregnant," Ailina said with her head low. "Hormones. Also stronger with my kind; stronger than I had anticipated. I won't be repeating that mistake. I'll be ready this time."

"Your kind?" Samuel asked. "So what, you're not human?"

"No, I'm human," Ailina replied. "Just more advanced. Think of me as--"

"Wonder Woman?" Samuel blurted. "That's what Achilla said."

"I find it irritating when you cut me off," Ailina said with a snarl that turned into a grin as she stroked her hair. "Keep doing it."

"No thanks."

"Why not?" Ailina asked with a pout. "Did I wear you out already?"

"So what did you want to talk about?" Samuel asked as he struggled to get the feeling back into his toes. He might as well keep her talking before he could make a dash for it.

"Oh right," Ailina said before pacing the room with her hands behind her back. "I did bring you here for that reason too. Your sister isn't in the best situation right now."

"It's the Marines," Samuel replied. "She knows it's dangerous."

"You're all so stupid," Ailina spat with a roll of her eyes. "She's not in the Marines. She's an agent for the CIA. Since I refused to join, they grabbed her instead, the slick bastards."

"Achilla joined the CIA?" Samuel asked. "She's...a spy?"

"Yep," Ailina replied. "Since she was sixteen. Though I doubt you could seriously count her high school years."

"She left the house at sixteen."

"Now you're piecing things together," Ailina said with her arms wide. "Don't be mad at her for not telling you. That kind of comes with the job. In exchange for her silence and participation, they promised to protect you from me."

"How do you know?" Samuel asked as his feet tingled awake.

"For a police chief, Greg Price is really oblivious to phone-tapping" Ailina chuckled. "It didn't take me long to figure out what happened before those agents cut me out. Good question, but I think you missed the most important part of what I just told you."

"What's that?"

"The CIA promised to protect you from me," Ailina said with a pointed finger. "And here I was preparing myself for an all-out brawl to get you, and nothing came. Not only was I able to get close to you, I was able to have you all to myself. I won't, but I could kill you right now, and not a single agent has come within a hundred yards of this conspicuous hotel with *your car* in the parking lot."

"How would you know that?" Samuel asked. "They could be waiting outside right now."

"Really good hearing," Ailina said as she tugged her earlobe. "I can literally hear a whole conversation about two football fields away; further if it's quiet out. I'm sure you noticed that with Achilla, right? You seem more observant than your parents."

Samuel remembered moments when Achilla would address him long before he was anywhere near her line of sight. It took him a while to figure out that she could hear him from far away. As she got older, she started letting him tap her shoulder before speaking. Samuel always had a feeling that she could still hear him coming, but he hadn't pieced it together. Now those snowball fights made a lot more sense. He took a deep breath and crossed his arms.

"When you're following someone," Ailina continued. "It helps to hear them from a further distance than they can hear you, but the reverse is a huge disadvantage, and that's why the CIA and the Feds have yet to catch me. Of course, they haven't really tried to kill me yet. That's probably a factor."

Samuel nodded his head as he looked for exits. Ailina seemed to read his mind as she stood between him and the door. She then covered her mouth and let out a slight giggle that made Samuel's legs shake. Something about the way she laughed always did that. It sounded just like Achilla's laughter, only without any real happiness to it.

"By the way," Ailina said as she bit her lip with a pitiful smile. "I heard what that girl said to you, and I thought she was a bit harsh.

You usually can't say things like that unless you're as good as I am. A man has to actually be your slave before you talk to him like one."

Samuel's jaw dropped as he lowered his head and clenched the bed sheets between his fingers.

"She'll learn that eventually just like I did," Ailina sighed. "But by now she's lost you altogether, right? You feel disrespected, and without any excuse to come back, you won't. She got what she wanted, but she has a long way to go before she can turn a man into a repeat returner. She has potential though. I kind of want to take her under my wing and show her the ropes, you know?"

"So you got past the agents," Samuel snapped while Achilla's warning about Trish ran laps in his brain. "So what?"

"Got past them?" Ailina replied with a sideways grin. "I'm good, but I'm not that good. If they were actually trying I would've killed a few before they all shot me to death. There were no agents to infiltrate. The CIA reneged."

"Achilla's being used," Samuel said as he stared down at his bed sheets. "And they're probably keeping her busy so she won't notice."

"That was a brilliant hypothesis," Ailina replied with a smile as she clapped her hands. "How did you figure that out so quick?"

"It's just a bait and switch, Ailina," Samuel said. "You should really stop assuming you're the only smart person in the room."

"Be that as it may, Achilla needs to know," Ailina said with her hands on her hips. "But she can't know that you know she's in the CIA because that could come back to hurt her and your family. Tell her about this rendezvous we just had. That'll be enough to tip her off."

"Why should I do anything you say?" Samuel asked.

"Oh, I love that you asked that question," Ailina replied with a slight shudder. "Please, argue some more--"

"Seriously, why not just ask the CIA--"

"And...you just turned me off," Ailina replied with a shaking head. "They're an organization that hires agents to lie and manipulate people for the sake of their country. What makes you think they'll tell you the truth?"

"They don't have to," Samuel said. "If I let them know--"

"I know where you're going and forget it," Ailina said. "Nobody will notify your sister of a thing. They'll just cover their tracks. Or worse, they'll take Achilla further away and bog her down with assignments until she forgets about her family altogether."

"Achilla wouldn't forget about us," Samuel said with a frown.

"You'd be surprised at what effective brainwashing can do," Ailina replied as she walked to the door. "Get dressed, go home, call her."

"And if I don't?"

"I won't kill you," Ailina said over her shoulder. "But your father works in criminal defense, and sometimes he gets a little too close to some shady characters. No agents means no protection until it's too late."

"Why would you care about that?" Samuel asked. "You tried to kill him yourself."

"I already told you that if I wanted you all dead, you would be," Ailina replied with a cutting glare. "You know, I had fun last night, but your father was a much better listener. She didn't have to say it, but Trish might be right. You're hot, but you seriously lack boyfriend skills."

"I lack…what?"

"Goodbye, Samuel."

Ailina shut the door and Samuel sat in bed with his arms crossed. He had no reason to believe that anything Ailina said was true. For all he knew, Achilla was in Iraq. Samuel rolled his legs out of bed and stood on his tingling feet and wobbly knees. He then stumbled and sat on the bed before reaching down and grabbing his clothes. He shook his head after he checked the clock on the night-stand. It was nine in the morning and he never called home. His parents were going to kill him long before any CIA agent could step in.

After Samuel pulled into the driveway at home, he hadn't stepped two feet away from his car when his mother stormed out of the house in a baggy t-shirt and sweatpants. Brendan trailed behind wearing a button-down shirt and jeans. Samuel lowered his head as he thought of an explanation. Judging from the last time he told his parents about Ailina, telling them about last night was a big no-no. Sam stood in front of Samuel with her hands on her hips as she glared at him with dark brown eyes like his own. After seeing Ailina last night, brown eyes were a refreshing sight.

"Mom, I--"

"Where were you?" Sam snapped as she smacked Samuel across the face so hard that his cheek burned.

"That's enough, Sam," Brendan said as he held her back by her arms.

"No," Sam snapped as she ripped her arms free before pointing at her son. "He needs to explain where he's been."

"That I actually agree with," Brendan said as he stared Samuel down with his arms crossed. "Samuel, why were you gone all night?"

"I...um..."

"Spit it out, son," Brendan said. "You don't want me to hit you next."

"I stayed out all night with the team," Samuel muttered. "We got carried away."

"You smell like that body spray these girls are wearing," Sam said with her arms crossed. "You were messing around with one of those little fast girls, weren't you?"

"Yes," Samuel said. "What do you want me to say, Mom?"

"I knew it," Sam said to Brendan. "I knew all this attention would get to his head. Those girls are relentless, Brendan. I know how they can be. If we're not careful, he'll get trapped. They're not like when I grew up. They are *treacherous*!"

"Did you use protection, son?" Brendan asked as he raised his hand.

"Of course," Samuel said with a frown. Then he remembered his night with Ailina. He was pretty sure that there was no condom then. Did she do that on purpose? Samuel's heart sunk through his ribcage at the thought of impregnating the woman who tried to kill his family. He shook his head and focused on his parents. Right now, they were his main concern.

"Well at least there's that," Sam sighed before pointing a finger at Samuel's chest. "Was it *your* protection? Please tell me you didn't take hers."

"Yeah, Mom," Samuel replied. "It was mine."

"OK," Sam said as she nodded her head at Brendan. "He listened to you at least."

"He has to listen to both of us, Sam," Brendan replied before turning to Samuel. "You're grounded for a month."

"Huh?" Samuel blurted and stepped back. "Just because I had sex?"

"Because you stayed out all night without telling us where you were," Sam replied. "You know why that's not safe, especially for us."

"There's always the possibility that *she* might return," Brendan said. "And Achilla's overseas."

Samuel's parents didn't know how right they were. Not only did Ailina return, but she forced herself on him. He wasn't sure if what they did was consensual or not. He certainly didn't hate it, but he didn't want it either. Still, the look in Ailina's eyes and her raw strength compelled him to stay put. What was he supposed to do? Say no to the same woman he watched survive a head-on car collision and then throw his sister fifty feet *through a tree*? Yeah, he had sex with an older woman, but the thought that he didn't have it willingly made his eyes water.

The more Samuel thought about it, the more it seemed like a good idea to explain to his parents what really happened that night. He would love to tell them everything, but they were so busy controlling everything he did. He couldn't go here. He couldn't go there. He couldn't date this girl or that girl; even if he liked *that* girl or perhaps wanted to see both. Every decision that affected him was decided by them. Samuel felt teenage rebellion rising up in his throat like vomit. It left his mouth just the same.

"I'm eighteen now," Samuel said. "You can't ground me anymore. I'm a legal adult."

"Oh, is that right?" Brendan chuckled as he stepped forward. "Whose house do you live in?"

"Yours."

"Do you pay rent?" Brendan asked.

"No, but--"

"Who pays for your car?" Brendan demanded with a hard stare.

"You do."

"And who buys groceries and feeds you?" Sam chimed in.

"You," Samuel said with his head low and his fists clenched as that same rebellion made his heart pump through his chest.

"Then you're grounded like your father said," Sam replied. "We need to work on this attitude of yours, Samuel. You're getting a little too bougie for my liking."

"Can I have my cell phone?" Samuel asked with a slight snarl.

"Yes," Brendan said. "We'll need it to communicate."

"Good," Samuel said as he pulled out his phone and started dialing. He waited until the person on the other end picked up.

"Who are you calling?" Sam asked with a scowl. "We're not done speaking to you."

"Hi, Mr. Washington?" Samuel said. "Good morning, it's Samuel Johnson from Stratford, Connecticut. I've decided to commit to Duke...Oh no, thank *you*. Bye."

"What was that about?" Brendan asked as Samuel hung up the phone.

"Grounded for a month?" Samuel asked. "You got it. But I have a free ride to Duke and I know one of those *fast girls* who's going there too. I can ride with her in case you take my car away."

"Son, you don't play for a basketball program to get back at your parents," Brendan said as he rubbed his hand against his forehead. "You have to put more thought into it than that."

"If I get good grades at Duke, I can go to their law school," Samuel replied. "Or anywhere else I want. If I become a criminal defense lawyer like you, it might not help me much to work in the same state. God knows I'm not working under you."

"Samuel, can we discuss this?" Sam asked. "UConn's a great program."

"UConn didn't even scout me, Mom," Samuel replied.

"We can send them a tape," Sam snapped.

"Why would I do that?" Samuel chuckled. "None of these other schools needed me to send them anything. Let them scout guys from New York or Cali or, I don't know, everywhere else, and if I ever play them, I'll bust their asses!"

"Samuel!" Sam gasped.

"OK, excuse my language, but you know I'm right," Samuel replied before looking at Brendan. "Come on, Dad. How did you feel when Fairfield scouted you more than UConn when you were the best player in the state? Well, they're doing the same thing to me, but I'll be able to play against them and pay them back for it. Dad, I know you would've killed for the chance to do the same thing!"

Brendan's eyes flickered with the competitive fire that Samuel could recognize in any current or former ballplayer; the fire that wanted to prove wrong anyone who doubted him. Samuel had that same fire and he looked back, hoping to speak his language and appeal to the heart of a winner. Brendan closed his eyes and sighed as he covered his face; the sign of a lawyer's unwilling submission to a good argument. Samuel suppressed his grin. It worked. Sam whirled on Brendan with a wide-eyed expression.

"Brendan!"

"He makes a good point," Brendan replied.

"Brendan. Johnson," Sam growled. "He can't go all the way to North Carolina."

"Honey, it's his decision," Brendan said. "We've got to let him make it."

"I don't believe this," Sam replied. "We never do this! We never make *executive decisions* about our children."

"It's not up to us," Brendan said with a hard stare. "He has to choose his own school, Sam, and he did."

"Mom, isn't this what you wanted?" Samuel asked. "Come on, you've been riding me about not choosing a school. Well, I chose one, and you said you'd support any school I chose."

"You did tell him that," Brendan muttered until Sam glared at him.

"All the way to North Carolina?" Sam demanded at Samuel

with her hands on her hips before lowering her head. "Are you sure?"

"My mind's made up," Samuel said as he walked past his parents to the house. "But while I'm under your roof, I'll respect your rules. I'm grounded for a month. If you excuse me, I have an All-American game to prepare for."

"Brendan, say something!" Sam said to Brendan as Samuel closed the door behind him. He strolled up their spiral staircase to his bedroom with a blue carpet and wallpaper. As he threw himself onto his bed's blue comforter, he stared at the ceiling. There was another reason he applied to Duke. Should Ailina ever come looking for him, she'll never have to harm his parents in the process. Samuel pulled out his cell phone and scrolled down to Achilla's number. If he told her about last night, she would go ballistic.

Samuel recalled the last time Achilla fought Ailina. The look in her eyes was inhuman. Samuel wondered what would have happened if Achilla won that fight. Would she have been able to control herself and stop? The thought of trying to calm down a bloodthirsty Achilla made Samuel put his cell phone away as his parents knocked on his bedroom door. They would try to persuade him to stay in Connecticut, but he had no intention of budging. He pulled out his cell phone again to tell his teammates the good news.

The following Monday at school, Samuel received high-fives through the hallway from all of the guys. Most of the girls smiled at him and touched his arms. Samuel spotted Trish. She fluttered her eyes as she approached him from across the hallway. When she tried to hug Samuel, he walked past her with the grace and agility of a boxer slipping a knockout punch.

As the students in the hallway pointed and laughed at Trish, Samuel approached the one girl in the hallway who wasn't gushing all over him. She had tan skin and black shoulder length hair and wore crisp, white, sneakers that matched her blue and white duke t-shirt and blue jeans. Lauren was her name, and they shared AP Calculus together. Samuel leaned against the lockers as she fiddled with her lock. When she looked up, she adjusted her black-rimmed glasses that magnified the thin, hazel eyes under them.

"Lauren, what's up?"

"Ugh, if you want me to do your homework for you, forget it," Lauren snapped. "You're like the fourth ballplayer to--"

"Nah, nothing like that," Samuel said with a wave of his hand. "I don't know if you've heard, but we're going to the same school next fall."

"Really?" Lauren said with a smile before coughing and straightening her face. "I mean, good. Duke's a good school. You made the right choice."

"Why don't we grab something to eat and talk about it?" Samuel asked.

"You'll have to meet my parents first," Lauren replied.

"No date," Samuel said. "Not yet. I'm grounded. I was thinking just meeting during lunch. I'll pick you up at class."

"Um…OK," Lauren said as she stroked her hair. "What about Trish?"

"Done with her," Samuel said. "She's not my type."

"Good," Lauren replied with her chin raised. "I always thought she was racist. It's like she just flaunts her privilege for everyone to see, and she's not even that smart--"

"Let's not talk about her anymore," Samuel said as Lauren closed her locker and they walked down the hall. "So have you decided your major?"

"Education," Lauren giggled as she stroked her hair some more. "You?"

"Criminal justice," Samuel said as he spread his arms wide. "I'll be the best attorney the world has ever seen. Watch me. "

Chapter Twenty-Three

ACHILLA JOHNSON:21

Samantha Johnson:44

Being a widow was not easy for Samantha "Sam" Johnson. As a career woman in her mid-forties, Sam knew she would find ways to keep busy. Planning a curriculum for an entire school district and then managing a school of her own as the new principal for Central High School in Bridgeport would take up most of her time. As much as her parents wanted her to go to school and earn a lucrative career at some fancy company in New York City, Sam stuck to her passion, and her love for children and education never wavered. She now earned the six-figure salary that her parents always wanted her to have. She just did it her way and the way that God accepted.

Not her parents.

That was how Sam always lived; even as a little girl. Her mother nicknamed her "Ms. Thang" because she argued with everything she told her; refusing to wear dresses until she felt like wearing them, and only if they were of her choosing; refusing to tell the teacher when boys picked on her, opting to pummel them until she had to be pulled away and sent home. Sam was a rebel in every sense of the word, and she never accepted what anyone told her to do unless she agreed to it. Only her parents could somewhat control her, and that was because they paid the bills, something her father reminded her of every time she fought with him.

When Sam started her first day as an English teacher at Central High School, she vowed to never depend on her parents again. She and her father were cordial toward each other while she lived in his house, but she moved out as soon as she could. She told herself that she would live her life her own way and not give a damn what anyone thought; especially when she started dating Brendan Johnson. When Sam told her father that she wanted to bring him over for dinner, he flat out refused. No defense attorneys were allowed in his home. Sam decided that she wasn't allowed in his home either. She would continue to see Brendan, and if her parents shunned her for that, then so be it. They would just have to shun each other.

After months of coaxing from Brendan and Priscilla, Sam changed her mind and invited her parents to her wedding. Brendan convinced her that no man should be denied the chance to walk his daughter down the aisle. Priscilla chimed in with how her mother died and that she would never have a chance to invite her to anything. How could Sam be so selfish? Sam sent the invitations and waited until she looked out into the church pews in her white dress looking for them with tears in her eyes. Her mother didn't show. Neither did her father. Sam never forgot that. It only pushed her to live her life the way she wanted regardless of what they thought.

Sam vowed to never stop pursuing her passion, and that was not going to change even after her husband's death; especially knowing that her husband wouldn't want her to stop. Sam had never met anyone outside of her college professors who was actually happy to hear that she wanted to be a teacher like Brendan. He asked so many questions about dealing with students and addressing their needs that it made Sam smile. He supported her with the sort of ferocious loyalty that was uncharted territory for her. He made her feel like she could do anything. When she had a rough day with the students, or when her school's politics bore down on her, Brendan always reminded her that she was strong enough to get through it. Such loyalty was one of the main reasons she married Brendan; that and the fact that he was so handsome in a suit that it made her jaw drop.

Those moments sustained their marriage and fueled a love that grew stronger every day. Now they only made Sam weep. She always thought about Brendan's faithfulness when she came home from work, and that was when her loneliness would set in. It usually hit her when she opened the front door to their new house and couldn't hear the basketball game on their big screen television or smell the T-bone steaks pan searing on the stove as he was prone to do when he wanted to surprise her with dinner. Steak was Brendan's specialty. He seasoned them the same way every time with a special dry rub that was passed down through his father's side of the family. He then added a side of steak fries that he bought at a store owned by one of his childhood friends and sprinkled them with seasoning salt. It made Sam's mouth water the second she smelled the aroma walking through the door, but it was never a surprise. Sam knew when Brendan had his days off or came home early. Still, she appreciated his consistent effort; especially now more than ever.

The loneliness hit the hardest when Sam entered their master bedroom with cream-colored carpeting and décor and a bathroom attached. When she showered and slept in her bed she remembered that she no longer shared it with the greatest man she had ever known, and that made its coldness even more profound. She could no longer make love to him. She could no longer stay up late and eat ice cream while they watched music videos or late night talk shows. They could no longer laugh at their old memories when they went out on date nights together. They could no longer go to church and worship together. Brendan was gone to be with the Lord, and Sam was left here on earth to sleep with herself.

Sometimes she cried herself to sleep. On especially long days, she was too tired for even that. So she just slept and dreamt about the day he proposed to her inside Carmen's Soulfood in Bridgeport. She dreamt about how they dropped Samuel off for his first day of kindergarten. Her favorite dream was a combination of Samuel's graduation from Stratford High School and Achilla's from Loomis Chafee. Sam never forgot the proud smile on Brendan's face as he watched his children grow. He always bragged about them to friends and family alike. Samuel was always *my* son. Achilla was always *my* daughter. It was always *my son's playing for Duke and he's going to start.* It was always *my daughter's a Marine; a real tough one too.* Had Brendan known Achilla was a spy with top-secret government clearance who gathered intel and battled terrorists every day, he would have told the entire Fairfield County. Sam could picture it.

My daughter's a spy, he would say. *Yep, she's like Charlie's Angels.*

Sam would wake up every morning and drink her coffee alone, thinking about how Brendan promised her this house and followed through. He seldom made promises he couldn't keep, and he made no excuses. After living a childhood full of broken promises from her own father, Sam had never seen a man do what he said he would do as often as Brendan did. He never deviated from his values. He always gave honest and passionate counsel to his clients and expected that same honesty in return. Despite every opportunity and temptation to cheat while working on the losing side of the law, Brendan did everything with decency and honor. Sam believed firmly in her heart that her husband was with God, and after his funeral, she thanked God every day for taking him in; even if his death caused her to toss and turn in her cold bed and spend her mornings alone. If it was God's will, then she just had to bear the burden.

Sam spent a lot of her time in prayer. She prayed for Samuel, hoping that he was staying safe in North Carolina. Sam never missed a Duke game and watched from her living room, sometimes yelling at the television the way Brendan used to. She prayed that he never got hurt. She prayed that he never got distracted by parties, drugs, and women. She prayed on her face that he would remain the pure, simple, yet brilliant son she raised. Judging from his phone-calls home, he was doing just fine.

She prayed for Achilla too and with much more fervor. Ever since she moved into their house, Sam suspected that Achilla was more than just a victim of abuse. She saw the pictures from Brendan's investigator. She noticed the clues in Achilla's language that she had been abused and brainwashed with some weird ideology.

Sam taught enough abuse victims to identify one on sight, and Achilla was a textbook example. Still, there was something deeper, darker, and fiercer to Achilla's personality than anything Sam had ever seen.

Sam wondered if Achilla was possessed by a demon.

She knew that deep down, Achilla was a good person. Achilla had a smile that could cheer up anyone after a long day. She was loyal to her family and particularly protective of Samuel. As much as she refused to admit it, Sam also knew that Achilla loved Dahntay. She pretended to lack tenderness, but that was only to protect herself from getting hurt. As a woman who acted the same way before she met Brendan, Sam was not convinced by her ploy.

No, Achilla was anything but heartless and selfish. She hurt when her family hurt and worked to alleviate their pain. She felt guilty when she made mistakes and tried to correct them. She mourned her father's death as much as anyone else. Though they broke up years ago, Achilla's face lit up like a streetlight when she saw Dahntay at the funeral. Sam saw that look. It was the same one she always gave Brendan when they were dating, and she knew that cold women were incapable of it. Achilla was always a good girl and she had grown into a good woman. Still, Achilla's tendency toward darkness and violence disturbed her.

When Sam watched from their old doorstep as Achilla fought Ailina Harris, she didn't just see the anger of a daughter fighting for her family. There was a sort of untapped rage and bloodlust in the way she moved and spoke. The longer she fought with Ailina that night, the less human she appeared. The very force behind her blows increased until they shook the ground. Eventually, there was no protective, righteous anger in her eyes. Only the fight and the desire to kill remained. It kept them alive that night, but Sam never forgot how little she recognized her. It was like watching two evil spirits engaged in combat over her family as the spoils of victory.

She recognized Achilla even less when she came back home for Brendan's funeral. Sure, she was a taller, fitter, and a more striking beauty, but it was her demeanor that threw Sam off. The Achilla who watched basketball games with her father, had girl talk with her mother, and cried when she broke up with her high school sweetheart was no more. Someone else stared back at Sam through those intense green eyes the day she arrived at her doorstep with Sandy. It was as if there were two different spirits living in the same body engaged in a civil war, and the good Achilla was holding on by a thread.

Sam was losing her only daughter.

That day when she watched her attempted suicide, Sam knew it was Achilla's way of trying to purge herself of evil. Achilla was trying to save the world from herself and prevent the darkness inside of her from lashing out and killing her loved ones. Judging from the blood on Achilla's sneakers (Sandy wasn't the only person to notice that), Sam could tell that Achilla had done something so vile that she would struggle to live with it for the rest of her life. When life looks that bleak, killing yourself becomes an option; especially when you believe that you're the problem.

Of course, Sam suspected that Achilla's state of mind resulted from Ailina's influence. Everything bad in Achilla's life was somehow related to Ailina. Sam never claimed to know what the devil looked like, but if he resembled Ailina, it wouldn't surprise her. The very thought of her face with those glowing green eyes sometimes gave Sam nightmares and cold sweats in her sleep. Sam had never met Ailina before the night she came to kill her family, but she heard enough stories from Brendan to know that she was evil. Brendan always told her that something about Ailina made his stomach turn and that even his stories of deception, manipulation, and abuse didn't quite do her any justice. He warned Sam to run away if she saw anyone who remotely reminded her of Ailina. Much like her parents' demands, Sam refused to obey. She promised herself that if she saw Ailina, she was pulling her hair out. She deserved as much for treating Brendan that way.

Sam could handle herself in a fight. She grew up with two cops who taught her how to box and lived in a city that gave her ample practice. Still, she underestimated Ailina's destructive power. When Sam watched Ailina lift her husband by his throat, it didn't occur to her how unnatural it was for such a thin woman to lift a man like a bag of oranges. All she cared about was protecting her family. She jumped into the fray ready to take her down, only to get snatched up by her neck just the same. When she gripped Sam's throat, her strength was jarring and impossible for a man let alone a woman. As she looked down Ailina's arm, Sam saw a look in her eyes that haunted her for the rest of her life. They didn't just glow in the dark, they dilated and smiled as she squeezed Sam's neck even tighter. Sam struggled to breathe and wracked her brain to think of something; some way to survive. Her heart raced as tears streamed down her face at the very thought that her family might not make it. The look in Ailina's eyes told her that it was just a game for her. They were objects for her use and amusement; toys that could be broken on a whim and replaced. Sam grew up in a family surrounded by violence. She married a husband who worked with dangerous criminals. Sam was no stranger to living with threats on her life on a daily basis, and she was fearless enough to handle it. Ailina was different. In the presence of Ailina, Sam felt like only God could help her. She now believed that it was only by His grace that her family survived. Sam prayed that she would never have to feel so hopeless again.

As of late, Achilla's eyes looked more and more like Ailina's. Even when Achilla smiled her bright smile, her eyes were cold and hard like green grapes left in the freezer and forgotten. When she came home from another random outing, Achilla's eyes were so intense that they made Sam's heart skip a beat. She was changing for the worse, and Sam could see it coming. Sam could see her turning into Ailina, and she could not afford to subject her family to that hopeless feeling again.

So she dropped Samuel off at the airport when Achilla snuck off for the last time. Sam knew she was up to no good, and she didn't want her son to be there if and when she came back. As much as she prayed for her, Sam no longer trusted her. She offered to take Sandy with her, but she refused; claiming she could reason with Achilla. When Sam returned from the airport, she wasn't surprised to find Sandy laying in the foyer unconscious, vomiting blood onto the wood floor. As strong as Achilla was mentally and physically, nobody could fight a demon alone, and that demon was driving Achilla's decisions. Sandy just happened to be in the way.

Poor Sandy. She was so damaged yet warm and kind. Sam had plenty of students like her, victims of sexual abuse who don't know who to trust but are simultaneously searching for someone they can rely on to protect them from the world. They sometimes learn to protect themselves with violence (i.e.: Achilla), but Sandy wasn't there yet. Instead, she found her protector in Achilla. She was adamant that Achilla was her savior, and maybe she was at one point, but she was no longer that person. Sam wouldn't know how to explain it to Sandy, but it wasn't Achilla who hit her that day. It was her demon that struck her and left her there to die. She had to assume that the next time she saw Achilla, she would be talking to that demon from this point on.

Sam kneeled and wept for Sandy before she called 911. She prayed for her in the ambulance all the way to St. Vincent's Hospital. When they arrived, they had to wheel her to surgery to repair the internal bleeding in her large intestine, and Sam sat in the waiting room and prayed for her recovery. One of the doctors spoke to Sam and compared the damage to getting hit in the gut by a bowling bowl traveling at 80 miles per hour. He said he was baffled by the force and focus of the impact, but Sam wasn't. He may have never seen an injury like this one before, but Sam saw Achilla's strength first-hand in her own driveway. Only a monster like Ailina could walk away unharmed. On the bright side, the doctors predicted that Sandy would make a full recovery. Had Sam found her any later, she might not have made it. When a blonde female doctor, Doctor Rice as she called herself, questioned Sam on who did it, she told them the truth.

"It was my daughter," Sam said as she rubbed her hands on her jeans. "No question."

"Your...daughter?" Dr. Rice asked with a frown while she shoved her hands in the pockets of her gray scrubs.

"That's right," Sam replied. "Nobody else is capable of something like that."

"Mrs. Johnson--"

"Miss," Sam sighed with a raised hand. "My husband's gone. He died before he arrived at this hospital."

"Yes, I remember," Dr. Rice said. "I was there. My condolences and apologies. Ms. Johnson, one of my coworkers compared Sandy's injury to a bowling bowl at 80 miles per hour, right?"

"Yes."

"Please forgive him," Dr. Rice replied. "He hasn't worked in this emergency room before. I've seen every kind of freak accident, beating, and animal attack that's come through here for the last thirty years."

"I'm sorry, I don't mean to be rude, but what is your point?"

"My point, Ms. Johnson, is that I've seen this kind of injury before," Dr. Rice whispered as she stepped closer. "Was it that cop that went missing, Ailina Henderson, I believe?"

"Harris."

"Right, Ailina Harris," Dr. Rice said with a nod of her head. "I see you're familiar with her. If it was her, you can tell me. Nobody likes to talk about her. When you've…seen her work, it could make you afraid of the repercussions. But if she's back, every form of law enforcement in this city needs to know. The last time one of her boyfriends came to the ER, he looked just like this girl. I'm old. My kids are married with children of their own and they live far away. I have nothing to fear if she comes after me. You can tell me."

Sam had never heard anyone outside of her family speak of Ailina before. Judging from Dr. Rice's hard expression, an expression that Sam always held when someone called their home with a death threat, Ailina had quite the reputation at this hospital. Sam suspected that Dr. Rice was a brave but misguided person. Had she seen Ailina's eyes, her face would be wrought with fear.

"It wasn't Ailina," Sam said. "It was her daughter."

"I thought you said--"

"I should clarify for you," Sam replied. "Achilla Johnson is technically my step-daughter. Ailina is her real mother. I just raised her."

"You mean your husband had a child with *her*?" Dr. Rice asked with raised eyebrows.

"You sound shocked."

"Yes, I am," Dr. Rice said. "How did he survive long enough without losing a limb?"

"God only knows," Sam sighed and shook her head. "But she did break his arm when they broke up if that counts."

"I'll have to report Achilla Johnson," Dr. Rice said. "I know how you must feel about her, but I'm obligated; especially if she's anything like Ailina."

"Do whatever you have to do," Sam sighed as tears filled her eyes. "Even my baby girl isn't exempt from the law."

"Understood."

"Is Sandy able to have visitors?" Sam asked.

"Yes," Dr. Rice said as she turned and walked back into the ER. "I'll show you her room."

Sam thanked God under her breath as she followed Dr. Rice to a room across the ER. Sam found Sandy sitting in bed wearing a white gown with her curly, dark brown hair flowing down to her shoulders as she held a remote control. When Sam entered the room, she noticed that the television was silent, and Sandy wasn't even watching it. She just stared out at nowhere like a dazed child who just entered the new world. She didn't look at Sam when she walked around to the side of the room to a pink chair and crossed her arms over her sky blue Columbia t-shirt.

"Sandy, how do you feel?" Sam asked as she sat down and pulled her chair close to the bed.

"It hurts to breathe," Sandy replied with a stone straight face.

"One of the doctors said you had some internal bleeding, a bruised abdomen, and a couple broken ribs," Sam said before turning up a weak smile. "I know this sounds strange but compared to some of the other people Achilla's fought, your list of injuries is pretty short. You probably don't feel lucky, but you are. Trust me."

"She wasn't trying to hurt me," Sandy muttered. "She knocked me out so I'd get out of her way."

"Get out of her way?" Sam asked. "Well, I'm not surprised that she got rough with you. That girl always had a temper, and her strength--"

"Your daughter's a murderer," Sandy said with unusual curtness.

"I've been around enough killers to know one. They have this weird look in their eyes, and ever since she found out her dad died, she had that look. She said it was best for all of us if she left. I tried to go with her. God knows why."

So Sandy noticed the look in Achilla's eyes too. Sam didn't know what worried her more; the fact that Sandy called Achilla a murderer or the fact that Sam wasn't surprised. If Ailina was any proof, Achilla was born from the stock of killers. She and Brendan tried their best, but they knew after her night with Stanley that they were fighting an uphill battle. Marty was one thing. Kids fight and sometimes girls beat up boys, even if the beating is severe. However, the damage Achilla did to Stanley was unnatural, and her next fight with those two girls at Stratford High was just as bad. Achilla's cruelty in a fight lent itself to murder down the road. Sam tried her best, but she knew this day would come. She leaned forward and held Sandy's hand.

"It's because you still see her as the woman who saved you from a bad life," Sam said as she squeezed Sandy's hand and maintained her smile. "That's why you wanted to go with her."

"She's not that anymore," Sandy said. "She's lost."

Sam nodded her head and waited as a couple tears streamed down Sandy's face. She then took a box of tissues off of the counter behind her and handed them to Sandy. Sandy waved them away without looking at them. She didn't wipe her face either. She just sat there and let the tears drip from her chin.

"I never thought of it until now," Sandy said as tears still streamed down her face. "But I want to go to college."

"OK, well, did you graduate high school?" Sam asked.

"No," Sandy replied. "I want to go to your school and finish my senior year. Then I want to go to college."

"I can arrange that," Sam said with a nod of her head. "Whatever you need, but it'll be a challenge."

"I don't care," Sandy replied. "It can't be harder than what I've already been through."

"Well there's some truth to that," Sam sighed. "Sandy, I have to ask. Where are your parents?"

"At this point, my mother's sitting right next to me," Sandy replied with just about the least amount of affection someone could have for claiming a new mother. Sam lowered her head. It was clear that Sandy never had a family and was searching for one. As Sam got to know her better, she realized that her childhood was as hard as Achilla's. Abandoned by her parents, she moved from foster home to foster home until she turned eighteen. During that time, she had to look out for herself any way that she could. When she couldn't fight to survive, she used her body as a bartering tool to get her needs met. Men and women alike sexually abused her in nearly every home she lived. As a result, Sandy knew more about sex, drugs, and violence than most adults by the time she was fifteen. Of all of the sad stories Sam heard as a teacher, Sandy's was the saddest. Sandy may have needed a mother at some point, but it was too late for that now. If she had a family, she would be halfway out the door. She was a woman now, and she needed to be strong like one.

"Sandy, I appreciate that you see me as a mother, but you've only known me for a few weeks," Sam said in a low voice. "I think you have attachment issues. If you need my help, fine, but I'm going to help you become self-reliant."

"Yeah, maybe you're right," Sandy said.

"Can I ask you what you want to go to college for?" Sam asked. "You have to pursue a major, right? So what's your major?"

"Psychology."

"You want to be a psychologist?" Sam replied. "That's a good field, Sandy. I like where your head is--"

"I want to find Achilla and bring her home," Sandy replied. "I can't do that without understanding how she thinks."

"Sandy," Sam said with a frown as she sat up. "Oh Lord, Sandy, no--"

"Even if I have to arrest her for murder," Sandy continued with a hard stare out the door. "I can find her. I know I can."

Sam's throat tightened. Achilla's actions hurt Sandy more than she anticipated. She had to stop her from hurting herself. Chasing

Achilla around could only result in turmoil. The next time Achilla hit her, Sam might not be there to call an ambulance.

"Sandy, I won't help you ruin your life," Sam replied as she released Sandy's hand and crossed her arms. "I won't help you live your life based on Achilla's actions. Now she's my daughter, and I would give my life for her, but--"

"Then why can't I give mine?" Sandy replied as she looked at Sam for the first time with a crazed look in her hazel eyes. "Why can't I give mine like you would, huh? I can find her, and I will."

"This is more than attachment issues," Sam said as she rose to her feet. "You're obsessed with her."

"So what if I am?" Sandy replied without breaking eye contact.

"I thought you and Samuel--"

"He was sad about your husband, and I wanted to make him feel better," Sandy replied as she looked down at her lap. "So I did what I'm good at to give him a distraction. He's a nice boy, so I wanted to help him. That's all."

"That's so *self-destructive*," Sam said with her hands on her hips. "You can't live like this. You can't keep living like you don't matter, Sandy. You have to overcome this!"

"I have to bring Achilla home," Sandy sobbed as she pounded her bed with her fists. "I have to bring her home!"

Sandy slapped herself in the head three times, and Sam tried to grab her arms and tell her to stop. Sandy flailed and knocked Sam back against the counter top, and Sam grunted as her back throbbed from hitting the counter. Sam fought many girls in high school and college, and she always won; even against women twice her size. With the exception of Ailina, no woman had ever overpowered her like that before.

No wonder Sandy survived her blow from Achilla.

A strawberry blonde nurse in blue scrubs stepped in to pull Sam away, and a pair of security officers rushed past them as the nurse pulled Sam out of the room. Sam watched as Sandy fought with the security officers. The bed rattled and the officers cursed and grunted as Sandy punched and kicked until one of them slammed her on the mattress.

Two more security officers rushed into the room to grab her legs, and Sandy wailed out when they shackled her arms to the bed. Sam shook her head as Sandy tried to break free of her restraints until they tightened them and pinned her down. As the security officers walked out of the room, one of them with a fresh black eye, Sam overhead what Sandy kept repeating over and over, and it brought tears to her eyes.

"I can find her," Sandy moaned. "I know I can. I can find her… I know I can….I can find her….I know I can…."

It looked like Achilla's demon left its mark on Sandy as well. All Sam could do now was pray for her. She was learning that in a world where people like Achilla and Sandy come to her doorstep looking for shelter, prayer provided all of the answers. She just wished that God could spell things out for her a little more. She asked God why. Why did it have to be her? Why did He want her to bear the burden of being a widow with a son hundreds of miles away and a daughter who disappeared? No, she did more than disappear. It was obvious now that Achilla was as dangerous as she feared she would become.

What was Sam supposed to do? What could she have done better as a mother? What mistakes were made? Was it because of that night with Stanley? Sam still kicked herself over letting her go on that date alone. Was it because they let her leave for boarding school without asking any questions? Sam was so caught up in Achilla's academic success that she didn't see the obvious in front of her. She didn't think anything of Achilla's refusal to come home during the summer, claiming that she had to stay on campus for work and sports. She didn't think anything of Achilla's choice to join the Marines when she could have gone to any school in the country on a full ride; even a military school that could have given her a higher rank after graduation. Why didn't she notice all the signs that Achilla was living a secret life, a possibly deadly one full of espionage and murder? How could she miss that? What kind of mother was she?

Sam prayed for forgiveness. Perhaps God was showing her all along and she refused to listen, blinded by her refusal to hover and control Achilla like her parents did to her. Sam told herself that she would not copy her parents' child-rearing. She would never tell Achilla what to do with her life. She encouraged her children to be motivated go-getters, but only in the fields and careers that they chose. Once they made that choice, Sam was in their corner, pushing them to never give up or slack off; or at least one of them. Samuel needed encouragement sometimes. Sam never had to lecture Achilla about motivation. If anything, Sam found herself suggesting that Achilla slow down, but she never suggested too hard. As long as Achilla brought home straight A's and basketball trophies, she could work as much as she wanted and take as many martial arts classes as she pleased. Sam never guessed that Achilla was training to be a lethal fighting machine right under her nose. She never suspected that she would join the CIA and hold people at gunpoint, among the countless other things she hid from her. Now a casualty of Sam's ignorance and Achilla's secrecy was lying in a hospital bed going crazy. Sandy's injury wasn't Achilla's fault. It was Sam's, and she decided right then and there that she would she make it right by helping Sandy any way that she could.

When the nurse gave Sandy a sedative, she finally fell asleep. Dr. Rice informed Sam that Sandy had to stay in the hospital for three more days so they could evaluate her physical health and mental state. So Sam drove home alone and lived alone for the time being. At least she would have some company when Sandy returned.

Every day Sam sighed and lowered her head as she entered a house that was too big for her. With a dead husband, a son in college, and a daughter on the loose, Sam wondered if it was about time that she sold it. She could move into a smaller home in Bridgeport not far from Central High. With any luck, she could walk to work and Sandy could walk to school. Sam plopped onto her living room couch and grabbed the remote. She seldom watched this thing when Brendan was alive. She might as well get some use out of it. She caught a syndicated sitcom before nodding off to sleep.

Sam jumped awake in a pitch black living room. Her heart pumped out of her chest as she stared at the shadowy figures of her furniture. When she fell asleep the television was on. She remembered nodding off to the laughter of a live studio audience. Sandy was still in the hospital.

So who the hell turned off her television and all of the lights?

Whoever did it had to know Sam was in the house. Maybe it was a burglar. In this neighborhood? Forget it. No, somebody came here with a different purpose in mind. It must have been whoever shot her husband. Sam stared across the living room in the general direction of where she hid her revolver. If she could get to it before he found it, he was in for a world of trouble; the eye-for-an-eye, Old Testament variety. Sam lay still in the dark for a few moments before she slid her leg off the couch. If there was an intruder, he had to walk through the dark too, and he didn't know this house like she did. Sam rolled to the floor without making a sound. She was going to crawl to her closet, get her gun, and blow him away.

"You know," announced a voice that made Sam gasp as her heart nearly jumped into her throat. "If you were in actual danger, that would be a good maneuver. Fortunately, I mean you no harm, and I've already removed your gun. I'll put it back before I leave. Promise."

Sam froze and looked around. That voice sounded familiar. It was soft with an edge to it and a slight Boston accent.

"Calm down, Samantha," the voice said. "You have nothing to fear from me today."

The more the voice spoke, the more Sam trembled.

"Ailina Harris?" Sam mumbled.

"Yep," Ailina replied.

"What are you doing in my house?" Sam snarled as she looked around. "You've got some nerve coming around here."

"Oh, relax, I'm sure Achilla explained everything about that night," Ailina said with a chuckle that carried throughout the living room.

"She explained what you told her," Sam said. "I don't believe it."

"Not exactly accurate," Ailina sighed. "She figured it out on her own."

"Get the hell out of my house!"

"Look, I get it," Ailina said. "I do. We once screwed the same man, and then I came back and held that man by his throat. I'm not welcome, so I'll leave. I just wanted to tell you something about Achilla."

"What have you done to my daughter?" Sam demanded.

"*Your daughter?*" Ailina growled.

That was when Sam saw them. The green eyes that haunted her in her sleep glowed from the corner to her right and floated toward her. Sam hopped to her feet and stumbled back but the eyes were too fast. They stood in front of her until Sam backed away toward the window on the other side of the room. When Sam fell, the clouds outside parted, releasing moonlight into the living room. Ailina stood just a few feet away wearing a black t-shirt and gray sweatpants with black sneakers. She wasn't wearing gloves this time. Perhaps she was telling the truth about not killing her.

"Let me make this clear to you," Ailina commanded as her eyes glowed like tea candles and pierced into Sam's face. "Achilla is *mine*. I gave birth to her, *not you*. Just because you housed her for a few years doesn't make you her real mother."

"I did more than *house* her," Sam shot back. "I fed her, clothed her, raised her. All you did was abuse her, and Brendan and I had to work ourselves to the bone cleaning up your mess."

"I taught her how to survive," Ailina snapped.

"You taught her how to kill!" Sam shrieked as tears burst from her eyes. "Now look at her! This is your fault! You did this to her! You ruined her!"

"Ruined?" Ailina screamed back. "Ruined, are you serious? You're the one who tried to domesticate her and turn her into something she isn't!"

"A good girl!" Sam retorted. "A good woman!"

"Your pet!" Ailina roared with a voice that made the window above Sam's head tremble. "That's all she was in this house, and I'll be damned if I watch her turn into anything like *you*!"

"I am a good mother!" Sam growled. "And unlike you, I taught her right from wrong. Achilla is no pet. I love her as if she were my flesh and blood."

"Yeah, sure," Achilla shot back. "Because you couldn't have a daughter of your own, you had to take mine?"

A lump grew in Sam's throat. How did she know about that? She decided to ignore Ailina's comment as nothing more than a snide insult. She couldn't possibly know that much. Could she?

"I didn't take anyone," Sam said. "Brendan and I rescued her from you. Women like you don't deserve children. All you do is damage them and then women like me have to piece together whatever's left--"

"You're so pathetic," Ailina spat. "All you did was soften her up."

"If I made her so soft, why haven't you killed me yet?' Sam replied. "You're afraid of what she'll do if you touch me. You weren't afraid when she was just a girl. She's gotten stronger than you, hasn't she?"

Ailina's eyes glowed like the green clouds in a bad storm, but Sam spoke anyway. If she was going to die, she might as well go down verbally swinging.

"She wouldn't be that way if it wasn't for *us*," Sam hissed as she pointed at her chest. "You haven't really fought until you've fought to protect your family, but you wouldn't know anything about that. A woman like you couldn't possibly understand what it's like to defend someone you love, even with your bare hands if you have to. Achilla learned that from us because we were the first ones to love her, not you. We were the first ones to defend her when she needed defending, not you. We were the only people who fought for her, *not you*! You've done nothing for her. *Nothing!* We did everything. *Everything!*"

Ailina's eyes glowed until she sighed and rested her face in her hands. When she looked back up, her eyes looked no different than Sam's.

"I didn't come here to argue about who's the better parent," Ailina said with a calm voice. "Frankly, I couldn't be bothered, but woman to woman, I think you should know that Achilla's changed. She's not the girl you want her to be."

"Oh, so she's the girl you want her to be then?" Sam asked with her arms crossed.

"Actually, yes," Ailina replied. "She's developed her fighting instincts, and I couldn't be more proud. I'd be happier if I wasn't sure that she'd come looking for me next."

"Why would you be proud of that?" Sam snarled. "What kind of sick woman *wants* her daughter to kill people?"

"You know nothing about us," said Ailina with a sneer. "You never did. You thought you could help by coddling her, but you're wrong. It's in Achilla's nature to fight and kill, and I nurtured that seed early on. After that, it just grew on its own. She needed a little push here and there, but I think she's got it."

"You're saying she ran away to be a murderer?" Sam asked.

"No, she could've done that from your house," Ailina said with a shrug. "She actually ran away to keep you safe while she kills everyone in her path. She still has your...feelings I guess. The only reason I let her come back here was that I hoped she'd turn around and kill you herself, but you can't have everything you want, right?"

Sam shook her head as tears flowed down her face. So it was true. Achilla was out there killing people right now. She was more than a murderer. Somehow, someway, with all of their effort to turn her around, Sam and Brendan raised a serial killer. No. Ailina raised a serial killer. Sam was too late, no matter how hard she tried. She curled her lip at Ailina's grin. How could she stand there and be so smug when she was responsible for the deaths of Lord knows how many people?

"You're evil," Sam replied as she wiped her eyes. "You're the devil."

"You know you're not the first person to tell me that," Ailina laughed. "I'd take it as a compliment if I actually thought those things existed."

"You've made your point," Sam muttered. "If you wanted Achilla to be some killing machine, you've succeeded. If you came here to gloat, you've done that too. Just please, leave me alone. Just go and never come back."

"Nope, I'm not done," Ailina said with a smile as she wagged her finger. "You should also know that you're going to be a grandma."

"What?" Sam asked with a furrowed brow until she watched Ailina caress her midsection. It was well hidden, but there was a bulge there. Ailina was pregnant? No, she was more than just pregnant. Sam squinted harder at her baby bump and realized that Ailina was at least six months along. What did that have to do with Sam being a grandma? When Sam pieced two and two together, she rose to her feet with her fists clenched and her jaw tight.

"You're catching on," said Ailina with a grin on her lips. "You know I heard your little tirade about *fast girls* that morning. You should really loosen the reigns a bit. I can personally attest to the fact that your son is very much a man."

Ailina and Samuel? Why didn't he tell her? How could he hide something like that from his family? Sam's eyes clenched shut. Of course. The last time Samuel mentioned Ailina to his parents, she almost killed them. This time he decided to protect everyone.

Sometimes raising a good kid backfired at the worst moments.

"How?" Sam growled. "What did you say to him?"

"I didn't trick him, if that's what you're asking," Ailina replied. "But if it makes you feel better about his innocence, he wasn't entirely a willing participant in the matter."

"You...*raped* Samuel?!" Sam choked at first until her voice changed into a demand. "You raped my baby?!"

"Rape is a strong word," said Ailina with a shrug. "Futile resistance just happens to be a big turn on for me, and he has a natural talent for it."

Sam's mouth dropped open when she thought about Samuel, the sweet boy with a brilliant mind and a smile as wide as his ears, pinned down and forced upon by this monster. Samuel was a sensitive boy growing up. He used to cry at the slightest thing. He got tougher from playing basketball, and he had a few girls here and there, but he was still her little boy. He was still the good-hearted, mild-mannered boy she raised who wouldn't hurt a soul if he didn't have to, and this *thing* targeted him? Sam ground her teeth at how helpless he must have felt confronted by Ailina, how he was probably wondering where his parents were, where *Achilla* was. He needed someone to protect him, but no one was there.

How could Ailina do that?

Why did she always attack people who couldn't defend themselves?

Sam's body shook until the words left her mouth on their own.

"You raped my son," Sam growled with bloodshot eyes. "He was just a boy. A good boy! And you just *violated* him?! Why would you do that to my boy?!"

"Again, he was hardly a boy," Ailina replied. "Someone had to teach him what men are supposed to do. You never showed him his place, so I did it for you. You should be grateful. Because of me, he's now fully a man."

"He's my boy!" Sam roared as her hands trembled at her sides. "How dare you! How dare you touch my son, you fucking bitch!"

"More compliments?" Ailina replied with a flip of her hair. "Unlike my daughter, I kind of like that word. You know when a bitch is in heat, male dogs for miles come running to screw her? She has her choice of men without raising a finger and they all beg for her. That's a lot of power to give to a woman. I'd be a fool to turn it down, really."

"You won't get away with this!" Sam snarled as she stepped forward. "You won't get away with hurting my son!"

"Not a good idea, Samantha," Ailina said with hard eyes. "I didn't come here to hurt you, but I won't take kindly to an assault."

"Well, come on then!" replied Sam as she charged at Ailina with a raised fist. She didn't care anymore. She didn't care how strong she was. She didn't care that she almost killed her last time. Someone had to teach her a lesson. Someone had to stop her. Nobody, nobody, *nobody* got away with hurting any member of Sam's family; not Brendan, not Achilla, and definitely not Samuel. Ailina was going to get hers. Period.

She swung her fist at Ailina's head, but Ailina didn't even duck. Sam could see her fist about to connect with her left eye. That would be a start. Her throat was next. After that, she was getting her gun and--

Sam jolted to a halt when a hand grabbed her wrist; a hand so large that it enveloped half of Sam's forearm. Sam's neck hairs stood on end and she froze without even attempting to pull herself free. She looked at Ailina, and both of her hands were at her sides. Sam's mouth turned raw when the hand grabbing her wrist lifted her off of the floor and turned her around.

Standing in front of her was a man taller than Samuel and at least twice as wide. His shoulders looked like shoulder pads and his chest popped out like two pillows stuffed under his white t-shirt. His hair was shaggy and black and his jaw as square as a kitchen table. But his eyes caught Sam's attention the most. They glowed green just like Ailina's, but stronger. They made Sam's body go limp as she hung suspended in mid-air.

"Not her, *Bampàs*," Ailina said from behind Sam's shoulder. "Please leave her alone."

"Explain," the man rumbled with a voice like a Metro-North train.

"She's had one kid in over eighteen years," Ailina replied with a slight tremor in her voice. "After years of fertility treatment, she failed to conceive again. That's why she was so happy to take in Achilla in the first place. She'd be a great mother if she could bear a child, but as it stands she'll only waste your seed. I promise I'll find someone more suitable. I just need more time."

"You'd better," the man said. "I'm getting impatient, Ailina. We need to get started. Don't forget your purpose."

"I know," Ailina's voice turned soft and mousey. "I won't."

Sam frowned when the man's eyes flickered and stopped glowing. She noticed Ailina's tone when she spoke to him. She never thought Ailina would be afraid of anyone, but she feared this man. Ailina also called him *Bampàs*. Wasn't that Greek for Dad or something? So he was her father? The man lowered Sam to the floor and glowered at her with his hands on his hips.

"You will keep your hands to yourself," the man barked. "My daughter will finish what she has to say, and then we leave."

Sam stared at the man as her heart raced. Her feet lost all sensation and her thighs trembled at his voice. It took all of her might just to stay on her feet. His voice was so…awesome. Sam's ribcage trembled at the sound.

"Do you understand me?" the man growled.

"Yes," Sam breathed as her heart jumped. "Yes, I do."

"Good," the man replied before turning and walking away. Sam held her chest and dropped to her knees. She had met men from all over the world. She married Brendan Johnson. Still, nothing she had ever seen compared to the man she watched walk out of the living room with a back the size of one of her whiteboards at school. Sam struggled to catch her breath before looking up at Ailina.

"You're welcome," Ailina said. "I guess being half a woman worked in your favor this time."

Sam continued to stare at the man's frame as he stood in the foyer. No one, not her husband, not even her athletic exes in college, had that many muscles in their back. Sam shuddered when he stretched his arms and scratched his head. Every moment made his shirt pulsate like catfish in a shallow stream. How was it possible for anyone to attain a build like that?

"That'd be my father," Ailina said. "Ares."

"Ares?" Sam asked as she watched him sit on the stairs in the foyer.

"Yep," Ailina replied before narrowing her eyes and stepping in front of her to block her view. "You can stop undressing him with your eyes now. He's no longer interested in you."

"I wasn't--"

"Whatever," Ailina said with a wave of her hand. "Judging by your little outburst, I'm sure you figured out that I'm pregnant with Samuels' children."

"Children?"

"Yeah, this part Achilla doesn't know," said Ailina with a wide smile. "I think I have twins this time. Exciting, huh? I'll get them a couple matching outfits and everything!"

Sam looked down at the floor. They got lucky with Achilla, and even she ended up going crazy. Now Ailina had more? She had twins? Without Brendan to save them, what would become of them?

What would become of the world around them with Ailina as their mother?

"You look thrilled," Ailina quipped before turning to walk toward Ares. "So, that's all I came to tell you. Later, Samantha."

"Wait," Sam said with a low voice. "What are you going to do with the children? Are you going to treat them like you did Achilla?"

"You really do have a soft spot for kids," Ailina replied. "Why don't you just worry about yourself?"

"Just answer the damn question," Sam demanded with clenched eyes. "I just need to know. How will you treat the children?"

"That depends on how they turn out," Ailina replied with a look over her shoulder. "Every child has different strengths and weaknesses. As a teacher, you should know that."

"OK," Sam said. "What was Achilla's *strength* that made you abuse her so much?"

"Battle," Ailina said. "She's a warrior, born and bred. Your law enforcement will try its best to stop her, but they'll all fail. Her instincts are too sharp, she's too strong, and she will get more dangerous by the day. You should feel grateful. You're probably the only person alive right now who is safe from her wrath."

Achilla's wrath? Sam shook her head. She prayed every day that she would never hear statements like that. She never wanted Achilla to be known for her anger, for her ability to kill. Still, her inner voice told her that she knew this would happen. She knew it when Marty's parents called her, threatening to sue the Johnson's for the hospital expenses Achilla incurred on them after beating down their son. She knew it when Achilla survived Stanley's overaggression by replying with her own overwhelming power and efficiency in a fight. None of her victims were innocent, but they were victims nonetheless. Sam knew this would happen when she woke up one morning and realized that Achilla had more victims than friends.

"You're right about one thing," Ailina continued. "She's stronger than me, but it has nothing to do with your parenting. Achilla's body and mind are predisposed to combat. She was destined to surpass me. She takes after my father more than I do, actually."

Sam's eyes wandered to Ares as he rose to his feet. His very presence filled the room like smoke from a gas fire, and every muscle on his body bulged like it had a life of its own. Yes, it made sense. Achilla had a commanding demeanor. Achilla had muscles on top of muscles even as a little girl. Much like this man, she was built to fight. How could Sam miss that for all these years?

When Ares looked in Sam's direction, his eyes forced her to look away. They emitted that same Harris bright green glare, but they were intense beyond measure. As amazing as Achilla was, Sam had a feeling that she was no match for this man. Sam had no proof of that. She just knew. One look into Ares' eyes and she knew he was unstoppable.

"You should see your face," Ailina said with a cackle. "Looks like you understand. Yeah, my dad's way too strong for Achilla. The males of our kind always are. You'd better pray to your god that I don't have a boy."

"Ailina," Ares demanded with a voice that shook the windows and made Sam gasp. "We're leaving. Now."

"Coming," Ailina replied with her head low. Sam flinched at Ailina's response and looked at the floor again. When she looked back up, they were gone. Sam stood up and ran around her house, checking every nook and cranny. They disappeared as quickly as they came. Sam held her head in her hands as she paced the kitchen in the dark. She always feared that Ailina would come back, but this was much, much worse. The image of Ares' eyes popped into her head again and Sam sat down at the kitchen table.

Sam was no stranger to danger. She was no stranger to men. Still, this Ares made her hands and knees tremble in such a confusing way. One moment she told herself that he was dangerous, deadly, not to be trusted. The next, she had this desire to run outside just to see if he was still there so she could get another look at those intense green eyes that made her legs wobble. She hadn't felt that way about a man since she was a teenage girl with a crush on a gang leader, but this was even stronger. It was like his very presence created a yearning for something she never knew she wanted until he walked into the room.

No. She mustn't think that way, not about this man. He was evil, and her better nature knew it. She felt sorry for the next woman who met him though. She wouldn't stand a chance. Sam took a deep breath and dropped to her knees; mostly to talk to God, partly to keep herself still. She no longer thought that Ailina was the devil. If anybody walking the earth could earn that title, it was Ares.

Sam's only answer to this situation was prayer. Prayer was the only weapon that could defeat the demons that constantly attacked her home. Sam lowered her chin and closed her eyes as she prayed for strength. She prayed for wisdom. She also prayed for a battle plan. Sam now realized that a war was brewing and that her family was on the front lines. She could only hope that Achilla was on the side of good when it mattered most. From the look of things, they were going to need her more than ever. Sam prayed that Achilla would survive long enough to stop them. Without her, it was impossible.

Chapter Twenty-Four

ACHILLA JOHNSON:21

Achilla sat in the cushioned seats of an airplane terminal wearing blue jeans, blue and red sneakers, a gray hoody and a blue, red and yellow Denver Nuggets fitted cap that rested over her hair and sent it flowing down her back like a black cape. She surfed the internet on her laptop as she waited for her plane. For the past three months, she was a security officer at Denver Hospital and a server at the Tavern, a bar in Lodo just across the street from the spot where she met Sidney Christie. She kept a low profile, collected tips at the Tavern, and pretended to be too weak to restrain the larger patients at the hospital. Nobody suspected a thing when she quit out of the blue. Leaving her apartment was a different story, but threatening to tell HUD about her landlord's illegal practices (namely trying to convince Achilla to have sex in return for a rent-free apartment), was more than enough to get out of her lease. As for Sidney Christie, well, that was the easy part.

She wondered how long it would take before they found his body in Aurora.

Achilla lowered her head as two U.S. Marshalls with obvious gun bulges under their navy blue and navy green t-shirts passed by.

Law enforcement in the U.S. was a joke compared to Achilla, but Colorado was especially simple. It might as well have been the Wild West. Achilla was sure that she could have stayed and staged Christie's death as self-defense, but she had no intention of being seen. Her enemies had yet to catch her trail, and Achilla wanted to keep it that way.

When Achilla's plane to Seattle arrived, she reached to close her laptop before she saw a blip on the FBI website; where she, of course, hacked into their network. It was a newsflash about a murder in the Denver-Metro area that fit the *modus operandi* of a string of murders in Boston, Philadelphia, Pittsburgh, and Cleveland. Sidney Christie was found dead in a reservoir in Aurora. No prints. No weapons. However, his throat was cut open, and his limbs were twisted in ways that no man could pull off by himself. The local police told the media that it was a nationwide gang phenomenon; a group of gangsters ran into his home and tortured him to death. The Feds knew better, but they most likely wouldn't tell anyone but the CIA. One of the intra-office bulletins read:

"The Mantis Strikes Again. Meeting in five minutes."

Achilla smirked and shut her laptop before grabbing her gym bag and her boarding pass. Mantis had a nice ring to it. A praying mantis was silent but fierce. It could blend in with the grass until it was time to strike. Achilla saw that in herself. At first glance, she looked no different than any other tall black woman with dark hair and green eyes. Some might assume that she was a model, an athlete, or just a working woman who liked to stay in shape. Nobody would ever look at her and see a serial killer. Only her victims could see that, and they were in no position to blow the whistle. Achilla grinned as she strolled past clearance and boarded her plane before she set her cranberry red headphones into her ears.

Obie Trice's "The Setup" blared in her ears when she found her seat and leaned her head against the headrest. As Achilla looked out the window, she watched the sun rise behind the cumulus clouds. Denver's elevation made the sun and the clouds look so much bigger, and she preferred that view over any other city. Achilla sighed and watched with a smile on her face until an older gentleman sat next to her.

"Sir, I have a random question for you," Achilla said without turning her head as she patted his knee.

"Sure," he replied with a strong Denver accent that sounds like the word shirt without the "t" at the end.

"When you hear praying mantis, what's the first thing you think of?"

"Well, not to sound sexist," the man said with a shrug. "But hell hath no fury like a woman's wrath. You know what they say about the female praying mantis, right? "

Yes, of course. After the female praying mantis mates with its male partner, he tries to run away. He tries to survive long enough to find another mate. The female allows none of that. She strikes him dead with one blow and eats him. She then moves on to her next male mate and does it again. That fit Achilla too, and she was glad that she let Dahntay go when she did. It wasn't right for him to stay so close to her; not when there was a strong possibility that she might eat his head. That fate was reserved for Xerxes' men. She told herself over and over that Dahntay deserved better than to get caught in the crossfire.

"It's OK," Achilla said to her neighbor as she turned her head and winked at him. "That's what I thought too. It's a lot better than Gumby anyway."

"I'm sorry, what?"

"Oh, nothing," Achilla sighed as she placed her headphones back on. "Just making fun of an old friend."

"Hm, right on," the man replied before grabbing a magazine and opening it. *Right on* was the Denverite way of expressing disapproval or approval depending on what you said. Considering his body language, disapproval was the obvious context. Achilla looked out the window again as she wondered how her mother and brother were doing and how Sandy was holding up. She closed her eyes as she imagined her mother's house filled with all the people she loved eating dinner together. She imagined the salty aroma of fried catfish with collard greens filling the room as her father sat at the head of the table with his bright-eyed smile; bellowing his laughter at one of Samuel's jokes. The thought of her father's face made Achilla set her jaw and glared at her own reflection in the airplane window.

As the sun rose above the skyline but not quite high enough for true daylight, her eyes flickered like a broken neon sign. Achilla learned that her eyes glowed in the dark during moments of intense focus; like when she saw in the dark for the first time. As she got better at it, her eyes dimmed until she was invisible in the shadows at night. Still, during moments when her thoughts wandered to her father's death, Achilla couldn't help herself. She took a deep breath and relaxed her body until she saw the glow in the window's reflection fizzle out. She then leaned back and closed her eyes; pretending to sleep just in case her eyes started glowing again. Such a phenomenon would be impossible to explain without exposing herself and difficult to hide on an airplane.

When she arrived at Seattle-Tacoma International Airport, Achilla found a bathroom where she pulled her hair back and tested a pair of dark brown contacts in front of the mirror. She had several colored contacts: brown, dark brown, blue, hazel, gray (She seldom used gray. It was too easy to remember). Today she blinked back her dark brown contacts and looked in the mirror at eyes that reminded her of her father's. She then took them out to save them for later. She smiled and lifted the blue fitted cap off of her head and shoved it into her bag before she released her hair and smoothing it over her head. She sighed as she pulled off her shirt, grabbed some deodorant, and dabbed her armpits as an old woman gave her a dirty look in the reflection. Achilla shrugged and reached into her bag for a navy blue long-sleeved t-shirt, a navy blue and lime green fitted cap, and matching sneakers. Achilla grinned at herself in the mirror as she pulled the cap on her head and adjusted her brim before changing her shirt and sneakers.

Fitteds were her kryptonite. She may have to stop after a while before someone picked up on her fetish, but she would collect one from each city if it had one available. Perhaps when her mission was over, she could show them to Samuel. Achilla straightened out a stray strand of hair before zipping up her bag and walking out of the bathroom.

When she left the airport, she hailed a cab and found a hotel on Alki Beach. As she carried her bag toward the door, she noticed that Seattle was a sharp contrast to dry and sunny Denver. While the occasional storm visited Denver and passed through, Seattle's clouds hung in the air like permanent residents, and they surrounded the city with a cool mist. Still, there was something pleasant about so much moisture in the air. It was like enjoying a refreshing drink that never emptied. Had Achilla not come here for her mission, she might have stayed a while and let the water kiss her skin for a bit.

With a set of fake passports and IDs, she registered under the name Simone Pratt. Achilla wouldn't stay there long. She just needed a night to plan out her strategy before she found a location that better suited her needs. After entering her hotel room, she didn't even bother to unpack. She sat cross-legged on her orange and white-sheeted bed as she opened her laptop.

Her next target was Darvin Francis. He grew up in Seattle before attending Washington State University. He then became a corrections officer at the King County Juvenile Detention Center. Go figure, his specialty was trafficking young boys, but according to Blue Eyes' records, he had charges of kidnapping underaged girls as well. He was found not-guilty and worked as a security officer at New Future Academy; a charter school.

Achilla frowned.

He got a job at a charter school? How did a man who was charged with kidnapping minors get hired to work with kids? She would investigate that later. For now, her main focus was finding Darvin, eliminating him, and getting out of Seattle. After him, her next target was Jordan Milton, a former Mormon pastor who lived in Salt Lake City, Utah with a string of child pornography charges. Blue Eyes couldn't save him like he did Darvin. He served time before he got a job as a math teacher.

Again, at another New Future Academy.

Achilla noticed a pattern. Though she was considering heading out to Portland, Oregon first, now she knew she had to go to Salt

Lake City to dig deeper into this charter school. Achilla groaned at the thought of going anywhere near Utah as she set her laptop down, rolled off her bed and banged out a set of handstand pushups on her fingertips. After six thousand, she somersaulted to her feet before stretching into a full split. She closed her eyes as she meditated on her plan. She would trail Darvin, figure out his routine, and find the best place to lure him in; perhaps a bar or his favorite nightclub. Knowing his history, he might hang out by a few playgrounds. Where he spent most of his time would determine her approach. She could look like a naïve woman who put herself in just enough harm's way for him to perceive an easy target. Or she could be a seductress looking for a good time with no strings attached; wearing her red dress and red bottom heels for the night. Achilla shook her head. She liked the red dress, but she had to expand her horizons and get a new one. Much like her fitteds, it would only establish a pattern after a while, and Achilla couldn't afford to get caught until she finished what she had started.

And she would finish. Achilla would stop at nothing until she got them all. She was going to destroy Xerxes and his operation. She would kill any CIA agent in her way. As for Ailina, Achilla would make her pay for all the pain she caused. Ares was the one obstacle she had to figure out, but he was not exempt from Achilla's rage. Her revenge was nonnegotiable. Achilla stood up and grabbed her android phone out of her bag and put the earphones over her ears. She bobbed her head and paced her room as Tupac's "Ride on Our Enemies" blasted through her ears mentally preparing her for the next step of her mission.

From this day forward, Achilla only had enemies. She had no friends. No family. No love. All she had was hatred and revenge and she would clutch to it like a child to its mother's breast. The only refuge from Achilla's wrath was death. Darvin would find his refuge soon. Eventually, so would Xerxes. It was just a matter of time and persistence; both of which Achilla possessed in ample measure.

Achilla performed eight thousand body squats and held a fifteen-minute plank before showering. She then threw on jeans and a red t-shirt that was just baggy enough to reduce the catcalls she might encounter in the nearest mall. She would not meet Darvin tonight. Achilla was shopping for a new dress; maybe something purple or teal. She would then find matching heels and earrings and figure out what to do with her hair so that she would know exactly how she could appeal to him. He would have no option but to notice her. Achilla would make sure of it.

She wanted to look good for her targets. Her brown velvet skin, steel toned legs, and hills-for-hips would be the last image they would ever see before she reeled them in. The mix of her favorite perfume and shampoo would be the last scent they would ever smell; sweet but smoky with a hint of come hither. If they were lucky, her cashmere lips covered in strawberry lip gloss would be the last flavor they would ever taste, and her hungry thighs, warm and tight like a leather glove in the winter, would be the last sensation they would ever feel. Achilla was going to make damn sure that it was the best night of their lives before it became their worst; before she inflicted the kind of tear-jerking, throat-scraping pain that made their minds throb even faster than their piston pulsating hearts. She took her time before she finished them just to make sure their senses ran the gamut, and the price of killing Achilla's father left a lasting impression that haunted them even in the depths of hell for all eternity. With her headphones in her ears and her hands in her pockets, Achilla looked straight ahead as she left her hotel room. It was time to get to work. Only God Himself could stop her from completing her mission. So far, He hadn't even tried.

Perhaps, for once, they were on the same page.

Epilogue

CHIRAQ. That was what they called Chicago because of the sheer number of its murders. Every day on the news, someone got shot. Every night, someone lost a loved one. Someone cried. Someone swore revenge. It wasn't the whole city, but it was enough to be a common occurrence.

So the dark-skinned man with dreads tied on the floor in front of Achilla would barely register on the cops' radar. He wasn't an innocent mother or child caught in the crossfire. He was a well-known pimp and gun runner to them, and they didn't care if he died. In fact, a couple cops had already tried to kill him, but he was nimble.

But he wasn't nimble enough for Achilla or, to him, Officer Valdez.

Achilla leaned against the living room wall inside of a house in Chicago's Bronzeville neighborhood. As far as Chicago neighborhoods go, this one wasn't so bad. There were certainly more dangerous parts of the city, but it was enough to keep its residents on their toes. Posing as a cop around this part of town wasn't too hard because no one batted an eye when they saw Achilla walking down the street. Staying inside for weeks until her skin lightened up, adopting a Chicago Latina accent, and wearing brown contacts every day? That was the hard part. As her captive struggled with his restraints in the middle of his tan-carpeted floor, Achilla breathed a sigh of relief that she no longer needed this cover or the uniform she stole.

"Your name's Dominick Harding, right?" Achilla asked.

"Fuck you, bitch!" Dominick snarled before he spat at her feet. "Fuck y'all cops! All you do is bother us black people when we're just trying to survive--"

"How about I drop my act and you drop yours?" Achilla sighed. "My name isn't Valdez, and I'm not Chicago PD, so you are not a victim of police brutality tonight. Oh, and you not just trying to survive. You have lots of money, Dominick. Xerxes pays you handsomely."

Dominick's eyes lowered.

"You're the Mantis, huh?" Dominick asked. "Aw, shit. I should've known you'd come here."

"Then you know why I'm here," Achilla said as she stepped forward. "You're going to die, Dominick, but if you cooperate with me, I'll make it quick."

Dominick struggled with his restraints again until Achilla kicked his gut, making him grunt. She then rolled him over with her foot.

"Dominick, please pay attention," Achilla said as she pulled a knife from a sheath on her left side. "Your last words moments should be productive."

"You're in the wrong city," Dominick said. "This is his hometown, and I'm his best friend."

"Interesting," Achilla said with a cocked eyebrow before looking out the window. She could see the skyline from Chicago's West Loop from here. She always found it beautiful, but it just couldn't replace Denver's mountains. Achilla sucked her teeth as she tapped her foot on Dominick's shoulder.

"Yeah, you fucked up," Dominick said. "He won't let you leave this city alive. Cops, feds, everybody's on his payroll. You should've stayed in your lane, bitch!"

Dominick spat again and hit Achilla's shoulder. She curled her lip at the saliva on her uniform before shaking her head.

"Well you have been productive," Achilla said as she dropped her knee onto Dominick's chest, making him groan. "But you've now talked me into torturing you."

"Wait, I can tell you where he is," Dominick replied as Achilla raised her knife.

Achilla stopped and cocked her right eyebrow at him.

"Please continue," Achilla said with a nod of her head. "Don't keep me in suspense."

"Look, he has a spot in River North, and he should be back for some conference for his charter school," Dominick said. "Does that help?"

"It does," Achilla replied. "Thank you for your cooperation, Dominick."

"All right," Dominick said before exposing his neck. "Go ahead."

Achilla rolled her eyes before stabbing his ribs. Dominick screamed out, but she clamped a hand over his mouth.

"Did you really think this was going to go slow?" Achilla asked. "You have brutalized and killed hundreds of little boys and girls. For them, making you suffer is the least that I can do."

Achilla worked on Dominick for an hour until he finally died. She then left his body inside for the police to find. If Chicago was Xerxes' town, then it was hers too for a while, and he was the one who wouldn't make it out alive. Achilla stared at the Chicago skyline as she waited at her bus stop down the street from Dominick's house wearing a red Chicago Bulls t-shirt and black sweatpants. She carried her cop uniform in a gym bag that she adjusted right when the bus stopped in front of her. Achilla swiped her CTA card and walked all the way to the back. As she sat with her bag on her lap and looked out the window at her brand-new city, she grinned a little. Her mission was almost complete, and she was ahead of schedule.

Soon, she could see her family again, and they'll be safe and sound.

Acknowledgments

As always, I would like to thank God for giving me the talent to write, my creative writing professors Kim Bridgford and Pete Duval for teaching me how to refine that talent. Thanks to my loving parents for instilling in me the work ethic required to pursue my dreams, especially my mother, Felicia Coble, who always encouraged me; my father, Tom Coble who always pushed me; and my grandmother, Elene Crosby, who always corrected my grammar. Thank you to all of my friends who supported me and even beta read my work. You are appreciated. Without any of you, this would not have been possible.

This, and all of my writing, is in honor of my grandfather Philip E. Crosby. You will always be loved and missed.

Made in the
USA
Lexington, KY